SON OF THUNDER
BOOK ONE: A GATHERING OF COMPANIONS

A. K. Ishaya

Note for Librarians: A cataloguing record for this book is available from Library and Archives Canada at www.collectionscanada.ca/amicus/index-e.html

ISBN 1-4120-6858-4

Printed in Victoria, BC, Canada. Printed on paper with minimum 30% recycled fibre. Trafford's print shop runs on "green energy" from solar, wind and other environmentally-friendly power sources.

TRAFFORD
PUBLISHING™

Offices in Canada, USA, Ireland and UK

This book was published *on-demand* in cooperation with Trafford Publishing. On-demand publishing is a unique process and service of making a book available for retail sale to the public taking advantage of on-demand manufacturing and Internet marketing. On-demand publishing includes promotions, retail sales, manufacturing, order fulfilment, accounting and collecting royalties on behalf of the author.

Book sales for North America and international:
Trafford Publishing, 6E–2333 Government St.,
Victoria, BC v8t 4p4 CANADA
phone 250 383 6864 (toll-free 1 888 232 4444)
fax 250 383 6804; email to orders@trafford.com
Book sales in Europe:
Trafford Publishing (uk) Limited, 9 Park End Street, 2nd Floor
Oxford, UK ox1 1hh UNITED KINGDOM
phone 44 (0)1865 722 113 (local rate 0845 230 9601)
facsimile 44 (0)1865 722 868; info.uk@trafford.com
Order online at:
trafford.com/05-1769

10 9 8 7 6 5

THIS BOOK IS DEDICATED TO:

My mom, Ann,
who taught me what it is to love the arts, especially the written word,

My dad, Marvin,
Who was the first to teach me of the joy gained by teaching others
to believe in who they are,

Maharishi Krishnananda Ishaya,
Who never compromises when it comes to sharing the truth that being one with God is
not only natural, but the easiest thing in the world,

And my Teacher, Gauri Ishaya,
Whose Brilliance consistently sees the truth of who I am
and never, ever lets me forget how beautiful that is.

IMPORTANT NOTE:

Though the following story features persons and places from history, it is not factual. According to historians, many of the events mentioned occurred in different times, in different places, with different people. Indeed, some of the characters could not possibly have been in the places they were at the point in history during which this narrative takes place. Again, this is not a factual account.

Nevertheless, it is absolutely true.

PROLOGUE:
GOLGOTHA

He *was dying.* Painfully, ingloriously dying.

Or so they thought.

Oh, it was true enough that his body was dying. He'd been nailed—*nailed*—to a cross at wrists and ankles; hung out to wither under an unseasonably hot sun like the most monstrous criminal while indifferent soldiers gambled for his belongings beneath his feet. He had been here for hours, forced by the lash to carry the instrument of his death; watched by the laughing, festival crowd come to see if the Messiah would this day save himself as he'd allegedly saved others.

The answer to the crowd's question was "No". He would not save himself at this juncture. Such was not his to do.

Officially, the crime for which he was being executed was treason against Rome. Yet, the true purpose of this drama was far greater than the simple removal of his "disruptive" influence from Empire and Synagogue—far greater, even, than most who followed him might ever come to understand, even if they did manage to live out their lifetimes.

As he'd told Governor Pilatus when he'd sought to set him free: "Were this not my time, a league of angels ten thousand strong would come to save this body, and neither Rome nor Judea could stop it. But it is my time, and you cannot prevent Death's arrival. Fear not, and tell your good wife also to have no fear. What is is as it must be."

Poor Pilatus. His countenance remained impassive, but his skin had blanched to alabaster. How could the prisoner possibly know of his wife's warning, given in the privacy of their chambers, to "bring no harm to this holy one"? Upon hearing his words, the Governor tried all the harder to find some way to free himself of the responsibility for ordering the body's death—but like the need for the death itself, his part in the play was unavoidable.

The crowds were not so great as they had been earlier; he'd not been as entertaining as they hoped. This far into his execution, he should be raving, begging, delirious —or dead, as his poor companions, ranged to either side of him on their own t-shaped crosses, finally were. But the connection with the True Being he had accepted while praying for freedom from this task filled him as never before. The initial shock of the heavy nails piercing his flesh had only pushed him farther from identification with his body and more deeply into true Identification.

Not, mind, that he was completely unaware of the body. He felt the throbbing protests of arms, wrists and feet at this enforced attempt to defy gravity, was aware of the fullness of bowels and bladder and their refusal to soil both him and the cruciform as they properly had the right to do. He felt the pain of the spear wound in his side, a result of the soldiers' growing agitation. How could this weakling who'd refused to fight their abuse in the dungeons now be so stoic—no, brave—in the face of such hideous suffering? Could not he end their growing unease by having the grace to bleed out and die?

Well, soon enough the body would accommodate their wish, and then he would discover if he could truly do what he'd come for.

He had lived lifetimes and lifetimes to come to this point. True, many times, the traumas of birth and living obliterated his awareness so that he lived his span in ignorance and misery. Yet, between each life, he fully remembered his calling. He remembered that the day would come when humanity would at last be ready to awaken to the consciousness of being the Cosmic One, remembered that he would be the catalyst that would change the very nature of creation in this Golden Sphere of existence. And when the day came that he realized it would be *this* time, he withstood the trauma of birth to be nurtured by this desert land of visionaries and prophets.

With the help of ones likewise prepared before their births, he grew and learned, first in his homeland of Galilee, then in places far from home—Egypt, Britannia, Persia, and in the high, secret places of the Indus Valley's incredible mountains. He learned the ways of the very ones who'd defined his Task eons before; indeed, he sometimes learned at their feet, unaware that some of them had embodied solely to foster his awakening.

And here was the culmination of that work: his body hung on a cross of wood by shipwright's nails, dying by inches.

No, it wasn't that he was unaware of the body's pain, not at all. It would have been inappropriate to wholly ignore its trials while one still inhabited it. It was only that he was so identified with the hugeness of the unbounded One that the body and personality alike were but miniscule particles of concern floating in the greater Life's wholeness. The notion of treating them as if they were important above all else, to act as if *he* would cease to exist without the body and personality, was now both strange and ridiculous to him. No longer was he an infinite being playing the part of an awakened man and son of God called Jeshua bar Josef. He was, in every part, the Never Born and Never Dying, the infinite, ever-whole One...

Jeshua quaked as the True Being of the Son of Man within him grew beyond Infinity and filled with the effulgent, imperishable song of Perfection. Yes! *He* was inviolable, not only as an aspect of the True Being, but as the personality and body. What he had done for Lazarus he could now do for himself, of himself. He would fulfill this mission and thus trigger the larger mission's accomplishment.

Jeshua tried to laugh through the ringing hymn of his recognition, but instead heard his mouth cry out in pure gratitude the word "Father" and what sounded like "spared". He could at last leave the vagaries of time and matter behind, could plunge into the depths of the Unbounded and exult in his new splendor. He could become in truth what he now was in his knowing...

...But not yet.

Jeshua snapped back into the personality he'd carried throughout this earthly sojourn so abruptly that he gasped. He was suddenly again aware of the crowd below, once more heard the guards throwing the sticks to pass the time. Though he felt no real pain, the heaviness that sought to at last lay his body into the dust from which it was formed pulled his vision downward, so that he might see what he must see.

Below and before him, as close to the foot of his cross as the guards would allow, were a number of his followers. Along with the women the twelve had jokingly dubbed "The Mary's," stood his own belovéd mother Mary, her countenance still. To her left stood the one people would someday call "the Magdalene," she who had gloriously blossomed from the soil of fear's excretions to become the most beautiful of blooms, and whom Jeshua loved more than any woman grown upon this earth. Her usually expressive face was also still, so much so that though her eyes glistened, he honestly could not tell if they did so with sadness or joy.

To Mary's right stood John, the youngest of his closest companions, his face filled with horror and dismay, but of the rest of the twelve Jeshua could see no sign... No, wait... There. As far back in the crowd as they could get and still be in the crowd, stood James and Andrew, their faces aged by despair and furtive terror. Jeshua's heart went out them and their unknowing, went out to their belief that all was lost. He wanted to cry out, "Take heart, my brothers, all is well!"

But there was no need. Soon enough, the sky, the trees, the mountains themselves would shout his triumph.

John and Mary held to each other amidst the other women's weeping and stared up at the heinous sight before them—and though, with lips so cracked by dryness it must surely look like a grimace, this time Jeshua did smile. Of all those he'd had the honor of calling student, his own mother had best grasped the truth of what he'd said. She had proven herself more than worthy of the devotion The Marys showed her.

And his heart filled to bursting as his eyes fell on young bar Zebedee! The boy's face was pasty with sorrow and fear, but the terror that had scattered the twelve upon his arrest had not outlasted his faith for even a day. The youngster stood boldly forth for all to see—and the Romans and everyone else be damned! *He* would not hide away in some hole, not while his Teacher still lived!

This one, of all the companions, had the best chance of fulfilling the task the One would set him. Indeed, he might even be the key to the completion of Jeshua's great Task, not only on this world, but eventually on many others.

Jeshua heard a kind of chiming in his ear, like the sound of small waters dancing against diamond rocks, like the music of groups of angels singing softly to each other. The True Being's joy swelled within him; the time had come at last. The body would finally be allowed to give up the ghost and die; yet, this apparent ending would bring the new beginning that would eventually awaken humankind.

Jeshua gazed at Mary, filled with the rapture of his success, and directed her with his eyes to look at young bar Zebedee.

"Woman," he said in a voice so strong that the guards stopped their gaming and jumped up to stare in shock, "behold your son!"

Mary beamed at him as if he'd responded to the question she had spent her life seeking the answer to as Jeshua turned his gaze on John. The tears the boy had so stoically held back now fell freely, as if he finally realized his Teacher meant to die on this wretched cross.

"Rabbi, Rabbi, please..." he choked out, but Jeshua stopped him.

"John bar Zebedee, Little Brother—*Boanerge*," he said, and all the focus of Heaven itself was in his voice, "behold your mother!"

John gazed long into Mary's eyes, then looked at his Teacher and nodded. He would, in the face of Death Himself, see to Mary's care.

Jeshua's smile became a wide, crack-lipped, grin and his body let forth a long, relieved sigh. He looked to the sky, aware of the True Being's pull on his soul, aware of that same soul separating from the body. He heard music all around him, the sound of a thousand, thousand Singers, all exulting at what they could now, at last, call the One's accomplishment on Earth.

"It is finished!" Jeshua bar Josef cried, and his voice rolled and echoed so that every animal, every plant, every part of the earth stopped to heed his joyous declaration. He was free! He was free, and this universe would know freedom because of it.

Mary still stared at her firstborn, her face brightly mirroring his joy, and Jeshua saw with jubilant assurance what lay in her future. Magdalene, too, smiled up at him through tears...and now Jeshua saw the sadness that lurked just behind her smile. But the joy was in her, too, a radiant sun throwing rainbows through thin clouds. The fullness of that day still lived in the future, but she, like Mary, would someday *be* the Truth.

John, however, leaned against his new mother and sobbed inconsolably. His head was bowed by the weight of his sorrow and his despairing stance said he could not at all accept the necessity of this fate his Teacher had come forth to meet.

"Little Brother."

Jeshua said it so softly that none but these chosen three could hear it.

John looked up, the question in his eyes showing through the misery written in every line of his face. Jeshua smiled tenderly at the boy.

"Trust that all is well, John. And remember—I love you always."

ONE

Now, *as always, the* candlelight was a comfort.

John bar Zebedee sat, empty wine cup in hand, and enjoyed the lively yet calming flicker of the flame before him. As the last glow of daylight slowly faded to full darkness, the room became a place where silence and stillness were remembered as a celebration, an appreciation, Home.

While the flame spirits entertained themselves with their dances of warmth and light, John brushed his fingers along the table his Teacher had built with his father as a boy of twelve summers. This was the last carpentry project Jeshua bar Josef had undertaken before being called forth by Destiny to do the work that must be done in every age by those who agree before their births to do it. Made of one of the hardwoods that had been carried westward over miles of sand and stone by donkey and cart, its grain and craftsmanship were flawless, something a very rich man would gladly have paid a full day's wages for so he could impress visiting personages from Rome and Greece and Tyre.

This table had never seen a rich man's house, however. It had been the focal point for dining, meeting and play in the home of Josef bar Heli and his wife Mary, had spent its life in a village so small and backward that one once wondered what good could possibly ever come from it. That one, called Nathaniel, had found the answer to his scornful musings, and even now (to the chagrin of the authorities) traveled far and wide to tell others what good had come from "Nazareth".

John felt as though if he turned his head just the right way, he would see the others' faces, smell the warm aromas of food and drink, hear the velvety steel of the voice that had defied both law and custom to share the will of the One with the world. Though they'd been naught but tiny glow bugs against the brilliant daystar that was their Teacher, each of Jeshua's twelve companions had more than once occupied tables like this one; had received meals, shelter and other gifts from his followers.

Indeed, back when he first knew himself to be part of something truly earth-changing, John often took for granted the gifts they'd received. To his youthful mind, bestowing such on his Teacher—and his companions—only made sense. He'd considered the women in particular just a little dense for their fawning awe of Jeshua, assumed their gift-giving was due more to his Teacher's charisma than any true understanding of his message, and thanked them for their efforts as a Roman General might...with the nonchalance of one who knows he is superior to those who serve him.

Even now, he vividly recalled Jeshua's reaction when he noticed his attitude.

"Do you truly think your place in this quest is greater than those who joyfully give in the best ways they can, Little Brother? Truly?"

Jeshua stared at him as if he'd grown a second head, and the chill in his voice could have frozen the water of every well in town. That coldness was reflected in his expression as he took in the rest of the twelve; suddenly, they seemed unable to look him in the face.

"If any of you believe your place is assured because you seem closer to me than these others, know this: that greater closeness is only an appearance. There is no one, not one, who is more worthy to me than another because of what they think or believe or do. I care only for what you are—and that was determined by the One long before you chose to play at being the separate ones you can never be in truth."

Jeshua lovingly took the hand of the woman who stood closest to him and turned again to John. "Hear my promise, John bar Zebedee. Those who give all because they have it to give, who give without thought for their place among those who see and judge, they will reach the perfect rest of Heaven before ever you do."

That incident had taken place almost twenty years ago, when John, with less than twenty summers behind him, still carried what Matthew jokingly called "the stench of youth." He was by far the youngest of the twelve; his longish mop of curly brown hair still glimmered with deep auburn highlights instead of being threaded with the barest hints of silver, and only the lightest fuzz covered his naïve and innocent chin. In fact, he hadn't yet reached his full height: he grew another two inches the year after Jeshua charged him to be son to his mother.

At the time of that rebuke, John was sure his ears would never again be a color other than flame red, and he made sure from then on to always show respect to those who honored Jeshua and the twelve. Still, it was years before he truly felt the sense of his Teacher's words.

John shook himself back to the moment, smiled into the dimness, and rose to clear the table of the cups left behind by those he now taught in remembrance of his Teacher. Then, before Mary could return and yet again nag him, he lit the rest of the lamps. Though his mother knew he enjoyed the dark of the evening this single candle permitted, she still seemed to obtain great amusement from teasing him about it.

"This is not a tomb we live in John, but a home. It needs more light."

John, in turn, would roll his eyes and tease her about "women who fear what mere shadows might bring," while slowly circling the room with the small torch.

Of course, in Mary's case, his words truly were only teasing. She'd conquered more shadows in this lifetime than most others might do in ten.

Lamps lit, John stepped onto the porch of the home he shared with Mary on the outskirts of Bethany and reveled in the quiet of the crisp, dry, midsummer evening. Midway through Jeshua's ministry, Mary's second-born son, James, had purchased this house with its two bedrooms, small alcove and unusually large living and cooking areas—all with considerable bewilderment.

"I am a practical man, not prone to frivolous purchases," James had said upon meeting John and Andrew in Capernaum while doing business for the family's carpentry shop, "and I know full well Jeshua will never live in that house, for he walks the prophet's path. Still, when I saw it, I knew I must buy it...though I know not why."

People had often found themselves saying, "I know not why" when it came to dealing with Jeshua bar Josef—yet even now, many joined the name and cause of the man who'd defied Synagogue, State and even the seeming intractability of death. John supposed it was good that so many—including his own brother, James—had willingly given up even their lives to publicly state what they believed Jeshua's mission to be. Yet more and more these days, he wondered if they truly grasped what his Teacher had said.

Indeed, did he?

As the day sky's last hint of azure faded into star-punctuated blackness, a familiar, and of late, increasing sense of frustration crept into John's awareness. He was no longer the seventeen year-old boy who'd unquestioningly relinquished all to follow Jeshua. As he thought of James and the others, the man John had become was acutely aware that something was missing in his life. More, he strongly felt that missing thing was something he must do, a thing of extreme importance that would affect far more than the small corner of the world he lately felt more and more confined to.

Until recently, that feeling had come and gone, only to once more leave John with the peace that came of knowing he did his Teacher's will. His promise to be son to Jeshua's mother he gladly fulfilled, and not alone out of a sense of duty. His years with Mary had been ones of almost unmitigated joy; not only had he discovered the origins of Jeshua's sense of humor and love of telling a riveting story, but the Light his mother shared simply by being "Mary" was ever and increasingly a wonder to behold.

Additionally, and even more importantly, there was the work they'd begun doing with selected students after his early travels with Peter and James. John delighted in sharing the techniques—the Practice—Jeshua had given the twelve and others of his closest students in secret. Like those closest companions, John and Mary's students willingly accepted that *they* might be the miracle and frequently gathered to discover the depths of their own wholeness. Not by worshipping Jeshua as something unique, but by using a method that would allow them to experience what he was.

Yes, John had gained much satisfaction through teaching others to know their true Selves—and could even boast of finally having a properly luxuriant beard. But the growing sense of "what now...and when?" dogged his heels ever more insistently, and all his attempts to discern the cause behind it led only to his saying, as so many had of their relations with Jeshua, "I know not why."

John glared at the imperturbable stars as if they could answer his questions but chose not to and found himself (as he often did of late) mumbling aloud in the wry hope some passing angel might deign to explain things to him.

"I know not why so many have risked all they have to share the good news of my Teacher's existence with the world...while I still stand on the porch of my mother's house, comfortable and safe."

"Yes you do," a richly amused feminine voice said from the darkness. "'Tis only that you want to forget that you are saddled with the care of an old woman—one who, no less, teases the oh-so-enlightened Master about talking aloud to himself where he might be heard...and suspected."

John's mouth twisted with a wry grin as he turned toward the mother he had adopted on Golgotha seventeen years before.

Mary of the House of Josef finished the easy climb up the rise to their house and set her empty basket, once full of bread, next to the door. Using the traditional Zebedee family greeting every son offered to mother and eldest married sister, John tenderly took Mary's hands and briefly touched his forehead to the still-soft skin of her fingers.

Mary was no longer a young woman by any means, yet the sparkle in her eyes, the spring in her step, and the radiance of her countenance put many a woman thirty years younger to shame. John could well see how Josef must have fallen completely under her spell upon seeing her for the first time. Indeed, he himself had fallen utterly—and embarrassedly—in love with Mary on their initial meeting, only to be further mortified by Jeshua's teasing wink.

But it wasn't her physical beauty alone that caused men and women alike to stare admiringly at her; it was Mary's *beingness* that stilled their busy hands and engendered respectful, even joyous greetings on the streets and in the market. John had the constant sense that if the body enclosing his mother's spirit was suddenly stripped away, he'd find nothing but pure, dazzling, unblemished Life in its place. Jeshua had charged him with taking care of Mary, but it was her light, and lightness of being, that carried him through when the companions feared Jeshua's crucifixion had brought his work to naught. In fact, this evening Mary seemed bright enough to cause the flowers to mistakenly open in their desire to enjoy the radiance of her morning sun.

"Good Eventide to you my mother. You are late."

"Blesséd Eventide to you, my son—and does that mean you've allowed your dear old mother's dinner to fall by the way while yet again being caught up in visions of finding your true destiny?" Her beatific smile was mischievous.

"Has it been so obvious, then?" John asked as he ushered her into the house and took her cloak. He kept his tone light but didn't feel that way at all; he was dismayed his mother had so easily *seen* him.

Mary, her smile suddenly gone, turned and looked at, then through John, but there was no less lightness to her when she spoke. "It shows when you begin to question aloud—in all seriousness—your chosen purpose, dear one. Though, even if you did not speak your concerns to the stars, your discontent would show, to my eyes at least. But in truth, it has shown for months. More than one has commented on it."

Mary walked to the table her firstborn son had made with the father who had loved them both beyond all measure and patted the back of the chair closest to her.

"Sit," she said, then followed her own order and waited for John to comply.

"Let me heat some water first and get you something to drink," he said, suddenly and inexplicably reluctant to talk about his experience. Mary shook her head.

"*Sit*," she said again, in her "I'll brook no argument on this matter, John"-tone.

John sat.

Mary peered into his eyes a moment, then looked down at her folded hands as if she meant to study every line and callus she'd gained through fifty-odd years of carrying out the usual duties of wife and mother. John could only stare in amazement: though her body sat still as stone, he had the overwhelming impression she shouted "Joy!" from the rooftops and danced in the clouds. The light he'd sensed a few moments before grew even more apparent; the room was actually bathed in a soft white glow that made the yellow of the candlelight seem weak and dingy.

"Tell me what you know," Mary said, her voice suddenly sounding as if it belonged to the Ancient of Days.

Her words were no ordinary request for information, but the opening of an honored ritual, the call from one soul to another to remember its place and purpose in the cosmic dance that is Creation. John looked at his own hands, clearing away his awareness of being merely "the son of Zebedee", then closed his eyes. He spoke to himself the simple phrases of the Practice Jeshua had taught him so many years ago and dropped into the omnipresent Silence of his being, into the one true Self.

Within moments, memories that had been buried beneath the layers of that Stillness began to surface. They were John's own experiences, ones that came from this life, not another. Yet, so far as his mind was concerned, until this moment they'd never happened. They had been deliberately obliterated from his awareness, excised until he could come to this place, at this moment, with this person, to reawaken them...

He, Peter and James were huddled on the ground on the outskirts of Jerusalem, lying in the damp chill of what would prove to be the night of the twelve's last supper with Jeshua. Jeshua had brought the three of them here, leaving the others farther outside the garden of Gethsemane. He'd said he wished to pray to the One, to discover what was to come next on this glorious journey...but John felt a strong sense of apprehension. Jeshua seemed so preoccupied, so unsettled; never had he seen his Teacher thus in the three years of their companionship. It was as if a thin but tangible shroud lay between Jeshua and his knowing, as if he could only faintly hear the voice of the One.

Indeed, though John's nineteen year-old heart could never fully credit such a thing where his Teacher was concerned, Jeshua seemed afraid.

He wanted the three of them to tarry there, to hold vigil during the hour he would be in the garden; but it was *very* late in the day, early in the morning, actually, and John was so very tired. Twice he started guiltily awake when Jeshua came to check on the three of them, twice he felt something akin to panic at the tone of...of desperation in his voice. Yet the moment Jeshua departed back into the garden, John fell asleep again, his Teacher's impossible fear completely forgotten.

In fact, John slept now and dreamed...or thought he did.

He stood at the edge of a high grove, the likes of which he had never seen: there was nothing but dazzling, heartrending beauty as far as he could see. The trees, the flowers, the blades of grass fairly exploded with rich, full, iridescent greenness; every plant was vibrantly alive, radiant with what seemed to John to be actual intelligence. He felt as if he could call to these beings and they would joyously answer, if only he knew what language to speak. The air was so crisp and alive that breathing too deeply might cut his lungs, yet to not breathe every breath as deeply as possible seemed like an affront to the spirits of the Air, a refusal of the fullness of life they offered.

John had been gifted with recognizing he dreamed even as the dream went on since early childhood: not only could he affect such dreams' content, but they possessed a kind of luminous clarity that was more vibrant than his waking experience. "A budding visionary," his father was fond of saying, in a tone that plainly bespoke his opinion of the uselessness of such a talent.

Well, the clarity and sharpness of this dream was more vivid than anything John had ever experienced. In fact, the sense of aliveness was so great that he was soon convinced he did not dream at all.

So, how had he come here?

John let his sight range further afield; the grove led to a valley that was at least several leagues wide. It could easily take several weeks of steady walking to come to the high, knife-jagged mountains that enclosed the valley, yet, John could also see its far end as if it was but a short walk away. The climate must change enormously as one went higher up: the place where he stood supported both familiar fruit-bearing trees and exotics he never imagined could exist, while the upper reaches held cold-weather vegetation. Snow traversed the valley's rim; at those elevations summer was no doubt short, if ever it truly came at all.

John heard a sound, turned, and hastily backed up, startled almost out of his wits.

A large buck stood before him, his snow-white muzzle presented for his inspection, his soft brown eyes focused directly on his. It was the largest creature of its kind he'd ever seen—taller at the shoulder than a horse—yet his stature was as graceful as something from the angelic realms. Like the vegetation, this buck emanated an almost human level of intelligence, and John again felt a pang at not knowing his language.

"Good Morrow to you, Sir Buck," he said a little shakily, but with the dignity befitting conversation with such a kingly being. He tentatively reached out to pet the creature's muzzle; the buck didn't resist. "Well, then, where am I to go? I know this is no idle visit, that I am here on the Emperor's business, so to say. Are you to be my guide?"

"No. Actually, he was mine."

John grinned at the familiar voice and turned, ready to greet Jeshua with a saucy comment—but what he saw froze his voice in awe.

Incredible brilliance filled and surrounded Jeshua, as if a hundred suns had collided with each other, but still maintained the individual integrity of their own radiance. Yet, unlike the transfiguration John had witnessed with Peter and James on the Mount of Olives, this brilliance was not solely Light. He could clearly see Jeshua's body, knew if he grabbed the hand hanging relaxed at his Teacher's side he would find a hand *to* grab; and for some reason, that was far more awe-inspiring to John than the experience on the Mount. Though he resisted falling to his knees, the word, unbidden, came to his lips and spilled out of his mouth.

"Master!"

Jeshua smiled and answered the question in John's mind as if he'd voiced it aloud. "This experience is greater to you than the one on the Mount, Little Brother, because you truly see for the first time that this brilliance is possible for you. It is possible for any who are willing to become what they truly are."

Jeshua grinned and shook all over, as a wet dog might do, and the Light dimmed slightly; he seemed more like his ordinary self to John's eyes, if not to his dazzled heart.

"It is impressive, is it not?"

The buck, whom John had completely forgotten in his surprise, pushed his muzzle into his back and propelled him toward Jeshua. Still grinning, Jeshua caught the projectile and hugged him with the fervor of one who thought a loved one lost at sea, only to discover he had come back safe, his own prodigal son returned to life.

And John, as always, melted unabashedly into his Teacher's embrace, feeling yet again the inexplicable sense that he returned to one he thought he had somehow betrayed, only to find it had never been so.

Jeshua pushed at the unruly curls that dangled in John's eyes and held him at arms' length to survey the futility of his handiwork.

Then his smile turned sardonic.

"*'Master'?*"

"I, well, that is...I... I meant..."

John was sure he blushed all the way down to his waist. They'd had *this* discussion before. Jeshua, while well aware of his public stature, would tolerate no worship by his closest friends. Indeed, doing so was one of the few things that would truly annoy him. John could almost hear his Teacher's exasperated voice saying for the thousandth time:

"My friends, I am neither your 'Lord', nor your 'Master'! I am worthy of respect only because of my greater experience in knowing the One, and I am worthy of being heard only because I willingly give all I have gained to others. The surrender I seek from you should come only from your willingness to experience what I Know. And in truth, you do not surrender to my personal self at all, but to the One within the center of each one's heart."

John *had* forgotten in that initial moment of witnessing Jeshua's glory (he often did, though he tried not to show it); but it was as Jeshua had said. Seeing his Teacher in this luminous ordinariness filled John with the sense that he, a common man, could become That as well; inevitably would if he gave himself the chance.

Truly, *that* was awe-inspiring.

Jeshua affectionately tousled John's hair as if he clearly saw his student's realization, then stood back, his smile fading. "Your way will not be overly easy, Little Brother—though there will be times when, to your mind at least, it will seem too easy. There are things I want you to do John, things that on the surface will sometimes make you seem as a coward, to yourself and perhaps to others."

Jeshua began walking through the grove at a leisurely pace, eyes on his feet as if every step was a thing wonderful to behold, as if his body was barely heavy enough to stay moored to the earth. When he stopped, he looked around like a lover filled with boundless praise for the beauty of the belovéd that surrounds him at every turn.

"As you know, John, my task on earth was not merely to heal the sick of body and heart, nor was it solely to proclaim that God is alive, well, and loves us unconditionally. My earthly mission is part of a much larger one, one that affects all the universe.

"You know what I have taught you, Little Brother, know that those techniques are an especially effective means for leading any who desire to forget this dream of pain and strife and remember their boundless freedom. But tell me, have you ever wondered why you are so much younger than the others of the twelve?"

"I have wondered, I must admit it, Rabbi...and I am ashamed to say I've had some pride about it, thinking I must be very special to be thus honored so young. Maybe more special than the others."

"Yes, well. I do recall a question from certain members of the twelve and their families concerning who might be allowed to sit at my right and left hands in Heaven," Jeshua said, his voice dry as dust. John blushed at the memory of that folly as his Teacher went on. "The reason you are so much younger than the others has many answers, but the one that is of importance here and now is that you will be able to withstand the rigors of the journey you must make."

John's eyebrows rose in surprise. He was going on a journey? Without Jeshua, which he clearly sensed was what his Teacher was saying? "But..."

Jeshua raised a hand to interrupt his interruption. "It is a journey you promised to undertake literally eons ago, Little Brother, so this world would at last complete its climb back into the fullness of the One's embrace. But it is by no means the only part of this great Task you agreed to carry out, nor the first."

They came to the end of the sloping grove (impossibly soon it seemed to John—perhaps this was a dream after all) and stopped before a lake that looked to rival the Sea of Galilee, despite the fact that John could easily see its far shore. He set aside his consternation long enough to stare in amazement: the water appeared to boil as if it sat in a gigantic cauldron heated by a million logs. Steam rose from its roiling surface and John's heavy robe was soon wet with humidity and perspiration; yet though the evidence of his senses was overwhelming, his youthful curiosity demanded more tangible proof of the water's state. Jeshua's strong hand stopped him as he bent to dribble his fingers in it.

"The water does indeed, boil, Little Brother, and then some. To get too close could lead to a very unpleasant experience, to say nothing of what would happen if you fell in." He pointed with his other hand. "What do you think of that?"

Growing quite close to the lake's edge was a surprisingly healthy tree—but what truly made it remarkable was its size and color. It stood at least ten times Jeshua's height, its burl-covered trunk easily twice as wide as he was tall. Its branches formed a canopy that could comfortably provide shade for twenty or thirty people to lie in, and every one of its thousands of hand-sized leaves was luminously golden. As with the other foliage of this place and the king buck, the golden tree shimmered with intelligence, even sentience. It took in John's presence as a wizened old man or woman might (and he could not decide which gender it was), as if deciding if he was worth its time to acknowledge.

"This is Vanaspati, John, the Tree of the World," Jeshua said, reverently touching one of its leaves in unmistakable greeting. "Vanas is the life-core of our world, the source in physical form of that part of the Earth that grows without humankind's conscious intervention. You could say it contains the heart-seed of Earth and Her children, that it is the source of our true nourishment. Indeed, you could say many and far loftier things about Vanas and they would all be true.

"For a very, very long time, Little Brother, humanity has suffered from a deep forgetfulness. Humankind, including most of these ones we work with, has forgotten the importance of simple being, of allowing the One to invariably direct them as It will. We have remembered, honored and emulated the way of the Father—humankind has *done* much and will do more—but rarely have we simply *been* in symmetry with our doing.

"Rarely have we honored the Mother, and this unwillingness to be Source in addition to expressing It allows darkness and emptiness to grow out of balance, to seemingly take on a life of its own. It causes us to cast ourselves out of Eden in the mistaken belief that God would have us suffer for a sin God knows nothing of.

"What you've agreed to do, John, is to care for the Mother until the time comes for her to be Lord of this earth in balance with the Father. You have agreed to do whatever it takes to awaken all people to the value of simply being That, so that the dream of evil's existence can at last fade into the unreality that it actually is."

Jeshua laid a hand on John's shoulder, and though the brilliance in him still shone bright, his eyes held sadness. "My time on earth grows very short, Little Brother. Though I would have it otherwise, the "I" of me will not determine the outcome of my work there. Many of you received special instruction from me, and all of you watched me demonstrate that love is something to give to each and all in every moment, without conditions. But now there are trials I must go through at the hands of those who yet sleep, so my part of this work may be successfully completed.

"Many of you will be severely tested by witnessing those trials, John...and more than a few of you will fail that test."

TWO

John's *heart quailed at* Jeshua's words. Then he grew angry. His Teacher was the Son of God, for Heaven's sake; surely no one would dare attempt to harm him!

He desperately wanted to say as much to Jeshua, to reassure the Reassurer, but the words froze on his tongue. Son of God Jeshua surely was, but right then he looked like a messenger who, upon seeing an enormous host of enemies in the distance, has pledged to tell what he sees, regardless of his desire to spare his companions ill tidings.

"When I face my trials, John, many whom you now call brother will forget the power of what I taught and scatter like so many birds alerted to the cat's presence. All but a very few will either forget the Practice I taught them—or carry it to their graves. Even the many who now embrace my broader teachings will misunderstand and use them ill, for there is much, much more to what I taught than a mere three years of study can fully impart. In truth, only those who have previously walked the Wheel of Existence as fully conscious beings will come to fully understand my teachings at this time, and they are few indeed."

"Then was all you said, all you taught us, naught but words, Rabbi? Is not Heaven on earth possible for every man?"

"It is possible for every human to experience love as their normal state of being, John, and it will be so far sooner than if I had not come to this earth. It is only that that awakening will take time for most, for they believe in a time-based universe and are not yet ready to instantly remember their wholeness. Most of them cannot truly imagine wholeness even in my presence, which is the Presence of God.

"Those few who have walked the Wheel in Fullness before, who've once more come to this earth to do this work with us, did so specifically to help plant the seed of love's true value, but it was never their task to make all the world fully manifest that energy at this time, any more than it was my task to establish a Heavenly government on Earth. In truth, Little Brother, a large part of the work of bringing my greatest teaching back to humanity will belong to you. With time and the help of others, many of them not yet born, your part will be accomplished."

Had they been back in Jerusalem, John knew he would have been frightened to the point of tears by Jeshua's words. But here in this place he felt, with a kind of pride and growing maturity, the sense of an Elder's understanding. He was one who had fully walked the Great Wheel, he knew, and soon he would have the chance to do more than simply anchor love's energies to the earth. He would be able to actively help the Good grow. John had many questions, but at that moment, Jeshua pointed upward.

"Is that not a perfectly awe-inspiring sky, Little Brother?"

John looked where his Teacher pointed and gasped. He'd always loved the gigantic, snow-white clouds of Judea that gave the sky such an effect of depth, which awoke in him notions of finding that place from which he might one day stand and survey the universe. But the splendor of this sky, with its dancing rainbow-hued clouds, made Judea's skies seem like something a bad artist had painted with dirty pigments; its beauty engulfed John until he felt as if he and it were one inseparable thing.

He turned to Jeshua, his heart rejoicing—and discovered that he was also the boiling lake, the great tree Vanas, and the air between them. He was *Jeshua,* and he knew in that moment not only what his Teacher was, but what his life was truly for.

"Rabbi, have I been transported to Heaven? Surely this cannot be Earth!"

Ah, but what is 'Earth' John bar Zebedee?

Jeshua's eyes twinkled as John blinked away surprised tears of joy. His Teacher did not move his lips, yet John heard him as clearly as if he did. And what are you? Are you a body, your persona, your name? Or are you something far beyond that? Are you truly only 'the creation,' John, with no say about how that which is around you is affected? Or are you also the Creator, creating what you desire so you may know ever more of your Self? 'Have I not said, ye are gods?'

Jeshua continued to speak, his lips now moving with his words. "Vashti—this place—exists both as a physical location on each of the earths, and as a location in the spiritual realms. Masters from all universes confer here to arrange the fulfillment of the Seven Tasks the One has set so humanity may awaken to its wholeness.

"You, more than any of the twelve, understand what the Practice I taught can do, John. And yet, though you desire to awaken that deepest knowledge in others, you sense, too, that humanity is not yet ready to step into the Fullness it fosters."

John nodded, realizing for the first time that he in fact *had* wondered how people would ever come to accept their right to be one with the One if, as was too often the case, Jeshua's very existence had not convinced them.

"Your portion, Little Brother, if you should decide to take it, will be to make the journey to the physical version of Vashti, there to hold the purity of Practice in the Stillness until humanity is ready to use it. When that time comes, you will go forth and teach those who are ready to spread this knowledge and thus give to all the means to awaken the Stillness within them.

"Only by that awakening will the balance of the Mother's energy reintroduce itself into the world, and we, as the Father/Mother, be able to again create as we did in Eden."

John nodded again, excited and deeply honored by being given such a task "How will I find Vashti, Rabbi?" he asked. But Jeshua only shrugged.

"I have no idea. Since I'll not be there with you, but seeing to other aspects of the One's business, the how of finding Vashti must be yours to discover."

John was shocked to his bones by Jeshua's words.

What could his Teacher possibly be thinking? Yes, he was sometimes conscious enough of his intuition to actually follow it, but his ability was by no means consistent enough to fulfill so great a task as this. Not by any means.

John's sense of maturity and understanding dissolved like so much smoke; his beardless, suddenly grief-crumpled face looked even younger than it usually did. "Rabbi, I do not think I can do what you ask," he said miserably. "Are you sure one of the others will not be better suited than I? Peter perhaps, or Matthew, or even my brother? I—I fear to fail you."

Though he saw it coming, John couldn't duck the smart smack Jeshua delivered full on the crown of his head. The blow didn't hurt in the least, of course; still, he blinked like a kitten who's just taken a paw from his mother. Jeshua's face held an almost comical mixture of exasperation and love, but his voice was sharp when he spoke.

"Not one valueless, ineffectual fool did I choose to be amongst my companions,

John bar Zebedee, not one! Peter's, Matthew's and the others' portions are different from yours because you will *listen* to the Voice when it tells you not to travel and proselytize in the public squares. Your portion will, in many ways, be larger than the others' and so slower to digest, but you will have the patience to let it develop as it must without taking hasty action; you will let your task come to you. And that, John, makes you strong as very few who live upon this earth are strong."

"But—"

"No, Little Brother! Do not let the youth and inexperience of your body fool you into believing the task set for you is too difficult! The One will be with you in many forms if you will but be open to the help It offers. Trust, John, even if the form the help takes is unexpected or looks on the surface like a hindrance—" Jeshua suddenly smiled, "—or seems impossible. If you keep to the counsel of your Unstruck Heart, you will recognize that help when it comes and each part of the task will be easily completed.

"Believe me, Little Brother, I am not mistaken in my companions. Each of you will do exactly what needs doing, even if you do not live to see the results."

Though John no longer despaired—how could he in the face of Jeshua's assurance? —he still felt entangled in his doubts. The task his Teacher had set him seemed so large. How would he ever find this Vashti? Where would he even begin to look?

Jeshua peered intently at him, almost as if willing him to relinquish his fears, then his countenance lightened. He briefly laid his hand against John's cheek, then placed his forefinger between the boy's brows. He spoke so softly he seemed to talk to himself.

"I think, dear one, that this is too much for one so young to take in right now. There is a life you must yet live, after all, and you will only be distracted by the question of 'when, when, when?' if you know what your future brings. So for now you must forget all you've heard—but I promise," Jeshua said, cutting off John's budding protest, "the forgetting will last only for awhile.

"Upon awakening from this dream, Little Brother, you will recall having quite a different one, one that was pleasant enough, but otherwise unremarkable. As for this meeting, let it bury itself so deeply within you that even your body forgets it. When the time comes, the one best suited to do so will trigger this memory...but in the intervening time, you will wait and, save for some small adventures, live your life as a teacher to those who live close to your home."

Jeshua looked toward the distant mountains on the other side of the huge valley, his eyes glazing slightly; then he nodded and turned his attention back to John with a small smile. "And so you do not grow too bored, I will even give you a responsibility to fulfill, one that will make the waiting easier for your heart and keep the fullness of what you know alive. All will be well."

Jeshua removed his finger from John's forehead, then took the boy's face in both hands and kissed the spot between his brows with all the tenderness of a mother kissing her only son goodbye. John again saw sadness lurking under the brilliance of his Teacher's light and felt his own chest tighten, but the oppressive apprehension he'd felt in Gethsemane was gone, replaced by a peace that seemed bigger than the universe.

"The world calls us back to finish this play, Little Brother, and we'll not have the chance to talk again for a long while. Though you will not remember this conversation for some time to come, do remember this: there is nothing to fear, no matter what the appearances may show you. You are my belovéd one and you will never fail me, no matter what you do. Go forth, John bar Zebedee, and give peace unto those you meet, just as I offer my peace unto you."

The dream began to fade, not to darkness, but light. John was aflame with the brilliance of it, as if he was being transmuted into it, as if he would never again know density. Surely he'd now float through the marketplaces as Jeshua always seemed to do, not walk like a mere heavy-footed mortal.

He felt Gethsemane's cold, hard ground beneath him, heard through his sleep-muddled ears the sound of Jeshua's footsteps and—though they were yet some ways away—what sounded like the footfalls of many people approaching. Momentarily, his eyes would open and he would forget this experience in Vashti had ever happened. Yet, he could not feel sadness or loss, only a sense of Calm.

The approaching footsteps grew louder and one of the others, probably James, shook him further into wakefulness. The call to come back again to the heaviness of earth was a mandate John's mind and body could only obey, but he was still enough in the dream to hear Jeshua's last words:

"Remember, Little Brother. I love you always."

The candle on the table was half its original size. John opened his eyes to find his face wet with tears and Mary beaming at him. The brightness of and around his mother seemed at least twice as intense as it had been earlier.

"Did you see it too?" he asked.

Mary nodded but did not speak, and he noticed through the enormous smile she wore that her face was as wet as his own.

John rose and paced around the room, running his fingers through wavy hair that in seventeen years had been suffered to grow well past his shoulders. He literally vibrated with the energy of this long-past/brand new encounter with Jeshua; he felt like his cells were racing from place to place, trying to find a way to escape from skin that had suddenly grown too tight.

"All this time, all these years...and I remembered nothing. All the times I wanted to go forth and proclaim the news of Jeshua's life as Peter and Matthew had done. All the times I asked myself why I did not. And now, at last, to know there was a reason."

Certainly, the urge to go had come to John often enough, especially right after Jeshua's crucifixion. Yet, save for a few forays with James, Peter and one or two of the others, whenever he'd seriously considered taking his own ministry road-ward, a strong sense of warning told him he must not do so. John lost more than a little sleep wondering why he, of all the companions, should be thus prevented. Wondered more than once if his reticence was only cowardice.

And when Saul-become-Paul of Tarsus began preaching in the very cities where he'd previously brought so many of Jeshua's followers down—well, that had particularly rankled. Some snickered behind their hands, saying John no longer believed Jeshua's message. He had forsaken his Teacher's mission, they said, and claimed his defection as proof that Jeshua had been naught but a mountebank and charlatan. John held his tongue well enough in the face of such accusations, but many were the nights when an eavesdropper would have heard Mary calling on his youthful self to focus on the truth instead of the distractions of others' claims and rumors.

That had been a bitter time, and even knowing now that his reticence had a good—

nay, excellent—reason for existing did not keep the ghost of that bitterness from filling John's throat. He wanted to curse Jeshua for the unfairness of not being told in the beginning what his place would be, wanted, in truth, to punch something, just as he would have as a younger man.

But the One knew, his mother had seen enough tantrums on this subject in his youth; she deserved better than to witness one now.

"John." Mary's quiet, amused voice suddenly cut into his thoughts. "My Jeshua was accused of many things, but behaving for the sake of pleasing the crowd was not among them. After all, how do you know seeing your anger is not exactly the thing I need to step at last into the One's Fullness? Would you keep me from my destiny?"

John sighed. Jeshua's oneness with the Unbounded had been so great that he never spoke except with Its voice, nor acted except by Its hand. More, he taught over and over that if one knew and lived in the Stillness, he could commit no wrong in the eyes of God. So, John silently spoke one of the phrases of the Practice which Jeshua had taught him and let it float through his mind, to have whatever effect it would.

Instantly, his entire body tensed as the ghost of his bitterness came fully to life. Anger, shame and even betrayal flared and burned along his nerves. His heart felt like it would spew the blackness of that ire all over the room, would taint the whole world with its rancid stench—

—But then, just as suddenly as they'd appeared, the thoughts and feelings dissolved. John was swallowed by a Silence so complete that he had to keep himself from slumping in relief. Mary smiled.

"Hmm, yes. It can still be a bit of a shock when the One moves through without hindrance, especially when it feels like you no longer own the self you think you are. But then, allowing the One to become all we are *is* our ultimate purpose, is it not?"

Her tone grew brisk. "So then, my son, you have finally awakened to the true vision of your night in Gethsemane and know now what your mission is. What do you think?"

"I think...this is a great deal more than I'd have ever expected, Mother." John took a rueful breath. "And though I hate to admit it, Jeshua was right. Perhaps I was more patient than the others, but knowing his intentions for me most assuredly would have made things much harder. Still, it is a relief to know my recent discontent has a cause."

Mary nodded. "Good. When will you be leaving?"

John blinked stupidly and his eyes went round. "Leaving? For Vashti?"

"Actually, I was thinking of Greece."

John's mouth opened and closed like the fish he and James used to pull from his father's nets as he realized that Mary did not speak in jest. He sat down, exhaled heavily and stared at her as if Jeshua had again smacked him atop his head.

Mary smiled and went into the kitchen, only to return a moment later with wine, bread and fruit. She daintily poured the wine; John drank, then gripped his cup like it was his sole hope of rescue from the edge of a high, sheer cliff. Mary laid her hands on his.

"For seventeen years, John, you've fulfilled your promise to do whatsoever Jeshua asked to help awaken the One in everyone. You've stood by those of us who had no calling or inclination to cry of Jeshua's existence from the rooftops as if he was the one and only Messiah, even when your mind told you you did wrong. You've taught those who wanted to understand his teachings to be lights unto themselves and the ordinary world of children and laundry, plows and vineyards and shepherding.

"Now the time has come for you to prepare the way for the future by fulfilling the task Jeshua spoke of in Vashti. Now, your pledge calls you forth to do what you promised to do in a different way, my son."

John looked into his wine cup as if he expected to find something of great interest, then picked it up and savored its remains, thinking irrelevantly that the one who'd made it most certainly knew how to bring out the One in it.

"I made to Jeshua another pledge, Mother, one that also means a great deal to me. What shall we do about that?"

Mary looked startled as she realized what he was talking about. Her merry grin returned. "Are you speaking of your obligation to me, my son?"

"Of course I am." John said it more sharply than he meant to, but his mother's unseemly cheerfulness suddenly irritated him. "You are my Teacher's mother—and mine as well, by his behest. He left your care to me. I cannot simply walk away from that commission as if it is of no importance."

John began to pace again as his mind gathered more objections. "More, there is a tremendous amount of business to take care of before I can leave our students behind. It will not do to simply throw a sack over my shoulder and disappear. And to Greece, no less? You saw the look of Vashti's sky, Mary. It cannot possibly be in Greece, nor indeed, anywhere on this earth. No. I'll not go off on some wild goat chase, hoping against hope that the universe will show me the signs and wonders I need. I must first discover a way to find this Vashti...and I absolutely will not leave until I have you and our students properly prepared and situated."

John stared a challenge into Mary's eyes as they narrowed; she might well be as obstinate as Jeshua ever thought to be, but he, by the One, would be just as stubborn until she saw sense. Never had he invoked a grown son's right to demand his mother's obedience, but if she insisted on defying him he most certainly would do so now.

Mary sucked in a breath as if holding back an unsavory retort, but made no attempt to keep the sarcasm from her voice when she did speak.

"My poor, poor child! So much *you* must do, so much *you* are responsible for! Pray, where has my innocent, trusting son gone?"

"Mother, you listen to me—"

"No, John, you listen to me." Mary's voice was calm, but her look was sharp enough to slice meat. "You've claimed dissatisfaction with your lot in Bethany these many months, with teaching those who ask for the tools to fully know the One. But now that your chance to change that lot has come, you tell me your responsibilities are ever-so-much-more important. You stand here, ready to invoke the law to hide your fear of going where your soul would send you. Your mouth speaks Jeshua's words readily enough John bar Zebedee, but your heart seems to have forgotten the meaning behind them!

"'I will do whatever it takes.' Each of us who became Jeshua's students vowed a vow to the One Itself to be lights unto the world in whatever ways the One would have it. Do you now tell me you've changed your mind, that you would rather protect your small self from failing your soul's mission? Do you forsake your vows?"

John stared hotly at Mary for a moment longer, then sat and gazed into his now empty wine cup. The mirror his mother's words presented showed him a self he didn't like at all: that of a man grown comfortable with his exalted position. Was he exempt from certain forms of growth because he was called Teacher? His Teacher had not been, and he now called John to take up the scythe and bring in the harvest, just as his brother and others had. Would he now risk cutting himself (or being cut), or choose to remain safely in Bethany?

John suddenly felt like the nineteen year-old who'd feared he could not fulfill his Teacher's task for him. Still...

"Mother, I will do as my Teacher asked; you know I will. But the matter of your wellbeing is still of concern to me. Yes, yes—I know you have other sons who would happily take you in...but that was not reason enough for me to forsake you seventeen years ago and it is not reason enough now. Mary, my pledge to be son to you came of my love for my Teacher, but I willingly serve it because of my love for his mother. I must see to your care before I leave; my heart will allow me to do no less. Even Jeshua —especially Jeshua—cannot fault me for following what my soul knows I must do. I will not leave this place until I know your care is in hands I can trust."

The joyful equanimity Mary had displayed all evening returned as John came to his inevitable conclusion. In fact, he felt sure her face must hurt, so wide had her smile become. Despite his concerns, she looked like a sixteen year-old who's only worry was which shawl she should wear to her best friend's wedding. She squeezed his hands, her face so luminous that John almost felt the need to close his eyes; it seemed to him that the room itself filled with light, fed by the radiance that shimmered from beneath her skin like a lamp lighting the way to the end of a long, long road.

"John! Dearest one! After this night, neither you nor any other in this world will need to have a single care for me," she said at last.

As his brow furrowed in surprise, then worry, the woman John had happily called mother for the last seventeen years laughed aloud.

"Oh, my son, do you not see? I have been greatly blessed... I am going Home."

THREE

John's understanding of Mary's statement and its meaning was perfect—but so was his mind's desire to disbelieve her. It wanted to discount her claim, to dispute her surety; but as the room itself exploded with the Light his mother's being could no longer contain, the truth John's heart already knew silenced every argument aborning.

If she so desired, Mary could now choose to remain in this body eternally. If she wanted, she could not only cease to grow older, but could grow ever-younger, until she displayed the age that best reflected the eminence of her fully remembered wholeness. She could choose to walk the earth and heal the many hearts and minds made sore by their forgetfulness of their True Selves, just as Jeshua and the other Masters had.

Or she could do as she meant to: expand until her human form could no longer embody the largeness of her enlightened spirit—she could go "Home." Mary, with her humble, joyful, single-minded focus, had awakened the ability to do what Jeshua promised they all would someday do.

Mary, like her son before her, had become the Christ.

A fleeting sense of loss and the thought, how I shall miss her laughter, skittered through John's mind like a field mouse seeking safety before the hawk finds him, but the urge to dash forth and cry out the news of the fulfillment of Jeshua's promise overwhelmed all hints of sorrow. The knowledge that his mother intended to release her spirit from this plane and be about the One's business in other venues made complete, even comforting, sense.

Because that was so, John was surprised when a question escaped his lips.

"Why, Mother? Why must you forfeit your earthly vessel and leave those who yet need healing behind? Why can you not stay and continue doing our Teacher's work with those who still seek to know the Light you now know?"

The brilliance in the room suddenly dimmed and a shadow crossed Mary's face; she instantly turned her vision inward to face the sudden twinge of uncertainty that tried to gain a foothold and drag her from the knowledge of her wholeness. John made no attempt to speak, but held to his own Center as the conflict between Mary's self and her Self took place, doing his best not to judge what the outcome should be. One moment passed, then another, and yet another.

And then, suddenly, the dimness dissolved.

The room shimmered—blazed—with Mary's Life Force. Everything was haloed with Radiance: the furniture, the lamps, even the walls. John looked at his hands; they too glowed with her Light. Every trace of fear and doubt he'd ever felt dissolved from his being, leaving him engulfed in ringing, joy-filled wonder. Mary smiled brilliantly.

"Thank you," she said simply, and John knew his question had not been his at all. He'd asked it solely so she could face and relinquish the last of her doubts.

They sat in companionable silence and enjoyed the beauty of Mary's Presence. John clearly heard the constant paeans of praise that hid within the usual croaks, squeaks and bellows of the night creatures outside; time, space and the underpinnings of separation now seemed invisible to him. He felt as huge as Creation itself. He wanted to stay that way until he truly became what he now only experienced, would cheerfully have done so...but he knew he could not, not yet. Now he must reluctantly break this silence so the next part of the journey could begin.

"Well then, Mother, when will you do this thing?" John's voice was rusty, like he'd been silent for hours, not a mere fraction of such.

Mary shook herself as if she, too, had to make the effort to speak. "Tonight. At Midnight." Not quite three and a-half hours from now. She stood. "But there is business we must attend to first, so we need to go now. Gather what you will need for your travels, my son...and pack thoroughly. When we leave this place, there will be no returning."

"Where are we going?"

"To Miriam and Martha's house. They expect us—" she smiled suddenly, "—or they should, if Ephraim's young scamp delivered my message to gather the students."

John rose, all hesitation gone. Whatever his earlier reactions, Mary's requests were now no less binding than Jeshua's would have been, and for the same reason.

He entered his room and knelt before a trunk Josef had built several years before Jeshua was competent to work with awl and chisel. Although the wood was not as fine as that of the table, the workman's love for his work showed in every joining of joint to joint, in the perfect mating of every seam. On the lid was a carving of a hawk in flight, surrounded by billowing clouds in an endless sky that made John think of Vashti. Though somewhat worn now, the detailing had at one time been so fine that a certain small boy could've felt the wind rushing over the majestic creature's wings.

Inside the trunk were all of John's robes, including those that would withstand the harshness of winter, and a water jug he'd carved while still working the family's fishing boats, useful now only for its sentimental value. John placed them on the foot of the bed, dug through the other odds and ends that had gathered over the years, and gave a small "hmph" of triumph when he found what he sought.

It was a small, richly detailed wooden fish threaded with a leather string to make a necklace. Jeshua had carved it one night as they sat in the gathering room of a rich merchant, enjoying a welcome respite from the lumpy, insect-besieged fields they'd spent most of their nights in on that expedition. He'd worked as if he couldn't care less how it looked; yet, when he finished, the fish was beautiful and perfect, a laughing, lively thing. He'd handed it to an awed John, the only one of the twelve still awake.

"Keep it, Little Brother," Jeshua had said, playfully ruffling his flustered student's hair when started to hand it back. "Think of it as a gift for one who will be among the greatest of the fishers of men." Then he'd laughingly told the merchant how he'd invited Peter and Andrew to join him. John had kept the fish, of course, as a reminder of his Teacher's and his own purpose.

Recently, and somewhat to his consternation, some of their students had begun wearing cruciforms as a way to declare themselves "Christines". Though most wore the symbol in recognition of what Jeshua had transcended, John noted more than a few —too many—saw it only as a sign of his apparent suffering.

No, he would stay with the sign of the fish—it better suited Jeshua's sense of humor.

John pulled the necklace over his head, quickly rolled the robes and an extra pair of shoes into several cloaks, then wrapped two wool blankets from his sleeping pallet around it all. He rolled the resultant bundle in an oil-soaked piece of wool; one never knew when the weather might turn, and putting on cold, dry clothes, no matter how short a time they might stay that way, was definitely preferable to donning cold, wet ones. He tied a wide leather thong around the whole bundle so he could carry it over his shoulder and reverently lowered the lid of the trunk, knowing he'd never see it again; Mary came from the kitchen and handed him another oilcloth-covered bundle.

"There's bread and dried meat, dried oats, wheat and millet." The grains could be eaten as they were, or with hot water added to make a mash. John wrinkled his nose.

"You know I hate millet," he said plaintively, slinging the second bundle over his shoulder. Mary only smiled archly.

"Faugh. You are an enlightened master—you love everything."

John snorted but made no other comment; Mary, the now ever-present smile touching her lips, looked in appreciative silence around the small abode that had been such a perfect home for so many years. John likewise looked about and remembered all that had passed between these walls. He felt a wave of fondness for the memories, a touch of sadness for leaving, and more than a little uncertainty: Where will this journey take me?

"Mother, we'll need a light to see by," he said as Mary prepared to blow out the last lamp in the house.

"Was there a light in my hand when I came home this evening?" she asked, and John realized, as she doused the lamp and unerringly strode through the blackness to open the door, that she had not, in fact, had either lamp or candle, despite the dark, rocky, pot-holed terrain. "Fear not. I can see the road perfectly well—and so will you."

The lighter dark of the night sky cut a rectangle into the black of the room's walls; John made for it, hoping he hadn't left any chairs out of their usual places.

The moon was a mere sliver, too new to lighten the darkness that enfolded the landscape around them, but Mary seemed more bright and exquisite by the second, almost unbearably so. When she turned, John could only shake his head at her still-expanding brilliance.

"Take my hand."

John did so—and gasped. The night-darkened world gradually brightened until the trees, fields and trail all looked as they would have at midday. But the lack of townsfolk walking the road, the sounds of night creatures continuing to sing , and the black and starry sky that still hung above this Noontide all betrayed to John's suddenly uneasy stomach the strangeness of the scene. Surely, it told him, this was no sight meant for mortal man.

Hand-in-hand, they walked down the trail and away from the house: away from the small, well-tended garden, away from the prosperous little orchard, away from the home that had been the core, the base, of their lifeworks for these seventeen years. John was surprised to discover he didn't have to work very hard at resisting the urge to look back. Yes, he loved all aspects of the work he'd been blessed to do. He loved each and every one of the seekers who had come to them, loved watching students who'd seemed wedded to struggling suddenly brighten with the understanding that they were in truth the One playing at being something other than That. He'd been privileged over and over again to watch as the sleeper began to awaken.

But that chapter of his life was well and truly finished. A new, larger version of the True Life was about to begin.

The journey to and through Bethany was short and silent, for of course, he and Mary walked through a marketplace that at this hour was free of the usual throngs of merchants, hawkers and buyers. The town was not totally quiescent: strains of softly-played music and raucous laughter wafted by as some Important Person entertained guests in the hope of extending his connections.

One of the local priests hurried by, his mouth drawn in disapproving lines as he recognized them, and as always, the greeting brought a sigh to John's lips. While some of the clerics had at least been willing to hear John out, if only for the sake of ridiculing him, most were afraid of—though they would say "angry at"— John and his ilk. Still, and fortunately, most of the violent reaction to Jeshua's teachings that plagued many cities had so far passed Bethany by. John prayed that would continue to be true.

And speaking of ridicule, John thought ruefully, as he and Mary rounded a corner only a short distance from Miriam's house: there on the step of the community washing well, useless legs stretched out before him as he wrapped them in tattered strips of cloth, sat Prochorus.

Prochorus, so far as anyone knew, was originally from Rome. He had been a soldier, proud of the many campaigns he'd been part of in fifteen years of service to the Empire. His first tour of duty in this arid, wild land had been some years ago; John had heard it whispered that he'd been one of the escorts for Jeshua's infamous audience with Pontius Pilatus. But his second tour had brought him in contact with the intractably violent fervor of the Zealots. Their ambush had left two soldiers dead and Prochorus without the use of his legs.

John knew of that particular attack—and like every Jew, knew of its results: the new Governor ordered seventy-five people of all ages pulled off the street and put to the sword. To Rome, such was the worth of three Roman soldiers compared to the lives of the local inhabitants, while to the Zealots, such slaughter was merely the price of war, a new reason to fight the tyrannous Caesars.

The Empire, with all due haste, declared Prochorus a hero for his service to the higher good—then just as quickly forgot him. Or perhaps he refused its help. Whatever the case, he was now naught but another dirt-covered, crippled beggar, as tattered as his old cloth wrappings. Though none knew how he'd come to Bethany or why he remained in Judea at all, he nevertheless now lived here, moving himself about on a low, rickety cart and sleeping wherever he could find shelter when the weather was bad. As often as not, the first merchants to set up in the market found him here at the washing well, petitioning for alms and food.

They rarely gave him either. The beggar's manner was so bitter, his criticisms of their wealth versus his poverty so offensively expressed, that any inclination they felt to help him was, three times out of four, eliminated by his own mouth.

Prochorus's legs were by no means the only things that were crippled.

And for some reason, the man had a particular hatred for all things "Christine". The way he railed at them, using language in the presence of the women that would make a fisherman blush, one would think Jeshua's followers, not the Zealots, had caused his injuries. To Prochorus, the Christines were scarcely worthy of giving alms to such a one as him, beggar though he was. Any offer of aid that came from a follower of Jeshua bar Josef was most likely to result in being spat at, violently cursed, or even threatened with one of the knives he always carried. Returning the Roman's threats did no good; he would only laugh at the local men's anger, offering up such gory descriptions of what he and his weapons were still capable of that the offended ones usually and hastily realized they had urgent business elsewhere.

It never seemed to occur to them that sufficient numbers might conquer the beggar...but then, perhaps they, like John, sensed something in his demeanor that made it clear that, though they might manage to kill the Roman in the end, he would drag as many as he could into Death's Realm with him.

"Who goes there?" Prochorus snapped as John and Mary entered the square, just as if he still guarded the gates of some city. One hand was poised above his legs, wrappings held loosely between his fingers, but the other was suddenly down by his side, no doubt grasping one of his weapons. There was the slightest hint of fear in his gruff voice as he squinted in their direction; John remembered that though he saw only silent, sunless daylight, to Prochorus it was still the dark of night.

John reached for his mother, meaning to save her from the assuredly loathsome greeting the beggar would inflict on them when he discovered their identities, but Mary had her own ideas on the matter. Though she usually ignored Prochorus and his ravings, this night she approached him as one might a long-lost friend. The light around John grew brighter, reminding him that this one could no longer be affected by mere angry words; would never again be thus affected.

"Good Eventide to you, Marcus Prochorus," she said, answering the Roman's challenge just as if he was still a soldier on guard duty instead of a bitter, crippled beggar. "It is Mary, widow of Josef bar Heli, and her son John bar Zebedee." Hands outstretched to show she carried no weapon, she walked to the side of the well where Prochorus sat.

John's brows rose as he followed Mary at a distance, staying within the beggar's sight so as to give no impression of being a threat. No one had ever called the Roman anything but "Prochorus"—that is, when they weren't trading far more colorful names with him. From where he stood, he could see both their faces perfectly; surprisingly, though his mother no longer held his hand, the daylight state remained with him.

If Mary hoped her light, wholeness and gentle approach would cause Prochorus to act in kind, then surely she was disappointed. As always happened when some one of Jeshua's followers had the nerve to speak to him, the beggar's face contorted with anger and he spat on the ground as if he had taken a bite of spoiled meat.

"What do you want, whore? Is not your daytime whining about your bastard son enough? Do you now come to me in the night too, to spout your drivel and ruin my dreams? Away from me! Get away, you shriveled wench, or my knife will send you to be with your so-called savior!"

During his and James's growing up years, it seemed as if, at one time or another, Zebedee, son of Ezekiel, had been boisterously irate at everything. His sons, in turn, learned early to express their own opinions loudly, caustically, and if necessary, with fists. Jeshua was alternately amused and exasperated by the brothers' tendency to defend their views with their father's ire.

Their insistence that he call fire down on Samaria for refusing him and the twelve, however, had been the coup de grâce, one he'd responded to by jokingly (and yet with utter seriousness) giving the brothers a surname perfectly designed to remind them of their folly. James, albeit sheepishly, got both the joke and the point, and took the rebuke with good grace. But John, with all the seriousness of a proudly devout and much younger man, took the name as a personal failure, a sign that he was not disciplined enough to earn his Teacher's full respect. He waged battle against his temper, even once becoming physically ill from stuffing down the urge to beat half-to-death a critic who threw pig's blood at him...but his students now knew him as an at times stern, but gentle man.

This insulting behavior by the tattered, ruined beggar, however, stole the joy of Mary's awakening clean away from John. The gift of daylight faded more and more toward dusk with each insulting word Prochorus spoke—and when he actually called her a "daughter of pigs", it blanked out completely. John stood in Bethany's usual evening darkness, seething with the urge to kick the beggar senseless.

All at once, his mother ceased watching Prochorus (oddly, though it was again dark all around him, he could still see her clearly) and looked at him.

John's face grew hot. Mary smiled, not with understanding, but with the same exasperated amusement Jeshua had evinced during the Samaritan incident. He forced himself to turn his attention toward the utter nonjudgment of the Silence within; soon, the scene once more grew daylight bright. Mary nodded as if satisfied, then delicately crouched before the beggar, close enough to touch him.

"Do I ruin your dreams, Marcus? Really?" she asked. The exultation that was now her entire being carried clearly through her voice, yet her question contained no trace of mockery.

Although John detected no physical movement, it seemed to him that Prochorus shrank from Mary's closeness as if he feared it, but stared into her eyes as if he couldn't look away. He answered her question like a man surprised by his own honesty, when what he'd intended was to lie.

"Yes. You do haunt my dreams," he said, his voice almost a whisper; but it gained in strength and gruffness as he continued to talk. "You people—the nonsense you talk will be the death of all of you! 'Peace is true strength!' Bah! What stupidity! This world is one of war, and the Empire is great because it understands that. Your Zealots understand it, too, even if their cause is hopeless. But you people! You smile and praise that fool who put the lie to his own words—and die like sheep, just like he did! If he was so great as they said, why'd he not bring down Rome with his 'peace'?"

John shook his head. He'd heard this all before, for it seemed to be the only reason Prochorus had to explain his hatred for Jeshua's followers. And yet, as he listened to the angry words this time, he was surprised to also hear an unexpected note in them, one he couldn't quite put his finger on.

If Mary noticed it, however, she didn't say so; instead, she reached for Prochorus's hands.

The beggar started and almost pulled them away, but then seemed to notice his fear. With a determined look that said, "Do your worst", he leaned against the well, feigning nonchalance. Mary turned the grimy hands over and John was again surprised by the Roman's expression: genuine curiosity filled his features. Mary peered at Prochorus's palms for many moments, as if she meant to tell his fortune...but when she finally looked into his eyes, she told not his future, but his past and present.

"The condition of your legs is no hindrance to hand or mind, Marcus. Why then, when you were injured, did you not return to the scribing you still love? Certainly your old master would have you in his house, for he loves you as a son and would gladly train you as a new Master to his apprentices, crippled or not."

Now Prochorus did snatch his hands away, his expression full of shock; he tried to push away from Mary, right through the stones if need be, his face holding something close to panic.

"How do you know that? No one here knows I was a scribe, not even those who were in my own corps!"

Mary merely shrugged, and spoke as if she hadn't even heard his question. "If returning to Rome is more burdensome to your heart than you desire, Marcus, there are many merchants right here in Bethany who would be glad for the services of a good scribe. Would not your wife have wanted you to continue in the work you so loved, rather than mourning her memory by shunning it? Is being a beggar on the streets so much more desirable than your joyful memories of her?"

Prochorus sat slack-jawed before Mary, his vision abruptly turning inward as memory overwhelmed him.

Though he stood off to the side, John saw in his own mind the merry, dark-eyed woman who had been Prochorus's wife, beheld the young scribe's delight at hearing they would soon have their first child. He felt Prochorus's pride in being recommended to Rome as an excellent and conscientious scribe, felt his satisfaction at knowing his good work honored his belovéd master's teaching skills.

He felt all Prochorus's joy crumble away scant months later with the death of his wife and baby from fever...then he was again alone with his own thoughts, watching the beggar's face as it threatened to crumple under a grief too crushing to bear.

John wanted in that moment of seeing what fueled the man's bitterness to walk to Prochorus and lay a comforting hand on his shoulder; wanted to give him the chance to let his sorrow have its voice. But as long habit dictated, Prochorus throttled his grief; as long habit dictated, the beggar let the emotion John was most familiar with take him over.

Prochorus cursed at Mary, screaming with such viciousness that spittle flew from his lips. John was amazed (and he admitted, somewhat impressed) by the variety and combinations of curse words the man knew. If anyone in the neighborhood didn't know the he'd once been a soldier, they were certainly being disabused of their ignorance now.

And they were not happy about it. For a while, the almost eerie stillness of John's sunless, day-bright night was overrun by the usual noises of day—though in considerably cruder form—as doors opened all over the square and shutters were cast aside. People yelled for the beggar to curb his tongue, lest they should come and give him "something to curse about!" But Mary merely stood and watched the former soldier, likewise more impressed than offended by his language. The smile that played about her lips was coupled with a depth of compassion that must have made the angels jealous to see.

At last, Prochorus ran out of curses and slumped sullenly, as if worn out by his tirade. The street once more fell silent. The beggar went back to tending to his leggings, refusing to speak to or even look at Mary. She gazed at him a while longer, then smiled and started toward John, obviously ready to continue on to Miriam's house.

Suddenly, she stopped and spun back.

Mary stared at the top of Prochorus's slightly balding, dirty pate, her face as astonished as if he'd blessed her in Jeshua's name. She closed her eyes, but tears leaked from beneath her lids and coursed down her face; when she opened them again, her visage held such pure, naked wonder that John actually blushed. He felt as if he viewed a thing too intimate to be seen—as if he'd walked in upon his mother and found her naked. He thought of looking away, but could not, in truth, bring himself to do so; the glory that blazed from her mesmerized him.

Beaming at Prochorus with heartbreaking tenderness, Mary oh-so-gently, almost hesitantly, laid her hand atop the beggar's head, ignoring his cursed protests and near-frantic attempts to push it away.

"Marcus Prochorus, all that can be given unto you do I now give in the name of the One and in the name of he who is my Teacher. Be you blessed by those blessings."

She walked to John, holding out her hand as she did so.

"Come, my belovéd son; Miriam and the others await us."

John took Mary's hand and obediently followed, elation expanding out from his heart as he realized what she had done.

Behind him, Prochorus muttered at "the nerve of that whore," then spit on the ground.

FOUR

The *day would come* when, depending on the authority sited, she would be known as the prostitute redeemed by Jeshua's grace, as the adulteress who was on the verge of being stoned to death by her furious accusers. That is, until Jeshua tersely reminded them that only the sinless have the right to punish, and (though the point is often lost) that they are sinless because they choose not to punish. She would be known for washing Jeshua's feet with the most expensive of perfumes, then using her hair to dry those feet in weeping humility. She would go to Jeshua's tomb three days after his crucifixion to find, first to her horror, that his body had been taken, and then to her soaring exultation, that he was the one who had taken it. History would, in times to come, call her "Mary Magdalene."

But in all truth, Jeshua always called her Miriam.

Prochorus's curses died away as the two for whom Night had become Day made their way through first one tight, yet well-kept alleyway, then another. This neighborhood was old, almost as old as Bethany itself. It had once boasted many fine and opulent homes, but the rich had long since abandoned it to build larger, more modern structures worthy of their stature. Most of the magnificent old buildings had fallen to ruin or been cannibalized, and in their place stood the not-quite decrepit homes of those who could still claim enough wealth to avoid being called paupers.

Such neighborhoods were not always kept this clean, for this part of town was home to many for whom cleanliness could not be the first consideration; yet the people here took great pride in being good stewards to their surroundings, for many of them spent their evenings at Martha and Miriam's, learning to walk the quiet way of the Practice.

John walked alongside Mary as they rounded several more corners, awash in an ever-changing flow of thoughts and feelings. The honor of witnessing her tête-à-tête with Prochorus still filled him with wonder so strong he could taste it like a sweet and savory portion that satisfied both heart and soul.

A wave of anger fleetingly passed through his Silence: how could Mary be so selfish as to leave them now? Could she not see the value of staying with them at least a little while longer? Fear too, still made its presence known, and uncertainty. True, he had no doubt he'd done what Jeshua wanted him to do these last several years, but would he succeed in following his Teacher's will now?

John's thoughts came to a standstill as they came upon a sudden opening in the maze of jammed little house fronts: an oasis of floral and arboreal beauty greeted them, a true miracle in this neighborhood. Many of the old homes had fallen to ruin, yes; but some had found owners who willingly preserved and appreciated the beauty so carelessly left behind. Miriam's house was such a place.

Of course, the house was not Miriam's at all, for women had no right to own property in Judea if any adult male relative still lived. Rather, it belonged to her elder brother Lazarus, the same Lazarus Jeshua had raised from the dead after four days. Lazarus was now a successful vintner who lived outside the city, but he and his wife, Eliora, often came to keep company with those who followed Jeshua's Way. Lazarus fell in love with, bought and renovated the house and its gardens, then gave it over to his sisters' use. Martha, widowed these last eight years, also lived there; she and the youngest of her three sons occupied the west wing.

Miriam waited for John and Mary in the garden, her greeting smile rivaling the sun that now lay resting contentedly in the universe's arms. Even after most of twenty years, John's breath caught at the sight of her: though autumn approached for both the season and Miriam, her burnished chestnut hair still blazed copper with the highlights that came of being often outdoors and her gold-flecked brown eyes glowed. Her nose was a nose of the Levant, yet so softened in its curve that it enhanced the fullness of her lips and the firmness of her slightly clefted chin. She was tall for a woman, standing only half a head shorter than Jeshua had and a few inches shorter than John; her full, statuesque figure well-matched the beauty of her face. Though she was several years older than John, she, like Mary, carried herself like one years younger. By any stand-ard—be it Roman, Greek or Syrian—Miriam of Midjel was a devastatingly lovely woman.

Even more wondrous than Miriam's physical beauty, however, was the hard-earned dignity that suffused her being. Her stateliness made one want to pay her the homage one might a visiting queen. Yet along with that dignity came a level of...earthi-ness...she had never lost, even in all her years of plunging into the heart of the One. Miriam was a wholly paradoxical combination of ethereal, stained-glass brilliance—and robust, womanly sensuality; if John had fallen fully and completely in love with Mary on first sight, he had fallen fully and completely in lust with Miriam.

Those feelings cost him dearly in those early days, for he was sure he should be far more virtuous than his burning senses revealed him to be. After all, one who had been redeemed as Miriam had, from what she had, should not be subjected to the panting deliberations of a seventeen year-old compatriot. Worse, his sense of closeness to his Teacher suffered, for he was convinced Jeshua would never countenance such a fail-ure. Certainly, no other teacher would. Yet struggle as he might, John couldn't force his scandalous thoughts about Miriam out of his mind or loins. Finally, he'd approached Judas for advice, too ashamed to talk to the others and too afraid to say anything to Jeshua.

Judas snorted at John's embarrassment. "Well of course you're attracted to her, lad; look at her! What man living would *not* be attracted to Miriam? All of us are, though none save maybe Matthew would dare say so. Why, I'd not be surprised if even Jeshua has had his temptations."

John started to protest such a ridiculous notion, but Judas waved his objections aside, a man talking to an inexperienced boy. "You mark my words, lad. If they could talk Jeshua into it, those pious jackasses—our brothers—would evict Miriam from our company faster than a blink. They take umbrage at her presence among us, and not solely because a woman has no place in such work. They wish Miriam gone because of their mortification at their bodies' reactions to her. But I say again, you'd have to be dead—or an angel—not to want her. 'Tis as natural as being man born of woman.

"So, then, Little Brother," he said, raising a brow and ruffling John's hair in imitation of Jeshua, "you can either drive yourself mad worrying about your natural response to such beauty..." he fell back into his own voice's cadence, "...or you can enjoy the incred-ible gift God so graciously puts before your daily sight. I know which *I* choose to do."

Judas paused thoughtfully. "And if being in Miriam's presence becomes too great a burden, lad, then go and tell her what you feel. She'll not think your dilemma particu-larly offensive, I'll wager. She is by no means oblivious to her effect on men."

John's eyes widened and he blushed scarlet. "You mean, ask Miriam to *be* with me?"

"No, dolt," the older man said, giving him a don't-be-an-ass-clout. "While she might not to laugh in your face, she would surely refuse you, which would be her right. I meant that speaking your true feelings to the one you feel towards sometimes gives relief where thinking on it and talking to others cannot. You have seen how Jeshua does it, John. He says what needs saying in whatever way it comes to do so—and let the world be damned if it does not like it. Which the priests most assuredly do not. Jeshua holds nothing of his feelings back if they need be known, even if the world thinks him possessed of devils. Do you think, then, he would ask us to stifle ours? Never."

John did eventually talk to Miriam, stammering out his dilemma with ears so hot he feared his hair might catch fire. He looked at his feet the whole time, terrified she would laugh at him and even more afraid she would tell Jeshua. She did not laugh, but gravely thanked John for his honesty and for thinking her enough of a comrade to be worthy of such. And if she did later speak to Jeshua, well, he never saw fit to mention it. The desires had not completely gone away, but a lot of the guilt around them had, and that made them profoundly easier to deal with.

John sighed. Despite what history would say—was saying—he still sometimes missed Judas and his earthy honesty; in some ways, he and Miriam had been a great deal alike. And the body, he considered wryly, still has its own ideas about what is right and proper. Even now, as she hurried around the small pond and, twinkling at his discomfort, gave him a quick but thorough hug, John could not but feel a twinge of purely physical desire for Miriam.

Turning from John, Miriam took Mary's already extended hands in her own. They did not speak, but merely stared into each other's eyes for an eternal moment with identical, small smiles—then suddenly fell giggling into each other's arms with a delight so immense it was palpable. Not for the first time, John felt he beheld one soul that inhabited two bodies, one that took boundless joy in even this paltry version of reunification.

"Oh." Miriam stood absolutely still, her eyes growing wide, and John knew she now surveyed the strange day-lit night just as he and Mary did. She held Mary at arms' length. "Well! Gili said you had news, but—oh! This is wonderful! What Jeshua must think! What joy there must be among the Wise Ones this day!"

She hugged Mary even more tightly, her laugh ringing into the garden's brilliant night, then tugged at her hand like a small child going to market to receive her first artisan-made birthday present. "Come inside; the others are waiting."

They started toward the house, and since he was still holding Mary's other hand, John followed along contentedly, part of a jubilant human daisy chain.

The three of them entered into the candlelit dimness of Martha and Miriam's spacious, high-ceilinged community room. It was full of people, including men and women of several nationalities and even children. Everyone sat or lay with their eyes closed, experiencing the profound inner quiet that came of doing the Practice. Some even snored lightly—or not so lightly: Hosea was in the corner, mouth open, his intermittent snorts, honks and rumbles issuing forth from the heart of the One with great enthusiasm.

"*Jeshua, amen.*"

John spoke quietly, but his voice nonetheless echoed through the large room. Everyone immediately began to stir, even Hosea, who'd seemed so deeply asleep. Eyes popped open, yawns sighed, bodies stretched luxuriantly. Smiles and looks of surprise wreathed many faces as they caught sight of or felt the Life force radiating from Mary. Martha, who'd entered from the kitchen as the three came in the door, gave quick hugs all around, her calm face showing surprise and an extra dollop of her usual exultation only when she hugged Mary. She had long since chosen to take the "best part", to discover the Self Jeshua had once teased her about forsaking for the sake of obsessively making her outer surroundings acceptable. Martha now glowed with the joy of letting the One in her heart decide when things needed doing.

Everyone stood and silently greeted John, Martha, Mary and Miriam with hands pressed together at chest height, acknowledging both of the arrival of their Teachers and the unbounded One they represented. The others deferred to Mary, who returned the students' gesture then offered the same to her three co-teachers. The four took chairs at the head of the room and everyone else ended the greeting, situating themselves on pillows, chairs, the floor, or along the walls. John smiled at the new students' attempts to discover the source of the strange brightness that filled the room.

For a long time, Mary simply sat and gripped her chair's arms as if she feared she'd float out of it if she did not. Then again, perhaps she might, John realized. Jeshua could make his body lighter than air—or at least lighter than water; perhaps the same was now true for Mary. His mother gazed at each of the sixty or so faces she'd grown to know so well and love so much as if memorizing them. They, in turn, looked eagerly, joyously, tearfully or even fearfully back, wondering why a special meeting had been called. Her eyes locked on one face in particular.

"Hosea. Why are you crying?"

As was the custom, the man she spoke to stood. The large, squarely-built laborer, who, among other things, traveled to farmers' fields to put seeds in the soil in the spring and pull their fruits from the ground in the fall, rubbed work-worn hands across his tear-streaked face, doing his best—and failing miserably—to control his heaving chest. He looked more like a child lost than a man full grown as he stood and sobbed for several moments, too overcome to speak, but finally, he looked up, his eyes full with pleading.

"Rabbi," he said, using the honorific he would never dare speak to any woman in public, lest he be accused of heresy and she convicted out of his mouth, "I know what you mean to do, I know. Why must you leave us? Why?"

Though Hosea's understanding was great—he was, in fact, one of their most focused students—he simply could not fathom Mary's decision to remove herself from their company. He had witnessed the horror of Jeshua's crucifixion; to lose another teacher seemed more than his heart could bear.

Nor was he alone: many of the advanced students burst into tears as they caught Hosea's meaning, and fully half the people in the room (those who didn't look hopelessly confused) held looks of fear or grief or even anger. Cries of "What do you mean?" and "What has happened?" threatened to swallow the calm that had filled the space only moments before; John felt sure when they heard *two* of their teachers were leaving, some would depart this night's meeting and never return, certain they were being abandoned.

Mary seemed not to notice the turmoil, but motioned Hosea closer, her eyes on him alone. He stumbled blindly forward, falling to his knees as he reached her. Sobbing once more, the burly man grabbed her hand and held it to his cheek as if he needed proof she was still a being incarnate; Mary ran her fingers lightly through his curly, silvering hair and leaned her forehead against his, her quiet voice touching him alone. Then she raised her head and smiled as if every person before her was her most belovéd.

"Listen to me. Listen, and I will tell a story from days more ancient than you can imagine, from the time when days where still a thing most new to the universe."

The room immediately fell silent, bathed in the glow of Mary's peace. People shifted in their seats or on the floor to get more comfortable, and the children eagerly came forward and sat as close as they could get. Mary's stare grew intense as the need for History to speak through her swallowed up her natural softness; many in the room gasped when her voice again split the silence.

"The other teachers and I have spoken before of the fact that Earth is not the only, nor even the first, of humankind's homes. We have said that the stories of Adam and Eva, though mythical, are also true. Now I will tell a story from the beginning of humanity's existence. It is not a factual story, either...but make no mistake, it too, is True.

"Not long after humankind made its home in the universes that make up this Golden Sphere, some of the souls who had chosen to embody in gross physical form became curious. What, they wondered, would happen if humans gave up the memory of being one with the One? What would happen if there was an empty place in the heart where God was meant to be?

"Their answer came quickly. The appearance of emptiness, the appearance that one could be separate from the Fullness of God—could be god without God—quickly took on a life of its own. As it grew within individuals' hearts, everyone within that Sphere began to fight. They fought with themselves, they fought with each other, they fought with the earth and Heaven. Soon, they came to believe that the war between wholeness and emptiness, between good and evil, was real and necessary.

"The angelic ones became concerned. If something was not done, every soul in this now tainted universe would be swallowed up by the belief in emptiness. Indeed, their forgetfulness might even contaminate the higher worlds and thus make devils of angels. To prevent that outcome, they asked the One to destroy this Sphere of Existence.

"This the One refused to do, for It knew the harm that concerned those in the higher worlds was impossible. After all, what can contaminate the One if there is only the One?" Mary smiled at the children, who laughed at the obvious sense of her words. "...And yet, the One saw the necessity for some kind of intervention, for though they did not realize it, the angels' fear of corruption had created it. They had already come to believe that Perfection could go wrong, that there could be war between the eternal and the impermanent. And so there soon was war...but that is a story for another day.

"The One, as is the One's way, instantly cognized a solution to the problem: It would neither destroy the lost ones nor interfere with their free will by forcing Its Self upon them. No, instead the One would find a way to reawaken the hearts of those who had forgotten themselves so they would once more realize they were only One.

"Having decided that, the One went to Immortal Beingness to see how such a thing might be accomplished.

"'It will not be accomplished Self of my Self,' Immortal Beingness answered tersely, for It found the notion of trying to convince the contaminated beings to reaccept their Oneness ridiculous. "Simply destroy the Sphere and let us create it anew. None will be lost, after all, for they are our Self.'

"The One, however, remained unwilling to destroy our universe. "'I sense in this an opportunity, Self of my Self, something that could change the very nature of how we manifest. I would see that opportunity come to fruition, if it is possible. Indeed, I would do what I can to make it possible.'

"'I see. And what would you have me do?' Immortal Beingness asked as if it already knew It would not like the answer. And It was correct; It did not.

"'You must create a physical body for me so that I may enter into that Sphere and reawaken the forgetful ones' memories of the truth.'

"The One and Immortal Beingness discussed—nay, argued—the matter for eons, Immortal Beingness insisting that it could not be done, the One arguing that it must be possible, 'for we are Omnipotent. We can do everything.'

"Immortal Beingness would have thrown up Its hands and shook Its head had It had them. As it was, It simply mumbled away, saying unto the One, 'I will see what I can do, Self of my Self. But we have yet to successfully translate the Fullness of Being into the physical in any of the golden spheres. The aspect of you that embodies—especially in that universe—may have no more understanding of what it is than the beings who are already there. You could well fail in your mission before it even begins.'

"The One was not daunted, but only answered, 'I know you will succeed, Self of my Self. This thing is Destined.'

"Immortal Beingness worked long on the problem of creating a perfect vessel for the Fullness of the One to embody in—though of course, in Heaven, no time passed at all. Finally, all was ready.

"'The body rests in Para, the Source Universe of all our Golden Spheres. Your essence should be able to enter that pure place without being corrupted. And if you do not remember who Are (as I expect), Divine Mother will at least be there to help you, so that your mission may yet be accomplished.'

"The One nodded Its acknowledgement, but Immortal Beingness looked unhappy. 'You will really do this thing?' It asked at last.

"'I am not leaving here, you know," the One answered exasperatedly. 'I cannot leave, I am Everywhere. The outcome of this task is assured, Self of my Self. What then, is the source of your reluctance?'

"Immortal Beingness looked away. 'Perhaps that Sphere's taint has reached here, for I feel a dimness about this task I have never felt with any other. I have looked into that Golden Sphere, and truly, it is tarnished. There are endings there, and suffering in those endings, because of their belief in emptiness and separateness.

"'Listen to me, Self of my Self: if things go as they should, you will be able to enter the hearts of those ones and heal them from Para. But if they do not go as they should, *let the sphere go.* Destroy it. Make no attempt to enter any lower spheres of existence as your Self...and certainly do not enter that one. We simply cannot guarantee the strange malady affecting it will not swallow up your awareness of who you are. Granted, the One cannot be harmed...yet there is something too strange about that place. You must not take the risk, Self of my Self.'

"The One considered Immortal Beingness with a serious mien, for Its light *was* dimmed from Its usual splendor; It almost seemed as worried as the angels. 'Very well, Friend Self; I will do as you ask and not leave Para. I will make the attempt to cure that Golden Sphere only from its confines, and let it teach Us what it may from there.'"

Mary stopped talking to sip at a cup of water Miriam gave her. Someone coughed, but that was the only sound to be heard in the large room as they waited for her to continue.

"The One did arrive in Para with Its essence intact, but as Immortal Beingness predicted, It had no memory of who It was, nor of Its reason for being there. Though Its perfectly formed, magnificent body was that of a fully grown man's, the One's knowledge of that around him was wholly lacking. He stood and looked around in wonder, naked and beautiful in the midst of Para's shining beauty, and was completely unaware of being either one with or a thing apart from what he saw.

"'Greetings, Aleph, and welcome.'

"The Voice spoke in a tone that was like the ringing of a million beautiful chimes singing many different, yet harmonious hymns. Aleph, which means 'The First,' and was the One's Name in this place, turned to find Divine Mother standing before him, but he did not know it was her. He pointed at a flower.

"'What is that?' he asked, his innocence as pure as that of a newly-born babe.

"Divine Mother patiently and lovingly answered that question and every other as Aleph moved through all the stages of becoming human, as he asked, each in their turn, 'Why?' and 'How?' and 'What is its Purpose?' Thus did Aleph go from being completely unaware of knowing anything of physical existence to knowing himself to be a being both separate and eternally One, the Master of Para and all universes along with Divine Mother.

"He roamed the expanse of his domain, first with Divine Mother at his side, then with just her presence beside him, always learning, always awakening to more of his power. His sojourns grew ever longer and took him ever farther from the place of his first arrival, but he always returned to share with Divine Mother what he found and sometimes, still, to ask his questions.

"Then the day came when Aleph went out from the Center place, out from the Great Hall of Music where the First Song and all the lesser Songs of Creation have their being, and he did not return.

"Divine Mother went out from that place also, to all the places she knew to be his favorites: to the Eternal Mountain of Light and the Sacred Grove; to the Boundless Ocean of Milk where the Dream of Creation is forever dreamed, and to the Splendorous Garden of Peace. Aleph was in none of them.

"At last, Divine Mother came to the western edge of Para, to the Cliff of the Universes. This was the place where she could see all humanity's deeds acted out in every eon, a place Aleph had never cared to visit. Yet, when Divine Mother climbed to the grand plateau that was The Cliff, there he sat. Naked, golden and beautiful, he stared out at the scenes of humanity being human; Divine Mother walked to Aleph's side, gracefully settled beside him and took his hand. He did not look at her, but continued to stare outward.

"'I have to go there,' he said at last.

"'I know.'

"He turned to her, his eyes serious. 'The Spark of my being is planted, but things have gone beyond what a mere and distant spark can do. I promised Immortal Beingness I would not enter that Golden Sphere, but I must go among them to be the Flame that brings the Spark back to full life.'

"Divine Mother smiled serenely. 'I knew that, too.'

"They stood and faced each other, and she laid her hand on his heart. 'Remember who you Are,' she said, 'and teach them of me. That will awaken the Spark most quickly.'

"'I will remember,' Aleph answered gravely, not knowing what Divine Mother knew: that he would, in fact, choose to forget his Self and walk the same paths human-ity walked so that his compassion for them, and thus his ability to awaken their hearts, would be greater. She looked out at the multifarious scenes before them.

"'I will help you thus in this task, Aleph: when the time to go forth into each Earth is at hand, I will always go before you. I will bring your physical existence into which-ever Earth you choose through the Pure Memory that is my Body...or from the Seed that makes fertile that existence, for not always will I be only "mother". More, I will stay after you go from each of those Earths, to see that the Flame you light has a chance to catch.'

"Aleph stared at Divine Mother, dumbstruck. Her choice would vitally affect how quickly this Golden Sphere reawakened, but she had no obligation whatever to offer such a gift. Love, he knew, and love alone, motivated her decision.

"'Thank you,' was all he could think to say, but he raised Divine Mother's hands to his chin, then bent his forehead and touched it lightly to her fingers, as if to say 'always will I surrender to the fullness of your wisdom'. Divine Mother nodded, but as she once more turned her vision outward to stare off into her own future, a cloud formed behind the joy that always shone in her eyes.

"'The day will come when I will forget who I Am as I join in this dance to reawaken the souls in that Golden Sphere, Aleph. When I will seem to be many instead of One. Pro-mise to remember who I Am, so that all of my Self will be able to again unite. Promise me you will not forget.'

"'I will remember. I promise,' Aleph nodded, his heart almost too full to speak.

"Para's Sun dimmed next to the brilliance of Divine Mother's smile. She pulled Aleph to her and kissed him tenderly, then kissed her finger and touched it to the place between his eyebrows.

"'Go then, belovéd One. Be that Flame to light your Sparks. Go safely and be well...'

"...And so it is," Mary said, using the ritual words to bring the crowd of enthralled students back to the present moment. "So it is that Divine Mother always precedes the One into every Earth; so it is that She always follows the One from it. As I now do. The Flame is lit, my own, and now burns brightly to light all this earth. My work here is done."

Mary turned toward John and lovingly caressed his brow, just as Divine Mother had done with Aleph. She grinned at Martha and Miriam, then winked at Lazarus, who had come to the front of the room as the story ended. She squeezed their hands and smiled teasingly at their tear-stained faces, then looked down at Hosea, who'd sat at her feet through the whole of her story. Though tears still streamed down his face, he nodded.

"Hosea, dearest one, here is my promise: soon you will find your fear of losing your Way was not warranted. Indeed, you will soon find yourself telling others what I have so often told all of you: 'I am but a guide, not a Teacher, though 'Teacher' you may call me if it pleases you.'"

Hosea's eyes went round at the implication in Mary's words, but though he shook his head in disbelief, his eyes shone.

Mary looked back at John but grabbed Miriam's hand. "Do what Miriam tells you," she said, fully his mother in that moment. "She will guide you in what will come next better than any other can." John's glance briefly flicked to Miriam's surprised expres-sion as Mary continued to speak. "And thank you, my most belovéd Son, for choosing to be my son for this time. Know that your way will be bright and the Flame will light many, many more Sparks because of what you do. Blesséd art thou, most holy one."

As one, John, Miriam, Martha and Lazarus paid homage to Mary: kneeling, they brought their foreheads fully to the floor, arms stretched out before them, palms laid flat. When he came out of the bow, John's face was soaked with tears, his throat too tight for him to more than whisper the "I love you, Mother," that was on his lips. Mary heard it, however, and again laid her hand on his face.

She looked joyously out at the murmuring, sniffling, awed crowd as her body transformed into Light before them; soon, her boundless Luminescence filled, yet extended endlessly beyond, the confines of the room, its radiant Light so tinglingly intense that it almost made one squint.

Almost. In truth, Mary's sudden brilliance fed the eyes, not hurt them.

In moments, no human figure at all remained; the sun-bright sphere that had been Mary of Josef bar Heli's House rose from its chair and floated to the ceiling, creating sharp, shadowless clarity in every nook of the room and on every face in the crowd.

"Remember who you Are, belovéd ones. Remember and become Me once again," Mary said, and her voice was the voice of the Music of Creation.

"Remember: I love you always."

FIVE

All the students save Hosea and his wife Ada had finally departed, leaving Martha and Miriam's common room quiet, but by no means empty, these two-and-a-half hours after Mary's Ascension. Those who were left, John and Miriam, Martha, Lazarus and Elior, Hosea and Ada, sat at the dining table, sipping one of the excellent wines from Lazarus's vineyards and basking in the residual glow of Mary's realization. Each was lost in his or her own contemplations, yet none of them was ready to leave behind the camaraderie created by what they'd witnessed.

John sipped at his wine and marveled at the excellence of the vintage. He marveled, too, at the fact that Lazarus was the sponsor of such. When the companions first met him, Lazarus had been a successful young merchant. Though amiable, he'd been even more earnestly pious than John, serious to the point of asceticism. Now he was one of the best vintners in Judea, with wines known to please even the prickly Roman palate.

Ah, the paths Jeshua's presence had changed!

Lazarus and some of the others finally broke the silence and began discussing the night's events. John pretended to listen, just as he had before the students finally left to break the quiet of the neighborhood's night with their speculations on what it all meant, but his thoughts actually ranged far from the discussion at hand.

I should be happy, even overjoyed. Why then, do I feel such a sense of dread?

John turned his attention inward to seek the source of his distress, but each time he felt close to catching the answer, it slipped away like a small lizard avoiding a young boy's clutches.

He certainly couldn't attribute this feeling to Mary's Ascension. When he thought of that still-fresh event, his heart expanded so much that he felt the need to take hold of something heavy, lest he should float into the ethers as she had. Nor could he sense any great trepidation about his upcoming journey. Confusion about how he was to find the hallowed Vashti he had in abundance, but fear of seeking it, or the fear he would fail to find it, was blessedly absent from his thoughts...at least for this moment.

He turned toward the students' reactions to Mary's Ascension. Most of them couldn't stop talking about how it changed everything, how they now wanted to know the One above all else. Some, however, had slipped quietly into the early morning darkness with thoughtful frowns etched on their faces. John suspected any sleep they got would be fitful at best, full of speculations on how something so "impossible" could have happened. And yet others bore looks of dismay that told John they'd need time and patience to take in what they'd witnessed. That is, if they chose to continue with the Practice at all.

He tasted that awareness, but knew such possible losses were not the cause of his unease. He would regret losing otherwise promising students, yes, but in the end that was a matter for them and the One to decide.

No, whatever the source of this feeling of—well, doom—it could not be laid at the door of recent events or decisions.

Like John, Miriam appeared to listen to what the others had to say, but a cloud lurked beneath her seemingly attentive stare just as it did his. Her mind was also on something besides the current conversation. Every so often, she would catch his eye, then quickly look away as if she saw something she did not want to see; still, it took John a moment to identify what was so unusual about her expression.

Why, she is as discomfited as I am, he thought, and the realization surprised him, for he literally hadn't seen such a look on Miriam's face in years.

John was suddenly tempted to call her unease to the others' attention, to badger her into revealing what was wrong, thus forcing the shadow to move and restore her usual equanimity...but he could hardly fault Miriam for her disquiet when he felt the same way.

"Do you know where you will go, Rabbi?"

John came out of his reverie and stood with everyone else to give hugs and, in his case, say final goodbyes, to Ada and Hosea. "I know I shall go to Greece, Ada. Mary wished me to do so, and for obvious reasons I shall fulfill that request. After that, however...well, the One alone knows what is next for me." He looked toward Miriam, but she still would not meet his eye. In fact, she seemed even more nervous than before.

"You will travel alone?" Hosea asked.

"Yes."

"Oh."

The burly laborer hesitated for a moment, looking as if he might burst into tears for the second time that night, then suddenly grabbed John up in a bear hug that would have cracked ribs in a less sturdy man. John was deeply touched and a bit amused by his student's unabashed display of affection. Though his essential kindness fairly stuck out on him in lumps, Hosea usually refrained from such public demonstrations, as any proper Judean man should.

"Go safely then, Teacher," the big man said, his voice cracking. John stepped back from the embrace and surreptitiously gasped for breath while Ada, too, gave him a good hard hug, with sniffles and tears into the bargain. He couldn't help but think, still amused, that it was a good thing she was such a small woman; his ribs felt well-bruised.

The two bid the others Good Eventide and stepped out into the night, talking quietly; Lazarus yawned hugely and turned to the elder of his two sisters.

"Will Martha need help cleaning up?" he asked with more than a bit of teasing in his expression. She was still well known for her hatred of a messy room.

"No," she said drolly. "Martha is going to leave the cleaning to the morrow...and she is going to sleep in, to boot."

"Decadent woman," Lazarus said in mock dismay.

"Why, thank you, brother. It seems I've grown after all." Martha gave a slight bow of her head, then twitched her nose at him and grinned.

"If you can sleep, more praise to you," Elior said in her straightforward way, "for I more intend trying to sleep than actually doing so...this has been a night to remember." John and Martha could only agree as Lazarus nodded and took his wife's hand.

"We too, then, shall take our leave of you all," he said. "I've a very full day ahead of me and unfortunately cannot sleep in as my dear sister means to. Tomorrow's business with the Tyrian buyers cannot be left to Saul, excellent foreman though he is." He hugged his sisters and was turning to say goodbye to John when Miriam spoke.

"Lazarus, Elior, wait... Please, do not go yet."

The four of them stared with raised eyebrows. Miriam stood, eyes wide in her face, her agitation so great that she actually wrung her hands together. She looked for all the world as if she might burst into tears—that is, if she didn't dash from the room first.

"Jeshua's Heart, Miriam! What is the matter?" Martha went to her sister's side and put an arm around her shoulders. "Blessed be, child, you are shaking! Come, sit here at the table and tell us what is wrong." She tried to lead Miriam to the closest chair.

"No!" Miriam said sharply, throwing off Martha's embrace and stepping away.

She took a breath and tried to bring herself back to center—though not with complete success. Her panic lessened, true, but it still seemed to sit just below the surface, ready to flare again at the slightest provocation. Though she'd been unable to hold his eyes earlier, Miriam now stared at John as if an invisible rope connected them.

"There is a thing I must do that I have no wish to do. I...need you, Elior and Lazarus, to stay. I need you to be with us through this thing...else I fear I will not do it."

A chill skittered over John's skin, then crawled under it to grab and constrict his heart. He suddenly knew the dread he'd felt all evening was about to make far more sense than he wanted it to. Miriam again spoke.

"I will need a shaving stone, and also a cutting blade."

"There is still a stone in Aaron's room," Martha said, speaking of her eldest son, who was a seaman for Young Joseph, son of the Arimathean. As she bustled away, she instructed Lazarus to get the blade she kept in the kitchen, while Elior, who knew Martha's house as well as she knew her own, went with him to fill a bowl with water. Only when the two of them were alone did Miriam's eyes again waver from John's and seek her tightly clasped hands. He wanted badly to reach out to this one who'd been so much a friend and partner over these seventeen years, wanted to lay a comforting hand on her tensely-held ones and tell her all would be well.

But—though it shamed him to admit it—he was suddenly afraid to do so.

Lazarus returned with the blade; Elior and Martha were not far behind with shaving stone, water and soap. Miriam bowed her head and turned her vision inward, using the Practice as Jeshua had taught them; John clearly felt the One's Stillness enter her being and tie the pieces of her splintered composure together, saw all traces of agitation depart from her face. The strong, sure woman he'd trusted for years had returned...

...But he was the one who felt like bolting now.

Miriam once more looked at him, but as she spoke, John experienced the eerie impression he listened not to her, but Mary. Or, more accurately, it was as if both women now shared one body, just as he'd often sensed their two bodies shared one soul.

"John, the journey you go forth on will be a long one, one with trials to overcome. Mostly, these will be small things, no matter what their appearance. Yet, though the purity of your heart is as great as any who ever walked with Jeshua on this or any earth, there are still some aspects of your humanity you refuse to accept as perfect.

"If you allow your heart to be distracted by these few things, by the conflict between what is right to you and what is not, you will fail in your mission, despite Jeshua's reassurances that you cannot. More, you will do so by your own choice. I can do nothing to help with the last of these challenges, dear one, but with the first of them, I must."

Miriam turned to Martha. "Sister, please shave off John's beard and cut his hair to here," she said, indicating the nape of John's neck.

If Martha was dismayed by the order, she didn't show it; only nodded as Lazarus pulled a chair from the table for John to sit on. Miriam turned away, sat at the table and again closed her eyes, disappearing into the Silence even as It responded to her by embracing the whole room, a Lover returning to Its Belovéd.

It was not a long business for Martha to do as instructed; a widow with three sons quickly learns to handle the squirminess of small (and later, not so small), impatient, almost-cooperative boys. Indeed, it was often her wont to give Jeshua's beard a tidying trim when she could get him to sit still.

"Well enough to let your hair grow until it must be carried like a train behind you, Jeshua," she would say, her awe momentarily waylaid by her womanly sensibilities. "Still, you need not look like an utter vagabond when you go before the people."

Jeshua always meekly and amusedly submitted to her ministrations.

The room's cool air hit John's face as Martha shaved off the last of his once-luxuriant, hard-earned whiskers; he wiped his now clean chin with the wet towel Elior offered and wondered what he must look like. He knew how he felt—like the shy, pious (if quick to anger) seventeen year-old who, with all the pride of a pup allowed to run with the dogs, had dropped his set future to follow Jeshua, James, Peter and the others.

Just as Martha finished, and before Lazarus could say "*Jeshua, amen*" to bring her out of the Stillness, Miriam's eyes snapped open. She approached to within a few feet of John, her look inscrutable. The others waited, ready to do whatever she asked.

"Stand," she said.

John did so—too quickly it seemed, for he suddenly felt dizzy. Then he blinked in bewilderment. The dizziness must be interfering with his vision: though he stood to his full height, he looked slightly *up* at Miriam.

He looked down to get his bearings and his breath caught in shock: his body possessed a slender gawkiness it hadn't had in years. He didn't simply feel seventeen; he *was* seventeen years old again!

John's heart beat thunderously as bewilderment escalated into fear. What in Jeshua's Name was going on? He looked up, sure his eyes must be wild with distress, then choked back a cry; no longer was Miriam the still-beautiful but older woman he knew.

No, she was Mary of Magdala, the whore who'd been tended by servants and showered with the licentious attentions of any man who could pay, be they simple laborers or Roman generals. Her face was painted in the fashion of the Roman ladies of Court, and the reek of her was that of expensive perfume, womanly musk and the sweat of those she'd coupled with. The smile she wore as she posed before the pious boy John had suddenly, impossibly become was an invitation, a promise—and the sure death of his soul.

Only once had John felt such panic that his legs carried him away without his mind's volition. *He* would gladly have stayed by his Teacher's side in Gethsemane to face death by sword or cross, but his body's terror had taken him on a three mile run that had left him, panting and shivering, in a distant wheat field. He felt that same panic now as he faced this Miriam who'd he'd seen and desired in his youthful fantasies, the one he'd repeatedly taken against all honor, and against all his vows to be as pure as he thought Jeshua would demand.

"No. Do not touch me," John said, his voice cracking with fear and regained youthfulness. He hastily staggered back and only kept from falling over his chair because Lazarus's steadying hands held him up. He was vaguely aware of Elior and Martha's looks of confusion, yet this younger self knew with utter certainty if this too-real apparition touched him, all he'd gained over the years would be as lost as he'd feared his life had been at Gethsemane.

Lazarus still held him. In fact, Lazarus would not let him go. As a young man, the vintner had been not just slender, but skinny, able to amaze even Jeshua with his gustatory feats. Though he was by no means oversized now, he had filled out in his middle age. He now carried a light, softish covering of fat—stretched over sword-hard muscles that the calm part of John knew he had no chance of besting.

That did not stop his panicked, youthful self from trying, however. John twisted frantically in the "older" man's arms and managed to free his shoulders, only to have Lazarus grab him back and wrap them around his whole upper body.

"What is wrong with him?" John heard him say between grunts, but it sounded as if he spoke from a distance.

"Just hold him as still as you can," Miriam answered, and though she stood directly before him, her voice also seemed muffled.

John's terror escaped through his lips as a cry, but the moment her too-soft hands touched his face, all his struggling stopped. The painted, perfumed Miriam smiled her victory, slowly bent her face to his...and kissed him squarely on the mouth.

Rarely was John disturbed by the images and feelings that flowed through as he lived his life and did the Practice; indeed, it had been years since he'd felt any need to seek the meaning behind any seemingly negative movement he experienced while exploring the realms within. The intensity of what he encountered now, though, flayed his dearly-held sense of solidity. As the heat of Miriam's kiss overtook his seventeen year-old body, he became aware of—and his loins responded to—every lustful thought and fantasy he'd ever had of her or any other woman. Suddenly, that which John had never wanted seen or even hinted at was exposed to the sight of Self and God...

...And not just to God, for the whore had vanished. The Miriam of his adulthood was suddenly there, watching his thoughts and observing his reactions. Heat again engulfed John's body, but this time it belonged to shame and mortification. This was a place he must not go...

No, John, Miriam's thoughts traced patiently through his mind, *you've hidden this in the shadows of your shame long enough. Let it at last be* seen.

The fantasies passed through more and more quickly, yet remained utterly clear to John's view. They featured women of every kind, ones he'd known for years and others he'd but met in passing...but mostly they were about Miriam. Each one grew ever more prurient, ever more violent and hateful, until finally, he committed acts so heinous that the most depraved of men would gladly have put him to the sword. But the worst of it was, even though he tried to tell himself he was appalled at doing to her what no maddened beast would, John's much younger body made it abundantly clear that he enjoyed Miriam's growing helplessness and terror. He believed that mad self's excuses for tainting her thus and reveled in the jealousy and hatred that seemed to fuel them.

Oh no; not seemed, that mad self suddenly said. *You denied that jealousy many times, you swallowed it and hid it away like the coward you are. But* we *know. You felt it toward Peter, felt it toward Andrew, felt your own brother James—and especially,* especially, *you felt it toward your Teacher...*

It was true, another part of John's mind thought. He'd loathed Jeshua, hated him without limit. For his fame, for his relationships with the others of the twelve...and most of all, for his closeness to Miriam. He *thanked* Judas for betraying Jeshua, was glad he'd suffered on the cross. His only regret was that he himself had not driven in the nails...

No! Never did I feel these things, Miriam, never! John's youthful mind wailed across the trace between them. Never have I felt that way toward our Teacher! I swear it!

Instead of the comfort he hoped for, however, Miriam traced to him a question.

And if you did feel these things, John, what then?

To find such malevolence inside was more than John wanted to bear, but, he could no longer deny the brutal truth of the intent behind even the mildest of these new and ancient fantasies. He'd not dreamed the most violent of them before only because he'd never allowed his mind that far into his own darkness. Though he'd believed otherwise, in truth his corruption was as great as that of the most evil of men. The boy John had again become wanted to turn away from what he saw, wanted to forget the horrible disappointment of discovering this truth about himself.

He wanted to forget the Light he'd thought himself so dedicated to, sure he didn't deserve to know such magnificence...and the emptiness responded to his wish, offering, in the place of John's lustful yearnings, the solace of ignorance.

This is the only freedom, it said. *This way—or death—is the only way you will ever escape the horror of what you are. Better to die than live with the unbearable knowledge of this boundless hatred for those you thought you so loved, no?*

No, John, Miriam suddenly traced.

No. Do not try to run from this shadow, but look more *closely at it. The emptiness can never control those who look into the face of their illusions and accept them as such. Yours is the power to dissolve this, dear heart—but to be the light that sees it for what it is, you must look at the shadow, not your fear of it.*

Despite all she'd seen, John felt from Miriam only the greatest compassion, the greatest confidence, the greatest love—and the complete unwillingness to let him choose anything but the truth. He hesitated for a moment more, then did as she asked.

Grace met his willingness, gently stealing into his mind and heart, and the realization that he was witnessing, not becoming, the horrible scenes his shadow showed him filled John's awareness. As he again stood within the heart of the Self that watched all from the silent Calm, he remembered how, through the power of Jeshua's Practice, all thoughts and feelings, no matter how "unacceptable," invariably dissolved into true Emptiness, into the Completeness which needs naught, being All Things. Using its techniques, John looked his shadow in the face, embraced it...

...And felt his seventeen year-old self revert to the full-grown man he actually was.

He acknowledged that, though he'd told himself his periodic thoughts about Miriam were merely amusing side trips away from his present-moment awareness, he was in truth still ashamed of having them for her or any woman. And yet, those thoughts, like all things, were part of the Wholeness; only his judgments against having them gave them the power to entangle and wound. All that John was, shadow included, gave him the peculiar qualifications he needed to help those who came to him remember their true Selves—just as every being was so qualified through his unique experiences.

The visions began to fade, and as they did, Miriam's voice—or was it Miriam's?—whispered through John's soul like a fresh breeze.

This is the power of the Mother, John. She stands silently within her Self, watching what appears to be, while yet always knowing only the Good of what truly Is, knowing only what Good is forever possible. Every one of us embodies the Mother's Heart, just as we possess the fullness of the omnipotent Father. And so we, too, have the power to see truly and awaken Truth.

Thank you, belovéd, for choosing to remember.

A sense of lightness, both of feeling and brilliance, stole over John until he soon had no thoughts at all. No sound, no Miriam, no self existed for him; he experienced only the awareness of the silent ever-joyous, Witnessing Self.

Then, even that awareness drifted away into undifferentiated Light, pure Being...

John's return to worldly perception was so subtle that for a long time he seemed to be naught but a floating thing, a mote of wood in the center of the ocean, with his body as the faraway shore.

Eventually, though, his growing sense of solidity told him he was indeed more than merely the Silence. He lay on a sleeping pallet with a pillow beneath his head; a warm hand that had the mild roughness of one who has no servants held one of his. A set of fingers rested lightly on his bare foot, while yet another set idly combed their way through his nape-length, curly hair. He frowned slightly: his face seemed unusually cool and his pillow warmer than was warranted by his face being on it. His other hand twisted up, searching, only to find a clean-shaven cheek and chin...

...And like the cats the Romans had brought with them from Egypt, the memory of what had brought John to this place padded softly across the ground of his awareness.

Ah then, here is the shame, he thought, his peace dimming away all at once. For he somehow knew both the hand in his hair and the thigh on which his head lay were Miriam's. And recollection of her wholeness or no, he had no idea what he would possibly say to her.

SIX

John *started to rise,* but Miriam laid a hand on his shoulder, forcing him more by intent than strength to remain where he was.

"Do you know, John, what my reaction was the first time I saw Jeshua?" she asked, her normally rich voice rough with disuse. "The first time I saw Jeshua, he was walking along the road by the house where I lived and did my work, and I thought he was the most beautiful man I had ever seen. Not because he was so comely, though he was certainly built well enough. No, it was because I saw in him that thing I sometimes saw in the richest of my customers—and few of them, at that.

"'There is a man so whole that not even Caesar himself could cow his heart,' I said breathlessly.

My handmaiden giggled like the silly thing she was, but I saw absolutely no blemish in him. His dignity was so great that it seemed as if he rode, not walked, along that dust road. The first time I saw Jeshua, I thought he would be a most fell conquest to make, and I wanted him as I had never wanted a single other thing in my life.

"You know the nature of my fame, John, and my fortune. Many reviled me and would gladly have seen me stoned as the harlot I was, true. But my use to some—in both Synagogue and Legion—made me fit to keep and keep well. I had handmaidens and a slave, a eunuch who was brought to my house by a Roman general as a favor gladly given. Many men gave me their favors then, but I was always expected to return them in whatever coin they desired. And some desired very strange coin, indeed.

"Still, I always paid without complaint, because I knew full well there was nothing else for me. I might be rich and famous, in my way, but make no mistake: my place was to give all my body would give, for as long as it would give it, to any who would pay the right price. For do you know, John? Everyone has a price. When I saw Jeshua walking outside my garden, I knew he too, had a price; more, I knew I could pay it and that he would let me.

"So I sent one of my maids to invite him to the bench where I sat beside my favorite pool, and he willingly followed her.

"Of course."

The pictures that came to John as Miriam talked and continued to play with his curls were not his imaginings of her memories; just as with Mary and Prochorus, he *saw* what Miriam remembered. The connection they'd made during his experience had left an opening between their minds. It was thin as a thread, true, but he suspected either of them could now awaken it if need be, and wondered if it would last.

Miriam went on. "I kept my eyes down and listened to Jeshua's approach with growing anticipation and the full expectation that, just like the rest, he would be in my bed within the hour. I remember thinking he must be a hunter, so light was his step upon the ground. I was more excited than I had been in years, for even coupling can be boring if there is no heart shared in it. And though I would have sworn otherwise, for I had my favorites, in truth I had not shared my heart with another for many, many, years.

"Suddenly, Jeshua stood before me. I wanted to keep my eyes averted to heighten his suspense at meeting me, but *I* could wait no longer. I raised my eyes, looked into his face, and...what I saw, there, John, what I saw.

"There are no words for the cold shock that blew through my being. This man stood before me and looked into my eyes with tenderness such as I had never known—yet the strength of lions was also there, cracking open a heart that had no notion it was closed. All the love I felt for others who had touched both my body and my heart, all the love I pushed aside lest it should interfere with my life, went out to Jeshua in that moment. Everything I could have given I wanted to give to him, even if it killed me to give it.

"'Good Noontide to you, Miriam,' he said, and smiled.

"What was left of my composure fled like a frightened rabbit flees the fox. All the clever lines I used with my other patrons turned to dust. All I could do was clutch at my robe and speak exactly what was in my heart, naked and unvarnished.

"'Come into my house, Master. Come inside, and I will give you pleasure, pleasure and rest,' I said, only scarcely aware I'd called him 'Master'. My voice sounded strangled in my ears and all my life spilled out of my heart with those words. Suddenly, nothing in the universe held any meaning, and nothing ever would again unless he came to me.

"But Jeshua looked into my eyes, saw my beauty, saw my desire—and refused me.

"'I am already in your Heart, Miriam; I always have been,' he said with a smile. 'I've no need to come into your house.'

"At first, I was too stunned to do more than stare at him in astonishment. But then I grew angry...and then afraid." Even now, John could hear the echo of the shock Miriam felt at that moment. "Never had any man I wanted refused me; what could Jeshua possibly see that could cause him to do so? But if I was stunned by his refusal to be with me, John, I was even more shocked by what he next said.

"'Many are the men who gain their selves by taking you, Miriam, but there is nothing you can give me that you have not already given simply by existing. I love you for all you Are and have always been, dearest heart of my Self. All I want for and from you is for you to become my Self in your own awareness.'

"I asked him several times to come into my house." Miriam laughed derisively. "In truth, I all but fell to my knees and begged him to come into my house. But Jeshua refused each time, explaining with the patience of the mountains that his Love for me was not the love of those who sought to take, only of one who desired me to remember my Self.

"Finally, he stood and laid his hand on my cheek. I kissed it and held to it as if my life depended on it. I thought to ask him once more to stay, but his eyes held my tongue still in my head. He smiled. 'Soon enough, belovéd, you will come to my House,' he said.

"Then, he walked away from my garden...and from me. And from me."

Miriam was again silent. Then she sighed. "John, when Jeshua walked away, the life I knew was forever ruined. I hated him and wanted him dead—even as I pined for him and prayed with all my heart no harm might ever befall him. From that moment on, I could not lay with a man if I loved him less than the favors he could give me. And at last the day came when, taking naught but the clothes I wore, I left my house and all it stood for.

"Even so, it was many months before I finally became one of Jeshua's followers. Others have asked many times why it took so long for me to do so, once I knew my heart, and my answer always was that I delayed because I yet feared giving up who I thought I was, whore though she be. But that was not the truth, John. I was never brave enough to say the full truth of it."

Miriam stopped playing with John's hair and he knew she wanted him to sit up, to look at her. He lifted himself from the pillow of her legs to find her eyes danced with joy even as they brimmed with tears, and the look of wonder she gave him brought tears to his eyes. Whatever she might say next, he was suddenly certain his would not be the only heart healed. The giver would also receive the gift.

"The reason, I did not come to Jeshua right away, John, was because for all those months before I finally surrendered, I was insane with the grief of his refusal of my body. For all those months, my nights and most of my days were haunted by such dreams and fantasies of Jeshua as the ones you had about me.

"Never have I told that story to any other save Mary—not even these ones who love me so unconditionally," Miriam said softly, nodding toward, Martha, Lazarus and Elior, "for I too, was ashamed, you see? I truly had become 'the woman with seven devils'. Your shadow-dreams showed you doing things with me that I did not merely dream of doing, John. I did them, more than once, with people who had no value to me save that found in the silver given. There was nothing you could have shown me that I did not wish on Jeshua before he became my Teacher. Never could I have found you wanting."

Face still solemn, Miriam lightly kissed John on the forehead, and leaned back; then she smiled, brightening the entire room with her Light.

John smiled back and looked around. Martha sat at the head of the raised pallet, her hand still holding his. She beamed at him and her sister like she often did her boys —with a mother's burgeoning pride. Elior sat at the end of the pallet, the mother's smile as much on her keen, slender, dark-eyed face as it was on Martha's. Lazarus sat in a chair behind her, grinning his relief at John's return.

"Ohhh, graciousness," Miriam stretched and groaned. "Help this old woman up, John. Her agéd legs are stiff from having a certain gentleman sleep on her lap."

John stood, stiff in muscle and bone himself. Grabbing Miriam's hands, he drew her gently up, brow skeptically raised at her self-designation as an "old woman", and looked her over thoroughly.

"Good," he said at last.

"What?"

"I am again taller than you. Being beardless is bad enough, but the idea of spending the rest of my life staring at Lazarus's chest would be more than I could properly bear."

Miriam chuckled as Lazarus snorted behind him, while Martha "tsked" with a pursed-lipped smile. Elior, however, made no effort to stifle her mirth; she sincerely believed a good, loud cackle was the most ladylike thing in the world.

"You've a handsome enough face, John," Martha said, rubbing her own legs. "Indeed, beardless suits you quite well, now that the baby fat is gone."

"Well gone," Lazarus teased, rubbing his wife's stiff shoulders and getting a happy groan for his efforts.

John made ready to deliver a retort to his old friend, but frowned instead. "I thought you had important business that required your presence at home."

"And so I did," Lazarus answered smugly, looking toward the women. "Yesterday."

John's eyes widened in alarm. "Yesterday? ... Just how long have I been...?"

"Well, let me see." Lazarus made a great display of thinking over his answer, just as he often did when telling some story about something Jeshua had done. Or might have done, John thought wryly. Lazarus did love a good story and was not above adorning things even more than the average person of this region did. "You collapsed—or so it seemed to us at the time—at slightly after fourth hour yesterday morning...and it is almost Noontide now. You have been out for not quite thirty-two hours."

"Which means you must be ravenously hungry," Elior broke in, "and this room has entirely too many people in it for its size. So let us adjourn to the main room, and you can tell us what you experienced, if anything. And if you so desire."

She said the last almost as an afterthought, for as usual, Elior expected the truth, the whole truth and naught else but the truth, which was also what she told. John admired the trait enormously, especially since she'd acquired a certain level of tact over the years.

The five of them crowded out of the room—Miriam's room, John belatedly realized, still shaking his head. After all these years, the seemingly arbitrary shifts in time that occurred when one entered into the Presence still amazed him. True, the occasional "stretching" of time that came of being in the Stillness made it easier to get work done, but coming out of It with so extreme a loss of duration, ecstatic to mind and being as it was, always made John feel as if he had somehow misplaced some part of himself.

Which, of course, he had. The part of him that needed time to exist, what the Greeks called the persona or ego, did get displaced. To purposely step into the Silence fostered by doing the Practice must seem to that self like insanity...or attempted suicide. Still, John would not give it up for anything in the universe: not riches, not fame, not safety.

John's mouth fell open as the group entered the large common room and Miriam steered him toward a table laid out with a sumptuous feast. He saw lamb chops and fish, boiled eggs, several kinds of bread, figs, apples, grapes, and Martha's spiced lamb, barley and vegetable soup, which he was known by all to be very fond of. There were also, naturally, two kinds of Lazarus's famous wines.

"Welcome to your going-away feast, brother," Lazarus said, laughter lacing his voice over John's amazement.

"Thank you, thank you all," John stammered, his voice choked with appreciation as he looked from face to smiling face. "It is beautiful. I only fear I'll be unable to do justice to such a wonderful—and large—repast."

"I daresay, you'll not have the chance if you just stand there with your mouth open," Elior said, piling food on her plate. John wondered how the woman stayed so slender; she could consume quantities that would've stifled a younger Lazarus. The others more reservedly followed her lead, while John protested that he really wasn't very hungry.

"Well the rest of us are hungry, John bar Zebedee, for we sat vigil with you through most of your sojourn," Martha said. "You may choose not to eat our cooking on your final day among us if you wish, but I, for one, could readily eat a Roman mule, and I intend to do my best to prove it!" The others chorused their hardy agreement.

"With women, Little Brother, it is often best to recognize the voice of the One within them and cooperate fully...else they will nag you to death," Jeshua had once joked. John merely smiled as the women piled numerous comestibles on his plate and once again acknowledged his Teacher's wisdom: he soon discovered he was hungrier than he'd expected, a result, no doubt, of healing so thoroughly entrenched an inner shadow.

At Elior's insistence, he spoke of his encounter with that shadow, gratified to realize that he felt no sense of embarrassment at speaking of so intimate a matter. Truly, he had faced and accepted what it had shown him.

The conversation turned to the others' recent experiences. John listened with particular interest to Elior's surprisingly shy, yet sure description of how, for the past several months, she'd not been just seeing the One in herself, but was more and more frequently focusing on It first and foremost, even in the midst of distracting situations. Miriam and Martha listened with one-pointed attention to their belovéd sister-in-law, their own Stillness palpable.

Elior fell silent, smiled tentatively at Lazarus, and turned to the others.

"Have you any advice?" She asked diffidently.

John took a sip of wine, then unhurriedly wiped his mouth. He looked at Martha, who smiled broadly, then at Miriam, who merely raised a brow. The room was thick with the Presence of those Masters who had gone before them: Abraham, Solomon, Zoroaster, and many, many others. John sent greetings to them all and felt the joy of their acknowledgement and approval.

"Elior," he said at last, the sense of the ancient ritual deep in his voice, "What do you know?"

Elior stopped her inner fidgeting and smiled at John, all the softness she usually hid beneath her acerbic wit clear in her face. "Rabbi, even when I seem to be unaware of experiencing It, I know the One's Presence is within me. No matter what I am thinking, no matter what I am feeling, no matter what I am doing, I experience the One forever Watching all that I am I am, and allowing me to watch through It's Grace, always."

John nodded. "I see. So, then, are you ready to teach those who come to you the Practice Jeshua gave us?" he smiled as Elior's mouth fell open in surprise. "Well, you've certainly worked long toward that goal, and there is need. What say you, dear sister?"

Lazarus leaned forward like a spectator at Coliseum; Martha held her hands to her lips, prayer-fashion, as if trying to refrain from speaking out of turn. Miriam sat, Stillness radiating from her. Elior, after taking in each of them in turn, slowly nodded.

"Yes, Rabbi, I am."

John smiled, all his pride in this, Mary's student, shining through. "It is well, then. Walk in glory, teacher of the Way. Share the One's Practice with those who ask for it and offer the love of the One to all you meet in whatever ways the One would have it. By Jeshua's grace and that of the Ancient Ones who came before him, I am overjoyed, Eliora, to acknowledge your inclusion in the community of teachers of the Practice."

For a moment John had an impression of angels' wings flapping; then there were simultaneous squeals from Elior and Martha, the scrape of hastily vacated chairs and the flurry of women's skirts whirling as hugs and congratulations were shared. Lazarus, managing to look overjoyed and abashed at the same time, gave his jubilant wife a thorough kiss, then frowned as he caught John gazing at him.

"What?" he said, though his voice indicated he knew perfectly well what John would say. John did so anyway.

"This group needs four Teachers, my friend," he said, opening up the old argument.

He knew Lazarus would protest, that he would say that as a businessman with workers, a family and buyers to care for, his time was too pinched to well serve those students who would come to rely on his "wisdom, such as it is". John knew he would protest that he could not possibly be present in the ways those students needed, not enough to properly honor the Teacher who'd loved him enough to bring him back from Death's own House. John made ready to counter his old friend's arguments, determined to this time to talk him into becoming the fourth teacher the community needed.

But Lazarus surprised them all. He stared thoughtfully into his wine cup as if seeing within it the memories he now spoke of.

"Do you know that after Jeshua brought me back, there were many who would not speak to me, who would cross to the other side of the road or hide their faces when they saw me coming?

"People I had known all my life, people I had always respected, feared me, John. They thought Jeshua's 'feat' was the ultimate of witchcraft. It was the most painful thing I'd ever experienced, death itself notwithstanding."

Lazarus's hand covered Elior's as she touched his arm in loving concern; his eyes were haunted as he looked at John. "I was a fairly well-known merchant by then, well on my way to making a goodly fortune. I was rich enough to pay the dowry of women of many good families, yet I had to beg Elior's father to let me gaze upon, much less say 'Good Morrow' to her. With all that, do you know what I wanted most in the world, brother?

"What I wanted most in the world was to forget I had ever known Jeshua. I wanted to forget I'd died of a fever and been brought back from death. I wanted to be nothing but a simple merchant again.

"Yes, yes. I know the One is all One; I've known it for years. I know some would long ago have asked me to be Teacher had I been willing to take the office upon myself. But what I wanted above all else, John, was to be perfectly, enthrallingly *ordinary*."

The others kept their silence, waiting for Lazarus to work his way through to his own conclusion. He stared at his callused hands, nodding very slightly, then straightened and took a deep breath.

"And do you know? I have done what I sought to do. I have again become, not just 'the one Jeshua raised from the dead' but simply 'Lazarus, a vintner of fine wines.' I have given joyfully, both to the community at large and to this one, and taken care of my sisters' needs when they had such. I know the One within me has been pleased. Now, however, I have grown to a new willingness, and would be more to our Way than just a financial and moral support; I would join more fully in Jeshua's mission.

"Yes. I too, would teach others the Practice."

No one cheered at Lazarus's acceptance, but John sensed that a thousand thousand souls who would live in future times would experience the One sooner than they otherwise might have. What John felt as he nodded toward his old friend—and by the quiet reaction, the others did too—was a strong sense of a perfect choice, elegantly made. Jeshua and Mary must be well pleased.

As they finished the meal and cleared the table, the five of them discussed who else among their many students might be ready to teach the Practice to those who sought a new Way of being. The names of several possible candidates came up; some they discarded as having potential, but not the temperament, though that might come later. Others had the temperament, but lacked enough experience of the Silent One.

Two names, though, came to the lips of each of the teachers: those of Hosea bar Eliran and his wife, Ada. All agreed they were ripe for further attention; that they not only knew, but knew they knew, the Witnessing One within. Additionally, their willingness to do whatever their Teachers or their Souls might ask showed a dedication to becoming one with the One that many advanced students still struggled with.

As if in response to their assessment, the subjects of the Teachers' discussion opened Miriam's front door and entered the house, beaming like happy children.

This was no breach of etiquette. Miriam and Martha were always available for any who needed them, for they believed no one should ever be alone with their fear, pain —or even joy—because they feared disturbing a teacher. John and Mary had the same policy, and though not officially teachers until now, so did Lazarus and Elior.

"Good Morrow, everyone." Hosea and Ada spoke to the entire assembly, but their eyes never left John. Indeed, they seemed relieved to see him.

Both were dressed to travel, with packs on their backs and water skins hanging at their sides; suspicion ignited in John's gut at the same moment that Miriam made a coughing sound. He decided against looking at her, sure she stifled laugh.

"Rabbi, Ada and I have talked," Hosea said with all the hastiness of a boy trying to talk his parents into letting him do something he was sure they'd refuse. "Indeed, we talked all day yesterday and all of last night. We prayed to the One and entered the Silence, and our hearts are set.

"Teacher, we would go with you on your journey."

"Oh, my," Martha said, eyes wide, an equally wide smile breaking out on her face. Elior and Lazarus looked amazed and remarkably pleased. Miriam had her back to everyone, shaking as if she did not want them to notice that she laughed uncontrollably at some joke that made sense to her alone.

John was *not* laughing. He suddenly realized that he'd expected—hoped—to travel alone on this mission, responsible for none but himself for the first time in his adult life. After all, though he had no doubt Hosea could fend for himself, Ada stood less than five feet tall. She was Hosea's wife, true enough, and thus his responsibility, but both were his students. How could he not feel responsible for them?

No, having them along was absolutely out of the question. John made ready to give that response, looking for a way to tactfully explain it.

He never got the chance.

"Of course you will travel with the Rabbi," Miriam said through her grin as she turned to face them. "Your presence is more than welcome."

John gaped at Miriam, his face a parody of shocked disbelief. She merely grinned more broadly, as if daring him to refute her claim. Irritation—no—anger, washed over him.

"Miriam, may I speak with you in the kitchen, please?"

Miriam followed demurely behind John as he decided to go outside; he suddenly realized he preferred a more private venue in which to vent his ire.

Which was profuse. He was more than a little tired of being entangled in what was looking more and more like a female-sponsored conspiracy to drive him mad. First, Mary had all but ordered him to search for a place that had no apparent route (yes, yes, Jeshua had told him to seek Vashti first, but that was beside the point). And now Miriam, who'd caused him more strain in the last thirty-six hours than any ten men had in the last fifteen years, was deciding for him who should go with him on this questionable quest.

"Pray, Miriam, what in the name of God are you thinking, to tell Hosea and Ada they can come with me?" John said through clenched teeth, leaning far closer to Miriam than was proper. Better that than make the whole neighborhood privy to his business by speaking in full, thoroughly irritated voice. Nor did his certainty that Miriam was highly amused help matters. "You have no right to make such decisions about this journey, especially since you are not undertaking it! I have had enough of every woman in my life telling me what I shall and shall not do, and with whom I shall do it, do you understand?

I am going on this journey alone, and I will thank you not to invite half of Bethany to go forth with me. I have had a mother—nay two, thank you!—and do not need another."

Miriam listened to John's rant with an expression that, if not serious, was at least not so full of the amusement she'd earlier displayed. When John finally ran down, however, she did smile...and it did not interfere with the terseness of her reply one jot.

"It is a good thing indeed that you do not seek a third mother, John, as I have no children for a reason. Therefore, if you would stop acting like one long enough to let go of your idea of what this grand adventure *should* look like and ask the One what is best, you will realize that my answer to Hosea and Ada was absolutely correct."

She crossed her arms and waited. It took him a thoroughly irritated moment to do so, but John stepped back from Miriam a pace, closed his eyes...and found himself back in the memory of his vision of Vashti, listening to Jeshua's instructions.

The One will be with you in many forms if you will but be open to the help It offers. Trust, John, even if the form the help takes is unexpected, or looks on the surface like a hindrance. Or seems impossible...

John sighed and opened his eyes, calmer but no happier. Miriam took his face in her hands and leaned her forehead to his.

"John," she said, and though the voice was very much Miriam's, he was surprised to feel more than just her essence radiating from it. "You have been through much in these few days, things that stronger men, by the world's reckoning, would find unbearable. You have borne this burden beautifully and will bear others with just as much grace—*but*.

"Though you have seen them only as students, Hosea and Ada can also be belovéd, trustworthy friends. Take them with you, dear one, and do not be afraid to show them all of your heart. They have the strength and the love to bear it and all of you will come out ever the greater for it, whatever your self's insistence that it wants this glory for its own."

Miriam leaned back, her eyes serious behind her smile. "Trust, trust, trust, John. More than any of the twelve, that has been your strength. It has never yet failed you, and it will not fail you now, dearest. Trust your heart."

John kept his eyes on hers, on the incredible beauty she'd always been within and beyond the comeliness of face and body. "I have a request," he said after what seemed an eternity. Miriam's look was questioning; he swallowed. "I would kiss you goodbye."

Miriam smiled, her astounding beauty making him slightly dizzy—or perhaps it was the audacity of his petition that did it.

John had always believed that to kiss a woman in the manner he now kissed Miriam, not as mere friend, but as man to woman, would surely cause him to lose all track of the Witness, even if only for a moment. Such was not the case, however. Rather, he became even more aware of his Self, and of hers, and of the illimitable beauty of both. He felt the wonder of his desire of years fulfilling itself utterly and forever and knew Jeshua's words were true: a longing satisfied from the Heart of the One fulfilled the One.

John stepped back and caressed Miriam's cheek. The wonder grew larger, then turned to awe.

"Miriam. You are the One's Perfect Expression, just as Jeshua was...Indeed, you are Jeshua's double!"

Suddenly, John understood a number of things about Jeshua and Miriam's relationship he previously had not...but more, he comprehended the feeling he'd had whenever he saw her and Mary interacting. They literally *were* one soul in two bodies;

both were Jeshua's double. For this Sojourn, their single, seemingly separate soul embodied the fullest Feminine Expression of God, just as Jeshua had been the perfect embodiment of the Divine Masculine. Yet, John also suddenly knew his Teacher had manifested within himself the fullness of the Feminine without it in any way diminishing his masculinity or the two women. Miriam nodded, proud of his comprehension.

"The Mother lives not alone in the female body, John; She must not. Each being is born on this plane with a purpose: to fully embody both the male and female within themselves until they are perfectly balanced. But some who come to the earths agree to do more. These ones consciously agree to be templates of perfection for the human mind and heart, so that every other part's journey to Remembrance is made easier.

"That is what Jeshua accomplished, John. He completed the male half of the healing by fully accepting the Mother. Mary, who is also my 'other half,' so to speak, has further healed the ancient breach that caused those in the physical to believe they could make the Complete incomplete. What she and Jeshua have done fulfills one part of the cosmic purpose. What you go forth to do will facilitate the fulfillment of the rest."

Before he could ask any questions, Miriam brushed her fingers against his lips, a wistful look fleetingly touching her features.

"It is time for you to go," she said. She slipped around him to start back into the kitchen, but John stopped her.

"I will fulfill Jeshua's mission—your mission—Miriam. This I pledge to you."

"Isha," she said suddenly, turning back, a slight frown on her face.

"What?"

Miriam's expression was stern, but her eyes had the faraway look of one listening. "That one is 'Jeshua' to you, yes, but where you go, he is also 'Isha'. Find the path that Isha traveled, John, and finding Vashti's location is assured."

Miriam stared through him for a long moment more, then gave his hand a squeeze, once again herself. They continued into the house.

"Hosea, Ada, it is time for us to go."

John picked up his bundle, which had grown heavier since his arrival. Obviously, Martha, ever the loving mother, had added to his supplies. He hugged Lazarus, then Elior with a deep sense of gratitude, comfort and just a little sadness. He held Martha, who actually cried on his shoulder, then gently turned her face toward Miriam.

"Love her, belovéd; take care of her. She is very advanced in her Understanding, it is true, and she is strong, stronger than most men. But still, she needs her sister."

Martha grinned through her tears at Miriam and nodded. "I will. I promise."

John hugged Martha again, then turned to Miriam, at a loss for words. What could he possibly say to this one, who had seen his very soul and loved him truly and unconditionally for so long? Who was who she was? What words could possibly be adequate?

"Miriam—" he began, but she shushed him by again laying her fingers against his lips. Her smile held not sadness, but a hint of joyful, knowing impishness.

"I will see you in Vashti, belovéd..." her gaze went distant for a moment, then her smile grew unmistakably mischievous.

"...if not before."

SEVEN

"*Where* to, Rabbi?"

"Tyre, Hosea. First we go to Tyre, then onward to Greece."

The business of making their way back through the maze of somewhat ramshackle homes was slowed by numerous well-wishers and curious gawkers. It seemed everyone who'd not been on hand to witness Mary's miraculous departure now wanted to hear the story, either for the sake of upliftment, or in the hope of somehow catching John out.

"Master, is it really true?"

"Thank you, Rabbi! Thank you, and travel well!"

"Master, your blessing upon us, please!"

"Teacher, Teacher, please do not leave us!"

All this and more John heard above the hubbub of the crowd. He caught glimpses of familiar faces, along with those who had previously taken no interest in Mary, her adopted son, or their work. While he was gratified to see those he knew, John simultaneously wished there were not so many people present. He wished he had gotten away yesterday morning, before the crowds had heard of Mary's deed. Like a young merchant ready to go forth on his first solo caravan trip, he was suddenly impatient to leave Bethany behind—but it seemed as if just passing through the packed alleyways would take forever.

Hosea and Ada likewise seemed excited as they called out greetings and goodbyes to those who knew them, their eyes bright with the promise of what might be...but John also sensed that Ada, especially, was nervous about the upcoming journey.

He shared her uneasiness. Hosea had been to many a town and slept along many a road, as was the wont of wandering laborers...but had she ever done more than the basic traveling any woman did when her family visited various festivals and synagogue ceremonies? Had she even traveled more than a day or two from Bethany since moving here? If the journey became arduous, which was far too likely, would she grow in strength or wilt under the strain? Whatever Miriam's (and Jeshua's) assurances to the contrary, the only way John could answer those questions seemed far too perilous.

Despite the delays the crowds presented, the three travelers finally made it into the open air of neighborhoods where homes were farther apart and better kept. Only a portion of the alley dwellers still followed, but this by no means meant the three went unnoticed. Everyone they passed, from merchants' boys to women tending their homes and children, seemed to know of their upcoming journey, and the growing throng either called out blessings or stopped John to ask blessings for their homes and families.

As always, John gladly gave the blessings requested, but he suddenly found the practice, not absurd...that was too strong a word...but curious, curious and unfortunate.

"The idea that you are not able to heal the sick and raise the dead, that you see miracles *as* miracles...now, that, my friends, is strange!" Jeshua would say with genuine amazement, as if such an idea was foreign and shocking to him. John thought of Lazarus's desire to be ordinary and shook his head. Of all things, bestowing blessings—and knowing oneself worthy of bestowing blessings—*should* be ordinary, he thought.

John's ruminations were interrupted by their arrival at the square where the washing well sat. As had been the case with the other places they'd passed, the travelers found themselves before a crowd. This time, though, the throng's focus was not on them, but on what was happening at the well itself—namely, a sizeable commotion. Many people, including students who'd been present for Mary's Ascension, were shouting angrily, some at others in the multitude, most at the one who was the real focus of attention.

As if I need to ask who that might be, John thought ruefully. Who but Prochorus could cause such an uproar?

"What goes on here?" Ada said, standing on tiptoe in a futile attempt to peer over the multitude. Hosea pushed through the crowd to see, but as Ada started forward, John placed a hand on her shoulder and shook his head. He'd no desire to experience the further delays that would surely ensue if they were recognized.

Ada seemed only mildly disappointed at not being allowed to wade into the ocean of bodies, but they didn't have to wait long for Hosea's return. The burly laborer practically shoved people aside as he worked his way back to them, garnering many offended exclamations. John stared; never had he seen his good-natured student so angry.

"Husband, whatever is wrong?" Ada cried, grabbing at his forearm. Apparently, she'd never seen him this upset before, either.

"That...beggar," Hosea answered shortly, making the word a curse. "A good thing it is that I follow of the Way of the One, else I would gladly break his useless, ill-born neck!"

Ada gripped her husband's arm tighter, as if to cajole him to calm, but John only raised a brow, his voice dry.

"Oh? And how is the Witness?"

Hosea's brows beetled upward in momentary dismay, but he promptly took the question as the invitation it was. Ada, too, turned her focus onto the Silent Witness within, and John noticed with some relief that despite the intensity of the turmoil surrounding her, particularly her husband's, she easily found and settled into her Center. Perhaps she would manage the upcoming journey after all.

Those closest to them quickly felt the results of their focus on the Stillness, albeit unwittingly: their raucous speculations about what might be happening became less fraught with anticipation and more filled with, if not the desire for peace, at least not the hope of violence.

"Well?" John asked the big man.

"I...am still angry, Rabbi...but I am watching the anger as well," Hosea said at last.

"And were you aware of the Witness even before I reminded you to become more conscious of its Presence?"

Hosea frowned thoughtfully, his gaze still turned inward. "I...think so."

John's own brows drew together as he stared sharply into his student's face. He was worried over Ada's ability to handle the tribulations of their upcoming journey, but perhaps his concern was for the wrong member of their little band.

"'I think so'? I think I am aware of the Silence? Hosea! You have done the Practice far too long and know the One far too well to merely *think* yourself aware of the Witness in the midst of situations like this. Whether you feel sadness or anger or fear or even joy in this moment means nothing to me, but I would not have one who lazily thinks he is aware of the One during his experiences accompany me to market, much less on this journey! Did you not see how this crowd changed as you chose to watch your experiences instead of entangling yourself in them?"

Hosea nodded, a bit shocked by his Teacher's indignation.

"Our very lives may depend on whether you consciously choose for the Witness, or merely hope it bumbles upon you because someone manages to point your inattention out, Hosea bar Eliran. So either know you are consistently watching—or turn around and go home! Is that clear?"

John let his baleful stare include Ada, but she only nodded, her tentative smile a promise of her willingness. Hosea dipped his head in agreement.

"Yes, Rabbi, it is clear."

"Good." John's ire calmed immediately, having served its purpose. He looked toward the well and sighed; he'd hoped to avoid this throng, not find himself in the middle of it, but... "Then take your wife's hand and let us see what Prochorus is up to now."

Hosea hesitated as if he wanted to protest such a plan, then, instead of merely taking Ada's hand, drew her close. His heavy baritone filled the air as he cried for those before them to make way.

He only had to call out a few times: word of John's presence flew ahead. People moved aside as the Red Sea must have parted before Moses; the noise of the many died to awed murmurs. John felt an occasional touch on his shoulder or robe, while those who were students paid him the usual hands-together reverence. Within moments, he stood before Marcus Prochorus, who, as always, sat leaning against the washing well. As he'd done with Mary, the beggar sneered, then spat close enough to John's foot to make his intent plain. The crowd's murmurs again took on an angry tone.

"So, the ringleader of the culprits dares to show his face, does he?" he drawled.

John smiled, a little sadly, and answered mildly, "So, you chose to refuse my mother's blessing, did you?"

The crowd's anger grew as John's question was repeated. Opinions of the local priests notwithstanding, refusing a blessing from an obviously holy prophetess seemed no less blasphemous to them than cursing Jehovah Himself would have been. Prochorus reared back as if he'd been slapped, as if John had insulted his honor, not the other way around.

"'Mother'!" He spat the word as he had his saliva. "You dare to call her 'Mother'? Hypocrite! You no more considered that one 'mother' than you do the Empress! These gullible fools might believe your outrageous tale, but I do not! 'Ascended'! What dung! Were not you getting enough followers to suit your tastes, Zebedee? Did you and that Jerusalem whore decide you needed a better story to bring more fools to your little sect?"

The air around the well swirled with the crowd's increasing fury; many of those closest to the Roman began cursing and even spitting at him while a few cooler heads tried to restrain them. John said not a word, only continued to stare at the beggar. Prochorus yelled over the crowd's heckling, seemingly oblivious to his effect on the fast-developing mob and what they would do if he kept on.

"Yes! You and that whore did plot this, didn't you? You used that old woman to further your ends! Tell me, holy man, did you cremate her after you killed her, like the Easterners do, or did you choose instead for a nice, secret, late night burial?"

For the briefest of moments, the crowd froze in shock, as if they could not believe anyone would make so vile an accusation.

Then all hell broke loose.

The fury in the air exploded into violence as those closest to the beggar broke free of those trying to restrain them and lunged forth. Prochorus was ready for them: with arms grown strong from years of hauling his half-useless body from place to place, the former soldier caught up the first of his attackers and used the man's momentum to lever him over his muscular shoulders. The man suddenly found himself swimming in the well, spluttering in shock, as two more attackers fell to the ground, holding jaws and noses. A fourth was on his knees spewing forth his breakfast, but soon, more angry men than the beggar could possibly stop surged forward.

Prochorus did not seem to mind; he just smiled fiercely and drew his knives. This mob might literally tear him limb from limb, but his look clearly said he thought the cost worth the price. Death would feast on more than just his soul by the time this was finished.

John was aware of none of this.

At the moment Prochorus spoke his accusation, John's mind and senses were completely overtaken; he was transported beyond the noise and jangle of the angry crowd. He stood alone before the washing well in a now empty square...

...But no. He was not alone, was not even himself.

John again stood in the daylight brilliance of a few nights before, again saw Prochorus at the well—but, this time he saw the scene as *Mary*. A Calm so full it was almost unbearable descended on him; a Power too huge to ever be mistaken for a mere personal self filled every portion of his awareness. Earth-shattering awe bloomed in John's heart: was this what his mother had become before her Ascension? Was it what Jeshua had been? It seemed impossible, too huge even for their greatness. Yet, the sense of "yes" he felt was just as impossible to deny.

Before his mind could register the shock of this realization, his view shifted. John suddenly saw, not just Prochorus's memories, but the deepest truths of Marcus Prochorus himself—all from within the beggar's own heart full of hopes and dreams.

And what a dazzling sight it was! Even in the midst of his most virulent tirades and darkest ruminations, the soul that lived beneath the leering, cursing, bitterly defiant cripple in truth loved the world with the kind of passion that would surely have set the earth aflame had it existed between man and woman. Marcus Prochorus loved laughter, loved truth, loved others—loved. Though his mind could no longer admit it, his soul still saw and joyfully praised the wonder of the world's beauty, be it found in the fairness of a woman, in a blossoming flower, in a drop of rain lit by the sun's brilliance...or in Mary, mother of the man he so bitterly maligned at every chance.

Though he'd derided her "idiocy", Prochorus had admired, no, loved, Mary's goodness and good nature, just as he'd loved her son's. He had indeed been one of the escorts who'd brought Jeshua before Pilatus, but unlike his cohorts, he'd seen the golden heart that lay beneath "the Jew messiah's" seeming cowardice in the dungeons. He'd actually had the chance to briefly speak to Jeshua, had sensed he was far more than the mere prophet of a conquered people. Prochorus had come to believe that Jeshua could re-awaken the love he'd once felt for Life, the love so cruelly sundered by his family's deaths.

Nor had that desire been ruined by his later experiences: even now, in the midst of being killed by it, the deepest self of Marcus Prochorus desperately wanted to believe in humanity's beauty. He wanted to believe that every man, given the chance, would evince such goodness as Jeshua and Mary displayed. John now knew, as Mary had, the value of blessing such a one; if ever a man existed who was worthy of life and wholeness, that man was Marcus Prochorus. But would Prochorus ever again believe it?

Would he live to again believe it?

John snapped back to full awareness to find himself on the ground and in danger of being trampled by the melee taking place around him. The sounds of cursing, breaking pottery, and even the occasional clash of steel on steel, assaulted his senses from all sides. Several men lay crumpled around the well, most with well-bloodied faces, but two of them lay far too still, surrounded by women frantically trying to staunch their blood as it seeped into the hard-packed earth. One of Prochorus's knives lay a few feet away, mutely testifying to how the injured had gained their wounds.

John's eyes followed his ears to the source of the greatest clamor and found the one he sought. Several men held Prochorus under the waters of the well, screaming deprecations as the crowd cheered jubilantly, while another group held down a mightily struggling Hosea. Of Ada, John could see no sign.

"Stop it! I said, STOP IT!"

John's voice cut through the noise like a gale through tattered sails; he jumped to his feet, snatched one of the men holding Prochorus's shoulders, and flung him aside as easily as one threw away a dirty rag. The sudden, towering fury in his face clearly proved that, though given in jest, Jeshua's surname for him and James—*Boanerges: the Sons of Thunder*—was well chosen.

Those closest to John actually ducked and cringed as if they expected to be inundated by torrential waters or buried by a falling mountain. They backed hastily away, both from the grimness of his expression and from the lightning-hot vibration that throbbed in the air for a dozen feet around him, yet the utter Calm that had claimed him when he'd become Mary budged not at all. The men who still held Prochorus no longer had him completely submerged, but he was still far enough in the well for small waves to swell as he coughed up water and phlegm.

"Let—him—go. Now."

The men couldn't comply fast enough. Somehow knowing John would take any other treatment amiss, they lifted Prochorus out of the water as gently as their haste would allow and set him, still coughing, on the step that ringed the well. John looked out at the crowd, including those of his students whose clothing or faces showed the dishevelment of their recent activities. No one seemed inclined—or able—to return his stare.

"Ada!" he called.

"Here, Rabbi!" He heard from the back of the crowd. He smiled briefly, gratified she'd had the sense to get away from the fray instead of trying to help him or Hosea. Hosea also stood again, staring at his Teacher in elated disbelief. John let the sternness go just long enough to wink at his companion.

Then he knelt before Prochorus. The beggar had stopped coughing and, as he'd done with Mary, pretended to ignore John's presence, wringing out the ragged clothes he wore as if it was the most important task in the world. To one who did not know him, he gave the impression of uncaring bravado, as if what had just occurred was no more unusual than the sun rising in the morning. But John did know him now, knew him quite literally as he knew himself. He knew Marcus Prochorus's real dreams, the depth of his desires and the fullness his grief. He knew the truth and the beauty of his heart, just as Mary had, and could not but love it.

That did not, however, stop him from looking at the beggar as if he were some particularly vile form of vermin.

He grabbed the Roman's chin hard enough to make bruises and directed his eyes to his own. Prochorus, in turn, grabbed John's arm as if he meant to throw it off—or break it—but froze. His arms were still remarkably strong, even after his battle and near-drowning, but they were not as strong as John's stare, which held him in place as surely as any rope could do. The throng watched the scene, afraid to make a sound.

"Marcus Prochorus, two nights ago my mother and I came upon you, sitting in this very place. She came to you in Joy, ready to move on into the fullness of the One that each of us is, and in her boundless love and compassion, in her ability to see the truth of all your deepest dreams, she gave you a gift.

"You were healed, Prochorus. She knew it, I knew it, and most importantly, you knew it. You could have stood upon your legs and walked, had you so desired. You could have gone back to your home country or to any other place on your own two feet and once more taken up your profession as scribe, the profession that not only brought you joy, but also your late and belovéd wife."

The crowd murmured, shocked that one so...lowly...could actually read and make figures, while Prochorus blanched at having his secrets so casually published.

"You refused Mary's gift, Prochorus, a gift she'd never been able to give so fully until that night. You were so busy nursing your anger and disappointment at what you thought of as Jeshua's failure that you rebuffed his legacy, who stood before you in the flesh.

"Yes, disappointment. When you came here on your first assignment as a young soldier, you met Jeshua. You saw his bravery in the face of your comrades' tortures and tauntings and wanted to believe he knew the Truth. You could no longer have such faith in your own gods, for they'd taken your wife and son away, but you wanted to believe they were alive and well somewhere, and you expected Jeshua to prove your hope by escaping his fate on the cross." John's voice took on a wheedling whine, imitating the beggar's self-pitying demeanor. "'But Jeshua did not escape, he died...and then the gods took my legs from me.'

"Did you respond with even a portion of Jeshua's bravery? No. You became a parasite. You became a parasite who wanted so much to wallow in your anger that you ignored your wife's dying plea to someday remarry and continue the scribing you loved. You became a parasite who hated a dead and disappointing messiah so much that you spat on the gift his greatest student gladly offered you. You became a parasite who hated the world so much that you tried to get others to taint their souls with your murder."

John released Prochorus's chin and stood as if he held something repulsive.

"Truly, Marcus Prochorus, you are a coward."

John walked from the well and the cripple at it as if Prochorus held no more interest to him than a piece of refuse on the ground. The multitude gave him a wide berth.

"You bastard!" The beggar screamed at his back. "You bastard! You think yourself so great, but you and your ilk are as much parasites as I could ever be! If I could walk, I would chase you down and cut out your lying heart, you scum, you bastard, you stable filth! If I could walk—"

John spun and pinned the beggar with a stare that threatened to burn him to dust.

"Then *do* so, Marcus Prochorus! Get up on your feet and *walk!*"

The air instantly grew thick with the power of John's command. It seemed as if a strong wind blew, yet the air was as still as that inside a tomb. People shifted uneasily; some even cried out.

Prochorus gaped for a long moment, as if he couldn't quite believe what he'd heard...but then, with a shout that could have been heard in Rome, he suddenly jumped to his feet and ran straight to John, laughing and crying all at once.

John, his own eyes bright, caught the beggar in his arms before he could prostrate himself and held him in a tight, welcoming embrace. The Roman crumpled to his knees, his great, heaving sobs echoing off the walls of the baked clay buildings around the square.

"There then," he said when Prochorus calmed enough to look into his face. He drew the former scribe and soldier to his full height, feeling as he'd often had the impression Jeshua felt about him, as if someone he loved dearly had finally come home. "Let there be no more of hatred for you, Marcus Prochorus. Let there be only the one who dreams of men as better than they seem and knows that dream is true. Will you do that in remembrance of the ones you loved so much in the secret chambers of your heart?"

Prochorus wiped at his dirty face and nodded, lips pressed together as if he feared to trust his voice.

John embraced him again, then walked to where the most grievously injured still lay. The crowd gasped at seeing the impossible, for the men suddenly rose, free of the results of Prochorus's considerable skill with a blade. John looked about at their awe-struck faces, saying nothing with his mouth, but nevertheless making his message plain; many of them, especially those who'd most actively sought Prochorus's death, abruptly realized they'd neglected this day's work long enough...and perhaps it was time to rectify that situation.

Soon, none were left in the square save John, Prochorus, Hosea and Ada, and a few students of the Way who still stood discreetly by. John picked up his walking staff, which had fallen to the ground during the battle.

"So, then, my friends, shall we continue on? We still have far to go and too much of the day is already gone." He turned, ready to make the word deed.

"Zebedee...wait," Prochorus said, his cheeks suddenly crimson beneath his grime. His manner was that of a man, long unused to politeness, suddenly rediscovering its value "I know I have not the right to ask any such thing of you, especially in light of my past behavior...yet if I do not, I will be forever haunted by it. If you and your companions would have it, I...would travel with you and...learn more of this Way that has given me back my legs. I...if even one of you does not wish it, I will not go...I ask only that you consider it."

Prochorus hastily retreated to the well, trying not to look too eager for an answer, and began clearing away the now-useless cart and ragged clothing that were his only possessions.

"Well?" John said to his other two companions. Ada's reply was prompt.

"If we cannot see and forgive the true heart of one thus healed, what use will we be when we meet those who may have done worse things than Prochorus? There is Destiny in his desire to accompany us, Rabbi; I think we should say 'yes'."

"Hosea?"

Hosea's face twisted in a scowl. "I like the man not at all, Rabbi. He strikes me as one who but seeks a convenient way to return to his homeland—and even some who Jeshua healed reverted to their old ways. I wish I could feel as my wife does, that the beggar has given up his animosity toward us, but in all truth, I feel it is more likely that he will turn upon us at the first trial; that we'd travel more lightly without him."

Hosea paused and sighed as if there was more he knew he must say, even though he did not wish to. "And yet, though I wish to Jeshua's heart it was not so, I too feel Destiny would travel with us. What I want is not important; what Destiny would have outweighs it. If you say he is to go, then so be it, Rabbi—but I, for one, will keep a close watch on our supplies!"

"Hmm. I also feel Destiny's Hand is thick in this business," John said thoughtfully, "I've done so since Mary and I first saw Prochorus at the well. Yes, he must accompany us." He smiled. "It is not given me to know which way his heart will take him anymore than it is you, Hosea—but that is no great thing. I know not which way your hearts will lead you, either."

John motioned Prochorus over, ignoring his students' shocked expressions, then turned to one of the young brothers of the Way as if sizing him up. Yes, he would do.

"Timothy."

"Yes, Rabbi?" The youngster said, his eagerness to serve practically sluicing from his pores as he approached.

"Would you take Prochorus to your home? Let him wash himself, and give him clothes and provisions to get him as far as Tyre? Martha will see you are repaid for it."

"Gladly, Rabbi!" The young man said enthusiastically, beckoning Prochorus to follow.

"And Timothy?" John called after them. "Please hurry."

He returned Prochorus's grin as the young man led him away.

EIGHT

...Ah well, it could have been worse, John thought, as they made their way along the dusty, cart-scarred road that would take them to Tyre.

The four, of course, had not been able to hurry from town, certainly not once word of Prochorus's healing got out. As soon as Timothy led the former beggar away, John was besieged by those seeking healings of one ailment or another.

He obliged as many as he could—and quickly gained a bone-deep understanding of why Jeshua had healed so few during his ministry, compared to the numbers that needed healing. That is, beyond the fact that Jeshua's ministry never had the purpose of healing bodies in the first place.

So much unwillingness to let go of our pain, John thought sadly, as he saw the inside selves of the many who asked for his help. Some would literally rather have died than forgive some slight given as much as thirty years earlier! They were so bent on being "right" that their bodies had literally twisted into knots to accommodate the wish of their minds. The stubbornness of humankind—and more, what it was being stubborn for, amazed him. Though he could hardly credit it, he now had even greater respect for Jeshua's unlimited willingness to teach the same lessons over and over and over again.

That John now seemed to have the ability to heal was, oddly enough, no great source of awe to him. He realized, as he futilely tried to wave away the dust of a just-passed wagon, that he'd always been able to heal others; it was just that such healings had generally been subtle. Yes, once in a great while, someone would report having had some obvious defect or sickness heal while in the presence of the teachers. But John, at least, had never sought to be a healer, because he'd realized early that healing one's illnesses became unimportant once one established full awareness of the Self. And that, paradoxically, led to physical healings. "Which is just as it should be with dreams of reality," Jeshua would say.

If healings occurred in John's presence, they were usually incidental, a symptom, if one could forgive the choice of phrase, of the healed one's decision to accept, even if only briefly, her oneness with the One. This afternoon's healings had been intentional choices on John's part, true, but he took no more pride in them than he would have the sun's choice to rise. He gladly attributed this new ability to Mary's "memory" and knew not at all if it would remain with him. What he did know was that the moment he'd challenged Prochorus, he himself had risen to a new level of Wakefulness. He'd gained a new, greater sense of responsibility for the world's wellbeing.

The latest result of his handiwork walked a few yards ahead of John and Ada, ill-concealing his childlike glee at having useable legs for the first time in seven years. Prochorus bounced on his toes at about every fourth step, as if checking to make sure the spring was still in them, and smiled broadly every time he looked down at some passerby. Hosea walked a little behind them—and as far from the former beggar as he could; still, John was pleased his companions had accepted the necessity of the Roman's presence, even if it was not their first preference.

Or, as Ada had put it: "It is not a matter of liking him, husband, but of accepting what my soul says must be."

"And your soul tells you this one must come on this journey to make it as unpleasant as possible?" Hosea had asked gruffly.

"It tells me his presence will be extremely important...though it is, as usual, silent about the 'how' of things." Ada had then smiled charmingly (a tool John suspected she used often and well), distracting her husband from further argument.

John knew Hosea's position was no less painful for its prevalence in human society. He had, as John's student, sworn to offer Light to everyone, and had done so for the most part. That he found himself unable to do so now could only be painful in the most literal sense: no hell of some mystical future could be worse than having the soul want one thing, while the mind and body experienced its opposite.

While Hosea struggled to perceive Prochorus as something other than the bitter vagrant who'd accused his Teacher of murdering his own mother, any stranger on this road would only see a man of forty or so summers, making his way to the next town. Washed and clean-shaven, with the hair of his slightly balding pate trimmed short, John could well believe Prochorus was some enthusiastic scholar exploring the land of the foreigners on behalf of his Emperor. If anything, the lines of care that gave his face its craggy character enhanced the intelligence that shone in the Roman's eyes as he delightedly watched all that took place on the road before him.

This was the man Hosea must come to see, John knew...and only he could bequeath his past perceptions to the One that would make that possible.

Yes, I have indeed set Destiny's hand in motion by healing this one, John thought, and wondered where it would lead.

Ada strode steadily along beside John, her mouth and nose covered by her shawl, her step still strong after four hours of brisk walking. He felt both the fullness of her focus on the Stillness and her joy in being so close to her Teacher—though she was as yet too shy to say very much now that she finally did have him mostly to herself. He remembered to ask if she'd journeyed far from home before; if, for instance, she'd ever been to any of the festivals in Chorazin or Capernaum. Her answer surprised him.

"As a matter of fact, I've traveled to both Capernaum and Chorazin frequently, Rabbi. My father's eldest brother lived in Capernaum, and since they were very close, we went there each autumn to 'fill this large old place', as my uncle would say." Her sudden sardonic smile looked out of place on her usually cheerful face. "My brothers, sisters and I learned early to walk long distances, but in truth, I was never so fond of it as they were. I was glad when I married and no longer had to go out quite so often."

"And what of Chorazin? Do you have relatives there also?"

"Chorazin is where Hosea goes for the annual Roman census."

"Ah." John nodded his understanding. Amazingly, though they often did as much as the men to increase the family's fortunes, neither Rome nor Judea considered women important enough to tax as separate entities. Before marriage, they were regarded as the father's tax responsibility; after marriage, the husband's. Tax-wise, their value was half that of the man or less.

It was a fact many a household rejoiced over at year's end.

Shortly after sundown, the tired and dusty party—even Prochorus's enthusiasm was subdued—arrived at an inn outside Ramah. The owner moodily showed them to one of the long tables common to less prosperous lodgings and brought them ale. A timid, unsmiling girl, no older than thirteen by the look of her and obviously the man's daughter, brought a large pot of stew from the kitchen and served them.

Or tried to. She stared at John with such fascination that she very nearly ladled the steaming stew into Hosea's lap. He caught her attention and avoided disaster by gently directing her hand back over the plate; the girl blushed almost purple and apologized profusely, barely hearing Hosea's good-natured reassurances.

Unfortunately, her father did not hear them either. He fiercely berated the cowering child as he approached from his place near the kitchen, clouted her across the head as soon as he was in range, then dragged her into the kitchen, leaving the companions and the rest of the inn's patrons to wait for their dinners in shocked silence.

As sometimes happened when someone expressed strong emotions in his presence, John suddenly saw the motives behind the innkeeper's actions. He believed the girl was trying to attract John's—indeed, every man's—attentions, especially now that she'd begun showing signs of growing into womanhood. He often and loudly declared the girl's existence a bane, yet, along with beating her for various imagined infractions, he'd taken to telling her how no man would ever want her to wife. But then, that only made sense: his plans did not include ever letting this freely-gained slave out of his control.

John shook his head as the companions began picking at their food. Not all the One's gifts were a joy when hearts such as this one's existed.

Finished with his latest round of vilification, which the patrons could clearly hear from the kitchen, the man drug the girl back to finish serving the others. She did so, stiff with humiliation, then rushed from the room, giving him as wide a berth as possible.

"He's the one who needs a good thrashing, not her," Prochorus murmured angrily, shaking his head. "No one should be allowed to treat another, especially a child, like that."

"How would you have treated her, Marcus?" John asked in an equally quiet murmur. He was surprised by the Roman's vehemence, especially in light of his history with the women who came to "his" well.

"I do not know," Prochorus said, as if perturbed that he'd been heard. "Differently, that is all." He suddenly blushed as if he also recalled his past behavior. "In truth, I would do many things differently, if Chance would allow it."

John smiled. "Yes, well. History has a way of changing Itself, Marcus, if the One —and one—truly desires it."

Prochorus gaped at him for several moments, then self-consciously applied himself to the adequate meal of lamb stew, unleavened bread, and what he eventually pronounced to be "a truly horrible ale".

Save for the occasional soft comment between Ada and Hosea, the four ate in silence, the sounds of the warm room filtering into their awarenesses as the dust of the road had filtered through their makeshift veils. John was glad for the dearth of conversation; it gave him the chance to enter more deeply into the Stillness with his eyes opened. As the four finished eating, the inn master's daughter returned to clear away their rough wooden plates. Though he fully agreed with Prochorus's assessment of its quality, John said "yes" when she offered more ale. The girl avoided his gaze as she timidly poured, careful of every drop lest she should be disgraced twice in one evening.

To feel thus so young! he thought, seeing in the girl's posture the depth of her resignation to the belief that such treatment would always be. Suddenly he spoke, and though his voice was pitched so only those at the table could hear him, it sounded in his ears as if he pronounced the words to all the universe.

"Child, do not despair. No matter what he would have you believe, your life will not always be like this."

The girl started and looked sharply at John, then glanced in her father's direction and shrank as if trying to become invisible. She made as if to back away, but he grabbed her hand and smiled, fully aware of the innkeeper's hard scrutiny and not caring one jot.

"Please sir," she practically whimpered, fear clouding her eyes, "I must go back to my duties. My father—"

"No, Little One, no... Rachael. Do not run from this answer to your prayers, but look instead into the face of the truth I show you. You will know joy in your life and peace in your heart, for the One walks where you do and would even now give you all you desire. You will have Its blessings, and no one, no one, will stop them lest you choose not to accept them."

The girl blushed, but she continued to stare into John's eyes. Finally, she nodded and straightened, her face full of wonder. "Thank you," she said shyly. "Thank you, Master."

John chuckled. "Not 'Master', Little One, just someone who hears the One's voice and shares It with those who are willing to hear."

Rachael nodded again. She smiled tentatively at each of the companions, garnering their smiles in return, then walked back to the kitchen, her step light. She passed by her father, her sleeve brushing his as if she'd forgotten his existence.

John had not forgotten it, however. He caught the man's eye, his look clearly saying if he valued his peace he'd not scold the girl this time. The innkeeper scowled after her, but made no move to follow.

"Was that true? What you said to her?" Prochorus asked incredulously.

"Why would it not be, Marcus? Is not the One aware of every time and space? Have we not already established that as true today?"

Prochorus sat in thoughtful silence for many moments, as if some amazing notion had just occurred to him. When he again looked up, his eyes shone. "Then...it would be possible for me to someday be as you? —Not that—I mean, I don't expect—I mean—" He closed his mouth, obviously at a loss for words.

Probably for the first time in his life, John thought, stifling a smile. But he said, "Yes, it is possible, Marcus. Indeed, it is impossible that it *not* be possible..." he let the smile show, "...with a little Practice."

John stood, noting that full dark had descended outside the inn, then stretched, yawned widely and blinked owlishly. "Hosea, Ada, I am going to bed. Would you be so kind as to teach Marcus the first technique?"

It was a good thing Hosea had only just begun sipping his ale, else he would surely have watered the patrons at the next table with the horrible brew. Ada's eyes looked like they intended to pop out of her head and run away.

"But—but Rabbi!"

"Yes, Hosea?"

"You know Ada and I have never taught another...we haven't permission to teach!"

John allowed his mouth to quirk in the barest of smiles. "And who, exactly, gives students permission to teach, Hosea?"

"Why, uh...oh." Hosea flushed scarlet, but Ada had gotten over the initial shock of John's request and now smiled broadly. In fact, he had the distinct impression of someone rubbing her hands together in anticipation.

"Wait," Prochorus said, looking from John to Hosea to Ada and back again, "I wanted you to teach me, especially if they are not even sure they know how..."

John waved him off and looked at Hosea. "Is that true? Do you not know how to teach others the Practice? Am I mistaken in your abilities, Hosea bar Eliran?"

Hosea swallowed hard, but shook his head. "No Rabbi, you are not."

"Then feed this lamb, and let his spirit learn to soar as yours has. I will speak to the innkeeper about using the small room off this one, and you and Ada may sleep there as well. Marcus, you and I will sleep in the Common Room—that is, if you sleep at all."

He looked again at Hosea and Ada. "Trust in what you Know, my own. Marcus, do as they say, and you will indeed be on the Path that leads to what you seek, and more."

John spoke briefly to the sullen owner, handed him several coppers to hold the space, then made his way to the common room where many had already settled for the night. He unrolled his cloak and extra robes, made a bed of them on a thin straw mat, lay down, and wrapped his blanket around himself. Surprisingly comfortable, he closed his eyes; his breathing quickly slowed and his muscles immediately relaxed.

But he did not go to sleep. These days, John rarely slept more than three or four hours a night. Rather, years of habit awakened as soon as he closed his eyes; he began speaking the phrases of the Practice to himself, quickly bringing his body to a much deeper state of rest than sleep itself could ever foster.

Normally, he would let the techniques take him where they would, would allow the Practice to guide him to whatever understandings might await him in the Spirit realms. Indeed, these days, he always entered into the Radiant Being of the Originless Now, to bask in the unbounded One's joyous Silence.

Tonight, however, John had different plans. He desired to discover Hosea and Ada's level of skill, to determine if they were in fact ready to teach the Practice; yet he also knew his presence would hinder such an effort, particularly under these circumstances.

So, he was going to take a walk.

The notion of consciously attempting to move beyond the bounds of his physical shell excited John deeply...and made him very nervous. Oh, he'd tried taking walks beyond his body before, but while he'd always been able to do so while dreaming, he'd only rarely managed it while awake. Mary, Miriam, even Martha, seemed always to have had conscious control over one or another of the so-called miraculous talents that had, until quite recently, eluded him, but John's attempts to manifest such abilities had usually turned out to be naught but excellent tranquilizers, putting him straight to sleep.

In the first few years after Jeshua's resurrection, such failures were a source of major frustration. He lost many moments of peace wondering if his inability indicated some fundamental unfitness to be a teacher of the Way.

Mary actually laughed aloud at the notion. "They are not your talents to use yet, dearest. In fact, they are not your talents to use at all. When they are—if ever they are—it will be by the One's Grace. And then they will come as easily as taking breath."

Like healing Prochorus. Well, we shall see, then, Mother, if it is time for this talent to manifest now, hmm?

John focused on the inside of his body, treating it like a room he'd never explored. His awareness moved into and occupied more and more of his being, until he felt as if there was only a body, simultaneous with feeling there was only Self. He stood up...

...And looked back at his prone form, still lying in his makeshift bed. Though he didn't know why he knew it to be a good idea, he took a few deep breaths, just as if he was still in his physical body. He looked around the room. It was brighter than it should be; the two candles sitting atop the mantle gave off the luminescence of ten times their number, so that he saw the decorative designs on the blankets some of the sleepers wrapped around themselves.

John walked to the door and reached to open it—and was thoroughly startled when his hand passed right through it.

This is *not* a physical body, he reminded himself with an inner snort, then walked through the door and into the dining room. Hosea, Ada and Prochorus had already adjourned to the rented room, so John followed.

"...is our natural state," he heard Ada's sweet voice finish as he stepped into the room. The three of them huddled around a small table, for though a fire blazed merrily away in the small hearth, the room was not yet warm. The half-dozen candles they'd lit made the room bright enough to rival daylight to John's enhanced vision; additionally, he could see their individual life forces with a level of clarity he'd previously only sensed.

Ada was a small oval of silver radiance that filled John's heart with gladness; her gift lay in calming any storm, be it created by weather or people. Hosea's blue-silver light, though more subdued, made of him a sparkling star much like the one that had proclaimed Jeshua's birth. Prochorus's bright yellow light was the dullest of the three, yet its newfound clarity and aliveness shouted to all the universe how different he was from the cripple whose life had consisted of waiting to die only a few hours before. It also revealed the man's delighted curiosity in all things and his willingness to go wherever he needed to satisfy it.

Prochorus nodded at Ada's comment. "Many of our philosophers also say that. Granted, our gods are capricious, but I think we are not quite so fatalistic as you Jews. We Romans assume that, whatever their vagaries, they took pride enough in their work to at least create things right, not form them to be in immediate need of repair."

"It is not that God created Adam and Eva imperfect," Hosea replied, bristling a bit at Prochorus's flippant manner. "It is only those who followed, Adam and Eva's children, whose perfection was supposedly blurred."

"And we of the Teaching of the Way do not believe that, as I mentioned before," Ada said, her voice a soothing and surreptitious reminder to Hosea that Prochorus was a student, not a critic. John watched with satisfaction as Hosea caught her hint, chose more deeply for the One and instantly became more centered.

"Ah... Then I was mistaken in my understanding," Prochorus said thoughtfully, unconsciously responding to Hosea's deepening Stillness. "This pleases me, for I thought it tragic indeed that a whole culture could be based on what is wrong with one instead of what is right and beautiful."

Hosea nodded in surprised agreement, and John could see in his life force that he realized his own change of heart had fostered the former beggar's softening. "Yes. The Practice teaches that though we come into this world perfect, with the potential to be great in all things, we lose our awareness of that faultlessness practically while we are still wet from birth. We then act, not from that perfection, but from the belief that we—or something—is wrong."

"Mmm, yes. I have seen this. I've watched men whose hearts were stout and true ruin their lives by making choices they knew to be wrong, even when it pained them and those they loved. Faugh! My own experience tells me such choices feel like no choice at all when we make them. But why should that be? Does your teaching answer that?"

John smiled to himself as he remembered another's answer to the same question...

"You see, my brothers," Jeshua had said as he and the companions sat in a field during their second summer together, "we are not born as one man, but two.

"First, we are the true Self, the soul that is perfect, pure and inherently holy. This Self is the purest form of the originless, absolute One and leads to It. Then there is the self that speaks in many voices, the one we believe is us. In truth this self is only a phantom, one that has no substance we ourselves do not give it.

"The soul is born into this phantom self and brings with it the knowledge of what it wishes to be and experience on this earthly stage, while the phantom self is an empty slate, the means by which we learn to fit within our world. It records all things and is a most excellent learner.

"This is a good thing, for we would otherwise repeat the simplest tasks over and over, yet never learn how to be in this world...but the problem is, the phantom self is too good a learner. When something happens that is intensely painful, pleasurable, or simply repetitive, it becomes part of the phantom self which we believe we are. From then on, when something happens that might only be *like* the first experience, the phantom self will react as if it *is* that experience. More, it will do so even when you know it is not the same and do not want to react to it as you have before. This is why men often find themselves doing or feeling things they know make no sense."

Quiet prevailed as the twelve tried to wrap their minds around their Teacher's revolutionary concepts. At last, Peter spoke up, his manner, as usual, lending a bit of an edge to his question.

"Yes, Rabbi, that is all very well. Still, it seems to me that those who cannot stop themselves from wrongdoing are simply weak or lazy. Why do they not simply refuse to do what they do not want to, if they really do not want to do it?"

Jeshua considered Peter's question, then: "Why did you sink when I told you to walk across the water to me? You did not want to, did you? Pray, were you then too weak?" He raised a hand to forestall Peter's answer. "The correct answer, Simon, would be 'No, Jeshua, I was not too weak to walk to you.'"

The others chuckled at Peter's confounded look and Jeshua grinned at his most stubborn pupil.

"There is the necessity for faith, yes, especially when you do not yet know the One as your self. Faith will make possible every step that must be made for you to remember the Truth—indeed, faith, when fully accepted in the self, will make possible every creation you could ever dream of bringing into manifestation.

"Yet, faith is a neutral thing: it can apply to whatever you choose. For far too many, their patterns of faith say this thing or that is not allowed, is not possible. Their faith is lodged in the phantom self's tendency to remember what did not work. Peter, your phantom self's faith that you could not walk on the waters ran deeper than my Knowing, which I by no means doubt. That, and only that, was the reason you could not walk to me.

"Pray, then, should you—or anyone—be punished for following beliefs you gained when you could not yet talk? Should you be refused the One's joy because you've learned through experience that you are not worthy of it?

"Our belovéd Father and Divine Mother say 'no'. The Practice of the Way of the One allows you to relinquish the misguided faith that there is anything you cannot be, have or do. Indeed, it ultimately allows us to relinquish the phantom self, which in truth has no purpose once the soul learns to walk the earth."

"...So then," Ada said to Prochorus as he slowly nodded his understanding, "the techniques of the Practice work by bringing together—in a way specific to who you are—the two personas, or minds, we carry within ourselves."

"*Two* minds?" Prochorus asked. Ada smiled, clearly seeing the comprehension that lurked just below the surface of the Roman's confusion.

"Yes," Hosea said, motioning with his hands as if to create a picture. "Have you ever had the experience of talking to yourself as if you were talking to another? Those are the different selves within you, talking one to the other, often as if both exist apart from you. The Practice brings these selves together by giving each one something good and true to focus on, and that allows us to rise above the our phantom self's picture of the world. Once that happens, we remember the Wholeness that we are in truth, and how to once more act from That instead of from what no longer serves us."

"The first mind within us measures time and space," Ada said. "It sees the parts within the whole and names them. It measures and moves, one step to the next, and makes manifest our ideals. It wants its world to make step-by-step sense. You could think of that mind as the male self, the persona that defines why good is good and bad is bad."

"The other mind is the one that sings, that feels and cries and laughs. It sees all things at once," Hosea continued, picking up the thread. "It notices beauty, appreciates the wine, speaks without words, and acts without thought, while yet knowing exactly what best to do. It sees the picture of what can be, yet also senses when a thing does not serve us.

"That is the female self, the persona that notices the world, not as separate, unconnected pieces, but as a thing whole and entire. It channels the One's Fullness and gives It to the male persona as possibility, so the male mind may create in the world."

John well remembered how the twelve responded to the notion of having a "female" mind...

"I have no female self in me!" Nathaniel snarled, garnering grumbling, offended agreement from the others.

Jeshua only smiled. "No, Nathaniel? Why do you walk with me? Do you see something in me you also desire to have? Andrew? Jude? Matthew?" They each looked into his eyes and nodded. "That 'something', my friends, is the richness of the Feminine within me. When it is fully awakened and balanced with the Divine Father, only then do you experience the fullness of God, which is both—and neither—Male nor Female.

"The dark faith of the phantom self has long made it wrong for the Mother to work in balance with the Father. Indeed, it attempts to make it wrong for the Mother, the self in us that feels and intuits, to exist. Because of this imbalance, we actually believe we can fail the One. We perceive all we see as potentially sinful, constantly guard ourselves against receiving our own joy and punish our own and others' souls with lack and sickness and pain and death. But when both minds dance in harmony, we step into the realm of the Silent Witness, straight into the heart of the One and Its illimitable beauty. We soon experience the One, even as we go about our day-to-day business.

"With this Practice, my brothers, you will each of you again know that dance and become one with the One; you will know and accept the joy that is your unlimited birthright. More, as you remember that the wholeness of the Father and the Mother is all you ever were, you will share that Oneness with others..."

Ada explained to Prochorus exactly how to do the first technique, and how, especially, to make it specific to his own understanding. Then the three of them closed their eyes to give him his first experience of what the Practice was like.

John was pleased, pleased in the extreme with his new teachers' performances. Hosea in particular had shown how well he knew the One by his willingness to begin accepting Prochorus as he now was, rather than as he'd been. His natural kindness has found a place to rest in Marcus's house, he thought,

Better than his change in mind about Prochorus, though, was his change in his belief about his own abilities. He hadn't quite believed it when he'd told John he was ready to teach, but now he knew he was. It thrilled John to know these ones were, through their service, well on their way to 'doing all that I do, and more', just as Jeshua had.

Well, then. I can go back to my sleep roll, John thought. It has been a day of many events for me as well as the others.

Taking a moment to be proud of his feat of walking about without a body, he turned to go back the way he came—

—And was instantly flung from the inn like a stone from a catapult.

Suddenly, John was hundreds of miles above an Earth that had become a speck of dust in a black velvet ocean. As he gained speed, a bright silver cord, the cord that connected his spirit to his body, became a string, then a thread; the sudden fear that it would snap and block his return to his body engulfed his awareness.

As if to confirm his fear, the thread began to fray.

Stop, stop! John yelled to the universe, then: Jeshua, help me!

John thought he heard a chuckle; then he jerked violently and sat up on his bedding, panting hard. He was back in the Common Room of the inn; the candles on the hearth were a third shorter.

He lay down and let his heartbeat relax back to normal. Carelessness—or arrogance —was most assuredly not a good thing if one was going to travel without one's body. Still, John took a moment to recall and appreciate—now that he was safe—the amused, reassuring chuckle.

"Thank you, Jeshua," he smiled, then closed his eyes and joyfully entered the Silence.

NINE

John *returned to earthly* consciousness while the dullest shade of cobalt still stained the eastern sky. He quietly rolled from his blankets into the early morning chill, repacked his clothing, and tipped from the Common Room to enter the warmth of the inn's dining room. He was unsurprised to find other patrons already awake, most of them eating a breakfast of some unidentifiable grain. He looked for something warm to drink, but wrinkled his nose when he found it: it was the ale. Deciding he simply could not countenance such a hideous concoction warm, he settled instead for a cup of hot herbed water.

The owner of the inn was nowhere to be found; young Rachael and a patient-souled, harried-looking woman tended the guests. The beauty that had once been something to behold still lived in the woman's face, but her vivacity had long since been worn to a kind of melancholy waiting that made her seem older than her years. That didn't stop her inner Beauty from being easily seen if one had the eyes for it, though; the budding Fullness John beheld in the girl was definitely the gift of this one, who could be naught but her mother.

It looked as if neither of them had gotten much sleep. Someone had to tend the fires, after all, and make sure the morning meal was properly prepared. Since the innkeeper seemed disinclined to take on such lowly tasks, the two of them probably took turns turning the logs throughout the night, then worked together to prepare and serve breakfast.

John smiled and nodded a friendly greeting to Rachael when she caught sight of him. She responded by beaming back, tugging her mother's sleeve and pointing him out ...all with the excitement a girl her age usually displayed. The child might cower and stammer in her father's presence, but she clearly felt no such fear of her mother. Even through her tiredness, the woman's love for her warmed the room as much as the fire did.

The mother briefly examined the subject in question, nodded a tired "Good Morrow", then turned back to the guest before her, trying to ignore her daughter as she cajoled her to drop everything and greet John personally. When ignoring Rachael didn't work, she spoke softly to her and firmly shook her head. The girl, not to be balked, laid a hand on her mother's arm, her look growing petulant.

John smiled. He knew that expression well, for his youngest sister had often used it with great success on her parents, sisters and brothers. The mother's long-suffering look showed she was likewise familiar with the expression—and that this time, at least, she would surrender to the tactic. Hitching the heavy pot higher on her hip, she approached John with a warily neutral expression.

"Good Morrow to you sir," she said, her voice as neutral as her mien. "My daughter would bid me speak with you, for she says you gave her a wondrous gift last night."

"Good Morrow to you, Eleanor of the House of Gideon bar Jacob," John replied affably, pointedly acknowledging her father's former guardianship rather than her husband's current authority. "In truth, I but spoke to your daughter as the One would have me do. And if she would have it, I would do the same for her mother."

Surprise replaced Eleanor's neutrality; she glanced quickly at Rachael, who, likewise amazed, shook her head.

"I did not tell him anything about you Mother, I promise! Not even that you were here! You see? He is a holy man, just as I told you! Perhaps he is even a prophet!"

"Hush, child. Stop yelling like a market hawker before you disturb the other guests." Though the woman's words scolded, her voice carried mild amusement, not the harshness of Rachael's father. Rachael, in turn, looked only mildly abashed.

"It could be, of course, that my husband mentioned my name...but he did not, did he? Nor did any of our regular patrons." Though her expression was tempered by experience, Eleanor now stared at John with the same fascination her daughter had shown the night before. "Do you know? I have worked in this inn for thirteen years. In that time, I've met many others said I should be honored to meet, but far too often it would have been best had they remained unknown to me. Your countenance, though, seems as familiar as a pleasant dream that stays even after awakening."

The woman set the heavy cereal pot on the corner of the table, sat down, and stared into John's eyes for a full minute, looking for all the world as if she half-expected the reason for her feelings to write itself upon his forehead. Then suddenly, she blinked, took a deep breath, and turned to her daughter.

"Rachael, go to the storeroom and pour out a cup of the red wine from Bethany—you know the one. Such as this deserves better than that throat-searing ale." She looked again at John. "Rachael said you had friends with you last night. Are they still here as well?"

"This one is," Prochorus answered huskily from behind her before yawning widely.

"Two cups then, daughter. Warmed?" John nodded yes; Prochorus preferred his cool.

John observed the Roman as he sat and introduced himself to Eleanor with surprising graciousness. He looked five years younger than he had last night and smiled his "Good Morrow" to John with a lightness that had not been there even immediately after his healing. Plainly, the Practice was already showing positive effects for him. John smiled back as Eleanor finished speaking.

"See to it, Rachael. And stay with the wine as it heats, child! It will not do to scorch it."

Rachael protested at being sent away, sure she would miss some Very Important

Conversation, but Eleanor simply gave her the look all mothers seemed able to give rebellious children (no matter what the "child's" age, John thought wryly). The girl dragged off toward the kitchen, mumbling at the unfairness of it all. The mother briefly smiled after her, then turned again to John, her expression serious.

"My Rachael tells me you promised she would be free of this place. Is that true?"

"Not precisely. I told her she would know joy in her life and peace in her heart. And I say again, it was not I, but One greater that spoke."

"Hmm. Be that as it may, Sir, I nevertheless thank you for whatever you said to her. It has been too long since I saw my girl so excited about anything—especially herself."

Eleanor looked shamed as she spoke, well aware of the cause of her daughter's unhappiness. She sighed and looked off into the distance.

"My mother died when I was still a girl. As the eldest daughter, I took it upon myself to care for my father's household, and so more than once gave up the chance to marry before my twenty-fifth summer. Mind you, that was no burden, for my father was a generous man who loved his children fiercely. Also, in truth my interests lay elsewhere besides caring for home and hearth as a good wife should do. I desired to be a Healer; my joy lay in being consecrated to the work of the Lord as my mother's eldest sister had been. My father's house was easy to care for and, despite my unmarried state, my life was full and well-blessed.

"Then Hiram came along. He was young and handsome then, full of great dreams of building a fine inn and leaving a legacy for many sons. I fell straight in love with him, and though my father disliked him (and I had always trusted my father's sense about these things), I ignored his warning that all was not well with Hiram. We were married after a short courtship."

She shook her head and sighed again, as if the folly of her choice had just now occurred to her. "Hiram wanted sons, oh how he wanted sons. It was everything that was light and hope in him to have sons. But I had Rachael and only two other girls, both stillborn...and then I had no more children at all. He blamed me, of course, for I should have been sure to have a boy, but here was this...this girl...and how was he supposed to create his fame and fortune with that?

"From the day we buried my third baby, Hiram would have naught to do with me, except as a man does with a woman he owns: to treat her as servant and brood mare—though, of course, this mare would have no brood. And well, you see how he treats my daughter. Not his daughter, but mine."

John saw Prochorus shift uncomfortably, both at Eleanor's words and her look, for a kind of horror had come into her eyes as she spoke, as if she'd just fully realized something she could hardly credit—and did not want to know.

She looked around as Rachael returned, cups of wine held in one hand, two bowls held in the other. The girl glanced worriedly at her mother as she competently set everything on the table and ladled out generous portions of cereal. Eleanor, not far from tears, remained silent; her folded knuckles were white with the tension that filled her body. She seemed to age as she spoke again, her voice trembling slightly.

"Rabbi, you told Rachael she would someday know happiness. This I want for her more than I want my own life. But if she remains under my husband's 'protection' she will never know even the chance of joy. I would therefore ask a boon of you, good Sir.

"When you go from this place, take my daughter with you."

Prochorus wrongly swallowed the gulp of wine he'd just taken and began coughing raucously, while the cereal ladle clattered to the floor and Rachael, equally dismayed, threw her hands over her mouth as if to stop a scream.

Eleanor went on hurriedly. "I said before I was once a Healer, that I stopped in the practice when I married. But never have I lost my sensitivity. You are a holy man, Sir, as Rachael said...and yes, I see in the Life that swirls around you that you are also a prophet of great and Godly stature. I trust that your Way is honorable, that Rachael will be safe with you as she would be nowhere else. And so I ask again, will you take her?"

"But, surely she is too young! And you know not even where we go!" Prochorus protested roughly as he recovered his breath and voice. "Do you realize that if she goes with us you might never see her again?"

Eleanor blanched but did not budge. "Though she does not yet look it, she *is* old enough, for she celebrated her fifteenth birthday just this month past. And though I might never see my belovéd child again, if she stays here, it is certain she will never use the talents that rest within her soul. I would rather have my Rachael gone from me forever than helplessly witness the fate that awaits her if she does not go." Eleanor's voice cracked on a sob. "My husband must not be allowed to use her for...his own purposes."

John shuddered and his heart cried out at the anguish that welled from both the girl's and the woman's souls, for he had no doubt of Eleanor's meaning. And yet, how could he say yes? To be responsible for his adult students as they made this journey would be problematic enough; how could he possibly care for this child who had no experience of the world whatever? He simply didn't have the expertise, and said so.

"What of the others who travel with you, the woman and her husband? Surely they have raised children," Eleanor said, still unwilling to be thwarted. And it was true: though Ada looked far younger to John's eyes, she was actually only five years his junior. She and Hosea literally married the day she came of age and had the first of their children, twins, ten months later. Their elder three children, all girls, were married and had young of their own, while their youngest, a boy two years past bar mitzvah, was a smith's apprentice to Hosea's cousin.

"Rachael is a good girl, sir, and pious in ways that go beyond what Synagogue merely teaches. She will mind well enough, and she is strong and healthy, so she can help with whatever chores will need doing."

Eleanor's eyes were pleading. "Please, Rabbi, please. Will you not at least consider it?"

If Miriam had thought herself amused by Hosea and Ada's additions to this journey, this would surely cause her to double up with mirth, John thought. Yet, he could not but love this woman's incredible bravery; truly, she offered up her greatest treasure. He took the others in by eye—Hosea and Ada had appeared just before Eleanor made her request—and they adjourned to the small rented room to discuss the matter.

Surprisingly, there was very little discussion to be had. All agreed it felt right for the girl to become part of their company, even though there were definitely considerations.

"Two that I can think of," Prochorus said worriedly. "How will the mother talk her husband into letting her go if he is so bent on keeping her here? Your culture frowns somewhat on strange men spiriting away young unmarried women."

"And the other concern?" Hosea asked, his own countenance apprehensive.

"The other concern is to my mind more important: does young Rachael want to go?"

"And even if she does, would it truly serve for us to bring her along?" John asked. "We are not merely speaking of her never seeing her mother again, my friends. The dangers of this path will be many and varied, from meeting those who will seek to do harm for what they think they can take from us, to those who will desire to harm us for being 'Christines', regardless of whether we claim that designation or not. More, even if we discover Vashti's location, the process of entering it may prove to hold dangers that make violence by mere humans seem tame. I will go forth no matter what the danger; for myself, there is no turning back. But are we sure this is the Way this child should walk?"

As John spoke, they all knew he was again giving each of them the opportunity to forsake the quest and return to whatever lives they might wish to find—and he saw that each of them meant to continue with him.

A sudden and terrific din erupted in the dining room; benches crashed and crockery shattered. A man's rough voice raged incoherently as a muffled cry and shrill "no!" rang out. The four rushed in, then stopped in shock.

Hiram bar Abiel stood at the center of the tumult, cursing drunkenly and tightly grasping Rachael by the hair. Crumpled against a table behind him was Eleanor, her expression dazed and terrified as blood streamed from her nose. Rachael struggled against the innkeeper and ineffectually pushed at his chest to get away from him—then gasped as he jerked her hair hard enough to snap her head back and pressed the blade of a large knife against her throat. The inn's patrons stood frozen, too shocked to act.

The innkeeper's mouth twisted in an ugly, inebriated smile when he saw John.

"So. You thought to take th' little whore with you, did you?" he slurred, jerking Rachael's hair again. She cried out and grabbed at his hand; he struck her in the face with the knife hilt. "Thought you'd steal 'er away from her rightful place, hah? This is *my* property, do you hear me? Mine! You do not discuss with it what it wants!"

John opened his hands, almost as if making a plea, and focused on the One as he spoke to bar Abiel, trying to reach below his madness to send healing to his tortured mind. The innkeeper's angry, blood-red eyes tracked him; if pushed, he would slit the girl's throat and dance over her body.

"I had no intention of taking your daughter without discussing it with you, Hiram bar Abiel. Forgive me, please, if I gave that impression. It is only that I needed first to discuss with my companions the possibility of her going. After all, what good for me to speak to you if we did not want her along?"

Bar Abiel's face only hardened more. "You'd like me to believe that, eh, 'holy man'? I know what you are! Yer all alike! Think you can come to this useless pigsty of an inn —*my* inn!—and take my property without so much as a 'by your leave'! You think since a few people take y'r curséd orders, you should get honor from everyone!

"Well, not from me! Not from Hiram bar Abiel! This is my property—and that! And that!" The innkeeper's knife hand swept grandly around the inn and his voice grew louder as the insanity that lurked just below the surface came boiling to the fore in his drunkenness. Rachael's eyes rolled up as he again laid the blade against her throat and pulled ever so slightly, causing blood to well. "I will do with this whore as I please, d'you understand? As *I* please! I'll cut 'er throat out before your eyes if I want! I'll—"

Prochorus moved so swiftly that John barely felt the wind of his passing before finding himself with an armful of swooning girl. Roaring with rage, the Roman snatched bar Abiel by the chin, lifted him to his toes, and used the knife, hilt-first, to give him the thrashing he'd wished on him the night before. Hosea started toward him, intending to pull him off bar Abiel, but never made it: John stepped forth at the same instant and tripped the big man, then smiled cheerily down at his appalled expression. He turned just as Prochorus jerked bar Abiel's head back and positioned the knife behind his ear, intending to slice deep; Ada, Eleanor and the other patrons cried out and hid their faces.

"Marcus. Enough."

John's voice was utterly mild, yet even the most obstinate soul would have been hard-put to ignore the power behind it.

Prochorus blinked as if suddenly awakening. He looked down at the well-beaten innkeeper and the knife in his hand as if seeing them for the first time, then released bar Abiel, who collapsed to the floor in a bloody heap. Feral gleam still in his eyes, he backed away, his chest heaving from his efforts.

John held out his hand expectantly. For a moment, Prochorus stared blankly, then realized he wanted the knife. He handed it to John and their eyes locked.

"Jeshua would simply have taken the knife from the man," John said, his voice still as mild as a warm spring day.

Prochorus started, blushed and turned shamefacedly away.

John went to Eleanor. Both her eyes would be black by the morrow, if not sooner, but she nodded that she and the still-sobbing girl were all right. He turned to Ada, who offered an ashen-faced smile, and to Hosea, who avoided his gaze.

"If you've not already packed, do so; we leave within the half-hour," he said shortly; but his voice gentled as he turned to the girl. "Rachael, are you coming with us?"

Rachael's sobs caught in her throat and her teary eyes widened in near-panic. Never had she been allowed to make even moderately important decisions, yet now she was being asked to make one that would change her own—and her mother's—lives forever. She looked pleadingly at Eleanor.

"Mother? Will you not come, too?"

Eleanor slowly shook her head, and though tears rolled down her face, her voice was firm. "No, dearest daughter. I cannot. I know now my Way lies elsewhere, not with yours...and I will follow it fully for whatever is left of my life. Take no concern for me."

"But, Father..."

"Will bring her no harm," John said with utter assurance, not even bothering to look at bar Abiel. "Eleanor of the House of Gideon will follow her path, and it will take her to the highest heights because she follows it. What you must now do, Little One, is listen while I tell you what my companions and I seek. Then you can decide whether or not to follow your own Way while the door to It stands open."

John explained exactly what their mission was, leaving out none of its uncertainties and possible dangers, then finished by nodding toward bar Abiel.

"Know this, dear one: no matter what path you choose, no injury will ever again befall you or your mother at that one's hand. I promise." He heard Hosea's derisive snort and Ada's sharp admonishment, but chose to ignore both...for now.

Rachael still looked frightened, but the more John had spoken of their journey, the more the sad, downtrodden little girl had stepped aside and the young woman she would become opened to accepting the mantle of responsibility for making her own choices. John had seen such sudden shifts many times in the last seventeen years, especially in those students of the Practice who were just coming of age, and always it filled him with a sense of awe. That this one, who'd yet to even gain the means to enter into the fullness of her Self, should begin to awaken so quickly filled him with the same sense of Destiny—and humility—that he'd felt in welcoming Prochorus into their party. Whatever her choice, at the very least, Rachael was taking the first step toward manifest-ing the fullness of adulthood; and if she chose to join them, that step would be toward awakening the fullness of her Self.

The girl and her mother beheld each other for several moments, then fell into a long, fervent, sob-filled embrace. Eyes still brimming, Rachael turned and nodded.

"Yes. I will go with you, Rabbi."

The company walked the whole day, making excellent progress along the dusty road. They said almost nothing when they stopped for lunch, and John cautioned them to waste little time on talk when they stopped for the night. The morrow would come early.

He hardly needed to make the recommendation. The intensity of the last two days had finally caught up with Prochorus; he was too tired to be interested in anything but a short dinner and a long rest. Ada was also glad to quickly crawl into the bedroll she shared with Hosea, for she'd spent the day comforting the soul-shocked Rachael, whose sniffles and sobs frequently broke the quiet of the walk. Rachael, exhausted by her morning ordeal, fell into the sleep of the dead almost before her body was fully prone. John knew that would complete much of the healing for the girl.

As to Hosea...well, Hosea scarcely looked at or spoke to his Teacher, and rolled into his blanket with a barely civil "goodnight" to his other companions after dinner. John let that be as it would and laid his own head down with a relieved sigh.

Well, I told Mary I wanted more adventure in my life, he chuckled, but I never thought I'd experience five years worth in five days!

They awakened, ate and were walking through the chill morning air long before Nature's recalcitrant child, the Sun, deigned to make his daily ride across the heavens. The only sound to be heard was that of gravel crunching underfoot as the sky faded from the blue of deep, deep ocean and the orange and clear gold of dawn, to settle at last into the brilliant silver-blue of full day. John reveled in the silence, and as he had at the inn, again gauged his companions' emotions.

He looked at Prochorus. The Roman was still ashamed of his behavior of the day before, yet also still wanted to defend it, for he felt bar Abiel thoroughly deserved the beating he'd received. John drew even with him.

"So, Marcus, what do you think of the Practice?"

Prochorus was quiet for several moments, as if trying to find the best way to say what he wanted.

"It is too easy," he said at last, choosing honesty over tact. John smiled and hoped he would always choose thus. Prochorus continued. "The first technique is this one Ada and Hosea called Praise, and it is certainly simple enough to use—"

"But it is too simple?"

"Well...yes. Oh, they explained well enough how praise is among the highest of powers, being less powerful only than gratitude and love. But why is that so? How could something so simple, yet so supposedly powerful, be ignored so consistently by so many? Even our priests and oracles? Such a thing seems impossible."

John smiled. "It is ignored because it is simple, much like water is simple to a fish. Because the water is always there, the fish doesn't recognize it as the source of Life. Thus do too many of us feel about praise, the distinction being that men do not die as quickly of being out of praise, so to speak, as fishes do from being out of water. But die we do.

"Our very beings are made of praise...and of gratitude and love as well. The universe itself is nothing more than a constant, glorious song of Praise. When it is consistently experienced, the universe—and our lives—easily and joyously maintain themselves."

"And this simple little phrase allows that to happen?" Prochorus remained skeptical.

"Absolutely. Marcus, that simple phrase, spoken exactly as it is taught, is not just a simple phrase—it is what we are. It... Well, what was your experience? That will tell you more than my words can."

"Well...the first few times we did the technique, my mind went quieter each time I said it. In truth, had I not experienced it, I would never have believed such silence was possible." Prochorus smiled at the memory, then frowned. "But last night, my mind was as noisy as ever, if not more so. The thoughts never seemed to cease. I feared I was doing something wrong, but Ada assured me such was not the case."

He said this last as if he wanted confirmation; John gave it to him. "Ada spoke truly. To have thoughts while doing the Practice is not a failure, but a boon. Remember, using the Practice clears the phantom self's record of life by taking the mind straight into the Stillness. Every time you use any technique of the Practice, you enter into Rest and the body heals. The thoughts that come up as that healing takes place, be they one or many, mean some part of the phantom self's history is cleansing itself, that one will be more able to respond to what comes rather than react to it."

"Let me see if I understand this," Prochorus said after a moment. "When I use the phrases of the Practice, I enter the Silence of my Being. When I enter the Silence, my being becomes quiet and is allowed to rest, and so, to heal. When I...that is, the phantom self of me, is healing, then thoughts come, and that is as it should be. Is that correct?"

John nodded, smiling at the aptness of his pupil, but Prochorus still frowned. "But why is that so?"

"Because, to the mind, entering the Stillness is the most natural and pleasant thing in the universe. The body's joy, however, lies in healing itself, in becoming ever more able to move and experience. When you notice thoughts as you are doing the Practice—or emotions or physical sensations, for that matter—movement, the movement of healing, is taking place. By re-speaking the technique upon noticing those movements, the cycle continues, and you heal more, and heal more quickly."

"But does that mean I will never again have only silence when I do the Practice?"

"As you continue using the Practice, Marcus, you will have all kinds of experiences. Soon enough, you'll experience naught but your Silent Self, not only while doing the Practice with your eyes closed, but in the midst of living your daily life."

John suddenly grinned. "Indeed, you'll come to experience It even when you're in the process of slitting someone's throat."

TEN

Prochorus *stopped so* suddenly that Rachael, who walked but a few feet behind, bumped into him with a startled squeak.

"What goes on here?" Hosea asked from the front, his irritation of the last day and more plain in his voice. John signaled the others to continue on and laid a hand on the Roman's shoulder.

"Well after all, you are somewhat new to all of this, Marcus," John smiled, replying to the *I failed* that was so plainly written on Prochorus's face. "Listen to me: what happened yesterday, or five years or a hundred years ago, is past. There is neither merit nor goodness in focusing on what should or might have been. In fact, the only question you can ask about the past that has any value whatsoever is, 'What am I focusing on now?'"

"That is all well and good, but—"

"No, Marcus. If the self is crying or cursing, well and good. If we let it, it will cleanse us, then pass on. And if laughter comes to uplift us, wonderful. But it, too, will eventually go. It is only looking back at our choices and assessing their value that stops our awakening. Expressing sadness or mirth—or yes, even anger—is what makes us human, and the offspring and Joy of the Unbounded. By using the Practice with our eyes open as well as closed, we come to know that. We begin to trust that the Voice of the unchanging One guides us to act exactly as we need It to...and It does. We truly learn to 'take no thought for the morrow,' and experience the glory of our wholeness in every moment."

"And that is how it is for you?" Prochorus asked after a long moment. The skepticism was back in his voice, so he must feel better about what had passed.

"Let us just say... I grow better at listening every day," John laughed.

The group walked on as early morning made its way toward noon, and John continued to assess his companions' states of mind. Just as he expected, Rachael was far better this morning. With the typical resiliency of the young, she had had her cry (not the last, true, but enough for now) and was busily being fascinated by everything around her. He'd have Ada and Hosea give her the first technique when they stopped for the day; he was keenly interested in seeing the girl's response to the Practice.

Ada, as always, was both soothed and soothing; she innately recognized that all was well, no matter what things looked like. The ease with which she seemed to accept and thus heal her trials made John wonder, not for the first time, if most women's natural tendency to watch, then act made them better suited for the spiritual path than men. Of course, it might just be that they'd just attracted those kinds of women in Bethany...but Hosea's frown seemed an excellent argument in favor of John's theory.

There is a man who is not happy with his Teacher John thought. But that was just as well, for he'd no interest in dragging a pedestal all the way to Vashti on Hosea's behalf. He knew, of course, the "why" of his student's upset, but...

"Hosea, will you walk with me?"

Hosea fell in step beside John, practically bursting with the desire to speak, yet he seemed to be waiting for John to do so first. John, in turn, spoke of everything but what he wanted to hear. This went on for a good half-hour before Hosea at last snapped out:

"Rabbi, how could you leave Rachael's mother with that madman? He tried to kill his own child, for Jeshua's sake, yet you left her behind with no protection!"

"Mmph. And that is something I should not have done?"

"Of course not!"

Hosea didn't shout, but his attitude did. He stopped in the middle of the road, dust settling around his feet in swirls of gray. The others also stopped, taking in the confrontation with concerned eyes.

John stared at the ground for a long moment, as if fascinated by the patterns the dust made on his shoes, while the birds sang gaily in the late morning coolness, beautifully illustrating his comments to Prochorus on the value of praise. When he looked up, however, his face was as hard as Hiram bar Abiel's had been.

"Hosea, be clear on this: my reasons for my choices are the One's and no other's. I have no more interest in your moral considerations about what I should or should not do than a cat would have for a mouse's feelings about being the cat's dinner. What business is it of mine if Eleanor chooses to follow her Way as she does? None. Her moral considerations do not interest me, either."

John turned on his heel and continued down the road as if he was finished with the subject forever.

Hosea was livid, his already large eyes bulging. "Is that all you have to say? That woman is in danger, and all you can say is, it is none of your business? The welfare of others is always our business, Rabbi; to say otherwise is disgraceful! We must go back!"

"Then do so, if your heart calls you thus," John shrugged, throwing the words over his shoulder. "Mine calls me to Greece, not back to Ramah to watch a woman tend her dying husband."

"What...?"

The entire party responded with dismay as John again faced his student. "Had you considered the 'why' of my actions from your trust of the Stillness in you, Hosea, you might have understood long before now that the moment Marcus moved to stay bar Abiel's hand, that poor entrapped soul chose at last to free itself of the self-hatred it has felt for most of its life in the only way its ignorance will allow. Though I did not know it at the time, that is also why I stopped you from restraining Prochorus, and stopped him from committing murder.

"Bar Abiel will experience little, if any, pain in his last days—and more importantly, no taint will fall on Eleanor because of his death. Her tender care of one she has every right to hate will convince even the most suspicious soul of her righteousness. Had I even an inkling that any other outcome might come to pass, we would still be at that inn. But since I trusted the One's intentions and made no assumptions, we are now on the road, where we belong.

"That, Hosea, is the value of innocence."

John gave his student no chance to reply, but turned to the now crying Rachael and gently explained to her the Nature of the Soul, explained how, when it could not fulfill its life's mission, it would choose to leave the body so it could later start anew.

"Believe me, Little One, you did not cause your father's choice. Only he could have done that. Trust that all is well, for your mother, for you, and even for him. His soul will find what it seeks, for it can ultimately do nothing else."

To Hosea, John said nothing more; best to let him work out his own salvation, so to say. Would he choose a new set of thoughts and feelings to hold to, or would he watch everything from the Stillness and let them naturally pass, as all inner movements will, given the chance? Well, they'd know soon enough. John saw Prochorus nod thoughtfully.

"So then, my action was a necessary thing? It relieves my mind to know that."

John actually snorted as he wiped a tear from Rachael's cheek and handed her into Ada's comforting embrace. "Yes, well. Do not depend on consistently receiving explanations for the One's ways of moving through you, Marcus. Many will be the times when you will never understand Its motives."

At about an hour past Noontide, the companions suddenly stopped. Someone on the road behind was calling to them.

"Whatever in the world?" Ada said, interrupting John's reply to one of the many questions about the One and her own experiences that she'd finally been bold enough to ask. The others turned as well, but only saw a fast-approaching cloud of dust.

"Rabbi, wait! Wait for me!" The voice cried again, and a moment later, a mop of black hair, a forehead, and a pair of brown eyes crested the small hillock behind them.

John refrained from slapping his forehead as he suddenly realized who it was; surely, the One's sense of humor must be in full bloom.

Oh, it was not that Timothy bar Arioch was unintelligent or impious; in fact, he reminded John of himself at nineteen when it came to matters of the spirit. But Lazarus liked to say that the unmindfully exuberant young man who'd helped ready Prochorus in Bethany was an angel sent to earth, "one without any apparent understanding of the social graces." Only Timothy's unshakable innocence had saved him from many a thrashing at the hands of some offended stranger. To say nothing of his friends.

Timothy stopped before John, panting from what had been a very long run indeed. The dust of the road covered him from the top of his thick hair to the bottoms of his sandaled feet, making his grin seem that much brighter. Despite the million or so reminders from Miriam that it was inappropriate, he was yet again allowing his life force to blend with whoever's was close by, just as very young children did. Still, John could see out of the corner of his eye that the others grinned back at him; it was hard not to in the presence of such unabashed ebullience. Rachael seemed especially charmed, a sentiment that, by his look, Timothy was only too glad to return.

"Good Noontide, Rabbi," the young man said merrily, just as if he'd been with them the whole time and had just now remembered to speak the day's greeting. "I have come to be on your journey with you."

"Indeed?" John crossed his arms and stared until the youngster's grin wavered, then disappeared. "Pray, and by whose authority did you make such a decision, Timothy? Or did you simply decide on your own that your place was on this journey?"

Hosea turned away, his own troubles forgotten in his amusement, while Prochorus covered his laugh with a contrived fit of coughing. Timothy's expression was one of purest mortification; he suddenly looked like a puppy who'd been caught doing something guaranteed to result in his being tied up behind the house.

"I... that is, my Teacher... Rabbi, you'll not send me back, will you? Please, I wish to go where you are going!"

John stared at him for a few moments more, his expression losing none of its severity. Truth to be told, he was enjoying Timothy's chagrin far more than was strictly warranted. Had Jeshua so enjoyed taking him down a peg or two when he was that age? No, impossible. He'd always been a little less presumptuous and a little more prudent...well, hadn't he?

"You said something about your Teacher?" John asked.

Timothy hastily dug through the small travel bag that hung over his shoulder, then with a little cry of triumph, pulled out a piece of folded parchment and handed it to John. John unfolded the note—slowly—and read what it had to say.

> *Dear One,*
>
> *I send you our ever-enthusiastic Timothy. I found him at his mother's home the night you left, fairly frightened out of his wits at the realization that his head and heart were full with the vision of following Jeshua's 'disciple' wherever he might go. I did not have to think long on whether or not to send him: the One's scribing was written all over him, so that even his voice seemed that of an older self. Therefore, in my stead, I give you the responsibility of being Teacher to my student, if you will have him.*
>
> *I heard from him—and at least a hundred others (smile)—about your deed on Prochorus's behalf, and that he has joined your party. This pleases me more than words can possibly convey, both for the sake of the women at the washing well (smile), and because I sense the wondrous possibilities this journey will no doubt bring out in him.*
>
> *I close this letter, then, with two suggestions: first, let the Roman teach Timothy to fight, style of such to be at Prochorus's discretion. And second, tell Timothy not to stare at the girl so; else he will surely end up falling into a ditch (smile).*
>
> *I say again what I said at our parting, belovéd one: travel safely and be well. I will see you in Vashti.*
>
> > *In Remembrance of Jeshua's Heart,*
> > *Miriam*

John refolded the letter. Miriam had not actually written it herself, of course, for like many, she had never learned to scribe. Probably Lazarus, or more likely his eldest daughter, Hannah, had written the letter to her dictation. He shook his head, a small smile of amazement on his lips. How had she known about Rachael? Probably the same way he'd assessed Hosea and Ada's readiness to teach, or...well, no. Not exactly the same. Miriam tended to simply know things, usually without the help of elaborate adventures.

John looked sideways at Timothy. Miriam's recommendation held great weight, of course, but...

"Timothy, why are you here?"

"Rabbi?" the boy asked. John repeated himself as if talking to a slow learner.

"Why—did you—come—here?"

Timothy blushed and pursed his lips as if he wanted to say something sharp in response to John's manner, but then looked at the ground. When he again looked up, the "older self" Miriam had written of was suddenly and clearly present in his eyes.

"Rabbi, when I helped Prochorus find clothing and supplies to make this journey, the feeling came on me that I should have been preparing to go forth as well. But I set it aside, thinking I was just caught up in the excitement of helping another go forth. I thanked Prochorus for letting me be a part of his journey, and watched as he went out the door...then I cried like I had lost my own heart for the rest of the afternoon.

"I knew I'd made a mistake by not going with Prochorus to ask to join you, but at the same time, the idea of asking my Teacher to let me go terrified me—what would she think of a student who followed another Teacher, even you? And how could I leave my mother? What would she say if I left on a journey that might take me from her forever?

"Later that night, very late, there was a knock on the door of our house.

"'I missed you at meeting tonight, Timothy. May I enter?'

My mother appeared from her room and bid Miriam sit in her favorite chair while she took another, and the two of them just watched me cry for a long time. Miriam was smiling—but it wasn't a cruel smile, not as if she was laughing at me," Timothy said suddenly, looking at Rachael as he spoke (oh no, John thought, concealing his own smile; Miriam would never laugh at another).

"When I finally stopped crying...well, or at least stopped crying so noisily... Miriam asked me why I did not follow you, 'as your heart and mind called you to?' My mother's eyes filled with tears as I spilled out my fears, but she nodded as if she'd always known my path would lead me from her.

"I hoped Miriam would say I should stay home with my mother..." Timothy suddenly shook his head. "No, that is not true. I hoped she would say something, anything, to make my way plain, be it praiseful or scolding. I simply did not trust my own heart, Rabbi."

"But Miriam did no such thing, did she?"

"No. She asked me what I knew in my own heart," Timothy said like a child who's heard the same question a thousand times. That surprised John not at all, for all the teachers lived by that rule: Never tell a student a truth he already knows—no matter how ignorant of it he thinks he is.

"Hmm. I see. So then, Timothy bar Arioch, what do you know?"

The boy straightened, his usual light-heartedness suddenly replaced by the fullness of his conviction. "My place is with you, Rabbi. I would follow you as far as the One would have me go."

"That may be very far indeed, Timothy. Perhaps even to the ends of the universe itself," John replied, once more staring intently at the boy. This time, Timothy neither blushed nor turned away, and John smiled. "Well then. Come along; Tyre is still a goodly way off."

And yes, Miriam, we will assuredly have things to say when we meet again in Vashti...

"*Has the Rabbi* taught you the Practice yet?"

"No, but Ada and Hosea will teach me as soon as we find an inn for the night."

"Then let us reach an inn very soon!"

John sighed. Neither Timothy nor Rachael had ceased to speak for more than thirty seconds since the young man had joined the group. It seemed no subject was too far beneath the notice of either to be unworthy of at least a half-hour's discussion. Ada, bless her heart, walked between the two, serving as chaperone; John wondered how she could abide their perpetual chatter, awareness of the Silent Witness notwithstanding.

Of course, they shouldn't be talking at all. Both Ada and Rachael should have been at the back of the group, speaking to none but each other or a male relative. And Hosea, as said male relative, should have been walking near the women so as to shield them from the unseemly attentions of the other men.

He wasn't; having chosen to again be the witnesser rather than the author of Life, he now walked beside his Teacher, periodically rolling his eyes at whichever grandiose claim Timothy made in that moment.

Like his father before him, John was defiant enough to find such customs a little ridiculous. Much of Zeb bar Ezekiel's social rebelliousness had been trained (beaten) out of him, but when he'd noticed such tendencies in his youngest son, he'd been loath to force John's conformance just to save him from the local fishwives' gossip. A fact which often made Mother throw up her hands in despair, John thought, smiling at the memory of an incident featuring him, his cousins Ruth and David, the best gown of one of the city's most prominent wives...and a very old fish.

As afternoon approached evening, John began thinking about finding an inn for the night. Though they covered far less ground as a group than he would have traveling alone, all in all, their pace was good enough that they should reach Tyre in a couple of weeks. Still, he wanted to find an inn on the other side of Antipatris so they could start the morrow's journey even closer to their desired destination.

John turned and carefully walked backwards along the dusty road to mention his intentions to the others...but caught sight of Prochorus, who walked at the rear of the small group, staring with ill-concealed favor at Timothy and Rachael. John slowed to let the others pass, and began walking forward as the Roman approached.

"You seem captivated by those two," he said by way of greeting.

"Hmm? Well, yes...I suppose I am at that," Prochorus answered, showing no embarrassment at being caught out so, as John would frankly have expected. Who would ever believe this same man had tried to orchestrate his own death only three days before?

"The lad wears his second best robe to travel in, you know. He gave me his best when I cleansed my smelly old body in his mother's house. They gave me food as well, also their best. You did not ask that of them, yet they insisted I take it." A touch of sorrow tinged the Roman's voice, and his eyes gleamed. "My own son, had he lived, would be only a year or two younger than Timothy. I suppose I am thinking I could have had such a son, and that little Rachael is just the kind of girl he would bring home for his mother and father to meet."

Suddenly self-conscious, he snorted, a vestige of his usual crustiness returning. "Listen to me, talking of ghosts like some old woman."

John smiled. "Perhaps, Marcus. And yet, your praise helps lay those ghosts to rest, so you can create something greater out of the energy thus set free."

"Hmph. Is that how your Jeshua did it?" Though he tried to keep his tone curt and disinterested, John could practically see Prochorus's ears swiveling on his head so he might better hear the answer.

"In part."

"Hmph," Prochorus said again. Then: "Ada and Hosea told me the technique of Praise is so powerful that if I use it on a regular basis, I will surely come to be immersed in the Silence, know 'true enlightenment', as they put it. Yet, there is more to the Practice than just the technique of Praise. Why? What use having more than one technique if one is all you really need?"

"It is true we only need the first of the Practice's techniques to eventually awaken our awareness of the Silent One," John answered. "Yet, while all of us are born knowing the truth of what we are, it is a very rare soul indeed who remembers that fact even into their eighth or ninth summer, as Jeshua did. For most of us, the phantom self's talent for making up highly convincing stories about who we are and should be—and how we are failing at it—makes remembering our Selves much slower than it has to be."

"You make this phantom self sound like some sort of demon that actively fights against us," Prochorus said incredulously.

"It can sometimes seem that way," John shrugged. "In actuality, however, it only has the power we give it. Then it uses that power to protect itself—and remember, we believe it is us—by telling us that anything that might eliminate it will destroy us."

"And the different techniques help us bypass this belief?"

"Precisely. More, they speed and smooth the process of awakening. The Practice of the Way is a gentle path, Marcus. After all, how could the One, who is forever well-pleased with us, desire it to be any other way? So then. Hosea and Ada told you how Praise works...but did they tell you what the technique is specifically designed to do?"

"The Praise technique heals my ideas about how I experience my life. It helps me be at peace with what it is right now, just as it is," Prochorus answered.

"Yes. If our feelings about life are distorted by the belief that there is something wrong with our experience of it, we will react as if we expect life to treat us that way —and as if we deserve it. Jeshua said we must 'love our neighbor as ourselves', but if we love not ourselves, loving our neighbor will be impossible."

Prochorus frowned. "But will not loving ourselves make us think less of our neighbor? Will we not become like Narcissus, who loved himself so much that he was cursed by the gods with pining away when he saw his reflection in a pool and realized he could never acquire his own loveliness?"

"My goodness, Heaven must have been greatly amused over that piece of folly!" Ada said, joining the conversation. "My own experience, Marcus, has been the opposite of this—what was his name?"

"Narcissus."

"Nar-siss-suss. Mmm. For me, loving my life, loving who I am just as I am, allows me to love others more. After all, if I, as a child of the All-Knowing One, acknowledge the perfection of my life's experiences, how can they not be perfect? That is what we remember by using the Practice of Praise."

"Very well, I can understand that," Prochorus said. "But then, what does the Practice of Gratitude do? What does it heal?"

"How did you feel about Jeshua's followers before your healing?" John asked suddenly.

Prochorus snorted contemptuously. "I thought they were cowards and idiots. It seemed to me many of them were no better off than I—yet they ran about with insipid smiles, trusting in 'Jeshua's grace' and nattering about how all was well when it surely was not. I thought if everyone followed your Way in earnest, mankind would soon become as crippled in its strength of purpose as I was in my legs.'"

"Yes, but did you ever know any Christine to go hungry? To have no place to sleep if they needed it?" Ada asked.

Prochorus looked thoughtful. "Now that you mention it, I cannot say I remember even one going without help...if they were willing to accept it."

"And if they were not?" John smiled, aware Prochorus was remembering how many times he'd pushed away the locals' help. "That is what a lack of gratitude will do, Marcus. When you see the world outside you as something to ridicule and reject, you will always find a reason to do so. By doing the Practice of Gratitude, we remember how to accept the gifts of wonder and beauty the world has to offer. And the universe can do naught but create more for us to joyfully accept."

"But surely, one cannot be thankful for everything," Prochorus protested. "I certainly was not thankful for being a beggar on the streets."

"Do you know what Jeshua said before he called Lazarus forth from the tomb? 'Thank you Father, for I know you hear me always.' Jeshua did not see decay or death, but focused only the Life that pervades all things, if one but has the eyes to see."

Ada continued, "The Practice of Gratitude heals our belief that anything is ugly or wrong in the world. And that includes how we experience our bodies, which are but the costumes we wear over our Selves while we play at existing on this plane."

"Truly, Marcus," John said, "Gratitude is the magic key to answered prayer. And yes, you are expected to be thankful for all that comes, for you are its all-powerful creator."

They walked on to the sounds of the breeze wafting through the grasses, the birds and insects singing in the fields...and Timothy and Rachael's everlasting conversation.

"I do not know. It seems impossible," Prochorus said doubtfully. "To affect myself with a simple technique I can barely accept, and that only because recent experiences indicate it might be possible. But to actually use this to affect the world? Jeshua could do it perhaps, and you," he said, looking at John. "But I?"

"Marcus, the wonderful thing about the Practice is that we never have to use mere words to convince others of its power. As soon as we stop for the night, Hosea and Ada will give you the Practice of Gratitude, so you can discover for yourself if it really does what our experience teaches us it does."

An hour later, the six of them reached the outskirts of Antipatris and The Inn of the Seven Tales. The sky was still light enough to find an inn at the far end of town, but staying here would give Ada and Hosea time to settle before teaching Prochorus and Rachael. Rachael and Timothy looked about the large dining room with mouths agape —the first time in hours either of them had been quiet. John wondered if their throats would be sore in the morning, and amusedly chided himself for at least half-wishing it.

They had reason to gape: not one, but two fireplaces bookended the room, with the one farthest from the patrons already ablaze. Near the hearths lay several woven rugs that looked to come from nearer the shores of the Nile than those of the Jordan, and the innkeeper was either a friend or patron of a wonderful artist, for despite their simple materials, the tapestries on the walls were of excellent quality. Each sturdy chair had stuffed pads, further bespeaking the inn's success. John espied several doors on the ground floor, indicating private rooms, while a stairway led to a balcony and floor beyond; probably the innkeeper's family quarters. The aroma of chicken and other dishes being cooked by one who knew their business made mouths water all around.

"Rabbi, this seems a very grand place," Hosea said uncertainly beside him. "Are you sure we will want to pay what it surely costs to stay here?"

"Yes," John said, his manner almost curt. Then he turned and laid a hand on Hosea's shoulder. "Trust, my friend. Our place this night is here."

Only a few customers occupied the inn at this time of day, but two of them immediately caught John's eye. Though the cut of the first man's clothing was Roman, he was a Jew and a very wealthy one. He sat alone at his table, drinking some beverage whose quality was undoubtedly miles above the ale at Hiram bar Abiel's inn. Save for a brief look in their direction, he ignored the travelers, preferring instead to stare at the fire.

His apparent fascination, however, covered a state of desperate boredom which gripped him bone and sinew; though he had perhaps twenty-five summers in all, it seemed to John as if he'd already seen too much of the world, and seen it wrongly.

The other man stood at the rich man's elbow, his skin, in this light at least, as black as night and smooth as combed velvet. His clothing was simple, yet he wore it with the elegance of one born of high estate. 'Regal' was the only word to describe him, even though he was quite clearly the servant, and more likely the slave, of the one sitting.

Though his demeanor was calm, the servant stared at the party, especially John, as if he had never seen anything like them in his life. John found himself nodding to him as their eyes met; after a moment's consideration, the man nodded back, a small, confidential smile lighting his face.

As he had grown in his awareness of the One, John had many times come across people he knew, even though he had, in fact, never met them in his life. Well, he not only knew this one, but sensed this recognition went far beyond that of again meeting one who'd shared wine or small talk in some long-past life. They were brothers, he and this dark stranger: brother scribes, fellow acolytes, old warriors who had been comrades in arms. Together, they had triumphed over every trial, regardless of whether they'd lived or died. Yes, in this life, the man was a slave, surely part of the spoils of some Roman conquest; he was in no way free, by Roman or Jewish law, to choose his own road.

Nevertheless, John knew, and knew unequivocally, that when he and his companions departed The Inn of the Seven Tales, it would be not six, but seven, who continued on the journey to Vashti.

ELEVEN

John *felt a tug* on his robe and looked down to find a boy of six or seven summers peering up at him with a friendly but serious look on his cherubic face.

"Pleasant Eventide to you, good sir," the boy said earnestly, immediately and accurately marking John as the leader of the band. "My name is Jacob bar Salem, and I welcome you to The Inn of the Seven Tales. Do you know why it is called The Inn of the Seven Tales? I do. Can I tell you about it?"

John smiled at the boy and squatted so they were face to face. "Greetings to you, Jacob bar Salem. I would be honored to hear why this is called The Inn of the Seven Tales. First, however, my companions and I would speak to the innkeeper about staying for the night. You would not happen to know the innkeeper, would you?" he asked, having no doubt the boy was very well-acquainted with him.

The boy confirmed it by answering that the innkeeper was his father, "And would you like me to go get him?"

"I would appreciate it very much, Jacob bar Salem."

The boy did what counted as hurrying for most young boys, making a winding path around and under several tables before finally exiting through a middle door at the far end of the large room. Ada laughed delightedly.

"Well! That one certainly knows how to treat a customer, no? Shall I take this as a sign that his father loves what he does?"

The innkeeper soon appeared with his son in tow. He was a bit portly and his curly hair had more of salt than pepper in it, but his face was still youthful, giving the impression that he laughed frequently and spread that laughter whenever he could. Radiating an attitude of confident welcome, he started to give a spirited yet cultivated greeting to his guests...but it died on his lips as he and John got a good look at each other.

"Well, Jeshua's Heart! John bar Zebedee! Or should I say 'Rabbi'?"

The innkeeper quickly closed the distance between them and caught John up in a hardy, backslapping, embrace. He saw Hosea and did the same, then literally swept Ada off her feet as she squealed a joyous greeting. "Welcome to my Inn of the Seven Tales!"

At the mention of John's name, the rich young man's head snapped around so abruptly that his drink sloshed over the edge of his cup to stain the table; his eyes were suddenly alive with interest and his scrutiny of the group intense. The servant calmly reached over and mopped up the mess he'd made.

"Well! And Jeshua's Heart to you, Eli bar Jehosophat!" John said joyously. "Or should I say 'bar Salem'? Blessed be, how long has it been? Ten years? No, more like a dozen! I'm glad to see you've prospered so—both in your business and your family."

Bar Salem smiled proudly, taking his young son by the shoulders and pulling him forward. "Yes, you've already met my Jacob, eh? He is my third eldest. I've an older son and daughter, two younger girls and, as I learned only yesterday, a child on the way."

"That would be blessing enough from the One, even had you not this wondrous inn to look after," John laughed. "And the change in name?"

"Well, as a matter of fact," bar Salem said with the slightest hint of a blush, "I decided upon it not long after we last saw each other, the day my Amirah found she carried our firstborn. I wanted to honor my time with Jeshua, for I learned more of what I could be in those two years than most could hope to learn in two lifetimes. Also, it bespeaks my wish to be within myself the Peace he always was."

Bar Salem grinned at the other companions, who returned cheerful greetings of their own as John introduced them. The innkeeper called to a young man to bring several bottles of the inn's best wine and motioned them to sit at one of the large tables.

"So then, my friends, tell me what your Way has been. But not all of it! I doubt a month of nights would be enough to explain these dozen-odd years. Tell me instead what brings you to Antipatris after so long. How fare the blessed Mary and beautiful Miriam and Martha? And how is that scoundrel Lazarus? Tell me, does he waddle like an enormous duck or have his inner fires kept up with his amazing appetite?"

John enjoyed telling his old friend of his adventures, not only for the sake of the story's beauty, nor for the sight of Prochorus's eyes filling as he heard about Mary's Ascension for the first time. John enjoyed telling of the company's' journey for the sake of again observing Eli's reactions. "Let no secrets fall young bar Salem's way," Jeshua always joked, "for if questioned, everyone will know all and know instantly." The years had put no lie to his words: as John and the others talked, Eli's face shaped itself into numerous, often comically readable expressions. Happily, the openness that was the source of such suppleness had not diminished through bar Salem's years of living.

John finished, leaving behind an echoing Silence that vibrated in his soul as hugely as the silence that held the room. Eli unashamedly sniffed and wiped his eyes on the hem of his not entirely clean apron, while Ada laughed a little self-consciously at her own sentimentality and likewise wiped her face. Prochorus more discreetly did the same, while Rachael seemed wholly unaware of her tears and stared at John with undisguised awe. Despite the endless flow of words she and Timothy had exchanged, she had not until now known exactly who the "holy man" she walked with was.

"My friend," Eli said at last, "truly have you honored this house and its family by your coming. Allow me to return the wondrous gift you have given with my own humble one: I would be greatly honored if you and your companions would eat and stay this night at the Inn of the Seven Tales without cost."

Ada clapped her hands to her cheeks and Timothy and Rachael grinned, but Hosea's eyes rounded in alarm. "But Eli, there are six of us to house and feed this night! Surely that is too much even for a friend to offer!"

"Ah, old man, but this friend would gladly offer a week of such nights if it would help in this great task."

"Nevertheless," John said, forestalling an argument before it could start, "six is a few too many for even your prosperity to stand, Eli, especially for the sake of your growing family. Though I thank you most lovingly for the offer, my friend, we cannot possibly allow you to make so great a gift to us."

"Then I would be honored, sir, if you would let me pay the innkeeper on your behalf, for I have no such constraints on my finances."

Everyone turned at the sound of the new voice. The rich young man stared down at them, his expression conveying an odd combination of assurance and deference; the servant stood just behind him, his expression impossible to read. John stood to greet the young Jew properly, keeping his smile on the inside. This one, he thought, was very used to hearing "yes" for an answer.

"Good Eventide to you, sir, and all our thanks. My name—"

"—Is John bar Zebedee, I know. I overheard Master bar Salem speak to you. Forgive me for eavesdropping, sir, but when I heard your name I could not help but listen. Truly, it is both an honor and my good fortune to meet you, especially since I was on my way to the city of Bethany to find you."

"And you would be?" Prochorus said, and John realized he stood at his shoulder as the young man's servant did his, suddenly very much the bodyguard. The Jew briefly perused the Roman, then returned his attention to John. Both Prochorus and Hosea bridled at the slight, but the young man either did not notice or didn't care.

"I am Joshua Matthatus, of Caesarea. My father, Joses Matthatus, is a merchant of some renown; his ships trade goods between all the coasts and Rome. In fact, his fame is such that he and his family have even been recognized as citizens of the Empire."

Matthatus looked like he expected the company to be impressed, but John only nodded noncommittally and bid the young man to go on.

"Our family has been successful for many years, well able to afford whatever we desire, so I was allowed to study in Athens, the true Home of Wisdom. I've studied well the parchments of the Greek, Roman and Persian philosophies; my teachers tell me I have the mind to become one among the great wise ones, which I would find suitable indeed. Yet, lately, I find something is missing from my studies, and though I have repeatedly examined my teachers' words, still I have not found what I seek. It has all been very frustrating."

John heard Prochorus's small, unimpressed "hmph," but the young man, caught up in his narrative, paid it no attention.

"Then, while I was in the port city of Samos on my way home from Athens, I heard the story of the Christos. I vaguely remembered hearing of him when I was but a boy, and I remembered that many said he knew the secrets of life and beauty and truth. Thus, when I heard of him again, I thought, 'there, perhaps, lie the answers to my questions,' and I determined right then to learn more of his philosophy.

"It was no easy task, but I finally discovered you were still in Judea, so I set out, hoping to find you there. And wonder of wonders, here you are now, standing before my very eyes, just as if the gods themselves called you to me." After once more failing to receive some comment, the young man asked into the awkward silence: "Did I not hear you say you head to Tyre, where you will then seek a ship to take you to Greece?"

"You did," John nodded. "My Way calls me thus."

"Yes, but...would not it be easier to sail for Greece from a port that is closer? Surely, whatever supplies you need can be more cheaply purchased here."

"Perhaps. But that would not be what is next for me to do," John answered with a slightly rueful smile. "Though I do not at this time know why, the Way points us toward Tyre first for a reason. I will therefore follow, for never does it do to ignore the will of the One if one truly desires to make his way light."

"Pray, why is such of concern to you?" Prochorus asked.

This time, the Jew gave Prochorus a slow head-to-foot survey, then followed it with a slight sneer, like a cat flipping his tail at someone it had no use for. "Do you allow all your people to carry on so toward their betters?" Matthatus asked reproachfully.

John smiled slightly, even as his arm shot out to stop Prochorus from treating the young man with the level of disrespect he so sorely deserved. "I suppose I would not allow them to behave so, Joshua Matthatus—if they were in fact 'my people', and were in the presence of such betters."

Matthatus's face went from affronted hauteur to closed resentfulness at John's retort, but he seemed to realize responding angrily would likely quash any chance of gaining the favor he sought. The servant displayed the smallest of smiles; John continued their conversation as if he had not just given substantial insult.

"So, then, Master Matthatus, you said you were on your way to Bethany to seek me out. My question is, what exactly do you seek?"

"Why, I want to learn from you, of course! I want to understand everything you do, so my studies might at last make sense!" The merchant said this as if it should be obvious to the meanest intelligence. Indeed, he spoke as if he thought John would no more refuse his demand than his servant would.

"Hmm. Well. Though you can in one night learn the basics that will lead you to what I know, Joshua Matthatus, to fulfill the depth of what you ask of me requires more time and—well, not effort—but focus, than a single evening of communing together at an inn on the roadside can ever begin to bestow. And as to having what you studied make sense, well..." John shrugged, his expression almost comical. "...I myself grow less sure with each passing year that 'sense' is what life is, or is even meant to be, about.

"My advice, therefore, is that you continue to Bethany and seek out the teachers I have worked with these last several years. Martha, widow of Uriah, and Miriam of Midjel in particular have a deep knowing of what Life is truly for; they will be more than able to guide you, and at a pace suitable to your experience..." John smiled. "Yes, working with them would be the best path to take if you truly wish to learn the Christos's viewpoint."

If Matthatus's smile froze as it became plain that John did not plan to drop everything and teach him all he knew, the mention of Martha and Miriam turned that smile into a highly offended scowl.

"You would have me learn the Great Truths from women? Are you mad? I sought you out because I want the one who knew best the one who knew! I most certainly do not mean to learn from someone who learned second or third hand! And you surely cannot think me so lacking as to deserve the insult of being taught of such important matters by women! How dare you even suggest it?"

"Hmph. I daresay, boy," Prochorus snorted before John had a chance to reply, "your years of studying with your philosophers have been useless. They've certainly not given you enough sense to know when you've been offered a great boon—nor how to speak with the respect due a true better."

Matthatus bristled and his hand went to the hilt of his short sword. "Perhaps not, but I'll not be spoken to thus by one such as you, be sure of that!"

The tension in the room abruptly increased as Marcus stepped forward and Matthatus's servant changed his stance—reluctantly, John thought—as if preparing to defend his master. Before things could degenerate into a melee, however, Hosea suddenly chuckled.

"You really do want to take your hand off that sword, lad," he said, not unkindly. "Our Marcus is learning to be a man of peace—but you know how these old soldiers can be. When they find themselves before some lad who thinks a few lessons from the local master makes him a warrior, they just cannot resist...helping him improve his style."

Matthatus's gaze flicked toward Hosea in surprise then flicked back to note Marcus's strong arms and confident demeanor. His conflict was clear: should he continue forward and thus save face, or back down and possibly save something far more important?

Fortunately, the young man's philosophers had taught him some sense. He slowly removed his hand from his sword and relaxed back to his full height, then turned from Prochorus as if he was a formerly interesting toy, now grown too common to regard.

Would that he could have done the same with John.

Though Matthatus's potential reminded him of Matthew's once-buried brilliance, his pride (like Matthew's) hid that truth from his own heart as thoroughly as disbelief could have ever done. Even though his desire did in fact belong to the soul of his being, he had no idea that was the case. He believed he sought—and only needed—to satisfy his mind; that he only needed *information* to have *understanding*. Young he might be, but Joshua Matthatus was as jaded as an old publican. His insolence, left unchecked, would surely be the death of whatever true desires his soul might possess.

That was something the One was not going to allow. John suddenly advanced on Matthatus, his eyes blazing like the fire in the hearth as his words arrowed straight to the merchant's heart. Interestingly, his servant made no move to stop John's advance.

"Joshua Matthatus, you say you wish to learn the Great Truths; that you want to understand all I do. Tell me, does any part of your arrogance seek to 'understand' for the sake of fostering Life—or does it wish to carry such knowledge into the realms of dead rhetoric only so it might seem wise to others?

"You claim your teachers saw in you the makings of one of the great philosophers, yet I tell you now, they were wrong. Your supposed education and awareness of your high station long ago ruined any chance for true understanding. They will never allow you to express the humility required to make further spiritual progress under *any* master. Even had you lowered yourself enough to continue on to Bethany, I doubt that either Martha or Miriam would have taken you as student—and I certainly will not.

The young man had fallen back a step, his eyes full of dismay; John shook his head as if reconsidering. "Still, I would not cruelly leave bereft one whose soul, at least, truly desires to understand the truths your conceit never will. Therefore, before my companions and I depart this place, I will impart what little I can of the understanding you claim to seek.

"The first thing for you to understand, Joshua Matthatus, is that a true Teacher never acts solely for the sake of humiliating another. When the teacher instructs the student in a certain way, his only purpose is to awaken that one to his oneness with the One.

"The second thing for you to understand, Joshua Matthatus, is that no one is unworthy of honor, be they man or woman, Jew or Gentile, young or old. That is, if they are humble enough to listen with their hearts rather than their useless training.

"And the third thing for you to understand, Joshua Matthatus, is that the women I would have sent you to were also students to my Teacher, and closer to him than many of us who daily walked with him. Even when we insisted that they knew not what they were about, they trusted Jeshua without question and bravely spoke their knowing forth. Indeed, they even now give that gift to any who will accept it, while you purchase useless 'knowledge' like a man collecting coins he will never have the willingness to spend. Those women have more knowledge of the One in their smallest bones than you will ever experience, Joshua Matthatus, and that is what your arrogance has discarded."

Matthatus stared at John in white-faced shock, his rounded eyes and tightly pursed lips revealing his body's struggle not to shake in the presence of this one who'd simultaneously revealed and shattered the soul-deep longing he'd scarcely known he had. John kept the steel of his gaze on Matthatus as if looking for what the young man's paralyzed mouth could not say. Then, finally:

"Hmph. Perhaps it is that you do have some modicum of potential. Perhaps, hidden beneath that superior demeanor is one Miriam and Martha can do something with. Tell me, Joshua Matthatus, could such a thing be possible? Could it be that your heart, rather than your understanding, desires to run your soul?" John again shook his head. "Perhaps, perhaps not. But know this: neither Martha nor Miriam have time for 'authorities'. They only take students who seek Knowledge, not 'understanding'. If you would have any hope whatever of gaining their guidance, best you should decide, and quickly, which you want."

Matthatus stood frozen for several moments more after John turned away, then jerkily made his way to his table. Waving the servant to stay where he was, he grabbed up his cloak; the red-orange glow of early evening briefly filled the room as the inn's door opened, then closed behind him.

John walked to the hearth at the other end of the room before the others could speak. His body shook with the fire that still flowed through him, yet his skin was broken out in gooseflesh. He felt four sizes too big for his body, felt somehow abraded by the intensity of his call to the young merchant's deepest self.

Happily, the slightest shift in focus quickly brought the Stillness that always lived beneath all sensations more fully into John's awareness; he basked in Its Fullness and let the rhythm of his breath make its way back to normal. After a long moment, he stepped away from the mantle and smiled wanly at Eli bar Salem.

"My friend, if you would simply bring the whole lamb to the table for dinner, I would be eternally grateful."

The dinner was a sumptuous one: in addition to chicken pie, there were three different soups and a homemade fig wine which Hosea pronounced excellent and John studiously avoided. They also enjoyed roasted yams and vegetables, and finished the meal with a sinfully luscious apple tart. The company met Eli's wife Amirah and their other children, and young Jacob at last got to tell how the Inn of the Seven Tales got its name. This lay featured a group of visiting Greek philosophers, a gaggle of Jewish clerics and an illicitly drunken contest to decide which culture told the best tall tales —and it had Eli's mark stamped all over it. John would ask later if it was actually true.

Also joining the company for dinner, at John's behest, was Joshua Matthatus's servant, who introduced himself as Haifata Adan. John noted with some amusement the companions' varying reactions to Adan's presence: Timothy and Rachael surreptitiously stared at the African as if they feared he might suddenly try to savage them all, while Hosea looked as if he couldn't decide whether to be happy or offended by a slave's addition to the affair. Ada, after a few moments of uncertainty, and with her usual cheerful aplomb, was soon treating him as if they'd always been friends.

Only Prochorus responded to Adan's addition with true indifference, as if it was the most natural thing in the world. But then, perhaps to him it is, John thought, realizing (not for the last time, he was sure) how different the ways of a once well-traveled soldier's likely were from a fisherman's from Judea. The African ate in near silence, but when he heard young Jacob's story of the Seven Tales, he regaled the wide-eyed boy, his siblings, and Rachael and Timothy with the tale of his first lion hunt.

"Sir."

Everyone save John turned at the sound of Joshua Matthatus's voice as if surprised. John was not surprised; he'd felt the young man's hesitant approach long before he reentered the inn.

"Sir, please," Matthatus said again when John did not immediately respond.

John stopped staring into the cup of wine he'd nursed through the evening and turned; the young Jew looked not at all like the pompous youth who'd stumbled from the inn several hours before. His hair was thoroughly mussed, as if he'd doused it with a bucket of water then pushed it back from his face with his hands; his clothing was disheveled. Joshua Matthatus looked as if God Himself had stripped away the lifetime of complexities that overlay his soul and left naked vulnerability standing in their place.

"Sir...Rabbi. I...have had time to consider what you said to me. My life has been as empty as you say...but until you spoke, I did not even know it. Now I do, and...and I want to know, Sir, to truly know what you know. That means more to me than anything else, Rabbi, even life itself."

John considered the young man's words, then sipped at his wine. "And what would you have me do about that, Joshua Matthatus?"

The merchant's son bowed his head. "If you wish it, Rabbi, I will continue on to Bethany and seek out the teachers you mentioned—if only to ask their forgiveness for my insolence—and hope one of them deems me worthy to be their student."

"But?"

"But I...but if it be your will, Sir, I would rather... Please, Rabbi...will you be my Teacher?"

Matthatus's question echoed through the center of John's being and filled the bottomless well of absolute Stillness that held his soul within It. A long, narrow tunnel of focus extended out from that center, into and through Joshua Matthatus, who, John knew, was also absorbed.

The Silence grew, exploded and sent John whirling backwards...and back...and back again, to Time's beginning. With each backward leap, John observed an ancient past and experienced the memories of each of the other times this one had sought him out as Teacher. He saw all the times this one had faithfully maintained his/her focus on the goal to become the One and saw all his/her failures as well—both the minor ones and those that had led to the student's dissolution.

"Joshua Matthatus, do you realize, truly, what it is you request?" John asked as his vision focused on one incident in particular. His voice sounded strange to his ears, as if not he, but another spoke. "Do you know that when you ask me to be your Teacher, you ask the One within me to guide your understanding? Do you know that if I say 'yes', I will expect you to surrender all your willfulness to me in trust that my knowing will guide you safely to the Goal, no matter how strange and frightening such guidance may look? And will you, this time, hold my life in your hands with respect and honor, not dash it upon the stones of Fate's capricious whims?"

John watched as his questions dove into the young man's awareness, watched as a flash of comprehension came tantalizingly close to surfacing, only to swirl away.

"In all truth, Rabbi, I do not know all that I ask, though even now I would tell myself I do," Matthatus replied. Yet, I do know I am willing to discover what you mean, to become all you would ask of me. My only prayer is that my courage never fails me."

John turned his attention to Haifata Adan. Gaze determined, he stared first at John, then at his master, as if he sought to remember something he knew was vitally important. Though the African might not fully realize what he saw, his soul assuredly did.

"Before I can accept you as student, Joshua Matthatus, there is a condition I would impose on you."

"By your will, Rabbi."

"Free your slave. Immediately."

Both Matthatus's and Adan's eyebrows rose in surprise, but the young man did not hesitate. "Though he was a gift to my father from the Emperor himself..." He turned to the servant. "Haifata Adan, I give you your freedom before these witnesses, for God's will speaks through this one...and in all honesty, because it pleases me to do so."

John smiled. "And I, Joshua Matthatus, welcome you as my student."

The connection that always exists between Teacher and student, no matter how many miles or lifetimes distant, once more awakened; as it was with all his students, John would have at least some awareness of Matthatus's inner experiences for the rest of their lives. Joshua Matthatus was, in a very literal sense, now a part of John, and vice-versa.

He received the young merchant's embrace, then turned and nodded to Haifata

Adan. Though Matthatus seemed unaware of it, John noticed the African reacted to his sudden change in fortune, not with surprise or delight, but with the comportment of a man who'd never considered himself owned.

There is royalty in that one, at least, if not royal blood itself, he thought as the room and the people in it snapped fully back into his awareness. The others, especially Ada, welcomed Joshua and Adan into their midst.

The rest of the evening went to teaching the newcomers, including Adan and Joshua, the Practice, but John later had a chance to talk with the former slave. Part of gaining his freedom included receiving money enough that he might, if he chose, make passage back to his homeland, but John was not surprised when Adan asked more about his quest. When he finished telling speaking, Adan gazed at him for a long time.

"In my land, I was the son of a prince. I had many wives and children, many cattle, and a Way the others followed, even my own father," Adan said, confirming John's suspicion of his status. "I have been gone from my homeland for eleven years now, the spoils, as the young one would put it, of Rome's conquests. Yet, though Rome and this captured nation's son might tell you differently, in truth the path I walk is no man's save the gods'.

"Had it been my choice, I would be long dead, and many of Caesar's men with me. But for reasons of their own (and who knows the reasons of the gods?), it was convenient for me to remain alive, even as my people died and were captured around me to be made concubines to the Romans' tastes."

Adan's expression was unfathomable as he took a sip of wine and stared into the hearth fire that reflected dully off his ebony skin. "A slave by name have I been, but never a slave within myself. Now, by the laws of Rome and your Judea, I am 'free' to choose what I will do with myself. But this freedom too, only seems to be. While I would return to my homeland to find if any of mine escaped the Romans' harvesting, my gods tell me my way will not lead me there again in this life."

"How do you know this?"

"How did you know what to say to the young one?"

John shrugged, and Adan nodded knowingly. "The gods alone know how it is so, and that is enough for me. This they know as well: I traveled with you as you spoke to the Matthatus, as your soul entered the Deep Lands. The gods recognize you as one who is close to me as a brother would be close. They tell me my journey lies in whatever direction yours does, perhaps wholly, perhaps in part. That is, if your companions would have a 'Nubian' travel with them...but then, we should let them decide that, no?"

Adan smiled as if he already knew what the outcome would be.

John's answering grin told the African his knowing was correct.

TWELVE

The *eight companions left* The Inn of the Seven Tales at sky's first light laden with breads, nuts, dried fruits, wine and Elisha bar Salem's profuse thanks.

"Would that I could go with you, John bar Zebedee," Eli said fervently as he stood with his wife to bid John and the others safe journey. "Yet, I know my place is here with my family and the blessings of the One they give me."

John hugged his old friend, bowed over Amirah's hand and tousled young Jacob's hair. Unlike his siblings, the boy had risen with his parents to see the companions off.

"You've spoken more truly than you know, Eli. Some of us go forth to light the sparks that awaken our brothers—usually gladly," John smiled. "But do you know? Those who stay behind and hold the flame steady for all around them, as I also did with Mary...well, those of us who go forth cannot wish great enough blessings on you for your faithfulness."

The rest of the companions murmured their agreement as John leaned closer to Eli and Amirah and laid his hand on Jacob's shoulder. "When the time comes, and if young Jacob wishes it, send him on to Lazarus in Bethany," he said, too softly for the boy to hear. "His will be a great part to play, one that will help many know the One's Heart."

John leaned back and clasped the youngster's hand. "Be good to your mother and father, Jacob bar Salem. They always and only mean the best for you. Eli, Amirah, farewell. The One be with you in your every endeavor."

Bar Salem and his wife nodded their thanks, eyes wide with wonder as they looked at their second-born son.

The group walked along the dusty road to Tyre, their loads made lighter by Joshua's horse and Adan's mule. John watched Matthatus, Timothy and Rachael from behind; Timothy and Rachael talked only slightly less than they had the day before, while Joshua mostly listened. At Ada's insistence, they'd conformed to proper protocol for the first few miles, but now walked unchaparoned while Hosea and Ada kept pace ahead and earnestly discussed the deeper meanings of the Practice with Haifata Adan. They, like John, had quickly seen Adan was no mere—now former—slave. No matter what it might look like on the surface, his understanding bespoke the touch of the One.

Prochorus walked next to John, looking...well, grim, in truth.

"So then, Marcus, is that to be the look of you all the way to Tyre? Do you not fear your face will become permanently stuck so?"

Prochorus's scowl only grew deeper. "I know full well I am the last one who should speak thus of another...but I trust that young one not at all." He pointed with his chin toward Joshua Matthatus.

"Perhaps that is because he is not to be trusted," John answered.

"You do not trust him, Zebedee?" The Roman looked shocked. "But then why—?"

"I did not say that, Marcus. I trust Matthatus implicitly, but my trust can only encourage. It can do very little to make him trust in his own soul, for he knows not what it is. Any more than you know your own soul."

"I—but I know I desire to be on this journey!" Prochorus protested, flustered by the scrutiny John suddenly turned on him. "Do you not trust me?"

"Again, I said no such thing. Listen to me, Marcus: until one knows he is the Power of the One that rests within, the ability to trust or be trusted is questionable. This is not because of some inborn flaw we must overcome despite ourselves, as some would have us believe. We cannot trust or be trusted because, as Jeshua said from the cross, we literally know not what we do. How can we, when we know not what we are?

"We think our doing *is* us, and we define the whole of our worth by that doing and how others value it. And yet, the habit of thinking of ourselves as what we accomplish is naught but one of many ingrained beliefs we begin developing from the time we are born. Like the tracks formed by a fast-flowing stream, our beliefs channel deeper and deeper into our beings, until our notions and behaviors habitually reflect those traces.

"While it is not our fault we respond to certain things in certain ways, any more than it is the river's fault it follows certain flood traces, it *is* our responsibility to choose whether or not we will live in those 'tracks of being' without conscious consideration or choose to recognize the truth of the Selves we are beyond them. Unfortunately, many believe it takes considerable effort to change the paths we flow in; in frankest truth, very, very few feel they can muster the required effort." John suddenly smiled. "Or, more accurately, very, very few believe they are worth it. And so awakening to the Fullness has been effortful for most.

"You, Joshua, and Rachael have only begun your journey Home...but happily, you have a means for erasing your tracks of being that is far less strenuous than most. Indeed, you have the most effort-free tool that has ever existed."

"The Practice makes coming to a state of trust less strenuous?"

"As you are beginning to see for yourself," John nodded. "That is, if you simply allow it to do its work without 'you', so to speak. That is why Ada and Hosea admonished you not to try to make something happen, or have expectations of what the Practice should be or feel like when you do it. Acting as if your mind is somehow stronger than the power of your soul only slows your awakening...and makes your head hurt."

Marcus nodded ruefully, as if he'd already experienced the truth of John's statement. "But what if there is something specific you want to address?"

"Can the omnipotent, omniscient, omnipresent One be unaware of what needs adjusting within you?" John asked by way of an answer. Prochorus pursed his lips.

"In all truth, Zebedee, I do not know if there is such a thing as an omnipotent, omniscient, omnipresent One. In fact, I frequently doubt if there are gods of any kind, anywhere. It seems to me if they did exist, they would be less capricious and more careful about how their supposed creations' lives go. I do your Practice because I sense it does something for me, and to honor the gift you were able to give because of it. But I am not at all sure I believe in the Goal you say using the Practice leads to."

"Good. And even better if you do not believe it."

"What? But how can you say that?

"Oh, I will speak even more outrageously, Marcus: it makes no difference whatever if you believe the Practice is effective or not. Remember, the phrases of each technique describe what you are—the unlimited, unbounded truth of the One. Your being cannot but respond to them. As your own experience will ultimately reveal, simply by using the Practice, and regardless of your belief or disbelief, you will become the Silence."

Prochorus still frowned. "So? Then why this business of asking for a Teacher?"

Though the Roman's tone was gruff as usual, John detected a note of...uncertainty? No, better to call it concern—though exactly what concerned him was unclear.

John was slow to answer, letting his thoughts to make themselves plain at their own rate. Prochorus waited, allowing John's Stillness to take as long at It needed to form an answer.

"This dream we think of as our lives is a very enticing illusion, Marcus. Despite our stated wishes to be free of all the pain and misery we claim to hate, the truth is, most of us would be frightened out of our wits if it was suddenly replaced by the full awareness of being the perfect, unbounded One. More than one man has stood at the very threshold of Heaven, only to turn back and reenter the Fray when he realized he would rather sustain the fantasy he believed to be life as he knew it.

"It is not the Teacher's place to stop us from stepping off the Path if we desire to do so, only to be a beacon and guide who, by virtue of having become the Truth, constantly reminds the student of the illimitable Joy that comes of crossing the threshold."

"Yes, but...well, I find I cannot blame such ones for stepping back," Prochorus replied. "Your Jeshua suffered an awful fate to gain such 'bliss'."

John stopped and placed his hands on his hips, his exasperation plain. "Marcus! Jeshua's crucifixion was *not* the point of his trial on the cross. His resurrection was!"

"But most Christines say—"

"Then most Christines are wrong," John retorted. "Anyone who teaches that Jeshua's suffering was anything other than a means to a far greater end lacks a fundamental understanding of just what value he placed on this world, and that is so no matter what their title or previous relationship to him might be! Enjoy this world my Teacher could and did, for though it is an illusion, it is also God's creation. Yet he knew unequivocally that all that changes, even his own body, is fully and only a dream. Jeshua knew being one Awakened is the only thing of value.

"And as to having to give up one's life to know the Fullness—well, so far as I know, I am very much alive. That is, unless you have been too polite to tell me some highly distressing news."

"Hmm," Prochorus said after a moment, his amusement apparent. "As the evidence of my eyes—and ears—do not tell me otherwise, I must assume you are still amongst the living. But that look in your eye tells me there is more to this taking of a Teacher than simply having a guide along the way. What is it?"

"Yes, Marcus, there is. Asking for a Teacher is the ultimate act of trust for one who is truly ready to recognize their fullness as the One. It tells us that we choose, at last, to trust the whisperings of our very Soul. Taking a Teacher is our pledge to recognize that, unlike the phantom self, the Self never chooses to enter the Fullness alone, because there is no 'alone' in the Fullness. There is only One."

The group walked in relative silence for the rest of the day—Timothy and Rachael's perpetual conversation having become background—and stayed that night in a grassy field that was known to traveling merchants of every stripe.

Both John and Prochorus knew of a forking not far ahead, but it had been years since either of them had traveled it. Would it be easier to take the less-used but quicker route to Tyre, or should they go through Caesarea, as Joshua insisted? They spent the evening trading news and opinions with other travelers, especially the caravaners, to find out.

"You've women in your band?" asked a grizzled, ornery-looking old man who could probably travel these roads in his sleep. "Then take the slower, more crowded road, good sir. There's those on the lesser ones who'd kill you for a shekel and take sore advantage of those you value. We travel them, for we are many and well-armed, but your lot'd be in constant danger, unable even to sleep without risking attack in the night." The man didn't spit, but his distaste for those so cowardly as to make battle in the dark of the day was heavy in his voice.

"Would none of the caravans be willing to escort our group along the shorter road?" Prochorus asked, not quite ready to give up. "Certainly it would be worth it to us to pay for such service, and at least two of us are game hands with both sword and spear."

"Were we going that way, we would gladly take you on," one of the others around the fire said after looking to the grizzled caravaner, "but not all caravans are able or willing to accommodate women. Still, it is possible. I know of one that goes as far as Ptolemais, which would at least take you past the most dangerous part of the way. Perhaps you could ask their headsman for passage."

"Ha! Old Kalmis?" the older man said. "He'll not take these ones on, not if it'll slow him from taking as many trips as his horses can stand without falling over. To say traveling with him would be unpleasant would be stating the matter very poorly indeed!

"No, good sir, you take the longer route. Though it may seem slowest to you now, in the end it'll prove the quickest, if you take my meaning."

John smiled at the man's turn of phrase. "I do indeed, good sir, and I thank you. Caesarea it will be, then, and then along the coast to Tyre."

He and Prochorus stood to go, but the crusty one bid them wait, the sudden shyness in his eyes not at all native to his well-seamed face.

"Sir, my men are pleased to tease me about being a seer when it comes to deciding the best times to travel and trade, and I gladly let 'em, for my hunches are not often wrong. Well, I don't think my hunch is wrong now, either. You and your companion here've more to your countenances than the usual man carries about, and I feel sure you're healers of some kind.

"Though we, like your friend, are game hands with our weapons, we prefer not to use them if we can avoid it. And, well...I sense a blessing from ones like yourselves'd be blessing indeed. Would you be willing to give one for my men and our safety?"

John's answering smile was warmth itself as he fulfilled the request, and he and Marcus departed for their own camp amidst thanks and blessings returned.

His grin broadened as he espied Prochorus's expression.

"I've been accused of many things, Zebedee, but never have I been mistaken for a healer," The Roman blurted at last. "How can they ever have seen such a thing in me?"

"It fair takes the breath away, eh, Marcus? Jeshua said 'hide not your light under a basket,' but the truth is when you consistently touch the Unbounded, it quickly becomes impossible for the light to hide, regardless of how impure your history may have been. Your willingness to remember your Self gives you a glow those with eyes to see can see.

"So welcome back to the Land of Light, oh Candle Prochorus."

John laughed as the Roman discomfittedly crawled into his blankets for the night.

The next day found John walking largely without company. All said, he was pleased, for no one showed any serious signs of evincing animosity toward any other. He well remembered the bickering that went on between Andrew and Matthew, between Matthew and Thomas, and between Thomas and *everyone* else.

He was especially happy with the group's acceptance of Haifata Adan; though somewhat aloof by nature, he was quick enough to converse when approached, not only with Hosea and Ada, but with Rachael and Timothy. The more he talked with the youngsters, the more they warmed to the willowy African (*not* 'Nubian', John reminded himself, for the Bathshebites were from another part of that hot continent). And it relieved him more than he cared to admit that Prochorus's initial indifference had quickly been replaced by ready camaraderie—even if the thought that they might need the warriors to trust each other enough to fight as a team brought him no joy.

The port city of Caesarea appeared on the horizon early the next morning, a glowing, yellow jewel cloaked by the cerulean beauty of the Mediterranean Sea that stretched endlessly out behind it. Even from here, John could feel the bustling energy of the merchants, plebeians, peasants and soldiers who made Caesarea in no way different from any other port in the Empire. Several buildings towered above the walls of the city, their workmanship indicative of the latest in moneyed Roman and Jewish fashion. Many who passed the group were richly attired, not for Sabbath, as would be the case for a native of Bethany, but as if such were their normal mode of dress.

If Rachael and Timothy had thought The Inn of the Seven Tales a source of wonder, distant Caesarea went far beyond all they had ever imagined of grandeur and taste. They exclaimed and pointed at every little thing as it became clear to their view and whispered excitedly at the dress of the passersby, making their newness to the approaching city—and their small town manners—far, far too obvious for Joshua Matthatus's more sophisticated tastes. John suddenly found himself more than usually in the young man's company...

...And truth to be told, he was glad of it. He'd noticed a subtle competition for Rachael's attention, especially from Timothy, and wondered how soon he'd need to attend to the resultant headache. Having Joshua *here* meant postponement *there*.

For all his previous insistence that they travel to Caesarea and take one of his family's ships to Tyre, Joshua now seemed more nervous with every step. True, his soul had made the commitment to be student to his Teacher, but while his spirit was indeed willing, his mind was realizing the enormity of the choice he'd made. John could feel Matthatus becoming ever more lost in pictures of what his father would say about his choice to free his servant and follow John God Himself knew where. Indeed, we might well lose our first companion before we ever leave Judea, he thought.

Time to help the youngster look that notion in the face.

"Would you be freed from your obligation to me, Joshua Matthatus?" he gently asked.

"What?" Joshua's glassy stare dissolved, to be replaced by the confused look of one forcibly pulled into the present moment. "No! No...of course not, Rabbi. It is only that—"

"You wonder how you will ever explain this to your father. Are you the eldest-born?"

"No. I am the third of five sons, with a sister who is youngest of us all. But my eldest brother is dead at sea these last five years, and my second brother...has his own business."

Joshua's hesitation told John more than any words could about his father's relationship with his second son. The young man seemed almost ashamed as he spoke the next words, as if he thought it a betrayal to do so. "My father expects I will eventually take over the business, but now..."

"Yes, I understand the dilemma," John said dryly, remembering his father's reaction to not one, but both of his sons taking up with the vagabond prophet from Nazareth.

"Rabbi, asking you to be my Teacher was the most shocking thing I have ever done in my life. I truly had no idea I was going to speak those words until they were already out of my mouth. Even so, the moment I spoke them, my soul sang in my heart as a bird sings when he escapes his cage to find blue sky. I have no doubt here I have done the right thing ..." he pointed at his heart, "but still, I do wonder what I shall tell my father. He'd not be given to fancies even if the angels themselves presented them, and he is not given to forgiveness once crossed. Still, I love him and would cause him no pain if I can avoid it.

"As to my mother...I did not really realize it until now, but she has always understood and supported my desire to seek Truth, even as I know my father has not. I love her with all my heart, too, Rabbi, but this choice I've made..." Joshua's face clearly reflected his anguish. "Has not she suffered enough?"

"Have you considered asking Haifata Adan what he would do?" John asked. Matthatus's reaction was just what he expected.

"Ask my slave what to do about my father? Why that—that is ridiculous!"

"Hmmm...yes. Perhaps it is. Yet, remember, Joshua, before he was a slave of Rome, Adan was a man born free to a family known and respected amongst his people."

"Savages!" The young man sneered.

"As the Hebrews were 'savages' to the Egyptians?" John retorted, his voice sharp. "Or were you not taught enough of your own people's history to know that we were, even in bondage, largely left to enjoy our own culture and remember our own history? Are the Romans any less civilized, since you think yourself one of them?"

Joshua was silent.

"Only a fool refuses to listen to those who serve him, Joshua. After all, servants often know us best *because* we think them too unimportant to guard our tongues in their presence. Adan seemed to be a slave to your house, but if you look into his eyes instead of your ideas, you will discover that he served you because it served his gods and because he found honor in House Matthatus. Had that not been so, he would gladly have defied your father before his first moon under your roof and seen his life ended.

"Joshua, Adan served your father closely before he served you; I would speculate he knows exactly what to say and how to say it, so that you'll at least receive a true hearing. And more, given the chance, I believe he would choose to be friend to you."

John picked up his pace, leaving his newest student to find his own way past his personal forest of old beliefs.

The travelers, the horse and the well-laden mule arrived at the gates of the bustling city halfway through fourth hour of the afternoon. John's brows rose; he'd not seen this many Roman soldiers and Jewish guardsmen together since Jerusalem. They were being quite thorough in their scrutiny of those who entered the city, but they were also efficient: though the line was long, it moved quickly. John wondered what disaster or attempted one had struck what noble; the Zealots were still active.

Or perhaps they were not the sole cause of the sentries' thoroughness. The guardsmen in particular asked many questions about the business of those entering the city, as if they sought someone or something specific. They checked the shoulder bags of many and inspected the necks of all—seeking, John suddenly knew, a certain piece of jewelry.

The Jewish guards, at least, were looking for Jeshua's followers.

John's hand went to his neck; Jeshua's wooden fish hung beneath his robe. Someone, perhaps even one of his original companions, must be expected in the city, and the local priests wanted no part of it. Saul of Tarsus was by no means the only Jew who'd thought it his duty to extinguish all traces of the Christine threat by extinguishing the Christines. In fact, John had heard rumors that Rome herself was coming to consider them something more than a mere local nuisance.

"Rabbi..." Hosea began from behind him.

"Yes, Hosea, I am aware of the situation. Thank you."

"What situation?" Prochorus asked. Hosea explained, but it was Joshua who responded.

"Have no fear. My family is known in the city for our generosity to Synagogue, Roman citizens though we be. The guards will cause us no trouble."

Young Matthatus spoke truly; he was greeted like a returning prince out on his afternoon ride. None of his guests were given more than a cursory interview and—with the help of a bit of discreetly-passed silver—none were asked to bare their necks.

A full decade had passed since John visited Caesarea and he found he'd missed it not at all. The companions made their way through the myriad noises, smells and sounds, being begged to and hawked at and sometimes herded like cattle as first this passing group of soldiers, then this rich family's retinue, forced the more common folk to the sides of the streets. It seemed as if everyone yelled at everyone else, even the animals, and Joshua's horse did not appreciate the change in scenery. Adan had to calm the poor creature several times as he backed and tried to bolt at some noise or other. Rachael and Timothy's mouths were for once closed, their noses covered to protect them from the flying dust as their wide eyes took in the overwhelming sound and movement of the place.

John frowned a bit behind his own makeshift veil; the deadness of the souls that occupied this city that seemed so full of life weighed on him like a large stone in a small boat. He saw it in the poor and crippled beggars who asked for mercy and alms, saw it in the rich men and women, with their expensive clothing and painted faces. He saw it in the soldiers, whose suspicious eyes surveyed them as they looked for the trouble these visitors were no doubt here to cause, and in the priests, scribes and laborers who managed the city's day-to-day business.

Caesarea was thick with a life force that was choking to death in its own effluvia.

"How much farther to your home, Joshua?" John yelled over the tumult as Matthatus, Hosea and Prochorus moved the ocean of bodies aside largely by the brute force that seemed so common.

"It is on the other side of town, I fear, nearer the docks," Joshua apologetically called back. "Many are out today to shop and inspect new wares. It is not always so—"

"Master Joshua!" a heavy-yet-feminine voice called over the noise. "Master Joshua, over here!"

John was the first to see the pudgy figure's hand waving in the air, the sleeve of his simple tan tunic a flag flapping in a breeze. He and the two men with him pushed toward the group, moving people aside with the ease of long practice coupled with a complete willingness to cause offense. Which they are doing quite admirably, John smiled, as several women swung bags and even walking sticks at them with sharp, if unintelligible, slurs.

Soon enough, the men stood before the group and the caller smiled joyfully at Joshua. His face was more a series of strategically placed rolls of fat, punctuated by small eyes, than it was a structure with character and consideration about it. One of the other two, though younger and slimmer, had the same telltale lack of fire that told John they were eunuchs.

"Master Joshua, you return home earlier than expected!" The large man said enthusiastically, his dullness giving him an innocence that seemed odd on one so large. He noticed Haifata Adan standing at the back of the group with the horse and mule and also called out a welcome to him. Adan nodded the amiable acknowledgement of one greeting someone too feeble-minded to properly be called grown.

The eunuch's attention wandered to the others in the group and lighted on John's face. His childlike smile grew larger; John could not but smile back.

"Are all these ones with you, Master Joshua?"

"Yes, Artus, they are to be guests at my father's house for a day or two."

John plainly heard the silent, "If he does not throw us all out on the street," but the servant just as plainly did not; he was as happy as a boy at Festival at hearing such news.

"Ah, your mother will be pleased! Though she has not said it, I think she—"

Artus suddenly slapped a hand over his mouth as if belatedly remembering it was bad form to speak so indiscreetly of one's mistress in public, but Joshua only laughed and clapped the eunuch on the shoulder.

"Come then Artus. Let us hurry home so Mother will worry no longer, hmm? Or did she send you out on some special errand?"

The slave's brow furrowed as if he were trying to figure out a complicated sum. "She did send me out to shop, Master Joshua...but I can leave Rufus and Tarin to do it. I think she will find it more important to see you. Do you not think so?"

His face was both eager and concerned, lest he should make the wrong deduction. Joshua put his mind at ease and the group continued toward their destination.

"Nearer the docks" Joshua's home might be, but it was by no means at the docks, for John caught no whiff of the usual smells. The group escaped the bustle of the crowds with the help of Artus's tremendous bulk; they soon entered a quiet, well laid out section of the city where homes were large, grounds were beautiful, and servants were plentiful.

Joses Matthatus had done very well as a shipper of goods; House Matthatus was one of the most elegant in this neighborhood. A Roman hand had designed the façades: the polished stone of the portico and supporting columns was stylishly decorated with various scenes of Rome's triumphant history. Trees and plants from many different lands grew in symmetrical perfection so both the denizens of House Matthatus and their neighbors might be oft-reminded of the life they'd lived at the Empire's center.

"Your face has that sour look again, Marcus," John said, only half-teasing.

"As does my heart, Zebedee. I have no stomach for making another half a man for the sake of having safe nursemaids, and this half-baked play at being Roman offends me. Conquerors we may be, but never have we demanded a people give up their souls to become ersatz Romans...and if we have, then best we should stop it. The gods, if there be gods, must prefer variety."

John kept his eyebrows from rising in surprise. The depths of the former scribe's passion—and compassion—continually amazed him.

Joshua stood before the house, ready to enter. Though his back was to the rest of the group, John saw the fear and tension in his stance. Adan, who had given the horse and mule to a servant as they came up the walk, stepped beside him and quietly spoke. Joshua looked long into the African's eyes, then nodded and set his jaw. He turned.

"Please, my guests, come inside and be welcome in my home," he said formally, his smile genuine, if still somewhat nervous.

John turned and shook a finger at Timothy and Rachael.

"There will be no fainting with awe from you two, is that understood?" he said, his serious mien in no way hiding the smile in his eyes. The two young and thoroughly flabbergasted faces smiled back at him, some of their tension at the thought of meeting such rich people draining away. Ada chuckled.

"It may not be them you have to worry about, Rabbi, but me..."

THIRTEEN

A *man with the* airs of a head servant stepped forth as the companions entered a magnificent front hall, all his attention on Joshua Matthatus. He greeted the son of the House with a reverential obeisance, observing, as Artus had, that he'd returned sooner than expected. He likewise welcomed Joshua's guests with an elaborate bow—but then, noting their plain dress, turned quickly away, his desire to have no more to do with them plain. Like many servants, this one defined his value by that of the house he served—and these visitors did not suit House Matthatus's elegance.

His duty to propriety discharged, the headman started to order the other servants to see to the guests' needs...then noticed Haifata Adan. His carefully cultured poise slipped.

"By what right do you come in with the guests, Adan? Are you mad, or has your ridiculous insistence that you were once a prince of savages finally overcome your desire to live? Get to your proper post, now, before I tell the master of this breach!"

"Haifata Adan is slave to this house no more, Cristus, but a free man and a companion upon my way," Joshua said sharply to the headman. "He is a guest in my father's house and you will treat him as such, lest I report your unseemly behavior in the presence of these other honored guests to your master. Is that understood?"

The slave Cristus went as white as the house's columns. The others in the hall also froze, their shock evident in their expressions. Shaking with a combination of fear and fury, the headman practically brushed the floor with his bow, and voice strangled, apologized to the companions. Then—though he did not look into his eyes—he apologized to Haifata Adan, who nodded slightly, with dignified grace.

The other servants returned to their duties with sudden, noisy efficiency, aware of the wisdom of at least feigning indifference; whatever their feelings about Adan's sudden fortune, they valued their places and would wait to vent the ire they surely felt.

Joshua faced the companions and again offered a formal bow. "Please, be welcome in House Matthatus and know our home is yours. If you have need of anything, at any time, you need simply ask. Cristus, Hosea bar Eliran and his wife Ada require a room together; please see to it. Also, please make sure Mistress Rachael has a lady's servant to attend to her needs." Left unspoken was the fact that said lady's maid would be with Rachael at all times when she was not under Ada's auspices. Propriety was taken seriously in House Matthatus.

"As you wish, Master Joshua," the head servant replied, still struggling to reestablish his calm veneer.

"I think it would be best if I first talked to my father alone," Joshua said to John, looking toward Adan. "Haifata has given me some advice on how I can best handle him, if he is to be handled at all. Hopefully, he is right."

He bowed again and left the rest of the companions to be led to their rooms.

Or, more accurately, suites. John figured his was not quite as big as the house he'd shared with Mary—but only by a very small margin.

The room was well lit, blessed with morning sun even in winter. It held several closets of hard pine, each as beautifully engraved as his chest in Bethany, and the bed had an actual mattress stuffed with feathers. Hangings and rugs from several lands covered walls and floors, so a guest might never have the shock of placing his bare feet on chill marble. A fire burned gaily in a rounded pit near the center of the room, and beyond that hung a heavy, sienna-dyed curtain. The servant stored John's pack, then showed him the washing-bowl, heavy towels and deep, covered chamber pot that occupied the curtained alcove. No tiptoeing out into the morning cold for one's daily ablutions in this house!

John stepped through a pair of terrace doors as the servant departed, greatly impressed by the large garden that greeted him. Joses Matthatus might not give credence to the fanciful worlds, but he'd clearly listened to one who did: the garden boasted many fantastical sculptures of mythical creatures from Greek and Roman stories. In the park's center stood a small, round building that could only be a Roman-style bathhouse.

John stood on the balcony for several minutes, taking joy in the soft, clear air and the noises of a late summer evening, wondering if Joshua's meeting with his father would bear the fruit the young man hoped for...when suddenly, he yawned widely. He stepped back, intending to enter the Stillness and discern whether the bed was as soft it looked...

...Only to discover that the garden had somehow stretched into his room.

No, that was not correct. The garden had *become* John's room.

John bemusedly passed between two small trees which tangled together in a leafy green arch that had been a stone doorway but a few seconds before. The air was warm and moist, but not uncomfortably so; plants and flowers exploded with the riotous vibrancy of summer in full bloom. Everything wore halos of shifting iridescence, so luminous they seemed to be lit from within, but it was the clarity of the air and the weight he felt as he moved forth that told John he'd not fallen into some dream unawares. He'd entered, not into a vision, but into some version of reality other than the earthly.

Just as he had in Gethsemane seventeen years ago.

This garden stretched into the distance, but it was not one John could walk without equipment for scaling mountains. Perhaps a hundred feet from where he stood, its rich verdure suddenly fell over a cliff, to reappear miles away and effortlessly crawl up a series of steep terraces. In the furthest distance, a jagged expanse of mountains hazed purple against a sky full of stars too large and numerous for any sky John might know...a sky which, despite the day's brilliance, abruptly darkened to sudden, solid blackness.

John shivered. Wherever he stood (and he sensed it was not Vashti), it was closer to the end of the world than the end of day; he was on very high ground indeed.

"Hello, my belovéd son."

John spun at the instantly-recognized voice, for though she had only been gone a week or so, he felt as if it had been eons since he'd last heard it. Yes. Sitting on a long, low boulder, her smiling countenance seeming as bright as it had been during her last moments in Bethany, was Mary.

John cried out her name with a grin so large it took up his whole face and stepped forward, intending to give her a bone-crushing embrace. But Mary raised her hand.

"No, John. Do not touch me."

John stopped, surprised at how hurt he felt, not only at being thus rebuked, but at the sudden suspicion that entered his mind. "Is this then but a phantom, Mother? A common vision born of a fatigued imagination?"

Mary's gaiety only increased at her son's disconsolate reaction, her eyes holding a combination of joy, mischief and exasperation.

"Really, John. I would hardly call any vision *common*."

She slid along the boulder and patted it; John carefully sat next to her. "The reason you cannot touch me has nothing to do with this being an 'unreal' experience. This body does exist in this time and space," she pointed at his chest as she spoke, "but your other body, the one you left behind—just as in Gethsemane—is still standing on the balcony of that sinfully luxurious room in Caesarea. You are experiencing being in two places at once with a higher level of awareness than you did then, but you've not yet mastered the ability, nor come anywhere near doing so."

Wondering, John closed his eyes. All at once, his other body's eyes opened, showing him his room in House Matthatus as if he looked at it through heavy gauze. He opened the eyes of the body that sat next to Mary and her garden also appeared. The room in Caesarea faded as his mother recaptured his astonished attention.

"Though it may not feel so to you, my son, you are expending a great deal of energy to remain in this space. The life force of this place and of those of us who frequent it is much higher than either of your bodies is yet able to accommodate. If you touched me now, those differences in our levels of life force would scramble your circuits, and you would find yourself back in Caesarea before I have the chance to tell you what I must."

John nodded. Though he still felt mildly disappointed at not being able to hug her, what Mary said made perfect sense. Except...

"What is a 'ser-kuts'?"

Mary blinked as if startled, then smiled sheepishly. "Forgive me, John. That is a word from another time and place, one it is not yet appropriate for you to hear. I meant to say, your mind and being would become severely confused if you touched me now. In truth, at this stage of your development, there is a real danger in staying too long in this space, and so I must quickly deliver the message Isha gave me."

John's brow furrowed in jarring recognition: "Isha" was the name Miriam had used for Jeshua back in Bethany.

Mary smiled. "Yes, what Miriam said was correct. Seek the land where our Teacher is called 'Isha', for there is where you will be most likely to discover the location of Vashti. But at this moment, his message is simply this: 'Be ready, Little Brother.'"

John was on the verge of asking, "Is that all?" But Mary interrupted him.

"Yes, that is all for now, dearest. 'Be ready'. I said the word 'circuits' was from another time and space, but soon that and many other concepts will become part of your awareness. Be ready for what will come by opening your heart more, and even more. Be ready by redefining your ideas of what it is to be One with the One. Expect the unexpected and embrace it.

"You and your companions must give more time each day to diving into the Heart of the One, even if you have to stop traveling earlier than you desire. I cannot overemphasize the importance of doing this, John; it will serve you more than words can say. Indeed, it may make all the difference." Mary stood and stepped away from the boulder.

John started to follow suit—but a sudden wave of dizziness snatched his breath away and made him horribly nauseous.

"Oh dear... I have kept you here too long," Mary said with a contrite and somewhat pitying smile. "The apothecary of House Matthatus can give you a draught for the headache, but I fear only rest will cure the weakness—so be sure you take it. Next time, we will be able to keep you here longer."

'*We?*' John tried to ask, but every cell in his body, not only his head, now spun wildly, each in a different direction. His ears rang with the noise of a hundred buzzing things. He clenched his teeth to keep the nausea from exploding from his mouth as the luminously bright garden began fading. Mary's voice echoed as if she spoke from a long tunnel.

"Go safely, my belovéd son. Do more of the Practice—and be ready!"

John was back in his room in Caesarea.

Falling.

Only a lucky grab at the doorjamb saved him from crashing straight to the floor and cracking his head hard against the marble tiles. As it was, he was vaguely aware, shortly before the darkness of unconsciousness carried him away, that his knees and elbows would likely take a goodly bruising.

The first thing John became conscious of was a cold, wet cloth gently pressing against his forehead. Next, the sound of soft, motherly murmuring reached his ears and the smell of clean human filled his nostrils.

Then he became aware of the headache.

His lids fluttered open just enough to let in a hammer-blow of excruciating light, then snapped shut of their own accord. He thanked them for it.

Early in Jeshua's ministry, the rest of the companions decided it was time for John to experience the joys of excessive imbibing. It was something he'd always avoided, since he'd never been overly fond of wines or ales, preferring instead the fresh juices from which they were made. His way had always been to let his host pour him a cup, then nurse it throughout his visit. It was a habit that had for some reason irritated his brother, and John had no doubt James was the instigator of this particular initiation.

He didn't remember a great deal about the experience of being drunk—not after the third cup of wine, anyway. But he did, emphatically, remember the resultant hangover. He'd felt as if someone had propped his mouth open, tied him behind a racing chariot, and dragged him along the roughest, dustiest trail they could find, while occasionally stopping to let the other chariots in the race run over him.

"Do not worry, brother mine, you will not die from this," James had laughed the next day, his voice pleased and inordinately loud in John's ears. John remembered being sorely disappointed by that piece of news, for death could only have been a mercy.

He felt disappointed now, and for the same reason.

"Urrrgh," he said, managing only a garbled gargle instead of coherent speech.

"Thank the One, he is coming to."

John opened his eyes as fully as the pain would allow to find Ada's face above his, the cold cloth poised in her hand. He tried to sit up, but the tiny woman easily pushed him back; as Mary had promised, his entire body felt as if he'd spent a year continuously rowing in the galleys.

"What time is it?" He croaked, seeing the sun was long gone from the sky.

"A little after midnight, Rabbi," Ada answered, looking off to the side. Hosea came into view, his face full of worry as he peered at his Teacher. He held an ornate cup of what John sincerely hoped was not wine.

"I will not ask how you feel, Rabbi, for your groans are answer enough," Hosea said, "but can you tell us what happened? Your poor servant nearly went frantic when he came to gather you in for dinner and found you on the floor. We tried to wake you, but you would not rouse." He suddenly seemed to realize he held the cup and gave it to Ada.

"The apothecary said this would restore you," she said, as Hosea helped him sit up and Prochorus and Joshua entered the room. He shivered with distaste at the bitter draught and hoped it would require only one dose.

"Sir! Thank the gods you are awake!" Joshua said, his voice far too loud in his relief. "My father sends solicitations and will be gratified to know you are better. He would like to talk to you as soon as you feel well enough." The young man's face showed nothing, but he'd obviously done well enough to keep them out of the local inns this night.

Prochorus, who was a bit more conscious of the vagaries of a hangover, spoke more softly. "Are you all right, Zebedee? What in Hades happened to you? We thought surely you were dead when we first found you."

John told them about his experience, mentioning Mary's emphasis on their need to engage in the Practice for more time each day.

"Hmph," Prochorus said at last. "Like all oracles, the Lady did not say nearly enough...but it is never a good thing to ignore them. Doing as she says will definitely slow our progress, but there is naught to be done but follow her advice."

John nodded, then swore to keep his head still until the draught saw fit to have more effect. He spoke to Joshua. "Please thank your father for his hospitality; I am sure this would have been far less pleasant had the apothecary not been available to work his magic. I can ready myself to speak with him within the half-hour, if need be...but if he would have it, I would like an hour or two more to recover my wits."

"Oh, I am sure he will allow you that much time, Rabbi," Joshua said, admirably ignoring Prochorus's snort at his choice of the word 'allow'. He seemed eager to put his father in a good light. "In fact, I am sure he will be willing to wait until morning. I think it is just that he is anxious to meet you."

"Rabbi, would you like some dinner?" Ada asked. "We have already eaten and met Joshua's parents, younger brothers and sister. They are indeed a gracious and hospitable family." She smiled at Joshua, receiving an appreciative smile in return.

"Did Adan join you?" John asked.

"He was invited, Sir, by my father. He chose however, not to eat at table. He told me later it would not have done, that it would have been too great a shift for my family to make just yet, regardless of their good intentions. Truly, I believe he was right and was glad for his wisdom." Joshua looked more than a bit impressed.

"Hmmm," John said, remembering not to nod. His head did seem to hurt less, though his body still felt thoroughly exhausted. Ada suddenly stood.

"It is time we left the Rabbi to his recovery," she said decisively. "The danger, if ever there was danger, is past, and some food and silence (and Silence) are the best things for him now... So out, you three, out."

John watched amusedly as the tiny woman made shooing motions at the three men. They hastily made their retreats with well wishes trailing out behind them, but Joshua turned back just long enough to smile shyly and say, "I am glad you are feeling better, Rabbi," before letting himself be pushed out the door. Ada shook her head in mock-disgust, then smiled as she left behind them, promising to have dinner sent up.

It went uneaten, however. By the time it arrived, John was fast asleep.

A soft knock woke John a second time; the sun was well up and the birds in the garden cried out songs of summer's end to each other and the world. A muffled voice sought and received entry, and the door opened slowly, several pudgy fingers wrapping around its edge. A face that was rolls of fat peered around it.

"Would you require a shave this morning, honored guest?" the eunuch, Artus, asked in his simple contralto. He stepped around the door, a looking glass and blade in his other hand. Another servant held a large bowl of water and a cleaning cloth.

John didn't—quite—wince as he rubbed his chin.

"No, Artus, but thank you. A shave will not be necessary today." Nor on any other day, it seemed. The eunuch bowed respectfully and closed the door behind him.

He'd thought at first the trauma of meeting and dealing with his shadow with Miriam, had affected him; that the beard would grow back soon enough. After all, once it had finally begun coming in during his twenty-first summer, it had done so with great enthusiasm. But it hadn't grown back, not one whit, and that annoyed John more than it had a right to.

"You know how long it took me to grow a proper beard, Jeshua. This is not at all fair," he mumbled to the room around him, sure his Teacher could hear him perfectly well. "I ask you, Big Brother, what need is there for me to go beardless now?"

There was no answer, and John thought it would probably be sheerest paranoia to think the universe laughed at his frustration, so he put the issue out of his mind, made his way to the wash basin, and reveled in cleaning his body. If they stayed another day, he would definitely give the bathhouse a try.

Now though, there were other matters to attend to.

John dressed in a clean robe and called a servant to discover if Joses Matthatus was available. It was time to meet the father of the son.

One thing John could say for Joses Matthatus: the man took pride in his library.

Though no great reader himself, John looked with considerable admiration at the numerous nooks that held scribed rolls of one fable or speech or another, this business notice or that. The elder Matthatus had the writings of every philosopher of the modern age, along with those of ages past. So often did he require and desire things be put into the written word that he had not one, but two scribes on his household staff.

Like his son, Joses Matthatus was a comely man, tall and spare but by no means skinny, with hair a wavy steel gray that held only a few streaks of the deep brown it had once been. His bearing was regal, but John sensed it was a learned thing, that he'd made his fortune, or at least the bulk of it, with his bare hands and an extensive talent for turning a small profit into a large one. His visage, as Joshua had said, was that of one who had long ago left the fanciful behind.

Joshua's mother, Sarah, was also in the room. She was dressed in the latest fashion, her hair the color of henna and her eyes painted in the way of the Empire's rich. Her delicate face held the intelligence of a woman who had been suffered to learn to read and took the privilege seriously; like her husband, she held herself as nobility might. She, however, had been born to wealth, and, also unlike her husband, felt things deeply. John entered the study and bowed his head to Lady Matthatus; the elder Matthatus, back to the door, surveyed some notice concerning his trade.

At last he turned, his otherwise handsome face marred by a frown.

"Who are you?" he asked after Joshua introduced them in the proper manner and was dismissed. To John's surprise, he spoke, not like a parent who suspected his child was being lead astray by some charlatan, but like a judge who wanted to maintain a neutral mien until he knew what was what. Not that he has not already decided against me, John thought, noting the closed energy of Matthatus's life force. Still, his whole manner said he prided himself on waiting until he could ascertain to his satisfaction the truth of what was said about another. John could see why Haifata Adan's gods had bid him live as a servant under this one rather than die as a rebellious slave. Joses Matthatus was a fair and honorable man who, once all the facts were in, made his decision and stuck to it stubbornly, no matter what the cost. He was a steady man, used to controlling himself and his situations...

John suppressed a sudden smile as the Voice of the One made clear to him exactly how to heal and prevent the estrangements between father and sons.

"Joses Matthatus, just last night, you yet again turned your second-eldest son from this house without even a hearing because he years ago chose to follow his heart instead of following you in your business. You would not hear of his desire to reconcile with you, to tell you that the wares he once sold to prostitutes and plebeians are now sought by the rich and noble of many cities. That he now raises his sons with the same pride and honor as his own father and mother. More is the loss to you, for not only could his wares profit your business, but his joy would profit your heart."

Matthatus was thoroughly nonplussed. He'd been in John's room to ask after his condition when his personal servant called him into the hall to tell him Seth Matthatus wished to see him; there was no logical way John could know what had transpired.

John's heart went out to Sarah Matthatus as she suddenly stood, her expression full of shock. Matthatus hadn't mentioned the visit to her either, and she was even now realizing it was not the first time he'd denied her such knowledge. She approached John, graceful even in distress, and pleadingly laid her hand on his sleeve.

"Sir, do you know where my son is now?"

"Sarah!" Matthatus's tone was commanding, but she spun on him angrily.

"Pray, Husband, will you banish me if I do not do your will? Seth has visited this house more than once, yet you denied it even when I asked! You've naught to say to me!" She turned back to John, her eyes still flaming. "Joshua tells me you are a prophet, one with many abilities. I wanted to believe for his sake that he did not throw his life away for a pretender, for he is as headstrong as his father and has already decided to travel with you. I think now I can believe...but you must tell me, where is Seth?"

"He, his wife and your three grandsons are guests in the home of a friend on the eastern side of the city, the one with the bright red and gold banner that has hung in the garden portico since the mother of the house died four years ago."

"Joshua!"

Joshua Matthatus entered the room so quickly that he could only have been standing just outside the door. His face was apprehensive as he looked at his mother.

"Did you tell him of David bar Ruben's house?"

Joshua's confused frown was answer enough, but he completed it by saying, "No, I would have no reason to. Why?"

The silence stretched long as Sarah Matthatus again looked at her husband; he would not meet her eyes. She turned to Joshua. "My son, nothing would bring me more joy than to have you here with your family, safe in our home. But if it truly is your desire to travel with this prophet, know that you have my blessing, at least."

She hugged the surprised young man hard and long; then, almost sobbing, quickly exited the room without looking again at her husband. John heard her urgently order one of the servants to bring her cloak as the study door swung closed.

"How dare you?" Joses Matthatus shook with unaccustomed rage. "How dare you enter this house as a guest and bring strife to my family? Have you no honor at all?"

John shook his head, suddenly aware of the source of Joshua's pride. "Do you still believe the Hand of God does not direct this course, Joses Matthatus? What will it take for you to understand that Joshua's destiny is not the one you have chosen?"

"I have lost two sons already, and will lose no more if I can help it!" Matthatus said tightly, "and if that means seeing you and your friends put in the local prison, then that is what I will arrange!"

"You have lost one son, not two," John said exasperatedly. "The other would humbly and gladly come to you if you would let him. He would well and joyfully serve you and your business. But you let your wife go to him alone, too proud to accept that he made his way without you—just as your father was too proud to accept your choice!"

Well then. And perhaps an angel *has* finally come to him, John thought as the elder Matthatus's face went white with shock. He gave him no chance to recover.

"You never told anyone, not even your wife and sons, that that is why you are 'Matthatus', not 'bar Matthias', did you? That you would not carry the name of one who, rather than accept the son who'd made his own way, spurned him even on his deathbed. Must history repeat itself five more times, Joses Matthatus? Free yourself and your sons."

"Father," Joshua broke in pleadingly, "Never have I desired to take over your business, to be lost in wares and ships and numbers. Finding the Heart of God and is all I've ever wanted; there lies my destiny.

"You always taught us the importance of keeping our honor by keeping our word. I have given my word to follow this one wherever he goes, for he can help me find what I truly seek. Would you now have me forsake my honor by turning from this pledge?" Joshua's voice caught as if his heart was breaking.

"Please, Father, cannot I go forth with your blessing?"

Matthatus's face was still pale as he stepped from behind his worktable and stared at his son as if seeing him for the first time. Finally, he shook his head, not in rejection, but bewilderment.

"Joshua, I..." He turned from the younger man and shook his head again. "Leave me now. I...must think about this. Leave me."

John and Joshua started for the door, Joshua doing his best to hide a defeated frown. John stopped and turned to find the elder Matthatus running his fingers through his silver hair.

"Joses."

The elder Matthatus looked at John in startlement, as if trying to decide whether or not to be offended by such familiar treatment. John smiled sympathetically.

"If you hurry, you should be able to catch up with Sarah. It really would be best if you saw Seth together."

He softly closed the door.

Several hours later, John and Joshua still sat on the balcony outside John's room, their cups of wine warming in the afternoon sun. The young man shook his head.

"My father may have seemed shocked by all you told him, Rabbi, but by now he has let his training draw his understanding to a 'reasonable' explanation for your knowledge, just as I would have let mine. He will never accept my going forth."

John took a bite of a one of the sweetmeats a servant had brought only a few minutes before, aware he was in danger of becoming addicted to the things. But before he could—yet again—remind Joshua to focus his thoughts on his technique of the Practice, someone knocked on the door. John raised a brow at the young man and smiled.

"Please enter, Joses Matthatus."

It was Joshua's turn to raise his brows; he hastily came to his feet as his father pushed tentatively into the room. Sarah Matthatus followed behind him, her face managing to convey both joy and sorrow. Joses Matthatus did not fidget as he spoke only because he willed himself not to.

"A ship leaves for Tyre in two days to pick up products and supplies for trade in Corinth. I will send word to the shipmaster that you and your companions will be on it." For possibly the second time in his adult life, Joses Matthatus looked uncertain, but then his face softened.

"Joshua...take care, my son, and be safe...may you travel well and find what you truly seek." The elder Matthatus awkwardly but soulfully hugged his son, then stepped back and looked at John, his eyes misty.

"If you would be so good as to excuse us, Sir, my wife and I must speak to the cooks about preparing a special dinner for this evening. Also...it would honor us greatly if you and your companions would dine with us, our son, Seth, and his family."

Joses and Sarah Matthatus exited, once more leaving John and Joshua alone.

"Do you know, Rabbi? That is the first time my father has ever hugged me," Joshua said his eyes meeting his Teacher's. Then he burst into tears.

Nine days later, the companions landed in the port city of Tyre.

FOURTEEN

Tyre stank abominably.

In addition to its twenty oars, *Galley Matthatus* had masts to permit whatever extra speed the winds might provide, and served as the Matthatus family yacht. It boasted three levels; its four cabins, located at each end of the first level belowdecks, were as luxuriously appointed as the rooms in House Matthatus. The section between the rooms served as storage space for the luxuries this particular ship most usually traded, and the flooring beneath it was extra-thick so the guests' illusion that their conveyance was borne on the wings of angels would not be disturbed by the drumbeats that kept the slaves who actually powered the ship in proper rowing rhythm.

Ada's response to seeing *Galley Matthatus* shocked John and the others, even Hosea.

"I will not board that ship!" she said, pulling up so quickly that Prochorus very nearly ran over her. Her usually cheerful countenance was suddenly hard and closed; it was the first time in more than a year John had seen his student so upset.

She fairly snarled at the others' dismayed inquiries: did she fear the water? Was she prone to seasickness? Did she fear the rough-looking men loading the supplies and goods? Or sea monsters?

This last, asked by Timothy, garnered a withering glare from Prochorus; the youngster bowed his head, his zeal temporarily waylaid by an embarrassed blush. But none of the companions' concerns moved Ada to explain herself or start up the galley's gangway. She crossed her arms tightly and refused even to speak, except to say again that she would not board *Matthatus*, "not even if Yahweh Himself orders it."

John finally directed the companions, even a worried Hosea, to board, and instructed them to obey whatever Joshua or the shipmaster said. He was gratified to see Joshua take his designation as temporary leader as a responsibility rather than a given.

"Let us walk, sister," John said, holding out his hand.

Ada stared at it for several moments, her lips so tightly pursed they were pale around the edges, but she finally complied with her Teacher's request.

They wandered through the dock area, heading back the way they'd come. John took a moment to simply enjoy the bustle around him; the scent of the Mediterranean's salty aliveness brought back fond memories of his "fisher of fishes" youth.

He made no attempt to draw Ada out, for he'd noticed Hosea had held his tongue while the others implored her to speak. Pushing for explanations would no doubt only make her hold silent longer. Instead, he simply introduced the techniques of the Practice, confident she did the same.

"I have a half-brother, ten years older than me. He was the last-born child of my father's first wife, who died having him," Ada finally said when they reached a small grove. "My birth, like his, was hard, and my mother was ill for many weeks after. She told me that, while my half-sisters looked after her, it was Daniel who kept to me. Not because my sisters did not want the care of me," she said, to make sure John understood they had no untoward animosity for her, "but because they could not keep Daniel away. Even my father felt in his heart that it was meet for Daniel to have the care of me until Mother was well, and could not but let him away from his chores to do so.

"From the time he was very young, Daniel loved the Lord. Yet, when he came of age during my third summer, he declined to enter studies at Temple, saying he was Told to stay home awhile longer to teach the truth of God to me until I wanted to learn more for myself. When he went off to Temple three years later, I cried for a week. Still, I knew his work with me was done, for my desire to know the One consumed me just as it did him."

Ada fell silent as the two of them surveyed the scene around them. They stood on a small hillock, high enough to see the turquoise Mediterranean stretching to the horizon. More than the usual number of ships plied the water, looking very much like children's toys on the surface of a crowded pond. A light breeze carried the scent of late-summer flowers, and the Stillness that permeated the loveliness made it all the more enchanting.

It could not long assuage Ada's burgeoning grief, however. She turned from her Teacher as if ashamed to display her anguish, but John walked up behind her and gently placed his hands on her shoulders.

"Where is your brother now, Ada?" he asked softly, already sure of what she would likely say. Her tearful voice was brittle with bitterness.

"He was condemned to 'serve' on a galley like the *Matthatus*. Or perhaps he works the Romans' quarries, or is in the mines somewhere. Or else he is dead."

She stared out at the sea, arms again wrapped around herself as if she was cold. "We never did hear the full story, but three years after he entered Temple, Daniel and some of his friends were allowed out to shop for extra robes or some such. That same day, a group of ruffians had robbed, beaten and left for dead the son of some Roman noble, and the soldiers were out seeking suspects—and blood.

"When they came upon my brother and his friends, they accused them of the attack, even though there was no sign they'd even been near the part of the city where it happened. They beat my brother and his companions mercilessly, then threw them into the garrison prison; in fact, they brought in over forty Jewish men and boys that night. And all these years later—more than twenty years, Rabbi—those who are not dead are still slaves of the Roman Empire. That is, except for the half-dozen that died of their beatings that night. And do you know? They never did find the ones who truly did it."

Ada turned to John with tormented eyes. "I know it is the past I speak of Rabbi, that I should have let it go long, long ago. I have managed, since learning the Practice, to set it aside most of the time. But still, it sometimes scratches at my heart like a jagged stone.

"How can I dare board that ship as a guest of a citizen of Rome when my most belovéd brother could be one of the men at its oars? I cannot, Rabbi. I will not."

The tiny woman bowed her head and sobbed; John wrapped his arms around her and murmured comfortingly. Definitely improper, he thought with a small smile as a passerby "tsked" his disapproval. It was a liberty for even a husband to embrace his wife so in public—but John did not care. Jeshua, who as Judas had once said, was "one of the *touchingest* souls I ever met", often showed affection through hugs; John certainly wasn't going to give up the practice for the sake of another's code of propriety, not now.

His robe soon grew wet with Ada's tears, but other than asking if she used the Practice, which received a stammered "yes", John said nothing. She'd managed to evade this grief for years; letting it come forth could only be a good and healing thing. The Practice, after all, was not meant to diminish one's humanity, but to awaken one to the full beauty of all they experienced—and that opened them to their Oneness with the Source of all. John's part was merely to let his own stability hasten her healing.

As John entered more deeply into his own Stillness, a picture arose in his mind's eye. It expanded until it soon was no picture at all, until he was in it, watching its world turn around him, filling him lungs and heart and senses with delight and gratitude. As the scene disappeared, John smiled, planted a small kiss on the top of his student's head, and pushed her back so she was at arms' length.

"Dear one, your Daniel does not serve on a galley like *Matthatus*, nor in the mines or quarries."

Ada looked astonished, confused, fearful and hopeful, all in a space of about a second. She swallowed as if she was afraid to ask, then asked anyway.

"I do not know the place, but it is both fertile and remote from Rome's influence. Or remote enough. He lives with his wife on a small and prosperous farm they dearly love. They have five children, three grandchildren, and neighbors who honor them both for their generous hearts. Despite all that has happened—or perhaps I should say, because of it—he still devoutly loves God and nightly gives thanks for the gifts he has received.

"Truly, Ada, your brother is well, and he is blessed."

Looking into his eyes, Ada could not but believe her Teacher's words; her tears this time belonged to Relief and Joy instead of Sorrow and Bitterness. John again wrapped his arms around her and let her cry, then once more held her at arms' length.

"We must get back, dearest. Though I know Joshua will have *Matthatus* wait for us, we do not want to complicate the galleymen's departure. Are you willing to come?"

Ada was thoughtful, as if trying to decide if she would still be betraying her brother by boarding the ship. She sighed, then nodded slowly and solemnly. "I am sworn to go where you go, Rabbi, and since you go there, I must also." She blushed. "In truth, I would have anyway."

"But you are not happy about it."

"No, I am not. I'm sorry."

John frowned with mock-severity. "To apologize for your heart's true feelings is foolishness, Ada. Let us hear no more about it...but I do have one question for you."

"Rabbi?"

"Considering what the Romans have wrought in your life, it frankly surprises me that you are so close to Marcus and Joshua. Why is that so?"

Ada looked surprised. "Why should I be angry at them? They had no part in causing Daniel's lot."

"No. Nevertheless, many people would hate not just those who caused the one they loved pain, but all who were of their clan or otherwise associated with them."

Ada's look told John she could credit the existence of such attitudes and had even seen them, but the idea of acting thus had literally never crossed her mind. "Marcus and Joshua are each selves of their own, Rabbi. Whatever else their lives have been, they offer to others the best they can give now. It is that which tells me whether one is worthy of love.

"Even more, it is the heart of the One that tells me whether another and I are to play the part of friends or enemies for a time. For me to judge another on any other basis, be they Roman, Jew or Nubian, would be as silly as feeling sorrow for the feelings of my heart." Her tear-stained face took on an impish expression. "Do you not think so?"

For that, Ada received yet a third hug from her Teacher.

The routine aboard Matthatus established itself quickly. The days were given over to the companions' growing the acquaintance with each other and the Stillness, while the nights were broken by naught but day's arrival. Rachael, Joshua and Adan received the second technique, thus joining Prochorus in his knowledge; now, on this, the morning of the seventh day, the galley pulled toward the port of Tyre. John clearly saw the red-gold bricks of the city's many palaces and homes, even from two miles away.

Unfortunately, he also clearly smelled the stench of the city.

The smell of Tyre's decaying trash wafted across the waters like the cloud that had killed the firstborn sons of Egypt in the days of Moses; John's defenseless nostrils wished they could go the way of those hapless ones. The Romans might be pleased to think of Judea as an outback, full of "sand fleas and desert weeds", but at least they were *clean* sand fleas. Like the Romans, the Jews placed a high value on cleanliness; the priests' strictures on personal hygiene and the proper disposal of wastes had many times saved their people from the ravages of plague and social unpleasantness alike.

Prochorus came up alongside him, his face twisted in a grimace. "Gods of the East, but this place stinks! I remember my compatriots speaking of Tyre, but did not credit their descriptions half enough. You told Matthatus your Way takes you here of necessity?"

"I'm afraid so."

"Then let us hope necessity fulfills itself quickly!"

The Roman snorted as if he could blow the smell away from him like some projectile and walked away, easily keeping rhythm with the ship's roll and pitch.

The necessity would have to be quick, for *Matthatus's* master estimated it would take only three, perhaps four hours to take on the variety of wares and artworks that had recently become popular in other parts of the Empire, leaving them the chance to be away and on the vaster ocean before the afternoon sun could send itself to bed for the night. John felt a twinge of concern; what if his business here took longer? What if he missed this necessary rendezvous? For he was now certain his task was to meet some-*one*, a logical assumption in light of how many had already joined this venture.

Ah well, if the One desired that he meet with some aspect of his fate here in Tyre, things would be arranged. Still, he couldn't help but chuckle irreverently at the mental image that popped into his head: that of him triumphantly entering Vashti—with an entourage of three thousand.

Just as the men of their party had done from the beginning of the ship's voyage, John helped where he could to get *Matthatus* smoothly into port. Such help from passengers was common, and, if the person was not a personage, expected. While Prochorus, Hosea and Adan seemed well able to fit in wherever they went, John watched Timothy and Joshua with particular satisfaction.

Timothy, especially, enjoyed the camaraderie of working with the crew of the ship and it showed in his changed manner. Even after just one short week, he exhibited a level of maturity he'd never displayed in Bethany. Perhaps being treated as an adult by men he'd not previously known was giving him the ballast (John smiled at the term) he needed to truly learn to be in the world in addition to not being of it.

Joshua was also a joy to watch, but for a different reason. It wasn't maturity he needed, for in John's opinion the young man had more than a surfeit of that. Instead, the young merchant showed excellent signs of growing in his willingness to be a comrade, of dealing with others as equals who had value simply by virtue of being themselves.

It hadn't occurred to him that he might have to help with the ship during the journey; as the heir-apparent to his father's business, such a thing had never been expected of him. Upon realizing his companions would do so, however, he'd been quick to recover from his surprise and had gamely pitched in to help. Of course, it was taking some getting used to for the *crewmen* to treat him as just another passenger, but the men's respect for their putative superior grew day by day. If this trend continued, Joshua might well find himself with not just subordinates, but friends among the crew.

Matthatus finally came to rest at dockside; the master and his first mate walked down the gangplank to meet with merchants or their agents and haggle on behalf of House Matthatus to transport their goods. Ada and Rachael came topside, their shawls covering their noses in an attempt to keep out the hideous stink. They'd spent most of the last week belowdecks at the shipmaster's insistence. Still, to say he was not happy to have women—and comely ones at that—aboard his ship was putting it mildly.

"Though they are my men, good sir, and mostly trustworthy, I see no reason to tempt them with the wiles of women any more than I must on this voyage," he'd said to John, his brusque tone both ignoring and clearly blaming the Ada and a shrinking Rachael for any future transgressions. "So if you can, I'd appreciate you keeping them off the top deck as much as possible—or if you do insist on letting them come up, making sure your men keep them under control."

Ada took the insult in stride, her raised brow saying much about her opinion of the master's viewpoint and manners, but Rachael burst into mortified tears as soon as he was out of earshot. The older woman and a suddenly awkward Timothy tried to comfort her, but Joshua started after the master, his face livid.

Adan stepped in front of him. "It would be most unfortunate for you to make an enemy of that one," the African said softly, his manner, for him, quite urgent.

"No one who works for House Matthatus has the right to speak thus to its guests, and I intend to see he does not do so again!" Joshua answered hotly.

"Yes, but it would be better if you spoke to him in private. King of this ship you may be, but never does it do to insult the Governor in his own palace."

"And if you can approach him a bit more calmly," John said, picking up Adan's argument, "we can make arrangements that will serve the honor of both the women and the master's crew. That is all he is truly worried about, Joshua, despite his manner."

Joshua stared from one man to the other for several seconds, his expression still tense, then finally huffed and looked irritated. "You are my Teacher, Sir, it is true... and I see you are teacher to me as well, Haifata. Nevertheless, and with all due respect to you both, I hate it when you see fit to be right."

John laughed and patted Joshua's shoulder, while Adan grinned, revealing amazingly white teeth.

"Rabbi," Ada said now, ending his reverie, "what would you have us do? Shall we all go ashore, or should we wait here?" John couldn't decide by her tone which alternative she preferred.

"What do you think, Little Bird?" John affectionately asked Rachael, sure that she, at least, was eager to step on dry ground. The sea hadn't been at all gentle with her stomach.

"I think the stink of this place is horrible, Rabbi, but if it is possible, I would like to find some herbs to help me keep my food down on the rest of this journey, else I will be but skin and bones by the time we reach Greece."

John acknowledged the girl's concern, still smiling. Just as with Timothy, these last several days, miserable though they'd been, had seen Rachael begin to trust that she was indeed capable and worthy of being treated as an adult. But then, the value of the Practice tended to be more quickly apparent in the young, for they usually had far fewer tracks of being to erase or reroute.

"This is what we can do," John answered. "The four of you—for I want Hosea and Marcus to go with you—can seek out an herbalist to find what you need for the remainder of our journey while I tend to my business. And be sure you get enough for everyone, Rachael! Though the rest of us have not been at odds with Mother Ocean while sailing the coast, things might be different on the open sea."

"May Joshua and I go too, Rabbi?" Timothy asked, and John could swear his voice had grown deeper in the last week.

"I have been to Tyre before, thank you," Joshua said dryly, wrinkling his nose. "I believe I will stay here."

"I would rather you both stayed to continue helping the crew, if they desire it... but if you feel there is need to go, then do as your heart tells you."

Timothy looked thoughtfully down at Rachael, whose look told him his company would definitely be welcome, then back at John. He decided. "I was curious to see the city, but there will be other chances to see new places, and it is not something I need to do. I will stay and help with the loading."

"Very well," John replied neutrally, but he was pleased with Timothy's answer. "My business will be short, I hope. The One has not yet made my Way clear, but I am sure—"

John looked out at the docks as he spoke, but now he stopped and peered intently into the crowd. The others followed his gaze, trying to see what had drawn his attention.

Two men had entered the dock area and were still several yards from *Galley Matthatus*. Their coloring was similar to those around them, but there was a difference that would have marked them as foreign to this land even had their colorful robes not so sharply contrasted with the earth-toned clothing of the Tyrians. Their walk was both purposeful and searching, as if they knew why they were there, but knew not if they would recognize what they sought when they found it.

John knew they would.

As if reading his thought, one of the men looked toward *Matthatus*, his eyes finding John even at this distance. He grabbed the other man's arm and pointed, talking animatedly as they hurried toward the ship.

"Who are they, Zebedee?" Prochorus asked. His soldier's training served him well, as he was the first of the others to catch sight of the men.

"They are the reason we came to Tyre, Marcus."

The men reached the ship and found its master. One, a swarthy, middle-aged man who seemed to be naught but a series of large tubes joined together—and whose demeanor indicated that he, like Joshua, was from a family of some means—frenetically gestured toward the companions and began haggling for passage on *Matthatus*. His musical, accented baritone rose above, then fell below the noises of those around him so that John only caught part of what he said. The other man, younger, taller, and as lithe as the other was round, stared at John with unabashedly beautiful night-dark eyes.

The shipmaster vigorously shook his head and tried to walk away, but the man followed behind him, gesturing and cajoling like a dog who's discovered his boy has his bone. John started down the gangplank, calling Joshua to follow.

"I said it is impossible!" John heard the shipmaster say exasperatedly. "There is no room for you and your companion; the ship is full with guests already."

"Yes, yes, I know this, for we came all the way from Persia to be among them!" the man said, his accent thick beneath the melody of his voice. "You must allow us to board and speak to them so you may see we are to join you!"

"It matters none to me where you've come from," The shipmaster said, what little patience he had well past gone. "There is still no space for two more male passengers, for we've women aboard taking more than their share of room for propriety's sake. You cannot board!"

"May I be of help?" John asked.

The round Persian turned, his own patience worn fine, and his eyes grew wide. He bowed deeply and with considerable flourish; the younger man followed suit.

"Darshinika Baremna my lord," he said thunderously as he finished his genuflecttion. "And this is my companion, Erezavan Isvant. We have sought these last several months to find you, for the Signs tell us our Way can be found only with you."

"Please sire," the younger man, Isvant, said, his musical voice and manner far more diffident than his companion's. "Our dreams told us many months ago that one who could lead us where next we must be would come to these shores. We have been here for two months, waiting and searching, and the light of your being is greater than any we have yet encountered. Compared to them, your holiness shines from you with the brilliance of the Great Sun Itself. Surely, you are he of whom our dreams spoke. Will you not tell the master here that we must go forth with you?"

John gazed at the men; they returned his stare, each one letting him into his heart and being as much as he could. Both, he sensed, had received considerable training at one of the mystery schools that dotted the Persian landscape, but while Isvant impressed him as one who sought only to serve, one whose healing grace had the potential to be a great boon to any who came into the domain of his will, Baremna was more of a scholar who enjoyed knowing *about* much. Not that the larger man was incapable of experiencing what it was to be a sage, mind. Rather, it was as if he was not yet willing to embody the fullness of his being. But that would no doubt come with time.

"Your Way does indeed lie with us, Darshinika, Erezavan," John said at last, clasping each of the men's arms in turn. "Welcome, then, to the One's Journey."

The shipmaster was livid. He followed John and the others to the gangplank, still insisting there was no room for them. The ship had no replacement crew as it was, thank you very much, and he could not, would not, leave two more sailors, already hired, to wait who-knew-how-long for another ship back to Caesarea so these two could board.

"But they will not have to wait long," Joshua said suddenly. "I know for a fact that *Ariel* is due here in two days, and like *Matthatus*, will be in port but a few hours before returning to Caesarea. Since she is a larger ship, they will easily have space for two extra men. More, House Matthatus will gladly pay full wages to any two men who will forgo this voyage so these men may travel with us. Would that be acceptable to you, sir?"

John applauded Joshua's willingness to negotiate rather than simply give an order, but the master shook his head. "With due respect, Master Matthatus, we will still be two hands short, and that is two too many to safely run this ship to Corinth at this time of year. Such carelessness could well end in disaster if there's a sea change."

"Perhaps, then, we can squeeze one more each into the men's cabins; at least, I am willing to try," John said. He saw the master appreciated Joshua's willingness to pay men who would be idle, and in turn, appreciated his unwillingness to forfeit the safety of *Matthatus* and those aboard her by leaving the crew shorthanded.

"We can fit one more in our cabin," said Prochorus who'd appeared from nowhere, only to be seconded by both Timothy and Hosea. Apparently, they considered an invitation for one to follow John onto the dock to be an invitation to all.

"I worked on my father's fishing boat before going to the School. I can help as crew if you wish it," The younger Persian offered, starting an avalanche of similar offers.

The shipmaster scowled and rubbed his chin.

"The whole lot of you together'll likely not make one good sailor," he mumbled at last, conceding defeat. "But if you're willing to endure the discomfort of closer quarters, then so be it.

"Let them board."

FIFTEEN

"So then, Rabbi. What, exactly, is love?"

John turned in the crisp afternoon air to find Marcus Prochorus beside him at the starboard railing of *Matthatus*. They were five days out from Tyre, headed for Crete and the cities of Fair Havens and Phenice. After that, they would disembark in Cenchreae and go on to Corinth, Greece, and wherever else the One led them.

If the ship traveled a day or so to either east or west, they would see land...but that knowledge did not break the illusion of the ocean's boundlessness now. Now, there was naught to be seen of terrain, other ships, or even clouds. *Matthatus* was alone in a gently rolling, blue-on-blue universe.

John looked more closely at Prochorus. Never before had Marcus referred to him as anything but "Zebedee", yet the best he could say now was that the Roman was *trying* to be facetious. Skeptical expression aside, some part of him truly meant the title.

"'What is love?' What causes you to ask?"

"Something Hosea said when he and Ada spoke of the Practice of Gratitude."

"Hmm. And how has your experience with the first two techniques been?"

"Good enough, good enough..." Prochorus leaned on the rail and stared out at the rolling sea, "but I find I like using Gratitude much more than I do the Praise technique. Yes, yes, I know praise is supposed to be the fundamental song of the universe," he said hastily, mistaking John's smile for reproach. "But in all truth, I find it easier to feel at peace with the world around me than to accept my own foibles. That made me ask Hosea why we cannot use only those techniques that best seem to suit us."

"What was Hosea's answer?"

"He told me it was important to do all the techniques of the Practice I have—in order—because each technique builds upon the one before it. He said the progression from praise to gratitude to love is natural, that as you appreciate a thing, your thankfulness for it naturally arises, and when you feel grateful for it, you cannot but love it."

"And that made sense?"

"Yesssss... But that is the crux of my question. If using the Praise technique awakens love for the way we see our lives, and Gratitude awakens love for the way we see the world, what else is left? Why do we need a Love technique at all?"

This time it was John who stared at the unlimited expanse of ocean as he considered Prochorus's question. Then, finally:

"Marcus, why did you marry Lydia?"

Though John asked his question with great gentleness, Prochorus straightened as if he'd been struck in the back with a spear. He gripped the rail so hard his knuckles went white; his face twisted as first one emotion, then another tried to gain dominance. He tried to speak, but nothing seemed able to make its way past his lips, and though his body did not shake, his soul positively trembled with his effort to prevent its doing so.

While this went on, Ada quietly appeared and stood behind and to the right of him. John nodded, acknowledging the support her Stillness added, but did not take his eyes from the former scribe's face. He knew the story from his experience in Bethany of course, but now it was Marcus's turn to tell it.

"You know what a horror it is to watch the ones you most love die," the Roman said at last, his voice a strangled murmur. "You know how it hurts.

"My wife and baby were the life of me, Zebedee. All I ever really wanted was to love her, watch our children grow and someday be a happy old grandsire. Yet, the day we laid them to rest, I fought not to let my tears fall. Lydia's father looked as if he wanted nothing more than to fall into that grave and never get up, but not a single tear did either of us shed. Oh, we argued and blamed and ended a friendship that had brought us both joy, but we did not cry. Only the women seemed free to cry...but as I look at it now, they seemed as afraid of not showing grief as we men feared showing it. It was as if they felt they must wail so others would not think they'd wished disaster on Lydia.

"And do you know? The oddity of it is, I married Lydia because she thought it strange for a man not to cry. I did, you know, when my mother died, and when she told me she was with child. But when I blushed and apologized for being unmanly, Lydia laughed and said I was more a man, not less, for letting my tears fall."

The Roman, his eyes now brimming, swallowed hard, once twice, then shook his head again. John and Ada remained still and Still as he finally spoke, his voice thick.

"I...never realized...never told her...how very much I appreciated her for that, Zebedee...how very much. I never acknowledged how thankful I was to have such a treasure in my life...or how very, very much...I still miss her."

Prochorus's last words came out on a rattling sob, and the arms that so rigidly held to the rail collapsed. The Roman laid his head on them and cried like a man whose heart had shattered into dust. Or perhaps it is just finally breaking open, John thought. He laid a hand on Marcus's shoulder just as he'd desired to do in Bethany, gave in that mere touch all the comfort the other man had feared revealing himself would prevent.

After several minutes, Prochorus's tears ended; he stood and offered Ada, who'd moved to the rail to lay a hand on his other shoulder, a watery smile.

"So then, Marcus," she said softly, her pride in him tangible, "that is the reason for the Practice of Love. It heals all those parts of ourselves we feel we must hide if we are to be loved by others. Greater than that, however, the Practice of Love heals our belief that the One, both as Itself and in Its guise as our first gods, finds us unlovable."

"Our first gods?" he sniffed.

"Our mothers and fathers."

Prochorus's brows rose, his incredulous surprise causing him to snort away the remaining shards of his grief. "Hmph! That I find hard to credit, dear one. My father as Jupiter? That is a most unlikely characterization. Most unlikely!"

"And yet, that is precisely what I am saying. You remember how Hosea and I said that as we grow into adulthood, the unlimited potential born to us is masked by the habits we form to live in the world? Well, where do you think those habits first develop?"

"Think of it," John said. "We arrive in this world straight from the eye and heart of the One as perfect—but helpless—beings. We come from a place where our every need is met before we even realize it exists, from a place where we've known naught but Love Unconditional. Does that describe this earthly plane?"

"No."

"Indeed not. Yet our mothers and fathers, who come as close to fulfilling our greatest needs as the One can on this earth, are as gods to a helpless babe. So, what happens the first time we do not instantly receive what we need, as inevitably must happen, even if unintentionally? What happens the first time we do something that meets with 'God's' —our father or mother's—disapproval? Never does it occur to a baby to think the parent might be wrong, for how can God be mistaken? No, we feel something is wrong with us, that 'God has reason not to love me anymore.' And we try very hard to never again do what caused that disapprobation."

Ada continued. "Every one of us has something—or many somethings—we feel we must not display, Marcus. As you pointed out, it is not meet for a man to cry, or for a woman to avoid tears. Nor are the things we should not reveal necessarily bad things. For instance, did you know I am an excellent carpenter?"

Neither John nor Marcus responded to Ada's claim in words, but their eyebrows said everything that needed saying. "Just so," Ada smiled wryly. "Yet, from a very young age, I loved and understood the nature of wood and saw how things went together. And my hands were adept at reproducing what I saw with my heart's eye. So, of course, when I was seven, I told my mother I wanted to be a carpenter.

"She was horrified. She immediately told my father, who proceeded to sit me down and explain, rather sternly, that it was not meet for a girl to have 'manly' talents—and it certainly was not good to show them.

"I was crushed. I would never have picked up hammer and awl again, but for the complicity of my brothers. They cheerfully indulged my strange talent without my father's knowledge...though I think now he must have known and said nothing, for Papa missed very little. But do you know? Hosea and I were married almost five years before I allowed him to discover my ability. I was terrified if he found out he would cast me aside as an unworthy wife.

"That is the power our parents' or other respected authorities' beliefs have over us, Marcus. And they bind us not just as children, but as adults."

John nodded. "Marcus, we were created with infinite potential so we might someday become the Infinite. God is not mocked, nor does He mock us with abilities we then have no right to use. When we hide portions of our potential, be they tears or talents...

well, the energy of those parts of ourselves have to come out somehow. As often as not, that somehow lies in using others to fulfill those needs for us, or in condemning those who do not live by our rules of conduct. Every argument, every feud between clan, every war between province and country, is caused by our need to hide the parts of ourselves that, if allowed to flourish, will help awaken us to wholeness, joy, and Godhood."

"So, the Practice of Love allows me to remember that my hidden parts are also created by the gods, and are meant to be given forth. Is that correct?" Prochorus asked.

"Yes, by healing our sense that we are separate from and unworthy of the One," John agreed. "Such giving forth of all of ourselves is the true essence of love. Never do you give without giving to yourself, after all; nor do you share what does not already exist within you. You are everything you see to love, just as God is, and you can learn to love all you seem not to, just as God does. The Practice of Love reawakens that remembrance."

John shooed them away, stopping Prochorus's dive into what Andrew had, on Thomas's behalf, named the "Yes-But State", but not before instructing Ada to find Hosea and teach him, Joshua, Haifata and Rachael the Practice of Love. Then, smiling, he leaned on the rail and looked out at the cerulean waters' endless expanse.

"Words are wonderful things, my brothers—so long as you do not mistake them for the thing itself," Jeshua said over the tune of the wavelets that slapped against the boat the twelve had co-opted. "Like signs pointing toward the place you wish to go, the right words can direct you to the heart of the Self...but never will they replace the actual experience. In fact, the moment the Thing Itself is found, the need for words should —indeed will—be left behind."

"But what of the words of the Practice, Jeshua?" Luke asked. "Are we to give those up once we've awakened our awareness of the One within?"

Jeshua crossed his arms thoughtfully. "The words of the Practice do fall away... but only in the sense that, as they lead your awareness ever more immediately to the Real, you will focus more on That than anything else.

"That does not mean you should stop using the techniques, however! Just as a desert storm starts with the smallest cloud of dust, to soon engulf all it meets, so the truth of the simple words of the Practice will soon engulf you in Infinite Life. As you will soon discover, just when you think you've reached the greatest possible level of union with the One, there will be more to experience, and then more. Each time you use the Practice, you will increasingly embody as the radiant being of God. And even more importantly, you will make it possible for all who follow to find that Wholeness with greater ease. For that reason, if no other, you should admonish those you teach to use the techniques as often as possible, even after they touch the Face of the One."

"But what if our hearts are not in the Practice?" James asked. "What if we do not believe the meaning that underlies the words, or do not want what they say?"

"If one truly has no desire to do a thing, will he do it? Or will the universe itself arrange for him to have 'more important things to do', things designed to take him away from the Practice? If one has not true intent, he will not engage in any activity, be it washing clothes or regularly praying to the One. Conversely, those who know what they desire (even if they know not they know it) cannot but use everything that will help them find what they seek. They will follow the Path until it swallows them up and gives them all they Are..."

A low, distant, almost inaudible thrumming brought John back to the present, causing him to straighten at the rail, brows furrowed and ears cocked. He did not have to strain his hearing long; within moments, the hum became a rumble and the rumble a clamor. He turned this way and that, trying to find the tumult's source; surely, no man-made object could cause such a reverberating din. Yet, there was nothing on the water.

As he turned to again look in the other direction, he saw them. Five—no, seven—enormous birds flew in formation off the port bow, more or less toward the ship. At least, John thought they were birds, but he could detect no beaks, no feet, not even heads, really.

Timothy's question about sea monsters popped into his mind, for the creatures did not flap their wings, but slid effortlessly through the air at impossible speed. Their oblong bodies were a deathly shade of gray, their mottled brown and muddy green markings splotched on as if God had been in a rush to have done with them.

And the noise! It was inconceivable it could increase, yet it and the he birds grew and grew as they came closer, until John actually began to think they were not birds at all, but dragons...and more than dragons, for he suddenly knew they flew higher than any eagle ever could.

As they reached a point more or less parallel to *Matthatus*, the creatures' stomachs (or were they mouths?) opened and each dropped a half-dozen dead-gray, eggs. John watched them fall whistling toward the sea, unaware he held his breath. The first one hit the water...

...And exploded with a heart-stopping roar.

The eggs' earsplitting detonations shook the ship as if it was in a quake. Balls of fire as big as suns rushed forth from each explosion, turning the sea into a flaming hell of flying, mangled creatures. John grabbed the galley's rail to keep from crashing to the deck, but to no avail. He fell, scraping his knees on the rough, heaving wood. He heard screams all around him as he squinted against the sudden wind of the blasts, smelled blood, smoke, and impossibly, dust.

A fireball, half-again the size of *Matthatus*, rushed headlong toward it, promising horrible, searing death; John scrambled back from the rail, arms before his face, knowing the ship was dead already and shouting an inarticulate exclamation—"

"Ho, little fellow! Have a care before you knock me over!"

Hands grabbed John's shoulders and pulled him to his feet, then steadied him as he frantically looked around.

The fire was gone. *Matthatus* and the waters around it were calm; the sky was free of any objects, familiar or unfamiliar. John could again hear nothing but the sound of the ship's sojourn through the waves. He noticed he was shaking, took a deep breath, and turned to face his benefactor, an addition who'd boarded in Tyre just as one of the veteran sailors decided he'd enough of the master's cantankerous manner.

By Judean standards, John bar Zebedee was not considered a small man. He was quite a bit taller than his father before him and only an inch or so shorter than Jeshua had been. The man who stood before him, however, had every right to call him "little fellow"; he was huge, towering over John as John towered over Ada.

John looked up into the man's face and got another surprise: his tanned, wind-roughened features were framed by a heavy mane of waving, almost-white hair that was pulled back into a braid that fell midway to his back. He had no beard, but his chin-brushing mustache was likewise spun of sun-pale gold, while his brows and lashes were a little darker.

Particularly intriguing, however, were the man's eyes. They were as pale a blue as the noon sky and held a level of humor and mischief that, to one less trusting, could seem like imminent cruelty. In all truth, and despite the physical differences, they reminded John of Jeshua's eyes.

"Are you all right, fellow?" The large man asked in a strange, clipped accent, his expression concerned beneath the mischief.

"I—yes. I am all right now, thank you. I just had a turn," John said, aware it would be futile indeed to try to explain his experience.

The sailor nodded as if he meant to go on with his duties, just as John meant to go to his berth and allow the One, if it so willed, to clarify what he'd just experienced. But neither of them moved.

"You are the one the others call 'prophet', are you not?" The man asked at last, his curiosity apparent. "I am called Torer (it sounded like "Toorrerr," with a very soft "t"), but the others call me 'Tor'. You would think they could pronounce my full name, but that is apparently not so. You may call me as you wish."

"'Torer'," John said, pronouncing it correctly. "I am called John bar Zebedee."

"Or 'Rabbi', yes? I have heard the others of your party call you that. It means 'teacher' in your language, hey?" His jovial tone was just a shade impertinent. "And what is it you teach?"

"I teach of the One."

"Ah, yes," The big man said with an amused nod. "I have heard of this Jewish god who has but one child in the Heavens to help him with his tasks and responds to the news that there are other gods with violence and destruction to the rest of his children. He seems to me to be a lonely, selfish fellow, if you will excuse my saying so; not like the highest god of my people, Lord Odin." There was smiling challenge in the big man's expression.

John smiled back. "If that is indeed what you have heard, then you have been misled," he said, and when invited, proceeded to tell the big sailor what Jeshua had taught of the true nature of the One, how Its Wholeness was meant to consistently, easily and fully manifest in all people.

"I see." Torer looked thoughtful behind his amusement. "And did this teacher of yours teach how such easy manifesting might happen?"

"He did."

"Ah... Then perhaps I will wish to talk some more of this with you...Rabbi...if only to hear how such a thing might be possible..." The big man smiled crookedly as someone raucously called his name. "But right now, I am a man at work. After the evening meal, we two will talk more, hey?"

John laughed as he swaggered off to see to whatever needed his attention, then called after him.

"Torer! Never have I seen such a one as you. Pray, where are you from?"

For this, John got a proud answering grin from the huge man.

"From the far, far North. The place the Romans call Scandinavia."

Matthatus's master had irritably agreed to keep his men as much to the bow of the galley as their duties would allow for an hour each day, so Ada and Rachael could come topside and take in the air without the governance of their male companions. And as they did almost every afternoon, the whole group now took dinner on the top deck. This was not at all adequate to the men, but the women had assented to the arrangement.

"If we truly feel the need to come above for a longer time, Hosea, we can call one of you to accompany us," Ada had said to her thoroughly irked husband.

"Besides, being below means we have more time to do the Practice," Rachael finished brightly. She loved entering into the deep rest the Stillness offered and had stated her desire to consciously experience It in every part of her life as soon as possible.

That was something else the shipmaster was not thrilled about: each afternoon, the men of the party invariably stopped whatever tasks they were doing to spend an hour entering into the Silence. Though John had made it clear they would make themselves available if needed, Joshua had made it just as clear that the master's definition of need had best be dire.

Which brought up the third thing the shipmaster was annoyed about: many of the sailors had asked questions about the what and why of the companions' journey, and while some had distanced themselves upon hearing the answer, many of them desired more information. John allowed Hosea and Ada to teach the first of the techniques to the few who wished to learn, and to the Persians, Baremna and Isvant.

John's attention wandered to their newest companions now. Baremna was expounding spiritual theory to Adan and Marcus, his voice and manner unconsciously protective in its loudness, while Isvant sat talking to Timothy, Rachael and Joshua in his diffident way.

John cringed a little: though the young men were genuinely friendly in Rachael's absence and, in all fairness, Joshua seemed only to see himself as a friend to someone who just happened to be female, the budding rivalry John had seen on the road to Caesarea was now magnified by the swarthily handsome Persian's presence. With Timothy and Isvant, at least, the interest in Rachael was definitely that of young men trying to impress upon an attractive young woman the merits of their company.

John sighed, aware that such notions were new to both of them: though certainly of marriageable age, Timothy's much older brothers had designated him their widowed mother's guardian, breaking his betrothal to a smith's daughter in distant Capernaum shortly after their father died of brain fever. The move had caused considerable gossip at Timothy's expense since he'd made no objection to the breach, but both Miriam and Martha felt his apparent lack of interest in the fairer sex had more to do with shyness and the desire to more deeply know the One than any real lack.

And Isvant, with only a year more than Timothy's nineteen summers, had been apprenticed to his mystery school at barely ten summers old; until leaving there some seven moons before, he hadn't been within yards of any woman younger than his mother. To be so close to a woman near his own age was a novelty he simply could not disregard.

John was glad Rachael was so enthralled by the Practice.

Supper done, John made his way to *Matthatus's* stern. In wet weather, the sailors ate and slept in the storage area between the cabins immediately belowdecks; if Joses Matthatus or another merchant was aboard, however, they stretched greased tarpaulins between the railings and mast and prayed the rains, if any, were light. Torer stood slightly apart from the others, his body bent almost double as he rested his forearms on the ship's railing, but he straightened and smiled a roguish greeting as John approached.

"So, Rabbi. Have you come to convert me to your god?" he asked jovially.

"Not if I can help it," John laughed. "After all, could so great a Being truly require all of us to live in one small Room before giving us Its gifts?"

They talked for hours. Torer, who was few years younger than John, spoke of his homeland and shared some few of his adventures with, John thought with a private smile, a surprising amount of self-deprecating humor for a man who swaggered so well.

John, in turn, watched Torer's expression go from insolent merriment to the intense stare of a hawk looking to locate his prey in thick grass as he spoke of humankind's history and the many Tasks they'd agreed to fulfill to rekindle humanity's Awareness.

A chill ran up his spine; the Scandinavian's soul held such a balanced mix of light and dark that he literally could not decide which way such a one might go; even so, when the big man asked to learn the Practice of Praise, John readily complied.

After several minutes the Scandinavian opened eyes that glowed with surprise. "Is this what always happens, this—this quiet?"

"No," John said with a half-laughing snort, thinking of his frequent lamentations to Jeshua that his mind would never be Still. "Every experience of the Practice will be different, because our minds and bodies are always in different states when we do it. No matter what the experience seems to be, though, each time we say its phrases, we in fact touch the Stillness, causing our awareness of the One to grow. That is why we never worry about what happens while doing the Practice, but simply let the One carry us where It will and notice how our lives change when we are simply living."

They stopped talking long enough to watch the sun dip below the horizon, dragging behind it a shroud of dusky blue that gradually faded to velvety, stars-punctuated black. Torer asked questions about the companions' quest, some of which John answered with detailed explanations, others with only a shrug. The big man fell silent as the almost-full moon made her appearance and quietly reminded those with eyes to see that there was more to the universe than the ordinary magic of Day.

"Always have I been a man who sought adventures that would satisfy my senses," Torer said at last. "But as I have and watched you speak of your quest, a light has grown in you, as if the Sun wants to come out through your skin and brighten the night.

"That same Sun has come out in my heart as I have done this Practice of yours. It tells me I should see if this one god you speak of is also my Odin, that I should travel with you for a while on this great adventure to find this out." His sudden grin was wolfish. "Do you think, perhaps, I should do what it says?"

"I do not know Torer," John said, smiling at the man's audacity at inviting himself along on the expedition to Vashti, "but perhaps we can ask another." John looked toward the shadows. "What do you think, Marcus?"

Prochorus came forward, his demeanor that of the warrior he had been for so many years. The two men looked each other over speculatively, confirming John's suspicion that Torer, like Marcus, had done more in his life than simply "adventure".

Prochorus nodded judiciously. "I think this one would be as dangerous as they come in a fight, that he might well find this the journey of a lifetime...and I that I would rather have him on my side than not."

Something in Marcus's tone again brought a chill to John's skin as Torer smilingly bowed his head in tribute to the assessment; he cocked his head thoughtfully. "I trust Marcus's word greatly, but I must tell you, Torer, that this journey will be like no other you have made. It calls first and most importantly for you to explore the land-scape within your soul, not that outside it—and that is a journey that has ruined more than one the world called brave. Yet without it, the outer expedition is surely doomed. Think you that you are ready for such?"

The Scandinavian's humorous mien turned serious for the second time that night.

"Never have I feared any adventure Odin has put in my path...but never has He asked me to travel to His own lands. In honesty, I do not yet know if this way you go wants to be my way. I think I must give it some thought." His roguish smile returned. "Still, whether I go or not, I hope He makes your way a smooth one—and not *too* boring!"

"He would be an interesting addition to our party," Prochorus said noncommittally as the big man strutted toward his bedroll.

John nodded, his expression also neutral, as they started toward the cabins. After another moment, the Roman "hmphed" deep in his chest.

"What?"

"I like that one, that is all," he admitted grudgingly.

"As do I," John agreed.

SIXTEEN

John stood at what had become his usual place: at the starboard railing of *Galley Matthatus*. Today though, his eyes were not on the endless dunes of rolling blue-green waves. What he saw now, what they'd all seen since shortly before sunrise was the distant but growing raggedness of coastal hills. They were nearing the port city of Cenchreae.

I must be more eager to reach land than I realized, he thought, then shook his head and smiled. He'd spent the last hour trying to convince himself that if he squinted just a little harder, he would surely see the white stone houses dotting Cenchreae's hillsides.

After four weeks of little more than blue on blue, broken only by the claustrophobic gray on gray of the occasional drizzly, fog-bound day, all the companions were ready to set foot on dry ground; even Rachael was a touch impatient with having *nothing* to do but the Practice, much as she favored it above anything else. John's desire for change, however, came not from boredom; being on the water for this long was no hardship for a former fisherman. No, it was the steady shift from pleasant boredom to constant nightmare uneasiness that made him anxious to depart *Matthatus's* decks.

He'd had more visions since the one with the terrible exploding eggs.

In fact, they'd grown increasingly common, and though not all of them were hor-rific—some, in truth, had been almost heartbreakingly beautiful—each apparition filled him, heart and soul, with a frightening sense of portent, followed by skull-split-ting headaches that left him feeling weak and stupid for hours.

Two of the visions had again featured strange flying creatures. The first of them had had more of the dragon-birds, ones that flew even higher and faster than those in his first vision. And while they'd dropped no flaming eggs, the booming thunder that fol-lowed in their wake rattled John's insides for a full minute after they passed overhead.

The second vision featured a creature that looked to John like some kind of flying whale, but before he could get a clear view of it, it burst into flames and crashed to earth, shedding burning, screaming bodies as it went.

Disturbing as the visions were, John had, for the most part, been able to take them in stride, had even began to grow somewhat used to them...but then came the vision that showed him what Hell would surely have looked like had there been such a place.

Everything—land and sky, air and water—was utterly devastated. Not a tree or flower lived; only their husks stood silently by, twisting in a monstrous wind. Just as some of his visions had been filled with more living people than John could fathom, in this place there were more dead than he imagined could ever have existed.

Assaulted by unfamiliar, gut-wrenching smells, he'd stood aghast in the middle of the carnage, sure it could only have been caused by some hideous plague—or by some monstrosity whose ruthless brutality would make the cruelest Roman seem like the most benevolent of God's angels. The worst thing about the vision, though, was the ones who still lived amidst the horror. Their agony at being cursed with continued life as the flesh fell from their bones and their minds rotted away tore at John's soul, just as the people themselves tore at his clothing, pleading and crying for healing he could not give.

Because in truth, the only healing he could possibly comprehend as desirable for any of them was a quick death.

Upon coming out of that vision, John had stumbled to the rail, vomited up his entire dinner in less than a minute, and fallen to the deck, sobbing as if he would never stop. That tumult didn't last long, of course, for instead of trying to force himself to "calm," he'd engaged the Practice and let all his emotions pass at their own pace. But the episode had alarmed his companions and terrified the more superstitious of the sailors.

"Excuse me Master... I...may I join you?"

John barely kept the annoyance off his face as he turned at Erezavan Isvant's apologetically devoted appeal. He had observed the young Persian's interactions with the others—especially Darshinika Baremna—and did not at all like what he saw. Both Baremna and the young man had trained at one of their land's mystery schools and now used the Practice, but Baremna still chose only to know *of* the One. In fact, he'd grown increasingly and jealously aloof in the presence of John's awareness, prone to flinging subtle insults that had no effect save to make the other companions avoid him. Isvant, on the other hand, had so deepened his already intimate acquaintance with the Fullness that he sometimes seemed to shine with Its brilliance.

And yet, the older Persian had him convinced that he was the true proficient. The younger man had repeatedly backed away from what he knew to be correct rather than take the risk of speaking up; indeed, a single look from Baremna could instantly cow him and quell any threat of Certainty.

Now he stood before John, his almond-shaped, long-lashed eyes filled with fear; he spoke in a half-whisper lest Baremna, his "teacher", should discover he'd come to John because the older man had refused (that was to say, failed) to answer yet another of his questions. While he did not prostrate himself, his manner made clear he felt he should.

John was in no mood to accommodate him.

"Erezavan, you may speak to me only if you never again call me 'Master'."

Isvant's eyes widened in surprise. "But... Your light is too great to be other than a Master's, just as with the teachers at the School. Must I not then honor you as such?"

"Some might indeed honor me as a Master, Erezavan, but *you* may not call that."

Isvant first looked baffled, then mortified. "Forgive me, Maste—Sir, for offending you. I did not mean to... I only meant...that is...that was not my intent at all."

The youngster started to slink away in the face of so pointed a rebuke, but suddenly a ghost of desperate determination flitted across his face and stopped his retreat. "Sir, I do not know what I have done wrong, but if you would...I will do whatever is needed to correct my error. Will you tell me what I am doing wrong? Please?"

"Groveling, Erezavan, that is what you are doing!" John snapped. "You grovel like a well-whipped dog who is too stupid to leave a cruel master, even as the one who values you offers everything your heart could ever want. Unlike far too many, the mark of the One is written upon your heart in letters of fire and you perpetually hear Its Song of Glory, yet, all I've seen these many weeks is a man who diffidently dips his head and folds away his soul if he senses any possibility of disapprobation. Though yours is strong enough to hold up universes, you walk about like a man born without a spine!"

"But!" Isvant snapped to his full height as sudden frustration overpowered his unnatural humility. "Darshinika says a true student must be humble! He must set aside his own ideas and never question those who know the Truth! And I do not! Is that wrong?"

"Yes!" John retorted, pleased to see the young man finally standing up for himself. "Granted, if he would know Truth, a student must be willing to follow his Teacher's call, even in the face of his fears—but only if that Teacher has proven his own Fullness. If Darshinika Baremna has done that, why do you come to me with your concerns?"

Isvant turned from John's expectant glare.

"Erezavan, the student who throws aside his soul's knowing for fear of outstripping his 'teacher' is naught but a slave who lazily sucks at others' life forces in the hope of gaining the succor he doubts he deserves. Then he blames them for his failure to find God. Courting slaves holds no interest for me, and I'll have no truck with the one who stands before me. But—" John raised a hand to avert Isvant's next retort, then laid it on the young man's shoulder. "When you decide you are ready to set aside your false humility and fear of becoming God's Brilliance, then will I answer your questions, and gladly."

Silence descended on *Matthatus's* deck as John again faced the coast; the homes he'd only imagined clinging to Cenchreae's hillsides a few moments before were now solid and real. Isvant remained beside him, but John offered neither encouragement nor rejection. He could stay and ask his question or he could go; the decision was his to make, probably for the first time in years. If, for a change, he responded to John's intent rather than his own fear, he would choose what he truly desired. Or better yet, perhaps he would use the Practice and let the One choose for him.

After several minutes, Isvant straightened, took a breath and said in full voice, "Sir, I have a question to ask of you."

John smiled and turned. "And that would be, Erezavan?"

"I...well... Will you tell me of your visions? You see," he said hastily as John's brows rose, "for many years, I too have had visions and dreams. They are usually jumbled and strange, as dreams are, but their meanings are so clear I come out of them feeling as if I have been where they were. They are why I was sent to the School, for when they sometimes came true, my father...decided he wanted no witch in his home."

The pain of that rejection was still clear in the young man's voice.

"When I asked the Masters why such visions came to me, they said it was a gift, and that I should have no fear of them. But they do frighten me, for some of them are... horrible. I thought if one who carries as much Light as you also has visions, you could explain them so they would not be so fearsome—or even better, so that they might stop coming."

John sighed. After his hellish vision and its aftermath, Torer had approached Prochorus, unaware John was nearby. Unsurprisingly, the big man had decided to join the company, and as Miriam had suggested, he, Marcus and Haifata began training the others, even Ada and Rachael, in the rudiments of self-defense. The three warriors often spoke of (or more accurately, bragged about) their many exploits, and Torer quickly became known for his rakish sense of humor. Yet, when he spoke to Marcus of John's reaction to the vision, that good humor was nowhere in evidence.

"I have experienced many things that would cause a brave man to blanch, Roman, and never had cause to think myself a coward. But something like that I have never seen in ones not struck with wounds or fever. And even they...well, it is very strange, I tell you."

"Hmm. Would you part ways with us then, when we reach Cenchreae?" Marcus's voice was remarkably bare of what he might feel about the big man choosing thus.

"No, no; I will see this through," Torer answered a little too hastily. "This quest —your quest—calls me to it as well. It is only that...well, I wonder. Will we find ourselves following a madman? Will what he is experiencing happen to us?"

He has heart enough to face an army with nothing but a knife, but the thought of madness terrifies him, John thought. Prochorus was quiet for several moments—and that told John the episode had shaken him more than he admitted, perhaps even to himself.

Then: "One night, when I was still naught but a crippled beggar on the streets of Bethany, hating all that that one stood for, he and his mother walked by my way. His mother clearly saw in me what my heart truly dreamed of...yet when Mary departed this earth, I publicly accused bar Zebedee of murdering her.

"Almost everyone in the crowd gathered there sought to kill me for my insult, but he was the one who pulled my executioners away. Then, even as I still cursed him, he so clearly challenged me to choose for the Truth he saw in my soul that it healed my crippled legs in an instant. Even more importantly, it began healing this heart, which had been wounded for far longer than the seven years my legs were useless."

Prochorus shrugged. "I cannot see the future of this strange journey, Torer, but this I know: if John bar Zebedee does go mad, I will stay with him and try my best to see him as he saw me, until he again remembers who he Is. And if I should go mad, well...whatever may happen, I cannot but trust that he will hold me in my truth, for he has already done so, even in the face of having every reason not to.

"The Fates have made clear there is a part in this I'm to play, and I mean to play it to the fullest, no matter what."

John smiled at his memory of the gratitude he'd felt in knowing Marcus Prochorus in that moment and expanded on part of his reply to answer Isvant's question.

"Erezavan, this universe and all within it are like an infinitely large Diamond, one that constantly forms, removes and changes Its facets from shape to shape, from one to many, and from one place and time to another. Each of us, though fully the One, is also an individual facet of Its diamond wholeness; each of us is a unique and specific Aspect of It, with unique and specific abilities. The more fully we express as the facets we are born as, the more Joy the One experiences."

Isvant frowned. "The Masters at the School say something similar...but, Ma—Sir, how can something frightening bring the One joy?"

"How can Omnipotent, Omniscient, Omnipresence be frightened, Erezavan? Oh, at the deepest level of our understanding we know we are the One and can never separate ourselves from our Self; but we *think* we are separate, think we are at the mercy of our bodies and world.

"The ones who remember that joy is everything given, received and experienced also know there is no fearful appearance that truth cannot bring to wholeness. Why? Because there is nothing that is not at source the Great Diamond One."

John held his peace as a couple of sailors staggered by, freshly-mended nets in tow. They'd be stored away while *Matthatus* was in port and free of the need to rely on the fruits of the sea to fill the crew's stomachs.

"The facets of the Diamond you and I are have the gift of seeing beyond the likeness of Life that stands directly before our eyes, Erezavan, but it is not ours to determine if what we see is good, nor to decide that our gift must be bad if what it shows us offends. Each facet of the Great Diamond exists only to be like the Romans' aqueducts, conduits through which Its gifts express. Ours is to bring what we know to others—or not, as the One wills—and to Witness the results of doing so, without personal pride."

Isvant looked unhappy. "Then I must resign myself to these fearful dreams?"

"Oh, no. The One desires you be happy, always."

"But you just said..."

"Listen to me with your heart, not your head, Erezavan! It knows very well what I say, even as your phantom self tries to twist my words into a demand to suffer. As you awaken to your inborn wholeness, you'll begin to accept that all the facets of the Diamond that you previously thought worked against you, be they thoughts, feelings, situations or other beings, in truth act only to create your joy, for joy is all the Witnessing Self knows. And as you accept that, all nightmares will turn to beauty. The drama of Life will become a comedy, and you will take no care for whether you have strange talents or not."

Isvant shook his head. "But how will I ever come to such a place, Sir? Since childhood, I have feared others and my own talents. I have tried all I know, all that the Masters of the School taught me, to be rid of that fear, but when I look at others, I see only what they may say or do. And the visions have only made that worse. How can I ever change that?" Isvant blinked rapidly, as if trying to hold back tears; he'd no doubt been maligning himself for his "defect" for years...and creating proof of it by his belief.

"Erezavan, none of us can change our tracks of being by force of will, for we love them too dearly. The belief that '*I* must use my wits to survive in this harsh world,' is one of the strongest ones we have, and to the phantom self, at least, there is a kind of pleasure in proving that is so. But as you allow yourself to touch the One that is the core of your being, you will find you need not rely on *or* fight against your thoughts or judgments to live in peace and joy. Nor will you need to fight those of others. You will come to accept all that you are, as you are, often without even knowing when that acceptance came. Your gifts, no matter how they once seemed, will become the means of bestowing only joy.

"I promise you, Erezavan, you will come to know the truth of who you are, and that discovery will be as easy as lying down to rest in the Practice."

Isvant looked as if he desperately wanted believe John, yet still feared to do so;

however, he also looked as if he was willing to take the risk of following this path in the hope that he would finally find what he sought. And that in itself shows the greatness of your courage, John thought, for many others would have given up long ago and simply let their misery lead them as it willed. Yes, Erezavan would let his experience with the Practice to show him the truth... but right now, he had another question.

"You said I must learn to trust the counsel of my own soul if I am ever to know my true Self—but Darshinika is Teacher to me, he has told me so. He says I can come to Truth only by following his guidance; that a student who follows another's words will be forever banished from the sight of God." Isvant shivered at the thought of Baremna's threats being true, but his growing frustration made his jaw tighten. "He scorns me for being such a dolt that I do not already know the answers to my questions, and now forbids me to speak in his presence at all...but how can I know if I do not ask?"

Despite his potential, John wondered for the first time just how much time Erezavan had actually spent with his School's Masters...surely, they'd have admonished him against trusting one so untrustworthy if he'd spent more time in their presence, yes?

"Erezavan, your task as student is to listen to what your Teacher says, and better, to let his Stillness and his joy in being the One fill you until it is all you ever desire and choose to be. *Not* because you fear the withdrawal of his protection," John said sternly, "but because you trust that his guidance will lead you to what you seek. To follow a Teacher for any other reason is sheerest nonsense. And any 'teacher' who lets not the student recognize his bond to him in his own time, who needs to tell you he is your teacher, then uses threats to hold you, is no Teacher at all."

Isvant's expression went though numerous changes as he digested this information, to settle at last on a grimly furrowed brow. A moment later, he offered up a somewhat absentminded "thank you," and hurried to the cabins. John hoped Baremna had other students to dominate, for if the young man's look was anything to go by, he'd just misplaced this one.

Joshua confirmed John's suspicion as *Matthatus* pulled into port an hour later.

"He finally starts to act like a man instead of skulking about like a frightened mouse," the merchant said with vehement satisfaction.

"Whereas you noticed before that he did not?"

Joshua snorted. "If Caesar suddenly forgot he was Emperor and started acting like the lowliest drudge, they would call him 'Erezavan'. He was like a dog that tries to make himself small but is still always in the way. Just the sight of him made me want to kick him."

John stifled his smile as Joshua pursed his lips.

"But then, is that not the way of it with all of us at sometime or another, to think ourselves unworthy of what we truly want? Even I, who've never wanted for anything, have done so... Faugh! Even the priests tell us it is not good to be too happy, lest we should call the gods' jealous anger down upon our heads.

"Is this one of those tracks of being you speak of, Rabbi? Do some affect all of us, so that we think them normal and right?"

John nodded, pleased. "It is indeed so, Joshua. And it is why Jeshua chose to go through the crucifixion."

"But...how can that be? You said he did not die to redeem our sins, as some on Samos insisted when I talked to them."

"What those on Samos—and in Jerusalem, for that matter—fail to understand is that Jeshua was crucified, not as a punishment for what humanity may have done, but solely to prove that there is nothing one can be punished for."

"His resurrection."

"Precisely. Jeshua showed us that when we fully awaken to the Self, we can heal any damage to mind, body and world. Any belief, no matter how irredeemable it appears to be, can be made naught when you know the Truth. The death of the body is never the death of the Being or Its power, Joshua. Jeshua was crucified, not to heal our sins, but to prove they never existed in the first place."

"But... Are you saying, then, that even such a one as I can do the things Jeshua did?" Joshua asked slowly. John grinned.

"I am saying that as you increasingly remember who you are, it is impossible that you not be able to do as Jeshua did."

As had been the case throughout the voyage, the male companions helped the crew secure *Matthatus* and unload its wares. John did not join in the work this time, but motioned to Joshua to follow him to the cabins. Once there, he gathered in Ada and led the two of them to a trap door that was concealed by several crates and barrels.

"The other day, Joshua, you came to me, suddenly distressed for those you'd never before given thought or concern. You had always believed their misfortunes to simply be the way of things, you said, but had come to realize that that was not so. You wanted to know why the universe, if it is formed of unlimited good, allows such hardship to exist."

He nodded to Ada, "And you, dear one, have done well to hold to the Silence while knowing your brother once suffered as these below now do. Yet, you too still wonder why such things must be, if our God is a merciful one.

"Below lies the answer to your questions. Will you come with me? I will not fault you if you choose not to."

The two of them nodded compliantly, though Ada's swarthy complexion grew pasty; John grabbed the ring atop the heavy trapdoor and slowly drew it upward.

The stench of human flesh that had gone far too long with only the barest of necessities gusted up from the dim, damp, space. And this is a well-kept ship, John thought, wrinkling his nose, for *Matthatus's* captain suffered the slaves to occasionally wash their bodies, see the daystar and smell the fresh sea air. This practice was not entirely altruistic. True, Joses Matthatus might in fact be more compassionate than most owners, but it was also true that the reek of vomit, feces and weeks-old sweat wafting through the deck boards would certainly shatter the illusion of a gods-powered ship.

John stepped aside to let Joshua go before him, then handed a trembling Ada into the younger man's hands. He followed, taking care as he stepped to a deck that was slippery with water from the wash buckets that lined the starboard wall, and nodded a greeting to the master, whose large, kettle-shaped drum thundered in a stately rhythm.

He motioned Ada and Joshua forward. Both looked somewhat like marionettes as their hesitant movements brought them to each side of him; Ada got more than a few surreptitious looks and one scowling one from the drum master. She kept her shawl over her face, both for propriety's sake and to alleviate some of the air's thickness, but her eyes conveyed her distress at seeing men doomed to row out a large portion—or the rest—of their lives as her brother had once been condemned. Joshua's eyes were also a bit wide, but he managed to keep his emotions from showing too plainly on his face.

John laid a hand against the nape of each of his students' necks and pulled them a bit closer. "Tell me what you see," he said over the throb of the master's drum and the grunts of the rowers.

Joshua swallowed, staring at the men as if he could not look away. "I see...I see men who are made to live like animals, Rabbi, men I once thought of as naught but criminals who deserved whatever harsh fates they received, but whom I now see as men unjustly treated no matter what their crimes may be." He shook his head under John's hand. "I know many consider my father a merciful, even a soft, master, and that these men fare better than most. Still, no one should be made to live like this."

"And you, Ada?"

"I see men who are suffering too, Rabbi—brothers who deserve a better lot."

"You think they are unjustly treated, then? That it is unfair of the One to allow such a thing?"

Ada nodded. "Yes; yes I do."

John closed his eyes and focused his attention inward, not at all sure what he intended would actually happen, and was pleased to feel, rather than hear, his charges gasp in amazement. He smiled. "Tell me what you see now."

"I can still see the men as they row, Rabbi," Ada said, amazed, "but I also see the maps of their lives as clearly as if they were written in a book! I see the stories of what each one chose to experience before ever he came to this earth to play at being human!"

"And what do you see, Joshua?" John asked.

The young man answered in the manner of one who sees the truth of a thing, but wishes not to believe it. "I see that, in his deepest heart, every man here knew before he was born that he might—no, was likely to—end up in this place. But Rabbi, it cannot truly be that each of these men chose this lot...can it? And chose willingly? Why? Why would anyone's soul choose to live in such misery? I do not understand."

John allowed them to take in the enhanced scene a little longer, then lifted his hands from their necks and made for the ladder. They followed behind until they were again on the main deck, savoring the fresh air and blue skies.

"So, then, why would anyone choose sickness, or madness, or poverty, over joy and happiness? Why would God allow it?

"Well, what if you were God, dear ones? What If you were the uncreated, indivisible One for all Eternity? What if naught could mar your beauty or shake your Stillness and Perfection? Pray, how, then, would you experience yourself to be God?"

John smiled as they looked startled, then puzzled, but raised a hand to prevent Ada's attempt to answer. "Might you experience yourself as God by seeming to become many? Might those many seem to be separate from each other? Might you, as that many, live numerous different kinds of experiences? Perhaps you would choose to forget you had made the choice to be an unlimited number of separate characters. Perhaps you would forget the truth that you, as each of those characters, have the right and ability to stop enacting any role at any time.

"That is, until you Remembered."

The frown on Joshua's handsome face looked great enough to bring on a headache. "Do you say God plays a *game*, and we are but the pieces?"

"No. What am I saying, Ada?"

Ada's expression was thoughtful. "You are saying that we are God, Rabbi, and our 'individual pieces'—all the bodies, minds and souls—are Ours to do with as we please. That when we, as individuals, awaken enough to see that, our only desire becomes to awaken all of our 'selves' to the awareness of being Self."

"By letting them suffer?" Joshua asked, still incredulous.

John shrugged. "Sometimes the One in your heart calls you to take action. But mainly you help others awaken by being as much of the Light as you are capable of being, by simply standing in the fullness of the One's Silence, which is also Love. Consider this: because the two of you trustingly chose to follow me where you would rather not have gone, chose to hold to the Stillness and see what lay in their hearts, at least three of those men will be free within the month and another two within the year."

Ada shook her head. "Rabbi, I have heard you, Mary, Martha and Miriam speak of creation as the "Play of Consciousness," and I asked no questions because I thought understood. Yet, though I saw the map of life written in each man's soul, still I find myself asking, 'why ever would God wish to play thus?' Can He be so bored?"

John chuckled. "No, dearest. For God—and let me remind you it is our Self I speak of—the reason for this game is to discover the infinite joy that we are and experience it."

"Even the suffering?" Joshua asked again, still unable to accept such a notion.

"Hmm... Tell me, did you ever have dolls?"

Ada smiled slightly. "My sisters and I did, yes."

"Did your mother ever feel sad when one or another of the characters they played seemed to suffer some loss? Joshua, did your father grow angry when you or your brothers lost your imaginary battles?"

"...No..."

"Nor does Perfect Omnipotence. You see, our divine Mother/Father knows your choices cannot harm you. And though They would have every one of their parts remember they are but One Part, and so worthy only of Joy, They do not suffer when they do not. The One simply waits, ever patient, and rejoices as we awaken one by one."

"But then, if this is only play—and I am not saying I agree with you, Rabbi, offend you though that might—what is the point to doing anything at all? I feel if I accept your coin as real I will lose my purpose for taking this journey with you, lose my purpose for living at all. What then?"

"What is the use of love, Joshua? If there is always love to discover and enjoy, can you ever lose your purpose?"

John could see the young man's answer would only be more questions. "You will find your answers only by answering that question, and you will answer that question only by experiencing it for yourself. Let it settle within your being, my friend, and bring you its answer in its own way and time."

John smiled as Matthatus mumbled away; then: "And what have you to say, sister?"

Ada sighed. "I know not what to say, Rabbi. So I think I, too, will take your advice and let the One show me the truth of your words—if ever It is so inclined." She sounded more than a little skeptical as she added this last. John laughed and gave her a brief hug.

"I daresay, Ada, if your willingness is even one-quarter of what it has been, your answer will come swiftly. You will keep me apprised?"

"Of course, Rabbi."

"Good."

John smiled as Ada made her way to the women's cabin to collect Rachael and the rest of her belongings, but he felt just the slightest edge descend on his joy. His own experiences over the years told him that what he had said was true...and yet, would their next move easily present itself, or wait for him to find it?

And there was still the matter of the visions. Though his talk with Erezavan had done much to alleviate the young man's concerns, John still felt off-balance, wondering when the next one would strike.

Suddenly, he shook his head in amused self-deprecation.

I have trusted the Way Jeshua would have me walk thus far; it seems a bit late in the day to worry about such things now, hmm?

Still: "What would you have me do, Jeshua, Mother?"

John looked toward the heavens with more than a little drama, but though he asked the question lightly, he knew, too, that he meant it.

SEVENTEEN

John *strolled contentedly* along, relaxed for the first time in weeks as the companions wended their way through the city of Corinth. After spending the early afternoon walking from *Galley Matthatus* and the docks of Cenchreae, they now sought an inn that one of the crew recommended as fit for women. The shipmaster, curmudgeon to the last, long-sufferingly accepted Torer's departure, sincerely wished the big man good journeys, and invited him to seek him out if ever he wished to serve aboard a ship again.

Then, surprisingly, he thanked the male companions for their work.

"You each of you listened as if you actually had heads on your shoulders, not sacks of grain," he said gruffly, still amazed at their competence. "More, you did your share without complaining. Would that the hired men worked as hard and as willingly."

He'd then invited any and all to consider serving on *Matthatus* if ever the notion so struck them...and provided they brought no more women along to distract them.

John wondered again at the shipmaster's annoyance. Surely, there'd been women passengers aboard *Matthatus* before, and frequently. Indeed, Sarah Matthatus and her daughter, Judith, had sailed from Rome aboard this very ship but a few months before, and it was equally certain other dignitaries, guests of Joses Matthatus, sometimes traveled with wives, daughters and even small children in tow.

"Oh, he does not like that either," Joshua smiled when John mentioned it, "but it would be unseemly, if not dangerous, for him to behave rudely in those cases. Our companions, though respectable enough, are women of little consequence, and he suspects it will be some time before I again communicate with my father. Thus does he think it safe to be his usual surly self—on this matter, at least."

John took a deep and satisfying lungful of the Corinthian air. Despite being considerably larger than both Caesarea and Athens, he could feel in Corinth's topography its most ancient experiences, even those that had occurred before ever it was called "city". The spirits that made up the ground of this territory had long since come to terms with their place in the scheme of things, just as all beings, and perhaps even the stars themselves, must do. Though they were surrounded both by newcomers and longtime residents seeking to inspect newly-arrived wares from the city's two ports, the Quiet in the earth of Corinth resonated with the earth of John's heart.

"How far away is this inn supposed to be?" Prochorus asked over the rumble of the crowd. "Is it in this part of town, or farther in?"

"Closer to the other end, based on what Hayyim said," John answered, and received a muted "hmph" in return. Though they'd been walking all afternoon, he didn't mind being out longer. He was glad to again feel the solidity of land beneath his feet.

He also enjoyed observing the cosmopolitan Corinthians, many of them transplants from lands as far away as his own Judea; he smiled as Timothy and Rachael commented on the differences between these townsfolk and the ones at home. Erezavan, who walked as far from a sullen, taciturn Darshinika Baremna as possible, also seemed fascinated by the spectacle of a place so different from what he'd known, while Joshua blandly ignored it all, as the scion of a great House should do. Ada and Hosea were engrossed in a personal conversation that was wreathed in smiles, Prochorus and Torer maintained that air of relaxed alertness that seemed to come naturally to all warriors, and Haifata Adan, as usual, was unreadable.

All at once, John frowned, and his sense of peace abruptly curdled away. Rather than thinning out as they left the market, the crowd had grown thicker; the air held an ever more palpable sense of disturbance, one that had been present for some time. He cursed the disorientation his recent experiences had fostered. He was usually quick to notice when intrusive energies entered his awareness, but after the intensity of the last few weeks, he'd become so immersed in the peace fostered by Corinth's land spirits that he'd led his companions straight into the buzz of danger that now surrounded them.

"What goes on here?" Prochorus asked sharply, looking about as if he wished he had eyes all around his head. Haifata and Torer likewise grew suddenly alert, while Erezavan, who to John's surprise had needed little defensive training, also became watchful.

"Tell the others to stay close," John said, trying to locate the source of his disquiet—and a path away from it.

The group maintained their direction but tightened their scraggly circle. Suddenly, the throng thinned, bringing them face-to-face with the focus of the burgeoning trouble: a man stood atop a pedestal, loudly exhorting the crowd to action. John hastily changed course at the words "Jesu's sacrifice", but Hosea couldn't resist looking over his shoulder.

"Who does he remind you of, Rabbi?" he asked with a sardonic chuckle.

John had to smile himself; save for some slight physical differences, the speaker could easily have been Moses bar Josef, one of Jeshua's more fervent (in his own mind, at least) followers. He'd been a hawker of wares, and so used well his sense of drama to convey Jeshua's message—free of any understanding of the truth behind the words. Bar Josef believed his name, containing as it did those of two great Patriarchs, destined him to do great things in spreading Jeshua's "war against sin" to all the world, but he'd angrily left the fold when Jeshua publicly rebuked him for declaring himself one of Jeshua's "generals" and giving out "the Master's special instructions," which he'd made up from whole cloth.

This one's sincerity may be greater than bar Josef's, John thought, but his understanding certainly is not. Still, many in the crowd listened to him with rapt attention, their eyes aglow with admiration for his fervor.

"Listen to me! Jesu was led like a lamb to the slaughter so that you might be free! Do not ignore His call when He suffered so cruelly to save you, as the Roman monsters do! Else, when He returns to this earth in fire and righteous wrath, you will be among those who see his eyes of blood! You will be eternally damned and never know God's grace!"

"We must get out of this crowd now," John said urgently, for though many of those present responded to the man's words with fright or exasperation, the increasing sense of menace had not its source in any of them. He, Prochorus and Hosea formed a wedge, keeping the women between them, while the others stayed close behind and protected their backs. The man kept talking.

"I tell you, brothers and sisters, you must throw off the tyrannous yolk of your sins! You must throw off the yolk of those who crucified Jesu so they'd not have to face the corruption of their own villainous souls! Do not be like them! Turn you now to the one and only Son of God! Turn to the true King of the world, before it is too late!"

And suddenly, it was too late.

"Liar!" Someone bellowed off to John's left.

Within seconds, other calls of "Liar!", "Traitor!" And words far more venomous joined the mix of voices, all of them male.

Then the clubs came out.

"This way!" John yelled, raising his elbows to protect himself from the sudden, fear-filled jostling of the multitude. Chaos ensued as people were caught by the vicious blows of what seemed like hundreds of toughs swinging clubs with indiscriminate fury.

"They're soldiers!" Prochorus yelled, his dismay apparent even in this din. And it was true: though the club-wielders dressed like everyone else, they acted in concert.

John's sense of direction twisted away and disappeared as several people slammed into him, some with blood on their faces; men's and women's cries alike filled the air as they tumbled to the ground, either struck by the clubs or pushed by those who, in their panic, sought escape from or combat with their attackers.

"Hosea!"

"No! Ada, hold to me!"

John almost pulled the tiny woman off her feet to stop her headlong rush to rescue her husband, who lay, tangled on the ground with two people who'd crashed into him. He waded forth to help Hosea up; though his lip was bloodied, the laborer nodded, grabbed Ada's hand and motioned them to continue forth. John looked for the others: Adan and Isvant had managed to seize clubs and fought with considerable expertise and no small amount of ferocity; Marcus held his own with fists alone, though John knew he still carried the knives he'd so artfully used in Bethany. Joshua and Baremna looked harried but uninjured for the moment, and Torer, head and shoulders towering above the mob, flung his attackers about as if they were straw dolls.

"Rabbi, look out!" Rachael shrilled next to him.

John spun awkwardly, trying to get between the women and this newest threat, only to find a large, thick, club speeding toward his face. He raised an arm, knowing even as he did so that he moved far too slowly—

—And right at that moment, another vision took him.

"NO!" he yelled angrily as he found himself alone in the garden where he'd reencountered Mary. "No! Send me back!"

"Hello, my son." Mary stood before John, her usual unconcerned delight shining from her countenance.

"Damn it, Mother! You must send me back! The others—!"

He actually grabbed Mary's shoulders, fully intending to give her a good hard shake, but she effortlessly slipped from his grasp. Ignoring his agitation, she strode to the cliff-edge he'd noticed on his first visit to her garden.

"Mother—!"

Mary turned back, and though her expression was still joyful, her voice was as stern as ever Jeshua's had been. "Were you planning to follow, Boanerge, or will you just stand there, frustrated, angry, and useless to your friends?"

John could not but follow.

The rough little trail wasn't as steep as he'd assumed it would be; still, walking it without taking a dangerous tumble required enough concentration to prevent him from continuing his protests. In all honesty, that was a good thing, for he was embarrassed... no...mortified...by his behavior. He knew men who considered it their right to strike a wife or elderly mother, yet he'd never before laid a hand on Mary in anger, had never even cursed in her presence. That he should have done both now shamed him deeply.

But still and all! John grew angry all over again at the timing of this summons. If his body was in the usual state these visions engendered, he must be not just useless, but an actual hindrance to his companions' escape. How could Mary so callously indulge her whim to take him touring and laugh away their plight? Had her translation into this paradise taken away her compassion for the frailties of her still-human friends and students? Would Jeshua ever have been so uncaring?

"Isha," Mary suddenly said over her shoulder, reading John's thoughts as if he spoke them aloud.

He again felt a jolt at the mention of the name, but was too concerned about his friends to give it more than passing attention; indeed, his concern for them made even the thought of such a frivolity somehow vulgar.

It seemed to John they walked for hours, but at last they came to a small house that strongly reminded him of their home in Bethany.

"Mary, please," he said as she reached the door, "you must send me back to Corinth to help the others...or at least to not interfere with their ability to get safely away while my body stands frozen in trance. You must send me back!"

Mary turned, took John's hands and gazed searchingly into his face. Her expression held concern for the first time since Bethany, and John felt sure he'd finally pierced her ecstatic disregard for his friends.

He was wrong. "I begin to think Jeshua's charge that you care for me after his departure may not have been so wise as it seemed at the time, John. Perhaps you should have done more public proselytizing on his behalf, as his other companions did."

"Mother—"

"Shh." Mary laid her fingers against his lips, then stepped back as if to look him over. "My dearest son, your path has allowed you to grow most beautifully in the Way of the One...yet I fear now it has also left you sheltered from the larger world. I fear your abilities—and your trust—have been impaired because of it."

"But—"

"Though it has been more subtle before now, John, you have believed since this journey began that the welfare of your companions is your personal responsibility. You believe if they come to harm, it will be because you have somehow failed both them and Jeshua. Such is not the case, my son."

John sighed. "Mother, my companions are in the middle of a riot, one sponsored by the local Roman authorities, if not Rome herself. The ones who wield the clubs are skilled at hurting others and clearly have orders to beat anyone who had the misfortune of being in that crowd when they struck. Should I not be concerned for their welfare?"

"Can you not trust that the One is with each of them, even in the midst of a riot?"

"Of course I can!"

Mary shook her head. "'Of course I can...and yet...' your eyes say to me. Tell me John, where is the Silent Witness now? Where is the One?"

"Why, it is here, as always," he said, stung by the accusation in his mother's words.

"Yes, yes it is. But my question is, are you with *It* right now?"

"I will do whatsoever the One would have of me, Mother, you know that."

"This knows it, you mean," Mary tapped John's forehead. "But this is not so sure when it comes to risking the wellbeing of your friends." She tapped him on the chest, over his heart. "I ask again, where is your focus, John? Is it on the fullness of the One, or is it back in Corinth? Do you trust...or do you worry?"

John could not meet Mary's eyes, for they both knew the answer.

"My son, you must recognize—and let go of—your phantom self's need to keep your companions safe. Else, its fear of somehow leading them wrongly will stop you from completing this task. Their souls know what they seek and its risks; trust that the One will perfectly guide you and them to find it. Have no fear, John. Truly, all is well."

Mary's serious demeanor held for a moment longer, then her joyful expression returned. She kissed John's cheek. "Now then, dearest, come inside and have a drink."

John sighed again as she ushered him into the cottage, trying, at least, not to show that he still worried for his friends.

The house was not nearly as small as it had seemed from the outside; in fact, it was impossibly large. The main room was only slightly smaller than Miriam and Martha's, but its ceiling was low enough to give the place a sense of coziness, even with its pale stone walls. There was a rounded, Roman-style fire pit off to one side, but not so far off as to make one end of the room too cool while the other baked. Numerous chairs, pillows and benches marked this home as one where visitors were frequently made welcome. Directly across from John was a hallway with doors that lead to more rooms, and on the side of this room, furthest from the fire pit, was another door. Before it stood a long, rectangular table that boasted at least a dozen padded chairs; it was partly set for dinner.

"Is this where you stay?" John asked in amazement.

"This is my home, good sir, and you and your company are most welcome for dinner and more, if you are in need."

John whirled at the sound of the voice, for it was not Mary's, nor even female.

The man, an elder whose once-full head of hair now boasted naught but numerous bright gray wisps, introduced himself as Dareios Isaurus. Though his back was slightly bent from some inborn impediment, John sensed he had nevertheless been robust, even handsome, in his youth. He wore the garb of the locals, but the smiling eyes that met

John's confused ones were warm with greeting—for him and the rest of the companions, who crowded in behind him.

John looked his friends over carefully, but save for Hosea's busted lip, a quickly purpling bruise on Prochorus's left cheek, and Rachael's heartbroken sobbing, they all seemed unscathed, if disheveled.

...No. Not all of them. Timothy and Torer were missing.

"Forgive me, good sir. I must have taken a blow during the riot; my manners are not what they should be," John said bewilderedly, bowing slightly to the old man in an attempt to be gracious. "Thank you very much for getting us away from that onslaught and taking us in. We surely would have suffered far more harm had you not done so."

The old man looked perplexed, but Ada peered at her Teacher and nodded as if she suddenly realized what had happened. "Rabbi, Master Dareios did not come to us...you lead us to him."

"And you took no blow at all, though I swear to Jupiter I've no idea how you avoided it," Prochorus added incredulously.

"When Rachael cried out, I turned also—just in time to see the club of that thug coming down," Ada continued. "I thought surely it would leave you unconscious at the least...but then, instead of striking you, the man and his club suddenly jerked straight up into the air as if God Himself grabbed hold of it."

"You should have seen him fly, Rabbi! He looked like he'd been fired from a catapult," Hosea interjected with considerable satisfaction. "Then you grabbed Ada and Rachael's hands and marched through the crowd as if the attackers were not even there. Several of them came at us, but either turned aside at the last second or ran by as if they could not see us. Once we got away from the riot, you led us through the streets like you knew exactly where you sought to go and came to Master Isaurus's door. Then you knocked and entered, and now here we are."

"Except for Torer and Timothy," John said, looking about as if he hoped he was mistaken. This caused fresh sobs from Rachael.

"Puh-please, Rabbi, we must go back and find him!" she said, and John was somehow sure the "him" she spoke of was not Torer. "Those men were beating people so viciously, he must be hurt! We have to find him!"

She broke down completely then, the rest of her words unintelligible. Ada comforted the girl and gently reminded her to use the techniques of Practice to help her stay centered despite her surging emotions.

"Rabbi, may we search for them?" Erezavan asked. Baremna sneered at the young man's eagerness to gain John's permission to act, but Joshua looked equally ready to go forth. Hosea, Prochorus and Adan looked at him expectantly.

John turned to Isaurus. "Has this happened before?"

"The riots? Oh, yes. They have become almost common this last year and more, for the city's powers have come to perceive the Christine community as a growing threat. My friends and I help the injured when we can, only to have them go forth again. In recent weeks, some of them have not come back." A slight shudder took the old man, but then his eyes cleared and he looked again at John. "What do your friends look like?" he asked. "I have friends who know this city well and are quite good at finding those missing; you need but give me a description and I will set a search in motion."

John thanked Dareios, happy to have his help, but before he could describe the missing men, the door burst open and two women staggered inside. Another woman, bloodied and barely conscious, slumped between them.

"That fool Camon has provoked another attack," the taller woman said angrily. "He wants so much to hear himself speak that he takes no thought for the safety of those who come to see him!"

John's glimpse as she passed by revealed a tallish, sinewy woman of rather sharp expression, but even in this crisis he noticed her luxuriant hair, which was so light a shade of brown it was almost golden. She and the other, slightly shorter woman, whose lush, chocolate curls hid her features, barely noticed the companions as they laid the injured woman on one of many couches.

"They know what they are choosing, daughter, and you know many of them think it an honor to be abused for the Christos's sake." Dareios spoke with the resignation of one who has said the same thing to the same one more than once. "Are more coming, Ariadne?" he asked the dark-haired woman.

"How else?" she sighed in a slightly husky voice, her back still to the companions as she wiped blood from the woman's face. "Thomas and the others are bringing them."

"Do you know if any they bring are men, especially one of about twenty summers?" John asked as the lighter-haired woman went to prepare for the coming injured. He thought of Timothy, of course; he was sure he need take no concern for Torer.

"I cannot say one way or the other, I fear; Demeter and I needed to get this one to safety quickly." The woman called Ariadne straightened and turned, her brows rising in surprise as she realized just how many people were in the room.

Then her eyes settled on John.

John's reacquaintance with the ancient bond between himself and Haifata Adan in Antipatris, though moving, had been an easy thing, a pleasing surprise. But the surge of recognition that flooded his senses as he returned this woman's dark-eyed stare left him frozen in blank astonishment. He suddenly felt like he was drowning, like the blood that rushed loud in his ears had had all the air drawn out of it. His heart staggered in his chest and gasped for breath.

I *know* this one, John's soul triumphantly shouted as he looked into her—into this Ariadne's—eyes. He felt the same incredible joy he'd known when Jeshua first consented to be his Teacher... Or, no, not the same joy exactly, but... John couldn't find a comparison, but the power of what he felt shocked him beyond words—and brought with it an even more surprising twinge of apprehension.

The woman hastily turned back to her charge on the couch, but not before John noticed her widened eyes and flushed cheeks. He suddenly realized his own were quite hot.

"Two more of this party did not arrive here," Dareios said, oblivious to the exchange that had just taken place. "I was just going out to call a search when you two came in."

"Let me see to it," Demeter Isaurus said as she came in with a basin of water. "Ari, you can attend the injured, can you not? You're better at that sort of thing, anyway."

She set the basin beside the dark-haired woman, sparing a moment to stare curiously at her still-flushed cheeks, then turned to John to gain the names and descriptions of the missing. John decided the searchers would most easily find Torer and hoped if they found him they would also find Timothy.

As Demeter left with Prochorus and Adan, he realized that though her expression hid it, she was in truth quite attractive. More, despite differences in coloring and height, the two women undeniably favored each other, with their oval faces, exotic features and willowy, shapely figures. Both were daughters to Dareios Isaurus...and he'd not yet introduced himself or his company to any of them. Maybe I *have* taken a blow, John thought ruefully; this gentle soul had taken them all in and knew not even their names.

At that moment, several men came in with more injured to settle on couches and chairs; introductions were forgotten as the companions set to work helping the wounded. The men accepted their presence gladly, for it meant they could bring in more who needed aid—"far too many this time," the one called Thomas said gruffly.

"And what of Camon?" Dareios asked.

"Pah! He is a good one for calling for martyrdom, but seems to have no taste for it himself," Thomas sneered. He started out the door again, having received descriptions of Torer and Timothy and promising to find them, "if they've not already been arrested."

"Wait!" John called, and Thomas turned, his face full of impatient inquiry. John took out the carved-fish necklace Jeshua had given him. "I fear Torer could be dangerous if you approach him without some proof of your connection to us, so be sure you show him this when you find him and Timothy."

If they can be found, he thought, resisting the urge to go forth himself.

Thomas looked as if he had questions about a companion whom John could so readily refer to as dangerous, but kept them to himself.

For the next several hours, the Isaurus home seemed as crowded as the docks of Cenchreae. Many of those brought in were badly injured, for in addition to being beaten, they'd been trampled when the crowd scattered. John laid hands on the most badly hurt, healing what he could and frustrated by the fact that he did not have Jeshua's unlimited reserves of energy. He was discreet about it, knowing well how quickly word of such healings traveled. Under the circumstances, having the companions' presence brought to the attention of the authorities seemed imprudent.

John also spent a goodly amount of time covertly watching Ariadne Isaurus, unable, in truth, to long keep his eyes from her. Though she seemed quiet almost to the point of shyness, he sensed in her a single-mindedness that could turn intractably stubborn if provoked by the right cause. He was still taken aback by the force of his attraction and resistance to her; the few times their eyes met as she bound wounds and soothed those conscious enough to benefit from such care, he quickly looked away, his skin tingling as if he'd received a shock. Surely looking too long into this one's eyes would result in his soul being swallowed up—and that was something he simply could not afford.

And yet...how it *would* be to merge completely with another, even for a moment?

Afternoon crept into evening and evening rolled into night. Demeter, Prochorus and Adan returned when it was dark enough to require torchlight to see by; Rachael, who'd comported herself with amazing maturity through the hours, began to cry again, leaning on Ada and Hosea by turns.

At around eighth hour, Dareios, his daughters, some of the other rescuers and the companions, ate supper. There was little conversation, for many injured still slept on couches at the other end of the room and everyone was tired. Midway through dinner, John remembered that he still had not properly introduced himself and his companions and finally undertook to correct his error.

"You are one of the Twelve? You walked with the Christos?"

Dareios's cup clattered to the table and splashed the last of his wine onto his plate and clothing, while the others present whispered urgently to each other. Demeter, hand to her mouth, stood so quickly that she nearly overturned her chair. Ariadne stared down at her plate as if she'd just discovered it was filled with gold—and expected to be accused of stealing it. Even in the dimness of the candlelight, John saw her cheeks were ablaze. He acknowledged Dareios's question with a nod, frankly surprised his name had traveled so far, since it had been years since he'd done any public proselytizing.

The old man fluttered up out of his seat, apologizing profusely for treating John as a familiar; he offered him and his companions his family's own beds to sleep in, along with anything else they might ask. If he could come by it, he would get it, no matter what the cost or inconvenience.

"Neither I nor my companions seek to be worshipped, Dareios," John said, working to keep the exasperation out of his voice and ignoring Baremna's disbelieving scorn. "That is for the Camons of this world, those whose skill with words far outweighs their understanding of what the Christos truly taught. Please, Dareios, Demeter. Sit and let us tell you of our journey." He did so, with many welcome interjections from the others; then: "My friend, you have given *us* the greatest possible gift by taking us in and allowing us to serve those in need. Jeshua himself could ask no more of you, and I surely do not. But my thanks and friendship I do hope you will accept—as equals, not servants."

John looked at Ariadne as he spoke this last. She did not see it, for she still stared at her plate, but Demeter did and smiled despite her consternation.

Dareios's eyes filled with tears. "When I first heard of the Christos—a dozen years ago, it must be now—I felt for the first time in my life that it might be possible to know the true heart of Nature. I daily prayed that even a taste of his knowledge might come to me, and now I have been blessed to meet one who knew him personally. Is there more I could ask? There cannot be! Surely I have lived to the fullness of my days, to be so blessed."

"Ah, but there is always more, Dareios, if you would have it." John grinned as he told him of the Practice. "Will you allow us to teach you, your daughters and your friends as payment for your hospitality?"

Though their friends quickly agreed and both he and Demeter were eager to learn, Dareios considered it too good a gift to be given to their like. Ariadne remained quiet, but at one point, her eyes shyly met John's, and he knew she, too, desired to learn. Happily, after several minutes of wrangling and Ada and Hosea's gentle urging, Dareios at last agreed that he and his daughters would learn the Practice of Praise as soon as Torer and Timothy's fates were discovered and their other duties permitted it.

At around twelfth hour, Thomas and another man, named Alexander, returned to the house, their faces tired and grim. Like the other groups that had gone out searching, they had nothing to report on Torer and Timothy's whereabouts.

"One of the guards at the city garrison is one of us," Thomas said tiredly as he gave John's necklace back to him. "He was sure he saw no one like your Torer, but could not say one way or another about Timothy. Nor were there any on the streets who said they'd seen them. I am sorry." Everyone sat in gloomy silence.

"Rabbi, I have a thought." Ada said suddenly. "Is it not possible they headed back to the ship?"

Her words were met with Rachael's bleary-eyed but hopeful expression.

"*Matthatus* was not scheduled to leave for another day," Joshua said, excited by the possibility, "and Torer could surely find his way back to the docks from here. Perhaps they did go back to the ship."

"It is indeed possible—*but*," John said hastily when Joshua and Erezavan jumped up as if they intended to immediately go forth, "it will have to wait until morning before we find out. I have no doubt there are soldiers about who would love nothing more than catching two strangers out at this hour. I'll have no more of us go missing."

The young men slowly sat back down, their disappointment obvious, but John felt sure even Mary would appreciate his need to protect his friends in this situation.

Suddenly, the door rattled with a knock so loud it made those who could jump in startlement. Prochorus, Erezavan and Haifata instantly came to their feet.

"Soldiers?" Marcus half-whispered to Thomas.

"It could be."

"Well, we will never know if we do not look," Demeter said with some asperity.

She opened the door a crack...then opened it all the way, craning her neck in amazement.

Torer stood in the doorway, one arm wrapped around a barely conscious Timothy.

EIGHTEEN

"**Well?** *Do you mean* to stand there gaping like frogs in hot water, or are you letting us in?" Torer said, already pushing through the door as he spoke. Demeter hastily stepped back and beckoned the large man to deposit Timothy on an empty couch, still staring as if she'd never seen such a sight in her life—which was probably the case.

"Well met, Torer," John smiled, his relief evident.

"Likewise, Rabbi. Oh, he is not too badly hurt, Little One," Torer said over Rachael's horrified exclamations. "He is just exhausted. It has been a hard day of running to and fro." He sounded tired himself.

"Do you know what injuries he may have besides the black eye and cut?" Demeter asked. Ariadne was already sponging the injured areas, which were caked with dust.

"A few cracked ribs, if the bruise on his side is anything to go by. Also, he will have a good knot on his head." Torer pulled a makeshift hood from his own head, exposing his brilliant locks to further amazed scrutiny. Corinth might indeed be cosmopolitan, but a Scandinavian, especially one of his stature, was obviously still a rarity. "You will be glad to know the lad fought like one born to the art, brothers. That is, until he got angry."

"Why would that be bad for a warrior?" Thomas asked.

"He is not a warrior," Prochorus explained," but a young man who has but recently learned a few basic skills for defending himself. And one who fights in anger will always lose to one skilled, because angry men think only of hurting the opponent, not ending the fight."

Torer shrugged his agreement. "He saw one of the soldiers beating a young girl. That one will eat mush for awhile, I think, but it made the boy vulnerable. I took care of the ones who struck him down—they will not eat at all for a day or two! But it made us a bit too popular; the scoundrels had search parties after us the whole day. So, since I tend to stand out in a crowd, we had to take refuge as best we could."

John looked more closely at the Scandinavian and realized the darkness of his mustache, brows and face had nothing to do with the dimness. They were so dark because Torer had rubbed what looked like oily dirt into them. He'd no doubt also spent the day stooping his way to a height more comparable to the locals' stature.

"How did you find us?" Ariadne asked, stepping away from Timothy to defer to Rachael and Ada's ministrations.

"I heard your friends give a description of me to some others. Since we could not be sure they were friends, we followed at a distance. When they came to this place instead of the local garrison, I decided to take the chance that whoever lived here knew where we could find the rest of our company. It was a good choice, no?" Even through his tiredness, he managed a mischievous smile.

"Rabbi?"

John went to where Timothy lay. The boy's eye looked terrible, swollen shut and black out to the cheek, but John sensed no permanent damage. He was more concerned about the cut; it curved along the eye socket and would fester if not properly tended to.

"I am here, Little Brother," he answered, taking the young man's hand and easily offering him the nickname Jeshua had so long ago and lovingly offered him.

"Rabbi, are the others all right?"

"Yes, Timothy, we are all here, and only Hosea and Marcus received even a bruise."

Timothy was quiet for many seconds, as if his tired mind needed time to take in the information. When he finally spoke, his voice was thick with shame and grief. "Rabbi, I have failed you and my Teacher. I did not fight only to defend myself, but to hurt another... But when I saw them beating that little girl, I got so angry! I wanted to kill that man, Rabbi, and I...I tried my best to do so. I am sorry," he said a in a heartbroken whisper.

John's eyes filled, for he heard not just contrition in the young man's voice but the death of his belief that he, if not the world, was essentially good. He glanced at Ada, who tearily brushed at the lad's tangled hair. She too, heard it, and both sensed such a loss in Timothy would be as great as the loss of Timothy.

"Little Brother, do you remember when I told you what Jeshua did when he saw the moneychangers and sacrifice merchants selling their wares in the temple in Jerusalem? Do you think believed he was no longer good because he reacted with 'violence' over their desecration of a House of God?"

"No, Rabbi...but—"

"Was not that girl you protected the House of God as well? Timothy, simply stopping that soldier might have been enough; still, the Goodness that you are did not fail you."

"But...I do not understand."

"You may have wanted to kill him, Timothy, but the truth is, your Self only allowed you to do exactly what was needed to stop that soldier from defiling himself with murder. You served your goodness and his. You need feel no shame for that."

"But...what if I grow that angry again, Rabbi? What if I wish to hurt someone else?"

"Little Brother, what care have you for what may be if you stand in the Stillness of the One now—as I know you can? You've discovered the cost of losing your Self in your feelings by that experience. Take then, that lesson into the Silence and let what happened go." John laid a hand on the youngster's cheek. "And Timothy? Know that Miriam and I, and all of us, will love you always, no matter what you may do. Always."

Timothy seemed more like a child of nine than nineteen as he sobbed out his relief, but he nodded a firm "yes" when John asked if he was aware of the Stillness. Rachael, also crying, held to his hand like it was part of her own body, while Ada managed to hold the lad's other hand, dab at his wounds and comfort the girl, a talent she'd no doubt perfected through years of mothering her own children.

The young man's relief was no match for his exhaustion; his hiccupy sobs soon softened into the deep inhalations of sleep. John stood and was pleased all out of proportion to find warm approval in Ariadne's eyes for the brief moment they met. Then he looked toward the long table where they'd had dinner.

Torer sat straight up in one of the chairs—but he was fast asleep.

"Best we should find a pallet for him," he chuckled. "He'd be mortified if he opened his chin by falling off a chair."

Adan shook his head and smiled. "Not that one. He would simply make up a story of fighting off an army of ruffians to explain such an injury." The others chuckled.

"It has been a long day for all of you," Dareios said. "We have discussed it, and my daughters and I would be greatly pleased if you would sleep in our beds this night."

The companions protested such special treatment, pointing out that they had also seen a long day, but Ariadne nodded toward the few injured who still slept.

"It is no hardship. Our day will not end until these ones can go back to their own homes to mend."

"I will stay with Timothy," Ada said, and though she did not speak, John knew nothing short of the Roman Army would drag Rachael from his side. He nodded gratefully.

"We will take your gracious offer of beds, then, dear ones, with many thanks. I, at least, feel a week's sleep cannot make up for this day's excitement."

John and the others followed Ariadne down the hall where a total of five rooms awaited them. All were austerely decorated with a bed, writing table and wood closet, and as further proof that the Isaurus family was used to guests, all had enough extra straw mats to crowd in two or even three more, if needed.

"This one is mine," Ariadne said shyly, pointing out John and Marcus's space.

Prochorus thanked her with something closer to grunts than language and entered the room through a heavy curtain. John wondered at the lack of doors where they'd once obviously been, but did not ask about them. His eyes were frozen on Ariadne as if she'd suddenly appeared from Heaven—but his tongue was likewise paralyzed. She, too, seemed to be at a loss.

"Well...then...I..." Ariadne stammered, then took a deep breath. "Well. I must get back to the others... Sleep well, Master Zebedee." She hurriedly started away.

"Ariadne?" John called after her, his tongue suddenly uncleaving in his reluctance to see her go. She turned quickly, her face both hopeful and apprehensive.

"I...thank you...again...for your family's hospitality. I...we...that is, it is greatly appreciated. Greatly," he finished lamely.

Ariadne nodded—a bit disappointedly, John thought—and disappeared down the hall.

"Surely, I have lost all sense of my sense," he muttered, and firmly reminded himself that becoming involved—with anyone—would be the worst possible thing he could do.

And yet...and yet... John fell onto his pallet, sure he'd dream of Ariadne once the Practice finally carried his tired body into sleep.

A minor uproar greeted John when he entered the Isaurus's main room the next morning. Ada had discovered that one of Timothy's ribs was broken and decreed he would not be fit to travel for several days at least. And though the young man looked like he'd been in a brawl with his cut face, *two* black eyes, and the extra bruises that had become visible overnight, he was proving to be a very grumpy patient.

"I can walk, I am fine!" he protested—then made Ada's point by gasping and turning as white as the walls when he tried to rise. Ada "tsked" and with Rachael's help gently forced him back onto the couch.

"There, then, what did I say? We could not even carry you, even if Torer wanted to be your horse! That rib did not cause the harm it could have, but it could do so with too much jarring, so walking with it is out of the question. Your body needs to rest and heal, Timothy bar Arioch, and that is what it is going to do if I have to tie you to this couch!"

"Do not worry, Little Brother." John chuckled, stopping any further argument, if not Timothy's grumbles. "We are not in so great a hurry that we desire to carry you. If Dareios and his daughters have no objection, we will tarry here a bit longer—and you will enter the Stillness to get the rest you need to speed your healing."

Dareios and Demeter assented so eagerly that no one but John seemed to notice that Ariadne looked not at all thrilled at the idea; in fact, she avoided being alone with him for the next several days, something he greeted with mixed feelings. On the one hand, the more he watched as she cared for the last of the injured, ran the household with Demeter (both were widows), and was simply her quiet, competent self, the more he wanted the soul-deep connection he felt whenever he caught her staring back at him.

But on the other, his very desire to increase that connection only intensified the apprehension he'd first experienced upon meeting her.

They shuffled rooms after the first night so everyone could sleep comfortably, but the curtains were still a source of bemusement to John. On the companions' fourth night there, he met Ariadne in the hall as he headed last for bed and, largely to make some sort of conversation before she could bolt as she usually did, commented on it. Ariadne caressed the heavy fabric of the closest curtain and unveiled a small, heart-stopping smile.

"In his youth, my father was imprisoned for spreading 'seditious philosophical ideas'—or, as he likes to say, 'for attempting to open the closed doors of others' minds.' Naturally, he hated the dungeons and swore if he ever gained freedom and a home of his own, no doors 'would block the free flow of ideas' from room to room." She chuckled in the dimness. "Many were the times we fervently wished for them, though, for our parents were early risers and tended to carry on their debates at the tops of their voices."

"You and Demeter had rooms of your own, then?" John asked, aware he talked solely to keep her in his presence.

"No. We have brothers and sisters, two of each, who are now married and have children and homes of their own. Homes with doors at every room entrance, I might add." Ariadne's smiling gaze fixed on John's with a definite impish glint...

...Then she seemed to remember who she spoke to and blushed furiously.

But she did not look away. Heat flooded John's own cheeks, but he also stared, as unable to look away as she. He felt like he was floating, like his head lightly touched the ceiling. John's breath stuttered as his and Ariadne's essences flowed across the gap between them to touch, then meld into a brilliant column of life; he felt Ariadne's head nestle against his chest to rest directly over his heart and smelled the freshness of her hair and skin as if he held her in his arms. Her marveling look made clear that she shared the sensation, even though neither of them had moved an inch from their respective places.

Time and space telescoped, showing in a moment history of what they had been together; showing them the instant when their once-single, star-bright Life split and headed off in separate directions to fulfill different yet harmonious tasks. John knew beyond all logic and sense that each held the other's Fullness, even as each recalled, then instantly forgot what it was to Remember.

Drown I might, but I would be happy during every moment of it, John thought, his earlier apprehension the dimmest of shadows. And to his joy, he felt the echo of Ariadne's agreement, felt her soul's desire that this be so forever as well...

Suddenly, the bond broke. Wide-eyed and breathless, Ariadne jerked her life force away from John's and her hands shot to her cheeks. He blinked in shock, bereft, and it was all he could do to keep from reaching out to pull the connection back.

"Ariadne—" he said, his voice sounding strangled in his own ears.

"No. This cannot be. It is too sudden—too impossible. How dare I expect..."

Ariadne pushed against the wall of the suddenly too-narrow hallway as if trying to put as much distance between them as she could, then, shaking her head like a child who expects to be severely punished for committing a greatly desired wrong, dashed down it. A few seconds later, John heard the muffled thump of the front door.

Though he desperately wanted to follow, he didn't. Instead, he sank into a squat, back against the wall, and ran his hands through his curling hair. Mary had admonished him for living too sheltered a life, true—but that didn't stop him from passionately wishing he could be thus sheltered now.

More than one female student had been attracted to John during his years in Bethany, some quite obviously; nor had he been so saintly that he'd not been attracted to some of them. But acting on such urges, especially with the newer students, would have been unseemly at the least. And so, as he'd done with Miriam, he'd disregarded his desires, even after the women could have been fit partners by virtue of coming to know that they were attracted to the One in him, not just his persona.

Disregarding Ariadne was all but impossible. Yet as the echo of her words, "How dare I expect...?" ran through his mind, John knew it *was* impossible, that he absolutely could not allow such a thing to happen. His Way was chosen. He could not abandon it. If he entered into her life now, it would only, must only, lead to heartache. Indeed, he and the companions would be gone from this place in only a few days, perhaps a week, and Ariadne left behind. He had no business wanting to carry this attraction any farther than simple acquaintance. To do so would be horribly unfair.

But why am I here, if not to be with her? John's heart whispered traitorously. He'd not come to House Isaurus by accident, he knew; the inevitability their meeting and rightness of their desire—whatever Ariadne's protests might be—was almost as old as their Selves. To not be allowed to fulfill it, as seemed to be the case, went against all he knew of the One's Love and Generosity.

So why had It seen fit to bring his double into his life now?

The presence of one's double could make the process of relinquishing the phantom self infinitely easier—or infinitely harder. Mary had once described doubles thus:

"Imagine two loaves of bread made with the same recipe. Slices from one loaf will taste similar to slices from the other, perhaps almost identical. But slices made from the same loaf will be indistinguishable from each other in taste and texture, even if one's flavor is changed by the addition of meat, while another's is changed by honey. Doubles are the same loaf of bread split into two or more."

She'd laughed. "But of course, in the end, we are all the same Loaf."

The problem lay in the fact that, while doubles' personalities and life experiences might appear to be very different, they nevertheless shared the same soul, a soul that was forever and intensely drawn toward Union whether it lived in one body or many. Meeting one's double awakened that desire even more, but if one hadn't yet made peace with his Self's ways of expressing, or had not yet consciously chosen to awaken, the presence of a double, which was the perfect mirror the phantom self least wanted to peer into, could literally be unbearable. Doubles were either inseparable—sometimes miserably so—or they avoided each other at all costs; but once united, they rarely separated for long, save through death. Though it would have been nice, or more accurately, easier, if John and Ariadne had found each other's presence unbearable, this reacquaintance did not have the feel of wanting to end in instant and relieved separation.

No. Leaving Ariadne would not be a relief.

Indeed, though he'd often told himself nothing could attract him enough to make him give up his Path, to his horror, John felt as if he'd met the one person he would willingly throw the whole of Creation away for. He could find it in his heart to betray Jeshua himself for Ariadne. Or so it felt at this moment.

It gave him a headache.

"Rabbi? Are you all right?"

John's eyes snapped open (he hadn't realized he'd closed them); Hosea crouched before him, holding a short candle in a simple stone holder.

"What time is it?"

"About second hour. Rabbi, are you sickening? Do you need Ada to see after you?"

"No, Hosea, I...thank you, no. I am well enough."

Hosea's mouth turned down and he took a breath that was almost a sigh. Then he surprised John by speaking frankly, his usual reserve lost in annoyance.

"No, Rabbi, you are not well enough, I think...and it is unfair of you not to give Ada and I the chance to help, even if only by listening. Before we left on this journey, Miriam told us the time would come when the Teacher might need to be student—and that if the Teacher allowed it, the students might then become friends."

Hosea shook his head. "I could not credit it then; it seemed impossible I could ever be enough of an equal to speak to you thus. Now, though, I sense that what Miriam said may be true, and I feel we will both lose something important if we miss this opportunity.

"So I ask again: Rabbi, are you sickening?"

John sighed. Miriam had also told him Hosea and Ada could be worthy confidants, but he'd not taken advantage of their friendship, telling himself there was no need. Need there was now—but never in an eon would he have believed it would take this form.

"No, I am not sickening Hosea," he answered. "At least not of any physical ailment."

Then he mumbled as an afterthought, "would that I were."

Hosea blinked as comprehension flooded his features. "Ahhhh," he said, a sudden smile in his voice. "Ariadne?"

"Is it that obvious?" John said with some horror.

"Not to one who is blind, Rabbi," Hosea chuckled. "Though truth to tell, I was slower than Ada to see it. She said you looked lightning-struck when you saw each other, that she actually felt the connection between your souls awaken. But Ada always was more sensitive to such things than her thick-headed husband."

Hosea's grin faded. "Here then! Do you feel shame over such a thing? Yes, I see you do! Rabbi—John—I know you have been careful to walk the prophet's way, despite sometimes excellent temptations to step onto the path of the householder—and no, marriage does not cause a man to go blind! I still know a beautiful woman I see one, and I've seen plenty hunt you over the years."

Hosea chuckled again at the look on John's face. "My point is, whatever Tarsus's comments on the matter, never did Jeshua condemn either path. Ariadne could never take one such as you from your Way; you know too well the One's will leads only to Joy. More, I sense she wishes to know that, too. Have the two of you spoken? Have you told her what you feel?"

"Her Way is not ours," John said gruffly. Hosea raised his eyebrows and snorted to keep from laughing aloud.

"Have you asked her?"

"I have not...exactly. But I know."

Hosea snorted again, this time derisively. "Trust a man long married: there is no way to know a woman's mind without asking her directly—and sometimes not even then! Just when I think I've Ada's ways in hand, she throws a new grain into the dough and I find barley rather than wheat bread on my plate. It is not an intentional thing," he continued as John laughed in spite of himself, "it is just the way they are designed.

"John, you and Mary saved my sanity more than once by reminding me to trust the ways in which the One would have me experience my life. Now do I give the same advice to you. You must trust that what your soul desires is both right and good, that it exists for reasons that will serve you and our task. Then you must follow where it leads, no matter how odd it may look. Such is no strange thing for you, Rabbi; your doing so during the riot saved our skins! Well, and this situation is no different, save that it takes a form that you've not yet known. But be sure, my friend, wheresoever your desire leads, it will leave all concerned in Joy in the end. The One will have it no other Way."

"I... Thank you Hosea, for the reminder, and for your friendship," John said with genuine gratitude, though he knew his expression was still troubled.

Hosea peered at him for a moment longer, then smiled and spoke with complete assurance. "All will be well, John, you will see." The burly man patted his arm, then said his goodnights and returned to his room.

Surely, Divine Mother, you have blessed me, John thought, glad to the core of his being Hosea and Ada were with him. Still, what Hosea suggested was impossible, and both he and Ariadne knew it. How, then, could his heart be so adamant? John closed his eyes and wished, not for the first time, that he had Mary and Miriam's knack for hearing Jeshua's voice within. Perhaps he would explain why so cruel a joke should be played, especially on Ariadne.

A sudden sweet rush of spring air and floral effulgence that certainly had not its origins in Dareios Isaurus's hallway touched him, and John sighed resignedly. It'd do no good to keep his eyes closed; Mary would simply wait here with him until they spoke on this matter. At least, he assumed that was why he'd been summoned yet again.

"Fah! I never 'summon' any who do not first desire to see me, and well you know it."

John's eyes snapped open in utter astonishment. Not six inches from him, squatting as he did, was Jeshua, grinning fit to harm himself.

John stared at his Teacher for what seemed like an eon—and only barely restrained himself from cursing his name. Whatever his wish only a few seconds before, seeing Jeshua now brought him no joy. In fact, he realized he was angrier with him than he'd ever been during his tenure as his disciple.

"Good," Jeshua said suddenly, seemingly without reason. His grin turned wicked as he rubbed his hand against John's cheek. "Martha is right. Beardlessness suits you."

Jeshua trailed silently behind as John, still loathe to speak lest he should dishonor himself, abruptly came to his feet and marched down what looked like the same path Mary had earlier led him along. It was not the same path, however. Soon, thick trees surrounded him, revealing only a sliver of a sky that was full of brilliantly pastel rainbow clouds. The ground below him radiated a familiar, sentient aliveness, just as flora did and, he knew, the fauna would. He once more approached the lake that boiled like water over high flames and shortly thereafter, entered the presence of the vast, once-met, golden-leafed tree called Vanas.

John had returned to Vashti.

But it was a Vashti different from the one he remembered. Where before there'd been only field and forest on the other side of the impossibly large lake, John now espied a massive white edifice that surely surpassed Caesar's legendary palace in both size and grandeur. Though many details of its diamond-bright majesty were obscured by the wavering steam of the lake's heat, even from here, he sensed the building was in some way as alive as the rest of the land around him. Tiny figures entered, exited or simply stood in small groups before the structure's enormity; he heard, or thought he did, the musical buzz of their distant conversations. Just as Jeshua had been in the Gethsemane vision, all of them were dazzlingly alive with radiant inner suns.

And that only made John angrier than he already was.

He stood before Vanas in grim silence, fingers absently playing with the golden leaves, not quite oblivious to the ancient equilibrium that greeted the ever-so-much more transitory self housing his own eternal spirit. Jeshua stood beside him and waited with a Stillness that rivaled the World Tree's.

"What game do you play with me, Jeshua?" John asked when he finally felt he could trust his voice. "Have I not always served as you wished? Have I not willingly gone where you sent me and did what you asked with a full heart? Have I not?"

"You mean, 'Why her—and why now?'" Jeshua said dryly.

He didn't wait for John's response, but screwed up his face as if suddenly angry. "'What games do you play with Us? Have We not always served you fully and with glad hearts? Why, then, would you have Us now serve humans?'" Jeshua's angry expression disappeared as abruptly as it came. "Lucifer asked those questions, the first and only ones he asked as an angel. And do you know what the Mother and Father's Answer was, John? 'Because, belovéd, this is the part you agreed to play at this time.'"

Jeshua smiled at John's look. "Yes. Well. That answer gave Lucifer no satisfaction, either. Still, that did not stop it from being the truth. After all, that and, 'because you wanted it that way,' are always the only answers to 'why must this be?' that matter.

"John, you know the answer to your real question better than anyone living, but it is as Mary said: you've become entangled in what you think must happen through your self. You've forgotten that neither you nor any other is required to serve me or God or anyone, including himself." Jeshua raised his hands. "Yes, yes, I know what Mary said about pledges and comforts and purposes, but you know she did naught but reflect what you truly wanted then: a reason to go forth when common sense said you should not. But the truth, brother, is this: you need not take one more step toward Vashti if you've no wish to do so, nor are you ever required to deprive yourself of any experience because it might cause you to 'fail'.

"Do not you know, John? It is impossible to fail me."

John was abashed by Jeshua's words. Here stood the one who wanted nothing but his eternal and unshakeable Joy, yet after seventeen years apart, all he could greet him with was anger. He shook his head.

"With all that happened before we left Bethany, Jeshua, you could not have told me such would be possible, but I do find myself questioning my desire to go forth, and it does feel like a failure. I run into a simple distraction and immediately want to walk away with hardly a backward glance. How then, even knowing it is possible, can I think myself fit to do this task?"

Jeshua glanced sideways at his pupil and pulled thoughtfully at his beard, as had been his wont on Earth, and John suddenly and irrelevantly recalled that the habit used to annoy Martha to no end.

"He heals a crippled man, rescues a girl from a painful life of certain servitude, and shows his student her brother is well by becoming him—yet he thinks himself unwilling to fulfill the task he chose," Jeshua laughed. "John, encountering one's double can hardly be called a *simple* distraction, and you've scarcely made this a 'without a backwards glance' situation. Indeed, you seem bent on making it as difficult as you can.

"You fear you can go wrongly, brother, but what you or anyone else does can never affect the outcome of the One's plan. After all, it has already been fulfilled; only how long it takes those who play at being human to realize that truth is in question.

"You were given the task of finding Vashti and holding my teaching, John, not because you are inherently more worthy than the rest of the twelve, but because it was what you wanted and agreed to do. If that is no longer the case..." Jeshua shrugged. "God cannot suffer because of your choices, but so long as you think you can, or think that suffering has some sort of value, you will suffer. Yet, learning that suffering is never necessary is all I would have you know.

"So then, my belovéd brother, what do you desire? —Oh," Jeshua added with a smile. "And focusing on the One, which is something you've done precious little of these last two hours, might be of some use."

John flinched at the rebuke, all too aware he'd devoted most of the last several days to what excited his phantom self, not what enlivened his heart.

"What care have you for what has been," Jeshua said, once more flashing the wicked grin he'd so effectively used when walking the earth, "if you are standing within the Stillness of the One now, John—as I know you can?" He gave John a warm embrace and a kiss, then began walking backwards down the trail so John could still see his face. "It is good to see you again, my friend, even if you do not feel the same in just this instant."

"Jeshua..."

"Fear not what may be John, nor what already is. For what may be is not yet here and what is can always become what may be. Or not, as you wish."

"Jeshua, wait." John moved to follow, but Jeshua shook his head.

"We will meet again, brother, but for now I leave you with a question:

"Is it possible to be forced to choose between one's soul and one's Self? Answer that, and you will know what next to do."

NINETEEN

John *sat, eyes closed,* in the tiny community garden behind the Isaurus house. The companions had been in Corinth a week, and though Timothy's injuries were healing rapidly, Ada insisted they stay several days more to ensure his full recovery. Despite Timothy's strenuous objections, John had agreed, with Dareios's happy concurrence.

Having taken to heart Jeshua's remarks about his recent lack of focus on the Stillness, he'd been co-opting the small granite bench that fronted the garden's small, flourishing pond these past three days to sit in the fall sun and bask in his experience of the Practice. He had, as yet, no answer to his Teacher's last question, but each moment he spent simply resting in the One's Presence helped revive his recently lost equilibrium.

And perhaps that is answer enough, John thought, as he dove more deeply inward.

He made no attempt to control his experience. Rather, the words of the Practice floated up from his center of their own accord to effortlessly shepherd him to that place where thoughts, feelings, manifestations and identities could never intrude...then they drew him forth into Life's movement again. Like a sea turtle taking unlimited joy in sounding the depths of the ocean, but who yet finds occasionally coming up for air a meet thing also, John's consciousness alternately rested in the Silence for a timeless eternity, then slowly drew to the edge of mind, world, and their peripheral noise. He'd experienced such states with increasing regularity during his years in Bethany, but he had yet to be graced with *consistently* being the Unlimited Silence, as the great Masters were said to be. Truer for John was that he experienced and even knew his self to be one with the One's Presence even in the midst of strenuous activity. Yes, he was becoming the selfless Self that lived, moved and had Its Being only in the One...but if the last several days were any sign, that becoming might be a long time arriving.

With that thought, a sudden memory of Martha's description of the Practice as being like a brush that removed long-set, especially nasty stains from a garment floated through: "You scrub and scrub, that is, use the Practice, and when you step from the "tub" of its activity, the stain is lighter. Then you scrub and scrub again, and so on and so on, until at last there is no blemish left upon the garment of your being.

"But be warned! If you worry over why the stain is there, where it came from, or how long it takes to fade, the scrubbing will feel exactly like being pounded with rocks and drowned in the well. If, on the other hand, you simply relax, you'll find it washes quickly and effortlessly away.

"Which is as it should be," Martha suddenly smiled, "since 'tis God does the washing."

To John, the events of these last weeks, and of the last few days in particular, were definitely ones he would call Washing Well experiences. He felt like every belief he carried was being made visible, thoroughly scrubbed and, if useful, moved into the realm of knowing instead of mere believing.

"I would talk to you, bar Zebedee. Now."

Ah, and here is Darshinika Baremna to continue the scrubbing, John thought wryly.

He opened his eyes, and only the fact that he was completely swathed in the Silence kept him from "tsking" and shaking his head. Even now, with anger straining his voice, the scholar was trying to sustain his idea of how he, an "enlightened master", should look. His stance, the way he held his hands, even the self-righteous set of his face, reinforced his picture of himself as a stern-but-benign spiritual teacher who wanted naught but the best for John.

But beneath that thin veneer of civility was a man who sat on the finest edge of rage.

"How might I be of service to you, Darshinika?" John asked mildly, noting how Baremna bristled at being addressed so casually and, in his opinion, so disrespectfully.

"Why are you trying to steal my student—and why have you told the others lies about me?" Baremna haughtily demanded.

John yawned, sniffed and blinked, his deportment assuredly not that of the perfect spiritual master. "One cannot steal what was never owned, Darshinika...and was not deserved in the first place. Erezavan sought my opinion. I gave it. And would do so again."

John once more closed his eyes and so could not see the scholar's reaction, but he certainly could feel it. The ire in Baremna's life force spattered against his skin in searing waves of fury, and the ethers stank of his sense of insult at John's deliberate —and in his mind, ongoing—dismissal of his value, position, and intelligence.

Then again, Baremna's intelligence was the problem. Though he was, both in fact and potential, an adept of some degree, instead of allowing what he knew to be swallowed up by the Unbounded's Knowing and thus increased in ways he could not begin to imagine, he tried to control Infinity.

Rather than lauding Baremna's exalted status, the Masters at his school no doubt admonished him to let go of what his intellect said was "the end" so he could become the endlessness of the One. But such advice would only have angered one so adamantly convinced of his fullness; would only have become the basis of his need to own a student who'd never question his right to be called "teacher," and thus prove his worthiness.

But the student had questioned, and this...peasant who showed his mastery no respect, either, had spirited him away. Worse, he effortlessly received the veneration Baremna's phantom self so desperately sought.

The Persian's desire to pound John to a small, bloody pulp splashed against his skin like soiled water, but Baremna would not let his anger come forth. So deep was his phantom self's need to avoid looking unspiritual that, just as he had done since leaving Matthatus, he struggled to stuff away his ire, to be in control. John could practically see him looking up at the sky and taking deep, calming breaths as if counting slowly, could hear him recite some prayer under his breath. Baremna was on the verge of locking one more kernel of rage into the vast storehouse he carried within that rounded body, rage that would, with his abilities, eventually turn and rend him and others to bits.

Or perhaps not.

"I take it, Darshinika, you had nothing else of interest to say?" the One within John echoed up from his center of its own accord, like a contemptuous master dismissing a slow-witted servant.

The entire neighborhood heard Baremna's roar as his fury blasted forth and echoed off the surrounding houses. John tumbled backwards as the Persian slammed him to the grass and wrapped large, strong hands around his throat in a deadly grip…

…And at that same moment, the Silence that had swathed his awareness throughout their encounter saturated John's entire perception.

All sense of "other" wholly dissolved from his experience; his body, the ground he lay against, and the bench his legs still rested on all became one Thing. He was the hands that choked him, the rage that drove those hands and the blue sky that silently witnessed this violence. John was All…and No Thing at all. He was neither this nor that, here nor there —and he was all those things. Even as his head smacked hard against the damp ground, once, twice, thrice, he knew what it was to experience all things as good, to be truly neutral about the outcome of any event, even his own murder.

It was Bliss beyond bliss, Peace beyond all understanding…

A cry split the air, and the Persian's weight (John's weight) suddenly disappeared. Many hands (his hands) pulled him from the dust.

Hosea and Ada held him up while Torer, Marcus and Haifata restrained the still-raging Baremna. Demeter, Rachael, Dareios and Ariadne watched from behind them, their horrified eyes wide, while even farther back, Joshua and Timothy held tight to Erezavan's arms, cajoling him to calm. Smiling, John approached Baremna, who ceased straining to again get his hands around his neck.

"One day, Darshinika, not long after Jeshua taught the twelve the basics of the Practice, he told us that we had acquired an important ability, then asked us to guess what it might be. None of us could, though we certainly had guesses enough.

"'Be still and watch,' he said, and we thought he meant we should stop walking and listen to the world around us. 'No, no! I mean, be *still* and *watch*.'

"We walked behind our Teacher for a half-hour, trying to identify what he would have us know. Suddenly, Judas halted, his face as bright as a lantern on a moonless night.

"'Jeshua!' he said, because he rarely called Jeshua 'Rabbi', 'I can see myself thinking!'

"The rest of us stared at him like he was a simpleton and at least one of us spoke that opinion aloud. Judas, however, ignored our criticisms and kept talking, his voice full of excitement at his odd discovery.

"'I tell you, I can see my own thoughts! And I can see my feelings as well, and my body! It is as if I am but watching my life go by, rather than being the actor of it!'

"'You are possessed of devils,' Nathaniel said, for though they tried to deal civilly with each other in Jeshua's presence, there was never any love lost between them. Some of the others took up Nathaniel's cry and we all looked to see what Jeshua would say, sure that he, too, would admonish Judas. But Jeshua only walked to where Judas stood and looked into his eyes.

"'Do you see this from within yourself, or from without?'

"'It is as if I sit at the center of my self and watch. I am apart, but I am also experiencing this…whatever I am experiencing.'

"'But I have always done that; it is no important thing!" I said, and I admit there was a bit of a whine to my words. Jeshua's eyebrow rose as James, Phillip and one or two of the others murmured their agreement, but I was saved from his admonishment by Matthew, who suddenly brightened as Judas had.

"'Yes! We have all experienced this, even before we learned the Practice, I'll wager; that is why we've never noticed its importance. But think of the power of such a thing! If we know we are apart from our thoughts and feelings and actions, we can decide what we should do before we act. Is that not so, Rabbi?'

"'Yes—and no.'

"Jeshua grinned, patted Matthew and Judas's shoulders and bid us continue walking. 'To see yourself think and feel and act as you are doing so is indeed important, for it means you are starting to experience the Silent Witness. But I have no desire to see you use that ability to determine what you should do next. To give the power of the Silent Witness to the individual self would be like melting gold into staves to build a pigsty.

"'What I want, once you see that you can witness your life, is for you to surrender into the Witness even more and discover what Its nature is. Indeed, I want each of you to come to know yourselves *as* the Witness and Its Source, for only then will you move beyond this dream of being separate from the Unbounded.'"

John gazed into Baremna's angry eyes, still experiencing them, their owner and all else as himself. "You, Darshinika, have built a pigsty out of gold staves. Instead of being the Witness, which you know, you use your memory of It to decide what God in man should look like. And you wish dead one who does as you choose not to do.

"Yet even now, the Witness in you watches in perfect Calm; even now, you can step back from the swirling anger that fills this courtyard. You have the chance, even now, to know the One, not only know about It. Pray, Darshinika, will you not take that chance?"

The courtyard went still as everyone waited for the Persian to make his choice.

He spat in John's face.

Baremna shook free of the warriors, and though he did not again lay hands on John, the venom in his words—that John sought to make slaves of the companions, that he, not Baremna, was the liar—poisoned the air until all John's inner eyes could see of the corpulent man was a dark, muddy cloud of contaminated life force.

Finally, Baremna ran out of curses and turned to leave. He stopped before Isvant, who, with Joshua and Timothy, still stood somewhat apart from the rest of the group.

"Are you with me, you who trusted me to carry you—oh, how I have carried you!—for all this time? Or do you choose this impostor, to his doom and yours? Think carefully before you answer, Erezavan Isvant, for no matter what that spawn of demons says, you are *my* student! If you forsake me, you will be forever cursed in the eyes of God as a liar and blasphemer! Choose your path carefully!"

Timothy and Joshua stepped away from the two men, instinctively understanding that Isvant must choose his Way, free of interference from any other's life force.

The young man's swarthy face was pale and his eyes full of fear at the possibility that this one who'd walked with him since his childhood might speak the truth; for a moment John again saw the groveling youngster who'd feared scolding from his own shadow. Yet he saw as well the determined set of Isvant's mouth, saw how he stood straighter and straighter the longer he talked.

"I know your guidance helped me survive the rigors of the School, Darshinika.

I trust, too, that your desire led me to take this next step toward finding my fullness in the One. I am grateful for that, for never would I have undertaken this journey without it. But I also know now that because you needed to feel superior to someone, you coerced from me what should never be taken: my right to trust my own soul.

"So I thank you, Darshinika, for all you have made possible in the strength of your assurance; always will I be grateful to you for bringing me at last to my true place. But now my Way does in truth lie with Rabbi bar Zebedee and his companions, who have become mine. Though I hope you will continue forth on this quest with us, if you choose not to, know that I wish you well."

Isvant started to bow, then stopped. His eyes glinted, but not with humor.

"And Darshinika...you are *not* my Teacher."

For a moment it seemed as if Baremna might transfer his violence toward John to his former protégé, but he only shook his fist under Isvant's nose then stalked away.

"You mark my words, young fool! You will rue the day you chose to follow that demon on his insane quest! All of you will regret your choice, for he will be the death of you!"

They looked after the Persian until he disappeared from sight.

"Rabbi, are you all right?"

"Whatever happened to make him attack you?"

"Do you think he will come back? Surely he did not mean what he said..."

"Here, sit down so I can see what damage he may have done."

John let a thoroughly annoyed Ada lead him back to the small bench, the smile still on his face. His eyes found Ariadne, who returned his stare as she had not done since the night of their merging; the smile she offered in spite of herself was more welcome to him than food and water.

"Well, you will have a couple of lumps on your head," Ada muttered, and he winced as she touched the spots in question. She came around the bench and looked at his throat, then "hmphed". Producing a cloth from nowhere, she wet it with her tongue and began cleaning his abraded elbows, causing more winces. "You will definitely have bruises on your neck, too; already there is discoloration. How does it feel?"

"Well, enough," John grinned. "Though a little tight."

Ada looked sharply into his eyes, no doubt checking to see if he had a concussion, then quietly said, "John...you need not speak of what happened now, but I would be gratified, when it is appropriate, to know what brought this about."

John only smiled more broadly and laid a hand against her cheek, honored by her use of his given name. Apparently, Hosea had conveyed their conversation of a few nights before. "There is little to tell, sister. He asked why I was trying to steal his student and I told him. His many years of hiding his rage behind a benign persona shattered like so much glass. Rage which he focused on me."

"And that is something to smile about?" Hosea asked, for he'd leaned in to hear.

"No, but what I am experiencing is, my friends." He nodded past them. "That, however, will have to wait, for another requires help besides me."

Isvant, his swarthy face ashen, fell to his knees before John and grabbed at his hand like a frightened child might grab at his father's.

"Sir, have I done rightly? Have I betrayed my friend and mentor? Please, you must tell me."

The love John felt for Erezavan and everything else in that moment literally left no room for any other emotion. Yet, while his heart would gladly have comforted the young man, the One in him wanted only what would serve his growth.

"I cannot tell you, Erezavan, nor would I if I could. What I can tell you, and as I myself am yet again discovering—" John's voice was suddenly full of wryly amused honesty, "—is that any man who tries to live by his own understanding instead of trusting the One's is naught but a fool. Until you know you only hear, are and do the One's will, finding the best guidance you can by finding one you see is living that Fullness is what you must do."

Isvant nodded, but his eyes were still troubled. "But...do you truly think Baremna's attack was the will of the One, Sir?"

"Do you remember what I said aboard *Matthatus?* The One's Joy lies in experiencing; whether It is being attacked or kissed, It cannot be hurt." John ignored Ada and Hosea's poorly concealed grins as his eyes involuntarily flicked Ariadne's way. "But as always, my words alone mean nothing, Erezavan. Only your experience of the One will bring you to this realization—and right now, that can best occur only by using the Practice with your eyes closed."

Isvant gazed off into the distance, perhaps recalling the choice aboard *Matthatus* that had brought him to this juncture. Then, accepting the implicit dismissal, he bowed his head—though not submissively—and rose, his expression once more that of the budding power John sensed him to be.

John smiled after him, then said to no one in particular, "Erezavan is not the only one who could benefit from doing more of the Practice with his eyes closed, I think."

The garden cleared with admirable alacrity, but not before Ada took John in hand and sternly declared it would do him good to enter the Silence as well.

"Yes, it would, Mother dear, and I'd not dare gainsay you," he said, grinning at her suddenly dictatorial conduct and this firsthand experience of the "changing of the dough."

"That is wise, wise in the extreme," Ada answered back, her eyes twinkling. "Else, I might have to find a bed for you...right next to Timothy."

John laughed and reflected that having Ada and Hosea as friends was definitely a thing to celebrate, even without the amazing Joy of fully experiencing them as All One.

John did get in a good, long day of the Practice, followed by more full, long days of such. He also shared with Ada and Hosea, as best as words could, the incredible Oneness that had engulfed his awareness during Baremna's attack. They, in turn, had the chance to share their own experiences of teaching from and living with the Unbounded increasingly informing their activities. It was their first chance to really talk since being on *Matthatus,* and John vowed not to let so long a period between sharing befall them again. It was too important to Ada's, Hosea's and his own growth.

This evening, the day after Baremna's departure, the entire household enjoyed a quiet dinner, free for once of the Isaurus family's numerous friends and the companions' growing retinue of students and supporters. John crept from the house, intending to enjoy the warm night and the serenades of the creatures in the garden, but when he got there, he found it wasn't empty.

Ariadne stood before the small pond, apparently lost in thought.

John hesitated. Despite their silent exchange after Baremna's attack and his visit with Jeshua, it seemed foolish to cast off their pretended indifference now. After all, Timothy would soon be well enough to travel, and the companions would once more be on their way, never to pass through Corinth again.

He started to follow his thought and head back to the house, but at that moment, Ariadne turned and looked straight into his eyes. Though she spoke not a word, John suddenly realized she'd come to the garden specifically to find him.

John nodded a "Good Eventide", sat on his bench, and quickly found something of surpassing interest lying on the ground. Or tried to. Never had focusing been so difficult. Or, for that matter, breathing. He was devastatingly aware of Ariadne's tentative approach, of the soft, feminine scent that filled his head to overflowing; he passionately wished the all-embracing calm of the day before was more than just a memory. He might be willing to brave Death itself, as he had with Baremna, but facing this woman...

John's heart pounded so hard he thought surely Ariadne could hear it as she knelt before him, still without a word, then took one of his hands in both of hers and kissed it. They stayed frozen in that pose for what seemed like an eternity; when she finally spoke, her voice was choked with unshed tears.

"Master Zebedee, will you be my Teacher?"

John felt as if he'd again been slammed to the ground, as if Ariadne had wrenched his insides from his body. He sighed, but could not decide whether he did so in joy or terror.

"I cannot be your Teacher, dearest, you know I cannot," he said, his own voice a choked whisper. "Certainly it would be easier if such were possible. But Teacher is not what my place in your life can be, if there is to be any place at all."

John realized his cheek rested atop Ariadne's head only when he finished speaking, so natural...and yes, right...did it feel; he felt her shudder as his fingers, seemingly of their own will, stroked her dark, curling hair, then caressed her cheek. His other hand grew warm as tears fell on it, but when he lifted her chin she turned her face away.

"How can we possibly let this be, John? It is so...inappropriate...and impossible. Your Way takes you in a direction that differs from mine. And to so much as call you by your name, as I just now did, fills me with a sense of...of committing some breach for which God Himself will punish me. However can this be, in this time and place? One such as I cannot...to even think such a thing is...is wrong."

John actually snorted—and felt a thread of amusement bubble up as, in face of her resistance, his own arguments against allowing their attraction to go any farther turned to so many wisps of fog confronted by the warmth of morning sunlight.

"Why? Because I am one of the twelve who walked with Jeshua, while you are but a 'lowly' student of his Way? What makes you unworthy of being belovéd to me, Ariadne...of being with me?"

Ariadne inhaled sharply, for they both knew their feelings went far beyond being merely spiritual. John did not gasp at his audacity, but his sudden assurance that the level of intimacy a relationship with this woman would not just promise, but demand, made him wonder yet again why they had come to each other now. Why now, when he was about to enter into the most danger he'd faced since Jeshua's arrest all those years ago? He still had no answer, but...

"Ariadne." John turned her face toward his, jarred yet again by the shock of looking at the amazingly familiar Self that lay in her winter-dark eyes. "I do not know why this must be, or how it will manifest. I only know that, of all the things I may be to you,

I am not your Teacher. Whatever we are and will be to each other, it is a thing destined from longer ago than either of us can imagine."

John watched her nod in reluctant agreement, even as he frowningly shook his head. "Ariadne, it may be that the whole of our relationship will take place now, in this garden; that I will walk from here an hour from now, never again to be in your life. But as much as I have told myself that allowing this would be folly, that it can only end in pain, that I should, for propriety's sake, stay far from you and save us both...the truth is, I do not want to be 'safe' from you. Ever.

"Ariadne, if you would have me, I would be in your life for as long as you and the One will allow it to be so."

The sensations that coursed through John's body as, still sniffling a bit from her earlier tears, Ariadne tentatively brushed her fingers along one of the places on his neck where Baremna's fingers had earlier rested with completely different intentions, made him dizzy with longing.

"Ada spoke truly; you do have bruises," she said suddenly. "Why do you not simply heal them, as you did Timothy and Hosea's?"

They both knew she spoke to break the unbearable tension, but it was true: Timothy was still largely confined to Dareios' house for the sake of his ribs, but his and Hosea's cuts and bruises had healed days ago, leaving only a few pinkish areas to show there'd been any injuries at all. It was also true, though John had said nothing to Ada, that one of Timothy's ribs had done more damage than merely being broken, and that his actions had lessened that injury. That Ariadne realized this, despite his discretion, somehow did not surprise him.

"I can take no credit for Hosea's healing, Ariadne; his own awareness of the One achieved that. As to healing my own injuries, I can do so, in time, by entering the Silence, but I have not yet the ability to instantly heal myself by simply willing it so. Jeshua always said healing one's own body usually came late to the Awakening, with the ability to awaken from death itself coming last of all."

Ariadne nodded. John doubted she'd really heard a word he said, but some of the tension in the air had diminished. He took the hand that still rested lightly against his bruised neck and again looked into her eyes.

"I was never one to see the future, Ariadne, and I cannot see it now. But to avoid the path down which this love leads me is not something I am willing to do, for I feel to my soul it would only take some important good from us both.

"Still, if it is that my offer is unacceptable to you—or that another has claim to your heart (a notion which, to John's dismay, had only just occurred to him)—know that I will part from you with only the most amiable feelings, for I could do nothing else. What I cannot do is spend another moment not knowing what you would will of me.

"Please, Ariadne, will you not tell me?"

Ariadne gave a heartfelt sigh, then rose and walked a few steps away from where John still sat. The sounds of the neighbors going about their evening business echoed distantly around them, joining the night songs of the garden's true owners. Ariadne ran her hands through her dark, curling hair, as if trying to wash away her suddenly renewed tension—then suddenly shook her head and gave a gentle, self-deprecating snort.

"Though I have followed the Way of the Christos for years now, never have I forsaken the Divine Mother, for I always felt the gentle strength of Her power was what I most wanted to give in service to others. Also, I've in truth never believed God could be without His Bride and still be wholly God.

"Not long ago, I renewed my promise to gladly follow Divine Mother if She would guide me, for always I have trusted Her to take me to the highest in myself."

John stepped up behind Ariadne and laid his hands on her shoulders. She once more pressed her lips to his hand, then turned to face him, her solemn, exultant smile filling her with Divine Mother's Beauty.

"I think, John, I will trust where Divine Mother leads me now."

They slipped into each other's arms and let the quiet of the garden enfold them.

TWENTY

Jeshua's Heart, John thought, half of Corinth must be here.

He chuckled at the exaggeration, but was sure he was not far wrong. He, Ada and Hosea had taught the Practice to groups of up to ten over the last several evenings, but tonight it seemed as if members of every culture in Corinth crowded into the Isaurus's large living room. Romans, Jews, Greeks, and even a couple of Nubians—true Nubians, not people of Haifata's clan—were there, their noble dress and bearing attracting whispered comments. To see so many, of so many nationalities, coming together made John smile. Surely, Jeshua would be pleased to see how many sought to sate the Great Hunger.

Not that this sight alone caused his smile...and it is ridiculous that a man full grown should behave so, he thought. Many were his youthful self's fumble-tongued attempts to attract Miriam's favor, yet never had he felt as foolish as he now did in achieving the object of his desire. As Hosea had noted, John had chosen at nineteen to seek intimate relationship only with the One, and since no woman save Miriam had more than fleetingly diverted his attention, being madly in love was new to him. Still, the possibility that he would be traipsing about with this silly grin had not entered his mind at all.

Nor were his companions any help. He and Ariadne had been the object of numerous indulgent smiles—and several outright giggles from Rachael—as they enjoyed their newly-accepted love with many looks and the occasional shy touch: a hand briefly laid on a shoulder, fingers brushing against fingers. Demeter, who'd initially struck John as one for whom mirth was a rarity, was particularly cheered by her sister's new preoccupation.

"Not since Kyrillos was killed in battle have I seen such light in Ari's countenance," she'd said, stopping dinner preparations long enough to shyly touch John's arm and allow a reserved but delighted smile to light her own face. "Thank you for giving my sister's joy back to her, Elder. It has been too many years, and I missed it more than I realized."

John gratefully laid his hand over hers, aware such joy had long been missing from Demeter's life as well; though neither of the sisters had yet reached their thirtieth summers, she was also many years a widow, her husband long ago lost at sea.

John too, was grateful for this change in circumstances, and yes, for everyone's delight on his and Ariadne's behalf. Still, he was glad to be away from Dareios's house, daughter, and the others' amusement. This evening, while Hosea and Ada taught the new students, he and Rachael, Marcus, Joshua and Haifata, would repair to the quiet and privacy of Thomas's house, where John would share the fourth technique students of the Way of the One learned: the Practice of Compassion.

The group entered into the dimness of Thomas's cottage to find a lone oil lamp shining from the center of a rough-hewn wood table. Rachael, showing the ever-growing practical bent her mother had instilled and which, under Ada's fostering, had found a happy home, immediately located, lit and placed several more lamps, then stoked the smoldering embers in the small hearth, relieving the room of its chill and gloomy mien.

Here is the home of a man who is fastidious the point of cautiousness, John thought as he surveyed their surroundings. True, Thomas might have cleaned for their arrival, but John doubted it: this room had the air of belonging to one who needed everything to have and be in its own place. John wondered if the trait was native to the name, for as he recalled, the twelve's Thomas was just as fastidious as this follower of the Christos.

Or...well, no. Not quite as fastidious, John smiled. In his companion's case, the will to tidiness had always been more a desire than an accomplished fact. Wherever Thomas Didymus stopped, clutter soon gathered.

John's eyes fell on the sturdy door behind which the sleeping chamber lay. It was the reason he'd chosen Thomas's home instead of one of the many others offered. Small his house might be, but not much that wanted to remain concealed would leak through that thick and worthy divide. Yes, this would do nicely; none of the companions would have to shiver in the cold night air while he taught the next technique.

John opened the door, lamp held high, and found the chamber as precisely maintained as the rest of the house. He nodded approvingly at the small, low table sitting against the back wall and gestured to Adan, who silently handed him a white cloth bundle.

Since it had never occurred to him that he might teach once he left Bethany, John had gifted his ceremonial set for teaching the Practice of Compassion to Elior. After he'd explained to Dareios what he needed, however, the materials and supplies were quickly produced from within the local Christine community. This ceremonial set was not of entirely traditional materials, but that worried him little; the spirit, not the letter of the law counted most. Besides, this makeshift set was perfect for honoring this group's willingness to follow the One on what was certainly a most makeshift journey...

John's eyes suddenly narrowed as they fell on Prochorus.

"Marcus, you need to go back to Dareios's house."

The small group, which had been quietly talking among themselves, now gave John their full attention. Prochorus's eyebrows rose questioningly.

"Is there something you need me to get?"

"No. I will not be giving you the last technique. You must go back to Dareios's."

The others looked shocked, even Adan, who rarely seemed to experience any disturbance at the things John said or did.

"...May I ask why?" Prochorus's voice shook a little with dismay and insult at this turn of events. "If I have done something to cause you displeasure, bar Zebedee, I think I have the right to know it, have I not...?"

But John had already turned away and stepped into the smaller room, closing the door and Prochorus's inquiry behind him.

He sank to his knees, glad for the warmth of the thoughtfully supplied rug, inspected the low table for dust or other foreign objects—and of course, found none. He placed the bundle on the sleeping pallet and shook its contents onto it. The cloth, which he still held, was made of incredibly soft, excellent quality, white silk; happily, not all of Jeshua's followers had misinterpreted his caution to be willing to give up all to mean only the impoverished could enter Heaven. After all, how could a God who was all things ever insist that those He created in His likeness be indigent? Such a one would be a very poor God indeed...and yet, John sensed the day would come when the need to be *willing* to give up everything that prevented the full remembrance of the Unbounded Self would be distorted into the belief that poverty was a virtue—for those who were already poor, mind, not those who persuaded them to hold that belief. For a while, at least, the worldly would seem to succeed in distorting Truth to suit their ends.

John distastefully shook off the brief knowing, aware there was nothing to be done for it now, and carefully draped the silk cloth over the table's well-worn wood. He went to the door.

"Joshua, or one of you, could you please bring me a basin of water and a few small, clean, washing cloths? Also, get a second basin, to wash your hands and feet in before you enter this room."

"Do you wish it warmed, Rabbi?"

"At least somewhat, please. I've no desire to present this technique to people with apple-sized goosebumps on their flesh."

John smiled and closed the door on their giggled responses. One by one, he took the items from the bed, treating each as if they were old friends, not strangers he'd met only a few minutes before, and quickly set each one in its appropriate place. He surveyed his handiwork, almost satisfied...

...But what would he use to serve as a representation of Jeshua's Presence?

"Each of you is now part of a great lineage of Teachers," Jeshua told them when, very near the end of his time on Earth, he taught the twelve, Mary, Martha, and Miriam to present the Practice of Compassion. "Mind, I speak not just of Moses and Elijah, but of all the great Teachers, be they from Egypt, Canaan, or the far, far lands to North and East and West. Where and whensoever these Masters come from, my own, you sing this Ceremony of Thanksgiving to them, to honor their choice to step into the truth of God's Being. It is an appeal to those who know themselves as the Unbounded to help you surrender the control of your personal self to the greater Self of the One, and so purely transmit the Practice of Compassion and the essence of this Teaching to those you teach.

"The likeness you have practiced this ceremony with is that of the greatest of these Teachers to come to Earth, the one called by his people 'Krishna', and this is as it should be. The day soon comes, however, when I will move beyond this earthly experience..."

The companions and the women interrupted Jeshua's declaration with expressions of shock and fear. Some tried to deny it, to argue him out of such nonsense, but Jeshua merely shook his head. "No, dear ones, have no fear; I will not be gone from you in truth. It is only that I must join those who came before to take charge of this earth's Awakening.

"And when that happens, I charge you thus: let my likeness represent the Masters who have gone before, so that your charges may fall under the protection of the Christ Being. Let yourselves, by honoring my likeness, honor those who have found the Highest Consciousness of the One, who are, as the Masters would say in the true tongue, *Ishayas*.'"

"'Ishayas'? *Isha!*" The recognition blew through John like the thrill of angels' wings.

Strange I did not remember this before now, he thought. Then he shook his head, for it was not strange at all. Consistent users of the Practice soon relinquished the stress of trying to stay safe by remembering every piece of information they *might* someday need; when a memory came, it came at the perfect time—and the fact that John sometimes never discovered the why of a remembrance's timing was something he'd learned to live with, albeit with a bit of rue.

So then, "Isha" was not a name at all, not just a translation of "Jeshua," as he'd assumed. It was a title, just as "the Christ" was a title, a description of the state Jeshua had attained. Yet, it seemed to him Mary and Miriam had used it as a substitute for their Teacher's name, as if he had so united with the state that there was no longer a difference. Would everyone then, eventually come to be not just "Ishaya", those who worked for the Highest Consciousness, but "Isha"?

Well, would not all eventually remember they were the One?

And, to bring him back to the original question, what would he use to represent Jeshua's likeness? John did not have to use anything, he knew, but he preferred to. Having his Teacher's likeness for the ceremony more fully connected his heart to his profound love for him; and it reminded him too, of the love—and patience—he knew Jeshua forever offered him. Thomas had one of the increasingly ubiquitous Christine crosses on his wall, yes, but it spoke not at all to John's heart. He stretched, fingers lacing behind his neck...and smiled when he felt the leather cord that hung there.

Of course. He could use Jeshua's fish.

There was a knock at the door. "Rabbi, I have brought the water you asked for."

"Thank you, Joshua." Smiling, John opened it a crack so the curious young man couldn't see inside, took the bowl and towels, and carried them to a bedside stool. He stripped off his clothing, shivering in the chill, and washed, taking especial care to clean his hands and feet as he'd instructed the others to do.

Then he gingerly lifted the last item on the bed and looked it up and down.

The floor-length formal tunic, like the wrap that now graced his table, was made of fine, expensive silk; its intricate, gold-threaded embroidery and glaring whiteness bespoke the owner's considerable wealth, while its cut revealed its seamstress to be a native of Greece or its surrounding islands. John actually felt a mild sense of trepidation as its incredible softness slithered sensuously over his body; surely, to enjoy something so much must at least be a little decadent!

He smiled at his sackcloth-and-ashes heritage coming to the fore and remembered what Jeshua had told Miriam when she'd stated her intention of disposing of the many silk robes she'd received as gifts in trade for her services:

"Would you have others believe things have the power to cause sin? These robes have done no more harm by their history than you have, dear heart, for the Father-Mother never condemns and never will. Truly, these are fitting garments for the Bride of Christ—and that is how you must learn to see them. So, pick the one you most love and perform your Ceremonies in it."

Some of the other robes had been styled to suit man or woman, but the youthful John had turned down Miriam's offer to have one altered, preferring instead the fine-spun cotton robe his mother Salome had made. Slipping this one on was a definite treat, decadent or not—but then Jeshua would insist that such treats were his birthright.

John inspected the small table once more, then reentered the larger room.

"*Jeshua, amen*," he said softly into the dimness, noting with satisfaction that Rachael, Haifata and Joshua had entered into the Stillness. He waited until they returned from their far journeys before speaking. "If you've decided who amongst you should enter first, I will be ready in a few moments. Please remember to knock, and enter not until I have invited you. If you have not already done so, please wash your hands and feet before you enter the room—and leave your shoes off, for you step on holy ground."

John closed the door, settled onto one of two large pillows, and prepared to share the One's knowledge with whoever came. Though they might not realize it, the ones who entered this room were about to experience the most important event of their lives.

A knock came and John bid whoever it was enter; a nervous yet curious Joshua settled onto the pillow opposite him. The young man gazed at the ceremonial table, looking more than a little as if he expected to be tested and feared he might prove unworthy.

"You have questions Joshua—or should I call them worries?" John said, smiling.

"Yes Rabbi. I...that is...well...it is only that I am not sure I should take part in this ceremony. Or that I should even be traveling with you!" he blurted.

John raised a brow. "And you would think this because...?"

"Your altar has your necklace on it, the sign of the fish some Christines say represent your Teacher. But Rabbi, in all truth I am neither Jew nor Christine. Though my mother tried hard enough to remind us of our heritage, if I were to place any creed upon myself, it would be that of the Romans and Greeks. Theirs are the gods with whom I feel most at home, not those of my father's father, nor even of your Teacher, student to you though I be. How can I possibly accept your blessing if such is the case?"

"Hmm. I see. And why do you find the gods of Rome and Greece appealing?"

Joshua searched John's eyes, looking, John thought, to see if disapproval lurked behind his question, then shrugged. "Well, I suppose it is the fact that my teachers spoke of them as ideals of what we can be, even as they acknowledged their human qualities. The gods of Caesar appeal to me because they are not so perfect as the Jewish and Christine god, not so abstract and distant. I feel I can touch and talk to them, that despite—or better, because of—their capricious natures, they will truly understand my problems. I feel I can someday reach their heights as Prometheus did and perhaps even occupy those heights with them. With the god of the Jews and Christines, it seems to me that I will never reach perfection; that I will never be allowed to."

John nodded. "And what is your experience of the Practice thus far?"

"Awe inspiring," Joshua answered without hesitation, his eyes glowing. "It is as if I went forth hoping to find a muddy pond and instead discovered an unlimitedly pristine ocean. Even when many thoughts or fears come up, Rabbi, I feel like I am Prometheus, brought back to life and rewarded with godhood."

Joshua blushed suddenly, like one still unused to so freely sharing his heart with another; John pointed toward the ceremonial.

"What my Teacher taught me about the Practice, Joshua, is that it works because it requires no belief. Not in Jeshua, not in the laws of Jew or Gentile, not in God Himself. The principles of the Practice are what we are, you see; they are literally the building blocks of being. You will find what you seek by using the Practice because if the Path is true, you can only fall into the heart of your Self. That requires not belief, only experience.

"The purpose of this ceremony is to give thanks to all the Masters who, by walking the path to Flawlessness first, have made it easier for us to achieve the goal of Oneness. As one who has chosen to follow in their footsteps, it is my profoundest honor to perform this ceremony in your presence, for by doing so I also receive their gifts.

"I have no doubts about your fitness to continue, Joshua; whether or not you ever *believe* in Jeshua, or Yahweh, or any other god is wholly unimportant to me. The Practice will give you the experience of what they were, regardless. But what do you know? Do you still feel it is inappropriate to continue?"

Joshua's sight turned inward for a long moment, then he smiled. "No, sir."

"Excellent. Then let us begin." John started to turn toward the table, then stopped. "And Joshua? While I follow Jeshua's Way, I do not consider myself a Christine, either."

"What? But..."

"Would a God who created all infinity as One Thing claim only a single facet of that creation as his perfect Son, while relegating the rest to some sort of inferior status? For any reason? Would a God who is only Perfection be capable of experiencing what He created as so badly flawed that only the murder of that perfect Son could redeem it? The very idea is ridiculous. The only reason we suffer and cause suffering is because we have forgotten what we are. Jeshua's sole purpose was to remind us that we need only remember the Truth by coming to the Unbounded One through the one true Self.

"Joshua, my Teacher *was* the Way, the Truth and the Life...yet he gladly sat at the feet of masters from other lands, masters who likewise knew themselves to be the Way, the Truth and the Life. They taught to him the Practice which I now teach you; the Practice that makes the remembrance of our Self inevitable. Since my Teacher's teachers had many different faiths, it cannot be that only a certain few, of a certain creed, have the right to find God's Fullness and Grace. Nor did Jeshua ever teach such a thing.

"So, though I do indeed follow Jeshua's Way, I cannot, in good conscience, call myself a Christine, any more than Jeshua would have done." John smiled, remembering his earlier realization about "Isha". "Better to say I am one who is dedicated to experiencing the Highest Consciousness of the All-Loving One, just as my Teacher was."

Before Joshua could ask the questions plainly written on his face, John turned back to the table and grew perfectly still, as if waiting for the angels to tell him what next to do.

Then he began to sing.

For John, singing the Ceremony of Thanksgiving invariably drew him out of his self (or perhaps deeper into his Self). All sense of individuality dissolved into the vastness of Creation, to be fed again into this existence as physical being. He dimly heard Joshua sob as the passionate hum of the One's life force flowed through them both, felt the Masters fill the room; he saw and tasted, smelled and touched the full record of the young man's Being. As the song's power filled him, he wondered if his body would this time dissolve, leaving him no means to finish it, or would the song, having become all he was, simply vibrate in the air, thus allowing him to complete the giving of the gift yet one more time?

John's body did not dissolve away, not this time, but the last of the song reverberated off into the distance as if sung in a room that was far larger than the one he and Joshua occupied. As he'd done when saying goodbye to Mary in Bethany, he bowed deeply before the "likeness" of Jeshua, face to the floor, knowing it honored all the...*Ishayas*...who now stood with him. Though he stayed long in the obeisance ostensibly so Joshua could regain his composure, the truth was, breaking the ambiance of the moment was beyond his ability.

Finally, though, John did rise, to find Joshua gazing at him with unabashed wonder.

"It is impossible, Rabbi...but though I have never heard that song before, do not even know what language it is in, I know it!" he said. "I felt as though, if I could go just a little deeper into my memory, I could actually sing the words with you. How can this be?"

"That happens for a number of those who receive the Ceremony of Thanksgiving, Joshua. Remember, though we seem to be fleetingly existent beings, we are actually eternal, far older and more experienced than the mountains, trees or anything this world can show us." John chuckled. "In all honesty, it would only surprise me if one such as you did *not* at least partly remember this ceremony!

"So then, my friend, are you ready to receive the fourth of these techniques...?"

As was usually the case, each of John's experiences of presenting the ceremony was different. Rachael did not so much as sniffle, but when he finished and looked at her, his mouth almost fell open in astonishment, and the thought, who are these ones I have been blessed to walk this path with? leapt unbidden into his awareness.

A cool, golden glow that rivaled the brilliance of the largest summer moon shone about the young woman, cloaking her in a level of knowing Divine Mother Herself might have bowed down to in honest awe. John resisted his own sudden urge to bow in homage by reminding himself that it could be years (if not lifetimes) before Rachael would come into this fullness. Still, he noticed that the young woman took in the words of the Practice of Compassion with the kind of regal, yet humble bearing that told him she was at least vaguely aware that something within her had been awakened.

It took John twice as long to get through Adan's ceremony as it did the others', due to a series of small "disasters" that kept them both busy trying not to burst into giggling fits. It didn't work: the resultant outburst that came when John had to make a diving catch to keep part of the ceremonial set he smacked with an elbow from falling to the floor buried the ceremony in mirth for a full five minutes.

In his youthful, much more austere days, John would have been appalled by such desecrations of so holy a ceremony, but experience had taught him that the ways of the One were sometimes unfathomable. Indeed, he could not shake the impression that the witnessing Masters were just as amused at his unintended antics as he and Adan were.

As he had on first meeting Haifata Adan, John felt as if he'd found one who'd originally meant to ensoul as part of the Zebedee family but had somehow ended up in the wrong place. Whether friends or foes, their souls had long ago discovered and still held to the joyous side of their experiences—and Haifata's ceremony echoed this sense perfectly. And though he said afterwards that he knew not how, unlike Joshua, Haifata not only remembered the song, but could sing many of the phrases.

John once more stood alone in Thomas's room. Each of his charges now knew the Practice of Compassion and had instructions on how to use it with the other techniques; though it was past first hour in the morning, they still sat in Thomas's living room, eyes closed, lost in the depths of the Stillness. John removed the delightful silk and once more donned his own homespun robe; he doused the ceremonial candles with wetted fingers, mumbling and shaking his hand as he slightly burned one. When he started to clear the table of the materials he'd used as part of the ceremony, however, he hesitated; a small grimace marred his features as a niggling twitch grabbed hold of his mind.

"Surely, this can wait 'til the morrow, can it not?" he said, for it seemed only fair to finally give Thomas his room and bed back.

The argument availed him not; whatever would happen next should happen now.

Being careful not to disturb the others as he crossed the larger room, John stepped into the brisk night air. Ada and Hosea greeted him as he entered Dareios's almost empty front room, their faces aglow with the excitement of sharing the One, but he forestalled their report on the class's progress.

"Where is Marcus?"

Timothy answered, looking a bit worried on the older man's behalf. "In the room you, he and Haifata sleep in, Rabbi. He seemed very upset when he came in."

"Mmph. Could you get him, please? Tell him it is important."

Timothy, whose injuries were apparently healed enough for him to be unfazed by the lateness of the hour, bounded from the room. Prochorus returned with him, sullenly trudging in his wake to stop at the hallway's entrance. John decided not to provoke him by asking if he was using the techniques.

"You have questions, Marcus—" he said, echoing his earlier statement to Joshua, "—and a comment or two, perhaps?"

"So far as I know, Rabbi, I neither said nor did anything to warrant your treatment at Thomas's house," he answered with remarkable civility. "But if I did, I would know of it. Or is that one of those exalted secrets we peasants are not to know?"

There, John thought, fighting to stop his smile; that is the Prochorus I know.

"No, no, Marcus, it is not. It is only that, when the twelve learned to teach the Practice to others, Jeshua told us that though we might each teach many, some would learn the aspects of the Practice only from one specific teacher, or not at all. It was an agreement made between the student and teacher long before they were born, he said, and fulfilling it extended the growth of both. When I saw you in Thomas's house this evening, I knew you had made such an agreement, so I sent you back here. As honored as I would be to give you the gift of the Ceremony of Thanksgiving's beauty, Marcus, it is not mine to do.

"It is Ada's."

TWENTY-ONE

Hosea's *mouth fell open* in astonished delight, and Timothy's dark brows seemed set to crawl into his hairline. As experienced students of Jeshua's Way, only these two of the people in the room knew what an affirmation John's pronouncement was.

Ada, though dismayed, did not seem as surprised at John's assertion as the others might have expected, and that was no surprise to him. Her appearance at Prochorus's side as he'd expressed his grief for his Lydia told him then how quickly her trust in her inner Voice was growing, and it had only increased since then. John suspected that, despite her silence on the matter, she knew of her soul's agreement to perform Marcus's Ceremony of Thanksgiving—and her response confirmed his other suspicion.

"Rabbi, surely I am not yet ready to perform the ceremony for another alone! Hosea and I have not even been teaching for two months yet! It is far too soon."

"Faugh, woman!" Hosea snorted, perfectly conveying John's own opinion. "I've heard your voice ring out its tune enough in our own house these last ten years, and that even before you knew all the words! More, Martha's sharp eyes and sharper tongue made sure we'd someday be qualified to sing the ceremony for others. Well 'someday' is here, and what do you do when your Teacher offers you the chance to share this wondrous gift? You stand here like some frightened temple maiden and twitter nonsense about how you cannot do it! Faugh, I say!"

"And if it were you he were offering this 'gift' to, how would you respond?" Ada asked with atypical testiness.

"Just as you have, no doubt—but since my time has not yet come, I choose to malign your lack of bravery...and get your goat!" He grinned at what was obviously an old joke between the couple.

John laughed. "Ada, nothing I have seen on our journey has caused me to doubt your readiness to present Marcus's ceremony and teach him the Practice of Compassion. And beneath that veneer of 'I cannot', you know you are ready as well—no, let me finish. It is no surprise you are nervous about doing a proper job of this, dear one. Everyone is when they first share the heart of this Teaching. But know this: regardless of the outcome of this first attempt, the One, Jeshua and the rest of the Perfected Ones will be with you in joy and pride. As will I."

"Ada?"

Prochorus moved from his place just beyond the hallway's entrance, his face serious. He tentatively took her small hands in his, almost as if he feared his grip could hurt her. "I have neither your own nor the Rabbi's intuition in matters of Spirit; I fear I still must often trust my mind alone to trudge to my conclusions about what I should do. Certainly, I do not know if what he says about any 'agreement' is true. But I do know you and Hosea befriended me when my history gave you no reason to, and I know I can trust my heart to each of you as I have not done with any other for many years.

"Please, Ada, will you perform this Ceremony of Thanksgiving the Rabbi speaks of and teach me the Practice of Compassion? It would honor me more than I can say if you would. Will you do it?"

Ada looked at the hands that held hers, then pulled one of her own free to wipe away tears. When she looked up, her expression was humble with the miracle of what Marcus Prochorus was becoming; with what she, by her willingness to teach him, had fostered.

"It is I who would be honored, Marcus. Thank you."

They sat, side by side on the floor outside John's room. Though he had the impression that even Corinth's ever-vigilant land spirits slumbered at this late hour, the same could not be said of those in House Isaurus. The others sat out in the larger room as if they had no sense of the time; certainly, their animated conversations seemed to belong more to midday than nearly third hour past midnight.

But then, he was no better: he smiled and was being smiled on by Ariadne as they chatted of their day's experiences, she with her head resting on his shoulder. In such a happy circumstance, time was a thing his mind simply could not grasp.

"John..." Ariadne said, and he clearly heard her hesitation at addressing him so familiarly. She was still a bit uncomfortable with her intimacy with this personage, this direct disciple of the Christos who seemed more special than others.

John's face twisted with a small and sudden pang of grief; how sorely he missed the camaraderie he'd shared with his Bethany "family". Would he ever know such again?

"John...I have heard that once someone becomes student to a Teacher, the Teacher can always...feel the student's presence, always knows exactly what he or she is doing. Is that true? Can you feel what Ada is doing right now?"

Hosea had escorted Ada to Thomas's house and John had excused himself, intending in fact to observe Ada's presentation in the same way he'd observed her and Hosea at Hiram bar Abiel's inn.

"Yesss...I do tend to be aware of my students, Ariadne...but not to the extent you may have heard it is done. While I can sometimes clearly sense a student's state of mind if I focus on him, in general my awareness exists at a level below full consciousness. It is a bit like constantly hearing a barely audible sound."

"Oh. But is that not distracting?"

"No more than hearing the sounds of market while preparing dinner would be. Which is a good thing, I think. At this stage of my experience, if I were fully conscious of my students all the time, I would be too distracted to function in the world of men." John smiled suddenly, remembering an incident he hadn't thought of in at least ten years. "Such was not true of Jeshua, though. He was constantly and fully aware of his students, yet it never seemed to distract him. Certainly, he knew what I was doing and feeling often enough—and he'd no qualms about saying so in public!"

"Really?" Ariadne's smile quickened John's heartbeat and spurred him to explain.

"Yes. During the second winter of Jeshua's ministry, my friend Elisha bar Salem, a boy named Aaron and I created a manger for an exceedingly pregnant goat in the bed of a particularly irritating disciple none of us liked, a fellow named Zebulon. Eli and I entered in through the back of the house, hoisting the she-goat through a low window very gently indeed, while Aaron played lookout. Then we waited until the streets were clear of people before we made our escape, though since it was still fairly cool, wearing our cloaks to hide our faces did not arouse suspicion.

"That night at one of the Mary's houses, as we took the evening meal, Zebulon and his brother barged in without knocking, dragging behind them four young followers who had reputations for playing pranks. They accused them of our actions and demanded Jeshua make them pay for the damage done by the goat and her newborn. I kept my face innocent of expression and made the same outraged noises as everyone else, while Jeshua looked sternly at the boys—who, of course, fervently protested their innocence—and promised the situation would be rectified.

"Zebulon and the boys left, and after sharing a few comments, we all went back to our meal. I breathed a sigh of relief, thinking myself free of the fish net, so to speak."

"But?" his double grinned. John smiled ruefully.

"But. For a long time after they left, Jeshua was silent. He took a long sip from his cup of wine, his expression thoughtful. Everyone grew quiet, expecting him to go back to speaking on the subject he'd been talking of before Zebulon's interruption... But instead, he began to talk of how important it was for each one to take responsibility for his choices, how one must stand in his righteousness even when all else told him to sit. He spoke of how important it was to be always in integrity with the One and Its creations, 'since, after all, they are your own Self'—and he spoke of how keeping a secret from one's Teacher when one was not in integrity was difficult, if not impossible.

"'For instance...' he said. Then, to my eternal mortification, he relayed every detail of our caper to the entire room, even down to the very words Eli, Aaron and I had spoken to each other during the maneuver."

"Oh, my." Ariadne's eyes were round with ill-concealed amusement.

John chuckled. "Indeed. When Jeshua looked at me, my heart, which had already sunk into my feet, spilled right out of my sandals and tried to bury itself in the floor.

"'The others are as answerable as you are, John bar Zebedee, but they were not here to do what was needful and admit their deed. Since you alone had the opportunity to grow in joy, but could not bring yourself to choose properly, you, Little Brother who has chosen the Narrower Path, will be allowed to rectify Zebulon's situation by yourself.'"

John chuckled again and shook his head. "I can laugh at the memory now, Ari, but at the time it was not the least bit funny. It took me most of two weeks to clean Zebulon's house and make exchange for the damage done by working in his fields. But yes, I most assuredly learned that some Teachers can and do consciously experience the thread of their students' beings as part of their own."

Even as she laughed, John could sense Ariadne turning over the idea that a "chosen" one could do such things, and he was also pleased by the pleasure that filled their mutually shared field when he called her by her half-name as her sister and father did.

"You were very young when that happened, and not long in your Teacher's presence, no?" She at last said slowly. John shook his head.

"Ari, many students make the mistake of seeing Jeshua as some angelic soul who never experienced the concerns and feelings of normal human beings. They believe the God of all Creation, in all Creation, has no sense of humor or love of a good cry. When he was among us and discovered such overarching piety, especially in his closest students—well, let me just say that Jeshua was not above disabusing those notions with seemingly outrageous behaviors, for in that he truly was the Son of Man.

"And though I no longer play the kinds of pranks jokes Eli, Aaron and I did on Zebulon, I still enjoy hearing of them...and am not above perpetrating a small one now and again." His smile turned wicked. "As Ada, Timothy and Hosea can attest."

Ariadne considered this. "Then you are saying that, despite all you have learned and who you learned it from, despite what you are, you are in truth still only human?"

Something in his double's manner made John's automatic "Of course," freeze in his throat. She'd turned her face so it pressed against his upper arm; her warm breath caressed his skin as it passed through the fabric of his robe.

John's mouth went dry, and his body suddenly tingled with the overriding awareness of Ariadne's clean, feminine, musky scent; a warm wind seared through his stomach, chest and loins and roughened his voice with sudden desire.

"'Still only human?' Jeshua's Heart, Ariadne, yes."

He hadn't been aware of turning so they faced each other, did not know the moment when he raised his hand to delicately stroke the soft skin along her jaw. Ariadne captured the hand in her own and kissed it, then kissed his chin, nipped at his lower lip, and lingeringly kissed the exposed skin at the "v" in the neck of his robe. John's other hand twined into her luxuriant curls; his lips brushed her temples, then explored her ear, cheek and the softness of her throat. Ariadne's breath quickened as she returned his kisses move for move; there was no hesitation now as she murmured his name.

John's own breath grew ragged with the blaze of his longing to take their explorations further, yet he still remained aware of the inner, ever-silent Witness; realized Its Presence judged him not at all, but only increased his soul's joy in what they shared.

The Witness, in turn, noted John's response to his and Ariadne's increasingly urgent and pleasing investigations, noted his mind's surprise at his passion. It observed as that part of him "tsked" in sudden apprehension over where their embraces were quickly leading, watched as that suddenly fearful self told John with the same demand his body felt for continuing that "this must stop".

The Witness watched as John retreated from their embrace, his mind awhirl.

Though her own eyes still smoldered, Ariadne seemed neither surprised nor disappointed at John's sudden reticence. Indeed, it almost seemed as if she'd expected it —and recognized the reason behind it. After all, as a widow, she had experience in matters of men and women...experience he sorely lacked.

John looked away, his face suddenly hot with his discomfiture. He wanted desperately to say something, anything, but could find no words. Ariadne smiled slightly, kissed his palms, one and then the other, and stood.

"You came back here for a reason, John, and though I meant only to be simple company, I have interrupted your task."

"Ari—" he said, but she laid her fingers against his lips, her smile turning wry.

"No, John. I think the newness of...us...makes it necessary for me to be out of your way while you do what you meant to do," she kissed him lightly, "so, now I shall leave off being a distraction by leaving you be."

As she glided down the hall, John wondered if the newness would ever wear off... if there would be time for it to do so...but his heart shied away from such thoughts.

With a sigh that spoke a thousand words, he stood and entered the chamber he shared with Prochorus and Adan...and realized he had no idea how much time had passed. Had he indeed missed Ada and Marcus's first Ceremony of Thanksgiving? The notion irritated him, for unlike Jeshua, he couldn't travel back and forth through time.

For years, John had assumed that an ability, once manifest, would always be accessible, but that was not the case. Instead, one tended to experience periods of expansiveness, only to then experience what felt like periods of shrinking back. Jeshua swore such apparent contractions of spirit did not happen in truth; it was only that, as with new wine skins, it took awhile to stretch into and hold the new consciousness until it became ordinary. "But then, even that is only an appearance," he would say, "for Fullness can only be full *now*."

Being in Mary's presence before and during her Ascension had triggered that kind of expansion in John, filling him with the invincible trust of God. That unshakable certainty had made it possible to heal Marcus's legs and be in two places at once while at Hiram bar Abiel's inn—but in truth, John no longer felt that level of assurance.

Still, he wanted to see how Ada was doing.

"Help me with this," he murmured to the heavens as he closed his eyes, aware that Jeshua would have laughed and simply told him to know what he knew.

Ada's sweet soprano filled Thomas's sleeping chamber; she was not quite a quarter of the way through the ceremony. Marcus watched the event attentively, as if he might later have to report on what he saw, but John sensed both his soul's joy in the rite and his phantom self's attempt to keep him from experiencing such an 'illogical' emotion.

John "stepped" a bit closer to gain a better view of Ada's movements—then stepped back, surprised, as her soul sent a brief but delighted greeting to him. A second later, her conscious self also became aware of him, for she looked directly at him and smiled radiantly, the light of her heart center flashing out beyond the confines of the room.

Did she realize it *was* him, or assume it was one of the many Masters who looked approvingly on? John recognized many of them as the Masters who'd been outside the brilliant multi-domed temple in Vashti, carrying on the business of maintaining the myriad universes of the One's Creation. They greeted his presence also, though not with words...or not only with words. John had many, many questions he would have loved to ask, sensed that some among them would have enjoyed talking to him. But this was, after all, a time for sacred observance, not idle gossip. Perhaps another time...

"Boanerge!"

The urgency in the voice made John spin in startlement; Thomas's house popped from his awareness, literally leaving him in the middle of nowhere. After many tense moments of fighting down purely primal panic, he managed to remember himself back to his body, slamming into it as if he'd hit the ground from a great height.

John lay there for a full minute, too disoriented to move or even think. A sense of foreboding roiled in his gut; whosoever would seek him at such a time, in such a manner, by that name? He had to find the one who had spoken to him.

That one found him.

"Boanerge."

John jolted up, his eyes widening in surprise. Mary stood before him, not as a shimmering phantom or a vision in another world, but as a living, breathing woman. For a moment, he thought he must have somehow been transported back to Bethany, but Mary's look told him this was no time to comment on it. She actually grabbed his hand and pulled, urging him to stand.

"Come. You must leave this place, now."

"What? Why? Mother, wait! What goes on?" John's confusion was plain, but the urgency that had never been Mary's way made him start gathering his clothes and supplies.

"The Romans have discovered who and where you are and are greatly interested in laying hands upon you."

"Then we are all in danger," John said, rolling everything together with quick efficiency. "We must collect the others and get Dareios and his daughters to safety, for the soldiers will surely take their wrath out on them if they do not find us here. How long do we have before we must leave?"

"The others will not be going with you, dearest."

John stopped dead as he strapped together his bedroll, but he had no chance to argue; the doorway's curtains parted, admitting Hosea and Ariadne.

In other circumstances, the surprise that overran his companion's features would have been comical: Hosea's naturally large eyes seemed ready to take up his whole face and his open mouth could have accommodated a four-horse chariot. He stared at Mary only long enough to blink, then fell to his knees as if his legs were too weak to hold him up. Ariadne gaped, her consternation plain as she looked at each of them in turn.

"Mary! Belovéd Mother! You have returned from Heaven! Surely, we have been blessed!" Hosea started to rise. "Ada will be so glad to see you; I must call the others—"

"No, Hosea, you must not," Mary interrupted. "I called the two of you to this room only so what needs doing may be quickly done. John is in grave danger, and must depart from this place at once, but the rest of you..." She stopped, considered. "No. Actually, John, you are right, or at least partially so. Hosea, you—everyone in this house—must leave, and you must do so now. Then you who are John's companions must follow him from whatever safe houses you go to. You may even have to go separate ways for awhile..."

"But..."

"No 'buts', Hosea bar Eliran! The authorities know of John's presence and nothing would make them happier than gaining hold of him. That, however, is something the One will not allow if it can be helped, and so we must make haste."

John clearly detected the twinkle of delight behind Mary's seemingly sober expression as she turned and looked Ariadne over, aware she could have called any of the others into the room—but Ariadne just as obviously did not. She blushed and hastily turned from his mother's gaze, bewildered by the unrestrained Power and indescribable Beauty that radiated from this woman who'd appeared from nowhere.

Mary's mind, though, had already turned back to the issue at hand when she spoke.

"There are hiding places for you and yours in this city? Homes of friends where you can harbor yourselves and John's companions?"

Ariadne nodded as if she didn't trust herself to speak.

"Then you must gather what you need and go to them until the soldiers choose to seek my son elsewhere." She turned back to John. "And you must make your way from here to Ephesus."

"Then Greece is forfeit?"

"Oh, you will go there, but only long enough to find a ship to Ephesus. It will do you no good to stay there now; that would only lead to Rome, and it is not yet time for that."

John nodded, wondering when it would be time for Rome.

"Three others should go with you," Mary continued. "Young Isvant, Haifata Adan, and the man Thomas, who knows the countryside."

"No," Ariadne said suddenly. Mary raised an inquiring brow and she blushed even more furiously, but that did not deter her. "We cannot all leave here. If the soldiers find the house deserted, they will search the neighborhood and possibly the entire city. Demeter can lead the others to safety, for she knows more about which homes can best conceal them than almost any other; but my father, I am sure, will stay. And I with him."

So then, the journey, albeit haphazardly, again called John to it. He knew his life force revealed his anguish at how quickly events had turned, and saw too, the sympathy Mary felt for him and his double, so recently brought together only to be parted. Her smile held nothing but love for Ariadne, who sought to understand even as she fought back tears. No, Mary had not found this one wanting, but her words made clear her determination to see John safely away as quickly as possible.

"Dear heart, know that if things could be different, I would have it so for both your sakes...but John's Way calls him forth and it calls him now. He must go."

She turned to Hosea and stared as if she was surprised he still stood in the room. He jumped slightly, as if likewise surprised, and turned to do as Mary bid him...but then stopped, his face pleading.

"Mother, please, before we again part, may I at least kiss your hand?"

Even in the midst of this emergency, Mary found reason to chuckle.

"Kiss my *hand*, Hosea?" she replied with great but wholly feigned offense. "Have I become some dignitary who must needs be treated like a fragile piece of pottery? Faugh! I expect no less from you than one of your great, smothering bear hugs!"

She fell against the big laborer and laughingly wrapped her arms around his waist with childlike delight. Hosea returned the hug, his breath coming out in something close to a sob, stepped back with moist eyes and a large grin, looking as if he sought to freeze the picture in his mind, then quickly left, calling to Timothy, Rachael and the others.

"Mother, what of Torer?" John asked, turning back his desire to come up with reasons to stay in Corinth longer. "Surely he will be easily recognized by the soldiers."

"Fear not for that one, dearest," Mary said, dryly amused. "He not only knows his way around Corinth, but around people, so to say. No harm will befall him."

Mary turned to Ariadne as if she meant to say something more to her, but instead smilingly placed a hand on the younger woman's face and kissed her lightly on her cheek. Ariadne gasped and looked as if some frightening secret had been told to her, then returned Mary's embrace as if she hugged a loved one she'd thought lost.

"Go quickly now, my son; the darkness and the angels will slow the soldiers' progress but they will not do so forever." Mary hugged John as if she'd greatly missed being able to do so, then leaned back to impishly peer into his eyes and murmured, "And well done."

John didn't ask what his mother meant, only stared after her as she stepped into the hall, but not, he knew, down it.

He gazed into Ariadne's eyes as he settled his bedroll on his shoulder and listened to the commotion in the main room that Hosea and Demeter made as they herded the others into the night. She came and leaned into him with a resigned, quavering sigh. Their time together had indeed been short, shorter than even he could have feared.

"I hoped we would have at least a few more days," she said into his chest.

"I hoped we would have a lifetime," John answered, his throat suddenly as tight as the sail ropes he'd helped work aboard *Matthatus*. "I hoped it, even knowing my Way takes me elsewhere. I hoped, though I see it only now, that you would come with me. That you will come with me now.

"I want you with me, Ariadne. Please say you will come."

Ariadne went still in his arms; even her breath stopped. John knew she would find no reservations over what might be as she looked into his eyes, and in perfect reflection, her eyes showed neither fear nor reservation either. Yet, as they stood there, flowing into and through each other's beings as the ocean waves flow into and become each other, both knew what her answer must be, and knew it to be utterly right.

"I cannot, John. My place is here, helping with your friends and mine. My place is..." she leaned into his chest and began to cry.

How will we stand being apart, having found each other at last? John thought. It was insupportable, impossible...and it was, they both knew, what must be.

When they'd sat in the hall, John felt as if time had moved out from under him so that the moment between sitting against the wall and facing his double, between facing her and caressing her face, seemed never to have existed. This time, as he took Ariadne's face in his hands, he was super-aware of every movement, as if time had deigned to bestow the gift of eternity for this little while. He was aware of each part of each kiss as his lips brushed her forehead, lingered over each eye and nipped her nose and chin. He pulled her close and felt her allow that closeness as her arms encircled him.

John felt Ariadne's fingers play with the hair at the nape of his neck, reveled in knowing there was not a hair's breadth of space between them; her breath was hot on his face, then on his lips, then in his mouth as they kissed, truly kissed for the first time. The fire of his being reached up and out and entwined with her life energy, remaining wholly Self even as it became the larger Self that included hers. The Silence in each of them swallowed their love and rekindled desire, recreating it in a loop of eternal joy and beauty that flowed forever from one to the other and out into the universe.

When he'd finally kissed Miriam before leaving Bethany, it had been enough to kiss her once as man to woman. But John's heart, his body, his very soul insisted that what he shared here and now with Ariadne would never, could never, be enough. And yet, paradoxically, it *was* enough, just as the fullness of the One was always and ever enough.

It had to be.

The moment and the kiss finally ended; Time finished giving Its gift. John gently laid his fingers against Ariadne's cheek and nuzzled her hair. The desire to cry came into his heart and he let it, sobbing against her and hearing the echo of his grief in her tears.

When they at last entered the living room, everyone save Erezavan and Dareios were gone. Haifata entered the house a few seconds later, his traveling cloak and pack on, his countenance grim. John went to Dareios and embraced the older man.

"Are you sure it would not be more prudent to go into hiding with the others, my friend?" he asked.

"Yes. The soldiers have known us for years as people who help the injured and ill. In fact, Ariadne's gift with healing draughts is known and appreciated. My only regret is that we will not have the chance to learn more of the Practice."

Dareios searched John's eyes and lowered his voice. There was a smile in it. "Fear not, John of Zebedee; all will be well...and fear not for my daughter, either, good son. Ariadne well knows what she is about and can handle three times her number if it comes to it."

John nodded, but Dareios's reassurances couldn't take away the bitterness of leaving.

He once more reached for Ariadne.

"Heart of my heart," John whispered, his voice thick, "know that my soul will never forsake you; that I love you always."

His double nodded and gave him a last, brief kiss. He turned to Isvant and Adan.

"Brothers, our time in this good place is finished. Let us away."

TWENTY-TWO

Were *it not for* the relentless pursuit, this trek would be a pleasant one, John bar Zebedee thought wryly.

Rather than going out from Dareios's through the front door, the four men—John, Haifata and Erezavan, with Thomas leading—quickly but quietly climbed out the window of Demeter's room and into the small garden. They made their way through one of the homes adjacent to House Isaurus, stepped out onto the street, and held to the shadows, all at Adan's insistence. Though Thomas argued that the soldiers never scouted ahead when seeking someone, Dareios had agreed with the African.

"The one they seek is not the usual fugitive, brother, and Captain Patrius knows his politics. His Governor, if not the Emperor himself, would very much like to 'host' one of the Twelve, and his fortunes can only rise if his men make the capture."

Though he might now be a fugitive skulking in the shadows, John still relished the Stillness that permeated the land of this otherwise cosmopolitan city. Yes, it might well have been a most satisfactory place to live, he thought—and now, of course, he had reason to regret that he would never do so.

While not as serious as in other towns, the increasing violence in Corinth had the local Christines enough on guard that they'd already assembled an efficient underground network. Despite the early hour, the group walked by several homes, only to find some man watching the stars or some woman knitting by lamplight. These ones Thomas stopped and talked to, gaining information on the soldiers' location. He shook his head as they left one such house with provisions enough to feed them for their journey.

"They do not have the roads blocked, but Gorian says they are questioning travelers they deem suspicious."

"I trust that is not usual?"

"No, though it is not as uncommon as it once was. They seek those who are rumored to be Christine leaders more and more often these days—and when they find them they disappear, never to be seen again." Thomas's voice was bitter. "Apparently, the mines and galleys are not well-manned enough."

"It is late enough that travelers are already on the road, yes?" Adan asked, for it was just past fifth hour. Thomas grunted his assent, and the African "hmphed" in response. "It is unlikely that we will not be among those they think suspicious; we should not risk being seen if we can avoid it."

"We can. There is a stream at the edge of the city that sits in a small ravine. With the year so dry, we can walk all the way to the Isthmus Wall in it. We will have to cross a field to get to it, but once we do, we'll be able to travel without detection. But we must hurry; our danger increases every moment."

The four continued through the sleepy streets of Corinth for the next hour, occasionally coming upon the odd Christine sentry who calmly gave them news of the soldiers' whereabouts. At the second to last home they came to, they heard a disturbing piece of news: upon finding that John had left, the soldiers had ransacked the Isaurus home and threatened Dareios, telling the old man they would be watching them in the future to make sure they "aided no more enemies of Rome." If they found he'd given such help, it would go badly for both him and his "lovely little daughter." Their informant further stated that the "loud, portly man" who'd come with the companions had led the soldiers to Dareios's door.

She meant Darshinika Baremna.

Even in the dim light of the informant's lamp, Erezavan's shock was unmistakable. Apparently, it had never occurred to him that Baremna could behave so treacherously, even in anger. Both he and Thomas looked as if they wanted to turn back and check on their friends, and John's own stomach knotted with tension: with Demeter out hiding the rest of his companions, the "lovely little daughter" could only be Ariadne.

Instead of indulging in thoughts of turning back, however, he focused all the more on the Stillness and prayed that, as Dareios had said, they knew what they were about.

Only Adan, though as grim of countenance as the rest, showed no sign of wanting to take hasty action. But then, he'd seen his whole village either killed or enslaved by the Romans and had suffered numerous indignities at their hands over the years. Apparently, he'd found some measure of peace with what was.

Or, well, perhaps "peace" was not the word to describe his attitude, John thought, recalling the African's comments one day as they sailed for Corinth. "I trust, as you do, that the Gods will find it in their Way to balance the playing board of life, brother. And if it is that I am to be an instrument of that balancing, then I will be honored to do my part," he'd said. And for an instant, John had seen in the African's eyes the savage patience of one who, like a lion, knows the prey will eventually come to him —and will be ready for it.

They came to the field they would have to cross. Though it was still too dark to see the ledge that dropped to the creek bed, John could dimly perceive the ruins of the once-mighty Isthmus Wall, and beyond that, what looked to be a thick wood. Thomas pointed.

"The ravine is to our left, five, perhaps six hundred yards away."

"What of the forest, there? Is it a large wood?"

"Half-again a day's walk, perhaps. Then it thins out into meadow, followed by more forest."

Thomas looked toward the main road. It was becoming crowded with travelers and, based on the dull glint of torchlight on metal helms, was occupied by a number of soldiers. He crouched as if to make himself smaller and motioned to the others; John and Erezavan started forward, likewise stooping so they would be less visible.

"No," Adan said suddenly, still standing tall. "We must walk like men free, not scurry like mice seeking to escape a cat."

"But the soldiers will see us!" Thomas argued, stopping in his tracks. He crouched until he seemed almost to be squatting.

"Yes, for it is already too light for us not to be seen if one is looking this way. Still, even soldiers tend to make the obvious invisible. Would you draw their attention by acting as if you are what they seek?"

After a few seconds, Thomas shook his head and reluctantly stood. Adan neither hurried nor dallied, but maintained as stately a pace as the rough, recently plowed-under land would allow. The others followed, heading steadily toward the creek and concealment; John resisted the urge to look toward the soldiers by asking Thomas about what they'd heard from the last two lookouts.

"Do you really think they will keep watch on Dareios and carry out their threats?"

"In frank truth, Elder, I do not know. I have known Dareios Isaurus and his family since before his wife Zenobia died, and never have they been harassed for ministering to the sick and injured. If anything, the soldiers always supported them, for Zeni, especially, had a way with healing and no qualms about sharing it." He smiled slightly as he shared stories of Ariadne and Demeter's mother. "She was particularly appreciated for her potion to lessen the agonies of a head that had seen too many cups of wine; some of the soldiers grieved as much as we did when she died."

The smile faded with the memories. "But these new ones seem a colder and more violent lot than those who came before. Or perhaps our Way is seen as a greater threat to public order than it once was."

John considered this, then said, "That might be, Thomas. But it is also true that we find what we expect to, even when we believe we do not want it."

Thomas's puzzlement was writ large, but he had no chance to ask what John meant, for they stood at the edge of the ravine, staring at a creek bed that lay several feet below. In the decreasing dimness, John saw that the chasm-like furrow wound back and forth like a great serpent; it would screen them from the road and any pursuers.

They made their way into the rock-strewn trench carefully, for there was enough of a drop to break a bone if one landed wrongly. The creek was broader than it appeared, and at this point, at least, it was substantially deeper than the droughty weather would have suggested; John saw ripples and bubblings that indicated the presence of fish. The four men walked in silence to a growing serenade of sweet chirps, tranquil buzzes and sandals rhythmically crunching on the gravelly earth as the dimness of dawn's light crossed into the brightness of a typical cloudy autumn morning.

Truth to be told, the stress of the night's events told on the group; they were all tired. Even so, John could not but delight in the walk, for the Quiet that permeated the land in Corinth itself was even more pronounced here. Seeing nature spirits had never been usual for him in Judea, but this place was so filled with life that *seeing* was easier. Or maybe it was because of the Romans' strong tradition of worshipping the gods and goddesses of Nature. John stifled his mirth and thought of Ada as a flower deva acknowledged his scrutiny by plugging her ears at the group's noisy passage; she'd be thrilled to see so many sprites peeping out from their leafy, bright-colored clothing or leaping forth from the creek disguised as splashes of water.

John sobered at the thought of his companions. Were the soldiers also searching for them? Would the Christine community be able to hide them until things died down? He knew enough about the way his mother's mind worked not to accept appearance as fact, but she'd obviously included Isvant in this group to keep him out of Baremna's way. Was there another reason for his inclusion as well?

As if reading his mind, Erezavan suddenly turned, his face strained with more than fatigue. Ever since he'd heard about his former mentor's betrayal, he'd been withdrawn and disconsolate.

"I should go back, Rabbi," the young man said in a rush. "This is all my fault; I should not have humiliated Darshinika by choosing you over him. Perhaps if I go back to Corinth and face him, the Romans will stop pursuing the rest of you."

John shook his head. "Erezavan, even if such a thing was true—and it is not—I would not let you go back to Corinth now."

"But if I had not..."

"No. Darshinika Baremna seeks vengeance because the mirror of his own soul's knowing showed him the difference between those who choose to serve the One and those who seek glorification for appearing to do so. He could not accept what he found, and that alone is the reason he seeks to bring harm upon our heads."

"But, Rabbi, if I..."

"You did nothing *wrong*, Erezavan, not now, not at any time." John placed a hand on the Persian's shoulder and smiled. "So put the groveling one back to sleep and come along, hmm? I want to reach the woods before too much longer, so we may rest and discover what must come next."

Isvant winced and, smiling sheepishly, squared his shoulders and followed.

The forest finally sprung up around the creek slightly before Noontide. Though Thomas felt they could immediately leave the gully, get some rest, then travel in a more easterly direction to get to the main road, Adan declared they should not leave creek bed's confines just yet. Instead, he had them walk another half-mile in the waters of the creek, then climb the steep bank and walk in the direction opposite from the one Thomas indicated. When they came to a well-trampled clearing that looked to be a feeding ground for deer and other creatures, Adan had them head back the way they had come.

"What is the point of this?" Thomas finally asked, unable to keep the impatience out of his voice. "You must know no one follows us; the soldiers are undoubtedly still seeking the Elder in the city."

"Perhaps so, perhaps not," Adan answered in his imperturbable way.

Thomas only became more agitated. "Well, even if they are seeking us outside the city, they surely know we head to Athens. Why do we waste time trying to fool them?"

Adan seemed to take no offense at the question, but only said, "You do not hunt."

"I prefer not to kill living things," Thomas answered, still defiant.

"Mmm. Among my people, the question was not one of preference, but survival. The ones who taught me had a saying: 'the lion who eats best knows which way the deer will jump next, and the deer who lives longest is the one who assumes the lion waits in the grass.' The Romans are a very old and wily lion. They know the sea surrounds us to left and right. Perhaps, then, we head not to Athens, but to the west. Better to send men that way in case a ship awaits us. And better for us to have half a Roman patrol seeking where we are not than a whole one seeking where they expect us to be."

"To fear death is not our way," Thomas replied haughtily. "If the Christos wills that I should be captured, then I will gladly go forth, that His Cause may be strengthened."

"Hmm...and the lion grows fat."

"The Christos's will calls for us to make our way to Athens and find a ship to Ephesus, something I doubt the soldiers will allow should they find us first," John said, preventing Thomas's retort. "Best we should be cautious now to avoid regrets later, no?"

Adan nodded and turned to continue their journey. Thomas also went on, but he looked as if he still wished to argue what had now become a more important point.

John knew enough about the human tendency to see in others what one most disliked about himself to know that Thomas perceived his own lifelong caution as cowardice... and so saw the same in Adan. Yet, for all that the Corinthian bridled at Haifata's insistence on care, John enjoyed watching him trek through the forest with all his senses alert to any out-of-place noises or sights. To him, Haifata's caution signified not one who spent his life trying to avoid trouble, but one who avoided wasting energy by using it exactly where it was needed. That way, when trouble came, he'd have the power to deal with it.

The four men spent another half-hour following Adan's instructions. When he was at last satisfied they'd at the least be difficult to find, they continued in their original direction, crossing the creek over a line of protruding stones far from their first exit point. An hour more passed before they came upon a wall of tall, thick bushes.

"Here," Adan said tiredly after receiving Thomas's nod. "This place will do."

Using their walking staffs, they pushed the branches aside and crawled into what turned out to be a small, well-hidden grove. For a long time, none of them moved or spoke, but merely sat on the cool ground, breathing as if they'd run a long race. Even John, who tended to need very little sleep—a dividend that came of regular use of the Practice—felt like a seed gone too long without water.

Yet, though he was hungry and thirsty, what he wanted more than either food or water was rest. The others clearly felt the same way: Erezavan had already pulled his cloak around him, ready to curl up and sleep on the spot, and Thomas wasn't far behind.

Adan, however, insisted they replenish their bodies first to help them more quickly regain their strength. They followed his instructions willingly enough, but the supper conversation was decidedly less than scintillating.

John looked up. The trees formed a thick canopy whose shade undoubtedly kept the forest pleasantly cool on hot days, but here in the middle of a fall afternoon the air was chillier than was strictly comfortable. A light breeze blew the leaves around just enough for him to locate the sun and estimate the time: it was almost third hour. Another three hours would see dusk's appearance.

"We should rest here until mid-evening," he said. "It seems to me travel by night would be wisest, in case the soldiers are pursuing us."

"Very well. I will take first watch," Haifata said, but John forestalled him.

"No, my friend. I want you as sharp as you can be for the sake of your hunter's guidance. Best you should curl up with our companions here and experience more of the Practice of Compassion, even if you do not sleep. I am as used to long days as you, and can stand to stay awake for a couple more hours."

If Haifata had thoughts about arguing, they were only fleeting. "Very well...Rabbi," he said, smiling slightly. "But promise you will awaken me in only two hours. Practice or not, brother, you too, need rest."

"I solemnly promise, brother, I will awaken you in two hours," John grinned, feeling the slight disorientation of déjà vu. They'd had this conversation many other times, in many other places.

Adan pulled his cloak closer and lay down. Thomas and Erezavan were already breathing in the slow, deep rhythm that denotes slumber; John doubted if they'd even made it past the first of their techniques. The Practice could be the best of sleeping draughts if the One within felt that was what was needed. He considered walking the perimeter of their leaf-bedecked fortress, but decided against it. The bushes were thick enough to hide not only what was in the grove from those outside it, but what was outside from those within. It'd be useless to try to see if anyone approached; he would have to rely on his ears alone.

Or another would.

Both Jeshua and Mary had repeatedly insisted that humankind's so-called normal abilities were far greater than many could begin to imagine, for that was a fact known and practiced by adepts of every culture and age. Truncated though it had been, John's "trip" to see Marcus's ceremony had strengthened his confidence that that was so. He trusted more than ever that he could use those talents to the group's benefit.

Unfortunately, not all adepts use their talents with such selfless service in mind, he thought as he settled down, for though he'd said nothing to the others, they were in fact being pursued, just as Haifata assumed. John knew exactly how and by whom; the only question was, "How close are they to finding us?"

Happily, the answer to that lay as close as closing his eyes...

When John opened his eyes again, most of an hour had passed, but he felt considerably more relaxed about their situation. He now knew two things: the soldiers had come into the forest from the main road, and so were roughly a half-day's journey from their current hiding place. And, though they had no trail to follow, if John didn't find a way to throw their main pursuer off, they would find the fugitives wherever they might alight.

Darshinika Baremna had the talent to help the soldiers find them...and a channel through which to do it in Erezavan Isvant, whose countenance looked troubled even in sleep. The advantage the companions had, however, was that, though Baremna could read and manipulate Isvant's life force to, among other things, surreptitiously undermine the younger man's confidence, he could not accurately track him while he moved. Their pursuers would essentially have to guess where the four might be within a given (and fairly large) area, so they would be thin on the ground. Additionally, now that John knew Baremna was using Erezavan to home in on, he should be able to turn his ability against him. Perhaps they would make it to Athens without an unwanted escort.

Thus relieved of any immediate need for worry, John pulled his cloak closer and, after giving a thought and prayer for Ariadne, her family and his other companions, entered the all-embracing Infinite to experience the undifferentiated One.

John came back to full awareness to find dusk settling on the land—and Haifata staring balefully into his face.

Unfazed by the African's formidably disapproving scrutiny, he smiled sunnily, threw off his cloak, and gave himself the gift of a long, thoroughly satisfying stretch. Then he stood and let forth a belch that was just as satisfying in its own way, acknowledging both Erezavan's amusement and Thomas's rather shocked expression. It seemed he kept jarring the poor Christine's ideas of how an "Elder" should behave.

"Is any food ready?"

"I will tend to it, Rabbi," Erezavan said, and began sorting through of the ample provisions they'd been gifted with during their procession through Corinth. John turned to face his accuser.

"You promised to wake me at the end of two hours, so I might stand watch," Adan said, his sense of honor thoroughly insulted.

"Yes I did," John answered. "I suppose I must have lied."

He rummaged in his pack, pulled out a small pot Rachael had purchased in Tyre while seeking seasickness herbs and handed it to Isvant. "This meal we will have warm food," he said, and set about gathering up twigs. When he found his flint piece and began striking up a fire, Adan squatted across from him.

"This tendency to lie to your friends...it is a common thing?"

"Yes," John answered, not looking up, but allowing the amusement in his voice to match that which he heard in Adan's. "But I usually tell them that is the case the first time I do so, so they may protect themselves from future deceit."

"Ah, I see." Haifata laughed and shook his head. "I will remember that."

Dinner was pleasant, though quickly eaten, and the company quite acceptable. Erezavan's voice turned out to be as duskily beautiful as the rest of him; he softly graced them with a song in his native tongue as they made ready to leave their hideout. Soon, the four men were again on their way; as they walked, John asked about Ephesus.

Apparently, the city's Governor, though Roman, displayed an attitude toward the Christines that bordered on being openly sympathetic—largely, Thomas thought, because many prominent Ephesians counted themselves as members of the new sect.

"So long as we do not interfere with city business or threaten the Empire's ability to go about its lawful occupations, we are welcome to preach and gather as we will."

Such lenience was not a popular position among many of the city's officials or the army's commanders, but since the Governor was supposedly a nephew or cousin or some such of the Emperor himself, no one dared argue the matter, at least not publicly. Ephesus seemed an ideal place for a fugitive "Christine" to abide, at least for a while.

Even so, John found himself wondering what Mary really had in mind for him once he arrived. Whom might he meet this time to promote—or complicate—this journey?

He was saved from further speculation by the sound of Adan's voice in his ear.

"I had no chance to ask you about the Practice of Compassion, brother. Would there be time to speak of it now, or do I disturb your ruminations?"

"There is always time to speak of the Way of the One, brother. What would you know?"

"What is the purpose of this Practice? Why does it differ from the other three?"

Erezavan's triumphant exclamation at finding wood with which to make a perfect torch, and Thomas's earnest congratulations, reverberated ahead of them as John opened his mouth to answer Adan's question. Then he closed it. Though he had given the answer perhaps a thousand times before, as the fullness of the One filled him this time, he realized it was not his to give. Instead, he asked a question of his own.

"What was your experience, Haifata Adan?"

For many minutes, there was only the sound of their staffs thudding against the soft earth and the melancholy dirge of some night bird mourning the end of the days of sun and warmth. Then: "When I use the first three techniques, I am like a whale that dives into the deep of the ocean. I swim down and down and yet down again more, until I can see only darkness and hear only Silence. But then, eventually, just as the whale must come back up for air, so too, do I come to the surface of my being.

"When I give myself to the Practice of Compassion it is different. The whale swims down into the Silence, yes; but as the strength of his desire to stay in that holy place is touched by that Practice, he becomes a fish instead of a thing of the Air who pretends to be a fish... Perhaps that is why the Christines use that symbol to tell of their devotion to your Jeshua, yes? Are they, too, whales who seek to forever end the need to come up for air?"

"I cannot speak for all of them, brother, but I know that to be true for myself," John replied, captivated by the African's picturesque vision of how the Practice felt to him. "What you say describes the purpose of the Practice of Compassion perfectly. Whereas the other techniques carry us into the Deep, the Practice of Compassion allows us to remain in the waters of Life for longer than would be the case if we had only Praise,

Gratitude and Love. We have the chance to become so much a part of the Deep (though in truth there is no 'becoming', since the Stillness is what we are) that eventually, like the fish, we never need to seek the air.

"Not that we will not do so," John laughed. "So long as we humans believe there is something to be seen in the air, we will seek that something out. But once we are able to remain in the Deep, we can carry It with us, even if we choose to grow feet and walk amongst the creatures of the air again."

"Ah. Then the Practice of Compassion is structured differently only for that reason?" Adan asked, a smile in his voice. He'd caught the sense of testing behind John's query and seemed to enjoy having the chance to recognize aloud what he already knew.

"Again I ask, what was your experience?"

"...The first word of the technique is a foreign one to me, but it brought me to the Silence in a way the words of the other Practices did not."

"Yes. It is said that when we speak that word from the soul's purity, it protects the self from evil thoughts. But more than that, it opens us to the Source of Creation and makes creators of us. The first word of the Practice of Compassion is like an unplowed field that is ready for whatever seed we would plant, while the rest of the technique is the seed we grow in that field so that compassion expands within and from us."

"Hmm... but, if we correctly practice the first three techniques, we cannot but become compassionate. Or so does it seem to me. A special technique seems...unnecessary."

"Thomas?" John suddenly called.

"Yes, Elder?" The torches stopped their guiding dance as the Corinthian turned.

"What is compassion?"

Thomas answered without hesitation. "It is making allowances for others' weaknesses. After all, they can no more help being weak than I can help being the height I am."

"Mmm. Could you not help them overcome their failings?"

Thomas looked puzzled. "I? I am naught but a sinner myself. I would not be like the hypocrites who try to make others what I myself am not. Mine is only to lead them to seek the Christos. Once they experience His saving Grace, all will be well." His look suggested he thought John must be testing him, for surely he must know such to be the case.

"Already Jeshua's words become distorted, as is inevitable without a direct experience of the One within," John said quietly, shaking his head. "Far too many believe compassion consists of leading souls to some external savior who will then erase their flaws. They think they are inherently despoiled by sin, and so can never discover God's Wholeness within themselves, that the way to help another from the mud is to jump into it with them, to 'understand' their pain as if it were the truth of both.

"But never do they ask, 'What if this mud is actually quicksand?' Or better, 'Would Perfection create the corruptible? Would Omnipotence convince us the illusion of lack is real, then force us to escape from it?' The idea is senseless to one who knows the One."

"And yet, is that not exactly what your Jeshua did?" Adan asked with a frown. "Did he not go among the poor and the sick to be with them in their pain, as I have heard?"

"Jeshua did indeed go among the poor and the sick, Haifata—but never was he one of them, not even when he was being crucified. He never once gave anyone, not even the Pharisees and Scribes, the impression that they could not be what he was. After all, they *are* what he was, whatever their phantom selves' opinions on the matter.

"True Compassion is a combination of love and wisdom, Haifata. It never shows us anything but the reality that we are the One's belovéd Child in whom She is always well pleased. And that is true even when the help seems to look angry or uncaring. When we choose to see the Truth within ourselves, how can we not see others as whole?

"*That* is the truth Compassion forever sees."

"Very well, then," Adan said after a moment. "Let me put this as Marcus would, and you will tell me if I speak truly. With the Practice of Praise, we give appreciation to ourselves and the world. With the Practice of Gratitude, we accept appreciation for and from the world. Through the Practice of Love, we become the essence of appreciation; and the Practice of Compassion allows us to know that essence to be all that lives. Yes?"

John's night-veiled grin was mischievous. "What is your experience, my brother?"

The barest beginnings of a chuckle had escaped Adan's lips when the same sense of danger that had accosted them in Corinth assailed John. He grabbed the African's arm, shushing him, while up ahead, Erezavan abruptly stopped and drove his torch into the soft ground. Thomas, though confused, followed his companion's lead.

"You felt it?" John whispered to Isvant as he and Adan caught up with them. He could see the apprehension on the Persian's face as his torch fizzled to the barest glow.

"Yes. There are soldiers ahead."

TWENTY-THREE

Under the circumstances, there was only one action to take.

"What are you doing? We must be away, quickly!" Thomas hissed.

Erezavan put a hand on the Corinthian's shoulder and shushed him as John sat and closed his eyes, but it was the thickening Silence that strangled his further protests against such strangeness.

John dove into the center of his being, noting as a kind of afterthought that he could still hear the nearby night creatures. That they were oblivious to the drama taking place among the larger and supposedly more knowing human animals was a good sign, he realized; it meant those who sought them weren't as close as he feared. Still, how had he so misjudged their position? Had he done so? But no, he felt sure he hadn't.

Then suddenly, like a curtain being drawn back, John *saw* them.

They must have traveled at a steady trot to come this close so soon, but now they slowly moved in the four's direction. They searched thoroughly, swinging their torches in slow half-arcs; they checked both underbrush and tree limbs and stayed in sight of each other so they could signal when they spotted the fugitives. Yes, they were farther away than feared, but not nearly far enough away for comfort. At this rate, they'd be on them within the half-hour.

John opened his eyes to find Erezavan and Thomas waiting, each with very different levels of patience. Thomas fidgeted and barely managed not to wring his hands and bounce from foot to foot; Erezavan stood still, his gaze distant. John realized the young man had also extended his awareness to see what he might *see* and waited until the

Persian's focus was again on them before speaking. He received confirmation that there were indeed ten figures heading their way. Erezavan assumed they were soldiers and that they were not too close, but his talent did not yet extend to perceiving specifics.

"What should we do?" Thomas asked, looking around as if their pursuers might immediately appear and clap them in irons. John pulled his bedroll off his shoulder.

"The first thing you will do is get into different clothing. As it is right now, you are far too easy to detect." It was true: Thomas's Roman-cut robe was full-moon bright.

John handed him his second robe, quickly re-rolled his garments, and considered their position; they would have to be very careful if they meant to avoid the soldiers' searching eyes. He turned to Adan to ask his opinion on the best way to get past the patrol.

Only to find he had disappeared into the night, silent as a phantom.

"Where did he go?" Thomas's grating whisper was almost as loud as his normal voice. "Why in Hades would he leave us now? Is he mad?"

"Should we try to find him, Rabbi?" Erezavan's voice betrayed his own anxiety.

"No. I suspect he has not gone far and we have time yet before the soldiers find us. Let us wait for him here rather than forcing him to search for us."

The three sat still and waited—or more accurately, John and Erezavan sat still. Thomas strained to catch every sound, then jumped when he heard them. John was painfully aware of both his fear and his judgment against himself for feeling it; knew that when he gently reminded the Corinthian to take heart and use the Practice, he took his reminders for reprimands, for signs of even greater failure. John simply kept his awareness turned inward, trusting the One's "sight" despite his consternation at the soldiers' unexpected appearance. When they reached a certain point, they would leave whether Adan had returned or not.

"Rabbi... Do you think Baremna knows where we go and sends the soldiers to find us?" Erezavan suddenly asked.

"How could he do that? Is he some sort of seer?" Thomas asked.

"He...yes. Yes, he is."

So then, he is aware Baremna can *see* through him, John thought, but Erezavan's manner clearly indicated he did not want Thomas to know it.

"It is more likely he sent them to where we were," John said, looking out into the forest's shaded night. "I have no sense he can accurately track us while he is moving—no matter how strong his connections to his talent might be."

"What do you mean?" Thomas asked, but John held his peace. The sigh that escaped the young Persian's lips told him he understood his answer perfectly.

"What concerns me," John went on, "is that the soldiers come not from behind or to the side of us, but from directly ahead. Can it be we lost our way in the darkness?"

"No," Thomas said with surprising assurance. "We've used the creek to get people to safety before, though we've always left it immediately and walked to the main road. More, I have known these woods all my life. I know we head the right way, despite your Adan's insistence on trying to fool the soldiers with his hunting tricks." His tone showed he questioned the wisdom of following the African's advice now more than ever.

John was saved from having to reply; Adan returned as silently as he had left, coming upon them almost before they knew it. To John's amazement, he'd kilted his long robe into a tight knot so it would not brush against the bushes and make unwelcome noise; his velvet-dark legs were bared to his thighs. In place of the walking stick that reached only to his shoulder, he now carried a long pole that looked to be a full head taller than he was.

John looked closer; it was sharpened to a fine, long point.

Adan met his stare. "If we can make our way forth without having to use it, that will be well, for the soldiers no doubt outnumber us. Yet it gives me comfort to have a proper weapon at my disposal—that is, besides Marcus's knife."

John's brows rose in the dark. "Marcus gave you one of his knives? I am amazed."

"He made me solemnly swear that it and I would return whole." Even whispering, the African's amusement was obvious, but it soon turned to concern. "You know where the soldiers are?"

"Yes. There are ten of them more or less directly ahead, far too close and searching very thoroughly."

"Mmmm..." was all Adan said, but John sensed he was as surprised by the soldiers' position as he had been. The African grinned mirthlessly and nodded. "Very well. The Hunter seeks us. We will evade him if we can, and give him a good chase if we cannot. Would you have me be your guide?"

"Yes."

"Then tie your own robes in this manner and do as I do."

The process took only a few minutes. Thomas's frown was mighty, but he followed Adan's instructions and readjusted John's bulky winter-weight robe when the African deemed it too loosely tied. They also tightened the cords that held their bedrolls, packs and water skins so they were as close to their bodies as possible, since, "It would not do to tell them of our whereabouts by our noisemaking."

Adan retrieved his spear, which he had lain against a tree during their preparations, and started off at a right angle from the soldiers' approach. Erezavan followed, staying a few feet back as the African had instructed.

John made ready to go next, but felt a hand on his arm. Thomas frowned so deeply his expression looked like a caricature of human expression.

"How can you allow him to carry weapons? Will you let him do violence against the soldiers just to save yourself?"

John barely kept the sigh from escaping his lips; now was not the time to take up the subject of what constituted appropriate Christine behavior. "Thomas, I have traveled with Haifata Adan for many weeks, and whatsoever he has done he's always done as the will of the One. I trust his judgment implicitly. Can you trust me enough to honor his choice and mine until we are out of danger and may speak of this more fully?"

"I will have nothing to do with killing or with those who would condone it!"

"Nor will I ask you to, Thomas. Now, we must catch up with the others; let us go."

John stepped aside, motioning him ahead. Thomas glared for a long moment more before moving on, the promise that they would speak further on this matter plain on his face. Perhaps Didymus *has* a lost twin, John thought exasperatedly, remembering the other Thomas's stubbornness as he followed the Corinthian.

The four moved slowly, even though the soldiers were, at most, a quarter-hour away; Adan quickly and efficiently weighed every step in an attempt to minimize noise. John took consolation in the notion that the soldiers had probably been told how long it would take to find the coppice Baremna had no doubt *seen*. Hopefully, they had no real expectation of finding the four in this part of the forest, despite their careful search.

Thomas traded places with Erezavan, since his knowledge might help them find paths that would facilitate their escape; they walked one half-hour, then part of another before John called a halt and gathered in Isvant to again assess the soldiers' position.

They grew still, each extending his awareness into the night. Their pursuers now ranged behind them, still heading toward the grove they'd rested in. Another consolation: since Baremna was not with them, once they discovered the copse was empty, they would have to find the fugitives' trail without the seer's guidance. John wondered at Baremna's absence from the search party as he opened his eyes and they continued forth; had he been the officer in charge, he would surely have brought the Persian along. Could it be the patrol leader did not trust the foreign seer's ability? Such would not be surprising, considering Baremna's belief that no one truly respected what a great spiritual light he was.

Ah well, whatever the cause of his absence, John was disinclined to complain about it. The soldiers would not find them, not this night...

Sudden alarm overtook John's burgeoning relief as Erezavan gasped his own dismay; he sniffed the air and hastily extended his focus.

Though blocked from sight by trees and shrubbery, another squad of soldiers walked directly toward them, no more than two hundred yards away. Only the one in front held a torch, but just enough of its acrid smell had floated forth to make their presence known. John instantly looked ahead to warn Adan, but the African, with his hunter's sensibilities, had already heard their rustling approach. He stepped into the deeper shadows, his spear at the ready, and went as still as one of the trees. Erezavan gripped his dead torch like a club. John reluctantly shifted his own stance, walking staff ready. Thomas looked from one to the other of them, appalled.

"This is wrong, wrong! The Christos was a man of peace; we must not harm these others! Elder, will you not tell them to lower their weapons?" he asked pleadingly; but before John could ask Adan if they could escape without being detected, Thomas made up his mind. "I will turn myself over to the soldiers and distract them so you can get away," he said.

Then he made the word deed.

"Thomas, no!" John rasped after him, but the Corinthian was already crashing through the bushes and calling to the soldiers not to strike, he was unarmed. John started forward in the hope of stopping him, but Adan grabbed his arm.

"The soldiers will not believe he travels alone, brother. They will look for the rest of us when he reaches them. We must go now, or they will surely capture us."

They heard the startled yells of the soldiers, the clatter of swords being drawn and Thomas again calling to them not to strike.

They ran.

Though it seemed to John the time for stealth was past, Haifata admonished him and Erezavan to stay as directly in his wake as they could in their haste to be away. John marveled at the African: though he knew this forest no better than the two who followed him, when it came to negotiating the unknown terrain he was very much his own sort of seer. He seemed fully aware of which branches might create noise enough to attract a pursuer's attention, which stones would slow their progress or leave a trail, and he avoided them all. An hour, perhaps a bit less, should be all we need, John hoped, knowing the soldiers would be hindered in their chase by armor and swords.

He entered the Stillness and ran his body through the darkness, heedless of limitations of strength, stamina or perception. Nor need he take concern for Erezavan or Haifata. Mystery school adepts of Isvant's sort routinely learned to cede control of the body to Spirit and perform prodigious feats of strength and endurance, while Haifata had more than proven he retained his abilities, long from his homeland though he was.

Allowing for the unknown topography and numerous obstacles, they ran at best speed for slightly more than a half-hour, then slowed to a jog, still making it their business to stay quiet. When they finally slowed to a walk, almost an hour had passed; by John's reckoning it was close to eleventh hour. He estimated they had covered perhaps five miles of the rough territory and were well away from both groups of soldiers. Now they needed to find a place to get their bearings and some rest.

"There," Haifata said, pointing. It was another copse, one of real trees, not tall bushes, though there were bushes enough thrown in. It didn't offer the concealment of the one they'd stayed in earlier, but it would have to do. Adan walked the inside edge of the circle the trees and bushes formed as if looking for something specific, while John and Erezavan unslung their packs, loosed their knotted robes and sank to the damp ground.

A few moments later, the African joined them, his expression troubled.

"I hoped to find some sign of where we might be. Thomas told me of landmarks we should seek if we were separated, but I see nothing of which he spoke."

"Can the sky tell us where we are?" Erezavan asked, but his voice said he knew the answer was "No". The trees made it impossible to define their position by stargazing. John shook his head, realized they could not see his expression in the darkness.

"As Thomas pointed out, this is not an overwhelmingly large forest. And we have tools beyond those of mere physical reckoning with which to find our way. No, I am not especially concerned that we no longer have a guide to lead us...but I am concerned about the fate that guide has met trying to keep us from harm."

The three men prepared a small, cold meal in silence, each kept by the company of his own thoughts; when they settled down to rest, John again allowed his consciousness to extend outward.

Suddenly, with no transition at all between being within himself and being outside, he again occupied a large portion of the forest; he noticed, among other things, a small stream off to his left where many animals gathered. He became aware of two feelings as he perused the area around him: satisfaction at the realization that he already need not turn his awareness as deeply inward as before to detect the soldiers' presence...and mild disappointment at his abrupt shifts from "here" to "there". While he'd only experienced such during his experience in Hiram bar Abiel's inn, Miriam's expression of the same talent usually included consciously expanding into the world, like a bird taking flight: "With each flap of her wings, the world grows larger and larger, until she sees all of it in every direction."

Though it was useless to compare how their talents manifested, John still found himself wishing he had Miriam's sort of experience; it might prove to have advantages his way of *seeing* did not. Still, since their frantic run had put their pursuers far enough outside his range of vision that even if they knew what area to search, they'd not find them for some time, he could not complain too much.

Instead, he turned his attention more completely inward, enjoying the knowledge that all was well despite his surface mind's continuing clatter and clamor. John smiled:

no, experiencing the Silence did not always mean the mind *was* silent, but it did mean he could simply watch its blathering without *having* to act on its urgings.

Thomas's maneuver was at the forefront of the chatter that sporadically barged into his mind. The plethora of ideas the Corinthian had about correct Christine behavior constantly interfered with his realization of the very knowledge he sought. John found himself wondering if they, more than altruism, had guided his choice...but then, he'd wondered about that more than once in the last several years. In his experience, at least as many Christines used self-sacrifice to become worthy of the Grace God forever offered as gave naught but lip service to the Way in the hope that the universe would somehow be fooled. Either way, they were ignorant of the truth: that *they* were the Universe and required neither fooling nor bargaining with. After all, could God fail to give a gift that already lived in their hearts?

Not that all who chose such sacrifices did so from that mindset, he knew. But for those ones, like his brother, the sacrifice had in truth been no sacrifice at all. Interestingly, not one witness to James's execution had mentioned the blood and horror; they'd remembered only the light that shone from him even as his soul was forced from its home. James knew the body was naught but the One's tool, while Being was everything, and like Jeshua, he'd shared that truth despite Death's efforts to negate it, not to make his "valueless" self worthy of Heaven. Those who thought otherwise, like Thomas, missed the true point of his and Jeshua's lives—and deaths—in the most wasteful of ways.

"Brother, it is time we went on."

John opened his eyes. Haifata stood above him, his robe again kilted for travel; he came to his feet and adjusted his own robe while the African roused Erezavan. The Persian stood and stretched, then bounced around a bit, shaking his arms as if to get the chill of second hour's air out of his bones.

John hoisted his water skin onto his shoulder and realized it was less than a quarter full. Though he was glad for the lack of weight, especially in light of what their journey had been thus far, he knew he'd be wishing for its bulk once daylight came. With that in mind, he pointed Haifata toward the stream he had *seen* earlier. It was slightly off their desired trail, yes, but going there now would be worth their trouble later.

They made their way through the darkness as quietly as they had before their sprint to safety, heard the raucous laughter of the brook long before they reached it. When they came to the stream itself, Erezavan, whose water skin dangled in a way that showed it had been empty for some time, started to rush forward—but Adan restrained him. They heard no untoward noises that might betray the presence of unwanted company, nor even the normal sounds of the night's creatures; they'd all gone silent as the strangers approached their habitat. Or so John hoped.

When they again began to chatter and chirp, Haifata nodded them forth to quickly fill their skins—but as they turned back in the direction they wanted to go, a glimpse of what John thought was a figure flashed at the periphery of his vision.

"Did you see that?" he said, grabbing at Haifata's arm.

The African looked sharply around, spear held high, and Erezavan raised his knife, but it was evident neither of them had seen the apparition.

"Let us be away from so exposed a place," Adan said, hastily following his own advice.

They walked in tense silence, looking about as if they expected attack at any moment. Finally, Adan called a halt and went back into listening mode. He shook his head.

"Whatever it may have been, it is gone now. Either that, or we are being hunted by a tracker of extraordinary stealth."

"Let us hope it is the first and not the last," Erezavan said fervently.

"It may be it was only some creature who was frightened away from its watering hole by the strange animals, Haifata," John said apologetically. "After all, I saw it for less than a second and only out of the corner of my eye. Certainly, I do not now sense any presence beyond our own, and I have been diligently looking for such this half hour and more."

The African shrugged. "We are all tired from the last several days' events, brother; perhaps our minds are showing us ghosts of what we fear to find. Still, better that we speak of those ghosts than find they are real when we least desire to do so."

They continued to the northeast, pushing through the extra darkness the leaves provided as they blocked out the stars above. John repeatedly looked over his shoulder and even stopped, worriedly thinking he'd heard someone approaching from the stream. But of course, nothing followed.

Perhaps we are tired enough to be hallucinating sights and sounds John thought as he stopped yet one more time. Then he muffled an ironic chuckle as he turned to continue his walk. He'd been about to tell himself he was never prone to such things.

"Stop," he said suddenly. Night it might still be in the forest, but John now stood in Mary's garden with broad daylight blazing all around him. Surprisingly, he could clearly see Haifata and Erezavan, but wondered if they could hear him, since it was certain they saw not what he did.

"Oh, they hear you well enough," a smiling voice said slightly off to his right. "And this is not *Mary's* garden. Or certainly not Mary's alone."

The woman sounded a great deal like Mary, but there were enough differences in timbre and intonation that John knew it wasn't. He turned, curious...then quickly walked to where the speaker stood. He deferentially reached out with the intent of kissing her hand, but the woman smilingly snatched it away like a young girl who fears a boy's touch will somehow contaminate her.

"I think enough unnecessary homage has been paid to those who have gone before, don't you, young bar Zebedee? At least, that is what you told that lovely little flower of yours in Corinth, no?" The woman's smile broadened. "You treat the mother of the Son with enough familiarity; feel free to treat her mother in the same manner."

Anna of the House of Joachim peered impishly up at John, her pleasure at seeing him evident. Her resemblance to her daughter was more that of a sister's: this was no crotchety old woman he beheld. Though her eyes and hair were darker than Mary's and she was a touch shorter, they had, as young women, had the same physical dimensions— dimensions no man worth his virility would ever have called "unsightly". More, the fullness of Self that shone from Anna's countenance compounded the physical beauty she'd known in her prime as wife, mother, and adept in the way of the One. If Mary seemed always joyful, Anna's radiant bliss belonged to Infinity Itself.

Oddly, John had never met Jeshua's grandmother during her sojourn on earth; the few times their Teacher had gone to see the then-agéd woman, he'd sent the sons of Zebedee to their own mother to attend to whatever family matters they might have. In one case, that family matter turned out to be their father's birthday, which both the young men had forgotten in the excitement of being Jeshua's companions. Though, of course, he'd hidden his pleasure under his usual crusty exterior, Old Zebedee had instantly and delightedly assembled a neighborhood-wide celebration...and John had acquired the second hangover of his life.

Anna looked John up and down, her perusal seeming to miss nothing. Her smile expanded as her inspection came to his chin. "You *are* far more handsome when you stop hiding your face behind all that hair, you know."

"Umph. You have not called me here to speak of my lack of facial hair," John said brusquely, still annoyed by his beard's willful refusal to grow back. Anna merely chuckled.

"This is true enough, my son. The news I bring is of a far more serious nature," she said, not sounding very serious about it at all. "The Athenian authorities know of your escape from Corinth, courtesy of their spies in that city."

"How can that be?" John said, his consternation plain. "*We* have known of our escape for less than a day."

Anna's eyes twinkled with amusement. "Pigeons, well-bred and well trained, can carry information very quickly, dear one. Be that as it may, the Athenian Governor, like Corinth's, seeks to gain the credit for bringing you to heel and has sent enough soldiers in this direction to see that his desire is carried out. I, therefore, have come to speed your journey to the relative safety of Ephesus."

"What of Haifata and Erezavan?" His two companions stared at him with the puzzled concern that showed they could only hear his end of the conversation. "Since they cannot hear you, I need at least to tell them what we are doing."

Anna rolled her eyes in an all-too-familiar manner. "John! Will they not trust you to go where you must, as they have trusted you so far? Yes, they will. Now come, we have no time to lose."

John followed, aware that if the mother was even a third as stubborn as her daughter and grandson, arguing further would be pointless.

He couldn't tell if they went fast or slow, for he now walked in the broad, eternal, spring of the garden. He breathed in the riotous splendor of roses, lilies, sunflowers and many others he had no names for, espying colors on the ground and in the sky that were both familiar and impossible. He explained to Haifata and Erezavan what was happening and asked what they experienced—softly, of course. Whatever it might look like to him, their would-be captors still wandered in the forest his companions walked in.

"You truly cannot see the woman who walks beside me?" John asked at last, amazed that such a thing could be in light of Anna's magnificence. Both hesitated, as if they had difficulty finding words.

"I sense...something, Rabbi...a great Power, walking with us," Erezavan slowly replied. "But I could not have pinpointed its source if you had not said where it was. It feels as if it fills the whole forest, like my eyes see more clearly into the darkness because of it."

"I, too, feel a change in the air around us," Adan agreed, "but it has no position. It reminds me of a fast I took as a boy, when I felt for a while as if I walked both on the earth and with the gods...as if I was neither here nor there." The African shook his head, as if he felt his explanation was inadequate, but made no further attempt to elaborate.

Anna gazed admiringly at the two men. "Your companions have chosen you well, Boanerge. Surely they are worthy of this journey."

"They are that, Mother. I have been truly blessed."

The two of them walked along the garden path companionably, John taking note of—or "floating within" was a better way to describe it—everything the vision that now surrounded him revealed as they talked. This was the longest chance he'd had to truly appreciate the awe-inspiring sights, sounds and even smells of this realm.

"You are becoming more acclimated to being in two or more places at one time," Anna said when he mentioned it.

John raised his brows in surprise. "Am I in two places, then? Even though I can clearly see and communicate with Haifata and Erezavan?"

"Oh, yes. The vibrations of your earthly body and this one are beginning to match. That makes it possible for you to stay here for longer periods without suffering the fatigue and disorientation that plagued you in Caesarea and Corinth. That is not yet true of all the places you might go to, but it will become so, both as the need presents itself and as you let go the idea that you need do anything with your experiences or being."

Before John could ask what she could possibly mean—he found he had many questions about why his awareness and abilities still seemed to fluctuate so—Anna halted.

"This is where we part, dear one. You will be able to clearly see the path as long as you need to; not much farther, as it happens."

"Will I see you again, Mother?" John asked, sorely disappointed their time together was ending. Anna smiled so brilliantly that John's heart could not but reflect her joy; she took his hands and kissed each one as if he were her Elder, not the other way around. When she looked into his eyes, he clearly saw the origins of Mary's impishness.

"While I cannot say if you will see me again, my son—for that is ever up to you—know always that you are welcome in my house as if it is your own...since it is." She released his hands and turned toward Erezavan and Haifata. "Go safely, my sons, and trust always that the One leads you where you are most needed."

The men nodded as if they heard her perfectly. And perhaps they do, John thought wonderingly, for his companions' faces literally brightened as the light of Anna's Fullness briefly leaked from her world into theirs. John could easily believe sharing her ecstasy had been her greatest gift to others in her life on earth as well as in this realm.

"Let the blessings that you are in the One be ever with you, dear one, and know that Heaven is well-pleased. Be safe, John bar Zebedee, and go well."

John blinked as he again found himself standing in the darkness of the forest, but he could see the trail they must follow as clearly as if it was lit by light from the garden.

"Our way to safety is not long, brothers," he said to Adan and Isvant with a smile. "Perhaps we will have the chance to get some real rest before we continue on."

They still walked cautiously, but with a sense of confidence that had earlier been missing. The trail of light stretched between and stopped at the end of a channel of trees that were as neatly lined up as if a gardener had planted them thus a hundred years before. Relief washed over John as he noted the slightly lighter blackness of a starlit night sky at the end of the row; beyond that lay the safety Anna had promised. He smiled as the three made their way quickly and quietly to the end of the pathway.

Straight into an ambush of waiting Roman soldiers.

TWENTY-FOUR

Before *he could* do more than cry out an inarticulate warning, strong hands wrenched John's arms painfully back and cold steel pressed against his throat. Erezavan was likewise subdued, his knife bouncing soundlessly to the soft ground before he could raise it in defense. John didn't struggle; though he felt sure he'd come to no harm, prize that he was, he wanted to do nothing to precipitate his companions' abrupt exit into the next world.

Haifata Adan, however, had no intention of going quietly into captivity. He let loose a bellowing cry, freezing the soldiers long enough to let him spin from their grasps and back against a nearby tree. As his would-be captors surrounded him, he effortlessly snapped off a forearm-thick branch with an echoing crack, shortened his grip and stomped on the trailing half of his spear, breaking it off to something closer to sword's length, and sneered a savage, smiling challenge that dared the soldiers to come closer.

The soldiers did not rush the African; indeed, some of them actually backed up a step in surprise. This was not the usual weak, cowardly Christine, but a man warrior-bred and more than ready to fight.

"Hold! We've not come to arrest you, Elder, but to help! You men! Lower your swords!"

The voice spoke from somewhere off to John's left, and it was a second before he realized the last order was meant for the soldiers. They too, seemed unsure and hesitated to comply, desiring not at all to lower their weapons in the presence of one so plainly adept and so willing to prove it.

"I said, lower—your—weapons—now!" the voice repeated, and his tone promised they would answer to his sword if they did not immediately obey.

After a moment more of warily eyeing the African, the men did so—but none of them relaxed their stances too much. Adan did not lower his weapons, but after an eternally long moment, he relaxed ever so slightly and nodded almost imperceptibly.

The sword at John's throat withdrew; his arms were released so abruptly he almost staggered. He turned, thinking to ask several pertinent questions, but at that moment, one of the soldiers who'd not been after Adan stepped forth and removed his helm. John loosed a breath he didn't realize he was holding and clasped his arm delightedly.

"Thomas! Well met! We thought you lost."

"As did I," their erstwhile guide said, his usually dour countenance lighting as Erezavan clasped his arm in greeting. "But thanks be to the Christos, all is well now. Elder, Captain Iscariotus and his men are Christines; they've come to help us get to Ephesus. You must listen to him." He motioned to the stocky commander.

"Well met, Elder, good sirs. Thanks be you came upon us and not some of our fellows." Captain Amadeon Iscariotus gave a short, formal bow as he spoke, his voice reminding John of small rocks being shaken together in a leather cup.

John returned the courtesy while managing to keep his eyebrows from rising in surprise; was that surname common in this part of the world, or was the One's odd sense of humor again in play?

"My apologies for causing you undue distress," the Captain continued, "but we felt it easiest to get you under our auspices first and give explanations later."

"Well met, Captain Iscariotus. We, too, are most glad to have come upon you." Though we had some help, John thought, realizing at last why the soldiers they'd earlier come upon had at first gone undetected. He was glad Anna's promise had been fulfilled, but annoyed she'd not warned them their salvation would come in so unexpected a form.

Then his eyes flicked to where Adan warily stood, back still against the tree, and his budding irritation faded. Anna's reasons for such a strategy might very soon come clear.

"Captain, I have many questions, as I am sure you do...but ..."

Iscariotus's eyes followed John's. He nodded, again gave his short, formal bow and turned to speak to one of his men. Adan lowered his weapons as John approached, but his eyes darted back and forth as if he still expected treachery.

"Brother, may I help?" John asked quietly.

Before he could clearly read the emotion Haifata turned on him, the African closed his eyes and took several deep breaths; John could literally feel the heat of his struggle peeling off his skin as he battled whatever feelings held him.

He was about to remind him to take his struggle to the One...but at that moment, Haifata opened his eyes, dropped both the branch and his broken spear and stood to his full height. He turned his usual unreadable stare on John, utterly relaxed; the roaring ferocity which had filled the entire glade but a second before was gone as if one moment had suddenly been replaced with one that belonged not at all to the scene it now filled.

John summoned up a smile and clasped his friend's shoulder, but as they made their way back to the Captain, his thoughts were troubled. While he wanted to believe Adan had simply dropped into the Stillness to produce this sudden change, he had a strong suspicion, bordering on certainty, that he hadn't. The African had by no means let his emotions flow through and dissipate naturally. Yet no trace of their existence remained in his expression—or his life-force. Adan had mentioned when they met that he'd walked a Way many of his people followed; could that be the source of his sudden shift? Certainly, the calm he'd just called forth showed such might be the case.

And yet, what if it was not? What if, because of his need to survive in a world that considered him wholly expendable, Adan had simply grown better than Darshinika Baremna at quashing his more ignoble emotions? John knew Haifata would never intentionally endanger his companions, was even inclined to attribute his uneasiness to his recent experiences with Baremna.

But, what if, at some critical moment, Adan proved to be more danger than help?

Though John had seen the phenomenon for years now, the many different kinds of people Jeshua's teachings attracted still never ceased to amaze him. If his face clearly showed his history, Captain Amadeon Iscariotus, like Joses Matthatus, was a man who'd long ago renounced his interest in the fanciful. God Himself might impress Iscariotus, but not much else would...not unless it had a practical use. Not, mind, that he struck John as unimaginative. Rather, it seemed as if the need to survive, both on the battlefield and in the Empire's political arenas, had left him no time to waste on awe.

Yet, here stood this gravelly-voiced, sensible soldier, acclaimed by Thomas as a Christine and lover of Jeshua's Way. Though he'd been openly Christine almost from the time of Jeshua's crucifixion—over fifteen years—he was also considered a brave and intelligent officer, one trusted with the Emperor's business.

"I was just telling the others that we have clothing enough among us to disguise you as soldiers," Iscariotus said when John and Haifata joined him, Erezavan, Thomas, and two of his officers, "but I did not know you would have an African with you. I fear you will be somewhat hard to disguise," he said, granting Adan the same courtesy of speaking directly to him as he would any other freeman.

"You have charge over a full cohort of men, do you not?" Adan asked.

"Two," one of his lieutenants said, earning a stare from Iscariotus.

"Yet, you have no manservant to do your bidding?"

"Mmm," Iscariotus answered, his face thoughtful. "While it would be somewhat unusual to bring a manservant along on so short a foray, such things are not unheard of." The "unfortunately", though unspoken, was clear in the lifelong-soldier's tone.

Adan shrugged. "Then I am now your manservant."

Becoming soldiers was the work of only a few minutes for Erezavan and John, once they created a proper cowl with which to camouflage Adan. The short sword at John's hip felt strange to him; he'd never had cause to carry any metal weapon heavier than a knife. And I shall have to carve a new walking staff once we reach Ephesus, he thought, with a bit of regret for leaving behind the one he'd used for years.

The men were soon on the move, making their way to the main road the companions had so diligently sought to avoid, for "It will make us less conspicuous, one squad of soldiers among many," as Iscariotus put it.

"The Governor got word of your presence quickly, but we had no idea of exactly who you were," he said to John. "So he sent us along to Corinth at a high city official's request—not Governor Talun's, mind you—to help subdue any lingering unrest. Our true orders, of course, were to fetch 'this important Christine personage and bring him back to Athens for interview and subsequent transport to Rome'. I've no doubt if you hadn't made your escape, Talun would have 'lost' you by the time we arrived."

Though it wasn't unheard of for Roman soldiers to be Christines, John had never known of one so highly ranked and said so. Iscariotus nodded.

"I was stationed in Galilee two years before the Christos began to preach and stayed until the last few months of his life," he explained. "In all honesty, his words appealed not at all to my soldier's mind; to me his calls to 'turn the other cheek' in the face of abuse belonged to a coward. Even so, something about the man intrigued me, for I also sensed a great strength in him. It caused me no end of confusion, I can tell you."

"I can well imagine," John chuckled, thinking of Marcus Prochorus.

"So, I attended to stories of his activities and saw him in person whenever the opportunity presented itself, that I might understand the paradox he presented."

"And your opinion changed as time went on?"

Iscariotus smiled slightly. "Better to say I became willing to consider that he might know of what he spoke. I was not convinced his way had any practical merit, however, until I got word of a healing. You see, I knew Quinton Jairus and his girl, Eliae."

"Ah..."

"Yes. And that swayed me, I can tell you. We'd served together on many campaigns and he is as hardheaded as I am. If Quin confirmed the stories, they could only be true. Still, it was not until after I heard the details of the Christos's trial and death that I knew his Way was the way I would—and should—walk. He carried no sword, true, but that one most assuredly knew what it was to be a warrior."

The two men walked on, their conversation easily moving through many subjects. Iscariotus was a man of good breeding, a minor noble who'd gained his title through his own merits, for his family had been poor and plain-born. In the last decade and more, he'd managed to discreetly disseminate the Christine view—John found that, in Iscariotus's case, he tended to think of it as "Jeshua's Way", for unlike Thomas, he seemed to understand its true Spirit—to hundreds of people, largely through simply living it. In fact, many of his men had come to embrace it.

"I admire your success in balancing the two different ways of life, particularly considering the current climate," John said at last.

"Oh, do not think I have not had my trials, Elder, especially recently. Still, I have had an easy time of it, all in all, largely, I think, because I do not experience the tenets of Empire and the Christine Way as conflicting."

"Indeed?"

"No. As I mentioned before, I had the privilege of actually seeing the Christos when he still walked the earth—indeed, I must have seen you with him at least once! His manner with those around him was worthy of the best generals I have served under. Like them, he drew out his followers' excellence by consistently and earnestly giving of his, and I have done my best to model my actions after what I saw in him. Yes, I can clearly see that Rome and Christ have much of the best in common and need not be separate."

"Yours is an unusual stance, Amadeon Iscariotus."

Yes, it is. But I know it to be true, right here," he pointed at his heart. "I know this Way can only help my people achieve the greatest heights. No, it has not always been easy. I've had subordinates and superiors both question my loyalty, and more than one has sought to bring me low as a traitor to the Empire. Yet, never have they had true reason to even accuse, much less convict me." His hazel eyes twinkled with sudden, wry amusement as they met John's.

"Until today."

They stopped to rest just as the Sun decided to remove his shroud of Night and bless the earth with his brilliance for yet another day. John was glad of the respite; he felt as if he'd either been walking or running for the last thousand years. He, Erezavan and Thomas removed their helms with sighs of relief, glad to again feel the flow of air against their scalps. Iscariotus apologized for the necessity, explaining that soldiers in the Athenian garrison all wore their hair cut short; his own close-cropped, steel-gray mane was barely an inch long. The three kept their helmets nearby as the soldiers parceled out the morning meal, but Iscariotus's ten men, all Christines, seemed too much in awe of John to comfortably engage in their usual soldierly banter.

"How is it you found us so quickly? Last night, that is?" Thomas asked Iscariotus. "And how did you—" he nodded toward John, Erezavan and Haifata, "—find us?"

Iscariotus did not answer, but looked at the dark-haired man sitting to his left. Though considerably younger than his captain, his pale gray eyes held the look of one who'd seen many campaigns. He favored Iscariotus, but was not the Captain's son; he'd introduced himself as Lieutenant Egnatius Titus. Perhaps a sister's son or cousin?

Whatever he might be, he was not comfortable with the others' sudden scrutiny. Titus flushed discomfittedly; his demeanor, in that moment at least, was not at all like the raging confidence John was so used to seeing in the average Roman officer. He did not quite mumble his answer, but it was not for lack of trying.

"The Lady told us where you would be, and I told Captain Iscariotus."

"The Lady?" John asked, his interest suddenly sharp.

The Lieutenant's blush deepened, but his voice grew stronger. "For several years now, the Lord has blessed my faith by sending to me a woman who advises me about what is coming and what I must do. She comes only when I most need her guidance, never when I merely want it out of laziness," he added hastily, as if he thought John might judge such idleness. "At first, I was wary of her presence, fearing she might be some sort of siren trying to entice me from the narrow Way. But when I told her my fears, she solemnly promised in the Christos's name that if I would trust her, she would never lead me amiss; that by my faith, my Gift would always help others.

"Since then, the Lady has saved my life in situations that not just seemed, but were hopeless; last night, she directed us to the glade you met us in, and of course, I could not but follow." Titus's gray eyes suddenly flashed with defiance. "Is this not what the Christos would have, Elder? Did he not say all would someday do as he did?"

John smiled. "He did indeed—I was there when he said it. Obviously, Lieutenant, your faith in your right to know beyond what eye and ear alone may show you has been well-rewarded. More, my companions and I have been blessed by the strength of your trust, for I am sure it was your 'Lady' who led us to you."

Titus bowed his head at the acknowledgement.

After that, the soldiers were much less shy, their awe, if not abated, at least temporarily overcome by their curiosity about Jeshua. John resignedly set aside his idea of closing his eyes for few moments and answered questions until Iscariotus announced they'd be moving out, with the objective of reaching the main road before tenth hour.

The party departed the glade, taking at a pace that, while not strenuous, was by no means ambling. John again spent a good deal of time talking to Iscariotus about a variety of things, including the politics of the Christines' current state of affairs.

"This will be the way of things for a while, I fear," Iscariotus shrugged, "for some among us have not sense enough to know when to step forth and when to stand quietly."

"And you believe you do?" John asked.

Iscariotus snorted. "Not I! I keep no crystal ball at hand to know the mind of Caesar and his advisors. Nor do I claim any greater knowledge than my brothers about how to spread the Christos's message abroad. Still, I have eyes to see. Too many Christines act like children who stick a sharp stick in a strange dog's side, then call themselves martyrs when the dog bites. From what Titus says of the Lady and how she speaks to him, I have come to believe such was not what the Christos desired for his followers."

"Yet, you as a soldier know one must sometimes sacrifice one appearance of good to make room for another. Is that not what many Christines are doing?" John asked, aware he was taking the role of devil's advocate. Iscariotus's nod was thoughtful.

"Yes, some are, and with pure hearts. I myself would risk life and limb for what I know if I were so called—in fact, I have. But I also see many who act for the sake of defying Rome or family; or worse, for the sake of gaining the kind of prestige and glory the Christos himself shunned as vain. I cannot tell you why the difference in motive should make a difference, but it does. And my gut tells me selfish motives will ultimately cause more harm than good, even should the Christos's Word spread throughout the world."

John nodded and wondered if Iscariotus realized just how farsighted his assessment was. In fact, he wondered if *he* realized it.

By the time they came to the main road, John had spoken with each of Iscariotus's men. All spoke eloquently of their reasons for following their captain into the Christine Way, and the stories and insights that came of living lives so different from John's own fascinated him. After speaking with the last of the soldiers, the son of a Senator with only eighteen summers, he drifted to the back of the group, where Haifata Adan walked alone.

"You have been very quiet, brother."

"It is not my way to speak much before strangers until I better know their ways."

"That is not what I mean."

Since the near-battle in the glade and the discovery that the soldiers were allies, not enemies, the African had been withdrawn, even sitting apart from the others during the meal. On any other man, it would have been sulking—and on Adan it was utterly unnatural.

"Tell me what you know, brother," he said, his voice matching his small, grim, smile.

"...I know you were, and are still, greatly disappointed at not doing battle with these men; that you contemplated taking the fight to them even after we knew them to be friends," John answered, matching Adan tone for tone. "I know now, as I did not before, that your desire to take vengeance on Rome is so large that it fills you, bones and guts and gullet. That taking such vengeance is the greatest, perhaps the only true wish you have for whatever is left of your life.

"And I know, Haifata, that such a desire is a waste."

To one who had not come to know him, it might seem that Adan still held to his quiet, calm center as he always did; yet John knew it was not so. The African's eyes briefly met his before turning to look out into the forest...and this time John recognized the absolute despair he had earlier missed as he faced him in the glade.

"You spoke to Marcus of his wife and child's deaths by illness," he said at last. "Such a thing strikes a man to the core, brother. It leaves a hole in his center he can never fill. For good or ill, he feels always that he could and should have acted...but did not do enough. Better to die than be cursed with living when those you love have been lost so.

"How much the worse is it, then, to lose not just your wife and children, but your mother, your father, your sisters, brothers and cousins—all those you swore to protect and prosper? How much the worse when all you loved is destroyed or taken away and you alone still live, a slave in the midst of those who caused it? How much the worse, brother, to watch and wait, year after year, for your chance to give back to the monster what he gave to you...only to find you cannot become that which made him destroy and rend?" Adan looked at John with hollow, haunted eyes.

"How much the worse is it to know yourself to be a king who has become a coward?"

John wanted to reach out, to show some sign of the deep sorrow he felt on his friend's behalf—but he couldn't. Whatever his heart might feel, he knew any gesture of sympathy would be wholly inadequate to the task of assuaging his friend's pain; would in some obscure way actually be an insult.

In truth, John could in no way imagine the extent to which Adan had suffered. Yes, he'd lost James and Jeshua and far too many others to Rome's—to the phantom self's—thirst for conquest and control. But they, at least, had chosen, eyes open, to leap into the fray, and he'd had the Practice and the support of those left behind to see him through the hardest times. What must it be like to know you were the last of your people, to know you'd been spared because you were the last and the strongest?

John could have cried for the insistence glistening in Haifata's eyes that whatever was left of his reason for living was futile...but their conversation about the Practice of Compassion from the night before echoed in his mind. Though his tone was gentle when he at last spoke, his words were not.

"My brother, best you should decide which is more important: wallowing in your failure to exact the vengeance your dead past calls for, or continuing on this journey. For you cannot have both. If you truly feel your life will complete itself only if you avenge people who no longer care about vengeance, then part with us now and go with my blessing. Or, you can accept that your unwillingness to do battle with these ones who are our allies comes not from cowardice, but from your soul's knowledge of your true purpose.

"I care not which road you choose, Haifata, so long as it fulfills your heart...but we cannot have men on this journey who would waver from the path to kill old ghosts."

Adan's sharp intake of breath and frozen stance told John his consciousness had suddenly and catastrophically turned inward. Just as he had no doubt done in thoughts and dreams a thousand, ten thousand times before, this man who had once been a prince among his people yet again relived the abomination of destruction, rapine and death visited upon his village.

But this time, another stood with him, as none ever had before.

John watched Adan fall into the devastation of his grief, then watched the One in his heart pull him out of the madness a lesser man would have chosen to live within forever. He saw Haifata Adan dive into the Stillness he'd always held, and almost, almost become the greater Wholeness he himself sensed in the African.

Yet, even as he watched, John wondered. Would Haifata now choose to give up his desire to bring death and destruction to Rome, and in so doing discard the hopelessness that dogged his every step?

No, he would not.

John felt a rush of disappointment as Adan quite consciously chose to push the Wholeness away so he would not forget his desire for revenge; as he chose his wish to get even over knowing peace... And yet, there was something odd about the refusal. Just as when he'd suddenly shifted his emotions earlier, something about this choice felt strange and incomplete. It was as if Adan only took on the veneer of rejecting the Wholeness—but such a thing was impossible.

John suddenly knew understanding his connection with this man was important, perhaps even vital to what he sought. He tried to reach for the understanding, to take hold of what it might mean, but it slipped away, fading into the Silence to hide once more.

Adan shuddered once, his body rattling as if it would cause the Earth herself to follow suit. His eyes refocused and locked on John's.

"The others are waiting for us."

John nodded; there was nothing more to say. Adan had chosen life enough to continue the journey to Vashti, but both knew the battle was not over, only suspended.

Or was it?

They met two other squads on the road, and as Iscariotus had thought likely, their leaders, both lieutenants, spoke only to him or Titus, ignoring the rest of the men. In order to maintain the façade of searching for John and his companions, Iscariotus's men periodically examined those civilians they came upon, even searching a small merchant's caravan to make sure they hid no fugitives amongst the cloth bolts they transported to Athens for sale to the wives of the city's rich men. As they neared the forest's halfway point, three soldiers entered the roadway several yards ahead. Iscariotus stopped in the middle of a story and frowned as a tired, grizzled centurion approached.

"These men are not from Athens, but Corinth," he said warningly; then, as John nodded and made himself less conspicuous: "What news?" he called.

"None, sir," the centurion answered disgustedly, giving the barest of salutes. "We've squads throughout the entire area as far out as the stream to the west. They saw signs of the fugitives, but they've eluded all searches, even though between us there must be a full cohort out here. It is as if the gods themselves make them invisible to our eyes."

"If you have not found them, why are you here on the roadway?" Iscariotus asked in a tone that suggested he thought their appearance here a breach. The crusty veteran only shrugged.

"The Persian told us to come here. He seems to think the fugitives have left the forest, that we waste our time continuing to search there."

"He is with your group?" John asked, hearing the crash and swish of others' approach even as he asked. The centurion barely glanced at him.

"Yes, perhaps a hundred yards behind us."

TWENTY-FIVE

John *managed not to* peer worriedly over the centurion's shoulder, but he saw Adan hastily pull the drape of his cowl farther over his face from the corner of his eye. Erezavan stood behind Haifata, his life force radiant with the fear that Baremna would suddenly appear and again betray them.

Iscariotus nodded and looked bored. "Very well; perhaps the fugitives have made their way out of the western forest. Has anyone searched the eastern side of the road?"

"You'd know better than I what the Athenian soldiers are doing, Sir. Our orders were to search the western side."

Iscariotus gestured toward John and the others, his message as plain as if he'd spoken aloud: hide yourselves quickly. What he said was, "Then perhaps it is time we did so. The fugitives may have made it to the eastern side, either by accident or design."

John only half-heard the words, for he, Adan, Thomas and Erezavan were already heading into the wood, accompanied by Titus and another of Iscariotus's men. He did not look back as he heard the sounds that told him the rest of the Corinthians and Darshinika Baremna himself were on roadway, but broke into a quick jog as soon they were out of direct sight; the corpulent Persian would surely sense Erezavan's presence if they merely hid within shouting distance of the Captain.

They stopped only when they came to the edge of a small pond and could no longer hear even the slightest sounds from the road. John beckoned Erezavan to sit, then sat himself, facing the young man. He carefully extended his awareness outward to find Baremna's consciousness sweeping the forest like a hunting dog seeking a downed pheasant; the man's awareness rode forth on the same wave of fury that had caused their parting. Even from this distance, John sensed the acrid reek of the older Persian's hatred, coupled with his arrogant assurance of this time finding his quarry.

"Close your eyes and enter as deeply into the Stillness as you can," John ordered Erezavan and Adan, and because he had no desire to frighten the others, "Pray for the Christos to conceal us from our enemies."

"Should I try to make myself invisible to Darshinika?" Erezavan whispered as the others complied.

"Absolutely not. Simply do as I say."

John took the younger man's hands, entering the Silence himself; within moments, the illimitable One at the core of his being responded by surrounding Erezavan's life force.

"An angry man quickly becomes a defeated one if you respond without anger," Jeshua had once said after yet again facing down the Pharisees. "If you cast the Truth into the heart of what an attacker thinks to be his strength, it will scatter like so many frightened hens and you will walk free and unscathed from his intent to bring harm."

John allowed the cool solidity of his knowing to extend toward Baremna's awareness but made no attempt to affect the stout Persian's consciousness directly. Though he couldn't have conceived of how to do such a thing even a day before, he now subtly matched his energy with Baremna's and slid around it, grabbing the smallest part of it as he went by. Holding to Baremna's "captured" portion and continuing to shield Erezavan, he moved a portion of his own awareness to the southwest.

Erezavan, can you follow along my trail without jarring Baremna's consciousness? he traced. He felt the younger man's affirmative and was impressed by how easily Isvant found and flowed along the silver thread that tied John's life force to his body.

When he'd placed the younger man's phantom somewhat to the east of the creek where they'd first entered the forest, John unveiled Erezavan's—and his own—presence to Baremna's.

The stench of the older man's rage flared strong as he discovered Isvant's life sign and felt John's close by; the rest of his consciousness, which sought them here in the eastern forest, veered frantically away, hurrying toward their counterfeit location. That attended to, John then wrapped a superficial overlay of Elisha bar Salem, owner of the Inn of the Seven Tales, around the rest of Erezavan's self. Baremna would have a difficult time finding them when next they stopped to rest, at least until he discovered the ruse.

John opened his eyes to find Erezavan smiling at him. To his surprise, Adan also gazed at him, and though he did not smile, the gleam in his eyes made him wonder.

"We can go back now, our prayers have been answered," he said when he got the others' attention. They started back toward the road and within a few minutes heard the call that told them it was safe to come forth. Iscariotus's gravelly voice was positively cheerful when they arrived.

"First, the Persian seated himself on the road as if someone had offered him a chair and closed his eyes. I thought he might start snoring at any second, he was still for so long, but then he jumped up and cursed, looking like a man struck dumb with shock.

"'We have been tricked!' he yelled, and hastily explained that you were doubling back to Corinth, no doubt with the intent of making your way to Cenchreae to leave by ship. They practically ran atop each other trying to get down the road."

John nodded. "We should have the rest of the day before they realize their folly, if they do. Even so, best we should depart from here and continue toward Athens quickly. Darshinika Baremna is by no means as foolish as he chooses to pretend."

"Perhaps not, but do not depend on the centurion believing that once he realizes they really have been tricked. There is no love between those two."

Iscariotus's assessment was apparently accurate, for the group traveled the rest of the road to Athens without incident. They maintained a soldierly jog as they passed through several small-to-medium glades, a jog which, though he'd neither soldier's nor adept's training, Thomas gamely, if grimly, upheld.

John sighed. The Christine's act of heroism had surprised him as much as it shocked his companions. Truly, he'd grown enormously on this journey, for he'd discovered he had more courage than he'd ever have believed. Still, the Corinthian tended to do what he *thought* was right; he'd literally rather harm himself for propriety's sake than listen to the instincts that would—for instance—have told him to call for rest.

Fortunately, Iscariotus had not become a commander by being unobservant: John saw he kept a surreptitious eye on Thomas and broke pace several times so he might be spared the humiliation of fainting from exhaustion.

That night as they made camp, Titus, with worshipful demeanor, congratulated John on "so easily outwitting Baremna". John gave him only the most perfunctory of acknowledgements. Besides the discomfort he felt at being in any way worshipped, this most recent encounter had made it plain that, despite the apparent ease with which he'd fooled him, Darshinika Baremna was even more of an adept than he'd suspected.

Beneath that veneer of pomposity lived amazing depths of talent, and the strains of the last few days had forced Baremna to begin plumbing them, just as John had been so forced. Likewise, the Persian's desire to disgrace—no, destroy—John, and now Isvant, had grown and intensified, and this latest episode would only make his hatred more implacable. They had shaken him off their trail for now, true. But so long as they remained within the borders of the Empire, John had no doubt the companions would have to be wary. Their dealings with Darshinika Baremna were by no means finished.

The men at last arrived at the outskirts of Athens to stay in the home of a prominent city denizen who had the unwitting ears of many of the city's officials, while they, militant anti-Christines, had no idea of his spiritual inclinations. He welcomed both the soldiers and the companions happily, setting out an opulent repast despite the lateness of the hour; he greatly desired to hear of John's journey. Indeed, he wanted to know all about who John had been as a child, as a youth, and before and after Jeshua's sojourn.

Thankfully, gracious host that he was, he allowed his guests a day before diffidently demanding the story of their adventures.

Iscariotus and Titus stayed for dinner, but the Captain regretfully declined the offer to stay the night, citing his need to report to his superiors as soon as possible.

"Their esteem for me is not so great that I can dally a night with a rich citizen when I could just as profitably sleep in the barracks," he said ruefully. "Besides, the less attention drawn to this place, the better."

John thanked the Captain and Lieutenant, gladly bestowing upon them and their men his greatest blessings in Jeshua's name. As he watched them depart, he ruminated on the miracle that had brought them together.

If only there was enough time! he thought with regret. So *many* people he'd met on this journey would he have liked to tarry with—Sarah Matthatus, Dareios, Demeter, and especially, especially Ariadne; now he added Amadeon Iscariotus and Egnatius Titus to that list. He'd talked to both men about the nature and value of the Practice while on the road and knew that, had circumstances allowed it, neither would have missed the opportunity to learn its techniques.

But his chances of ever seeing any of them again were nonexistent.

Feeling somewhat melancholy, John lay down on his host's comfortable guest bed to take his sense of loss to the One...

...And was greatly surprised when the two soldiers returned the next morning. He was even more surprised when they announced that they'd be escorting him to Ephesus.

"But, how did you convince your superiors to let you initiate such a scheme?"

Iscariotus's rough face lit with a smile. "I told them I believed that, with the help of some of the Corinthians and perhaps even some sort of foreign magic, you'd escaped the patrols and were probably even now on your way to Ephesus. I argued that, as the commander of the mission, I should be allowed to go there and attempt to capture you before the Ephesian authorities bring you under their auspices."

"Were they not suspicious of your motives?"

"Oh, yes—so I used that as part of my argument. I insisted that because I am a Christine and so suspect in some eyes, I must be allowed to prove my loyalty. Any officer with my record would be within his rights to demand such a boon. And, since I emphasized the necessity for speed, I was allowed to depart immediately...as will we all."

They sailed from the port city of Piraeus with the turning of the tide; Iscariotus's father-in-law, also a devout Christine, owned three ships that regularly sailed the waters between Greece and Caria. They made the trip to the relative safety of Ephesus in clear, cool weather and relatively short order.

Only to find that they were expected.

To say John was astonished would have been the greatest of understatements. Captain Amadeon Iscariotus, loyal soldier of Caesar's army, devout Christine, and newly-made traitor to Rome, was as cautious as any seasoned officer would be, especially one so familiar with the political machinations that ran the Empire. He'd not even told Titus what ship they would sail on until they'd arrived at the docks to board her. Of course, Iscariotus's father-in-law and *Ares's* captain would have known; perhaps one of them had mentioned John's upcoming presence to someone else. But how could word have ever gotten to this one?

After all, he'd left Ariadne in Corinth.

John managed to shift his gaping stare from his double long enough to look more closely at the woman who stood beside her. She smiled and waved as if he'd just returned from a long fishing expedition, and though her presence explained how they knew where to find the men—and perhaps even how they'd come so quickly to Ephesus—it gave John no comfort.

What in God's name was Mary doing here? Granted, she had come to him in physical form in Corinth. Yet, now that he thought about it, that physicality, substantial though it seemed, had had to it a flavor of the ethereal, as if she'd formed her solidity out of particles of light with the express intention of dispersing them as soon as her business was done. Now, even from here, John sensed a solidity about his mother's form that spoke of permanence, as if she meant to finish living out this life just as any mortal would.

The notion both gladdened and troubled him.

John walked from the ship in a daze, his joy and trepidation setting waves of butterflies free to flutter in his stomach. He tried to smile, but was sure it looked more like a grimace; though their forest journey had left him little time to think of anything but escape, he'd had ample time to think once they boarded *Ares*.

The truth was that, mixed in with his grief and worry over leaving Ariadne to the ministrations of the soldiers, was a great deal of relief. He'd congratulated the One on Its wisdom in parting them so soon, told himself the hazards of the journey would help him forget anything but the need to focus on whatever was before him. But now that Ariadne stood before him, her night-dark eyes swallowing him up, all John's smug self-congratulations burned away like dry parchments thrown into fire.

Jeshua's Heart, what has Mary done? he thought.

He'd immediately sensed how deep Ariadne's Stillness ran when first he'd met her, of course, but her shyness had subdued the waves of power he felt flowing from her, so much so that even Marcus had made a puzzled remark about how her humble demeanor seemed, not unreal, but like a costume someone else had put on her.

That certainly wasn't the case now. John could neither deny the burgeoning power that lived at the heart of Ariadne's being or her increasing awareness of it. Mary saw his look and smiled even more broadly; as she and Ariadne closed the gap between the two groups, she slowed, giving the younger woman the chance to greet John first.

Ariadne's face lit as she stopped before John. She was a bit reserved and hesitant as she gave him a publicly proper embrace; even so, fire ran up his spine at her touch and he actually felt a moment of dizziness, so great was the sense of their life forces blending. He felt sure his hair must be standing on end.

"Well met, dear lady," he managed. He wanted to say more, but as his mind had left his mouth to fend for itself, he wisely decided to simply smile his pleasure at seeing her again and pulled her closer. How ever could he have believed being away from this one could be a good thing?

John finally stepped reluctantly back, aware that holding her too long would put his individuality in happy, mortal danger. Ariadne held to his hand a moment longer then, eyes a little wide, turned and solemnly nodded a greeting to the two soldiers. They smiled and offered chivalrous half-bows, as if they sensed her reticence to actually touch them, but Thomas, Haifata and Erezavan received enthusiastic hugs.

John turned to his mother, not at all afraid her greeting would be overly reverent.

"Well, met, my son," she said with her usual good humor as she hugged John tightly. "I trust your journey treated you well?—and I see you have acquired some new friends." She nodded a greeting to Iscariotus and Titus, all charm and smiles.

"Well met to you as well, Mother. It was indeed a good journey, though we had a few...unexpected moments...along the way." He nodded toward her undeniably corporeal form. "To see you here thus, however, makes all other surprises pale by comparison."

Mary shrugged and her smile grew impish. "There has been a small change in plans."

John made the appropriate introductions to Adan and the soldiers, amused at the surprised expression on Titus's face; he surely saw the resemblance between Mary and his "Lady". Thomas looked as if he might fall devotedly to his knees right there on the dock, and it was all John could do to stifle his chuckle at the thought of his reaction when he discovered just whose mother she really was.

"What news of the others? Did they come as well?"

"Ada and Hosea stayed in Corinth to support those who learned the first technique; and since she had not declared Timothy whole, he and Rachael stayed as well."

John grinned. "Imperious little thing, is she not?

"Yes. But you like strong women."

"It would avail me nothing not to," he laughed.

"Young Joshua waits with our host here in Ephesus to meet you," she said, and, turning to Haifata: "he seems particularly anxious to see you again, good sir. I think he has realized how much he values what you have given him these last several years and has missed you these last several days."

Adan nodded in acknowledgement, but since he'd again wedded himself to his odd calm, whether or not he was happy at Mary's news was not to be seen.

"What of Dareios and Demeter? And Torer and Prochorus?"

"Demeter and Dareios are safe enough; I made sure of that before I left," she said, and John breathed a sigh of relief. He hadn't realized how concerned he was for them until he saw Ariadne. Mary suddenly chuckled. "Torer also remains in Corinth, and I must say, the man's nerve is positively limitless. He actually went to the soldiers' quarters and introduced himself. But since he will wager on anything and take any chance to win a bet, he has become fast friends with many of them despite their previous encounter."

John laughed. Somehow, that didn't surprise him. "And Marcus?"

To his surprise, Mary's expression suddenly grew serious.

"Of Prochorus I have seen nothing. He disappeared the day you left."

"He is gone?" John couldn't have been more shocked if she'd told him Marcus was dead. A sudden sense of hurt and abandonment left a sour taste in his mouth as he realized that, after Ada and Hosea, Prochorus was the last person he would have expected to depart from their company...or would have wanted to.

Then he looked more closely at Mary. The twinkle beneath her serious mien told John there was something she wasn't saying, but her look made clear she had no intention of discussing it, not right now.

Very well; he would not argue the point. Mary undoubtedly had her reasons for choosing not to speak. But it had best be a good reason, he thought, as they made their way into Ephesus proper.

"You did not expect to find me here."

John and Ariadne walked through the crowded streets of Ephesus, only vaguely aware anyone else in the universe existed. Haifata, Erezavan and Thomas walked a bit behind; Mary walked ahead and playfully chatted with the two enchanted officers.

They didn't do so in any physical way, nor even look at each other as they walked, yet John and Ariadne touched. The joy that flowed between them was so pronounced that several passersby turned to stare, broke into smiles, then turned confusedly away as if they knew not why they'd done so.

"I thought when I left you in Corinth I would never see you again. And though I told myself it was for the best, the truth is, it...I was heartsick." John looked into her eyes. "Yet, in all honesty, belovéd, I know not why you've come now to Ephesus. Nor if it was wise."

"You are displeased to see me?" she asked with a smile.

John could only smile back as he shook his head. His eyes told her such a thing could never be possible in this or any lifetime. "It is only that, as Mary pointed out to both of us, your Way lies elsewhere, and we both assumed that elsewhere was in Corinth. To see you here, and with Mary...it is just that I am surprised...and I confess, confused."

"It was for her sake that I came," Ariadne said, looking at Mary's back. "When the soldiers came and discovered you had gone on, the leader of the guard asked my father if he was sure he did not know where you were. But of course, those who guide others' in escaping the authorities never tell those who stay behind where they go, lest we should be coerced into betraying them. So, even though they destroyed most of our main room and threatened to hurt Poppi, he had no answer to give save that you were trying to make your way out of Corinth before sunrise, heading most probably for Athens."

Ariadne flushed and her voice suddenly grew low and strained. "There is a look men sometimes get, one I have seen all too often in the marketplace when a woman who sells herself for money comes into their midst. The leader of the guards had that look when he turned to me. He said it would be such a shame if so pretty a girl was to come to harm because of Poppi's 'bad memory'.

"I am no child, John—I was once a woman married—and I was terrified. I've ministered to women who were taken against their wills, seen what it does to their souls. And I saw in that centurion's eyes that he had already made his decision. No matter what my father said, my fate was decided...and I could see by Poppi's face that he saw it, too."

"Did they *hurt* you?"

Thomas, Haifata and Erezavan had to dodge around John, he stopped so abruptly. Rage suddenly flared wildly in his life force; not since Jeshua's abuse and crucifixion had he felt such fury. For a moment, he again became the John bar Zebedee who would fight at the drop of any slight; he was the lowest of primitives, ready to go to war over this encroachment on his territory. For a moment, he wanted to jump on the next ship to Corinth, to find and pummel every one of those soldiers into pulpy, hard-to-find bits. For a moment, the slightest thought of giving his wrath over to the One seemed abhorrent to him.

That resistance lasted but a moment, though, for long habit quickly took hold.

John shut out the throbbing red haze that filled his vision and offered up his ideas of what should be despite his phantom self's reluctance. He looked into his double's face, knowing she saw what was truly behind his ire: his fear that he'd failed her by leaving. More importantly, John saw the phantom self's—his own and the soldiers'—ancient pull to twist the purity of the Father's Justice, which saw no separation and so forgave all errors, into the right to damn and make "enemy" that which seemed to be "other".

Ariadne's look, in turn, coming as it did from the Heart of the Mother, told John that she'd come to no harm, and laid no blame on him or them. He found himself offering what was left of his dark emotions to the growing Stillness at her center, to the purity of the Divine Feminine that saw only the truth that nothing was worth the loss of his peace. John looked into Ariadne's eyes and saw in them the Beauty that awakened Wholeness, and thus deflected all harm, by seeing only the One's Perfection always. He saw in her eyes the place from which all mercy emerged.

So then, he thought as his rage ever-so-gently transmuted into peace and the Stillness that was both and neither Father or Mother filled him. This is what it can be to know one's double.

"Very well then, heart of mine," he said, his sudden smile wryly appreciative as he brushed his fingers along Ariadne's cheek, "my soul is safe for yet one more day. I'll not speed back to Corinth to explain to those soldiers the nature of their mistake. Tell me what happened next."

Ariadne squeezed his hand and they walked on. "Just when I thought I would shame myself by pleading for the centurion to leave us be, another soldier entered the house. He told him a woman had come forth, claiming to know where the ones they sought were hidden. But they had to hurry, he said, for the fugitives were about to leave the city for good and all.

"'Where is this woman?' the centurion asked; she was just outside.

"He leered at me and said they'd be watching us, that if we served anyone else they considered enemies of Rome there would be repercussions. Then they left.

"I wanted to faint with relief or burst into tears, John. I wanted to stack every piece of what was left of our furniture against the door. Poppi held me, but he shook as hard as I did; we both knew how close I'd come to being the soldiers' entertainment, how likely it was I still would be, and Demeter with me if she was there at the wrong time. I wanted to hide in my room, to forget there was a world outside that could bring evil to our house—but something kept telling me I must look out the door, and quickly.

"The woman—your betrayer—was hurrying behind the soldiers as they rounded a corner in pursuit of the four of you...but how could she lead them if she was behind them?

"Then she turned so I could see her face.

"It was Mary, and of course the soldiers did not find you...but the next morning the stories were all over that she'd suddenly stopped in the street, smiled, and disappeared before their eyes."

Ariadne told how Mary later appeared in the garden and, after condescending to receive her own and Demeter's profuse thanks, asked many questions and told each of them many things. Awe overcame her features as she spoke, and John saw before him a young girl who'd at last heard something she'd wanted to hear for many years.

"She said my mother was well, that she was in the higher realms preparing for the next step in her awakening. I had wondered and hoped, for her death had been so painful, but to hear Mary say it...how could I doubt? How can I ever doubt anything she says?"

John suddenly smiled. "Ah. I see you understand what it is to have a Teacher..."

Ariadne nodded and dimpled. "Yes."

"...But there is more to this than you are telling me."

She stopped and faced him, her look turning serious. "There is. I am going with you to find Vashti."

John nodded and sighed; he'd suspected as much. He searched his double's eyes, then said, "Dearest, are you sure this is the Way you would walk? Are you sure you do not walk it because I do, rather than for your soul's reasons? For if that is so, you must know that I will refuse to have you amongst us whether your Teacher approves or not."

John braced himself to receive a defensive retort, but Ariadne merely nodded, her gaze clear as she returned his stare.

"When you left Corinth, John, I thought I would never see you again. I was prepared to live with that, to stay there, follow my Path, and enjoy my life as much as I could. But then my Teacher told me I had a part to play in fulfilling the Plan of the One and that I had to come here to Ephesus to do so.

"I cannot say I go to Vashti solely because of what my Teacher says, John; I cannot say you are not part of the reason. But Mary's words have awakened in me a longing to find all of the Truth, and I must fulfill it. Still, if you see that I serve only my own ends and not Divine Mother's will, I will turn away this moment and return to Corinth."

This is unfair, John thought, his heart constricting as he realized his double truly would accept whatever decision he made. How could he walk away from her again? How could he let her go back to Corinth, knowing what awaited her if she returned?

Yet, he could not, would not accept her as a companion just because he desired to have her with him; there was far too much at stake for such an indulgence.

"John."

He looked at Mary. She did not smile. "When you doubt your mind, which is ever a good idea, my son, then you must follow what your soul calls forth from the Silence. Your heart is pure, John bar Zebedee. You can no more choose wrongly in this than you can fail the One."

John nodded slowly and turned again to face Ariadne. Her eyes were wide with apprehension, but the clarity beneath that trepidation had not decreased one whit. Her willingness to trust, whatever the outcome, glowed from her being.

"Come with us to Vashti, Ariadne Isaurus."

They smiled simultaneously, and John realized he was leaning perilously close to her, certainly closer than was acceptable to the more respectable people of Ephesus.

He didn't care. There were none on the street save him and Ariadne—in fact, there was no street, no noise, no city. Only the two of them. He could not, for the life of him, keep his eyes off her lips.

Well, there was a way to solve that problem...

A discreet cough interrupted John's intention, and suddenly the street was again full of people, some of whom displayed either lewd smiles or prim disapproval. Titus, Iscariotus and Mary smiled indulgently, while Erezavan and Thomas made it their business to look elsewhere—in fact, the Persian was actually blushing. Haifata stood before them, his arms folded as if he inspected some item he meant to buy, but John recognized the great amusement that hid behind his trace of a smile.

"Starting a riot, in light of our previous history, would be a most unfortunate way to enter Ephesus. Do not you think so, brother?"

John sighed as if he was being put upon and Ariadne blushed and giggled. She turned to catch up with Iscariotus, Titus and Mary, but John stopped her just long enough to kiss her on the cheek—very close to the lips. He nodded to Adan.

"A proud son of Zebedee, after all, cannot too often succumb to the mores of those around him, lest he should become cowardly and beaten down by senseless propriety."

That made Adan laugh.

TWENTY-SIX

By *any standards, Corinth* was a large city, one that, in John's admittedly provincial opinion, had more than a healthy number of people trapped within its limits. The denizens of Judea, being a desert people, tended to base their cities' populations on the amount of fresh water available. Since everyone seemed to agree that what was available was not very much, even large Judean cities were fairly small, whatever the complaints of longtime residents of both Jerusalem and Caesarea to the contrary.

Ephesus was much larger and far more crowded than Corinth, its square, baked-clay buildings pushed together like crowds entering Arena. Though the companions enjoyed more maneuvering space by virtue of Iscariotus and Titus's presences, they still had to work to dodge the buffeting of the city folk.

Where Caesarea's land spirits were almost absent and Corinth's contentedly present, too many decades, if not centuries, of psychic battering from the Ephesians had left its land spirits in a state of pained, fitful slumber. John clearly "heard" their pleas for surcease from being treated as things rather than living beings—a call that was echoed by many of the city's inhabitants. No wonder so many proselytizers, including Paul of Tarsus, were attracted to this place. It was ripe for the energy that came of even the most superficial understanding of Jeshua's teachings.

Not long after leaving the commotion of Ephesus's center, John and the others found themselves before the home they would stay in. It was much like House Matthatus in grandeur, but he soon found its inhabitants were quite different: the front door swung open and Joshua Matthatus dashed out, followed by the cheerfully bustling owner.

"Rabbi! Haifata! Erezavan! Well met! You made it!"

Joshua skidded to a stop before John, grinning like a boy who's just received the present he most wanted for his birthday at again seeing his Teacher. He grabbed his hands and bowed low over them, then not only clasped Haifata's arm but heartily embraced him. Adan's brows rose, but he returned the welcome warmly, then watched bemusedly as Joshua and Erezavan enthusiastically pounded each other's backs and jabbered of their adventures. John smiled; the bored, arrogant youth they'd met in Antipatris had been replaced by a babbling young idiot. It was as if some of Timothy's exuberance had rubbed off on him—much to his improvement.

"Was it a hard trip, Rabbi? Certainly, ours was much quicker, thanks to Mary." Joshua grinned in Mary's direction and got her brilliant smile back.

"The soldiers gave you no trouble then?"

"None to speak of. Once they realized you'd escaped Corinth, they stopped searching the city altogether. I do not know if it was because Baremna did not tell them of the rest of us or because they thought we'd all left Corinth together. Surely they'd have sought us otherwise, for we would likely know better than the local people where you went."

"Baremna did know only three of us escaped," John frowned. "And surely, as angry as he was, he would have suggested you be used as hostages to lure us out of hiding."

Joshua shrugged. "As may be. I know only that once we decided to leave Corinth, it was only a matter of leaving. The soldiers paid us no mind at all."

John glanced at Mary, who still spoke with Iscariotus, seemingly oblivious to their exchange. She'd likely secured the companions' unmolested passage—but still. If Baremna had *not* told, well, why not? What could he have possibly gained by keeping silent?

John sighed. Whatever the answer might be, it apparently had no plans to spring into his head at this moment, so he turned to greet their host.

Iustus Karikos was a startlingly round, homely-featured man who'd made his fortune selling fine cloths and spices. In all truth, his build reminded John of Baremna, but his boisterously genial manner came so naturally that he could only smile and resist the urge to plug his ears. The lines around the merchant's mouth and eyes testified that he'd weathered both the joys and tragedies of life, but the lines caused by smiles far outnumbered those fostered by frowns, as if even in tragedy, Karikos had found time to laugh.

"Ahh! Here, then, are the weary travelers!" he said, his voice booming off the walls of his home. He kissed Ariadne and Mary's hands and clasped arms with the officers as if he'd known them for years, then bowed deeply as he turned to John. "Well met, companion of the Christos! You honor me and my house greatly by your presence! If you have need of anything, anything whatever, please but say so and I will see it is supplied!"

"Our thanks to you, Iustus Karikos," John returned, hard-put to keep a straight face, "and surely it is the other way around: if we can serve you, please do not hesitate to ask."

Karikos's thunderous voice made everything sound like a cheer at Arena, yet, he was truly touched by John's offer—even as he quickly waved it aside. "Yes, yes, I will gladly do so, good sir. But not today! Today, you need refreshment from your arduous journey." He beckoned them into his house. "Come! I will show you to your rooms."

Though House Karikos was not as opulent as House Matthatus, it was appointed with surprisingly tasteful tapestries, sculptures and rugs. It was certainly cozier than House Matthatus, a home instead of a showpiece to impress fellows and competitors.

Karikos himself showed them where they would stay. John again had his own suite, but he had time enough only to drop his bundles and clean up before being herded with the rest into the dining hall.

Once there, he met the merchant's wife and children...and was fed to within an inch of his life.

House Karikos did not spare the coin when it came to foodstuffs, and their cooks were truly masters. The company was prevailed upon to try some of everything, and though John avoided the shellfish out of habit, he did enjoy the beef and lamb and tasted the pheasant. He also sampled several kinds of grains and sauced vegetables, some of which he'd never seen, and even had a second glass of a sweet wine. He also enjoyed a pastry that was so light, sweet and fluffy, he was sure it had been baked with manna beseeched from Heaven.

Like Karikos, his wife, Thaleia, was a large, portly, homely woman whose good humor seeped from every pore. Though she was not quite as loud as her husband, she was well able to hold her own in their conversations—and their repartee made it plain their love and respect for each other had never been marred by a lack of wit. Their seven children, ranging in age from six to twenty, were likewise boisterous, though unfailingly polite to their guests; John thought of his youth with James and his sisters as he watched their banter. Here lived a family that knew each other's value.

As he carried on polite conversation with his hosts and answered the children's many questions, John observed Joshua. The young merchant played the charming, amiable dinner companion almost as an afterthought, thoroughly captivating both the mistress of the house and her two eldest daughters. The joy he'd displayed on again meeting John had not diminished at all; like Ariadne, he had grown enormously in his awareness of his Self. Joshua no longer sought to merely understand what he was; rather, he was beginning to sense the truth of his Being. The day fast approached when his only focus would be to serve by becoming as much of that Truth as he could. John couldn't ask for more in a student or feel more blessed by his becoming.

The meal finally ended. John begged tiredness as the children requested "just one more story", but promised to regale them again on the morrow. Indeed, he must be tired, for even the idea of again being with Ariadne could not stop his discreet yawns.

Unfortunately, there'd be no rest just now. He intended to get Mary alone long enough to speak with her privately— that is, if she ever left Iustus's table. Like Jeshua, she'd always loved good dinner conversation, and this crowd was well able to provide it. It would no doubt be some time before he'd have the chance to speak to her.

Ah, well. Lying down would be a bad idea, especially in his state, but adjourning to his room to sit in one of the plush chairs and get in a few of the techniques of the Practice would energize him. John leaned toward Ariadne to ask if she would see him later and received an answering smile that made his mind go momentarily blank with delight, then he excused himself and made the long walk to his room.

Only to find Mary there, waiting.

John's brows shot up. Not only did the trip from the dining hall to the guest rooms in House Karikos border on being an excursion, but when he'd left, Mary was just starting on her second helping of dessert as she conversed with Iustus, his eldest son, and Captain Iscariotus. It was impossible that she could have beaten him here.

Hmph. Corporeal she might once again be, John realized, but that was obviously no hindrance to her getting wherever she desired, when she desired it. Or was she even now in two places at once? The idea made him shake his head.

Mary smiled at her adopted son as he came into the room and took his hands in hers.

"You have questions, my son—"

"Yes I do. Mother..."

"—such as, what things have changed, and what does it all mean?"

"Yes, yes, I do indeed want those questions answered," John said, shaking his head impatiently. "But for now they can wait. Mother, where is Marcus?"

"Marcus? Why, he is here in Ephesus, staying in a part of town that is most unsuitable to one with any sense of propriety." Mary smiled wryly, "Or taste."

John frowned. "But why did he leave, Mother? What passed between the two of you?"

"Nothing passed between us, at least not directly," Mary answered, then raised her hand to forestall John's retort. "All I saw of Marcus was his back as he hastily retreated from the house where you performed everyone's Ceremonies of Thanksgiving. That he saw me I have no doubt, but he obviously had no wish whatever to speak to me."

"And you let him go?"

"Of course," Mary said tartly. "Chasing men down and forcing them to speak to me is not something I have any taste for, John; I leave those behaviors to their wives and mothers. I knew he would follow us to Ephesus, even though he wanted none of us to know it..." She smiled. "Well no, that is not the truth. He did not want *me* to know it."

Mary then gave John directions for how to find the former scribe.

Of all the things that had been said about John's Teacher—"lying, slothful, harlot-loving, Sabbath-breaking *traitor!*"—never had Jeshua bar Josef been accused of being fastidious. He'd stay hours in places even beggars refused to darken the doorways of, share food with people whose fingers were black with dirt, sit on rugs that hadn't seen sun, much less water, in years, and stand on floors that were cleared of scraps only by whatever bugs or animals might be present. Jeshua went where he would—and where he would often appalled even John's young, adventurous heart—for he had exactly one criterion for visiting a place: was there even one person there who wanted to remember the truth of who he was?

Here is a place Jeshua would have been completely comfortable in, John thought sardonically as he pushed through a rickety door that stood in the most dangerous part of Ephesus. He could only call the building connected to said door a tavern by stretching the description to its farthest possible limits; there was absolutely no danger the moon's silver glow or night's fresh air would contaminate the ambience of the space. The greasy hides covering its few windows beat back any hint of outside light or air, allowing the tang of dirty smoke, intoxicating herbs and unwashed human to permeate the room. Though he'd been a fisherman and so not particularly bothered by grime, John avoided touching the tabletops, lest he should find himself stuck to one.

The place was fairly crowded, but many of the patrons were in no shape to notice the arrival of a newcomer; John stepped carefully to avoid tripping over any prone, snoring bodies that might be hidden in the darkness. He became aware of the sounds of coupling coming from one corner of the room, and as his eyes adjusted to the dimness, saw the thin curtain that gave the house prostitute's customers line-of-sight privacy, if not soundproofing. A few men waited their turn to sample her wares, though not with any great enthusiasm.

Prochorus sat alone at a back table, head lolling on his forearms, back to the wall. A cup sat atop the table and several empty bottles littered tabletop and floor. One of his knives stood, tall and lonely, in the cheap wood of the table's center; Marcus's right hand rested close by, making plain his willingness to use it if need be. John noticed the tables closest to him were clear of patrons.

"Marcus?"

Though the Roman looked too drunk to stand, John did not have to call his name twice. Prochorus raised his head, revealing a grizzled and red-eyed countenance, then blinked owlishly and sat up in the rickety chair, his back rod-straight. In other circumstances, John might have smiled at the dignity Marcus strove to maintain, but to see his friend thus, here, in truth brought him closer to tears than amusement.

"So, Rabbi. You still live free. That is good to know," the Roman said, being as careful and dignified with his articulation as he was with his posture. "Pray, what brings you to this part of Ephesus?"

"I think you know." This time John did offer a little smile as Prochorus's head bobbled loosely in acknowledgement.

"Then you waste your time. I will not be rejoining our little adventure."

John searched for a chair that might see fit to hold him, eyed one of the bottles of wine and motioned toward it; Prochorus shrugged and yelled for another cup. It quickly appeared on a cloud of smell and dirt that was disguised as the wine master or, as seemed more likely, the owner of this...establishment.

John sniffed it, wiped it out with the hem of his robe and hoped that would be enough. He poured a cup, then cautiously sipped. Though it was by no means first-rate, the wine was surprisingly good. Prochorus watched the operation, then commented.

"The proprietor has several sons. They steal most of their wine from merchant's stalls and caravans. I hear he's lost a couple of them that way."

The silence stretched thinner and thinner between them, until the sounds of snoring, men's grumbles and the prostitute's moans were all they could hear.

"Will you tell me what happened, Marcus? I was under the impression we had settled things when I departed, only to discover you left Corinth the night I did."

"Nothing happened," Prochorus said gruffly. "I simply realized my time with you and the others was done, so I moved on. Do I not have that right?" He asked belligerently, "Or do I owe you what is left of my life because you gave back to me my legs?"

"You owe me nothing, Marcus, and would owe nothing even if I had raised you from the dead. But even a child would know your reasons for leaving are not true."

As if to punctuate John's point, a cacophony of grunts and squeals suddenly issued from behind the curtain, breaking the stuporous silence. Several patrons looked up from their drunken meditations as if hoping to miraculously catch a glimpse of the activities beyond the ragged partition, and one or two lurched over to join the line of men who waited their turn. John kept his eyes locked on Prochorus.

"You owe me nothing, Marcus, true; but will you not at least tell me why you left?"

Sometimes, the only way to bring an injured animal under one's protection is to give it the space it needs to decide on its own that the only desire of the one before it is to help. John did this now, holding the welcoming light of the One within himself.

The Roman's expression grew vulnerable; he started to slump like a man whose weight has become so great he can no longer hold himself upright. The Prochorus who'd been awakening during their journey, the one who rejoiced in the growth that had come of the Practice, sat before John, looking for all world like he wanted to lay his head on his arms and cry for some grief only he understood...but then his expression suddenly grew stubborn. The vulnerability faded and he berated his body back into its inflexible pose; he was once more the hard, angry, miserable Prochorus who'd spent his crippled life at the washing well in Bethany.

Almost. John clearly heard the mumbled slur that was Marcus's answer, but asked him to repeat it anyway.

"I said—" and the former beggar's voice again took on the precision only the very drunk can achieve, "—I do not choose to associate with either liars...or ghosts."

"Well, that is useful, Marcus, since we have no liars among us and I am no ghost."

John was shocked to his core to hear Mary' behind him, to know his mother was in a place like this—but his real surprise came from watching Prochorus's reaction.

The Roman cleared his chair so quickly that the bottles and cups on the table leapt into the air with him, only to slam to the tabletop and floor in clangorous disaster. He plastered himself against the wall, knife suddenly in hand, his face a mask of unadulterated fear, as if he thought Mary meant to spirit him away to some netherworld.

John stood away from the table to give his mother a clearer view. The tavern's patrons watched surreptitiously, almost as if they feared drawing her attention. So then, he thought, none amongst these ones was yet so dead that they failed to feel the life force radiating from his mother.

Mary made no move to approach Prochorus, only quietly surveyed him, the love in her eyes belying the stern expression on her face. John suddenly realized no noise emanated from any part of the room, not even from behind the curtain. In fact, it had been drawn back, and the prostitute, hair disheveled and robe wrapped haphazardly around her, stood staring, as still as every one else.

What happened next was nothing...and everything. Mary made no move, but both the silence and the Silence grew and stretched and filled the room. The air lightened until no smell of smoke or sweat remained; all the shadows seemed to fade away, even though the light didn't change at all. Though she moved not a muscle, John had the distinct sense his mother opened her arms to Marcus in welcome.

Slowly, ever so slowly, Prochorus's countenance changed. His rigid fear relaxed first into shame, then into sorrow. Then his face crumpled in pure contrition; his body folded in on itself until he sank to his knees and sobbed.

Marcus babbled incoherently as Mary knelt and cradled his head in her arms, but she apparently understood his words perfectly; she murmured comfortingly at him, a loving mother soothing a hurt child. Her tenderness inundated the room just as her Silence had.

"What you were in Bethany is as nothing, Marcus. Do not you see that that man no longer exists? There is nothing to apologize for, dearest one—no, no, listen to me, Marcus!" She made him look into her eyes. "There is nothing to apologize for. Not for any part of your life, no matter how soiled or evil you believe it was. Never have you failed me, dear heart, and never can you fail me!"

Though Marcus cried even harder in the face of her forgiveness, John smiled. He knew whatever guilt the Roman felt about his past was even now dissolving, that once it was gone, it would never trouble his mind again.

"Who is she?"

John looked down to find the prostitute standing next to him. She stared in riveted wonder as Mary soothed and comforted Marcus, her careworn features filled with longing. She felt John looking at her and looked into his face; an expression of shock, then amazement, overtook her features.

John smiled at her astonishment, somewhat astonished himself. He clearly saw the girl this woman had once been, saw the hope and possibility she'd once taken for granted—and suddenly *knew* the fullness of the beauty beyond the value of face that Jeshua had seen in Miriam all those years ago. He knew, too, that this woman, like Miriam, saw not a man who saw only what she could give him, but one who beheld her Self and loved her simply and exactly as she was.

Both of them beheld a miracle.

The woman covered her cheeks as if she blushed furiously and her eyes sought the floor as if she could not stand the truth she saw in John's eyes. But he knew she did not miss his words.

"Who are you, dear one? And who would you be?"

It took John, Mary and Prochorus over an hour to leave the tavern, for the woman, Johanna by name, begged them to stay and talk. John gladly complied, thinking, in all truth, of Miriam and what both she and he might have been had Jeshua rejected her.

As Miriam had with her house in Jerusalem, Johanna left the tavern with them, vowing never to return; John and Mary parted from her with the promise that she would be welcome to see them as often as she desired. They kept that promise: she regularly appeared at the Karikos home to talk with John or Mary and soon became friends with the other companions. Surprisingly, she also became fast friends with Thaleia Karikos, who saw fit to take the younger woman under her wing.

"After all, Elder," Thaleia said when John praised her generosity of spirit, for she was well aware of Johanna's past, "if the Christos saw worth in the ones others saw as unworthy, how dare I not? The way her life has gone is no fault of hers, or certainly not hers alone. And beyond all that, I like her!"

Johanna's desire to learn was as intense as any of Jeshua's original disciples' had ever been, and it wasn't long before she, Iustus, Thaleia, and their three eldest children became the first people in Ephesus to learn the Practice.

"I have sought this all my life without even knowing I sought it," she said through tears. "Never will I forsake it, never!"

After he and Mary put a still drunk and crying Marcus to bed, John kept his date to meet Ariadne in the hall outside the room she shared with the two eldest Karikos daughters. They sat on a folded sheepskin, he with his back against the wall, she cradled in his arms, back against his chest. They sighed simultaneously, then giggled.

"Tell me what you know," he murmured into her hair, swimming in the smell of violets. She grew still and he knew she closed her eyes to more deeply enter into the Silence.

"I know I am changing so quickly that I notice a difference every day...and cannot imagine how I lived my life before I learned the Practice, before Mary gave me this Stillness I scarcely knew could exist. I know I cannot imagine how I lived before you came into my life...and that I could throttle myself for wasting the time we spent running from each other like frightened children when first you came to my father's house."

"And yet?"

"And yet...well...this is something I only suspect, I do not yet know it...but I feel you are not the other half of me, nor I of you. We are each a whole thing unto ourselves. You complete me, John...yet never have I been incomplete. How can that be?"

"What do you know, Ari?" John said by way of answer, and Ariadne grew even more still. He reveled in holding her, gratified to know he could even now be a teacher of Jeshua's Way, one who saw this woman not just as his belovéd whom he wanted to please, but as one who wished above all else to remember who she was. He was sworn to see that she so learned, and so would learn by her learning, as all true teachers did.

Ariadne suddenly let out a frustrated sigh and shook her head. "I have no words for what I want to say, John, because I cannot quite grab hold of what it is."

"That is because you are trying, Ari. Stop it."

She twisted to see his face in the dimness, the "what?" written all over her face.

"We humans think we are in control of finding the Self, that our ability to personally will an answer into the open is a sign of our intelligence and value," he said. "But only when we give our power to the Unbounded One and relinquish control of our personal knowing to It, does true Intelligence manifest. Ours is not to make things happen within our souls, as one would plow a field or dig a ditch, Ari. Ours is to open to that which will bring us to awareness, to allow the One's Grace to awaken us from within. That is what we do when we use the phrases of the Practice.

"So then, dearest, tell me: did your Teacher truly give you the Stillness you now experience, or did she simply direct you to It by asking the right questions?"

Ariadne frowned. "She told me to notice—ah, I see. Yes." Her voice was bright with discovery. "I was crying in the garden the day after you left. Demeter tried to comfort me, but it was hard; I think she felt worse for me than I did for myself.

"Then Mary appeared—and Demeter completely amazed me by immediately falling to her knees and asking her to be her Teacher. Mary made her stand, then took her face in both of her hands and kissed her on the lips as my mother used to do. Do you know, John? I hadn't seen Demti cry like that since Taros was killed, but she also smiled through her tears, for though Mary said not a word, we both knew she'd said 'yes'."

"'*Demti*'?" John smiled. Ariadne's gasp was comical.

"If you tell her I told, I will never speak to you again," she said, but John heard her smile as well. "Anyway, Mary told us how the One never makes a Plan without our consent, if not our memory of giving it, and it sounded so sensible that we could not but believe her. Not that it helped me very much; in all honesty, I was not ready to let go the pain of losing you.

"Mary patted my hand and laughed. 'That is all right dearest, have your wallow. I certainly did when Josef left to deliver this piece of carpentry or that, especially when we were first married. But while you wallow, be sure to notice whether you are crying and missing John, or watching yourself cry and miss John. And when you find the answer to that question, ask yourself just who is crying, after all...and who is watching?'

"And John, it was as she said! I noticed the one watching was Silent and encircled by Silence. I assumed Mary had caused it, but I see now that is not the case. She simply directed me to notice what was already there, and my willingness made it visible to me."

John closed his eyes. He could feel Ariadne assimilating her new realization, and her willingness and depth astounded him. Yes, both she and Demeter were at least part of the reason Mary had chosen to again enter into corporeal existence.

From that night on, the ritual of meeting outside Ariadne's room was an established fact, so much so that, to their amusement, House Karikos's servants—courtesy of the Karikos daughters—took to preparing the space where they usually sat, supplying them with cushions, blankets and even the occasional pitcher of juice or wine.

Oh, they could have met elsewhere in the house; John knew Ariadne would readily have gone to his room and stayed as long as he desired. Nor did he sense that anyone, save possibly Thomas, would object. Certainly, the owners of House Karikos would say nothing: Iustus and Thaleia lived by the motto that the best way to enjoy God's gifts was through the body, yet neither of them could be accused of lacking spiritual awareness. They did the Practice with as much joy as they ate a meal, and that was great indeed.

So, if no spiritual or social repercussions would ensue, why did John not take Ari to his room of a night, that they might pass a joyous time together?

What it came down to, John realized with a certain amount of rue, was that he was a child of Judea and its mores. Son of the rebellious Zebedee, son of Ezekiel, he might be, and so inclined to flaunt some of the rules he'd grown up with—but he was not quite brave enough to go beyond a certain point. Also, self-honesty told him he still harbored some notion of following exactly in his Teacher's footsteps.

John sighed as Ariadne entered the room she shared with Ulessia and Dora Karikos, leaving him on the other side of the door yet one more time.

Sometimes, maintaining one's honor was a very frustrating thing.

TWENTY-SEVEN

Word *of John and* Mary's presence in the city spread like wildfire throughout the Christine community, and soon throughout Ephesus itself. After their first week there, the rich and powerful frequently sought them as fashionable dinner guests, while the sick and poor simply sought them. Iustus and Thaleia delightedly opened their home to anyone who desired to come to the teachers to learn and grow; people of all sorts, Christine and not, came to House Karikos to laugh and learn from Mary's stories, hear John speak of Jeshua's Way, and become part of the growing community of the One. They taught close to a hundred people the basics of the Practice.

Many of those in power were displeased by the companions' celebrity, but as Thomas had predicted, the Ephesian Governor was not one of them. In fact, Terus Flavius's attitude was more than John expected, for he wasn't merely neutral toward the Christine presence, but actively supportive of it. As he himself put it to John during an opulent dinner that boasted some of the richest of the city's businessmen, Christines all:

"Even our non-Christine merchants report they've suffered fewer losses by theft, and over these last several months, other crimes have declined as well. Consequently, my tax collections are higher and my city more peaceful. I desire naught else."

So it was that John had had free run of Ephesus this last month and more, unafraid of molestation by overzealous (or overambitious) authorities. This was not to say that he did not suffer a certain level of surveillance, covert and obvious; certainly he appreciated the local Christines' discretely protective supervision.

Having Ariadne there gave John's heart great satisfaction as well. It was an absolute joy to awaken each day, knowing her welcoming smile would be there when he broke fast in one of the many dining rooms, and it comforted him to know hers was usually the last face he saw before going to his own bed to rest and enter the Stillness.

Even so, the lengthening stay fretted John; he feared his true mission was being forgotten, or worse, abandoned. Mary succinctly disabused him of such a notion.

"Do not be foolish, my son; your mission is in no way endangered by this seeming delay. In fact, it will only be helped by it," she'd say. Then, as she had many times before, she'd refuse to answer any more questions, either about how it would help or why she had seen fit to return to earthly existence. That is, except to say, as she had on the docks of Ephesus, "There was a necessary change of plans."

Iscariotus and Titus departed a few days after John's arrival, carrying with them the knowledge of how to do the first two techniques. Both promised they would return as soon as they could, and Iscariotus was even considering asking for a change of posting.

"Truly, nothing would give me greater pleasure than staying here to learn more of this Practice. Never have I had a greater sense of closeness to the Christos—and 'Natus swears he can sense the Lady's Presence even more clearly." Lieutenant Titus nodded his avid agreement. "Still, I've gotten where I am by listening to my soul's call, and it bids me return to Athens to work with those of my men who would learn more of the Christos."

"Are you not concerned about your Governor's response to your failure to bring me to him?" John asked.

Iscariotus shrugged. "Flavius's reputation and connections are well known. That I was too late to liberate you from his auspices should not surprise him." He clasped John's arm. "Thank you, Elder, for all you have given me. Know we will meet again, and soon."

"Send my regards and blessings to your men, Amadeon. Be well."

As Titus and John exchanged arm clasps and goodbyes, the Captain turned to Mary, took her hand, and kissed it, never taking his eyes from hers. "Well met, dear lady. It has been an honor beyond words to spend time with you. Indeed, I only wish circumstances were different—for then I might well have spirited you away from this place." His expression was serious, but his eyes danced. "You will take care?"

"Of course, Amadeon, I can do naught else."

The Captain held Mary's hand and eye for a moment longer, then turned away, reluctantly it seemed to John. The two soldiers wished farewells all around and departed.

"Well, well, Mother," John said, his eyes twinkling as he watched after the two for a bit. "Amadeon seems well-smitten with you. I trust you've no plans to encourage him?"

"Hmmm..." Mary smiled, her countenance simultaneously thoughtful and speculative as she sashayed away. John laughed aloud, well aware she had won this round of teasing: he'd need both hands to pull his eyebrows out of his hair.

A few days later, Joshua, Erezavan and another regular, a young man named Stavis Querceron, approached John with solemn faces. After conferring by eye to decide who could best put forth their case, Erezavan asked what it would take to become teachers of the Practice.

That they asked surprised John not at all, for Mary had mentioned their whispered discussions on the matter. He was amazed, however, when Marcus asked to join them. John steepled his fingers contemplatively, then surprised them with his answer.

"Gentlemen, I am not the least bit interested in your being teachers of the Practice."

Erezavan was predictably abashed and immediately tried to apologize for overstepping some previously unknown boundary. Stavis said nothing, and as was becoming more and more predictable of late, Prochorus likewise held his tongue. But Joshua (also predictably) was not so willing to be put off.

"Why should we not be teachers, Sir?" he asked with all the hauteur of his upbringing. Or most of it, at least: his flushed cheeks betrayed his mortification at the idea that he might not be allowed to fulfill what had obviously become his dream. "Have we somehow led you to think we are not worthy of someday being teachers?"

John shook his head and raised his hands, trying to preempt Joshua's attempt to count off the reasons they were fit to receive such an honor.

"No, no, no—sit down and listen!"

The three younger men did as ordered, Erezavan and Stavis with wide eyes and Joshua with a wary frown. Prochorus remained standing. "I said I am not interested in your becoming teachers of the Practice, not that I would not train you to teach it."

"But..." John shook off Joshua's budding protest, his face stern.

"Understand this, all of you: those who teach the Practice do not play a role! They do not teach because they can impart the mechanics of the Practice—any fool can do that! They teach because they know themselves to *be* what the Practice leads to. If one does not consistently experience the stillness of the One first and foremost, then he has no value as a teacher. And that is true no matter how great his charisma or eloquent his speech. If he is that wholeness, on the other hand, he will teach everyone he meets with great beauty, regardless of whether they ever learn the words of the techniques from him or not." John glared at each of them. "Do you see the difference? Are you willing to become That, first, and teachers second, if at all?"

This time, it was Joshua who looked like he wanted to apologize for overstepping his bounds, yet his nod was eager. Erezavan also nodded, his expression serious. Marcus frowned as if trying to translate John's words from another language, then also nodded.

John looked at Stavis. "And what of you? What do you want?"

Querceron was second cousin to Thaleia Karikos, the second son of some local noble. He was three summers older than Joshua and worked with Iustus and Thaleia as a minor partner in their business, keeping faithful track of what came and went and for how much. Though finer of feature and tall and slender where she was portly, Querceron had the same good-natured homeliness as his somewhat older cousin. It turned out he knew Joshua from one of the Greek schools, for in the typical fashion of younger sons with no real prospects save the military, he'd been indulged to find his own faiths and follies. Though he and Joshua had not been close in Greece, he was now firmly a part of the cadre of young men, a welcome, strong, yet cheerful influence who had none of Joshua's former haughtiness to be tamed out of him.

At this moment, he looked a little like he'd just been caught stealing dessert from an honored guest's plate; he'd never seen the more austere of John's temperaments.

"I—in truth, Elder, I came along only because the others seemed so determined about this thing and I was curious to see what you would say," he said. He looked unhappy at having to tell the truth of it, but according to Thaleia, her younger cousin had always been truthful, no matter how it pained him, "because he's a face that is easier to read than a parchment proclamation."

"I see," John said. "And you have no interest in what these others seek?"

"I have no particular interest in teaching, Elder," the Ephesian corrected in his gently emphatic way. "Like Joshua, I have found more in this Practice than I ever hoped to; in fact, for all the time and diligence I put into knowing the deeper truths of my mind and soul, it feels as if I learned nothing of value in the schools in Greece. I would cheerfully give all I have—" he suddenly chuckled self-deprecatingly "—or perhaps I should say, all my father has, to experience the Fullness these techniques lead to. They are a boon no amount of riches can ever match.

"But in honesty, learning to teach is not for me, not now. And as to this great adventure...well, I wish you unbounded success, but I leave it to you. I've done enough adventuring in this life and want naught but to settle into my cousins' business and enjoy this Practice as much as possible while we have you amongst us."

Joshua and Erezavan looked disappointed by Querceron's answer, but after giving the Ephesian a long, intent stare that made him squirm, John nodded. Then he smilingly told the others that he and Mary had discussed how they could speed their growth in the Stillness and thus facilitate the completion of the companions' mission.

"I make no promises, but I will let you know when those discussions see fit to manifest as some sort of training. *If* they manifest."

Joshua and Erezavan thanked him profusely and bounded from the room, congratulating each other and chattering excitedly, while Querceron's frowning exit was subdued. Marcus solemnly nodded his own thanks—and left before John could stop him.

John frowned over it. Though he hadn't exactly been avoiding him, Prochorus had been distant this last month and more.

But speaking to him will have to wait, he thought, for he wanted to seek out Iustus and Thaleia to see if they knew of any dwellings where the group might live and enter the Silence for long periods each day. Since Ephesus boasted any number of diverting entertainments, it would be easier for everyone if such a place were some distance from the city. True, neither Erezavan nor Joshua seemed overly inclined to seek such distractions, but John knew enough about the vagaries of relinquishing one's phantom self to want to take precautions.

Husband and wife looked thoughtful when he asked, two peas in a pod in their expressions. "There is old Badadrian's cottage," Thaleia said slowly, "though I imagine by now it needs repairs to the roof at the least...and you may have to run off a few squatters."

Iustus nodded. "Hmm, yes. It sits four or five miles from here, near a small grove of olive trees. It was part of a larger estate, but the Romans broke it up many years ago, after declaring the original owners enemies of the Empire. I am told a caretaker tends it since Badadrian grew too old to do it, but I would say his visits are irregular at best."

"You will definitely want to look at it, Elder—and if you decide you want it, you just let us know. We will see that it is made fit for your use," Thaleia said.

John thanked them both, then looked thoughtful. "Might it be big enough for everything to be moved there? We have, after all, stayed long on your wondrous hospitality."

It took the Karikoses a moment to catch his meaning, but when they did, their eyes went wide with identical expressions of horror.

"Oh, no, no!" They exclaimed in one voice, "Here you may stay forever, if it suits you to do so, Elder, and we'll be most glad to have you!" Thaleia said; and Iustus went on:

"Never has anyone been more welcome in our home! The children think of you, all of you, as part of the family. Please, do not even take thought of leaving us!"

John smilingly gave them his assurances, though he was, as always, gratified and amazed at the generosity they and so many in the city showed toward the companions. Not that Iustus suffered by it, he knew. As was usually the case with the Christine community, many brought foodstuffs and other supplies to help with the expense of having guests so often; likewise, most Christines made it their business to buy wares from other Christines. Karikos's already successful business had only improved with John and Mary's arrival.

They managed to secure the use of the cottage and the lands around it within a couple of weeks; when word got out, a veritable parade of Christines came to John to request the privilege of readying it for the companions' use. Timothy and Rachael joined them from Corinth just as negotiations ended; this was as he and Mary had planned it.

"Timothy in particular has been preparing for this for some time," Mary said, "and since you performed Rachael's ceremony, you well know which way her destiny lies. Learning to teach will serve not only the two of them, but the world."

The reunion between the two youngsters, Joshua and Erezavan was a noisy, chattery affair, and soon after, John and Mary picked the day when they would begin training their charges.

Everything was flowing smoothly; the only splinter in the walking stick was Prochorus. The unease John felt about his participation in the training had only increased. Since they'd brought him home from the tavern, the curious scribe who'd had nothing but question after question about the Practice and all things spiritual had disappeared, lost behind a constantly furrowed brow and taciturn demeanor. Granted, Marcus had never been the jolly, hail-and-well-met type, but he'd never been one to bite his tongue either, especially if something bothered him. This quiet was abnormal.

True, he used the techniques of the Practice more diligently than ever, so much so that one of the more oblivious servants worriedly came to John and asked if the Roman was ill, "...For I have never seen a man so tired...naps all the time." Still, his process was grueling to watch. He seemed never to smile anymore, and his attention was often turned so painfully inward that he had no time for friends or conversation. For him to want to take the step of training to teach...

That night, after dining to celebrate Timothy and Rachael's arrival, John managed by some miracle to find himself alone with Marcus. The Roman tried to rectify that error as soon as he realized it, but it was too late: John called him back from his hasty retreat.

Prochorus returned, his face guarded. John spoke without preamble.

"Marcus, are you sure you wish to join the others in this training?"

Prochorus looked disconcerted, as if he'd expected a different question, but nodded vigorously. "Of course I am sure. I wish to do whatever will help me awaken to the One."

John folded his hands on the table, choosing his words carefully. "I said nothing to the lads, but the truth is, Mary and I had already devised a plan for training them when they spoke to us. We were waiting only for the others to arrive from Corinth to begin."

"Ah. So all your words about needing to be 'That' first were naught but platitudes?" Prochorus asked skeptically.

"Oh, no, Marcus, I was utterly serious. A teacher who does not consistently hold to the Stillness is no teacher at all. He takes a tool that is guaranteed to awaken one to his wholeness and makes it trivial. If he himself does not know the Fullness, he will not be able to share or even identify what the student will experience as his phantom self falls away. In fact, he may even lead the student away from the truth by calling his experiences of the One illusory. Such a one is potentially worse than useless.

"We want all of you awake enough to be able to hear and rely on the One within your own hearts because it can only make the journey easier. Besides, who knows what seeds we are meant to plant as we cross others' paths—or which of us will be designated to plant them? I certainly do not. I thought to make this trek alone and never expected we would come to Ephesus, much less teach here. There is a reason each of you joined this venture, and Mary and I strongly agree training is the best next step."

John steepled his fingers. "But I must say, Marcus, I am not sure such training is the best next step for you."

Though Prochorus stiffened and his face betrayed his desire to argue with the assessment, or at least ask why John felt as he did, he said nothing. John sighed.

"As it stands right now, Marcus, this will not be an easy process, not for you. A core part of this training will consist of spending hours and hours each day engaging in the Practice with your eyes closed, true. But speaking of what you experience will also be vital, for we must know that all of you are conversant with touching the heart of the One before we again set out. With your unwillingness to speak of what has so held you in thrall this month and more, I simply cannot see you finishing this. And be very clear: once we again set out, we'll not have time to play caretakers to those who cannot remain aware of the One, no matter how useful their other talents might prove to be."

"I know this, damn it! I am not some silly child or fretful little merchant who will fold into a lump at the first threat of pain!"

"That is exactly my point, Marcus," John said, hiding a smile. The Roman might take all the other arrows sent his way, but he would not, by God, be called useless. "Awakening to your true Self is not meant to be arduous—indeed, it should be joyous! But in these last six weeks, you've done naught but walk about, looking like your teeth hurt. Even the greatest masochist eventually grows tired of pain, yet if he has ill-used the thing that will stop it, he may throw it away, thinking it is the cause. That is what I see you doing with the Practice, and I would not have it be that way for you. Especially since it need not be."

"I will not fail in this," Prochorus insisted stubbornly, "I am strong enough."

John sighed again. "Marcus, the One does not need your strength; It has quite enough of Its own. It wants your joy."

Prochorus held to his stubborn bearing for a moment longer, then pulled back a chair and sat heavily. He shook his head, staring off into some unknown distance.

"Since I came back from that tavern with you and Mary, nothing has been the same for me," he said. "Since Mary forgave me for all I said—all I meant—in Bethany, everything I've ever said or done has marched before me to demand, "What will you give back to the universe? What will you be?"

Marcus ran his hands over his face as if clearing away cobwebs. When he again looked at John, his eyes gleamed with the intensity of his desire. "What I want is to be what *she* is, bar Zebedee; what you are. I want to be one who gives just because there is something to be given...without thought of whether the world will value me for it. If it is that I must complete the entire journey to my Self before I can do that, then so be it; I will study forever if that is what is called for. But when all is said and done, what I want is to share the Power behind this Practice with any who would have it."

Prochorus stood, straight and stiff as the soldier he'd once been, but his eyes eloquently bespoke his heart's desire.

"Please. May I join this training?"

"Well," John said after a long moment. "We'll not require you to complete the entire inner journey on this training, Marcus, only recognize and consistently choose for your Self. And as you will soon find, that is in truth no hard thing. After all, the One in you is here now, waiting only to be rediscovered. And the journey into Its depths, the joy of its discovery literally never ends."

John let his smile come from hiding as he reached out and clasped the Roman's arm.

"Welcome to our training, Marcus."

To celebrate the start of their training—and the end of their autonomy, for they'd be in seclusion for the next several months—Iustus and Thaleia invited the companions to dine at an inn owned by of one of their friends. The invitation was excitedly accepted.

"We'll stop for flowers on the way to dinner," Mary said as they left, "and perform the Ceremony of Thanksgiving at evening's end to celebrate the beginning of training."

The group, including the entire Karikos clan, started for the inn, called the Pheasant's Roost. Mary, Prochorus and Haifata walked a little behind; John and Ariadne walked together, saying little and enjoying each other's presence.

John looked smilingly ahead at his four youngest companions, who laughed and talked like old friends with the older Karikos children; all were dressed in the finery

Iustus and Thaleia had insisted they accept as gifts. Rachael in particular gladdened his heart: in these last few months, she'd gained both weight and height, filling out in ways that only enhanced the regal bearing fostered by her ever-growing Stillness. Right now, though, she was simply a giggly young girl, enjoying the company of her friends and oblivious to society's insistence on "ladylike" behavior.

Timothy too, had matured enormously; not so much in his way of acting, for his exuberant innocence still made him seem somewhat puppyish. It was more that, underlying that exuberance was a new level of stability. He now easily carried the fuller sense of Self John had first seen manifesting on *Matthatus*, and it gave him an aura of strength that would someday cause others to follow him without question. He was even growing a proper beard...well, soon, anyway.

Joshua and Erezavan were both resplendent in their new robes, their faces and life forces aglow with excitement over taking the steps that would soon make them teachers of the Practice. John smiled to see Erezavan talking with more than usual confidence to Ulessia, the eldest of the Karikos daughters; well gone was the painfully frightened and apologetic child he'd chastised for groveling aboard *Matthatus*.

Joshua sensed he was being watched: he suddenly turned and walked backwards between the Persian and Stavis Querceron, caught his Teacher's eye and grinned. The glow of the One in him was even brighter and more vibrant than it had been during their reunion. The Stillness within him was becoming increasingly palpable, but so was his delight in life. John decided he and Timothy had indeed somehow traded some of each other's traits, and the resultant change served both greatly.

"Ah, there is the woman I want to see," Mary said, motioning toward a flower stall a few yards away. She stepped around John and Ariadne to greet the woman by name and get down to some serious haggling.

It was a funny thing: Mary had never been one to pinch pennies and could not care in the least about the cost of things. She'd gladly pay any price a merchant might ask of his wares if she liked their quality, and as often as not gifted others with the fancies she bought before ever getting them home. But she loved the dance of arguing over the price of a thing and could bargain with the best of them, any time, anywhere, just as if she actually cared about the outcome. In fact, she'd been so well known for the talent in Bethany that crowds would gather to watch her in action whenever unwary merchants —or those who enjoyed the haggle as much as she did—passed through town.

John took Ariadne's hand, thinking to entertain her with her Teacher's joyful participation in this very human distraction, but another stall caught his eye.

"Come," he said, and pulled her along with him.

They came to a stall full of bracelets. Most were of brass or copper, but some were silver and a few were gold. Most of the designs were elaborate, made with combinations of metals or inlaid with semiprecious stones.

"Will you pick one?" John asked, suddenly shy.

Though her face remained solemn, Ariadne's eyes lit with delight. She gave his hand a quick squeeze, then looked appraisingly at the selections, showing off her own acumen at recognizing quality workmanship. Finally, she reached out to pick a pretty, delicate brass one. John shook his head and stopped her.

"That is not the bracelet you want, Ari. Pick the one that speaks most to you of me."

That made her smile. "And which one would that be, John bar Zebedee?"

John took his turn looking at the selections, his brow furrowed as if he was unsure of which to choose. Then he reached out, unerringly picked the bracelet she really wanted and slipped it on her wrist with a smug smile.

Ariadne gasped in surprise. "How did you know?"

John grinned. "You are my double, after all, Ari; on some matters our tastes are still identical."

Sapphires of two different sizes circled the slender, burnished silver band like deep blue stars, while a single, thread-fine wire formed silver glyphs that twinkled along each edge. Ariadne started to take the bracelet off, then shook her head when John again stopped her.

"Surely it is too expensive, John."

"Perhaps," he said, looking toward the stall keeper, who smiled at the lovers' byplay. "That is what this gentleman and I are about—"

John's voice stuck in his throat and his smile died as a sense of sudden, intense hatred—seeking him specifically—filled and tainted the air. He stepped before Ariadne and searched the crowd in near-panic, utterly certain it would hurt others without a qualm if it meant getting to him, but he could not, for the life of him, find the location of its source. Its venom seemed to come from all directions at once.

"Bar Zebedee! Look out!"

John spun at Prochorus's yell; at the same instant, someone jumped in front of him, blocking his sight and almost knocking him down. He heard screams and someone crying "No!" felt rather than heard the dull tearing "thunk" as the one before him grunted in shock. John grabbed for him as he fell backwards—

And knew.

Knew Joshua Matthatus would be dead before his body fully settled into his arms and dragged them both to the ground.

TWENTY-EIGHT

John tumbled beneath Joshua's weight like a man being slammed by a tidal wave; his wits spun out from under him as Joshua's life force fled the body.

This cannot be! John's mind gibbered; then, as anger welled up: This *will not* be! Joshua could not die, not like this!

John found himself in a dark tunnel, running, following after Joshua's retreating figure. It narrowed as he ran, closing around him until he had to duck, then crawl, to continue forward. He sensed Death watching and following, but surprisingly It had no malicious designs on him. I mean you no harm, It seemed to say, noting his presence, but you belong not in this place. You must return from whence you came.

Soon, John had to slither on his belly to move. With every inch forward, the increasingly claustrophobic blackness grabbed at him. His breath shortened to shallow gasps; his own life force weighed him down and tried to hold him back. But he did not stop;

Joshua Matthatus was ahead of him, taken from Life out of turn. He would bring him back or die himself in the trying.

Suddenly, John crawled no longer, but stood on a surface that was smoother and flatter than any he'd ever seen. There was light here, but its cool brilliance was sterile to the point of lifelessness. Iridescent sand, again cool and sterile, crunched under his feet and shot small hints of rainbow effulgence into the air, but he saw no landmarks to tell him where he'd passed, saw no distant views nor even a horizon to tell him where he headed. He had no sense he walked in any direction that would lead him to some place.

Hours seemed to pass, yet the scene before John remained the same. The quiet, though it did not sap his physical strength, drained his motivation; he had essence and identity still, but they were without purpose in this place. He kept walking only because he had not enough will to decide to stop. The landscape passed by and by, presenting naught but eternal, unending flatness...

No, wait. Something lay ahead, tiny in the distance.

John picked up his pace, his mind crying gladly out at even this minor contrast. As he drew closer he saw a rock, saw that something...someone...sat on it. Back turned to him, the figure, white as the light that surrounded it, looked upward as if it waited for something. It turned to face him, a smile on its face.

It was Joshua.

John blinked and suddenly remembered the marketplace, the cries of warning, Joshua falling into his arms, Joshua—

Joshua was dead. And John had chased him to this place, beyond corporeal life, determined to bring him back as Jeshua had Lazarus. He *would* bring him back—

—But Joshua was shaking his head.

"No, Rabbi, I will not go back with you. There is no need for me to go back,"

"Joshua, you do not belong here..."

"On *Matthatus*," Joshua continued as if John hadn't spoken, "after you took me and Ada to look upon the galley slaves, you told me that God was Everything, playing the game of being many disparate things. I asked you then, 'but if this is only a game, then what is the point in doing anything at all?' I said that if I accepted your coin as real, I would lose my purpose, not only for taking this journey with you, but for living. Do you remember what you then asked me?"

"I asked you 'what is the use of love?'" John nodded, "and said you could answer that question only by experiencing it for yourself. Have you then, answered it, Joshua? Truly?"

"I have, Rabbi," his student said contentedly, his smile bright. "The use of love is to accept and to give it, all of it, no matter what the giving appears to bring. The meaning of love is to give all you are so completely that you eventually fade from individual life and become the entirety of all universes, everywhere.

"The purpose of love on earth, Rabbi, is to become God."

Joshua smiled at his Teacher, the love he'd always been shining brighter than the sun now that it suffered no constraints. John felt unease in its presence, actually wanted to look away, but he could not.

"You always gave all of your Self to me in every moment, Rabbi, and showed me what it is to be brave enough to follow Love wherever it might lead. I knew I would die when I stepped in front of you; I knew it before I took the first step toward you. I had the chance to stop then, to let Prochorus or Haifata get to you first, and perhaps die in my stead. But I also knew it would not matter which or if any of us died, because really and truly, we *are* but one Being, playing out many parts.

"In that moment of knowing, I could willingly die of my love for you, and for Haifata and Marcus, because I knew true Joy in the face of what seemed the worst possibility. And I will carry that knowing forth to where I go next."

But *I* do not understand, John thought. The unease he felt in the face of his student's love insisted he had not given all at all, only thought he had. It told him Jeshua knew the same thing Joshua now knew and he did not. John knew the answer, but asked the next question anyway.

"Can you not now come back and show the others what love is for?"

And Joshua, of course, shook his head, then added, "What I now know is needed where I go more so than here. Here, they have you and Mary to show them."

"Then you must leave us." Again the bitter taste of the sense that he did *not* know welled in John's heart. Such a knowing should not cost, not like this, not like this.

Joshua had risen from his seat and was slowly walking away. Suddenly, he turned, ran back to John and hugged him with all his might, once more the exuberant boy he'd reunited with in Ephesus. John returned the hug, his throat too tight with grief to speak.

"Thank you, my Teacher," Joshua Matthatus whispered tenderly, and perhaps he saw the doubt in John's eyes, for he added, "Fear not, we will meet again. And tell the others not to grieve, for I will meet them again, too."

Joshua backed away now, becoming harder and harder to see, until at last, he completely dissolved into the air.

Even so, John clearly heard his last words.

"I love you, Rabbi. I love you always."

The first thing John became aware of was that he was sitting on the ground, surrounded by voices yelling and wailing. He became aware of dust and sweat and the sweetly metallic smell of spilled blood. His vision cleared only slowly as he sobbingly rocked Joshua's body back and forth, trying to deny what would not be denied.

Someone knelt before him; he looked up and saw Haifata. The African stroked the young man's hair and wept inconsolably, his face full of rage and helplessness. Marcus, his eyes also overflowing, stood bent over to Adan's left, pulling on something...pulling something out of something. The something came out, and John realized it was a knife, stuck in a man's body.

Darshinika Baremna's body.

John's head drooped and his sobs wracked him as if they might beat him to death. A small voice told him he shouldn't be so grieved, berated him for his grief, and Mary's reproach that he worried too much for his companions' safety also echoed in his mind; still, he heard himself snarl as someone tried to take Joshua from him.

"Let him go, belovéd. You have to let him go," Ariadne said brokenly, and though he shook his head and tried to pull away, he had no strength to resist her.

John felt other hands on him, heard Mary coax him away from Joshua's body in the gentlest of tones, and finally let himself be pulled free. Then Ariadne wrapped her arms around him and led him, like a blind, broken old man, back to Iustus Karikos's house.

John's head hurt from crying.

They were in his room, sitting on his sleeping pallet. That is to say, Ariadne was sitting; John lay with his head in her lap. A shuddering breath occasionally escaped as the ghosts of his sobs came back to haunt him, but he felt calm now, mostly cleansed of the grief of Joshua's death. Mostly.

In the midst of his crying, he'd found himself thinking of his brother.

He'd been in Bethany when James's followers came to tell him of his martyrdom, but he'd known of it the second it happened. At the moment that James had been executed, a brief but dazzlingly luminous flame had engulfed John, the fiery shock of it blazing out into the room and bathing the few stunned students who'd been with him, including Ada, in light. He'd tumbled to his knees, laughing and crying at the same time, shaking like a man with a feverish chill. Then, just as suddenly as it had come, the flash had left, as had the sudden and contradictory flow of emotions.

He'd known that what he'd felt had been but a mere hint of the infinite light James had become in discarding his body; knew there'd be no obligatory rebirth onto this plane of existence for him. James would be reborn only if he chose to return to the Fray. John had done his best to comfort his family, but had not shed a tear himself, not in sadness.

Joshua, John knew, had likewise moved beyond the requirements of the Great Wheel of Life, yet he'd grieved for him as he never had for James. Or perhaps he cried for them both, or even grieved on others' behalf. He could not be sure and it did not really matter. That was sometimes the way of things: as one became ever more liberated from his phantom self, he often healed more than just his own personal sorrows.

John released a deep, deep sigh. He would always love his student for his willingness to set aside his own ideas of who and what he was so that he might find the truth of his Being, but he'd never regret what Joshua might have been.

Joshua Matthatus had become what he might have been.

Still, he could not shake the sense of a shadow on his healing, the sense of incompleteness. John still felt anger, still tasted bitterness at the way things had happened.

Oh, not toward Darshinika Baremna, not really. Despite his growing jealousy and the insane and disastrous choice it had led to, the Persian had ultimately been naught but an instrument of what must be. That knowledge was also why John had quickly discarded the notion that Joshua's death might not have happened had he not provoked Baremna further with his ruse on the road to Athens.

No, John's anger, all of it, was for the manner of Joshua's death. Yes, yes, the young man's realization of the perfection of all actions was true and real, but the apparent truth that that knowing *had to* lead to martyrdom seemed unjust, a ridiculous waste of Life.

John wanted to turn more deeply inward, to immediately root the emotion out and throw it away like so much old trash...but he didn't. Instead, he turned his attention outward, sat up, and looked into Ariadne's teary face.

"Ari," he said, gently laying a hand against her cheek.

That was all it took to make her burst into the noisy, heartbroken sobbing he knew she'd mostly held back. John held his double—and was once more surprised at the depths of Knowing she so readily displayed. She cried now as if she had no sense of the One within, as if she thought Joshua had died with his body. Yet John knew she also experienced the core of utter Quiet that simply watched. That Stillness celebrated her willingness to relinquish her self's notions of strength, to fully express her grief, free of the fetters of that self's ideas of appropriate behavior. Truly, Ariadne's Fullness was closer to the surface than that of most others he'd met.

Soon enough, a pause, then a lull came in Ariadne's tears; then the lull became an end, save for occasional sniffles. John held his double at arms' length.

"Did you notice the Stillness in your heart even as you cried for our loss, Ari? Do you feel it even now?" He was purely the teacher right then, his face almost stern as he looked for more than the answer Ariadne's mouth would give. Her eyes still held sadness, yet as she nodded her acknowledgement, John saw, too, her wonder at the recognition that it was so.

"Good," he said, and the sternness was suddenly gone, replaced by a small smile.

All at once, and though her expression itself changed not at all, there was a change in Ariadne's look. Something more than sadness, knowing and amazement came into her eyes—and John felt by the sudden tingling heat that spread from his stomach to his loins and out into the air itself that she wanted him. He took a shuddering breath, aware his eyes mirrored back to her what he saw.

"Ariadne..." he said, but that was as far as he got; she wrapped her arms around his neck and engulfed his mouth with hers.

"My sons," John's father one day said when he was twelve, "if ever you are walking along the road, and you meet a woman, and she is crying, make no attempt—no, not even the smallest one—to comfort her.

"That is, unless you plan to marry her afterwards."

John's uncles had laughed, and his mother had playfully smacked her husband with the cloth she was using to clean the table. But he remembered the look that had passed between his parents: amusement, understanding...and something else. Now, all these years later, John experienced what his father meant as Ariadne's devastating shift from vulnerability to passion flung him heart, mind and body into the depths of his own hunger. He'd no will at all to stop and back away from her as he had in Corinth...and he had no wish for such.

Even through their robes, every inch of every surface where they touched was suddenly as hot as metal lying in the sun; John's mouth skimmed Ariadne's throat, savoring the taste of her skin, and moved slowly from jawline to chin, then back to her mouth, over and over again. Each circuit only made him want to touch those magnificent surfaces more, made him want to extend his explorations. His breath caught as his fingers tentatively touched her breast; his head swam as they moved with their own will, as if they knew exactly how best to captivate the marvelous treasure his searching had found. Ariadne let out a small, pleasured groan and his own voice rumbled from somewhere deep in his chest as she drew him closer with her increasing need.

John wanted nothing more in that moment than to follow his body's urgent demand to turn this joyful investigation into glorious discovery. Still, he pulled away to look into Ariadne's eyes, uncertainty suddenly shadowing his own.

Do you really want this? His look asked.

And his heart exploded with elation at the "yes" his double's smile offered him.

John knew not when or how it happened—but suddenly there were no robes to stop their tentative probings from becoming the pure and blissful unfolding of mutual pleasure. He lowered his body to Ariadne's and knew the utter rightness of being with this one; wondered how he could ever have doubted the goodness of knowing such beauty.

The elation John increasingly felt as he and Ariadne caressed each other with hands and mouths, as they slowly and inexorably joined as man and woman, was made even more magnificent by what happened between their souls. Time again shifted in his awareness, stretching into eternity as it had the first time they'd kissed. He was again blissfully, excruciatingly aware of every movement they shared; every part of him rejoiced as the power of their dance drew them deeper and deeper into each other, as Ariadne's heart and soul cleaved to his.

As their hearts opened and touched, playing and exploring, entwining with each other as their bodies did, their souls drew ever closer to oneness, ascending in a rising wave of pleasure, delight and completion. The exultation of what they were as their intertwined bodies swayed in the ancient rhythm of Life spread out from their joining and touched the air around them; their ecstasy grew and expanded, owning John in a way he had never known was possible. He heard as if from a distance his own and Ariadne's incoherent utterances, was aware of sharing the laughter that echoed their growing joy in sharing mind and body...

...And yet, all within John was the joyful Stillness that was the essence and Source of their shared movement. He knew in a new way the utter truth of what he'd often told his students: there is no place the One does not live, no act God does not revel in.

Suddenly, completely unexpectedly, every thought fled as John was wholly possessed by ecstasy. Every last bit of his life force was drawn into Ariadne's heart and fed back to his own through her soul as God greeted God in the heart of the Silence. A rapturous cry escaped his lips and spiraled away in bliss as his being exploded and dissolved into Ariadne's; he felt more than heard her own exclamation.

But only barely. As the Silence rushed into their soul-shattering consummation, as they joyously drowned in it and became the entire universe, their individual selves disappeared. Of, "John" and "Ariadne" there was no longer any trace.

They were One.

They lay together in the dimness of the candlelight's comforting glow, his head resting on her stomach. A blanket covered them, even though John still felt as if his skin was on fire from the inside out. He heard night's creatures singing in the Karikos gardens; their calls sounded like a celebration of life, of love, of sharing.

His own heart was so full it seemed too large for his chest. He was...well...not exhausted, exactly, but... John realized he had no words for what he felt, and that made him smile for some reason his Self did not deign to share with his conscious awareness.

Another thought, though, did occur.

"Paul of Tarsus is mad."

Ariadne's husky laugh vibrated against his face. "His way is different from yours."

"Until an hour ago, his way *was* my way. I was mad as well."

"It may be that you are speaking from a bit of a bias, John," she chuckled.

"Then may it always remain so."

Ariadne was silent for several moments, then: "Tell me what you know."

He smiled. "Not very long after Mary and I first began teaching, I made a comment to one of our students that showed quite well my ignorance of the ways of men with women and women with men. Mary was thoroughly exasperated and told me I was not only sheltered from the world, but from my own humanity.

"I was greatly offended; after all, if celibacy was good enough for my Teacher, it was certainly good enough for me... But of course, now, in light of certain recent discoveries, I would say that her rebuke may have been warranted."

Ariadne giggled and lazily twined her fingers in his hair. "I have heard Paul criticizes his followers for their attractions to each other. I've heard he insists that to even allow oneself to feel attracted, much less act on those feelings, is against God's will."

"I felt that way too, Ari. Despite the fact that most of Jeshua's twelve are married men, I always thought his words referred not to us, but to those not dedicated enough to focus only on seeking the One without such distractions. Indeed, I thought walking the prophet's way made me in some way more worthy than even the rest of Jeshua's companions...and I held to at least a vestige of that belief until I met you."

"A vestige?" Ariadne said, highly amused.

"Well, all right, more than a vestige," John agreed with his own chuckle. "But Ari, there are very few of us who do not need the intimate mirror and connection of another at some time in our lives if we are to fully know the One. Granted, the connection need not be that of lovers, but it does have to be intimate in the heart. Whatever my own refusal to admit that, the truth is we never begrudged our students the right to marry and walk the Path—in fact, Mary, Martha and Elior were notorious matchmakers.

"And do you know? Those matches often expanded not only the consciousness of the two who came together, but everyone around them. It was as if their light was made two, four—a hundred times brighter by joining together on their journey."

"But you did not have to have it so, John," she said, a frown in her voice. "You found and shared the One without the need of an intimate companion. What, then, could be the purpose of our coming together now?"

"Oh, I had intimate companions all right," he said, thinking principally of Miriam. "But they were of the heart, not the body. And I often struggled even with that.

Jeshua used to say it was never true that man, to fully remember God, must live always alone as the eunuch does. Be *willing* to give all you have and are to the One, yes. That is necessary and at times becomes manifest. But there is no one-for-all conduct, save that of surrendering to the Stillness Itself, that will magically make everyone recall the truth of what they are. I see now that I never really believed that."

"Hmm," Ariadne said, her fingers causing shivers as they grazed John's neck. "I cannot believe Mary merely admonished you on a subject so important, then let it be."

"Oh no, she certainly did not!" John laughed. "Though I must say in my mother's defense that unless I did or said something so amazing that she could not avoid making her point in a stronger manner, she usually did only admonish me. Her solution in that case, however, was to engage herself, Martha, Elior and Miriam in finding a match for me."

Ariadne laughed. "Oh, no."

"Oh, yes. I had no idea there were that many women in *Judea*, much less Bethany! But I resisted their efforts so strenuously—

"—Breaking many hearts I am sure—"

"—And took such umbrage at their meddling, that they finally saw fit to let it go. Or more likely, they realized things would attend to themselves. And so they have."

John rose up on his elbows and gazed into Ariadne's large, dark eyes, played with the curls that tumbled softly around her face. "Thank the One they did not pressure me into choosing a mate, else where might I be now? Certainly, the wait has been worth it, for the One has blessed me far, far beyond what I could have imagined. Even so..."

John looked away, suddenly shy. "I am...very new at all of this, Ariadne. I was so young when I chose the prophet's way that...well. Pleasing a woman is not an art I ever thought to have to learn. Will you be patient with me while I do? Will you teach me?"

Ariadne was quiet for so long that John wondered if she had fallen asleep. When he looked into her face, however, he found she was staring at him with the same look she'd had when she recognized the Stillness while grieving for Joshua.

"You are an odd man indeed, John bar Zebedee," she said, the wonder as much in her voice.

"How so?"

"Most men would never admit to not being absolute masters at every aspect of pleasing a woman, not even if they were the clumsiest creatures in the world. Yet here you are, a Teacher of teachers, asking for help about the most intimate of things." She lay back and stared at the ceiling, a broad smile on her face. "No, dear man. You are not the only one the One has blessed beyond imagining."

They fell silent, then talked, then fell silent, then talked again over the next two hours, enjoying their conversation and the music of night by turns—that is, until a loud rumble from Ariadne's stomach interrupted them. She giggled.

"Well, full as our hearts may be, our stomachs have another opinion on the matter."

They dressed and tipped out into hall: though it was past twelfth hour, it was wholly possible others might be up. A number of people had come to Iustus's upon hearing about Joshua, both to commiserate and to discover how so horrible a thing could happen "to one who seemed so blessed." They were, as Mary later said with a wry chuckle, "equal parts caring and callousness. I will never fathom why people think sharing their bigger and worse stories should make the bereaved feel better."

John hoped they met no one—and instantly recognized the source of his trepidation. He'd done no wrong by loving Ariadne, true. Still, he found himself blushing, and thanked the One that Demeter was still in Corinth. So profound an experience must leave some sort of mark, after all; even if no one else noticed, surely she would know what had transpired between him and her sister just by looking at his face.

And he wasn't sure he'd be able to survive the resultant tittering.

They hunted up bread, cheese and fruit and adjourned to a small table in a corner of the dining room. They ate in silence, alternately staring into each other's eyes, then bashfully looking away to peer out the window; the half-moon provided light and lent an extra sense of delight to an already enchanted evening, born though it was of such a tragic day.

They wandered hand in hand back down the hall, to come at last to the "T" that led to Ariadne's room. She looked that way, then back at John.

"I should go to bed. You will have much to do on the morrow, to attend to Joshua."

"Iustus sent a messenger on the first ship to Caesarea, bless his heart..." John shook his head. "His parents will be devastated."

He sent what blessings he could to Sarah and Joses Matthatus, recalling his mother Salome's reaction to James's death, even with her great awareness of the One. Ariadne nodded, lost, perhaps, in her own memories of losing her mother and her own and Demeter's husbands; the silence stretched between them until it became uncomfortable.

Finally, she kissed John and started toward her own room. He watched her go, his heart constricting.

"Ariadne," he suddenly called after her.

She stopped and looked questioningly at him.

"You don't—" John stopped, his cheeks suddenly growing hot. He took a breath. "My room is big enough for both of us."

Ariadne stood stock still for several moments. Then she smiled, came back to him and took his hand in hers.

TWENTY-NINE

John *walked through the* dusky outskirts of Ephesus, heading toward Iustus Karikos's home. He and Mary had postponed the training for three weeks, one of which was already gone. It was a good choice, for it gave the throng of Christine volunteers the chance to make repairs on the old cottage that they would otherwise have had to make with the training in progress. More, it had allowed him to attend to what needed doing in light of Joshua's death.

John sent another missive to Joses and Sarah Matthatus, and one to the companions in Corinth. Joshua's families, both biological and chosen, deserved to know all the details of his death. It would not assuage their loss, but neither would it leave them wondering for the rest of their lives what had actually occurred. Or so he hoped.

John also paid Governor Flavius a visit to clear up any confusion about Prochorus's part in the affair. This was no hard thing: as all the witnesses could testify, Marcus had used his knife only to save John and only when nothing else would stop the mad Persian.

He'd checked the next day to see how Marcus fared, ready to remind him to keep his focus on the Stillness, but there'd been no need. Since being accepted for the training, Marcus displayed a willingness to share himself that made his inner self positively glow. Not that his crustily cynical opinions of the universe were any less in evidence; John frankly hoped he'd never be able to say that. It was just that these days, Marcus only rarely tried to explain away the gentleness he often allowed to show. John wasn't sure Prochorus realized it, but the One's tenderness increasingly informed all his activities.

As to Haifata... John breathed in the crisp air that now held a hint of winter's coming chill and shook his head. His ongoing avoidance of John and the others worried him. Had this latest blow, coupled with his disappointment at not avenging himself on Iscariotus's men, finally taken his heart from him?

Mary as usual, had seemed unconcerned when he'd taken his worries to her. But that had been almost two weeks ago, and Adan still showed little sign of coming out of himself... *And yet she is still unconcerned,* John realized with a sudden and unexpected sense of reassurance. *Perhaps, in light of previous experiences, he could follow her lead and trust.* John smiled slightly, suddenly glad of his willingness.

Well, on that matter, at least.

He recalled the care he and Mary had taken throughout the rest of that exchange. Though Thomas's disapproving manner made clear that he—and probably everyone in Ephesus—knew of the change in his and Ariadne's relationship, Mary had assiduously avoided mentioning it, not even dropping the small, smiling hints some of the others had. He was glad of the courtesy, for he was in no mood for teasing about Ariadne, not even from her.

John entered the crowded, closed-in streets of Ephesus proper. With solstice approaching, the sun came ever later and left ever earlier each day. The Ephesians, too, went home earlier, blowing out their lamps by eighth or ninth hour. That is, except for the frequenters of the local taverns, the flesh dens...and House Karikos. Famished as he was, John had no desire to spend an extra half-hour fighting the throng, so he turned the bulk of his attention to flowing with his surroundings, and with only minimal jostling and dodging, found the route Iustus's eldest sons had shown him. Soon, he was once more alone, on the street and with his thoughts.

Truth to tell, it was not Mary's teasing John feared at all. No, the truth was, he did not wish to discuss his and Ariadne's relationship because he felt a nagging sense of guilt over their intimacy.

Oh, it was not at all like the anguish he'd put himself through in Corinth. In fact, most of the time, he was sure he must glow, so great was his contentment. And yet, every so often, he found himself brooding over what he and his double shared, including, now, his bed. When the guilt nagged him—and it didn't often, not really, he again reminded himself—it came as the fear that, while he'd gained unimaginable joy by loving Ariadne, he'd also lost something special by satisfying the needs of his body.

And it hadn't helped that he'd had no visions since the change in their relationship.

John hadn't noticed it at first; he'd been too lost in the euphoria of his new love, too busy attending to Joshua and preparing the training space, to be alarmed by the absence of something that often wasn't even pleasant.

By the fifth day, though, he did begin to wonder at the visions' absence, and by the seventh day, he knew they'd ceased. He told himself he had no reason to miss them, but the truth was, just as with his imagined specialness in walking the prophet's path, he'd come to see the visions as a mark of grace, and now that grace was gone.

A week or so after moving into his room, Ariadne, self of him that she was, asked if all was well, but he'd been reluctant to speak of his disquiet, telling instead some story about missing Joshua. She'd gazed into his eyes as if expecting more, but her willingness to wait was apparently as great as Mary's: she'd simply kissed him goodnight, then burrowed into their blankets.

John had never loved her more than in that moment: they'd cuddled together like happy children until she slumbered. But then he'd lain in the dark, his guilt again niggling at him. Still, since it was gone the next morning, he decided it must be unworthy of concern and told himself it would pass soon enough.

John entered House Karikos and cautiously stuck his head around the corner of the main room. It wasn't quite full, but it soon would be, he knew. Despite Iustus and Thaleia's continuing insistence that it was more than adequate, discussions about finding a larger location went on just as if the ones making those grand plans thought John, Mary and the others would spend the rest of their lives in Ephesus.

John was wise enough not to second-guess them: it might be that the One would move two of his companions to stay here once their training was complete. Or perhaps Miriam and Martha would be prevailed upon to send someone from Bethany. And of course, Mary might well choose to stay.

John's stomach rumbled loudly enough to lighten his head; he truly needed to eat. He turned to go back out the door—but at that moment, Johanna rounded the corner. John shushed her before she could greet him aloud and pulled her outside for an embrace; he was always happy to hear how she fared. The radiance one gained as the Practice healed the scars of life's vagaries was becoming apparent in Johanna; her once careworn face looked a dozen years younger than it had even a few weeks before.

She laughingly agreed, bless her, to keep John's presence a secret until he could feed his poor, pining body and he walked to the side of the house. He entered the gardens by the shortcut shown him by Iustus and Thaleia's second-youngest boy, Andrus, "the child the word 'rascal' was created for," as Mary laughingly put it, and started to creep through, thinking to avoid any students who might be wandering within its beautiful confines...but he stopped at the sight that greeted him.

Haifata Adan sat in the semi-darkness before a small pond, staring into its shallowness like one lost to the world. John's skin rippled with gooseflesh: numerous birds and small animals surrounded him, seeming to take no note of his existence, yet John could not help feeling that they remained past their day at Adan's behest, to pay homage to the one so recently lost. John backed away, intending to leave Haifata and the animals to their business, but of course, hunter that he was, the African heard him.

Adan looked up from his vigil and motioned John forth; though he smiled, there were tears in his eyes. As those tears spilled freely down his cheeks, he raised his hand to show John what he held: it was a small, elegant gold medallion, a favorite of Joshua's that he'd given Haifata upon his arrival in Ephesus. "A gift," as the young man had put it, "for one who has loved me through all that's been, even when I had no right to expect it."

John's own eyes filled as he handed it back and sat beside his friend to share his vigil: the large emerald in its center was surrounded by several small diamonds, the exact number of Adan's lost children, plus one.

"You see, brother?" Haifata whispered thickly, "You worried for my soul when I found I could not fight the Romans. But there was no need. Now I cry for all my sons."

By the time John finally reached the kitchen, it was well nigh ninth hour and he was very nearly invisible with hunger. Happily, he found a large platter loaded with victuals of many kinds; he promptly grabbed a loaf of dark bread and several slices of meat, one of which instantly found its way to his mouth. As he hunted for a clean cup to dip into the water barrel, he looked toward the small table at back of the room. Several servants surrounded Mary, who was cheerily dispensing advice and encouragement.

John smiled; how very much he loved this one who so willingly loved everyone else!

As the servants collected hugs and moved away, John's guilt over Ariadne again flashed through his mind. Truly, this is no great matter, he thought, once more embarrassed that it should bother him at all, but he grabbed a cloth to lay his food on and went to the table anyway, wondering how he could broach the subject and gain his mother's advice. Mary said nothing as he sat, just smiled and squeezed John's hands when he tried to look away, her gaze locking his in place.

All at once, the universe dissolved. A sudden rush of exultation took John's breath away as his heart expanded beyond all boundaries. His skin warmed from toenails to hair-ends; his soul opened and embraced and rejoiced at the entry of another's into it. His mother was not just with, but within him. They were one, mind, body and soul.

Just as when he and Ariadne lay together.

John was suddenly standing, his cheeks hot enough to ignite parchment. Tight with fury, he snatched his hands from Mary's grasp as if she were a crocodile seeking to pull him into a swamp. He could not have been more insulted had she stripped him naked in the street and offered his services to the den-crawlers. For her—for his mother—to enter so intimately into the deepest part of his being was reprehensible!

Eyes still on John, Mary leaned back in her chair, her expression wry.

"Yes. Well. Then you can imagine how I reacted the first time Jeshua did that to me."

John's ire gushed away as surprise and disbelief overtook him. "Jeshua? But..."

"My husband," Mary said, her smile reminiscent, "was a man who enormously enjoyed being a man. As you know, I was many years younger than Josef when we married, and though he belonged to the One heart and soul, he was not without...experience. He taught his much younger wife what it was to know the heights and depths of the One by so intimately sharing, and when he died, I did not believe there could ever be another with whom I could share my soul that fully. Or ever want to.

"One evening, shortly before his winemaking feat in Cana, Jeshua and I sat at table and I spoke of his father. I admit my tone was wistful, and while I did not speak directly of it, for it would have been a most inappropriate subject for a mother and son to discuss..." Mary grinned at the awareness that John considered it an inappropriate subject for *this* mother and son to discuss, "...the truth was, I missed Josef's touch. More than that, I missed the Oneness we shared whenever we touched.

"Jeshua, of course, was not fooled by my attempts to talk around the matter. He grabbed my hands as I did yours, looked me straight in the eyes, as I did you—and I took just as much offense as you did with me.

"'How *dare* you?' I said, all indignity and ire. I felt he had violated me beyond all possibility of redemption, that he had soiled what had been between Josef and me. Even knowing what my son was and what it would cost, in that moment, I actually considered throwing him out of my house and crying him dead to my heart."

Mary suddenly laughed and shook her head. John, though still offended by what had happened, warily sat back down, hooked, as always, by his mother's love of a good story.

"Now, you know it is true, John, that like all good mothers, I could quail any of my children's hearts with just a look—yes, even Jeshua's, for he was not always a saint as a boy! Well, I certainly gave him quite the look then!

"But this time, my son did not flinch. 'Mother,' my Jeshua said with his solemn face and laughing eyes, 'you love the One as well as any priest or rabbi has ever sought to do; indeed, you love the One better than they do, for you know It. You love the One as the angels themselves must, as my father did, as I do. So can it be that you truly think God brought the two of you together solely to give my existence legitimacy? Do you really believe sharing the ecstasy of God's union with another was meant to die from your life with my father's death? That it could only be shared in one way?

"'Mother! Can you truly believe experiencing such union can ever be a violation?'

"Jeshua reached out to me again, his look a demand. I wanted more than life to run from that room, but I could not do so; though I was literally terrified of taking my son's hands again, I could only trust that he in truth would never act to defile another.

"And, John, it was true! When Jeshua took my hands and we again became One, I knew my trust was warranted. There was no violation, no defilement and never had been. There was only rejoicing In the Unbounded Fullness."

The splendor that glowed from Mary's countenance made John blush, just as it had at Prochorus's well on the night of her Ascension. It still seemed to him only husband, wife, lover—or God—should see such naked vulnerability in another.

"'Mary,' my first born said, further shocking me by using my given name, 'sharing the love of the One between only two people will never do. The purpose of union between belovéd ones is to extend that Fullness beyond themselves, out into the entire world, without reservation. To do anything else is to fail to fully serve the One—and your Self.'

"From that moment on, I strove always to give, truly give, all of my being to everyone, just as I had willingly given it to Josef. It was not always an easy thing; sometimes fear held me so strongly in its grasp that I could not give just then. Yet, I was always willing to move beyond that fear. And you, John, must learn to be just as willing."

John spread his hands. "But Mother, how am I to do that? You are an Ascended one, able to extend the gift of your being to whatever extent and in whatever form you wish. This depth of...of bonding you speak of I have only known in one way... and I most definitely have no desire to share that with any but Ariadne."

Mary actually snorted, her expression amused. "Indeed, you feel guilty about sharing it in that way with her."

"It is nothing, Mother, it will pass."

"It is a great deal, my son, however much your phantom self would diminish its importance to keep you from taking it to the One," she retorted. "John, the problem is not that you feel guilt for loving Ariadne with your body as well as your heart! The problem is you've allowed your phantom self to tell you this one thought is fine to keep. 'It is no great thing, it will pass.'"

As Mary seized John's hands again, he twitched at the sudden realization that she'd offered the same kind of union they'd just shared for years. It was only that until Ariadne, he'd not recognized it for what it was.

"John, your reaction to what I've always offered should tell you this will not 'just pass', for you continually push your discomfort with it aside instead of truly looking at it. You still think it wrong to be lover to Ariadne 'despite your focus on the Stillness' because you have not yet taken this to the Stillness. Because you fear the One will not give you what you want, you let your phantom self convince you that this one thing need not be given over 'just yet', that you can attend to it with your own strength.

"But I say you must instantly give any thought that takes your peace, even for a moment, to the Stillness. And until you do choose to do that—well, do not you think it unfair to continue to share Ariadne's favors when you think it a sin?"

Sin. It was a word Jeshua never used when alone with his closest students; he'd called it a ridiculous, utterly false concept to him and to God. After all, if being separate from and in conflict with the all-powerful One was but a dream, how could one commit any act that could decrease Its Wholeness?

And yet, here was this word, reverberating in John's head. He did believe his love...no...that being Ariadne's lover...was a "sin", even though he felt more complete in her presence than he had since witnessing Mary's Ascension, since Jeshua's sojourn on the earth. How could such a thing be?

Dearest son! This worry is no different than any other, Mary traced as she released his hands. Truly step into the Silence and discover the gift It has to give you.

John did so...and completely relaxed as his conversation with Jeshua during his second visit to Vashti flashed through the burgeoning Stillness.

Is it possible to be forced to choose between one's soul and one's Self?

The phantom self seemed subtle only until one finally stepped away from it and saw that its voice was not one's own. As John saw the machinations Mary had spoken of, as he recognized, yet did not judge, that self's ancient drive to be god without God, they and his guilt gently dissolved. He again knew, just as he had on the night of his and Ariadne's first joining, that when one's true desire was to know the One, the journey to that knowing could never conflict with Its Will. The purity of that desire made all pure.

Mary's beingness once more threaded its way into his, but this time John didn't flinch away. Instead, he opened to it more and gloried in becoming one with one whose unity with the Being of God was known, accepted and entirely free of doubts.

Your day of freedom is coming too, dear one, Mary's "voice" laughed. Keep trusting, keep open, keep letting go of what you think you know...

John opened his eyes, feeling more at peace than he had since Joshua's death.

"Which also happened exactly as it should have," Mary said suddenly, her look firm.

John's sense of peace fell away. "I told him he could know the use of love only by experiencing it for himself, Mother, but I knew not what I was about. Oh, I was smugly sure I did and smug in my advice, but..." he shook his head. "All I can see now is that I let my unknowing lead my student to senselessly martyr himself."

"'*I*' did no such thing, John bar Zebedee," Mary replied with some asperity. "The One flowed through you exactly as it needed to, just as it did with Joshua. And his choice to give his life by saving yours was exactly that—his choice."

John shook his head again, still ready to argue—but the approaching sounds of several exclamations and a harsh "get in there," stopped him.

The kitchen door pushed hesitantly inward and Prochorus backed in, pulling Erezavan behind him. The younger man's face sported numerous scratches, his nose gushed blood, and his mouth was set in a furious line. Thaleia, Johanna and Ariadne fluttered in after them, making motherly clucking noises at the mess and, John thought, lamenting the abuse of his darkly beautiful face.

"What in the name of the One?" John stepped closer, frowning.

"The boy decided to get into a fight," Prochorus answered, forcibly steering Isvant to the chair John had been sitting in. Erezavan pulled away and sat, tilting his head back; John felt a tap on his shoulder and moved aside. Ariadne stepped up and none-too-gently wiped the young man's nose with a wet cloth, making him yelp and curse.

"Is it broken?" Thaleia winced with the imagined pain of Ariadne's treatment.

"It would serve him right if it was."

"Was I supposed to ignore their insults?" he asked angrily, his voice muffled by the nose and the cloth. Johanna appeared with a bowl and Ariadne rinsed the now bloody rag, turning the water scarlet.

"You could have been killed, Erezavan; those men had knives, for heaven's sake."

"And was I supposed to simply ignore them?" he asked again.

Suddenly they were all arguing with the young Persian, who argued back around Ariadne's ministrations.

"Would someone like to tell me exactly what happened?" John asked over the din.

Four sets of eyes turned to him, brows raised, as if fully noticing his presence for the first time. The fifth set continued to stare grimly at the ceiling as Mary watched him.

Marcus's voice held dry amusement. "I came into the fray a bit late, but it seems several of the 'faithful' blamed the lad for Joshua's death because of his previous association with Baremna. Erezavan resented their accusations."

"I was there. I went out when I heard the commotion." Ariadne's voice held no amusement at all. "He resented the accusations of a butcher's apprentice and two of his friends, all of whom were armed. While you, Erezavan, were not. You might well have found yourself following Joshua."

"They dishonored me. I defended my honor. I would do it again, even unto death." The Persian's voice was almost unrecognizable, as if anger was so new to it that it roughened his throat. Had his head not been tilted back, he would surely have spat on the floor to further emphasize his point.

John had eyes only for Ariadne as she capably stopped the nosebleed and saw to Erezavan's cuts in tight-lipped silence. Her curtness might hide it from the others, but her fear of losing another one she'd come to care about was plain to him.

Even so, he asked everyone but Mary and Erezavan to leave the room.

"This last cut needs attending to, John," Ariadne protested, but he shook his head and gently laid his hand over hers.

"It will be all right, dearest. Please."

Both he and Mary stifled their smiles as his double stubbornly finished ministering to Erezavan's cut, then very slowly tidied up, but at last she followed the others out.

John sat across from Erezavan and waited, saying not a word; Isvant stared sulkily down at his hands as if he never meant to speak. Still John waited, then waited some more, his willingness to be patient apparently boundless.

Finally, Erezavan sighed and closed his eyes; most of an hour passed as his bruised face went from anger, to fear, to tearful grief, to acceptance. Through it all, neither John nor Mary spoke; they simply held to the Silence.

"I believed what they said, you know," he said at last. "That is why I fought them. I thought it should have been me instead of Joshua who fell to Darshinika's knife, just as they did; that if I had not come on this journey, this would not have happened."

"Hmm. You 'thought'. And what do you 'think' now, Erezavan?"

Isvant's gaze went distant as he considered it. "I... I think the universe does not make mistakes," he said, then scowled mightily. "Even if I want to believe It does. I think if Baremna had not fulfilled Joshua's fate, another would have. Always a soul has more than one way to complete such a major lesson as Death in given a lifetime."

John glanced at Mary and raised a brow. "Indeed? Then you think a man's way is laid forth, that he has no ability to change it once he sets foot upon its path to fulfillment?"

Erezavan's look again went distant, as if he sought the right words. He began to speak of the choices a soul was born to make and fulfill with other souls, of the inevitability of fulfilling those choices in their chosen ways, including how one died. The young man's speech was erudite, brilliant, and letter-perfect; John could almost see the twelve year-old who'd been taught by both the compliment and the stick to carefully compose the 'correct' reply to some esoteric inquiry. His head had been bowed as the Persian gave his answer; now he looked into his face.

"And this is your direct experience, Erezavan? You know this to be what is?"

"Well, no, Sir...but it is what the Masters taught me and what I believe to be true."

John actually sneered.

"Faugh! Any parrot can spout intelligent words, but that will never be the same as Knowledge. You waste my time and your teachers' honor by uttering such drivel."

Well, we need no longer fear the lad is too docile, John thought as Isvant roared from his chair. Now the pendulum swings to the other end.

"That is not fair!" Erezavan yelled, hands fisted at his sides. "That is *not* fair! I have forsaken one friend to follow you and watched both him another friend die! I have shown you nothing but the utmost respect in all our dealings, yet, you speak to me like I am a stupid child! Why? What have I done to warrant this? What do you want from me?"

Prochorus burst through the door, looking as ready to fight as Erezavan did, but John shook his head to indicate all was under control. The Roman grunted disbelievingly, but backed—slowly—from the room.

The distraction seemed to give Erezavan the chance to see what he was about. Eyes still blazing, he picked up his chair, which had clattered to the floor, then slowly sat and clenched his hands together. John sat on the table before him, his voice gentling but his words implacable.

"What do I want from you, Erezavan? Certainly not what your phantom self's emotions of the moment and learnings of the past choose to spew forth. Look at yourself! You risk your very life to prove some useless point to people who'd not know Truth if you laid it before them on a golden plate, yet when I ask you to tell me what you know, you spout theories at me like a bladder leaking wine. Then take umbrage when I say as much. If you wish to be another whose theories mean more than truth, that is your choice—but you'll not do so as one amongst my companions.

"Now, Erezavan Isvant, *tell me what you know.*"

Isvant stared at John for an irate moment longer, then closed his eyes. Though it took some time, when the young man finally found the Stillness, he dropped into It with the ease of a hot stone falling through snow. In fact, such was his proficiency that, even though his consciousness touched into other realities, he effortlessly stayed There with his eyes opened. John shook his head. Erezavan seemed wholly unaware of how long it took most others to realize even the barest sense of their Selves with any stability.

"Joshua lives in another place, another world," the young man said, his brows furrowing slightly. "It is as if he always lived there, even as he lived here, as if his death in this world served to bring him more fully into that one. The Silence in him shines like a beacon to others...in fact... Can it be? It is!"

Erezavan's voice betrayed his wonder as he fixed part of his attention on John. "Sir! Joshua was born into our world only so he could awaken and share the One in that one! He helps many there remember, not as a student, but as one called Teacher. Truly, so short as his life seemed, he fulfilled all he came for."

John nodded as Isvant's eyes cleared. "So then, do you see there is more to your teachers' theories than mere belief could ever have shown you?" he asked.

Isvant nodded, suddenly ashamed of his earlier outburst, but John gently took his chin, careful of the fast-forming bruises. "That is good, very good. Still, there is one more thing I would have you do. If I say or do something that offends or frightens you, I expect you to say so—" he smiled crookedly "—though without quite so much vehemence, perhaps. Yes, there will surely be times when you will have to trust based on no more evidence than my word, but that never means you have no right to speak.

"What you must not do, Erezavan, is waste your power living some false definition of what it is to be enlightened; you must not. One Darshinika Baremna was far more than enough."

Isvant nodded, then suddenly seemed to deflate; not with dejection, but exhaustion. It had been a long day. John smiled sympathetically.

"Go to bed, Bright Light; let the Practice restore you. You've done very well this day."

John extended his other hand to heal Erezavan's wounds as the young man smiled at his praise like the young boy he'd never truly been allowed to be—but Mary's look stopped him. She stepped around the table and laid a kiss on the Persian's forehead; he smiled again, tiredly thanked them and left. John looked questioningly at her.

"Erezavan is not the only one who has had a long day, my son," she smiled. "And he was not the only one to experience the truth of what he feared was not true, hmm?"

"No, Mother. I can no longer deny the value of what I gave Joshua aboard *Matthatus*," John agreed after a moment. "Even so, the manner in which he died was..."

"What it was, John. As was Jeshua's chosen way to show us the truth of what we are. It is not ours to understand, and it certainly is not ours to change."

"Not even yours, Mother? Even you do not understand the 'whys' of the One's ways?"

Mary kissed his cheek. "Does a fish ask why the water exists? When you know yourself to *be* the One, John, know so fully there is only the One that you cannot imagine a 'One' or an 'other'...well, what need could you ever have to ask 'why' about anything?

"Get some rest, my dearest son, and know that all is well. Always.

THIRTY

The *next dozen days* went by in a haze of busywork. John awakened before sunrise each morning and dashed from House Karikos, only to return late in the evening, tired to the bone. Not that what he did was unimportant, mind; it was only that it seemed to be producing little in the way of immediate results.

For instance, the companions would start their training the day after the morrow. Yet, many details still needed working out, from procuring food for the next several months to creating space for what would now be six people, since Johanna and Ariadne had asked to join the training.

"We cannot argue with her dedication," Mary said of Johanna, for like Rachael, she spent every hour she could either doing the Practice or asking questions about the nature of the One. "And I most certainly want Ariadne as fully trained as possible."

This day, John arrived at the cottage shortly after ninth hour to confer with the volunteers on how to enlarge the women's room enough to sleep three; he'd already been out of Iustus's house for three hours by then.

"Elder, this old place will be hard-put to comfortably hold two on an ongoing basis," Jaresh, the foreman said. "Now it's to hold thrice that number? And confined to this property, with the cottage the only indoor space available for several months?"

"I fear that is exactly the case, Jaresh."

The foreman shook his head, his face reflecting his consternation, while the other volunteers muttered their dismay. "Well, then, we'd best do something," someone said at last, "else the lot of 'em'll be at each other's throats inside a month, Christines or no."

John disagreed with that assessment, for he knew the Practice would help keep things civilized as no other activity would, whatever the conditions.

He gave the trainees *two* months before they'd be at each other's throats.

"So, do you think we can prevent murder, my friends?" he asked, smiling a little.

Jaresh looked thoughtfully at the building. "I think so, Elder... Yes, I believe we can."

"Will you need more time?"

"I do not think so...well, only a few days, with so many working. Will that do?"

John thanked them and managed to hide his sigh until he was out of their sight.

This sort of planning had never been necessary, as even Jeshua's twelve had rarely done more than a few consecutive days of the Practice at a time. In Bethany, students continued living their day-to-day lives as they came to know the One, working ever more closely with the teachers as their experiences of the Stillness deepened. If, after a suitable period, a student showed the inclination and aptitude, the Bethany teachers acknowledged him or her as ready to teach. It was a slow process, and effective; still, Jeshua had repeatedly said that the more hours, days and weeks together one enjoyed the Practice with the eyes closed, the more quickly the belief in the phantom self dissolved, leaving naught but the Joy of being the One's inherent wholeness.

Giving these six such a chance could only be to the good, but would an instruction period of but a few months be enough? Would the companions come out of this knowing the One well enough to face the dangers this journey would present?

Ah well, at least the delay will give me more time to find supplies, John thought. And it would also allow him to finally spend some much welcome time with Ariadne, who was beginning to feel like a stranger who shared his bed. Even on the rare occasions when he arrived home early, John usually ended up closeted with Iustus and his cohorts until second or third hour. By the time he finally fell into bed, Ariadne was either long asleep or he was too tired to do more than kiss her goodnight and roll over himself.

Tonight was no different; John crept into their room past twelfth hour, only to find Ariadne already lost in that ever-so-private world all slumbering souls inhabit. She came to just enough to receive a kiss and pillow her head on his arm.

John smiled and admired his double undisturbed. He knew she was nervous about the approaching training—but then, even Timothy's exuberance grew somewhat subdued when it was mentioned. He could not blame them, not when he was more than a bit nervous about it himself. So, he simply reminded them to use the Practice to notice rather than become their nervousness.

Ariadne shifted and mumbled something unintelligible; John went still, breathing only when she settled back into slumber. Then he winced. The arm beneath her

head was doing a far better job of falling asleep than he was. But at least this sleepless-
ness is caused by enjoying the view, not worrying, he thought with another smile.

And winced again. He tried to move without disturbing the source of his enjoyment.
"John?"

Ariadne awoke with a start, no sign whatever of sleep in her voice. John usually required at least some transition time between being fully asleep and functionally awake,
but his double claimed to have always been that way.

"Oh, I am drowsy enough if you try to wake me as I am falling asleep, but I have
always been quick to wake up—" she grinned, "—and my parents got to be so, too, when I
was a baby. Both Momi and Poppi swore I could wake the dead with my cry."

Now Ariadne pillowed her head on her own arm, her dark eyes smiling as she laid
her free hand on John's cheek.

"I did not mean to wake you, belovéd," he said apologetically.

"I am glad you did. We've hardly had any chance to talk these last several days. I
feel like we are becoming strangers."

John laughed and kissed her. "Echo, echo, soul of me. I was thinking the same thing."

"Hmm. Well, it seemed you did not want to talk for awhile, and though I can see
you are better, time just has not allowed us to be together. Without one of us being dead
asleep, that is."

So, as he enjoyed the distraction she caused by running her fingers along his ear,
cheek and jawline, John told Ariadne of his doubts after Joshua's death, of his unac-
knowledged fear concerning their love, and of his experiences with Mary and Erezavan.

"I think...there is something I do not understand," she frowned after a moment.
"Before Demeter and I began following the Christine way, we studied many different
philosophers, trying to understand something of the soul's journey.

"In one of the writings we found, the speaker referred to what he called 'Night'. He
spoke of it as a soul-shattering experience and said he knew of no great one who had
not been challenged by it; that everyone who sought wholeness must eventually face it.
More, he said that only the few who had successfully done so could be called Masters.

"Is that true, John? Is that what the Christos went through at the beginning of his
ministry and in Gethsemane? Is it what you just experienced?"

Ariadne's gaze was serious in the light made by the small fire that always burned
in the hearth at this time of year. John opened his mouth, ready to answer, then closed
it. He crawled from their bed, donned his robe, and extended his hand.

"What?" she asked confusedly, but John only smiled.

"I think, my love, I am not the best person to answer your question."

Though it was past third hour, Mary's voice bid them enter almost before John's
knuckles finished rapping on the heavy door. He wasn't surprised. In the months before
her Ascension, She'd slept only rarely, usually for less than an hour at a time, and he'd
only seen Jeshua fall asleep once in three years. Despite his generally grumpy awak-
enings, even John only slept four or five hours a night, even in these busy times. This
was a benefit of the Practice, of course. If the deep rest it fostered renewed the body as
it cleared away the phantom self, how could one not need less sleep?

Ariadne and John padded into Mary's chamber to find her sitting in a large, cush-
ioned chair next to her bed, mending a thin shift that was like the one Ariadne wore

beneath her robe, only very much smaller. She smiled at their questioning stares.

"Iustus's youngest asked if I could fix her dolly's shift, 'for it gets very cold at this time of year, you know.' Thaleia could not do it and Katri's older sisters are of an age where such things are perceived to be childish nonsense." Mary sighed lightly. "Is that not often the way of it when we think ourselves all grown up? Ah, well, they will outgrow it soon enough..." She motioned them to sit on her still-made bed. "Now then, dear ones, what brings you forth from the warmth of your bed at so early an hour?"

Mary's gaze sharpened as Ariadne asked her question. John thought she might not answer, for it was not her usual way to speak on things her students had not at least had a taste of. He was mistaken, however; his mother sat back in her chair, mending forgotten.

"Night is the first—and last—experience of fundamental Doubt. It is identical to the doubt that runs through the mind as we begin to uncover the truth that we are more than ever we thought, but we perceive it as the Great Doubt that can stop our growth in its tracks. Night is the phantom self's strongest defense against our efforts to step beyond it; it comes to those who are closest to fully remembering the truth of who they are."

"All of them?"

"So it would seem, Little Flower."

"'Seem'?" John asked. Mary shrugged.

"What is not real can only seem to be, dear son; it can never exist in truth. Indeed, the day soon comes when Night will be so quickly recognized for what it is that it will essentially cease to be. Still, for those who do believe, Night assails them, sometimes for an hour, sometimes for a day or two, sometimes for weeks. Jeshua's Night lasted a mere few hours, just before and during his vigil in Gethsemane (for his desert ordeal was not his Night), while mine lasted the week and more before he was taken and crucified. And Miriam's...well, that was an agonizing business, to say the least."

John frowned. Was Miriam's story about the aftermath of her first meeting with Jeshua also the story of her Night? He'd certainly never seen, in the last seventeen years, any other vestige of what Mary spoke of.

"But why should ones so advanced experience such agonies?" Ariadne asked. John felt the echo of her quailing heart and knew her real question: would she have to experience Night before she could awaken?

"The phantom self's purpose is to be a power that is opposite but equal to the One," Mary said. "Such a thing is impossible, of course, but the phantom self does not know it and would not believe it if it were told. Those who believe in the phantom self think its dream of being separate from God is real; they believe they are the phantom self.

"As we enter into greater awareness, Night seems to use the body, the emotions and the soul itself to convince us the phantom self's impending 'death' is ours, in the hope that we will step away from truth. That effort is in actuality an illusion..." Mary smiled suddenly, "...though it certainly does not feel that way while you believe it."

"But if the phantom self is so strong, and Night so horrible, how can we ever hope to fight it? How can we ever come to believe we are not that?"

Mary put down her mending and set her chin in her hand. "You know the Silence, Ariadne, do you not? Of course you do, for you've described it to me. So enter into it."

Ariadne closed her eyes and did so; as her swirling thoughts slowed, then stopped, the room settled into a deeper layer of the already present Quiet. John's eyes caught Mary's smiling ones. They both knew an excellent student when they saw one.

"Now, open your eyes and tell me what you experienced."

Ariadne blinked. "Nothing. I experienced nothing...or what seemed like nothing..." she smiled. "Yet it was also full and unlimited and wondrous. I...it is hard to describe."

"It will become easier with practice. Did you have any thoughts?"

"Yes, at first, but..." Ariadne looked surprised. "But even then, it was as if they were phantoms, as if the Stillness was all that was real."

"And so It is. Our agreement with the phantom self's belief that being a separate, fearful, individual is real does not make it so, dear one. That is the knowing every Master comes to, the place where Night forever meets its end. The phantom self is not real, never was real, and can never be real. It does not die—" Mary grinned, "—it withers away from lack of interest. We do not forsake our joy in the One's creations as we awaken, but neither do we mistake them for something all-important. The body becomes what it was meant to be: a tool for sharing the truth of our Wholeness with those still asleep.

"Jeshua 'died' to the world long before his body's crucifixion, and in that lay all his power to affect the appearance of Life. By overcoming Night, he made it easier for each one who follows to know there need be no Night—nor even doubt—now or ever."

Shivers chased up John's spine as Mary suddenly turned her attention on him; she had the same fathoms-deep look Miriam had had before he left Bethany. "I will tell you this, Boanerge: what you recently experienced was not Night, only doubt. If Night does come for you, it will do so in a way you could never imagine. In truth, I do not know if you will be able to avoid it—or even if you should. But if it does come, you need only remember your Teacher's words, 'Be still and know that I AM God.'

"*Be* the Silent One, Boanerge, and all will be well...and if that does not work, take the help that comes when it arrives. Do not, for any reason, rely solely on your own strength."

Mary stared through John for a moment longer, then her face cleared. She stood, stretched extravagantly, laid a hand each on John and Ariadne's cheeks and kissed them. "After all, my son, our willingness to use the gifts of strength given us by our companions is what makes it possible to know Fullness in one lifetime instead of millions.

"So then. Back to your warm bed, my darlings. What is left of the night is short, and there'll be visitors to attend to on the morrow, at least one of whom is best met with a sharp mind," she said. Then: "And Ariadne? You did well to bring him to me; thank you for your willingness."

John almost protested the blatant misclaim, but his double's dimpled "Thank you, Teacher," stopped him. She was obviously thrilled by the praise.

"John. Be sure you let Ariadne help you as much as you help her. You will surely find much joy in doing so." Though she did not laugh, Mary's eyes twinkled.

John nodded and smiled back as he pulled the door shut behind them; Ariadne drew his face down to hers and kissed him.

"Thank you for bringing me to her," she murmured, her smile, as always, dizzying him as it lit the hall.

"Thank you for asking such an excellent question," he answered back, for he was suddenly certain most of Mary's discourse had been for him. "Did she answer it?"

"I think so..." Ariadne nodded, then smiled again, "...but I think by the time it becomes an issue, I will be too old to care."

And I think you underestimate yourself, my heart, John thought but did not say.

Hands clasped, they walked down the quiet hall and back to the warmth of their bed.

The sky glowed with the blue of a sun well-risen by the time John woke up. He lay there for a moment, looking out the terrace doors, and refused to believe he could have slept so long. But the shadows did not suddenly lengthen, nor did the birds' soft chirrups revert to their usual morning-just-barely-arrived raucousness, so yes, it must be late.

He rolled over, bumping against Ariadne. She groaned dramatically as she, too, noted the position of the shadows in the garden.

"We have slept too long," she said grumpily. "I feel more tired now than I would if I had stayed awake."

"Mmph," John agreed, equally disgruntled. He would have liked nothing better than spending a bit of time to cuddle and talk more of their discussion with Mary, but: "I still have things to see to before you and the others begin your training. I need to get up."

He made to crawl over his double with the intent of rousing the small fire pit so it could warm the room and their wash water. Ariadne, however, was not so tired; the arms that wrapped about his neck and her sudden drowsy smile were definitely an invitation.

"Ari, I must go; I am late as it is," John said, though he couldn't stop the chuckle... or the sudden heat that flooded his body. Her smile brightened to its full splendor.

"Did not Mary say I could be a help to you? Then let me help."

John laughed and let her have her way.

By the time they got to the kitchen, it was more than midway past ninth hour. The porridge, always the first thing made and the last left, was lukewarm and stiff. Ariadne wrinkled her nose.

"Bread and water for us this morning, I think."

"It is your fault."

"Yes. I know." Her smile was sparklingly wicked.

They'd just gathered the items of their makeshift breakfast, finding milk and a mixture of dried dates and nuts to add to the bread, when they heard a loud cry and the exclamation, "Oh, they will be so glad to see them!"

As usual, the main room was filled with an eclectic assortment of servants, laborers, merchants, and even two soldiers who'd somehow managed to go missing from their rightful duties without being noticed. Some called themselves Christines, but many claimed loyalty to other faiths or none. This was no hindrance to successfully doing the Practice or achieving the Stillness, of course. As Lazarus had once pointed out: "The One is supremely indifferent to the costumes we wear and the customs we claim. It only desires that we remember our Self is Its Self."

At this moment, no one was doing any such remembering, at least not with their eyes closed; they were sharing greetings and hugs with two of three newcomers. Just as John wondered if it might be Iscariotus and Titus, the third traveler, who needed no help to be seen, entered behind them.

John grinned as Torer smiled with arrogant joy from across the room.

Ariadne squealed jubilantly, causing Demeter Isaurus to look up and duplicate her joyful shriek. The sisters flew to each other, laughing, crying and fully understanding their wholly dissimilar conversations as only women, and sisters in particular, seemed able to do. Dareios Isaurus did not squeal, but the tears in his eyes and the mighty hug and kiss he gave his youngest child showed just how thrilled he was to see her again.

Demeter, whom John had once thought so aloof, grabbed both his hands and gave him a smacking kiss on the cheek, her smile shining with the brilliance of the autumn sky at seeing with her own eyes that he was well. Dareios was just as glad, but more deferential—and their reactions as Mary entered the room were of a piece. Demeter practically jumped into her Teacher's arms and Dareios became even more formal.

"You are late," Mary said, looking them over. She received a matching set of bemused looks, but her comment about expecting visitors floated into John's memory.

"We did not know we were expected," Dareios answered, "as our parting from Corinth was rather sudden. Ada and Hosea seemed to think we needed to be here by today, so we immediately packed and set off."

John looked surprised and concerned. "Are they safe? We heard the soldiers threatened you after I left Corinth. Did they fear they meant to carry out their threats? "

"No, no, Elder. All was well in Corinth. Ada and Hosea continue to work with the new students, and send their love. They will be here in a few weeks, as you expected. They are exemplary teachers by the way, well-loved, and I think at times, well-feared."

"That is good to know, Dareios, very good. But why were they in such a hurry to send you and Demeter here?"

As soon as the words left his mouth and even before the two of them began shifting nervously about, John knew the answer. Mary did too and grinned broadly. Ariadne's brows shot up in delighted disbelief.

"Um, well," Dareios said, "we discussed it with the two of them and they seemed to agree...that is, they felt you would also agree...I mean..."

"You have come to join the training," John finished.

Dareios nodded, but Torer chose that moment to speak up, getting the usual astonished stares.

"Ah, it is better than that, Zebedee! They are coming with us to Vashti!"

"Tell me, Mother, does everyone in Corinth and Ephesus plan to join this journey?"

John paced back and forth in Mary's chambers, where they'd adjourned to discuss this latest complication. "And for Ada and Hosea to send Dareios, of all people? Make no mistake, I would be grateful for his existence even if he were not the father of the woman I love, but he is by no means fit to undertake such a journey as this."

"Because of his deformity?"

"And his age, yes. It will be difficult enough to have four women traveling with us, much less a man who is almost twice the age of the eldest of us, for Jeshua's sake."

"Five. There will be five women with you." Mary's smile was more exasperated than amused at John's dismayed look. "John. Did you really think we would leave Johanna to teach without continuing guidance? For that matter, do you truly think we train these ones to spread the Practice, knowing as you do its chance of surviving undistorted in this time and place?"

John's face grew warm. Despite what Johanna's life had been, it had never crossed his mind that she might want to abandon Ephesus and trek through some unknown wilderness after an elusive goal. But why would she not? Ada, Demeter and Ariadne had been blessed with far easier lives, yet he'd never doubted their willingness.

And as for Johanna's fitness, or Dareios's for that matter, in truth, none of them save Marcus, Haifata and Torer were likely candidates for this journey—least of all him.

Even more jarring however, were Mary's comments about the future.

Yours will be to care for the Mother until Her time comes to be Lord of this earth in balance with the Father, Jeshua had said on his first visit to Vashti ...*though I would have it otherwise, the fullness of this Teaching, ultimately, is not for now, but for a time to come.*

The numbers of people learning the Practice, both here and in Corinth, had lured John into hoping, if not believing, that there was some chance for its continued growth. Yet, the overall life vibration of this world was far too low to keep the teaching's essence undistorted, and he knew it. Jeshua had planted the Seed, yes, but it would take life-times, if not centuries, for this Tree to grow.

But will no one in this time remember to hold the true value of this Practice in their hearts? Is the Mother so grievously wounded? A wave of sorrow filled John's heart.

"We teach our trainees, John, not so much to further the Mother's Will in this time and space, as to fortify them for the journey which will make awakening to It conceivable later on," Mary said gently. "Like you, each of these ones chose to make this attempt many, many eons ago; they can no more resist the draw toward Vashti than the stag can resist the scent of the doe. We, therefore, must make them as ready as possible, for as we both know, this journey will not alone—or even primarily—be physical."

"Yes. But what of these ones we teach the Practice now, Mother? What of Haifata?" For Adan showed no interest in joining the training.

"Just because a seed may lie dormant for a while, even years, does not mean it will not sprout when water finally comes to it," Mary answered. "These ones we teach in Corinth and Ephesus and Judea will be among the first to come to the Practice as it comes back into the world. Their knowing will stabilize its energy in a way that would otherwise be impossible. If they awaken fully now, well and good, but we teach them largely to plant a seed that will bear fruit in the time to come."

Mary smiled. "And as to Haifata, my son, trust that he does exactly what he must and that the One holds him in Its Hands."

She fell silent, leaving only the birds' joyous songs and the laughing passage of Iustus's eldest daughters to be heard. John sat next to her and, sighing, laid his head on her shoulder, just as he had as a much younger man. Truly, he could never in his wildest dreams have imagined what his recent life had brought him.

"So then, Mother, just how many will go on this journey? Should I expect more?"

Mary considered the question as if she debated whether or not to answer it, then: "How many besides you are coming now?"

John counted up the number in his head: Ada and Hosea, Timothy and Rachael, Erezavan, Haifata, Marcus; Johanna, Ariadne, Demeter, Torer and Dareios.

"Hmph. But Jeshua had not one woman among his twelve, much less five."

"The Mother's need was different when my son walked the earth. Now we feed the Seed with new soil."

John's eyes widened, then he turned to Mary, his look accusing. Despite what he'd felt just a few moments ago, he spoke of journeying to Vashti with his growing company as if there'd never been a question of doing so. Mary beamed and nodded knowingly.

"Good. You see that what is left of your phantom self cannot betray your soul's course... So, then," she smiled, nudged John off her shoulder and briskly kissed his forehead, "if you've no more need for nursemaiding..."

"'Nursemaiding'?" he said with mock-indignation, while Mary shooed at the air as if chasing away a fly.

"...then be off with you. Your mother has things to do and so have you. Let me know how it goes with your visitor, hmm? Or perhaps I will find out for myself. We shall see."

John hugged her and left with a smile. He felt the sudden urge to find Ariadne and give her a big, very public kiss, but resisted it; the day was already half-gone. They'd make time to speak every day from now on, even if only for the ten minutes before going to sleep. Meanwhile, best he should get to the cottage and see to the further changes...

John stopped and frowned in puzzlement. Who was the "visitor" Mary expected him to enjoy? Certainly, she did not speak of Dareios, Demeter and Torer. Beyond the fact that they surely could be considered no less than family, they were already here. John turned back to Mary's door, knocked once, and pushed it open.

"Mother?" he called, looking around the chamber.

But he got no answer; she was gone.

Though it was possible she'd merely stepped outside to enjoy Iustus's gardens, all John's senses told him that was not the case.

He shook his head in awe. His business might carry him outside House Karikos, but Mary's carried her far beyond the realms of human time and space.

THIRTY-ONE

John entered House Karikos's neighborhood, his smile still bright over the workmen's solution to suddenly having nine trainees to house.

His consternation had still been considerable when he'd arrived at the cottage, explained the change in situation to Jaresh and sheepishly thanked him for his patience.

"Hah!" one of the men said with a laugh, "You can credit that to his doing that Practice with his eyes open—else you'd probably be swimming in the creek!"

The others laughed, but Jaresh simply rubbed his chin absentmindedly and called the men into a huddle. He pointed toward a clearing that ended at the property's tiny creek. Several good-sized boulders inhabited the flat, grassy space, but even during winter, it would be within easy walking distance of the already-existent cottage.

"What do you think, Avros? Is it big enough?"

"Certainly, though we'll have to clear some of those stones."

"Well, and it'll need a decent space to meet in as well," another of the men said. "That cottage truly is too small for much more than sleeping."

John's mouth dropped open as he realized what they meant to do, and he started to argue against it. After all, the volunteers had spent more than enough of their time and money refurbishing *one* cottage; to build another from scratch seemed too much.

But Jaresh and his men only grinned like young boys about to carry out some gently nefarious plot, then insisted that the Lord had moved them thus. "And would you have us go astray by denying His will?"

John rounded the corner leading to Iustus's house, only to find himself in the midst of a sizable crowd. He snapped out of his reverie and quickly extended his awareness, all-too-vividly reminded of the companions' adventure in Corinth...but only excitement radiated from the thickening multitude. Whatever was on, he need fear no violence.

The crowd quickly parted to let him through, greeting him with a more than usual level of respect, then turned to their neighbors to whisper even more excitedly. John hadn't experienced such adulation since leaving Bethany, and it was jarring to again be thus set apart, especially by the notoriously nonchalant Ephesians.

"Elder! You have returned at last!"

John turned to find Thomas before him, his face aglow, and barely kept his brows from rising in surprise. The glowering, tight-lipped exits the Corinthian made whenever he and Ariadne entered a room clearly bespoke his displeasure at the change in their relationship. And yet, while he barely offered John so much as a "Good Morrow" when they saw each other, he'd apparently not been so uncommunicative with his double: he one day accosted Ariadne in Iustus's garden, accused her of a variety of spiritual crimes, then threatened her soul with the wrath of God if she did not cease her "reprehensible corruption of the Christos's chosen Successor".

At first, John had been unable to discover Ariadne's reply, for she'd only tersely insisted that she'd attended to matters and would say nothing more. But Marcus had been in the garden: he proudly informed John that Ariadne had responded to Thomas's diatribe with a tongue-lashing that left the man ashen with shock. John had seen little of the Corinthian since, but he still spoke to Mary and did the Practice with the larger group.

"Elder, it is the most wonderful thing!" Thomas said, grabbing John's arm to pull him toward House Karikos's front door. "He only just arrived after a very long journey indeed, yet he agreed to speak here. He will be so pleased to see you!"

"Thomas, Thomas, hold! You have not told me who it is you speak of," John said, digging in his heels at Thomas's uninformative zeal. The Corinthian stopped, looking as if he thought John should've divined his visitor's identity.

"Do you not know? Paul of Tarsus has come to Ephesus to preach the Good News!"

John smiled as he resumed the pace Thomas set, but not with joy. Despite the Corinthian's zeal, it struck him as unlikely that Tarsus would be "pleased" to see him again.

They had indeed met before, some six months after Paul's conversion, but it could hardly have been called a meeting between good friends. Paul had scarcely paid the still-youthful John the courtesy of acknowledging his presence; he'd preferred instead to focus his keen attention on the elder of the Zebedee brothers, as if James was the only one who would have information of value—or common sense. John's impression was that Tarsus thought he'd been allowed into Jeshua's company, not because "the Master" prized his devotion to God, but because he'd been diverted by his childlike innocence.

The brothers had felt the insult of it at the time, but they'd stifled their offense because it was useful to do so. John had always been the better of the two at reading people the brothers encountered in their travels, and James relied on him to identify those who faked conversion in the hope of gaining access to the "vast booty" the growing Christine community was supposedly pooling. Slighting John meant he could scrutinize Tarsus without being observed by the brilliant former persecutor.

In all honesty, John would have been glad to discover a charlatan hiding behind Paul's façade of Christine piety, for his distaste for Tarsus was at least equal to Tarsus's insolence toward him. But though the man displayed an appalling lack of tact, in all other ways he was the exemplary Christine. John had not found him wanting.

Thomas tugged John through the front door of Iustus's house, then shushed him as they entered the more than full living room. There was no need; no one had ever had to strain to hear Paul's voice, be he in the largest market or the smallest cottage. Thomas wanted to immediately bring John before Tarsus—present him, John could not help but think—but this he resisted, demanding Thomas not interrupt the older man's talk.

Since most of the people sat on the floor, it was easy enough to see Paul as he spoke with his usual charismatic authority on his understanding of the Christine Way. John had to admit the man could sway the hardest heart; as one trained to serve the Sanhedrin, Tarsus was a fluent writer as well as an eloquent speaker. As one trained by his experience on the road to Damascus, he was utterly convinced of the correctness of his understanding of what Jeshua taught. His energy was boundless, and he spared none of it as he traveled to and fro and spoke to others.

Mary sat beside Tarsus and appeared to listen with rapt attention, but John recognized the amusement that rested beneath that beatific look. Paul frequently referred to her "great sacrifice" as Jeshua's mother, yet he never once directly acknowledged her. That fact annoyed John just as Paul's slights had years before, and he wasn't alone: many of the regular students shifted restlessly at the not-quite-sincere compliments. Though her back was to John, Ariadne's growing irritation was plain. He was glad the talk was winding down: if he referred to Mary as "Good Mother," in that glibly reverent tone one more time, his double was going to give Paul's audience a shock. He wondered if Tarsus had heard the rumors about Mary's Ascension.

John slipped free of Thomas's chaperonage and headed to the Karikos's kitchen, having caught Mary's eye and agreed through nods and gestures to adjourn to its coziness, but it was some time before his mother finally appeared with Paul in tow. He'd not changed much in the dozen-odd years since John had last seen him, save that he had rather less and considerably grayer hair. His stocky body seemed a bit gaunt, but the flame of his intellect still curled off his skin like smoke off a smoldering log.

He quickly but methodically took in the room as if he could gain the measure of its owners by what he found, then looked at John in the same way, quite obviously comparing his picture of the youngster he'd been to the man he was now. Rather than sharing the embrace that was common to most Christines, Tarsus clasped his arm.

"Well met, John bar Zebedee. It has been too long, too long by half," he said in his boldly mellifluous voice. "You've grown up well I see—though you are an odd sight indeed without a beard. Do you take the style of these Greeks you live amongst, or are there other reasons to show your face naked in public?"

"There are other reasons...a long story," John answered with resigned equanimity. The man's manners had not improved one bit.

"Forgive our delay," Tarsus continued, "but your people had many questions concerning my experience with Christ. I felt I could not in good conscience leave the room without instructing the many who seemed so hungry for guidance."

"Would you like some refreshment, Rabbi?" Mary asked, filling the bud of awkward silence before it could fully flower. "Iustus and Thaleia Karikos have an excellent larder. Surely, you must be famished after traveling and sharing with the students."

Tarsus's eyebrows rose at Mary's choice of the word "students" but, though his curiosity was evident, he chose to keep his questions to himself. Instead he said, "Thank you, Mother, but I never take my second meal before sixth hour of the day."

"Even if you are hungry?"

Paul frowned slightly at Mary's tone. "I feel it best to take less food than others might, Mother, so that I will not be sluggish if I am asked to witness on Christ's behalf."

"Hmm. I see... Then may I at least offer you water, that your throat may be soothed? You were, after all, prevailed upon to talk long."

This Paul consented to as John directed him to the table. He tried to catch Mary's expression, but could detect no irony in her manner at all. She was the perfect traditional Jewish female, modestly serving the "head" of the house and his guest.

"How go your travels, Paul?" he asked as they sat.

"Well, quite well. We've traveled this round through most of the important cities, to Phillipi and Appollon, Athens, Corinth and Cenchreae, and we are not nearly done. The journey has been long, yes, but many have been converted through the Grace of Christ speaking through this humble servant, which is all that truly matters. As I pointed out to the Good Mother, it is a hard life, but a bit of suffering is no great thing. After all, if Christ could experience his trials with grace, I can suffer mine.

"Besides, as I recently observed in many of the cities I visited, too much comfort can be a trap for those who walk the Narrow Path. Fortunately, and save for a few exceptions, the people's obedience to Christ grows by leaps and bounds...and even those ones are repenting their unsuitable activities to express their faith in a more correct manner."

John looked mildly surprised at Paul's assessment. They had students from some of the cities mentioned, but he'd seen in them no impropriety. Or at least nothing outside their own cultural norms, which were often less stringent than Judea's.

They talked on many subjects, Paul freely expressing his opinion on most of them. John was amazed at the amount of detailed information the man had stored away, on so wide a variety of subjects. He tended to be more aware of the feel of things, giving little thought to the minutiae unless it needed attention. He wondered if this tendency was a particular expression of the One's gifts in Paul? Or was it that the older man still trusted his mind more than he did the Unbounded, despite his connection to It?

Granted, he spoke of the Christ Mind as something to be found within the self. Yet, though John sensed that Paul frequently experienced the One's Fullness, his manner indicated he did not believe It was inherent. To him the "Christ Mind" was a state to acquire as one did a piece of land. He expected his followers to find—or perhaps a better word was "earn"—The One's grace through prayer and correct living...grace which was also external to them. What might he experience if he learned the Practice?

Tarsus asked John about his journey and John told his story, stopping several times to fill in various details, emphasizing how the companions' use of the Practice allowed even the least spiritually-versed of them to grow with amazing speed. Paul nodded and made the appropriate sounds, but he seemed more impressed by John's dereliction in not more directly sharing the Good News with all he met.

In fact, he thought him scandalously lax in the area of witnessing on Jeshua's behalf. John listened to the older man's erudite admonishments but shrugged inwardly; he knew the rightness of his role in expanding Jeshua's teachings, and his interest in feeling guilty was as great as Paul's interest in hearing more about the Practice.

The conversation stopped as Mary unobtrusively refilled John and Paul's cups. Paul waited until she moved away, then leaned forward, glancing after her as if to make sure she would not eavesdrop on what he clearly considered a private conversation.

"I noticed many who had questions today, indeed many who attended the meeting, were women," he said, his gaze full of concern.

John's brows rose. "There is no strangeness in that, Paul, in Ephesus or Judea. More women than men have always followed Jeshua's way."

"That is true enough," he said forbiddingly, "but it seemed to me these women's demeanor lacked in genuine humility. More than one spoke as if she thought herself a leader, not a follower, and when contradicted by men obviously more informed, showed a less than proper level of deference. Truly, do you think it wise to indulge them so?"

John had heard about the incident that no doubt bothered Paul: one of his followers had all but called Rachael a liar when she described her experience of the One, insisting she must have confused it with a story she'd heard from someone—some man— who was truly, and more capable of, being aware. The young woman, in turn, had rebutted the challenge with such utter politeness and regal assurance that the man had been too tongue-tied to continue the argument.

Strictly speaking, it had not been appropriate for one so much younger, and female, no less, to address an elder man so directly. But Paul's implication about what such behavior meant made John pull back in annoyance.

"Why should we not encourage them? Does not the One recognize the call to Wisdom in women as well as men?"

"Of course, Elder, of course," Paul replied quickly, and John swallowed a smile at his use of the honorific, thinking of their previous meeting. Tarsus looked mildly frustrated, as if he felt he'd not spoken plainly enough—or considered John obtuse—so he went on.

"It is only that...well, it is not meet that women should think themselves as honored by God as men. As you yourself know, Christ called only men to be his closest disciples for the very good and sensible reason that it is in women's natures to distort God's Word. We need only look to Scripture to see what treacheries the female heart can hatch when left to create without proper guidance from strong men; it seems to me unwise to change the ways of the Master too much, lest his teachings should be made vulgar."

John knew it was impolite, but he could not keep the amazement off his face. He glanced at Mary to see if she heard the hostility that lay beneath Paul's smoothly-presented argument, but her attention was focused on arranging the flowers one of the servants had earlier brought in. Paul continued to push his point.

"Please do not misunderstand me, Elder; I would not accuse you of dealing ill with the vagaries of human nature your students display as they attempt to fit themselves into the Garment of Christ's Righteousness. It is only that, when the women in a congregation have too much authority, they quickly breed an extremely dangerous level of familiarity among the faithful. Before long, the entire community draws away from Christ, corrupting not only themselves, but those who seek them out in all innocence."

"And you attribute this to the women?"

"I have seen it."

John was by no means unfamiliar with the attitude that saw women as Lucifer's accomplices; certainly it was common enough. Peter's, Nathaniel's and even Andrew's ire at Martha and Miriam's closeness within the circle was often ill-concealed, and when

Jeshua was not present, open. Though the sisters scarcely required defending, being well able to hold their own in any exchange of effronteries, John and Matthew more than once found themselves at loggerheads with the others over the way they treated them.

He gave thanks that he'd come into Jeshua's company while still boy enough to have malleable ideas; it allowed him to appreciate (mostly, he thought wryly, as he recalled his response to having so many on this journey) the soul-deep value of the women who enriched his life.

What could he possibly say to such a one? The Tarsian sincerely believed his mission to keep the Christine Way "pure" was a matter of honor, a task to humbly perform on Christ's behalf for as long as he had breath. Yet he also truly believed that given the chance, women would destroy that legacy. Jeshua gladly harassed those authorities who demanded that those under their auspices believe what they themselves did not; but when he met the average man who was stuck in his notions, he more often than not simply planted the idea that there might be another way to see things, then left be.

Paul, however, was no ignorant provincial; he was an educated man who'd directly experienced Jeshua's love for all beings. Should John not then prevail upon him to at least consider relinquishing so ridiculous a conviction?

Just as he opened his mouth to offer a tactful rebuttal, the kitchen door opened.

"John? ...Oh, I am sorry. I did not know the Elder was still here."

John turned, and his breath left him in a rush. Ariadne stood before them in a white, floor-length gown. It was wrapped in the Roman manner, with part of it draping over her bare shoulders to hang down her back; her dark curls were swept up, exposing the long, graceful neck John so appreciated, and the coiled braid atop her head was strewn with small, luminous, periwinkle blue flowers. Though she wore none of the fancy paints many women in Ephesus favored, the perfect oval of her face glowed. She'd obviously taken her earlier irritation with Paul into the Stillness, for her countenance was as brilliant as if she was angelic, not human. Mary made some enthusiastically admiring comment as John excused himself, walked to his double like a man pulled forth on a tether and took her hands.

"I am reminded of a line from one of King Solomon's Songs: 'Thou art all fair, my love,'" he said for her ears alone. He stepped away as she blushed and dimpled, then said in a normal voice, "Why have I been so honored with this lovely vision, dear one?"

"If you will recall, Thaleia decided last week that we should finally enjoy the dinner we were to have before...the last time we were to start the training. Though, I know its beginning has been postponed again—"

"Only by a day or two."

"—and three more join the table, the meal has already been prepared and so we must go. Tonight." Ariadne's look said she saw that he was thinking of begging off the dinner—and that she wasn't going to let him. John laughed and squeezed her hands.

"It will be no hardship to attend, my love, so long as I can sit across from you and stare rapturously...but I fear you'll not receive the same reward." The robe John had worn for the aborted dinner had been drenched in Joshua's blood.

"You'll not have to wear any of your robes, dear man; Iustus has supplied a new one for you. That is, provided you are not averse to wearing the Roman style. He does not think much of the Judeans' cut of clothing." Ariadne leaned sideways to take in Paul and, though still looking directly at John, said loudly enough for him to hear,

"Will the Elder accompany us for our celebration? I have no doubt there will be food enough for many more than will actually attend."

John turned, intending to invite Paul to attend the dinner, but the words froze on his lips at the older man's expression.

The Tarsian had stared at the table throughout the lovers' exchange. Now he turned as hard a look on Ariadne as if she'd just committed murder and still held the weapon. His thoughts were clear to see: She has corrupted him and he corrupts Christ's teachings.

Ariadne froze in bewilderment at the hostility in his gaze; John felt her life force try to hide as deeply within her as the necessity of supporting the body that anchored it would allow. The protector in him wanted to spirit her from the room and spare her from the wrath that looked ready to explode from Tarsus's mouth at any moment... but instead he drew his double to the table and properly introduced her.

Paul nodded grimly, but neither stood nor acknowledged her in any other way.

John felt Ariadne's humiliation at being so disrespectfully treated and his own temper frayed; still, he made the invitation to dinner, using the most formal of addresses to make it clear that Paul would be an honored guest, worthy of the highest respect. That he did not feel that way was immaterial; he would not emulate his visitor's ill-breeding.

Fortunately, Paul's legendary lack of manners did not prevail; he declined the invitation, then, with somewhat more grace than he'd shown in greeting Ariadne, made his excuses and quit House Karikos with barely a "goodbye" to Mary. His supporters, including, John later learned, Thomas, trailed behind him, never to return.

John blew out a sigh that was equal parts sadness and anger. Ariadne stood close beside him, looking as if she couldn't decide whether to curse or cry. She did neither, but when he took her hand, she leaned, trembling, against his shoulder.

His second sigh was one of unadulterated anger. "That such a one could call himself a follower of Jeshua's and think it so!" he huffed. Ariadne shook her head.

"John, it is all right..."

"No, Ari, it is not. The one who's Way he so readily spouts of would never have treated a woman that way, and he is not within his rights to do so, either." He turned to Mary, who again seemed engrossed with her flowers. "Is that the future we leave Jeshua's Gift to, Mother? By the time we return from Vashti, his teachings will be unrecognizable!"

"Yes, my son. As a matter of fact, they will be." She looked up. "Still, do not underestimate the value of what Tarsus does."

"How can I not? And how you say that? Even as he spoke of you with elaborate words of honor, he disdained your knowing and treated you like the lowest of servants. And you allowed it. Indeed, you fostered it."

"Yes I did, and I would do so again, without hesitation or complaint."

"It was degrading and unacceptable."

"It was exactly what was necessary," she said sharply. Her face softened and she reached for John's hand. "Listen to me, my son: though what Paul of Tarsus teaches lacks the purity of what you will someday bring back into this world, his presence nevertheless has a place and value to this Task. The soul that plays that part is well aware of the harm some in future times will perceive his acts and words have done. It knows how what he now helps build will be twisted and vilified.

"Yet, what he teaches is palatable to many who cannot yet see the importance of the Mother's place. He reminds them of the value of surrender—to a decidedly male God, yes. But even that, if fully accepted, will lead to discovering and accepting the Mother, for as your own belovéd knows, the two cannot be separate in truth. Though he distorts much, the beauty of what Paul's soul intends will implant in hearts that have literally been without it for eons the concept that Love's Presence is meant to be freely accepted and given forth. They will reach the highest level of understanding they can yet achieve because of him."

She smiled suddenly. "Besides, my son, he *is* one of Jeshua's. Soon enough, he will allow my firstborn's heart to soften his belief—at least to some extent—that women cannot well serve God. Honor him, John, and know the Plan flows exactly as it should."

Even had Mary's words not moved him, the depth of the One from which they came would have. Still, John's capitulation was grudging. "Very well. I will suspend judgment, Mother—but only because of my trust of the One in you."

Mary's amusement was dry. "That is a good thing, my son."

"Yes, well. It is as well he does not attend the dinner, for I would surely have caused him insult if he had spoken such nonsense before of the rest of our companions."

"Perhaps so. Fortunately, you will be saved from the necessity of harming his feelings," Mary chuckled. "Ariadne's presence managed that feat with great effectiveness."

John smiled at the memory of Paul's affronted visage, but Ariadne looked stricken at her Teacher's comment. After a moment, though, she swallowed her dismay and managed a small smile as John pulled her to their room to help him prepare for the dinner.

THIRTY-TWO

The *companions came together* at the home of one of Iustus's associates, a senator who had business dealings throughout the Empire, Persia, Africa and even the lands of the Indus River. They were ensconced in one of five "smaller" dining rooms that graced the house; mouth-watering comestibles of diverse origins were spread along a room-length sideboard and tended to by servants who fulfilled their guests' every whim.

More marvelous than the dinner, however, were those who attended it: the companions positively glowed with the splendor of their regalia.

John did indeed sit across from Ariadne, admiring the delightful view she presented, and likewise felt confident the vision he provided did not disappoint. Though his robe was cut in the Roman style as promised, instead of the usual Greek-inspired decorative designs, embroidered Hebrew glyphs ringed sleeves and neckline, their threads of real gold glimmering against the brilliant white silk. Ariadne had pulled his usually unruly hair into a tight ponytail and braided it, displaying the supposedly comely visage she claimed to be so charmed with.

Ariadne had said that if John thought her beautiful, he would think the gods themselves had dropped her sister from the heavens. He'd taken her remarks as the bragging of a proud younger sister and a sign of her own modesty—until he actually saw Demeter.

Her dress was borrowed due to her and Dareios's late arrival, but the cut, from some unknown culture co-opted in the Emperor's name, displayed to excellent advantage the willowy, curvaceous figure Demeter usually hid beneath bulkier clothing. The soft, rich shade of red carried hints of gold that caught the aureate highlights in her eyes and in the flower-laced, dark gold hair she this night allowed to hang freely down her back. The soft material draped forward, displaying enough of the creamy skin of neck and breasts to catch and hold the admiring eye. Like Ariadne, the elder Isaurus daughter wore no face paints—but then, like her sister, she did not need to.

Well! And who would ever have guessed? John thought, his eyebrows arching appreciatively. Both the dress and the woman in it would make any man look twice... then have wistfully inappropriate thoughts. Despite his extreme satisfaction with his double's appearance, he was hard-put not to stare.

The other men in the company suffered no such constraints; John watched amusedly as Erezavan and Marcus subtly jockeyed to sit on Demeter's right, since Ariadne was so cruel as to sit to her sister's left. Erezavan was the lucky man, or so it seemed; but John thought Marcus, who sat across from her, had the better seat.

Then again, they all seemed to be blessed with such riches tonight. Johanna, looking somewhat astounded, sat to Prochorus's right, dazzling in a Roman-cut dress of sea green silk that complimented her olive skin and black hair perfectly. John smiled as she covertly stared down at herself; he could well imagine she never believed she'd ever find herself dressed in such finery, in such a home. Timothy looked thoroughly pleased with Rachael's modest-but-womanly sky blue dress and embroidered shawl, while Mary was likewise radiant in her own freshly-created gown, her tastefully-styled hair covered with a new shawl made of gold-embroidered silk that was fine enough to see through. Torer and Haifata, who'd also been invited to attend the dinner ("'Commanded' is the better word, brother,") were each dressed in the kind of splendor that would have made anyone think them denizens of some royal court.

The dinner was full of talk and laughter, the company's nervousness about the training overcome by their excitement. Only once did they grow serious: when Erezavan, with a catch in his voice, proposed that the training be dedicated to Joshua Matthatus.

As one, the group closed their eyes. John was more pleased than he could say to feel the room's boisterous ambiance gently deepen into Stillness, as if they all instinctively understood that that was the best way they could ever honor not only Joshua, but themselves. When they finally opened their eyes, more than one sniffle filled the silence. John, too, felt a sense of sorrow, but it was not alone caused by Joshua's absence.

Ada and Hosea should see this, he thought; they should be here with us.

Though he fully understood his newest teachers' desire to stay in Corinth awhile longer—and had been told by a most reliable authority that they did exceptionally well —John greatly missed the couple's still, calming, joyful presence. Two months parted was a long time, too long. He was glad they'd be gone for only a few weeks more.

It took some time for the gay mood to repossess the group, but when it did, they made the most of the celebration. A few days hence, they would have little in the way of social lives; the next several secluded months would see them spending large portions of each day entering the One's Presence to awaken to their Selves. John was still uneasy about the upcoming training: could these ones come to know the One well enough to focus on It in any situation? His recent experiences made him shake his head uncertainly.

"Stop brooding and enjoy the beauteous sights across from you."

"I was not brooding." John smiled down at Mary, aware they both knew he lied.

"It will work, you know, it cannot but do so. The ones who do this training and this task will prove more than strong enough for whatsoever the universe sends them."

"It is not fair, you know," John said after a moment, leaning closer to Mary to be heard over the din of the others' laughter and conversation. "You can enter into my thoughts at any time, but I cannot enter into yours."

"That is because I have no thoughts, my son," Mary said, still smiling.

All at once, John's own thoughts stopped as if they'd been sliced away.

He was suddenly in a space of Silence so vast, so cosmically immense, that he could find no aspect of "self" at all in Its immeasurable, radiant Wholeness. The movements of his body, his breath, even his life force faded as all sense of separation, of self, vanished. Just as he'd been in Dareios's garden, he was again No One, floating in the heart of No Thing...yet that no thing contained all the fullness and aliveness of all the movements in every universe. He still clearly perceived the room around him, but it, too was no thing, while yet being wholly Self; Time, space, movement—everything—was replaced by indescribable Joy. He was pure Awareness, the unbounded Eternal; he was the perfect, silent Eye of the One. He was the wonder of All Potential and Possibility, watching, watching and being...

John snapped back to the room with a jolt and sucked in breath like a man who'd been too long underwater. He knew, though he knew not how, that while his sojourn had seemed rapturously eternal, only an instant, far less than a second, had passed.

He looked at Mary in awe. He had not forgotten the marvel of her Ascension, not exactly...but he saw now that when she'd reentered the corporeal world, he'd automatically ascribed to her human traits and concerns. No, when she *chose* to return, he reminded himself, truly hearing his thoughts this time. Yes, he experienced Stillness to a greater and greater extent; always was It with him...but it was also true that the flow of day-to-day life still periodically carried him away. What Mary experienced, however...

She smiled. "In time, my son, the pull of that flow will grow weaker and weaker. Soon enough, you will find you simply ignore it, stepping into it only when you need to deal with the world in certain ways. And even then, you'll discern naught but Stillness.

"And so it will eventually be for all these who sit with us, and for all in this universe," she said, using her eyes to point out each of the companions. "Each will follow his or her Path to its end, and that end will be the utter Silence of the One. I promise."

Mary sipped at the excellent wine. "Now, be a good belovéd and take your beautiful lady for a walk. She looks as if she could use it, and this home has exceptional gardens."

John looked at Ariadne, surprised. She did not look to him as though needed a break, for she entered readily enough into the roaring conversations and laughed as gaily as the others. But she'd been very quiet after their encounter with Paul, hardly saying ten words as John readied himself for the dinner.

"Ariadne," he called across the table, interrupting a tittering, heads-together chat with Demeter. "Will you walk with me in the garden?"

Was that anxiety he saw flit across her brow? But she said "Yes," quickly enough—while also returning a covertly delivered elbow from her sister with a half-stifled giggle.

The room quieted as John came around the table and took Ariadne's hand in his. As she stood, he smiled down at Demeter and openly appreciated the sight he'd quietly enjoyed for much of the night.

"Before we came to dinner, Demeter, Ariadne told me you looked as beautiful as a goddess. May I say I wholeheartedly agree?"

"You may, and thank you," Demeter said, coloring at the others' fervent concurrence.

Enjoying the magnificence of the garden would have been easy even had the servants not set torches and braziers out at regular intervals: the moon was near full and the night reasonably warm. John and Ariadne walked hand in hand, enjoying the stunning sights and sweet smells of flowers that came from one of the indoor gardens. They relished the music of the night creatures and took pleasure in several small waterfalls that lived throughout the huge space, coming at last to a roiling pond.

Ariadne released John's hand and stooped to trail her fingers in the cold, swirling water, then stood, folded her arms and looked out over the portion of garden they had not yet walked. John noted the tightness in her stance now that they were alone.

"Mary suggested we come here. She seemed to think you needed the fresh air."

"Did she?"

"She did." John walked to his double and stood behind her, close, but not touching. "I thought it strange at the time, since you seemed quite content as you talked with Demeter and your father. It is not air you need, I think, but there is something, Ari."

Ariadne sighed and continued to look out at the garden. When she spoke at last, her voice betrayed her distress.

"I do not think I can do this thing, John, or that I should."

"Should not do what? The training? Vashti?"

"Any of it."

John knew the "it" included their union. The encounter with Paul had obviously preyed on her mind since the afternoon.

He wanted to comfort her, say all was well. He wanted, again, to give the Tarsian a goodly piece of his mind. Yet, when he spoke, his voice seemed aloof, even to his own ears.

"Ariadne, do you know the One? Know yet that It lives within you?"

She stiffened, somewhat insulted, he thought, by the condescension in his tone, but closed her eyes and grew still. Almost instantly—and rather stubbornly, he thought with a brief smile—his double touched the hem of the One's Garment, then wrapped Its Infinite Self around her.

John scowled. Just as with Erezavan, Ariadne's ability to touch into the Silence was amazingly strong...but she did not yet believe it. The danger with that was that her phantom self might well convince her she wasted her time attempting to know something so seemingly intangible. John had seen students quit the Practice, convinced they could never know what in fact had always been theirs.

But that was not going to happen here. He gently turned Ariadne to face him as she opened her eyes.

"Describe what you see—no, Ari," he gave her the smallest of shakes as she started to close her eyes again. "Describe the One to me as It is now, with your eyes open."

Tentatively at first, but then with growing certainty, Ariadne did so, her vision turning inward even as she gazed into John's eyes. The night air quieted around them and the waters grew silent even as they continued to bubble and dance. Even the clouds held still as Ariadne described the Source of all Being.

"Hmm," John said, enjoying the heightened peace that filled everything around them. "And how is the fear? What is the One's experience of that?"

"What? I—oh. I—"

"No, do not step away from It. Describe the feeling from that Place."

Ariadne nodded and again turned her attention inward. "The fear is, well, not gone, exactly. But I feel it like an actor feels the mask he wears during a play. I know what the mask represents, but it does not affect what I experience." She shook her head. "I did not truly believe that could be, John, despite what you and Mary said, but I realize now I've experienced the Stillness with my eyes open before."

John nodded. "It is vital to regularly do the Practice with your eyes closed, Ari, for that will speed your recognition that you are naught but the One whether your eyes are opened or closed. And once that is so, doubting your Self will be impossible—even when confronted by the firmest concepts of those who do not constantly touch the Stillness."

Ariadne turned her stare toward the ground. "But I do have doubts, John. I—"

"No, Ari, You have no doubts. Your *phantom self* has doubts...and it is not real."

"...But what if something happens on the journey and I am too afraid to act when I need to? John, what if Demti or my father gets hurt because of me...what if you get hurt? I am not a coward, to run from what must be done, but I feel like one, and—"

John bent to his belovéd's height and gently stroked her chin with his thumb. "The phantom self is but a handful of voices in your head that seem to talk sense, Ari; but in truth its words have no meaning." He knew she saw the Joy he himself had recently regained, knew she felt the reassuring fullness of the Silence his soul exuded. "The 'sense' the phantom self strings together happens solely by your agreement. You need pay those voices no mind whatsoever, beloved; only attend to the One."

"But—"

"Ariadne, there is no phantom self. *You* are not afraid of anything!"

John continued to smile as he held the Silence and her gaze; after a long moment, his double relaxed ever so slightly. Never is it only the words that fulfill, he thought, recalling how empty Paul's eloquent arguments on the proper place of women had felt.

"Well..." Ariadne said at last, resisting her own urge to smile.

"'Well...'" John grinned, mimicking her fast-dissolving uncertainty. She smacked his chest and let out a giggle as he drew her to him.

"You do not fight fair," she said, burrowing into him.

"Hmmm. Should I have let you wallow a bit longer?" he asked.

"Well, yes. A woman sometimes likes a good wallow."

John chuckled and drew her even closer. "Do you think I have not had the same worries as you, belovéd? That any of us have not? I am leading five women and several men with no more understanding of the lands we will travel than I into the-One-knows-what dangers...and yet, my "legitimate" fears do not matter either. Ari, the phantom self's views—on any subject—are useless, because regardless of how right they sound, they invariably block our ability to perceive the One's solution when It comes. What I learned from Joshua most recently and from Jeshua first, is that ours is to hold only to the One, to trust and let It do whatever needs doing through us."

A thought suddenly occurred as they stood delighting in the quiet and each other.

"Do you know, Ari? People think Judas Iscariot was a traitor to Jeshua and his cause. If this teaching lasts at all, the only way he will be remembered is as the man who betrayed the Son of God. Yet, had he not done what he did, would Jeshua have fulfilled his mission? What if Jeshua had changed his mind in Gethsemane and chosen against crucifixion? Would we then call him hero or coward? The means the One may use to bring Its Plan to fruition is not ours to judge, for we do not see the whole of the Picture. That is what I am still learning from Darshinika Baremna's choice and from Paul and Mary. I do not like some of what they have shown me, but when I look to the One rather than the phantom self's judgments, I cannot but trust that all is exactly as it must be."

John held his double at arms' length. "Dearest, I trust your bravery, your sense and your knowledge of the One. I gladly gave my life into your hands in Corinth and here in Ephesus, and I will gladly do so on the trail to Vashti. Yet I also trust that your heart knows which way it must go better than I do. If it is that you cannot do this thing, any of it, then I will not try to persuade you otherwise. If you know it is best to stay in Ephesus when the companions depart, know that I will love you all the more for having the strength to follow your heart.

"Ariadne, is that what you know?"

Though John felt sure of what her answer would be, he still found he held his breath as his double again turned her focus inward. An eon later, she turned her attention back to him, her expression serious.

"I will stay. Not for Mary or Demti, who is truly excited about the journey...nor even for you, John bar Zebedee. I will stay and see this through for my Self's sake."

"'All of it?'" John's smile was playful. Ariadne smiled mischievously back.

"I did say I am not a coward."

John laughed, then kissed her long, tenderly and thoroughly.

The sounds of the party abruptly grew louder as the terrace doors opened and Prochorus called to them in his battlefield bray. Ariadne laughed as every creature within a league fell into cautious silence; she returned John's kiss and nodded toward the house.

"Come, belovéd man. Our celebration calls us back to it."

John received one more surprise on the morning before the training began.

He sat, enjoying a rare free moment to eat breakfast and peer amusedly out at the squirrels' preparations for winter's inevitable, if late, appearance. All the women in the house had gone to market for "last minute, very important items" save Mary; she'd been off and away on some errand of her own long before sunrise. Jaresh and his men expected to finish the second cottage two days short of the two weeks they'd promised, so the trainees would only have to share the original for a few days. All was going well, quite well.

Suddenly, Stavis Querceron entered the room. John stiffened at the anxious look on the younger man's homely face.

"Stavis, what? Has something gone wrong?" Querceron had been giving his time to helping at the cabins whenever his duties with Iustus's business allowed.

"What? Oh, no, Elder!" he said in hasty reassurance. "There is no need for alarm; all is well. It is just that I..."

Querceron fell silent and ran his hands through his nearly blonde hair, once more looking like a deer who'd just been introduced to a lion. He blew out a nervous breath.

Then, finally: "Elder, I wish to join your training and your journey!"

"Mmm." John scrutinized him just as he had the day he, Joshua, Erezavan and Marcus had approached him; at that moment Marcus, Erezavan and Timothy entered the room, their brows rising in genuine surprise. Obviously, they'd not encouraged Querceron, as John had momentarily suspected.

"When last we discussed the training and our journey, Stavis, you seemed quite uninterested in putting yourself out to any extent. Indeed, I believe your quote was, 'I wish you unbounded success, but I leave it to you. I've done enough adventuring in this life and want naught but to settle into my cousins' business.'"

"Yes, yes, I did say that, Elder," Stavis agreed before John could say more. "What's more, I meant it at the time. But, well..." he grimaced as if he didn't want to say what he really meant, but: "since then, things have changed. Joshua's death changed everything.

"Joshua and I knew each other not at all in Greece, for we ran in very different circles. He came there seeking a way to live, while I sought a living that would not leave me relying on my father or brother. As the son of a man of wealth, I knew many rich men sent their sons to the schools; if I got to know some of them well enough, I might then gain a place in their family businesses." He laughed ruefully. "Of course, I would have saved a trip and some years by coming to my cousins first, but things go as they do.

"My surprise at discovering that I actually wanted what the teachers spoke of was tremendous, but though I immersed myself as deeply into my studies as I could, I also knew I could never make my living at it, for I am not cut out for the philosopher's life."

"As you made clear to me," John said.

"Yes, as I made clear to you. But as I also said, this Practice has given me more than I could ever have imagined. I know that with it, finding Truth is only a matter of time.

"In all honestly, Elder, I thought there was no rush, that I would have a lifetime to find that Truth." Querceron's eyes were pained, "Until Joshua was killed before my eyes."

"Since then, I have wondered and thought and asked myself many questions," he said, his words echoing the ones Prochorus had used when John questioned his desire to take the training. "And the answer is, 'I want everything that will bring me to Fullness...and I may not have as much time as I think'.

"Elder, I have thought long on this and lost more than a few nights sleep, but I know now nothing else will make my life complete. Though it is impossible that one who knew him only a short while could do honor enough by Joshua Matthatus, I would like to take his place, both in the training and on your journey."

John gazed intently at Querceron, taking in the Ephesian's words. He'd been aware of the usually cheerful man's pensiveness, knew that seeing Joshua's death had affected him as deeply as it had the companions. Even so...

"Marcus, what say you?"

Prochorus looked at the Ephesian with as much intensity as John had, considering. "He'll be able enough to defend himself if there's need, and he is good with the bow, which will prove useful for hunting."

"And?" John said, with a slight smile for the Roman's concern for defense first.

"And, I cannot fault his desire to seek the One. He seems always to have his eyes closed when the chance presents itself." He shrugged. "He is welcome, for all of me."

"Erezavan, Timothy?"

The two younger men had spent the most time with Stavis and they concurred with Marcus's assessment of his willingness to seek the Stillness. "And he finds it already as well, Rabbi," Timothy added, smiling at the still-apprehensive man.

"Hmmm. Well. Beyond the fact that such would be impossible, Stavis, in truth, I've no desire to replace Joshua," John said at last. "I will, however, welcome one who seeks to simply be and give his Self amongst others who seek the same. Would you be that person? Do you truly believe you are prepared to go forth, to the benefit of yourself and generations to come?"

"Yes, Elder. Yes I am." Querceron straightened as suddenly as he'd begun to deflate.

"This will be no pleasure trip, Stavis, no hunt to help a rich man's second-born son find his way in the world of men."

"Nevertheless, Sir, I would go with you, if you would have me."

John felt an odd and sudden moment of disappointment as he realized he'd have thirteen companions on this pilgrimage instead of his Teacher's twelve, but he shook it off with an inward snort and smiled.

"Welcome to our training and our journey then, Stavis Querceron."

After much argument of the "no, please, after you"-kind, the women duly took occupation of the new cottage on the sixth day of the training. They were glad to be out of the crowding of the smaller house—but appalled by the lack of space for preparing food. Mary explained that their sole priority would be entering the Silence, that volunteers had graciously agreed to prepare and deliver (or have their servants prepare and deliver) light snacks for the day and full but light suppers.

At the end of the second week, and much to John's delight, Ada and Hosea finally rejoined the rest of their companions. While he'd fully expected they would come to Ephesus with a much deeper experience of the Stillness, he was happily amazed by how much the Practice's two newest teachers had grown.

Ada, if possible, was even more brilliant in her trust of the way things should go. That slightest edge of impatience John had sometimes detected was gone, replaced by unshakably gentle strength. And Hosea! True, their growing closeness as the journey progressed had alleviated most of John's early concerns about the burly laborer's stability, but now he knew he need never take thought over whether or not he could trust Hosea's judgment and constancy.

"Well, and you can thank Mary for that," the big man said as he and Ada sat with John and Ariadne in one of the tents the men had slept in at the beginning of the training. He had had to put up with a certain amount of "I-told-you-so," teasing from the couple, but they were thrilled with the state of his and Ariadne's relationship. "We could never have learned so much so quickly without her day-to-day guidance."

John raised surprised brows. "Mary was there?"

"Of course," Ada said with a puzzled look for his and Ariadne's further surprise. "I grant you, we were surprised when she arrived and took Demeter's room after she and Dareios left, but we certainly appreciated her presence. She is truly amazing in her willingness to give, Rabbi—though not all of the students appreciated her style."

She chuckled, then frowned, but Hosea asked the question.

"Why do you look so surprised, John? Did not she tell you where she meant to go when she left Ephesus?"

"No, she said nothing," John said faintly.

"And she never did leave Ephesus, at least not to our knowledge," Ariadne finished, her expression equally astonished. "Ada, Hosea, Mary has been here with us. Every day."

The silence that descended was thick with the four's awe at looking the impossible in the face.

John thought of the times he'd suspected Mary to be out attending to the universe's business and wondered: had she sometimes disappeared because she needed to be in only one place at a time for the sake of her strength? Or was there some other reason?

Certainly, he understood his mother's silence on the subject; even after three years with Jeshua, John sometimes found himself fighting the desire to make more of this one who so completely held the power of the One in her hands.

"Well, my mother always was a woman full of surprises," he said at last, and received several wonder-filled laughs in return.

THIRTY-THREE

The *trainees quickly fell* into a routine. They spent their days entering the Presence of the One by using the Practice with eyes closed, then ate dinner and took time for various activities. When evening came, they joined together to speak of their day, share their growing comprehension of the Silence, and ask questions. These periods of interacting in the world, though limited, gave the trainees the chance to strengthen the habit of actively using the techniques and resting in the Stillness with their eyes open.

The companions were quickly learning to trust each other as most people never did, were even becoming comfortable with fully expressing themselves, foibles and all. They frequently reminded each other, sometimes vehemently, to focus on the One within no matter what they seemed to be experiencing, but all in all, they were settling in nicely.

Other than answering pertinent questions, John and the other teachers mostly left the trainees to make their own discoveries about the nature of the One. That way, they could discover the truth that they were, in fact, always teachers, and come to trust that they or anyone could access and share the wisdom of Silence within.

Most nights after the gatherings, Mary returned to House Karikos with Hosea and Ada, who undertook working with the students with contagious zeal. But midway through the third week, John moved into one of the two tents that served as additional spaces where the trainees could enjoy the Practice. That way, at least one teacher was always nearby to answer questions or give comfort as their phantom selves dissolved. Too, and though he suspected Jeshua would be highly amused by his sentimentality, John did not relish occupying Iustus Karikos's comfortable guestroom without Ariadne. Not that she would be in the tent with him; all the trainees' energies, at least for now, would be turned as much as possible from worldly distractions.

This night, a month into the training, John lay on his pallet at close to second hour in the morning, enjoying the warmth and crackle of the small fire in the center pit of the tent's earthen floor. His misgivings about the training had all but disappeared. He'd held the idea that the Bethany way was automatically better, because he'd believed it took time, and quite a bit of it, to awaken to one's awareness of the One. But every one of his companions was growing at remarkable speed, proving that fast and easy growth was not only possible, but natural. It truly was as both Jeshua and Mary repeatedly said: the more time one spent doing the Presence of the One, the faster one's growth.

"Yes, and do you know what is even more remarkable?" Mary gaily said when he shared his realization with her. "Fully remembering the One need not take any time at all. It can happen instantaneously and wholly without pain."

John smiled. One thing that was no different than in Bethany was his, Mary's, and now Ada and Hosea's, way of dealing with these students. They could either be patience itself when someone asked a question or needed reassurance, or they could suddenly grow knife-sharp tongues that would bring a student face-to-face with some knowing they either needed to enter more deeply into or have done with. John was particularly surprised at Hosea's willingness to point out the phantom self's stupidity, for he'd always been among the most reticent of the Bethany students to say anything that might offend another. Yet his insights, though sometimes incisive, were never delivered with the intent to harm—and that gentleness came through clearly as well.

This was not to say that the phantom selves of the ten trainees always appreciated being asked to step away from the safety of the familiar; all the teachers had angered them at one time or another. In fact, Ariadne had greeted John with angry silence for a full day after he insisted she look again at something she *knew* to be right.

Ten trainees. Well, and that isn't quite accurate, is it? John thought, smiling into the dimness. Haifata had taken to attending the evening meetings regularly, could often be found in the men's cottage, eyes closed, lost in the Stillness. Mary had also conveyed the news that he seemed always to be in her presence of late, asking questions, sharing observations and sometimes arguing with her answers in his quiet way.

That hadn't stopped John from objecting when first he'd begun coming and going.

"He should either commit to the training or not come to the cabins at all. To allow him free reign—by his own choice, no less—when the others do not have it is inappropriate. We would never have allowed it in Bethany, Mother, even with that loose format."

"Haifata is not 'the others,' and they themselves know it," Mary countered. "Granted, dear son, his is not an exception I would make with any other, but even your companions sense and accept that that one touches the One as naturally as breathing."

"Yes, Mother, but why is Haifata different?" John asked. The sense that Adan's connection to him was in some way as important as his bond with Ariadne again furrowed his brow. More, John felt sure Mary knew the answer. But she but only shook her head.

"Leave that one to his own, dearest," she'd said, "it will serve everyone in the end..."

"NO! NO! NOOOOO!"

John jolted upright, heart suddenly in his mouth as one, then another bloodcurdling shriek shattered the night. He burst from his tent, ran to the women's cottage and slammed through the door so quickly that he later could not recall coming to his feet or pushing the tent flap aside; the scream shrilled again as he entered.

Johanna, her face contorted out of all recognition by terror, crouched in the far corner of the main room, gaping at something in the opposite corner and doing her best to push through the back wall. Apparently, Rachael also saw whatever held her stare, for she stood just inside the bedroom door, shaking and wide-eyed, while Ariadne and Demeter unsuccessfully tried to calm them both. John turned toward where they stared just as the men burst in, all thorns and bristles, loudly questioning and ready to fight.

No weapon, however, could attend to this.

"OUT!"

John yelled so loudly it stopped all the men in their tracks save Timothy; he continued forward, obviously meaning to protect Rachael. John was having none of it: he growled, grabbed the young man's arm and flung him back toward the door.

Timothy stumbled, but instantly regained his balance, his face twisting with rage.

"You have no—!" he began, but John cut him off, his voice so full of command and venom it that echoed through the room.

"Go back to your cottage and continue with the Practice! Now!"

The others complied with widened eyes; even Haifata hastily retreated. Timothy glared at him for a long moment more, as if he meant to carry on the argument, but finally spun on his heel and left, slamming the door behind him.

John went to the women, placing his body between them and the corner Johanna, who had sunk, whimpering, to the floor, still stared at. Ariadne and Demeter still looked worriedly at her, but their relief at his presence was plain.

"Go to the men's cottage and enter into the Stillness," he said to the sisters. "I will come get you when I have finished with Johanna."

"Come on, love, we need to leave," Ariadne said to Rachael.

"No, Ari, Rachael needs to stay as well. Leave her be."

Ariadne's face was full of questions, but she and Demeter skirted out the door without arguing.

John ignored the opposite corner and turned to Rachael. "Tell me what you see, dear heart."

She shook violently, but still had enough of her wits about her to give a coherent answer. "It is...it is a demon, Rabbi."

"Are you sure?"

Rachael nodded, all out of words. John motioned her to sit next to Johanna, something she definitely did not appreciate since it meant leaving the safety of the room the creature did not occupy. He took her hand when she was situated.

"Are you using the Practice, Little One? Can you find the One even now?" he asked.

Rachael the made attempt, but the process was slowed by her unwillingness to close her eyes. No matter; John was confident she didn't need to, even if she was unsure.

"I can sense It, Rabbi...but it is so far away, so far," she finally said in a small voice. Tears spilled down her cheeks, but John squeezed her hand.

"It is all right, dearest, you are doing excellently. Let your focus rest as much on That as you can and keep using the techniques."

Rachael sniffed and nodded. Satisfied she was all right, John turned to Johanna and lightly placed a hand on her arm. It was as cold and clammy as death itself.

"Johanna," he said softly, making his love for her as evident as he could. "Johanna, look here at me, dear one, please."

"It wants my soul," she said, seeming to wail despite barely speaking above a whisper. "It comes to take me for all the things I have done." Her muscles bunched as if she meant to jump up and flee, but John again squeezed her arm to circumvent her hysteria.

"It is a literal truth, my friends, that there are no such things as demons," Jeshua once said. Then, with a wry smile: "It is also a literal truth that they nevertheless exist."

Jeshua explained his comments, but only after letting the twelve, Miriam, Martha and others of his closest students squirm a bit with trying to figure out what he meant. Now John had to do the same for Johanna. It would not be easy; unlike Rachael, she had no solid awareness of the One to soften the intensity of what she experienced.

"Johanna, look at me. Tell me exactly what you see," he said, speaking as if to a young, very frightened child. She looked at John as she spoke, but only for a second or two.

"It...I...It is a d-d-demon" she said, her words coming out in a terrified pant. "It is in the corner d-directly across from me. It is...huge...and it is smiling at me...it beckons as if it wants me to go with it. Something...it is covered with sores and something horrible drips from them...it keeps telling me...it keeps telling me...that I belong to it."

John nodded. As he'd hoped, though she was still frightened, speaking of what she saw diminished her panic. "Can you tell if it is male or female?"

"Male," she said without hesitation, and indeed it was, emphatically so. John sat back on his heels and blew out a thoughtful breath.

"Johanna, have you ever done anything wrong?"

"I have done everything wrong, Elder, everything." She looked at her hands as if she was suddenly too ashamed to hold her head up. That she had stopped looking toward the corner John took as a good sign.

"My Teacher would say you have never failed the Father, no matter what you have done. But he would also say if you believe in your deepest self that you have committed any wrong, the world will then show it to you in some form." He nodded over his shoulder. "What is that, Johanna? Why does it seek your soul?"

Johanna reluctantly looked over his shoulder, then turned her head away from both the demon and John, her face mournful. "It is Lust, Elder," she sobbed. "It is all the lust I had for men, the lust that led me to seek them out. Young and old, married and not. That I might lie with them. It is the lust that eventually trapped me. So that I had to seek them out to survive long after I had tired in body and soul of living such a life. Now it comes to destroy me for daring to think I can be something better."

John laid a hand on her cheek, forcing her to again look at him, then shook his head.

"I saw what your life had come to, Johanna, saw the pain of it. Pray, have not you punished yourself enough by how you lived? Why do you let this demon seek you?"

Johanna looked as if she wanted to protest the notion that she was allowing anything of the sort, but John continued. "When you chose to learn the Practice, your 'punishment' ended then, there and forever. You have heard this before, I know, but I will repeat it. The only reason the phantom self will sometimes show you the folly of something you have been and done while you are doing the Practice is because the causes of that folly are leaving you. Your demon is nothing more than that, Johanna. Nothing more. Tell me: have you used one technique since the demon appeared?"

"No, I...was so frightened that I could not even remember what they were."

"I thought as much. Unless you gain the habit of using the techniques in every situation, unless you learn to merely watch what comes, you will doom yourself to believing that what your phantom self shows you is real. You will slow your awakening enormously. That is, if you do not stop the Practice altogether and run away. Remember, dear one: with but very, very few exceptions, what you see and hear and feel as you do the Practice are but the ghosts of tracks of being that are dissolving. You need give them no more thought than you would the scraps you throw a dog at the end of a meal." John smiled slightly as Johanna silently mouthed one of the techniques unawares. Though she could not yet feel it, her emotions had settled. "How do you feel now?"

"I am still afraid, Elder...but it is not as bad...I no longer feel as if I must run or die...and the demon is gone!"

Johanna sobbed her relief as John held her, then: "Was it truly only a phantom Elder? Not a punishment sent to me by God?" she asked when she could again speak coherently. John made a face.

"Johanna. The One sees all you've done only as joy and perfection. How could It then punish you? Why would It punish you? That demon was indeed naught but your own creation." He saw Rachael's look of puzzlement out of the corner of his eye but raised his hand to forestall her questions. There'd be time enough for explanations later.

"I have never wronged the Lord?" The former prostitute said, almost to herself. Then shook her head sadly. "I want to believe what you say, Elder, but I have lain with so many men. Surely I've harmed some one of them or their families by my actions."

"Soon enough you'll take no thought of believing or disbelieving, dear one. Soon, you will know," John replied. "More, that knowing will come easily to you, like a blanket slipped over a sleeping child who did not yet notice she was cold. Once that happens, all who thought themselves harmed will also begin to heal. I promise this by Jeshua's heart."

John stood, pulled Johanna, then Rachael, to their feet, and smiled as they simultaneously yawned and blinked sleepily. Truly, this crisis was done.

"Will you be all right until I send Ariadne and Demeter back?" He received a pair of drowsy nods. "Good. Then go back to your room and sit close with each other while I go get them. Let the techniques give you what you need...sleep in this case, I am sure. We will talk on the morrow of what happened. And fear not that the demon will return; you have chased him well and thoroughly away."

John hugged each of the women, imparting a bit more Stillness to their hearts, then took his time walking to the men's cottage. He listened at the door to discover whether the others had followed his instructions or were talking of what they thought might be happening. He was gratified to hear no voices.

"*Jeshua, amen,*" he said into the dimness, then waited as the group stirred, stretched, sighed and otherwise returned to the present moment. Or to wakefulness, as the case might be; John estimated it was well past third hour.

"Ari, Demeter, you can go back to your cottage now; all is well. No, Timothy, you may not go. Rachael has likely already fallen asleep and I want neither her nor Johanna disturbed before morning. Fear not, brother, I promise you she is all right."

And I expect I'll be seeing you one on one soon enough, he thought, as he looked at the young man's closed and angry face.

He walked Ariadne and Demeter back to their cottage, thankful for their willingness to wait 'til morning to ask questions; he was as ready for rest as Johanna and Rachael. Demeter said her goodnights, leaving John and Ariadne to smile at each other.

They embraced, not saying a word, as if breaking the night's silence would somehow ruin it. Just before he stepped away, Ariadne kissed him, a short but thorough buss.

"There will be stories in the morning, yes?"

John laughed. "I promise. Sleep well, belovéd."

Ariadne nodded, smiling, and went inside. John stood a moment longer, looking at early morning sky and hearing in it the Song of the Cosmos just as he had since childhood.

Well, then, the training has begun in earnest, he thought, knowing the stars would not deign to respond and at peace with that fact. He made his way to his own bed.

"So then, the training goes well?"

"Yes, it goes very well indeed, Mother."

They were now seven weeks into the training. John and Mary walked toward Iustus and Thaleia's, the chill of the late afternoon air making their breaths come out in cotton-ball puffs, the road beneath them crunching with the extra snap of oncoming frost. John enjoyed the walk; he'd been as cloistered as the trainees these last few weeks, so frequently had the trainees come up against one obstacle or another and sought his reassurance. Still, he was very pleased with almost everyone's progress.

Of course, they'd quickly recognized that the very act of asking for help, something the phantom self could never do, often dissolved their fears before they even spoke of them. Also, because they could now describe the Stillness while in It, they tended to easily regain their equilibrium. John now felt comfortable with leaving Ada and Hosea to handle crises and questions; he could once more take time to attend students' meetings at House Karikos, enjoy some of Iustus and Thaleia's fabulous dinners...and periodically leave behind the trainees' usual meals of vegetables balanced by a bit of fish.

John smiled. *That* had been a discussion. Though light meals were easier to digest and so made it easier to enter deeply into the Stillness, it had been quite the task to convince the women who supplied those meals the companions wouldn't die from not having red meat at every meal. And he'd had to work almost as hard to convince the men that that was so; only Erezavan accepted the constraint with any equanimity. Indeed, Dareios actually threatened to leave if he couldn't have meat every single day.

Ah, the desires the mind would convince us are necessary for our survival!

"What of Dareios and Johanna?" Mary asked, as if picking up on John's memory of his belovéd's father. With Ada and Hosea settled in, she now came to the cottages only a few times a week, working with the students at House Karikos the rest of the time.

"Dareios does well enough. Oh, it has been hard for him to jump fully into the seas of his Self and trust that they will buoy him up even if his mind knows not 'why', and he sometimes drives himself and us crazy trying to 'understand', but I think he will do well enough in the end." He sighed. "Johanna, on the other hand, I am not so sure about."

Of the ten (or eleven) trainees, Johanna, Erezavan and Rachael had the greatest awareness of the exalted realms, those that existed beyond the merely physical. In its milder permutations, one simply became more aware of the beauty of the world: colors seemed brighter and sounds lovelier; one experienced scents and sensations more intensely. But for some, seeing angels and nature spirits, reading others' life forces and remembering the history of times outside one's current lifespan was common.

Becoming aware of the world that existed beyond physical sight was a natural aspect of awakening, an important step to knowing that there is, in truth, naught but the One. But experiencing that perception without an active awareness of the One often made it far too easy to mistake such experiences for signs of being fully awake rather than as byproducts of the awakening process. More than one searcher had gotten so lost in the beauty of the One's Garment that they never found the One Itself.

"And you fear that is Johanna's situation?" Mary asked.

"I do. The day after her experience with her demon, she came to me. 'The Lord has forgiven me, Elder, forgiven me completely.' she said. Mother, she was as happy as a girl who finds her betrothed is a handsome prince instead of a pauper, utterly different from the woman who'd crouched, terrified, in a corner the night before.

"She'd had a dream of meeting a sick old man on a road. The demon reappeared, again seeking her soul, and though she knew he would die, she started to run, to leave the 'useless, scabrous old man,' behind. But something changed her mind; she instead of abandoning him, she decided she would protect him, 'even if the demon killed me.'

"At that point, the demon transformed into an angel of unsurpassed beauty. He told her she was no longer a woman stained by sin, that he'd come to watch over her and would see she was brought straight to Heaven when her time came to part from this plane. She ended by ecstatically stating that she feels the angel's protection all the time."

"A wonderful story, my son," Mary said. John snorted.

"Faugh! She places God outside her heart now just as she did the demon then. But I have not been able to convince her that is the case; she will not listen."

"Do you fear deceit on the part of the 'angel'?" Mary asked.

John thought about it, then shook his head, "No. I think she sees truly, that it is in fact an angelic one. But as we both know, those of the celestial worlds usually show only what we bid them show us...or think we deserve."

He'd explained this phenomenon to Rachael, Ari and Demeter, who'd appeared outside his tent the morning after Johanna's ordeal. Rachael, though much refreshed, was also mightily confused

"Rabbi, you told Johanna she saw that demon only because she thought she deserved punishment for laying with men for money, that it was naught but her creation. But I have never been with a man for money or any reason. How can it be I saw her demon too?"

"Ah, but Bright Star," John asked gently, "did not you think yourself worthy of the treatment your father visited upon you?"

Rachael started to protest, but stopped. The frightened girl John first met in Hiram bar Abiel's inn might not have been conscious of her father's ultimate plans for her, but her heart was. She lowered her eyes in sudden embarrassment.

"My mother said his own sourness caused him to act so, but honestly, I did think if I had not disobeyed him by being born a girl, he would not have been angry."

Demeter's snort and comment were so wholly unladylike that both Ariadne and Rachael broke into astonished giggles. "Well, it is ridiculous," she said a little defensively, her cheeks reddening. John expressed his own agreement with a wink.

"Still, Rabbi," Rachael asked once she regained some control, "why would I see Johanna's demon? Or any demon?"

"The celestial realms and those who live in them are real, Rachael, as real as you and I. And yet they are not, for we also are not. We are all the illimitable One, which has neither form nor movement.

"The celestials' joy is to serve those who live as God in activity in whatever forms our Selves deem needful. Those who take the guise of 'demons' but show outside ourselves what we will not accept as part of ourselves. Of course, that is true of everything, for the universe exists solely to serve the One and Its creations. It is only that with celestials, the service is sometimes...spectacular. Yet, once one chooses to love that which the demon represents within herself, it can only transmute into a thing of beauty—then disappear."

"Forever?"

John shrugged.

"Well, but then...when we accept within us what the angels manifest, do they disappear too?" Rachael sounded a little like a child who fears to lose a favorite pet.

"Oh no, dear one." John took her hand in his and smiled. "When we accept within us what the angels manifest, we become them—and more."

John's attention returned to Mary. "Mother, I worry that Johanna lacks the willingness to let her awareness move from that which changes, even if it be an angel, to That which does not. She could well end up forsaking the training and the journey."

"Can she describe the nature of the One? Has she done so to everyone's satisfaction?"

"Oh, yes. She did so last evening, in fact."

They stepped off the road as a man with a cart and two donkeys passed by on his way back to Ephesus. When the noise subsided, Mary's voice held a shrug.

"Johanna knows the Silence and knows she knows it. Though you can and must continuously remind her to fully focus on the truth of her being, what road she may ultimately choose is not yours to worry about. Especially since she will ultimately choose the only road that truly exists. All you can do, my son, is trust that the One goes about Its business with Johanna in as perfect a manner as It does with each of us."

John made no answer as they continued along the crackling road. He was not happy with Mary's reply, but he could not argue with it either.

"So, you feel the rest of the trainees are making good progress?" Mary continued, apparently unaware of his reservations.

"Excellent progress, I would say...and I am more than pleased with Ada and Hosea as well. Their presence has added more to this training than I could ever have hoped."

Mary nodded and silence again descended for several steps. Then:

"That is good, my son, very good. For it is time for me to go."

THIRTY-FOUR

John halted abruptly, kicking a frosty plume of dust into the air, as taken aback as he would have been had Mary suddenly turned and slapped him with all her strength.

"You are leaving? Now? But..."

Though he'd known she would not go with them to Vashti, John had assumed his mother would stay in Ephesus at least until winter's end, until the companions finished their training. He sensed, too, that Mary did not simply mean to go to some other part of the universe on some temporary foray. This departure would be permanent, assuming such a one any longer believed in earthly notions of permanence. But permanent from the standpoint of the companions, surely. John's heart sank. For her to leave now...

He suddenly realized it was not his companions he thought of, but himself. Though she had in truth been gone only a short time after her Ascension, John had missed his mother tremendously. With her return, he had again come to enjoy and rely on her wise, reassuring presence; the knowledge that she again meant to leave left him feeling bereft. Mary came back to where John stood and laid a hand on his arm.

"You have no need for my presence anymore, dear one, especially now that Ada and Hosea are established; and there is business elsewhere I must attend to. In truth, I have cut matters closer than I should, necessary though I felt that to be. I cannot stay any longer, John. I must be fully about on the One's business."

John nodded, almost irritated by the calm Self of the One that watched his discomfiture from within. "How soon will you go?" he asked, bracing himself to hear she'd be leaving in a matter of hours, as she'd done in Bethany.

"I hope to stay until the trainees feel stable in their awareness of the Stillness, and Ada and Hosea know themselves to be competent to train them, but...that may not be possible," Mary answered, suddenly looking a bit uncertain. Then she lightly squeezed John's arm and chuckled.

"Fear not, my son, we've a bit of time together yet, I promise."

"Indeed?" he asked, gazing into her eyes as if he feared to see she told not the truth.

"Most indeed. Now come! Let us get out of this chill air so we may go and abuse Iustus's fabulous table."

John allowed himself a small smile as she grabbed his hand and pulled him along.

"What would you *know* of unseemly behavior?"

Timothy bar Arioch stood before John, vibrating with anger. John stared expressionlessly back at the young man from his place on one of the cushiony floor pillows in the main room of the women's cottage, inviting, he knew, even greater anger by his lack of response.

How very much he has grown, he thought, remembering the boy who'd joined them on the road to Caesarea. Most of the childlike softness in Timothy's face and body had disappeared, to be replaced by a fine ripple of muscle that was easily visible beneath his robe, especially around the chest and shoulders. He also now sported a light but proper beard and features that, in a few years, would be chiseled almost to the point of sharpness. But the essential gentleness and natural innocence that so endeared—and at times infuriated—people would always soften any physical appearance of sternness.

And he hadn't only altered physically. Timothy had grown ever surer of his ability to deal with the world around him these last months, far more sure than he'd been in familiar Bethany, with a doting mother and strong elder brothers. Others, John knew, would always see in him an openness that would offer comfort in the face of their worries and absolution in the presence of their mistakes. He was, by every measure, a man full-grown and respectable; had it only been a matter of teaching the companions to teach the Practice to others, Timothy could have forgone the training.

But that was not all there was to it. Something was still missing from the young man's makeup, and that something would be vital to the fulfillment of their task.

On the night Johanna had met her demon, Timothy had stalked from the women's cottage angry enough to fight. More, John later heard that he'd had plenty to say when the men returned to their small house, actually kicking a chair across the room in his rage at being treated like a child when he might have helped.

And the truth was his presence would have helped. Even under the circumstances, had he insisted on staying, John would gladly have let him, for the young man's Stillness would have supported Rachael at the least. But instead—and as he'd done more than once when dealing with John—he'd angrily left and ranted to others over his treatment. Weeks later, he still either remained petulantly silent in his presence or took every other word to him or Rachael as a slight, yet he said nothing to the source of his ire.

Was this refusal to demand to be treated as adults inherent to men of Timothy and Erezavan's generation? But no, that could not be. Stavis's younger brother Orron, who was as severe an irritant as had ever been taught to walk on two legs, regularly stated opinions on things he knew nothing about while evincing a passionate belief in his infallibility, and he was by no means unique. So, if it wasn't the generation, what made Timothy continue to bury his strength beneath the tombstones of false humility? Did being near Masters from so young an age cause it? Was there some other reason?

Did it really matter? Whatever the cause, John had had enough of it. Erezavan had forsaken his boundaries months ago and grew more Still by the day because of it. It was well past time for Timothy to move his stone aside...and John had no qualms about triggering that movement by using the one thing guaranteed to raise the young man's hackles right off his body.

It had been obvious for some time that he and Rachael were in love. John and Mary had discussed what, if anything, they should do about it, since Rachael's mother had so trustingly given the girl into John's care. Eleanor, no doubt, would be appalled by the freedom her daughter had to associate, even platonically, with unmarried men, but between the Practice and the male companions' unfailingly respectful treatment, Rachael had flourished, letting go nearly all the damage done at her father's hands. In the end, Mary argued they should let things proceed at their natural pace and John had agreed, well aware of the benefits to both youngsters.

In Rachael, Timothy had found someone who loved the One as much as he did —and loved doing the Practice somewhat more. Her one-pointed focus was truly an inspiration, for though Timothy was fully capable of being Still in any situation, he still tended to let the wonders of the world distract him, as if he thought it impossible to be both joyful *and* focused. His growth, substantial as it was, was nevertheless slower than it could be. With the example of Rachael's dedication, Timothy had done more of the Practice, eyes closed, in the last few months than he'd done in the previous year.

But that same dedication sometimes made the young woman a little *too* serious. Eleanor's daughter that she was, she could be as practical as bread—and to her, doing the Practice was the most practical thing in the world. John sometimes got the impression that, but for the others' scolding, Rachael would forego eating itself to stay, eyes closed, in the Stillness. Timothy, however, didn't let her grow too distant. His playful sociability allowed Rachael to enjoy the innocence of childhood she'd rarely known, and his gentle attentions had helped her discard the belief that she was ugly and unworthy.

Even better, both youngsters seemed to understand the underlying purpose of their relationship, whatever form it might take. John knew they would extend their growing love for each other and the One to all the world, since they gladly and regularly shared their experiences of It with each other and anyone they could get to listen. Yes, Rachael and Timothy's relationship would foster the growth of many...

...But John had just accused them of the exact opposite intention.

The two of them sat together every evening, and though they did not touch, as was proper, John easily sensed their life forces flowing together and mingling. Such sharing was not unusual: even strangers' energies would briefly intermix if they were of the same mind on a matter, and the life forces of friends and family almost constantly blended. John, however, had begun this evening's meeting by insisting they sit apart from now on and not be without a chaperone at any time.

Rachael had looked hurt and puzzled, but Timothy, his voice barely controlled, had asked why John suddenly demanded such constraints.

"I'll not have the two of you sneaking away to engage in unseemly behavior," John answered brusquely, knowing even as he spoke that his accusation was unwarranted. Though they might be painfully desirous of each other as man and woman, Timothy, unlike John, had strong beliefs about what was and was not appropriate courting behavior.

As he had just angrily pointed out.

His retort caused all save Mary and Demeter to find anything but John and Timothy supremely appealing to look at—and Demeter's interest in Timothy was suddenly all too intense. She practically levitated to her feet and, face a scant inch from his, irately defended her sister's right to behave as she pleased. Timothy yelled right back, using epithets that proved that, while he might know correct courting behavior, he'd no idea how to keep a civil tongue in the presence of women.

All at once, the whole room was awhirl, as if twenty people filled it instead of half that number. Ariadne and Johanna restrained Demeter, who showed every sign of wanting to give Timothy a good, hard clout, while Torer did the same with Dareios. Erezavan and Haifata held to Timothy, who, though his vision was blocked by Demeter, was still looking to give John a piece of his mind at the very least. Rachael sat on the floor, crying heartbrokenly, while Stavis tried to comfort her, and Marcus, bless him, stood in a corner, arms crossed, taking it all in and laughing like his sides would split.

"My *deepest* pardon!"

Silence suddenly and ringingly filled the cottage, as loud as the yelling and cursing had been a second before, as Mary's voice effortlessly cut through the pandemonium. "Am I to suppose that any one of you could describe the One at this moment? Pray, can any of you even find It?"

"But Rabbi, he—"

"My son goes forth to seek Vashti soon. At the One's behest, he takes companions with him. You, unfortunately." The chill of Mary's anger was palpable as she examined the trainees one by one; almost all of them avoided her eyes. "This journey will require things of you that you have never had to give. It will show you things that look to come of the One, but which will leave your souls adrift in unimaginable emptiness if you allow yourselves to be fooled...or distracted by your fears."

A sad little smile came to her face, as if she'd caught one of her children doing something they both knew was beneath them. "Do you not know how very much my son and I love each one of you? Timothy, do you not know it? Truly? We have given everything of our lives to see you reach the highest, yes, but do you not know we would gladly give all of eternity if it meant you would forever know the fullness of the One?

"We would. We *have.*

"Each of you who goes forth to seek Vashti chose John, not the other way around. You agreed eons ago to follow this path with him and do whatsoever it takes to make this journey—which is, in its turn, but a part of an even larger mission. Yet agreements are not debts. This journey can be forsaken with little cost to those of you who would now change your minds. Though it is very unlikely you will gain the fullness of the One in this lifetime without those to guide you to the Wholeness they've become, John and I and your own experiences prove that it is possible to come to know the Stillness outside the land of Vashti.

"No, dear ones, neither I nor my son would see any of you take a path you are not ready to walk. You need only ask to be released from this task if it is not truly in your heart to come forth. But know this: if it is that you have suddenly found this path is not yours, best you should step clear of it as soon as may be, so as to avoid the cost of ignoring your unwillingness. And if it is that you choose to continue forth...well, best you should begin to behave as if the One is *all* you want. For I guarantee you, the agony of failing your soul by your own hands will show your heart no mercy at all.

"Now is the time, my own. You must choose what you truly want."

One by one, the trainees sat and closed their eyes, their expressions pensive or sad or even frightened. It was odd, John thought. Though every one of his company had, in one way or another, asked to join him on this journey, he could see it had never occurred to them that that was the case. They did feel, at some level, that John had chosen them, and the realization that their own souls had brought them here astonished them.

Mary stared down at the trainees as they took their places, her face glowing with her love for each of them, even though her smile was still a bit sad. Then she sighed, sat down and closed her eyes.

And that was when John knew something was wrong.

She sat slowly, carefully, as if she suspected her strength would betray her if she moved too quickly. And she looked—no—*was* tired. She surreptitiously gasped for air; in fact, she was almost panting. Jarringly, and for the first time ever during their long sojourn together, John actually saw Mary's age.

Their conversation on the road to Ephesus came back to him. He'd thought her vacillation about when she would depart odd when first she'd told him she was leaving, but he'd dismissed it, thinking her desire to see some specific shift in the trainees was its cause. Now, with sudden and painful clarity, John truly realized why Mary had been so hesitant. This time, his mother would not depart from the human plane by Ascending, or even by simply disappearing.

This time Mary would depart by dying.

The meeting ended quietly, with each of the companions either coming out of the Silence and going to their beds, or gathering their blankets and moving closer to the fire. Haifata stood with Mary, for he would walk with her back to Ephesus as he did most nights. John turned to him.

"If you've no objections, brother, I would walk back with the two of you."

Mary raised a brow, but made no comment. Haifata scrutinized John in his silent way, which grew ever more Silent with his continuing participation in the training.

"You will stay there for the night?"

"Yes."

"Then if you do not mind, I would borrow the use of your tent so I may stay and continue in the Practice for a while longer."

He knows, John realized, but simply nodded and ushered Mary out the door.

Despite his concern, John rejoiced at the brilliance of the cold clear night as he and Mary walked. As always, he prized the razor-sharp clarity of the million, million stars and celebrated the beauty of their never-ending songs. Here was beauty no amount of worry could ever obliterate.

He looked aside at Mary as they walked, ambled really, at a pace that was utterly alien to his picture of his efficient mother. Even at this speed, she labored; John could not clearly see her features in the darkness, but he suspected her face was drawn as if each step caused her pain.

How had he missed this? Could he have been so blind? But no, that was not the case at all. He'd seen his mother only a few times in the last two weeks, all of them briefly. What little walking they'd done covered only short distances: kitchen to room, into the garden, main room to front door. No, he'd not been blind; Mary had kept this from him.

His thoughts went to the day-brilliant walk they'd taken on the night of her Ascension, to the luminosity of the life force that had lit Marcus's unknowing heart and made it possible for him to later heal the beggar with but a few words. Yet, even as his mind cried out at the unfairness of it all, his heart—and yes, something even deeper—told him to trust in the rightness of things. It was not as if Mary would die forever, after all, any more than Jeshua had. She'd already Ascended once, no?

John's attention snapped to the present as Mary rambled to a halt next to a thigh-high boulder on the side of road. She sat, her tiredness apparent, and coughed once, so lightly John could hardly call it such. Yet it was a sound he'd never heard her make except to emphasize some point, usually humorously. The conflict between his heart and head could no longer stay inside.

"Mother, why? Why did you choose to come back if it leads only to this?" The unspoken question also hung in the air: Why did you not tell me?

Mary sat for several moments with her eyes closed; John sensed the strength slowly creeping back into her cells. When she opened her eyes, he saw her features as if a dim light shone on her face. She sighed.

"The seeds that required planting in Bethany not only did not require planting here, but would have adversely affected the Plan, especially at this time. My return was not originally among the things we intended, you know; but when it became apparent that you meant to teach the Practice in Corinth, we saw a chance to create some new possibilities for Jeshua's "church", possibilities that will keep his true mission alive for some who might otherwise have forsaken it." Mary smiled at John's confused look and laid a chilled hand against his cheek. "Forgive me, my son; I know I speak of this as if you already have a point of reference from which to understand it, but that is the best I can do for now."

Some of her usual impishness returned. "Besides, it has been a very long time indeed since I died while fully conscious...and I find I am looking somewhat forward to the experience."

John frowned. Though he sensed Mary spoke the absolute truth, he also sensed an unaccustomed falseness to her words, as if she had not said all she meant. He looked into her eyes, and the sense was confirmed: fear—*fear*—looked back.

Mary looked away. "I speak the truth, John, you know it. Yet, it is also true that the body has its own imperative to survive. So, yes, there is fear in this experience, and pain and tiredness. And it has been long, long since I have had to deal with any of them.

"I sense, ever so slightly, the agony my Jeshua experienced in Gethsemane, John. I know it was made more difficult by his awareness that those he loved would grieve for him. He had the strength to overcome his desire to spare his friends and do what he agreed to do, and I too, have the strength to overcome your sadness. Yet...the fear that comes with this amazes even me, especially considering what I have already done."

Mary stared at the star-encrusted horizon, and John could tell she struggled with some decision. Finally: "Cruel it may be, but I would ask a boon of you, my son. I would ask for your blessing, have you tell me you accept my choice, so my Way might be made easier than my son's was..." her voice quavered, "...and I would ask your forgiveness for needing such support."

John gazed at Mary's hands. They had always been strong and beautiful, of a piece with the beauty of Mary herself. They were the hands of a woman who had borne and raised seven children, the hands of a woman who'd outlived her true love by many years and watched her firstborn die in the most painful, degrading way possible. Those hands trembled on her lap now, showing the signs of her increasing physical decline.

John took them gently in his and gave them a light squeeze, then took Mary in his arms. He embraced the hugeness of her heart just as he'd taken in the beauty of the clear, starry night—with joyful appreciation that he could truly be Mary's comforter for the first time in their relationship.

Like her hands, Mary trembled as she leaned against John, wholly accepting his warmth and stability in the December cold. As they had in the kitchen so many weeks ago, the fullness of their Selves blended in intimate yet wholly welcome Fullness. One age passed, and then another; yet John realized that even if he was with his mother every single moment until this was finished, he would miss her presence terribly, just as he had the last time.

Even so, when he leaned back and saw his own tears mirrored on Mary's face he knew they were tears of joy. In that moment, he understood his mother's choice to take this mantle on, understood the gift she gave to the universe. He knew now that, just as he'd not failed his Teacher in Gethsemane all those years ago, he would not fail Mary now.

"Mother," he said at last, his voice thick even as he smiled, "In our Teacher's name, in the name of the unbounded One, my blessing be upon you. Do what you must needs do."

When they arrived at Iustus and Thaleia's, John put Mary to bed and watched her fall into a restless sleep. He took the garden shortcut to leave the house: though it was wholly unlikely that Ada and Hosea had not noticed Mary's worsening health, he preferred to wait 'til the morrow to confirm any suspicions.

His mother had needed sleep as she had not in years—but that was not what John wanted. His feelings had been in a constant ebb and flow these last several hours, first to joy at Mary's choice, then to grief over what her absence would mean. He needed to move, to feel solid earth beneath his shoes.

The last thing he wanted to do was think.

John got what he desired: he meandered past fine homes and downtrodden abodes alike and walked where only the hardiest souls dared as he took the longest possible route to the road that led to the cottages. Once outside Ephesus, he stayed so fully in the Stillness while watching stars and sleepy nature spirits that he felt a renewed sense of equilibrium with his body and world when he arrived at his tent, a comfortable kind of tiredness. He'd be glad to finally lie down; it had been an eventful evening, to say the least.

John raised the flap, more than ready to crawl into his bedroll...then stopped and slapped his forehead.

Argh! Haifata sleeps in my bed this night!

Of course, he could crawl in and roll up in a blanket anyway, then wait until his chilled bones warmed. The idea didn't appeal to him.

Instead, John headed toward the men's cottage, hoping the smoke rising from the chimney meant the fire was a goodly one. He opened the door as quietly as he could; it was not unusual for the trainees to stay awake all night so they could get in as many consecutive hours of the Practice as possible, and if they discovered his presence, they'd keep him up, desiring to share experiences and ask questions. This was especially true of Prochorus and Torer, who were troubled by the inactivity. Or as Marcus had put it: "I love the Practice, but this lying about and doing nothing *all* the time palls."

John had advised the men to exercise—but not too much. True, the more slowly the physical system vibrated, the deeper would be one's entrance into the One's Presence, but a bit of daily exercise could actually speed the taming of the phantom self.

My robe will have to be my blanket, John thought, but at least he'd have a decent bed, for several pillows lay on the floor. And no one was up to disrupt his coming rest.

Or so he thought. Someone sat in the far corner of the room, his blankets causing him to blend into the darkness. Now he stood, uncovering his head so John could see him.

It was Timothy.

At first, the young man looked surprised to see John, but then his face closed, his anger over the evening's events still strongly apparent.

"Rabbi," he said, meaning it not at all as an honorific.

"Timothy," John answered, and waited. He could see the young man had more to say, even if he seemed unready to say it.

"We were going to wait until morning to tell you, but as you are here now, I may as well attend to it," he finally said, and John was once again, all in spite of himself, impressed with the man Timothy bar Arioch had become.

"Rachael and I are leaving."

THIRTY-FIVE

Timothy's *determined countenance* conveyed his certainty that he could rebut any response he'd imagined John might make to his announcement—but John chose none of them. He only gazed in Timothy's direction, more through than at him, then shrugged as if he'd just found the morrow's weather to be what he'd expected.

"If that is what you wish," he said, and walked to the fireplace to sort out bedding.

"Do you not want to know why?" Timothy's surprise—and the slightest edge of uncertainty—dampened his stern determination.

"Despite my promise to Eleanor to see to her care, Timothy, Rachael, though young, is an adult, and so are you. I assume you know your hearts well enough to follow them where they would lead. And I know you know the One well enough to listen to Its call, wherever you might be. I will miss you both, we all will. But if returning to Bethany is what you want, you've the right to go, just as Mary said. I can do naught but wish you a safe journey."

A long moment passed with no sound but pillows sliding along the stone floor. "Is there another blanket? Haifata uses my tent and I would not wake him shuffling about."

"Rabbi!" Timothy did not quite stomp his foot, but he suddenly didn't sound at all grown. In fact, he sounded more than a little like he wanted to cry. Argument he'd expected, perhaps even hoped for, but this seeming indifference...whatever this journey had made of him, he had no idea how to respond to being treated as an adult with neither debate nor fanfare, not by this one. John lowered himself to his makeshift bed, resisting the urge to groan over its softness, and patted the pillow next to him.

"Will you sit with me for a while, brother? Surely you do not plan to leave before saying your farewells to the others...and I find I have no wish to be alone just now."

John heard a surreptitious sniff as Timothy came to the pillows. They did not speak as they stared into the fire's welcoming warmth. John was glad the Silence within still matched the silence around him; the wariness that issued from Timothy's every pore pounded against him with as much warmth as the fire but was not nearly as welcoming.

He could practically hear the younger man's thoughts: now he will try to argue—but I'll have none of it. The Rabbi's accusations during the meeting were an irreparable insult, especially to Rachael. They would find their way back to Bethany and marry, and he'd not change their minds, no matter how persuasive his arguments, no matter how upset Miriam might be...

John's lips suddenly curled in a rueful smile, and he half-laughed, half-groaned. "Oh, Jeshua...you were right."

"What?"

John's smile grew. "Here, Timothy. I have a story, a gift for you to carry on your road back to Bethany. One evening, after our return from the North Country, we attended dinner at one of the Rachaels' homes. Jeshua was there, of course, and the twelve; also Martha, Mary and my mother Salome; Lazarus and Elior and a number of others. Miriam, though, was not present; for some reason she was late.

"Now, when we'd arrived in the city, one or two of Jeshua's more prominent followers came to us, all concern and venom over Miriam. They swore she'd gone back to her former trade in our absence, for she was rarely at meetings, and when she did arrive she was usually disheveled. 'And she has been seen leaving the drinking dens,' one of them added with scandalized glee.

"Jeshua listened and nodded, but his look seemed to say he could not care less. I was glad, for I was sorely offended on Miriam's behalf. After all, she had never shown the slightest hint of impious behavior in my presence. Still, by the time dinner started, she had not appeared...in fact, she did not appear for more than two hours after we arrived, and when she finally did come, she was not only flushed, but tousled.

"Everyone in the room grew silent as Miriam smiled and nodded a greeting to Jeshua, but his look was as forbidding as ever I'd seen it. It was obvious he was angry at her...and suddenly, I was angry at Jeshua.

He does not trust her, I thought indignantly, not at all. He never has, not in all the time he has known her. So far as I could see, he had found her guilty of the others' charges without even asking her about it, had decided to believe their rumor-mongering.

"And his next words proved it.

"'If you would call yourself one of my followers, Miriam, best you should have a chaperone. After all, we have none in our party who actively live as harlots.'

"Well. There I was, all fire and lightning at barely eighteen summers old and madly in love with Miriam; I could not believe Jeshua would publicly humiliate her so." John chuckled, mostly at Timothy's astonished look at John's admission about his Teacher. "Add to that the fact that Jeshua had been goading me for weeks, as if nothing I did or said was right, and I was well-primed. I'd repeatedly swallowed my pride rather than argue, even when I was sure he meant to hurt me, but for the sake of Miriam's pride...well.

"I jumped to my feet almost before I knew what I was doing and gave the room a taste of my fisherman's tongue—especially those I thought far too delighted by Jeshua's words—and suddenly, everyone was up, yelling and cursing. Some cursed at Miriam, others at me, some at whoever seemed to be close by, and...well, it certainly was noisy."

Timothy shifted uncomfortably; he could scarcely fail to notice the similarities to his own recent experience. John continued.

"Just as Judas and James stopped me from leaping over the table and punching one of Miriam's more self-righteous critics in his big, arrogant nose, I caught sight of Jeshua. He was leaning back in his chair, utterly relaxed, his hands wrapped around his wine cup as he gazed across the room with the slightest smile on his face. I turned to see what he looked at, and was shocked out of the rest of my senses...for he stared at Miriam.

"She had not moved when the altercation started, did not even seem to be aware she was its cause. Rather, she returned Jeshua's stare, her expression a perfect match for his...and *winked* at him. Then she put on a serious face as Jeshua silenced the room and gave much the same talk Mary gave all of you this evening.

"I do not mind telling you, Timothy, that I felt as humiliated and angry as a man could possibly be. I could not decide if I wanted to curse Jeshua or burst into tears. I *can* tell you that I wanted to crawl into a hole and pull the earth up over me, for to my mind, I'd been baited and used by the two people I loved most in the world—not to help others learn, I was sure, but for their amusement.

"And since I had no stomach for such treachery, I decided to leave that very night."

"But you did not leave," Timothy said slowly. John snorted.

"Not for lack of trying, and I thank you for being good enough to tell me you mean to, for I extended no such courtesy to my Teacher."

"You meant to walk away from Jeshua without saying goodbye?"

If it surprised Timothy to hear John's admission about Miriam, he was absolutely shocked by this. John blinked as he comprehended for the first time just how high a pedestal the youngster had placed him on. He'd come to expect such from those who knew him only as "one of the Twelve", but he'd assumed such idolization by his companions had long since dissolved.

"I was a boy, Timothy, younger than you are now," he shrugged. And Jeshua was, well, Jeshua. I did not feel I could face him, certainly not in anger—and make no mistake, I was furious. So I gathered my belongings and crept out the door without even saying goodbye to my own brother, meaning to be as far from Jeshua and Miriam as I could manage by sunrise. I knew I could return to my father's house, that he would be glad to have a son back to help with the business; so that is where I meant to go."

John chuckled again. "I made it as far as the outer wall of Rachael's house.

"'A perfect night for a walk, is it not, Little Brother?' Jeshua said from a low place on the wall where he sat.

"I meant to say nothing, to keep walking, but before I knew it, I was berating him like a Pharisee. I accused him of using Miriam to hurt me, of hurting her, of publicly humiliating me to amuse himself, and the One knows what else. Jeshua did not look at me as I ranted, but stared at the stars until I finally emptied myself out.

"Then he sighed. 'There are times, John,' he said at last, 'when I say and do things that seem unjust. They seem unjust to those to whom I speak, to those who watch, and even to the part of me that would have mercy on their feelings. There are times when those who witness my words and actions are convinced they are the ravings of a charlatan, an ingrate, a mad man. Yet I speak and act anyway, hoping all the while it will lead where it can instead of where it wants.

"'The day will come when I will speak thus to one of the twelve, and from that day on, that one will see me as an enemy. Indeed, he will eventually convince himself he does the best thing for Judea by giving the Son of Man over to meet with Death.

"'I know this, John, know I need only hold my tongue to avoid it—yet still will I say what the One would have me say, and joyfully. For if even one of you recognizes the mirror I offer and chooses instead to see himself as he truly is, my life will be worth what it costs.

"'That is what Miriam did tonight. She spoke no protest to my accusation, made no attempt to explain herself, despite the fact that even now some believe that what I said was true—which it was not. By refusing to let even me tell her what to believe she is when she knows the truth, she begins to accept herself as her Self. No one will ever take that away from her, John, no matter what might befall her, no matter who calls her what name.'

"Jeshua turned then and looked me full in the face. 'The day comes when you will understand the beauty of giving others such a chance to decide what they truly know, Little Brother...but Miriam and the future are not the true subjects of this conversation. The true subject is, what do you know now...and what do you want?'"

John stopped, amazement washing over him. He'd completely forgotten that Jeshua had warned him of his betrayal months before he told the rest of twelve what must be.

"Timothy, every one of the teachers in Bethany, including Miriam, has asked Jeshua's question, just as Mary did again tonight. Yet I ask you in this here and now, 'What do you know, and what do you want?' The time has long since passed for you to merely sit and bask in the Stillness like you would some sunny resting place. The One calls you to become That, to act from the Strength I see growing in your soul every day. You and Rachael together will light many others' paths no matter where you go—but how many others? I would have you touch the hearts of hundreds, but to do that, you must stay long enough to at least finish this training.

"I say again, Timothy, you are both adults and well able to find your Way; I will not stop you if It truly leads elsewhere. But will the two of you at least consider traveling this far on the journey to Vashti?

"Will you and Rachael stay?"

Timothy looked away, and John knew the young man was not yet sure he wanted to trust again. "You had no right to speak to us like that," he said at last, with no small amount of petulance.

"You have no right to believe the One would make you wrong for your love, even if what I said was true," John retorted. "That your phantom self might twist how you perceive your love, yes, that is possible. But never can what you and Rachael feel be inherently sinful, Timothy. You well know I mirrored only what you yourself feared, and you know Miriam would do no less."

Timothy nodded, willing to take in the admonishment. "I will have to think about it, and talk to Rachael," he said at last.

John nodded, careful not to let his relief show. He'd said much the same thing to Jeshua when asked to stay with him.

They took turns stoking the fire and talked the rest of the night. Timothy shyly spoke of his feelings for Rachael and John told more stories about himself, Miriam and Jeshua. He spoke as well of Ariadne, of coming to terms with his feelings about his relationship with her. Timothy listened, spellbound, one man heeding the words of another.

It would take the lad awhile to be comfortable with the fact, but John knew he had lost a mere student, only to gain another friend along the Way. It would not make up for the one they'd soon lose, he thought, but it did lighten the burden ever so slightly.

Mary's health deteriorated rapidly, as if John's blessing had indeed made it easier for her to give up the body and its fear of dying. Within ten days, she could walk only with help, and at the end of three weeks, she had to be carried from place to place. Her breathing sometimes became so labored that she had to speak in parts of sentences, and she often took to her room to rest. Where once she'd been robust, now she was thin and ashen, fast becoming little more than skin draped over bones.

At least, that is how the students at House Karikos saw her. John's perception of his mother was altogether different.

Whenever he was with Mary, all he could see was the indelible, almost blinding brilliance of a life force that had not been one whit diminished by her body's ailments. Oh, it was not that he ignored the degeneration of her body. Such a thing would have been impossible so long as he had human eyes. Rather, it was that John's true vision took his sight beyond what appeared to be, filling him with such joy that the students began to fear his mind was ranging outside the gates of reality.

Finally, Mary herself asked him to stop visiting her when most of the students were present, "so they will stop coming to me...with their concerns about...your wellbeing."

"Well, I cannot seem to help it, Mother," he'd answered sheepishly. "Your light, your life force, is so incredible right now...how can they not be as aware of it as I am?"

"As with any other miracle...if one is not ready to see it...it will cause fear. Said another way, my son...your bliss is distracting them." She'd patted him on the hand and grinned. "Come to me in the evenings...dear one...for you I will always awaken."

The two of them sat together on one such evening, almost a month after John had given his blessing. As had become their habit, they basked in the Fullness rather than wasting breath to talk, for though her deterioration had slowed from its initial blistering pace, Mary had grown too weak to sit up for more than a few hours at a time.

John came out of the One's Presence before his mother did and watched her until she opened her eyes and smiled. He had to take a breath: her radiance filled him to overflowing with an emotion he could neither call joy nor grief, but which seemed equally comprised of both.

"How long, Mother?" he asked, when he saw she had returned to the present moment.

"How long before...Ada and Hosea know...their strength...do you feel?" There was little need to be concerned for the trainees; though she still sometimes lost track of it, even Johanna was now able to describe her experience of the One with her eyes open.

"Hosea truly accepts his growth, but Ada, a little to my surprise, in truth, still doubts a little. Even so, it will not be long. "

Mary seemed to think about it, then nodded. "That long, then..."

If Mary's wasting sickness was hard for the students in Ephesus to take, it was even harder for the trainees. John had been shocked by how much she'd changed, and he'd known her to be ill, but when she entered the women's cottage, leaning on Haifata's arm, a week after he realized she was dying, the trainees' collective gasp spoke eloquently of their shock and horror. Several of them burst into tears; others frantically asked questions, as if seeking some solution that could heal her. John even received one or two furtive glances, as if they thought he could and should heal her—and why hadn't he?

Haifata helped Mary to the one chair that had arms and she explained the situation as clearly as she could. Dareios, being much older, took the news with some equanimity, but Ariadne and Demeter took it very hard. They'd lost their mother to illness, and this situation was far too familiar. Though Mary shook her head and promised she would always be with them, their tearful pleas that she reconsider her choice broke John's heart.

So, when Ariadne came to his tent that night and crawled into his blankets to sob grief-filled tears on his shoulder, He said not a word about unacceptable distractions; and though he told himself he should rouse her and send her back to her own bed when she finally calmed down and seemed ready to drift off to sleep, he found he could not.

John started to justify the lapse by telling himself he allowed her to be with him solely for the sake of her consolation—then suddenly snorted derisively and chuckled.

"Hmmm?" Ariadne said, already more than half gone. He kissed her forehead.

"Nothing, my love, I just caught myself in a lie. Go back to sleep."

The distraction caused by Mary's sickness was a concern to John, but it was by no means his only one—and soon, it was not his greatest one.

One evening, as they shared their usual visit, a knock sounded on Mary's bedroom door. John looked questioningly at his mother, but she expected no visitors.

The number of students who were perfectly willing to force themselves on Mary for their comfort more than hers gave Iustus and Thaleia cause to shake their heads in disgust and seek a solution. The Karikos children, glad to be of use, promptly volunteered to guard her against invasions—something that was very nearly a full-time job. John, Hosea, Ada and Haifata were automatic exceptions to the rule, of course, but Haifata had gone to the cottages with Ada and Hosea for the evening meeting.

John opened the door a crack, only to find Iustus's portly form standing before him, his face pasty with alarm and fear.

"Jeshua's heart, Iustus, what has happened? You look as if you've seen a ghost."

"No," the merchant said as he stepped into the room, panting, "but one was made this night, woe be to us."

John poured a cup of water; Karikos he looked like he'd run all the way from the front door, no small distance for a man of his girth. Iustus took the water with thanks, but refused to sit. For a moment, John wondered if something had happened to one of the trainees, but his senses told him that was not the case.

Iustus drained his cup and accepted another, then sighed heavily. His face was still grim and frightened, but he was no longer on the edge of panic.

"It is bad news my friends, very bad," he said at last. "Terus Flavius is dead, assassinated by one of his own guards."

"Ah," John exhaled resignedly. This was indeed bad news, and at the worst of times. Considering how long they'd been in Ephesus, and despite the benign Christine surveillance, John was surprised at least one attempt had not been made to spirit him away to the Athens, which he assumed still wanted him as a "guest". He attributed his continuing freedom to Mary's presence, yes, but also to the fact that those who wished him ill knew that Flavius, who'd obviously had more than a portion of the Emperor's god-like ear, was not one who's favor they wanted to flout. His influence must have been extensive indeed.

But not extensive enough. It had not saved him from the assassin's hand.

The knowledge that, with the Governor's demise, his fortunes must surely change now stared John ominously in the face. How long did he have before his inevitable arrest? Would the authorities be satisfied with taking him only, or were all the companions in danger? Should he spirit them away before the local authorities got to them? If so, should they continue the training elsewhere? Where? What of the local Christines who supported them? Were they now in danger as well?

John was bombarded as these questions and more crowded against each other in their quest to gain his attention. He had no answers to give, yet his mind demanded he answer now and answer correctly, lest his indecision should bring disaster down on everyone's heads. Uncertainty clawed at his insides, trying to induce him to hasty action.

John did not react, at least not in the way his mind exhorted him to. Instead, he introduced one technique of the Practice, then another, with his eyes open, and entered into the ever-silent One. Within moments, his spirit gently disentangled itself from his mind's noisy intensity and the clawing sense of needing to *do* faded softly away. Mary managed a grin.

"Amazing...is it not...how the One prevails...when we simply let it." And of course, that only made sense, for the One was not just the core of know-ledge but Knowledge Itself.

Iustus's gasp caught John's attention so abruptly that he actually spun about, afraid the Ephesian might be having some sort of attack from his exertions. What he saw on the stout man's face, however, was not pain but intense wonder.

John laid a hand on Iustus's arm in understanding, knowing he saw in Mary for the first time what John had been aware of for weeks: the incredible fullness of a life force so strong it could effortlessly enliven a thousand men.

With a catch in his breath that was more like a sob, Iustus stumbled to Mary's bedside and fell to his knees, reverently catching her hand to kiss it. Mary made no attempt to deflect the obeisance, but laid her other hand gently on his face. As he looked tearfully into her eyes, she further amazed both men by speaking in a voice as strong as if sickness had never touched her.

"A gift, Iustus Karikos, for all you have done for me, my son and his company. Truly, you are one of God's innocents; such generosity as you and your family have shown is rare even for those who would knowingly entertain angels. Know that you need have no fear of what might happen now or in the future. Know that, whatever may happen in the days and months and years to come, your family and their families will know only Prosperity, and they will prosper others' hearts and minds and souls by their knowing. This is the blessing I lay upon you in Jeshua's Name and in the Name of the One, Iustus. I know you will carry it with honor."

Iustus nodded dumbly, tears streaming down his face. He once more kissed Mary's hand and held it against his heart for several moments, then rose, hugged John and practically floated from the room. John looked at his mother, sharing her rueful smile.

"We need do so little to bring joy, my son. Merely by praising and blessing each other, we bestow power beyond our wildest dreams—and are empowered by that bestowal. Why do we so readily forget that?"

"So that, when we remember, our joy will be all the greater?" He'd meant it as a statement but it came out sounding more like a question.

"I know not," Mary shrugged slightly, her expression all innocence.

John laughed. "Faugh, mother, you *tell* not."

The two of them sat for a bit longer, enjoying their silence and each other, for John had the sudden sense that they'd not again do so in this lifetime. Mary's smile faded and her eyes took on a distant gaze, as though she looked beyond the room she sat in, to times and spaces so distant and wondrous that John could only imagine them. When she returned from her reverie, her face was serious and her voice again held pain.

"Listen to me...my son. In a few days...more likely, a week...Amadeon Iscariotus... will return to this house...seeking you."

"To arrest me?"

She frowned and shook her head. "That is not...clear. Or it is not his...intention at this time. It does not...matter. Whatever the case...you must let the universe...take its course. Do not attempt to...avoid him...or what he brings."

John nodded, butterflies suddenly fluttering. "As you wish, Mother."

"Good." Mary lay back on her pillow, breathing as if she'd just run a race. John again observed the pallor that lived atop the brilliance with which she'd blessed Iustus Karikos; he hung his head as grief washed through his soul.

"I had hoped to be here...until Ada and Hosea...remembered more fully...John...but I see now that...events will not...allow it."

"I had guessed as much, dearest mother, though I did not want to say it."

"Afraid it might...upset me?" Mary said with the barest of chuckles. But John shook his head, blinking back sudden tears.

"Afraid it might upset *me*."

"Ummm." She still smiled slightly. Then: "John."

"Yes, Mother?"

"I would be with...the trainees now. I have one more lesson...to teach them yet... before I depart...from this plane."

THIRTY-SIX

As it *turned out*, it was three days before John, Haifata and two of the local Christines found a litter they considered comfortable enough for Mary to ride the almost two miles it would take to get her to the edge of the city. Her departure from House Karikos was a tearful one: the students knew this would likely be her last foray out into the world once she returned from the training site. The Karikos family and servants were at the front of the crowd, all solemn of mien. That is, save for Iustus; he still saw Mary in her truth and struggled to keep the smile from his face.

The crowd that followed the group through the neighborhood was tremendous, and as they'd done with John in Bethany, they cried out to Mary their goodbyes, blessings and requests for such. By the time they arrived at market, however, only the most devoted few remained to keep company with them.

John understood their rapid dispersal. The new Governor, Piros Bardisus, was on record as being neither for nor against the Christines; like his predecessor, he recognized the value of maintaining cordial relations, especially with the businessmen, and was content to leave things much as they had been. He'd not instantly ordered pogroms against the pesky religionists, as some had hysterically feared, nor had he called on their leaders for advice and counsel, as some had hoped. But he had ordered the local soldiers to maintain the status quo and leave the Christine population alone.

Even so, though nothing had changed on the surface since Flavius's death, the air was full of...not fear, exactly...but...watchfulness. People, Christine and not, seemed wary, going about their business as if they expected trouble at any moment and wanted to be well out of its way before it found them. Some of this, of course, could be attributed to the natural caution most humans displayed in the face of abrupt change, but there was more to it than that. The soldiers walked the streets more boldly than they had before, and though their manner was polite, their demeanor was less so. It was a subtle difference, yes, but John felt sure it would soon become more pronounced. Bardisus, for all his good intentions, had not the Emperor's ear as Flavius had, and so by extension, had not his power to influence the less prudent of the city's anti-Christine officials.

Interestingly, in a city renowned for its decadence, those who seemed most likely to benefit from the dispersal of the Christine population were in truth among the most worried. Purges tended to be bad for any business, but the drinking dens, gamers and prostitutes were more than commonly susceptible to overzealous enforcements of law and order. After all, what citizen would want to risk being mistaken for a Christine traveling the streets after some alleged late-evening meeting? And how many officials would not take advantage of those who had no real voice to protest with?

No, this change could only create changes that many would soon find burdensome.

It was cold out this early afternoon, and the sky, which had been unseasonably clear for much of fall and winter, was dark and cast with heavy clouds. The wind, though not strong, was cold and wet. As they neared edge of town, where they would place Mary's litter on a small flatcart for easier transport, John found himself wishing they carried heavier cargo so their exertions might produce more heat.

Then again, he wished the "cargo" walked beside him as she once had.

A few miles later, the cart, with its single mule to pull it, rounded a bend in the road and came within sight of the cottages. All the trainees and Ada and Hosea awaited them; John had told them the day before last of Mary's request to come to meeting. He craned his neck and tried to get a clearer look at everyone; something about them was different.

"Hmph," he said as he suddenly realized what it was. Every one of the trainees was either in the finery they had worn the night of their dinner or dressed in some other suitably elegant robe. John peered at Haifata, brow raised; the African, who'd obviously been expecting his look, nodded in the trainees' direction with a slight smile.

"Demeter asked Ada to bring the trainees their clothing, and Thaleia, who would not see her and Hosea without finery for such an event, gifted them with new robes also."

"Hmph," John said again. He looked at his own world-weary attire, then back at Adan, suddenly sure the African's cloak hid the splendid robe he'd worn that night.

Adan laughed. "Fear not for your vanity's mortification, brother; Ariadne has yours."

"Ah... Well, then. I see no problem with their undue indulgence."

They halted before the women's cottage. John pulled back the blue woolen curtain Iustus had insisted on adding to the litter's covering to further hold the chill air at bay and rubbed Mary's bony hand as she sat with eyes closed, resting in the Stillness.

"Mother, we are here," he said softly. Mary opened her eyes and smiled tiredly. John drew her from the litter as easily as he would a small child, ready to carry her into the cottage, but Mary suddenly stopped him and spoke to the two volunteer litter bearers.

"Thank you...Avros...Jaresh...for all your help," she said, gaining surprised and delighted looks from the two men by knowing their names. Jaresh, the foreman of the volunteers who'd work on the cottages, bowed deeply.

"We would gladly carry you to the ends of the earth itself if you asked it, Lady," he said, his voice shaking with emotion.

Mary's smiled slightly as she locked eyes with him, looking, John thought, as if she expected a specific response from the man. But the former foreman only gasped, blinked and shuffled about in mute befuddlement.

"Great Souls...play small parts," she at last said cryptically. Her smile grew and lit her bone-thin face until she seemed again to be her old, mischievous self. She raised a frail hand. "Go always...in peace...my brothers. You have served...the One well." Mary looked toward the trainees, her smile tender. "Take me inside...my son...so we may all...sit and talk."

No dismayed exclamations greeted Mary this time, but John clearly heard the grief-stricken cries of the trainees' hearts as they saw how weak she was. As much as they might have tried to believe there was still hope, they now saw with their own eyes that she was dying—and more, that her time was very short indeed.

They'd placed her chair close to the fire, and one of the women had made cushions for the seat and armrests. Probably Johanna, John thought, for, to her surprise, she'd discovered a talent and joy for beautifying things in practical ways. John placed Mary in the chair and laid a wool blanket over her knees; the others solemnly filed into the room and found places to sit. Ariadne and Demeter sat on the floor to either side of their Teacher, and after looking to Mary for permission, Ariadne took a hand in both of hers.

John's throat tightened at the desperation in the trainees' faces, but he could not but smile as his gaze fell on Ada and Hosea. Even as tears touched her, Ada, as always, carried the joy that seemed to be her natural way of being. Hosea, unlike the occasion of Mary's departure in Bethany, was calm in his sorrow, a spire of Stillness in a raging sea of grief. They, at least, had come to truly accept the necessity of what she did.

The heaviness and silence in the room grew as everyone waited for someone else to speak. Finally, Mary sighed in exasperated amusement.

"Dear ones... I have already been...through my funeral...once today," she said, referring to the trip from Iustus's. "I will thank you...not to treat...this visit...like another."

"How not, Mother, when we see that one who was so strong even a few weeks ago is now a mere shade of the self she was?" Prochorus's voice was bitter with anguish as the others murmured their agreement; even Torer blinked back tears in the face of their impending loss. "How can we not?"

Mary seemed to stare at something beyond the room; John knew she chose her words with care, so that her explanation awakened understanding not just in the trainees' minds, but in their hearts.

"By accepting this...truth...Marcus. Despite what the...appearance...of my body... would tell you...I bring...glad tidings...not ones of tragedy...and loss."

The trainees gasped as Mary smiled brilliantly and the majesty of her Being—along with the clarity of her voice—washed over them. "When I was in Bethany, I told a story about Jeshua's task, and mine. Timothy, Ada and Hosea remember it, I am sure..."

And so the One buoys us up at need, John thought, for just as she'd done with Iustus, she continued on with no hint of infirmity. But that wasn't the half of it: not long after Iustus's visit, Mary had had some sort of seizure that had left her unconscious for hours and stopped John's heart in his chest. When she came to, she'd been unable to speak —had been unable to for the last three days. Her blessing to Jaresh and Avros had been as much a surprise to John as the strength of her voice was to the trainees now.

Mary again told how Divine Mother taught Aleph, the perfect embodiment of the One, to be fully human, spoke again of how She had agreed always to go forth before Him to sire or give birth to the embodiment of the One on all the Earths. She told them how some form of Divine Mother always stayed on the earth plane after the One's departure from it, until the Seed of Self-Remembrance was again planted within humanity's collective psyche; how, when that task was finished, She then moved on.

"And so I do...precisely that...now," she said yet again as exhaustion overtook her. "Because of...Jeshua's twelve...and each of you...that Seed will...indeed live...to grow bountiful Fruit...on this earth. My work here...is blessedly... joyously..." she pulled forth a wry smile, "and this time...truly...finished."

"Yes, but, Mother! When you went from us last time you were whole, not like this!" Timothy's sorrowful voice broke the trainees' silence. "Why must it be this way now? Why must you die?"

Mary did not answer, but looked at John with a small smile. Did she wish him to answer? But no; she leaned toward Ariadne, whose grief overfilled her face and posture, and whispered in her ear. Surprised joy flitted across the younger woman's features and the briefest of smiles brightened her face. Mary sat back, her look satisfied.

"I go forth...in this way...so that you may...remember...the most important truth... of this or any... journey. And remember it...you will...though perhaps...not right away.

"Nothing is...what it seems. Nothing that can change...is Real. No seeming loss... can touch your...souls no matter...how permanent...and irreparable...your phantom self...may tell you it is. If you can...remember...those things...even to the...smallest...extent...all of Heaven and...Earth...will come to your...aid when most...you need...it. For all...Heaven and...Earth...loves you...always. As I...love you.

"Remember that...my own. Remember...that...and you...will never...lose sight of...me."

Mary began to cough, lightly at first, then more and more violently.

Her last words were completely forgotten as her wasted frame began to convulse and fold in on itself. The trainees came to their feet with cries of denial and pleading; Ariadne and Demeter just managed to keep their Teacher from crashing to the floor. They tried to straighten her limbs as she shuddered and jerked uncontrollably, but the coughing was too intense, her muscles too tightly locked.

It went on and on. Ariadne, eyes hollow with despair, held to Mary's hand as the others stood helplessly by.

Finally, the coughing stopped.

Mary went still, her body completely limp.

No one moved or spoke. No one seemed able even to take a breath. John knelt by his mother, put a hand on her chest, laid his cheek close to her open mouth. Waited.

"No. No. Please, Mother, no," Ariadne breathed as Demeter wept despondently beside her.

John leaned back on his heels. Despite what Mary had just said, despite his own experience with Jeshua, his heart suddenly felt as small as a pebble. Surely, the sun in his soul would never shine again if he said what he must—yet he knew the others waited to hear it through their sobs, even as they prayed it was not so. John's voice echoed in his ears as if he was a hundred miles away from his own self.

"Mary is dead."

The trainees reduced the fire in the women's cottage almost to embers so a bier could be set up. John was at somewhat of a loss as to what to do next: had they still lived in Bethany, Mary would have been placed in the sepulcher her James had purchased some years after Jeshua's departure. They were not in Bethany, however, but Ephesus. Here, interments were for the rich and royal, not common folk and foreigners.

The problem soon solved itself, however. Though the local Christines had, out of courtesy, stayed away from the cottages throughout the training and John knew not how they'd discovered it, within two hours of Mary's death Davos Karikos, Iustus and Thaleia's eldest son, appeared at the edge of the property to bear messages of condolence and numerous offers to see to her needs.

Perhaps Jaresh or the other litter bearer—Avros, was it?—had not returned to the city straight away, and so had heard the trainees' grief-filled laments. Perhaps they'd seen Marcus, crying like a heartbroken child, run from the cottage to stay all night alone with his grief, to return only when the morning sun crawled wearily into the dull winter sky.

A hail broke into John's thoughts; he looked out the window and smiled. Iustus and Thaleia themselves waited a respectful distance from the cottages, just as Davos had the night before. They need not have worried; beyond the fact that one could not distract one from the Stillness without that one's permission, most of the trainees were still up, sniffling on each other's shoulders. Even the few who lay with eyes closed were restless on their pallets, prone to suddenly burst into tears or sit up and stare silently ahead. John greeted the couple and held Thaleia as she cried both her sorrow and comfort out to him. Iustus stood by, his countenance filled with shame.

"I thought she would be with us longer," he said, in a voice amazingly soft for his usually boisterous self. "In truth, I thought she would heal herself."

A smile tinged John voice as he laid a hand on the merchant's shoulder. "My mother was never one to regret her choices, Iustus, even when they seemed to lead to unwanted results or behaviors some would have deemed inappropriate. It would honor her memory and the fullness of the One if you would adopt such a policy for yourself; else the blessing she gave will be but idle words."

The portly man swallowed hard, then nodded and smiled tremulously; he pointed toward a longish wagon that, save for a folded white cloth, appeared to be empty. "With your leave, Elder, Thaleia and I would spare a place in our family's crypt for Mary. And if it is not too much to ask, we would also like the honor of readying her body."

John looked surprised, not just at the request, but at Iustus's admission that he and Thaleia had such skills. Many of the rich in Ephesus had come from lowly beginnings, but very few ever mentioned the nature of their shame.

"Oh, we were not always so rich as we are now, Elder, not by leagues and leagues," Thaleia said, mistaking John's surprise for inquiry. "There were times in my home village when sickness wore down even the death god Thanatos's relentlessness, but my family was always as healthy as the gods themselves. So, my sisters and I learned the art of preparing bodies for burial. The pay was small, but we needed all the help we could get to fill sixteen mouths." She smiled with warm recollection. "That is how Iustus and I met, for I taught him the art when he came to our city by way of hard times in another place.

"Please, I know you do not wish outsiders to interfere with your training, but if you could grant us this boon, we would be eternally grateful."

John took Thaleia's hand and nodded his permission; even had they not loved Mary so much, their touching humility would have guaranteed their loving care of her. Even the sky shows its approval, he smiled, as a stream of sunlight burst through the clouds and bathed the distant trees in shimmering, golden glory.

"Excellent!" Iustus said, his face brightening. "We thought you might not want the trainees distracted from their studies while we worked. Do you want us to take her now?"

John considered. Though Jewish custom, for very good and practical reasons, called for Mary's immediate disposition and he was less than easy with flouting it, not all the companions had such traditions. More, they'd come to love her as much like a mother as Thaleia and Iustus had. As he had. He slowly shook his head.

"No, my friends. If you try to take her now you'll have to fight every one of the trainees to the death. If you can work here, do so; otherwise, the women's cottage will be cold enough to hold her for a few days."

John couldn't resist a sudden, tear-choked laugh. "And have no fear of interfering; I daresay, your presence cannot possibly distract us more than Mary herself already has."

As it turned out, Iustus and Thaleia could do what was needful right there. Though the other trainees were in and out, Ariadne stayed the entire time, watching from a corner as they washed and anointed Mary's body. Dry-eyed in her grief, she'd not spoken since Mary's death except to repeatedly and sharply decline even Demeter's attempts to cajole her to leave her Teacher.

"It is all right dear one, leave her be," John finally sighed to her worried sister.

"But—" Demeter began, ready to argue, though not with her usual volatility; the dark circles under her eyes told John her own grief had allowed her little rest. On impulse, he drew her into a comforting hug and smiled a little as she stiffened with surprise, then burst into tears and slumped against him.

"You know I will not allow her to get too lost in her grief, yes?" John murmured as Demeter sobbed on his shoulder. "The best thing you can do now, Demeter, for Ari and yourself, is to enter into the Stillness. You must attend to yourself first, dear one, else how will you be able to help anyone else?"

He held her for several minutes more, until she finally sniffed and pulled away.

"Thank you, Elder," she said softly, her voice still tremulous.

John cocked a brow and laid a hand on her cheek. "'Elder'? From you, Demeter, I would prefer 'John' I think. After all, am I not yet close enough to your family for such a familiarity?"

"I...yes. Thank you...John,"

Demeter shyly displayed one of her rare and incredible smiles, and John was again struck by how beautiful the elder Isaurus daughter was, especially when she let her natural gentleness come out of hiding. Ah well, soon enough, the Practice would take its toll on the tracks of being that kept such smiles from habitually expressing.

It took all day, but Iustus and Thaleia finally finished their work and reluctantly bid everyone farewell. John entered the women's cottage, to find Ariadne still sitting vigil. He crouched before her, took her face in his hands and kissed her nose, noting how chill her skin was. She made no response at first, but then expelled quivering sigh.

"Why John? Why?" she asked, and the one who spoke was the fourteen year-old girl whose mother had just died, not the full-grown woman he knew.

"Because, Ari. Because."

It was no answer at all, he thought, yet Ariadne relaxed and nodded as if his words explained everything. Perhaps his soul had given the only explanation that truly mattered to her heart: that no matter what, everything was all right and would be well.

John again kissed his double and drew her to her feet, then found a corner with a couple of pillows to sit on and some blankets to wrap up in. He sat them down, her back to his front, and leaned into her hair with a tired, yet contented sigh. He closed his eyes and allowed himself to fully enter into the Silence.

Ariadne, too, finally allowed the One to begin healing her, for she curled around in his arms and cried until she fell asleep.

Late on the evening of the day after they prepared Mary's body, Iustus Karikos again called to John from outside the men's cottage. This time, however, the call drew a frown: the urgency in the Ephesian's voice was unmistakable.

John motioned the merchant into the cottage to dry off and warm himself, for a cold, sleety rain fell from the prematurely darkening sky. Iustus warmly but hastily greeted the trainees as he pulled off his oiled wool cloak, then grimly turned to face John.

"Captain Iscariotus has returned, Elder, and wishes to see you."

"Amadeon," John said, as the trainees murmured worriedly. "Does he come alone?"

"His lieutenant, Titus, came to the house with him. I saw no others when I left to come here, but that does not mean they were not there."

Or that they did not follow you, John thought—and he could see by the looks on Prochorus, Torer and Adan's faces that they thought the same thing.

Haifata and Stavis unobtrusively made their way to the windows, while Marcus adjusted his body to more easily reach for his knives. Torer simply came to his feet, confident he could handle any man, armed or not. Though he'd accidentally broken the blade of his knife, Erezavan also grew more alert, and to John's surprise, so did Hosea and Timothy, who made it their business to stand between the door and the women.

Instead of turning to one of them, however, John looked at Demeter, who sat next to Johanna and Ada on a pile of cushions, mending stopped in mid-stroke.

"Sister, will you go tell Ariadne she is needed here?"

Demeter, round-eyed and pale, rose and quickly left, with Torer rushing out behind to play escort. It seemed to take forever, but soon enough, tight murmurs and footsteps filled the air. The door burst open and the three of them entered with Ariadne in the lead, anxiety written all over her face. John was relieved. If no soldiers had stormed the cottage with all that rushing about, they'd not followed Iustus.

Ariadne went to John and grabbed his hands in hers. His heart ached at the sight of her: she looked tired and wan, yet only this had made her leave her Teacher's side.

"The soldiers are here?"

John nodded. "Iscariotus and Titus await me at Iustus's house. I must go to them."

The rest of the trainees' reactions to his pronouncement were unanimous: the room erupted with loud, frightened, angry protests.

"Are you mad, bar Zebedee? They will surely arrest you—maybe even kill you!"

"Rabbi, please, you cannot go to them, no good can come of it..."

"You must escape while you can, Elder; with Flavius dead, there is no telling how they may act..."

"Please, Rabbi, do not go..."

John barely heard any of them; he and Ariadne still held hands, still looked into each other's eyes. He knew, and knew she knew, a kind and level of harmony and connection that left him awestruck with its glory; as Ariadne's awakening in the One had deepened, so had their union. Long gone was the time when they only knew such depths when they united as man and woman. They experienced oneness often now, usually at the most unexpected and ordinary of moments, and always, it filled them with overflowing Joy, no matter what other emotions might float on the surface.

The tears in Ariadne's gaze threatened to waterfall down her cheeks, but the stubborn set of her chin told John that she recognized his necessity and was resolved to let it carry him where it must without arguing. He smiled, leaned his forehead against hers, then kissed her tenderly and lingeringly. He drew her into a tight embrace, his face burrowing into her violet-scented curls even as the warmth of her breath and lips caressed his neck.

The part of Mary's story where Divine Mother had demanded a boon as Aleph left Para came to mind: she'd asked him to remember her wholeness, that he might remind her of it when she forgot. Now John heard in his own mind Ariadne's demand of him:

Do what you must...and come back to me.

And his pledge, given just as Aleph had given his to Divine Mother: I will. I Promise.

"Best be sure that you do; you do not want me to have to seek you out." The smile in Ariadne's voice shone through despite the tears that thickened it.

"I will keep that in mind," John chuckled, even though his own voice was thick.

Then his brows arched and he stepped back, searching Ariadne's face to see if she realized what had just happened. But no, she seemed unaware that she had demanded and received his promise without either of them speaking aloud.

John turned to the others and the knot in his throat almost took him over. Their sorrow filled the room, yet each of them, even Johanna, sought, found, and was choosing to trust the solidity of the Silence within their souls as they met the Stillness in his.

"You will stay with them until I call you to Iustus's?" he asked Ada and Hosea, and smiled to see no hesitation in either of them. Indeed, the strength of their combined Stillness softened the fear in the room and filled it, to his eyes, with a warm and comforting glow. Mary *had* lived to see them come into their confidence.

John shared hugs and tears with everyone then, reminded each one of his or her most precious strength. He promised them all would be well...but did not say that the One's definition of "well" might leave him alive on this earth for only a short time more.

"Hold to the One, my friends; It will guide you in all things. Remember what you came here for, no matter what befalls." His eyes fell on each one of his companions, to again rest on Ariadne's face.

"Remember, I love you all."

THIRTY-SEVEN

Here is a man born to discipline, was John's impression of Amadeon Iscariotus when first they met. This one would have found success in any endeavour, despite starting with little education and a poor background, for he was as one-pointed as a hunting knife, wholly unwilling to let the unexpected push him from his chosen path. His demeanor with his men betrayed a profound impatience with anyone who allowed his emotions to drag him hither and yon; his respect for Lieutenant Titus's talent came solely from the fact that it had proven effective. Even his choice to become a Christine had appeared to John to be more the result of deliberation than inspiration.

John quickly revised that impression after witnessing Iscariotus's interactions with Mary. Though his manner often revealed only the smallest part of the vast amusement her odd flights of fancy inspired, the Captain's willingness to follow them and give back tit-for-tat told John self-control wasn't the trait inherent to his personality. No, Iscariotus's dominating trait was an almost capricious level of enthusiasm, and only his long habit of repressing his emotional nature in favor of forethought had kept that exuberance hidden during the few days he and Titus were at House Karikos.

No such restraint marred Amadeon Iscariotus's demeanor now. When John entered Iustus's well-lived-in study, the Captain greeted him, not with the usual soldierly armclasp, but with a full Christine embrace, one completely lacking in any kind of reticence.

"Well, met, Elder." Iscariotus's voice was as warm as his embrace, but there was sorrow in his countenance as well; he grieved deeply over Mary's death.

"Trust that my mother did exactly as she wanted to, Amadeon," John smiled. "There was in her passing no sense that she was victim to it, I promise."

"I had hoped to see her again, Elder, looked forward to it more than I can say," Iscariotus replied, his gravelly voice even rougher than usual. "No other's laugh ever lightened my heart so, and no other's words, no matter how wise, ever filled me with such knowledge. And it is sure I could use Mary's ready smile and wise words now, to lighten the shame I feel for the cause that brings us to your door."

"Ah, then. I am to be arrested."

Iscariotus looked away as if his shame could not bear to look John's equanimity in the face. "I am sorry, Elder, so sorry. The moment Governor Valerus heard of Flavius's death, he sent me to bring you to Athens. Though I hoped the new Governor would tell me your disposition was still under his auspices, Bardisus made it clear that, whatever my orders, he would not hinder their accomplishment—and that effectively ties my hands. I must do as Valerus wishes."

John nodded, but something in the Captain's manner told him he was not through speaking. Iscariotus lowered his voice as if he did not wish to be overheard.

"In all honesty, Elder, I prayed you would not come back here when you heard I sought you. I hoped you would realize the situation and attempt to flee, for 'Natus—" he nodded toward his lieutenant, who gave a small bow of greeting "—assured me the Lady would guide you to safety. Even now, I have no doubt that if you left this house immediately, you would manage to get away from Ephesus. Especially with the help of the Christine community, a head start of say...a half-day? And a knowledgeable guide?"

The significance of Iscariotus's suggestion was not lost on John...but neither was his recognition of what would happen if he and Titus were implicated in such a venture. Too, there was Mary's admonition. So, although he was gratified by the offer...

"No, Amadeon, we do not want to burn that bridge just yet. Indeed, I would rather we not burn it at all. Your—and Egnatius's—capacity to inspire your men is extremely valuable to the One. It would be impossible to fulfill that role if it was discovered you'd abetted my escape from Ephesus. No, we'll not go that route unless it is unavoidable."

Iscariotus sighed as if he'd hoped, more than expected, John to accept his offer. "Very well, Elder, but know that the offer stands open. Furthermore, if there is anything else you need, but say so, and I will do all I can to supply it."

"Thank you, Amadeon," John said thoughtfully. Then: "Actually, if it is possible, I would take advantage of your generosity right now. The rest of my companions are on a property some five miles from here, waiting to hear what has occurred, and I'd as soon word came to them from one who can answer the questions they'll no doubt have."

"Hmph. Yes. Well, I believe 'Natus can help with that—since he is not actually here."

"Well met, Elder," Lieutenant Titus said, the musical lilt of his voice, as always, at odds with the battle-hardened soldier his appearance presented. "I rejoice to see you again, though I wish it was under better circumstances."

John smiled in spite of himself. "To the One, all circumstances are the best, my friend, even if they seem dire to us...but what is this 'he is not here' about?"

"My uncle and Captain means I am not officially here," Titus answered dryly. "Officially, I am in Laodicea, seeing to family matters. Upon my leaving here that will in fact be true; however, I wanted to give my greetings to you, and my condolences, before starting for my mother's home. Lieutenant—excuse me—Captain Gaius Horatius is my uncle's second on this excursion, at Governor Valerus's behest. He accompanies the Captain to make sure you find no more sanctuaries before you are brought to Athens."

Caught by the spirit of the Lieutenant's tone, John looked around. "Is this Horatius invisible, or merely exceedingly small?"

"Captain Horatius and the six men assigned to me for this mission are no doubt heading for Ephesus at this very moment." Iscariotus's visage was bland, but the twinkle in his eye was unmistakable. "They were forced to take a later ship due to an unfortunate miscommunication on my part as to the departure time of *Ares.*"

"Ahh. My escape time, had I needed it," John said, realizing that, had he approved the scheme, Titus would have been the guide to facilitate his escape.

"Just so," Iscariotus confirmed. "Though in truth, enough ships were in Piraeus that they likely found it easy to commandeer transport. I expect you would have had four hours' head start, at most, before the Lieutenant—Captain—came seeking you here."

John looked at Iscariotus and Titus questioningly; there could be no mistaking their disdain for the one they spoke of. The officers proceeded to enlighten him.

"His promotion to Captain and Governor's First Military Aide is a recent one, acquired at the cost of a good officer's freedom—" Titus said disgustedly.

"—Although, for this mission, which is probably his first outside a palace Court in years, he is my subordinate. Much to his disappointment," Iscariotus smirked.

The three fell silent. Well, John thought, if he was not going to run, and he was not...he turned an appraising gaze on the two officers.

"So then, you say we have three or four hours before this Horatius appears?"

"I fear so, Elder, yes," Iscariotus answered, his expression once more somber.

"Hmm. We will have to wait, then." John suddenly brightened. "But I see no reason we should not wait in style. Have the two of you had dinner?"

As usual, the Karikos table was laden with delicacies designed to bring the palate to a high state of ecstasy, and John ate with gusto. He'd had little appetite since Mary's death...and this might well be the last time he'd eat so lavishly. The officers also ate with a will, happily offering praises to the cooks, servants and their host and hostess, who'd joined the three for a light second dinner.

"Best I should be away before someone we do not desire to discovers my presence," Titus said as soon as he finished. "Is the young one ready?"

Andrus Karikos would be his guide, for as Iustus put it, "He will be better able to elude watching eyes than any servant." His comment garnered a grave nod of confirmation from Thaleia that made John smile: Andrus was their second-youngest son, a bright and often mischievous boy who knew every shortcut and hideout in the city.

Titus bowed to Iustus and charmed Thaleia by kissing her hand, then turned to his uncle. "Have a care, my Captain," he said, his affection for the older man poorly concealed by his officerial mask. That young jackal Horatius has no qualms about attaining command by walking over whatever bodies get in his way; I'd as soon one of them not be yours."

"I have dealt with his type before, 'Natus," Iscariotus answered as they clasped arms, then embraced. "This old jackal has a few tricks of his own, and the help of the Christos to support his task. Worry not for me."

Titus embraced John in farewell, then took his message for the companions and

instructions for Ada and Hosea. To his delight, John also gave him permission to receive the next technique of the Practice and stay the night at the cottages, since the
others would likely keep him there too long for him to well begin his travels this night.

"And Egnatius?" John called after him, "though they will likely ignore you, please
tell everyone that they need take no worry for me."

After all, he could do a good enough job of that for himself.

They talked for more than an hour after Titus and Andrus departed, catching up
on news and sharing memories of Mary. John was gratified to hear mostly humorous stories; he couldn't imagine a more fitting tribute for one who'd taken such joy in living.

Where are you now? he wondered, searching with his inner sense for some impression of his mother's presence. To his dismay and sorrow there was none, had not
been since Iustus and Thaleia began preparing her body. After his mother's Ascension, Miriam and Martha's house had vibrated with the Light of her departure for
days, and even after leaving Bethany, John could vaguely sense her tweak the edges of
his awareness, subtle and hindsightish though they had been.

Mary's presence this time, however, was most notable by its complete absence; it was
as if she'd truly died and left the earth plane, just as any normal mortal would.

Why should that be? John wondered...but Iustus's proposal that they adjourn to
his study with a flagon of their excellent wine interrupted any budding answer. As they
stood to do so, the house steward appeared, his face apprehensive, and informed them
that a Roman officer and soldiers were at the door.

Iustus and Thaleia looked worried, but the portly man told the silver-haired servant,
Lantos by name, to bring the officer to the study. It was a good choice: they would bypass the main room and, for awhile at least, spare the students the shock of John's arrest.

Lantos shifted nervously. "I did invite him to the study, Sir, but the officer refused
to come. He demands you send the Elder out immediately, or he will arrest everyone in
the house on charges of treason against Rome."

Iustus's eyes went round and Thaleia put a frightened hand to her mouth...but
Iscariotus looked like he might explode.

"He did *what?* That—damned—idiot!"

He jerked a ring from his finger and stomped over to Lantos. "You tell that dim-
wit his Commander said to bring his ill-born carcass into this house immediately,
and if the dolt gives you any trouble, show him this!"

The steward took the ring and, eyes wide, bowed and started from the room.

"And quote me!"

"Yes, Captain," Lantos said without turning, a trace of a smile in his voice.

Iscariotus shook his head in indignation. "I do not care if he is the Governor's *son*.
No man under my command acts like a common ruffian toward honorable citizens!"

It took several minutes, during which John, Iscariotus, Thaleia and Iustus moved
to the study, but at last a tall, slender soldier dressed in full regalia, including his helm,
entered the room.

"My brothers, the souls you meet in your travels will be of three kinds," Jeshua
once told the twelve with amused seriousness. "The first kind will gladly run to you,
desiring at all costs to know the One they see in you. The second will run from you,
sure you mean to steal their souls and make them slaves. And the third...the third kind
will run *at* you, to take your power—or failing that, to destroy you. Listen closely to the

One's instruction on which you deal with, and you will save yourself no end of trouble."

Gaius Horatius was definitely of the third kind, John thought. Titus had referred to him as "that young jackal," yet he looked to be a full decade older than Iscariotus's nephew, three or four years older than John. His half-moon, coal-black eyes shone brilliantly in the room's light; when he removed his helm, his cropped, deep brown hair showed hints of approaching gray. He had a straight, patrician nose and a wide, sensuous mouth that, given the chance, looked as if it would produce a beautiful smile, but the lines around that mouth—and the coldness in his eyes—spoke of a man who knew not what simple joy was.

In fact, Horatius's expression implied that he considered any kind of joy, simple or otherwise, a flaw. This one loves neither the Empire nor anything else, John thought, only what he can take from them. His life force clearly showed that his pleasure lay in trading trust for treachery, openness for furtiveness and cooperation for machination.

Iscariotus had told how Horatius had gained his current position. He'd "proven" his predecessor's intent to bring about the Athenian Governor's ruin through conspiracy. The Governor, in turn, had offered the disgraced officer, who was but a year from retirement, a choice: imprisonment, slavery—or posting to Britannia as a foot soldier.

Horatius had no intention of being a mere governor's aide, however. He desired to rule over some portion of Rome, be it as Mayor, Governor...or, though he barely dared think it, kingmaker, one with the ear of Caesar himself. He'd worked long toward his goal, ingratiating himself with those in power and destroying those he could safely remove. With the instincts of a predator, Horatius saw he could use the current climate to his advantage and make his name by ill-using the Christine population, and he saw in John a perfect stepping stone, a prominent victim who would quickly increase his fortunes.

But John also sensed that he had a deeply personal distaste for him, or more accurately, for what he represented—not as a "Christine", but as a Jew. Or perhaps as both.

Be that as it may, and whatever Horatius's current level of favor with his Governor, no guards accompanied him as he entered the Karikos study. Despite his decidedly—and likely inborn—aristocratic conduct, the servant's quote had no doubt warned him his commander was displeased. Certainly, Iscariotus's face left no doubt that that was so.

"So then, Captain Horatius. Not only do you and the rest of the men miss your ship, thus arriving several hours late, but you enter the house of a citizen in good standing dressed as if for battle, after speaking to his servant of him as one would speak of a common criminal. Tell me, did your mother teach you such appalling boorishness, or do you come by the tendency naturally?"

Horatius turned bright red at the dressing-down, but John saw no fear in his face at being so spoken to by a superior. If anything, he barely managed to check his angry retort at being berated in the presence of civilians. When he answered, he spoke with all the hauteur of a noble who was determined not to let it appear that a mere, plain-born soldier, whatever his current rank, had any advantage over him.

"Had I known you'd arrived, Captain, I would have sought you out before starting here, so we could come together," he said, his voice—and the lie—smooth despite his ire.

"Yes, well I am here, Captain," Iscariotus returned, speaking as if he addressed one of slow intelligence, "and I entered the house without the fanfare of threats and intimidation. That looks less heroic, I suppose, but it is nevertheless an easily-learned art, one it would behoove you to apprehend."

Horatius practically sniffed as he took in Iscariotus's familiarity with those in the room. "Then you have arrested the Jew and explained the charges against him?" he asked, his expectation of a "No" obvious. "After all, that is why we came to Ephesus, not? He and all those who follow him, no matter what their rank, must be made to understand that Rome will not tolerate anyone who disrupts the peace of the State...not even if he claims to be the Son of Jupiter Himself."

"He does not claim to be the Son of Jupiter, nor does he seek to disrupt the peace of Rome," John found himself replying with the slightest hint of a smile. "And 'he' is named John bar Zebedee, not 'the Jew,'"

Horatius did not deign to speak, but looked at John as if he considered his existence worth less than the dirt on his boots. He fingered his sword hilt, the intent in his chill stare clearly conveying his desire to see that "The Jew" never made it to Athens. He'd dealt with any number of his victims in just this manner over the years, and ultimately found them all easily intimidated and gratifyingly weak, regardless of whether they'd initially simpered or snarled. He expected nothing different from this one...

...But he'd never before confronted the Stillness he saw in John's gaze.

John's complete lack of either challenge or capitulation literally froze Horatius in place for a moment as his phantom self's dismay threatened to drop his jaw in stupid astonishment. Here stood one who not only had not even the slightest fear of him, but whose Wholeness could effortlessly expose and dissolve the predator he thought he was without using a single word. Though the Power behind John's gaze offered naught but Wholeness, all the Captain's phantom self saw was death. Horatius hastily looked away, fully aware the challenged had routed the challenger. With just a look, John had uncovered him in exactly the way Iscariotus's insults had not; he had, to his mind, made him look like a fool.

In that moment, Gaius Horatius's distaste for John flared into hatred.

"Captain" he said after a moment of fighting to regain his composure without appearing to do so, "I have commanded the ship *Amycus* to hold to port until we arrive, since it has a secure hold to keep the prisoner in. Its master says we must leave before twelfth hour, however, or the tides will not again be favorable until tomorrow afternoon." Horatius's voice held sudden anticipation, as if he saw a chance to immediately avenge the insult he'd been dealt. "Shall I transport him to the ship now?"

Iscariotus looked at John. "When will they inter your mother?"

"The day after tomorrow. And she will be buried rather than interred."

Though he understood not at all the why of it, that desire was the last sense John had gotten before the Karikoses began preparing Mary's body. Thaleia and Iustus, in turn, had insisted that she be installed in their family chamber until a suitably elaborate coffin could be built; John surrendered to their demands and, in a moment of pure of mischief, thanked his mother for having the grace to die in December instead of July.

"The day after tomorrow. I see." Iscariotus folded his arms thoughtfully, then made his decision. "Then we will leave after the funeral."

"What?" Horatius said.

"We will have no need of *Amycus's* services, Captain, but will leave after Mary of Josef's burial. And aboard *Ares*, which is undoubtedly more comfortable than a barge."

Horatius frowned heavily. "This is most irregular, Captain. Surely Governor Valerus expects us to carry out his orders instead of dabbling in matters that do not concern us."

"Like everyone else, even the Governor has but one mother," Iscariotus returned. "And were he her only son, I would not begrudge him the time to give her a proper funeral, either. We will stay until bar Zebedee's business has been properly attended to."

"With all due respect, Captain, Governor Valerus and I are well aware of your... partiality to these people and their ways. While we have indulged your proclivities in the past, I hardly think he would be sympathetic to this current insubordination, especially in support of a declared enemy. " Horatius's voice took on an undertone of threat. "Do you truly think it wise to delay this prisoner's transport, given how long Valerus has waited to interrogate him? No. I say you must forsake this absurd bias and immediately remove him from Ephesus, lest it adversely affect you and your command."

He suddenly smirked. "After all, what care has Rome whether this criminal sees his mother buried...or thrown into a ditch with the rest of the rubbish?"

Iustus and Thaleia gasped at the viciousness of the insult, and even John raised a surprised brow—but it was the fury on Iscariotus's face that raised the hairs on the nape of John's neck.

"Do you attempt to tell me my duty, Captain Horatius?" he asked, far too calmly. "Why yes. I believe you do. Indeed, you seem quite sure your recent promotion gives you the right to question my authority in whoever's presence you please. I would remind you, however, that whatever your authority in Governor Valerus's court, for the duration of this mission, command belongs to me."

Iscariotus's calm suddenly acquired an implacable edge and he laid a hand on his sword in a manner that made Horatius's earlier gesture seem like a child's playacting.

"That is, unless you seek to openly dispute my authority. Pray, *Captain* Horatius, is that the case? You need but say so, and we will, as officers of equal rank, step outside to attend to your challenge before proper witnesses."

Everyone froze, for despite Iscariotus's "offer," it was abundantly clear if Horatius showed even a hint of further defiance, he would never make it outside to discover that having the ear of a Governor meant nothing to a dead man.

Horatius realized it too, and it quickly became apparent he preferred to conduct his battles on more rarified planes. His face went toga-white as he swallowed, shook his head and then, lest his superior should misconstrue—or ignore—his unarticulated refusal, not-quite-squeaked-out a "No, Sir," to Iscariotus's challenge.

Iscariotus held to his sword for a long moment more, then: "Excellent. Now, then, one of the men should return to *Amycus* and tell her master that we will not require its use. You will, of course, leave Miklus and Parras with me, to ensure the prisoner's conduct?"

The dismissal was obvious and insulting, but the still-pale Horatius could not but deferentially salute his superior and, eyes aflame, stride from the room. After a moment, a still-shaken Iustus shook his head.

"I always thought Roman officers, at least, were chosen for honor as well as talent," he said with uncommon heat; the quality of Horatius's comportment was such that he never even acknowledged the Karikoses' presence. "But that ill-born dung beetle is enough to make me think again! How was such a one was ever promoted to grave digger, much less Captain?"

Amadeon's gravelly voice was wry. "Unfortunately, Friend Karikos, the Roman Army sponsors an ancient and time-honored program, one designed to promote those who would otherwise be unfit for officerial status.

"It is called 'politics'."

Iustus and Thaleia smiled, but John stared thoughtfully after Horatius's wake. As satisfying as it had been to see the pompous officer cowed, he was not pleased. That one was used to presenting at least a façade of control, and it had been shaken twice in very short order by two he held in naught but contempt.

A sense of future disaster lurking ricocheted about in John's guts, just as it had with Darshinika Baremna. And the havoc this one might eventually wreak would make the Persian's destruction seem insipid by comparison.

Andrus Karikos returned from his mission as guide as John and the others shared the earlier-promised flagon of wine. Ada and Hosea would arrive first thing on the morning of Mary's funeral, as instructed—but the youngster also brought back a plea from the trainees: they wanted to attend Mary's funeral and, if he was still in Ephesus, see John one last time.

Iustus and Thaleia instantly added their pleas, as did Amadeon, but John refused the request, citing both Mary's insistence that the companions not leave the cottages until they were fully trained, and his own unwillingness to further distract them.

"Your argument makes no sense, Elder," Iscariotus said shortly. "If any of that lot had wanted distractions, they'd have long ago found something to do the trick. After all, it is not as if they are so far from entertainment that they cannot make their way to it... or create it themselves." His manner softened at John's perturbed look. "None among us knew Mary as you did, but we deeply grieve her loss, nonetheless. And it is a harder business for us, too, for we have not your understanding of things to give us comfort.

"Let your trainees come forth for this circumstance, Elder. My experience tells me it will better serve your goal to have this 'distraction' now than refusing their request would do."

John's resolve wavered. He could find no flaw in Amadeon's reasoning, since in truth he felt the same way. Still, there were other considerations, ones made even more valid by their earlier encounter with Horatius.

Simply put, sedition was punishable by imprisonment or slavery in the mines and galleys, and treason was punishable by death. If Rome considered John a danger, could not the trainees, his companions, also be? The thought that he might already have seen them—and Ariadne—for the last time in this life chilled him to the core; even so, would it not be better to keep them out of harm and Horatius's way?

John's expression must have given his thoughts away, or perhaps some of Titus's talent had rubbed off on his uncle, for Amadeon nodded acknowledgement of his concerns as if he'd spoken them aloud.

"I understand your reluctance to allow them forth, Elder. Our Little Captain hates all the Way stands for, and we gave him no reason to suddenly change his mind; he would have no qualms about harming your companions if he deduced their importance to you. Certainly, he has used that means of ruin before." Iscariotus sighed at his own logic...but then a sudden flash of the exuberance that Mary's love had helped to again awaken flickered in his eyes. He looked at John and smiled like a mischievous boy who has just discovered some new game to play.

"So...we will just have to see that he does not know of their importance, hmm?

THIRTY-EIGHT

*"**So** then. How do they fare?"*

John sat in Mary's room with Ada and Hosea who, as promised, had arrived with due alacrity on this, the morning of his mother's funeral. Thin though it was, this was the only room in the house that still carried some sense of her essence; John felt a sort of comfort in spending his last hours in Ephesus here. Hosea settled his large frame in a chair the servants brought from his and Ada's room, while Ada sat in Mary's favorite chair for mending a young girl's dolly clothes. John sat on the bed.

"Actually, Rabbi, they do better than we expected," Hosea answered after a moment of deliberation. John noticed the big man often paused before speaking these days, dipping first into the depths of the One's Stillness to see what It offered. "Mind you, that is not to say they've not had their ups and downs—Johanna, Stavis and Demeter seem most worried about you, while Marcus walks about like his heart is broken—but by and large, they are willing and well able to enter into the One's Presence with but a little prodding." He smiled. "And that Egnatius is quite the one! He came to the meeting the other night and fell into place like he'd spent the entire training with us."

"Safe enough then, for them to be on their own for a few hours," John said, relieved.

Ada and Hosea exchanged a look. "Well," Hosea said after a hesitant moment, "we didn't *exactly* leave them without leadership, Rabbi...we gave Haifata charge of them."

"And Ariadne," Ada finished with a small smile.

John raised a surprised brow, which started a quick explanation from Hosea.

"We all knew Haifata was something different when we gathered him and Joshua in at Antipatris, but the Stillness he radiates these days is nothing short of extraordinary. Being in Haifata's presence is like suddenly finding yourself in an empty desert when but a second before the neighing of a thousand frightened horses surrounded you. It reminds me of when you or Miriam or Mary tells one of the True Stories."

"Yes...but there is a strangeness about him as well," Ada said with a slight frown, "a missing...something I cannot quite put my finger on. I sometimes feel as if the only thing that holds him back from doing exactly what Mary did in Bethany is his own, quite conscious choice. Yet at other times, he is so right here, so simply human, that the question of what he is or is not does not even occur. He is simply Haifata, helping the others bring in water or wood."

"I tell you, John, I've found myself asking more than once, 'who is this one?' But no answer seems to be forthcoming," Hosea agreed, also frowning. Then he shrugged. "Still, the others respect and follow his advice; he will get them to Ephesus in good order."

John nodded, his sympathy for the confused tone in his teachers' voices complete. In truth, he felt a tinge of relief that someone else had perceived Adan's oddness. Mary's assurances aside, he'd begun to think he was imagining it.

"And what of Ariadne?" John asked.

Ada and Hosea grinned. "Our brood mother," Hosea laughed. "She has blossomed delightfully in these last few days, John. It is as if her Self has come out to be with us since she ended her vigil at Mary's side."

"Just to be around her is healing," Ada said, clearly conveying the joy Ariadne herself spread. "Oh, she is no more outward about it than usual, yet there is a new solidity to her, as if she suddenly knows what she is really about. The others go to her for comfort and reminders of their wholeness at least as much as they seek me and Hosea out—and as far as I can see, their trust is wholly warranted."

"Hmm. But might this only be...?"

As all of them knew, one sometimes manifested great spiritual expansion, only to find it was just a temporary experience. If the student was unprepared for the seeming contraction that followed, their self-judgment could be painful indeed.

"We will certainly keep an eye on her, of course, but I sense her Self truly is coming into its own," Ada said at last as husband and wife looked consideringly at each other.

"And quite a power that Self is," Hosea smiled.

The rest of the trainees were likewise doing well, though both teachers expressed concern about Johanna, "who is still too fond of her experiences, rather than the Cause of them," Hosea said with a frown. Timothy and Rachael, however, simply glowed with the more public expression of their joy in each other.

"They actually sit with their shoulders touching at meeting now...and Timothy even kisses her on the cheek," Ada said, sounding both amused and proudly mothering.

Torer, Adan and Prochorus had once more taken to training any who showed an interest in learning to defend themselves, "though only every few days, and only for a short time," Hosea assured him. Considering what had happened—and what yet might—John couldn't fault the warriors' desire to protect their own in their own ways.

"Now I come to the most important question, dear ones," John said when Ada and Hosea finished their report. "How have you fared in all of this?"

He scarcely had to ask: between Mary's personal attention and what they'd gained here in Ephesus, Ada and Hosea's wholeness shone forth like sunlight. John smiled as Hosea described his experience; he'd spoken with awe of Haifata's Stillness, but John saw naught but a mirror of the big man's own growing immersion in the All-Conscious One. The strength and compassion Hosea bar Eliran had always been now touched all who entered his influence. The trainees and students could well count on his wisdom.

And as to Ada, well! Description failed as John beheld the all-embracing hugeness of the diminutive woman's soul. She'd seen Ariadne's presence as healing, but what of her own splendor? It seemed impossible to John that others did not gape in wonder when they looked on her growing luminosity. When she described the One, he felt as if all the universe was naught but Stillness, while yet seeming to dance within It. The exultation that accompanied Ada's knowing was truly no less than miraculous.

That I could ever have doubted your wisdom, dear heart, astounds me, John thought with a smile for Miriam, so much loved and far too far away.

The three of them closed their eyes, resting in the perfection of the Silence for more than an hour, reveling in their shared love of the One. At last, Ada broke the Quiet and laid her hand on John's, her soft voice making the smallest of ripples in Its Immensity.

"And what of you, John? How fare you in all this?"

John squeezed her hand in return. "Well enough, dearest, well enough. Overall, I am at peace with whichever way things go; I trust the One walks with me truly." He smiled. "Besides, I've no choice but to fare well. I promised Ariadne I'd return to her, and I will...though I admit I know not if that will happen in this earth's time or another's."

"She is utterly confident you will return in this earth's time, whatever the others' concerns might be," Hosea smiled, his voice soft as if he too, wanted not to move the Stillness too much. "As am I, Rabbi. You will come back to us, John. The One will not allow us to be kept from this journey for too much longer."

John hugged him. "You told me all would be well with Ari and me back in Corinth, Hosea, but I did not quite believe you. I think, however, I will trust your knowing now."

John shared a tearful—but not sad—departure with those who'd become so dear, strongly embracing Iustus, Thaleia and all of their children in front of House Karikos. Each shone with the light of their own experiences with the Practice, especially little Katri, their youngest...and John could only laugh when, instead of demanding he promise to return, as most others had, they promised *him* he would see them again.

No matter what "all will be well" might ultimately look like, he could take pride in his part in this creation. This legacy would never be lost, not to his heart's knowing, at least.

The streets were lined with people seeking to see Mary to her final resting place. John was deluged by commiserating well wishers, but most of those present were curiosity-seekers who'd barely known the woman who lay within the lovingly-crafted casket. In truth, many were present only because they'd heard John once walked with the founder of this odd sect that had recently brought so much trouble on itself; they wanted to see if the reputed specialness of the Teacher somehow marked the student.

This didn't stop John from graciously accepting their condolences, hypocritical though they might be. He simply focused his awareness on the Silent One and watched with an inward smile as many who greeted him in all insincerity left with stunned or puzzled looks. Confused they might be by these encounters now, but some who'd approached as skeptics would find their way to Jeshua's teachings because of it. No, dealing with the throng was not at all hard.

It was seeing his companions that was difficult.

They stood scattered throughout the crowd in twos and threes, following John's instructions not to reveal they knew him any better than the other mourners did. Horatius, having taken it upon himself to personally guard him, stood beside John, his aversion to being around so many he assumed to be Christines souring his features, yet for all his love of intrigues, he was not nearly so observant as Amadeon Iscariotus. To John, the companions' greater grief for Mary stood forth like a bonfire on a night-dark hill, easily seen by any who actually looked; but Horatius seemed oblivious to it.

But then, those asleep often grew even less conscious in the presence of those who well knew the One; John had seen Pharisees and Sadducees who, though considered brilliant in the law and oration, were otherwise so spiritually bereft that Jeshua's direct attention could temporarily strike them dumb. Perhaps Horatius, who had not even that sense of spiritual things, was likewise struck with a kind of blindness.

Or perhaps he simply believed that only his captured criminal was important enough to warrant observation.

"My condolences on your bereavement, Elder. It is a great tragedy, a great loss."

John did not let his sudden apprehension show, but simply turned as Horatius did, just as if he did not know Marcus Prochorus would be standing before him. Haifata accompanied him, and John felt the truth of what Ada and Hosea had said: his Stillness was so great it actually seemed to dull the noise of the crowd around them.

"You honor my mother with your presence, brother, and I thank you for your condolences," John answered, aware Marcus's grief still weighed upon him. "Still, though it is a mournful thing for those left behind, I know Mary goes forth to the Greater One, and that her life and death were shared with naught but joy." Mischief entered his voice. "Indeed, knowing Mary, she would no doubt find so sorrowful a commemoration most amusing and laugh us all to shame for thinking her dead at all."

John saw the answering laughter in Haifata's eyes and knew he understood his reply—but he had to stifle his smile as Marcus's face displayed every one of the several responses he wanted to give to his detachment: he did *not* appreciate this attitude. He was willing to try, however: he closed his eyes, increasing his Silence; when he opened them again, the tears he'd so stolidly held back rolled unheeded down his cheeks.

But he smiled.

John embraced Prochorus just as he had many others that day—but with far more satisfaction; Horatius sniffed disgustedly and stalked away, tired of such effete displays.

Marcus stepped away from the embrace, watching after the Roman officer, then decided to play for the public ear. "Will you stay to teach us further, Elder?"

John also answered for the public, so both Marcus and Haifata would hear. "I fear not, brother. I leave as soon as the burial takes place, for my presence is required in Athens. From there, I know not where I go, though I assume it will be to Rome."

"We will come to you. We will help you escape," Adan murmured when his turn came to embrace John. The fierce resolve in his tone made it a promise not just to John, but to the universe—and this one, John knew, would walk through the Fire to keep it.

John did not want him to. "No, brother. Finish the training with the others," he murmured. Then, before Adan could follow his suddenly taut stance with a stubborn refusal: "Trust that the One takes me where I must go, and that our mission cannot be stopped. Your presence is valued by the others, my friend; you must finish the training."

Haifata stepped back, his face all defiance as he looked into John's eyes...but then the usual false/strange stillness settled over him. He did not speak, only nodded once before turning away to make room for others to offer their farewells.

John sighed. Adan would abide by his request for now, but he was well aware he'd made no promise to stay that course.

Each of the trainees managed to make their way to John through the crowds of curious and well-wishers. Save for Erezavan, who simply kissed his cheek with a gaze as trusting as a child's, the men asked how they could prevent his fate and the women asked for—or in Johanna's case, demanded—promises of his return. It wrenched his heart, for he felt all the emotions they laid before him, expressed or not.

Even so, he could only smile when Timothy and Rachael came forth with sad faces...but holding hands; and Torer's expression also brought a chuckle to his lips.

"Grief suits you not at all, my friend," John said.

"Hah, no it does not," the big man said, instantly abandoning the mask to reveal his usual roguish smile. "So, then, would it be better, do you think, if we simply came and got you from wherever the Romans put you?"

"Torer. Brother." John sighed, but couldn't quite let go of the smile. "If all the warriors in our party come to rescue me, how will the others deal with the Romans, should there be need? Demeter and Johanna and Ada are your posting now, my friend. You must consider more than my wellbeing."

There, that would give the Scandinavian—and the others, John hoped—pause. It was not that John didn't want rescue if such a thing became possible, but Torer's consternation told him the big man hadn't considered what might happen if they went haring off to save one who might, when they arrived, be well beyond their help.

By the time the procession reached the burial site, most of the crowd had gone back to their daily tasks, immediately forgetting Mary, John and the "Christine problem." The forty or fifty left, most solemn-faced or crying, came to get second or even third hugs, like small children losing their father to a lengthy voyage. John momentarily worried, lest Horatius or an Ephesian spy should be counting heads for future purposes, but there was no need: Iscariotus even now engaged Horatius and his most likely allies in conversation. And as for possible Ephesian spies: if they knew not who was closest to him by now, then his companions were surely in no danger.

As he turned back to the crowd, John's earlier concerns about the trainees' need for stoicism suddenly became his own: Ariadne stood but one person away, waiting her turn to be treated just as casually as the other onlookers had been this day.

Demeter came forward first, however, her gold-flecked eyes swollen from crying. For a long time, she simply wept on John's shoulder, overwhelmed by her sadness over Mary and her fear for his situation. When she was finally able to speak, her tear-choked voice was full of entreaty. "Tell me we will see you again. Promise me."

John smiled and tenderly squeezed her hands. "Ask your sister what I told her, dear heart...and make me a promise also."

Demeter blinked in surprise. "I...if I can, Eld—John."

"Promise me, sister, that you will finish this training. Awakened hearts as powerful as yours are greatly needed, and will, in turn, awaken many. Will you do that for me?"

Demeter peered sharply into John's eyes for a moment that seemed to stretch on forever, then straightened as if all her fear suddenly screamed away, as if she suddenly realized that what Mary had said of her was not only possible, but had in truth always been. Yes, Demeter would finish this training, her eyes promised, and in so doing, become the magnificent power her Teacher believed her to be.

"Jeshua go with you, Strength of the Universe." John said, the smile strong in his voice as he took her face his in hands and gently kissed her forehead. Demeter blushed and kissed his hand, then walked a little away to wait for her sister.

John's breath wrapped around his heart as Ariadne approached. How would he ever treat her as just another attendee?

He warily peered over her shoulder to see if Horatius watched them, but Iscariotus still held his attention—facing away from John. John spared a smile; he had the distinct impression Amadeon was pleased with his maneuver.

As Ariadne came into his arms, all impressions vanished. John was, as always, inundated by the fullness of what they were as the Silence curled around, through and between them in perfect purity. Their heartbeats, the flow of the blood in their veins, the rhythms of their life forces, slowed and synchronized as the love they shared, the love they *were*, calmed every sense of apprehension within and around them, stilling the air itself for several feet around them. As the Light that filled them awakened the eternal promise of what was and would always be, assurance filled John's soul. Even if Horatius were to come at them with sword drawn, John knew in that moment that, even if he took their very lives, he'd have no capability to harm them in any way. No matter how far apart they might be, no matter what befell his body, never again would he and Ariadne know separation from each other.

Never.

The embrace ended far too soon; Ariadne stepped back and gazed with dry-eyed but smiling solemnity into her double's face. He remembered Ada and Hosea's comments and smiled; surely, his mother would live forever so long as her students opened to the One as this one did. Ariadne nodded as if she divined his thought (which was wholly possible), then broke the silence between them.

"Remember what I said to you."

"Remember that I promised."

They looked toward Mary's grave, now freshly-covered; John's mind briefly flowed back to the awe he'd felt when the men who'd moved his mother from sepulcher to coffin reported that not only had her body shown no signs of decay whatever—impossible even in this weather—but the tomb itself had smelled of a breezy spring day in full bloom. Would the same be true if they exhumed Mary's body now? Would it even be there?

John shook his head...then his brow furrowed as another memory intruded.

"Ari, Right before my mother died, she whispered something in your ear that, even in the midst of your sorrow, made you smile. Would it be meet for you to tell me what she said, or was it meant to be only between the two of you?"

John's universe brightened as, in a repeat of that day's reaction, Ariadne's face suddenly lit from the inside-out.

"She made me a promise, John, just as you did."

John waited, wondering, while Ariadne's smile grew and suddenly turned impish.

"She promised me that this time, my husband and I would get it right."

From the viewpoint of Christines who did not actually live there, Ephesus's value to the Way was somewhat ironic. The city could and did boast of having some of the most decadent diversions in the known world—while also having one of the largest Christine populations in the Empire. In truth, the fact that the greatly lamented Terus Flavius felt safe enough to support the Christine population from his official position was more the result of his city's powerful patrons than his blood-relationship to Claudius Germanicus, for many Ephesian Christines not only had money, but the kind of influence that made even Rome attend them.

Word of John's arrest spread quickly, and local Christine leaders of every stripe just as quickly let Piros Bardisus know exactly how displeased they were about it. The most prominent of them demanded John's release, while making it clear that it would be worth the extra cost to transport goods from other ports if such came not to pass.

Bardisus, politician that he was, promptly summoned Captains Iscariotus and Horatius: they'd caused this crisis by asking leave to expedite John, let them catch the fire for his decision.

And catch the fire they did. *Ares* was lucky to make the tide, for the officers had to face the chagrin of every Ephesian entrepreneur who saw fit to speak his mind—and that seemed to be every businessman in the city. Though the outcome of the meeting was never in doubt, John was disturbed by the grim countenance Iscariotus presented on his return to the ship—and the smug one Horatius displayed. Amadeon had obviously received some troubling piece of information.

John was not, of course, treated as a criminal, but berthed in one of *Ares's* lavishly decorated guest cabins. Like *Galley Matthatus*, *Ares* was designed to hold passengers and goods, not prisoners. Nor even slaves: Iscariotus' Christine father-in-law had freed his some years before, then offered to hire any who would continue to work the twenty-four oars they'd previously pulled under duress. To his surprise, fully a third of the men took his offer, and even now, three or four of the freed men were crew on this voyage. The memory of Iscariotus's threat at house Karikos was still fresh enough for Horatius not to protest John's treatment, but John knew that should even the smallest chance arise, he'd show him what being a prisoner of the Roman Empire was really like.

Such had not happened and was not likely to; while John hadn't spoken to Amadeon yet, the meeting in Ephesus obviously had not affected Horatius's ability to bring him harm. He stood at *Ares's* railing as Ephesus dwindled away, the last of the day's golden light edging the gray flotsam clouds and layering the sea's surface, so that the ship seemed to float on a flaming sheet of aureate luster. Easy enough, with such a view, for John to set aside his worries about what might be warming on the embers of that one's mental fires until they needed attention.

Would that he could say the same for the rest of his thoughts.

She promised me that this time, my husband and I would get it right.

Though he and Ariadne had been lovers for months and closer by virtue of their connection than most husbands and wives could imagine, much less know, those simple words had caused two simultaneous and equal reactions in John. His heart had shouted with such sweeping joy that he knew the angels themselves sang forth the "Amen" that sealed his double's words in Eternity's records—and all the blood had drained from his face in shocked horror.

Happily, Ariadne took no offense at his reaction, had in fact seemed thoroughly amused by it. She'd simply stared into his eyes for a moment longer, kissed one hand, then the other with lingering fervor in lieu of kissing him, then strolled confidently away with Demeter in tow. John had wondered, not for the first time, how he'd ever done without her presence in his life, how he'd ever do without it now—yet the idea of being Ariadne's husband filled him to the ends of the hairs on his head with cold dread.

But why should that be? In all truth, being with her was like being with the part of himself he most enjoyed, the self that forever approached life with cheer, patience and gentle humor. Despite their different life experiences, his and Ari's temperaments were a good match, yet different enough that they always seemed to surprise each other, often delightfully. What they'd shared in these last several months had been so full that the idea of settling for less was utterly absurd to him.

So why did being merely belovéd to her feel so much safer than being husband?

"...But she insists I've got t' give up the sea, and I do not want t' give up the sea."

Three sailors brought John out of his contemplation as they swayed by. The youngest, a man about Timothy's age, complained to the others in fervent consternation.

"So, then tell her you'll not marry her. She c'n either take y' as y'are, or find another fool t' take to husband," the other sailor, a summer or two older by his looks, said.

"But, I do not want her t' find another husband," the youngster said, affronted by his friend's offhanded manner. "*I* want t' marry her. 'Tis only that—"

"You want t' be married an' be free t' do what y' want...like a man unmarried, hmm?" the eldest of the three said, amused.

"No! But..." the youngster carried their argument down the deck, nonplussed by the accuracy of older man's observation.

John burst out laughing.

Clearly, some reactions seemed to be built into the human heart...and the male's fear of losing his freedom if he accepted himself as husband, not lover, was as old as man himself. Yes, the phantom self might tell John otherwise, but the unbounded joy he'd tasted as Ariadne had made her declaration was the truth of what he really felt.

Though the sun had given both *Ares* and the world its farewell salute, what was left of its light still edged the clouds with fading pink lace. The golden sky faded toward blue-black as the ocean slapped her own surface into rough, bouncing shards of wetness. There would be no moon to gaze upon this night, for the air spoke plainly of the weather's intent to pour rain down upon the ship before midnight, but the sea's clean scent was pleasure enough. John happily let himself be lulled by its salty musk—he'd grown used, but not resigned to, how *human* densely populated Ephesus had smelled—and likewise let his heart warm as his awareness turned to the cottages outside Ephesus, to the one whose life force even now twined tenderly in his like a golden thread.

"Yes, Ariadne Isaurus. The One willing, this time we *will* get it right," he said at last, knowing he sealed his promise in Eternity's heart just as his double had done.

"Evenin'. C'n I join you?"

Despite the accent, John half-expected to find Iscariotus standing behind him, for the voice had the same gravelly quality to it. It was not Amadeon however, but a sailor John had seen calling out orders shortly before *Ares* set sail.

John nodded; the man leaned against the rail. Several minutes passed as both enjoyed the rhythm of the waves and the cheerful creaking that came with any healthy ship.

"My fool of a youngest follows y'r way," the man suddenly said. "Left our house six months past, t' 'walk in the Christos' steps,' he said.

"In truth, I do not understand his choice at all. He's a headstrong boy, always was. Hardly the type t' follow anyone. Bright too; knew how t' make his way in this world. He could'a easily took on as a merchant's apprentice and made his fortune—yet he chose poverty and worship of a god that seems soft and spineless to this old man."

"The lad was your favorite," John stated rather than asked. The man shrugged.

"He was—is, I suppose, for he is not dead." He scratched thoughtfully at his mostly silver beard. "Boy's as much like his father as a man could stand, and we'd many a' squabble over the best way t' do this or that. Still, we were friends, not jus' father 'n' son. Until this Christine foolishness came b'tween us. My ire was so great when he left, m'poor wife actually feared for my health. Still, in the end I could not call him dead t' his family. So perhaps I'm as weak as him." There was no anger in old sailor's tone, only sadness over his son's estrangement...and curiosity.

"I thought my boy—Jiros is his name—I thought he'd come to his senses soon enough, that he'd find these Christines too light a dish f'r his taste. I thought he'd be gone a month, two at most. But it's not been so. And now I find m'self wonderin', 'what is this thing got, that so smart a lad as my Jiros would stay with it long as he has?' After all, he never was one t' go into things lightly. And he is very much like his father.

"So I thought—just t' other day, mind—'Perhaps there's somethin' I'm missin' about this. Perhaps I should look into it.' And now here you are. Standin' on a ship I wasn't even supposed t' sail this week, save they needed a quick replacement. You might think it strange f'r me t' say it... but the gods brought us t' this place to talk. Or so do I believe."

"What would you have me say, my friend?" John asked into the silence the man left.

"Convince me my son follows a way good enough to've thrown away his life on."

John did not try to convince the old sailor, only spoke of his own experience. Though he did not speak directly of the Practice, he did emphasize the value of praise, gratitude, love and compassion, emphasized how consciously experiencing even a little of these helped one better know the richness of the One that made life worth living.

The man, Varanikus, listened attentively, his countenance thoughtful in the lamplight one of the crewmen had lit earlier; by the time they finished speaking, the clouds had deigned to step aside, allowing a star or two to shine down on *Ares*.

"Hmph. Maybe m' son follows no weak way after all," the old sailor said at last, "even if it is got no use f'r fighting or war—which, t' my mind's a mistake." He gave his beard another thoughtful scratch. "I'll think on what y'said, good sir. Who knows? Maybe in the end, 'twill be the father who follows in the son's footsteps, not t'other way around."

That conversation alone makes this trip worth what it might cost, John thought as he bid Varanikus goodnight. He would never know if the man followed Jeshua's Way or not, but it did not matter. As Varanikus had pointed out, the One had arranged their meeting, not Chance, and It would see to its outcome.

John stood at the railing a bit longer, filling his lungs with the fresh sea air; then he started aft toward his quarters. Hopefully, Amadeon would at last be available and he'd discover what had happened in the meeting with the Ephesian Governor.

A figure stood a few feet from the doorway, and though his features were at first too dim to see, his uniform made him easy to identify. Captain Horatius had obviously heard at least part of John's conversation with Varanikus, for his dark expression matched the darkness the shadows of a nearby lantern threw on his face. John nodded a 'Good Eventide 'and made to pass by the Roman, only to have him roughly grab his arm.

"If you think to corrupt the Court by speaking such pretty words, think again," Horatius practically snarled. "Iscariotus protects you now, Jew, but the day comes when he will be too busy saving his own neck to worry for yours. Your time is coming, rely on it. And when it does, I will personally see no lies are spread about *your* resurrection."

Though John's answering gaze was just as devoid of challenge as it had been at House Karikos, his reply was unequivocal.

"It has been eighteen years since the Empire foolishly tried to crush The Seed of the One's awakening, yet It only takes root in more and more hearts. Likewise, if this seed 'dies' it will only result in more being sown. They, in turn, will flower with the One's Knowledge until they cover the abandoned husks left behind by those who thought their earthly realms eternal. And neither the Empire nor any other will stop it."

John smiled, his look almost pitying.

"Has Rome not yet discovered, Captain, the futility of trying to kill God?"

He turned toward the doorway without waiting for an answer; despite the fact that Horatius had half-drawn his sword, John knew he had no desire to weather Iscariotus's or his Governor's wrath by committing murder.

And now he also knew he they headed straight for Rome.

THIRTY-NINE

"**Well** no, Elder, *that* is not entirely true. We do not go *straight* to Rome."

As expected, John had found Iscariotus in the stateroom usually reserved for his in-laws, a space that made the opulence of the owner's cabin on *Galley Matthatus* look cheap and paltry. John smiled to himself; the practicality of Amadeon's soul seemed to squirm in the presence of so much extravagance.

"We will put into Piraeus first, as originally planned, but we will not disembark. Instead, Governor Valerus will meet us at the ship while more supplies are loaded."

"Indeed? For one so highly placed to come to the prisoner is unusual, is it not?"

Iscariotus gestured John toward another chair and smiled grimly. "Not for this prisoner. Supposedly, the Governor is to interview you, then I, as the commanding officer of your escort, will deliver both his recommendation and you to the Emperor. Or so was I given to understand at Bardisus's meeting. Certainly, he made it clear that he merely followed the mandate of Rome," Iscariotus frowned mightily, "as delivered by me through Captain Horatius."

"Horatius saw Bardisus before coming to Iustus's."

"Yes. He received further orders from Valerus when he missed *Ares*, and I know of it only because the businessmen compelled Bardisus to explain your arrest. My orders when I left Athens were to bring you to the Governor, who would interview you at his leisure and eventually present you to Claudius as a surprise. While it seemed impossible that Rome knew not of your existence after all these months, I assumed he had knowledge he chose not to share with me. Under those circumstances, choosing to stay for Mary's funeral was within my authority.

"Yet, now I find there was a change in plans, and that Horatius knew of it. He made enough of a fuss at House Karikos to make sure he can truthfully tell Valerus he attempted to prevent my 'insubordination', but he made no mention of any change in orders. Nor do I believe he meant to."

"Now that cannot be a surprise to you, Amadeon."

"No," Iscariotus said, then sighed. "Unfortunately it is not. That one means good only to those who can help him fulfill his plans, and that only for as long as they can help him. Still, what could he possibly hope to gain by keeping me uninformed on this matter? I would have known of it as soon as we reached Piraeus, after all, and since Rome is as wary of offending the Ephesian Christines as Bardisus is, our delay was still warranted. No; there is still more to this than we are privy to I am sure, and I fear it will bode ill for us both." Iscariotus sighed again. "I admit Elder, this constant political maneuvering wears on this simple soldier's mind. I prefer to fight my battles more straightforwardly."

"I understand your aversion to duplicity, brother, as I myself suffer from the same malady," John answered with a small smile. "But if you would, Amadeon, please call me 'John.' You of all people have you earned the right to call me by my given name."

Iscariotus looked surprised, then pleased at receiving such an honor. "Well then, John, though this is worrisome, I cannot see where turning it inside out will bring us any closer to making sense of Horatius's machinations. And while he may have his plots to keep him full, I, for one, prefer tastier fare." His smile grew. "I suggest we take advantage of my father-in-law's pantry and settle our minds and palates with dinner. I know from experience that the quality of his larder is as superb as Iustus Karikos's."

Iscariotus pulled a long, ornate cord, and dinner arrived shortly after. The food was as good as promised and the wine worthy of Jeshua's grandest blessing. The mention of that fact led to entreaties that John answer Iscariotus's many questions about the Practice and its history. He did so gladly, sharing his memories of what Jeshua had said —"often as cryptically as possible,"—with Iscariotus, *Ares's* captain and his first mate. In the days that followed, he also gave Amadeon the Practices of Love and Compassion.

Just as with his departure from Ephesus, John's arrival in Piraeus was noted. He watched as ships already moored grew from so many indistinguishable specks to vessels with readable names. That is, they were readable to Iscariotus, who came up beside John and read off the ones written in the Roman and Greek scripts. *Daedalus, Uriel, Romulus*; all came from lands Rome now claimed as its own.

One berth held a ship of strange design: the carved figure that graced its bow was a woman with hair a little darker than Torer's and eyes the same startling shade of blue. Iscariotus read its name, *Cadeyrn's Fall*.

"That one returns from Brittania—and their tribes are giving us a run for our money, let me tell you. Despite officially now being part of Rome, they continue to fight as if they believe they can defeat us. To win in battle against them is to know you fought well. Despite their barbarous ways, I respect their warriors greatly."

Iscariotus then pointed out another ship, *Ariadne*, and told John a story.

According to the Greeks, Ariadne was the daughter of King Minos and half-sister to the Minotaur, a monster so formidable that Athens found it prudent to surrender to him the life-sacrifices of seven young men and women once every nine years. According to the legend, Ariadne gave the great hero Theseus a ball of yarn which, after he slew the half-human, half-bull in hand-to-hand combat, he used to escape the beast's labyrinth. Then she fled with the Athenian prince to become his wife and queen.

John could well see his Ariadne as a hero's deliverer; she'd seemed so confident of his return when they'd parted, so strong as she'd taken Demeter's hand and repeated the promise he'd made. She trusted utterly that he'd not abandon her as Theseus had accordingly done his Ariadne.

John hoped, not for the first time, that she was right.

Iscariotus let out a surprised exclamation. The ship was far enough from shore that it would have been hard to distinguish someone known from one unfamiliar—but even had they been closer, such a feat would have been difficult; the dock was full with people. The glint of sun on metal made John look more closely: soldiers milled amongst the numerous civilians, doing their best to make way for a litter that crawled toward the edge of the dock. Horatius came on deck and John's gut tightened; he exhibited the same smug smile he'd had when he and Iscariotus boarded *Ares* in Ephesus.

Ares was quickly and efficiently secured in its berth to the music of the crowd's murmurs. As the sailors and longshoremen yelled orders, acknowledgements and insults to each other, Varanikus stopped next to John and clasped his hand warmly, his weatherworn face less care-filled than it had been only a few days before.

"May your gods an' mine go with you, good sir."

"And may the same be true for you, my friend."

The older man shook his head. "I cannot say I'm ready t' embrace your way, but y'r words made sense. I'll be speakin' with m' wife when I return home and we'll see t'ge- ther if maybe the Christine's words there call t' us as yours did me."

He clasped John's hand again, then nodded to Iscariotus and walked away, yelling at one of the sailors to have a care with some piece of cargo—that is, unless he *wanted* to give up a year's wages to pay for its damage. John sensed Iscariotus's uneasiness as they waited for the Governor's litter to come to a halt.

"You are using the techniques?"

"Like they are my hope of Heaven." Iscariotus's mouth twisted in a wry smile. "Which they are. Come, my friend, let us meet Horatius's schemes face to face."

John accompanied him to the gangplank as the Athenian Governor came up. His guards walked before and behind him, their hands tense on the hilts of their swords, their eyes suspiciously searching the crowd. John wondered at the tight security, then mentally slapped a hand to his forehead. But of course. After Flavius, more than one official no doubt felt the sudden need to take extra precautions.

Despite Abunius Valerus's evident distaste for the throng, something about him made John hesitate to dismiss him as he so readily had Horatius. The man's intelli- gence fairly leapt from his eyes, taking on, at this moment, the same palpable curiosity John often saw in Marcus Prochorus. What he did not have, however, was Marcus's level of focus or wonder; the signs of Valerus's dissipating habits were as clear as coal marks on parchment. This one had spent his life believing the ruling class, blessed as they were by the gods, had the right to live as they would, and only now, in what John estimated to be his middle years, had he begun to recognize that the Universe invaria- bly exacts its toll on all who sleep and choose not to follow the rules they themselves made for Its existence.

He need not worry about an assassin's hand bringing him low, John thought; Death had already struck him from within and would make its coming presence known before the year was out, though Valerus would live somewhat longer. Did he know it? John decided it was unlikely. The Governor was an intelligent man, yes, but like many intelligent men, his ability to reason away that which might be unpleasant was well-developed. That is, unless the unpleasantness made itself so evident that it could not be ignored.

"So, Captain Iscariotus, Captain Horatius. You at last return with the Emperor's prize in tow." Valerus glanced toward the crowd on the dock, then looked John up and down without really seeing him. "He seems rather nondescript to inspire so enthusiastic a turnout."

"Cupid often goes unnoticed, Sir," Iscariotus said, bowing his head to the Governor in acknowledgement, "yet his arrows can overwhelm a man with love or hate, and by those emotions cause empires to live or die."

Valerus frowned. "Do you say this one is as powerful as the God of Love?"

"I say that what he bespeaks, through the grace of his Teacher, is that powerful."

"Ah. But is there naught of importance in the man himself? Is he, as some of his ilk are wont to say, only a messenger?"

"I think him to be more than a mere messenger, Sir, but in the end, it is his message that is most important."

"Hmm..." Valerus said, again half-looking at John. John, in turn suffered being referred to rather than directly addressed, both for Amadeon's sake and because, unlike Horatius, the Governor intended no direct insult. As was typical of the aristocracy, he simply assumed that "commoners," would be too awed by his stature to speak sense in his company, and so he talked around them. Valerus turned to Horatius.

"What say you, Captain Horatius? What is your assessment of this one?"

"He believes himself less important than the message he spreads, My Lord," Horatius answered, all ingratiation and reasonableness. "He has said so to me personally and I am inclined to agree with him."

"And what of his message? You had fears about its power to corrupt the people."

"I have seen nothing to decrease my concern, My Lord. In fact, it is even worse than we discussed. The message this man delivers is extremely dangerous, for it does indeed seek to usurp the power of Rome, as we also suspected. And as to its effectiveness...well, you need only look as far as this dock to see it. In fact, my Lord, the disease this message and its messenger carry infects even those who once showed loyalty only to the Emperor. It makes them willing to treat the prisoner as a guest instead of as the traitor he is. " Horatius looked at John with a shark-like glint. "When such is the case, the messenger should be considered as dangerous as the message—and treated accordingly."

Horatius related to Valerus Iscariotus's familiarity with John and the Ephesian Christines, and though he gave no details of the incident at House Karikos, told of his decision to delay their return to Athens for the sake of Mary's burial. He mentioned, as expected, his objections to such a delay, "which the Captain was influenced to ignore at the prisoner's insistence," he lied.

Valerus knew of Iscariotus's Christine leanings, of course, for he'd never attempted to hide them, but John now realized he'd purposely sent him to Ephesus, most likely at Horatius's instigation. This was no less than a report on Amadeon's loyalty, and it favored him not at all, despite Horatius's ostensibly sympathetic remarks.

"What have you to say, Captain Iscariotus?" Valerus asked, his expectant expression radiating disfavor when Horatius finished his account.

Iscariotus stood at attention, but looked directly into the Governor's eyes as he spoke. Valerus's brow twitched upwards ever so slightly at the breach in protocol, but Iscariotus's complete lack of arrogance was such that his budding objections to being treated as an equal by a subordinate faded into a kind of begrudging anticipation.

"I saw no reason to create more problems in Ephesus than were strictly necessary, Sir. As it was, we were called to Governor Bardisus's home to explain to the city's most influential citizens why we were arresting 'a man not under Athens's jurisdiction'. True, we had no obligation to explain ourselves and would have had any help we needed to subdue any unrest, but my experience in the field told me that the small delay in transporting the prisoner would pay for itself in trouble avoided. As always, Governor, my aim was to do what would best serve Rome. Never would I base so important a choice on any other criteria."

"So you have been heard to say many times, Captain," Valerus said almost gently, turning his gaze toward the azure clarity of the harbor. He turned back to Iscariotus, and the suggestion of gentleness vanished. "Yet if that is so, how could you proceed with your so-called 'small delay', despite the Emperor's direct orders that we have the prisoner in Rome as soon as possible? Or did not his communiqué impress upon you his astrologers' insistence that he arrive at Court by the new moon? Clearly it did not, since you disregarded it at the behest of one who denies the very godhood of the Emperor.

"Tell me, Captain Iscariotus, is that how you define serving Rome?"

The trap was well-sprung. Horatius smirked and awaited the results of his maneuvering with barely concealed delight, aware that Iscariotus's sense of honor would never let him blame an underling for his ignorance of any order, even if that underling had deliberately failed to inform him of its existence.

"I delayed our return despite the Emperor's written orders, for I felt at the time it was the best course for Ephesus and Rome." Iscariotus spoke without hesitation, showing no sign in voice or stance that his answer guaranteed his ruin as a commander, if not worse. "I take full responsibility for my decision, Governor, and I stand by it."

"Yes. Well, your decision also has a bearing on my fortunes, Captain, and I have no inclination to suffer the Emperor's wrath because of it," Valerus replied. Then: "Despite your protests to the contrary, I find your loyalty has been compromised by beliefs inimical to Rome's wellbeing. We've known for some time of your attempts to corrupt the men who serve under you with your Christine bias; your actions in Ephesus merely confirm our impression of your willingness to further its ends instead of the Empire's.

"Now pray, would it be wise of me, that being the case, to allow you to continue in any form of command? Indeed, considering the Emperor's probable reaction to the prisoner's late arrival, is there any reason I should not order you executed on the spot?"

The question was not rhetorical, John knew, but it was a cruel insult to Iscariotus's honor. To order an officer of his rank executed was to condemn him as a coward who had not enough nobility to take his own life when disgraced. Valerus's was a threat designed to degrade and humiliate, to destroy Iscariotus's pride.

Fortunately, it was not pride from which Amadeon Iscariotus operated.

"Though I disagree with the Governor's assessment of the situation, were I in his position and believed as he did, I would not hesitate to remove such an officer from command," he said, staring straight ahead, as was appropriate. "It would only be right, for the garrison's sake and for Rome's. And considering the circumstances, if it is the Governor's will that I be executed and my head delivered to the Emperor to show I have been properly punished for my decision, then that, too, would only be right."

Iscariotus hesitated, then again broke protocol by looking full at Valerus. "However, if that is to be the case, Sir, I would ask, indeed plead, for the honor of taking the sword to myself as proof of my loyalty." He again turned his eyes straight ahead. "But of course, the preference for this soldier's disposition is and must be yours."

The sounds of the water, the crowd's buzzing and the crew unloading cargo filled the sudden silence. Valerus stared at Iscariotus as if he saw a ghost—or more accurately, as if he'd just seen the self he'd been before the politics of power and expediency had inspired him to exchange his soul for his position. He'd no doubt dealt with others in this situation; an officer's plea to prove his honor with the ultimate act of loyalty could not be unknown to him. Yet, even though Valerus saw a touch of fear in his eyes, Amadeon's readiness to stand for what he knew was right, along with his growing knowledge that he was more, much more, than a destructible body and persona, was something Valerus had not seen.

In truth, the Governor looked like it was suddenly occurring to him that Iscariotus might be the better of them, whatever his own nobility and power signified.

"Very well, Captain," he said at last, his demeanor respectful. "If I am forced to order drastic measures, you will have the right to assuage your honor in the proper manner."

Valerus barely acknowledged Iscariotus's grateful nod before at last turning to speak directly to John. His expression automatically strove for the bored indifference of the better toward the lesser, but, perhaps due to his just-finished interaction with Iscariotus, this time he truly looked at the prisoner before him.

To his credit, the Governor managed to resist his sudden urge to look away as the radiant Stillness that lay behind John's look seized him, but his shock was still plain. Iscariotus's integrity in the face of ruin might be worthy of respect, but what he saw as he beheld this one...the poor man suddenly looked as if he needed to catch his breath.

"And what have you to say for yourself, oh messenger-of-so-dangerous-a-message?" Valerus said, attempting to be flippant in spite of his shock.

"Best you should not let him have anything to say, but treat him as one would a Siren—with complete and careful disregard," Horatius said contemptuously, giving John no chance to answer. His rancor at Iscariotus's refusal to grovel, and at the Governor's weakness in treating such a refusal as honorable, was clear in his voice. "I have seen this Jew corrupt the ignorant with just a few words. Indeed, I saw him take in one of the sailors on *Ares* within minutes, so that he now thinks his Way valid."

"I see. And so you think I, too, will be corrupted if he speaks, Captain? Like any simple sailor or ignorant townsman?"

Valerus's tone was mild; his look was not. Horatius's life force shriveled and hid behind a wall of fear and resentment, but not before John sensed his confusion at so blatantly exposing himself before one whose good will he still needed.

"I—no, My Lord. No, of course not."

"I thought not," the Governor stated dryly, staring until he was satisfied he'd sufficiently cowed his subordinate. He turned to John again, trying not to look as if he braced himself, and studied him as one might a disturbing puzzle.

Suddenly, he turned on his heel and started across the deck.

"You will come," he said, beckoning to John; then: "No, the rest of you stay here."

Valerus spared no attention for Horatius's deferential protests, but walked along *Ares*'s rail, hands behind his back, until they came to a point directly opposite the gangplank. He stared out at the brilliant aquamarine ocean as if he never meant to speak; the few sailors there offered quick genuflections and hastily made it their business to be elsewhere.

But the fact that they bowed to both him *and* John was not lost on him.

"Who are you?" he asked at last, in a voice much different than he'd used before.

John shrugged." John bar Zebedee of Bethany, a teacher of Jeshua's Way...and the messenger of a very dangerous message. To some."

Anger flitted across Valerus's face, but he found no provocation in John's expression. He sighed and looked back out at the sea. "Would that you had come here sooner," he said, half to himself. Then: "I read Pontius Pilatus's report on his dealings with your leader. He was, you know, severely chastised, for though Rome had paid only small mind to the rumors, with even officers returning to testify to his powers, they were becoming intrigued. The Emperor felt Pilatus should have sent your Christos to Rome, so he could assess the truth of the rumors, instead of having him summarily executed.

"I was not at Court when Pilatus explained himself, but certain of my...friends...

were. They said every line between his words bespoke his belief that the one brought before him was much more than met the eye, yet he did the expedient thing for the sake of avoiding trouble with the locals.

"Having both heard about and read his testimony, I was satisfied Pilatus acted as a coward. Now, however, I begin to wonder. I...look into your eyes...and see something that makes me want to tell you my every secret...or run and hide. How much greater must that urge have been for Pilatus, looking into the eyes of one you called 'master'? And how could he have condemned such a one to that fate? He must have been far braver than any of us imagined."

"The One's plan required fulfillment," John said in answer, "and Pilatus was among those who chose to help. He could no more have freed Jeshua than a fly could carry a man across the sky."

Valerus frowned heavily. "And am I, too, such a tool? Did you know it would come to this, as your teacher was said to have known?"

John's smile was somewhat rueful. "I have not my Teacher's gift of prophecy; I cannot say I knew this would happen. But I do know this: the One takes me where It will, just as It does everyone. For now, my way leads to Rome and I go forth willingly. Perhaps I will live, perhaps I will die, but the Silent One that works through me will assuredly leave Its mark upon whoever I meet, no matter what their rank.

"So yes, Governor, you are such a tool—" John suddenly grinned, "—but never assume that makes you a pawn. The One in us can never be led against Its will. Never."

Valerus's frown grew thoughtful, then he squared his shoulders. "Horatius speaks truly. You *are* a danger. But not, I think, for the reasons he would choose to believe. Were it my choice, I would keep you here for a few days more...but it is too late; Rome calls you to your fate." Valerus hesitated. "But..."

John waited for him to ask the one question he truly wanted to ask, the question that, though it would not extend his life, could change it utterly.

But he did not ask it. His phantom self, which he'd managed to hold at bay until this very moment, stepped in and sealed his lips. Abunius Valerus would not this day, nor in this lifetime, ask "What is Truth?" as Pontius Pilatus had before allowing the crowd to have Jeshua.

Instead he said: "They say Pilatus spends much of his time washing his hands these days, as if he seeks to wash the stain of your leader's blood from them. Tell me, will I end up trying to wash your blood from my hands?"

John gave him no answer, for he had none. What he did know was that, while the Governor had in truth long desired the Path, when finally he'd been offered it, he'd turned away—neither the first nor the last among men to do so.

John headed back toward *Ares's* gangway; he'd done all that needed doing in this place. Valerus, seeming to realize he was not ready for the answer to either the authentic or the specious question, followed at a slightly slower pace.

"Captain Iscariotus, you will stay here," he said when he and John reached the others. He looked unhappy at his own orders. "I have heard *Ares* is an excellent ship; perhaps it will deliver the prisoner in time to keep us both from the Arena.

"Captain Horatius, I charge you in the name of the Empire to commandeer the ship *Ares* as transport to Rome. Further, I charge you with the safe conduct of this prisoner to Emperor Claudius by the time specified in his communiqué." He raised a finger as

Horatius started to smile. "You will see that he arrives at Court unscathed—or I will see that your tenure as Captain ends unpleasantly. Is that clear?"

"It is, my Lord," Horatius said, suddenly looking less pleased with his triumph.

Valerus signaled his men to disembark; John and Iscariotus clasped arms.

"Jeshua's Heart be with you, Amadeon," John said, his heart sore for the officer. It seemed so inadequate a parting for one who had given so much on his behalf. Iscariotus's smile was sad for them both.

"And with you, John. May the Emperor have sense enough to see the truth of you—" John nodded, but did not mention that such a realization might be the very thing that would condemn him. "—As for me... I should have paid more heed to 'Natus's warning. Perhaps the young jackal has had his way after all."

Valerus started to follow his guards, stopped and turned as if he wanted to say something more to John, then shook his head and reentered his litter. It made its way through the parting crowd on the dock, Amadeon Iscariotus behind it.

John, Horatius, four guards and the ship's crew were left on the deck of *Ares*, with Rome awaiting them.

FORTY

The *first thing Horatius* saw to, of course, was the change in John's accommodations. He immediately ordered *Ares's* captain to prepare the smallest possible space in which to put the prisoner, and when the sailors charged with the task informed him it was ready, hurried belowdecks to inspect it, dragging John along to see his new home.

"This is too large. I want it much smaller," he said after giving it the most cursory of inspections. The shipmaster, who'd examined the space and declared it more than adequately inhospitable himself, balked.

"This is no prison ship, Captain, but a merchant transport with storerooms designed to hold goods enough to turn a decent profit. We have no smaller space to put him in." And would not if we did, his expression said.

"Then put more cargo in this one, if that is what it takes. But be clear: I want it no larger than it need be for him to sit in. Include a bucket as well, for he will not leave it until we reach Puteoli. And since we need waste no more provisions on him than we absolutely must, he is to receive only a quarter-ration of bread and a third-ration of water."

"But...but..." the captain began in an indignant sputter. Horatius's gaze sharpened and his voice suddenly turned dangerous.

"Captain, this man is a traitor, one who would destroy all Rome has accomplished without a qualm. Were it up to me, he would at this very moment be outward-bound on some galley, or gracing the mines, to spend the rest of his days working for the Glory of the Empire. Or, best of all, he would be dancing at the end of a sword in the Arena.

Since my superiors wish to have their own say about what is to be done with him, however, and I am loyal to Rome, I will do as they bid and take him to the Emperor."

His glare deepened. "But until we arrive in the Emperor's presence, I am the one you answer to concerning this prisoner's disposition. And what I tell the Court about that disposition will determine your future and that of your superiors. See to it that you make this space exactly as I would have it or I will see that you answer for giving succor to an enemy of the State. Do you understand?"

And so the space was made even smaller and John shortly thereafter laughingly shoved into it by Horatius's guards. In addition to the bucket, he was supplied with a thin blanket that would not have covered shoulders and feet had he been able to lie down. He was not; the space was just big enough to sit in with his legs crossed.

John quickly lost his sense of how much time passed. He knew only his own company and the closed-in darkness, for the cargo space had neither porthole nor lantern. He hadn't used his voice since being put here, for there'd been no one to talk to. Or more accurately, Horatius had ordered all but his caretakers to avoid him on pain of death—and even they were never to speak to him.

Ares's captain had other ideas about how John should be treated. He'd apparently ordered his men to bring full rations of bread and water when they could, and John had been thus and gladly blessed three times. More, and also against Horatius's orders, the men who delivered the food and water sometimes took the bucket and its contents away, returning it empty and occasionally even rinsed.

John corrected himself. He had used his voice during his confinement. He'd said "Thank you," to whoever gave him food or removed the bucket.

On the third day out, Horatius began making it his practice to daily stop by the makeshift cell and try John's tranquility with malicious threats of what would befall him in Rome. Not that they were more than an annoyance; John's ability to hold the Stillness made it easy to simply ignore the man until he finished his feeding and left.

In truth, John treated this isolation as a somewhat of a boon; since he often had his eyes closed and lived then in spaces beyond the cramped confines of body and room, the lack of light and room was no great trial. True, he'd spent most of these last months living at the cottages with the trainees, but it had been his place to see to everything from delivering food to mediating the inevitable disputes that came of having ten disparate personalities constantly in each other's presence. He'd had little chance to enjoy the Presence with his eyes closed, and this confinement made him realize how much he'd missed that. More, it explained why Jeshua had occasionally disappeared, leaving his closest companions to tend to their own spiritual wellbeing.

This was not to say that John was oblivious to his body's discomfort. His legs ached constantly, and his stomach and tongue protested both the lack and the sameness of the fare. And though those lacks saved him from worse, his nose still complained about the smell emanating from the bucket. The lack of water was particularly uncomfortable: his throat constantly felt dry, his tongue slightly swollen.

No, his immersion in the Stillness did not make his discomforts go away, but it did let him experience them without also suffering the usual fears about where they might lead—and that gave him a kind of freedom that even these conditions could not touch.

And oh, yes. The visions had returned to keep him company.

John, Iscariotus and the rest of the soldiers had been making their way toward *Ares* through a neighborhood that contained, not the homes of the city's successful, but those who worked for them. As they rounded a corner that led down to the docks, John stopped in his tracks, mouth agape at what stood before him.

It was a building, he supposed, but if that was so, God had surely changed His mind and allowed Babel to be built. The dark, rectangular spire was made of hundreds, perhaps thousands, of slabs of dark, shiny stone and literally touched the clouds; the winds scrabbled around its sides with shocked and whistling protests as it slammed against the unlikely obstacle with what seemed like hurricane strength. John could not fathom how the building stood, yet strong as they were, those winds could not clear the smoky gray haze that tinted the sapphire sky the tower speared up into.

With a shock, John suddenly realized the monstrous construction was not a storehouse: it held people, thousands of them, crowded together like slaves in a galley. Yet, he also knew those who lived in the spire were not slaves, but freemen with the right to live where they would. They *chose* to live in that cramped, swaying, windblown tower...

"Elder, are you all right?"

John's head whipped around; Amadeon was peering worriedly into his face. Horatius stared with suspicious expectation as John glanced back toward the spire, but it'd returned to the ethers from which it had manifested.

"I am...fine Amadeon...my attention was caught by a hawk."

Iscariotus chose to let it pass—at least until later—and they'd continued on to *Ares*.

Even though none had been as dark and terrible as before, John had at first been less than thrilled by the visions' return. Now, however, he found it hard not to look forward to them. He'd not met Mary or Anna or Jeshua, as he'd come to hope; though he'd visited many places, some known and some not, none of them had been inhabited.

But still, what places they'd been! Stunning in their varied, shimmering, beauty, heart-speeding excitement or soul-stilling peace, some had made John ache with the desire to stay in their hidden spaces forever. Yes, the vast majority of his experiences still consisted of the One's ever-welcome Silence, but he more than once had to admonish himself to approach each entry into the Practice without expectations.

The scrape of metal against wood made John look up; hopefully, one of the sailors was bringing extra rations. John agonizingly unfolded himself in case the man might be willing to take the bucket, which was as full as he could stand.

It was no sailor at his door, however, but Horatius, come for the second time that day. Guards behind him, he entered the room holding a kerchief over his nose and mouth; his raised lantern splashed eerie shadows against the walls.

"Get up," he said harshly; then, once John struggled to his feet, his legs protesting the sudden use: "If you were expecting the sailors to bring you something to eat, you will be disappointed. We have...disciplined...both the man we caught bringing extra food to you, and his Captain, for disobeying my orders. And to punish you for your dishonesty in accepting such favors when you knew them to be against my wishes, you will go without food until we reach Rome, and your water ration will be cut to a sixth."

"Very well," John answered calmly, if rustily.

Horatius's lips pursed angrily at John's enduring refusal to offer him the deference he bullied from others...but then a small, reptile-cold smile encroached upon his face.

"Now, then. I have recently discovered that Governor Valerus neglected to ask you certain questions concerning your crimes against Rome. Since the Emperor must know what threat you and your Christines present, I will now ask those questions. If you do not answer to my satisfaction... But of course you will. After all, it would be a shame if things became...unpleasant for others because you refused to cooperate, not?"

Not to you, John thought. Horatius's intent to use the unlucky men of *Ares* regardless of any answers he might give, to avenge his fury and gain the submission he sought from John, was clear on his face.

With the suddenness of a large wave swamping a small boat, rage tightened John's muscles from foot to scalp. Here stood one whose hypocrisy would shame the most callous Pharisee. He invoked and used the name of Rome for his own selfish ends, while laughing at the likes of Amadeon Iscariotus, who truly stood for his homeland's ideals. He looked a Way that sought joy for all in the face, spat on it in contempt, and reveled in whatever harm he might cause others by choosing against it. It was as if he despised Life for Its aliveness and sought Its demise simply because he could.

Though Gaius Horatius looked the part of the patrician, with no strand of hair, no item of his uniform out of place, it was John, dirty, disheveled and fetid, who drew himself to his full height and stared aristocratically down on him. The guards actually fell back a step as his voice thundered off the walls; to one who could see such things, the room suddenly exploded with the radiance of the sun as he pointed at Horatius like a king reproaching a recalcitrant subject. The same flame-bright halo that had graced Jeshua's head the day he'd cleared the temple of the moneychangers ringed John's head; he felt its brilliance and knew his eyes blazed with it.

"Beware, Gaius Horatius! Beware! For though you claim to men to serve the spirit of Rome and its people, she too has ears to hear and eyes to see, and she knows you have no more love for her than you would for a hired woman! Beware! Just as you've called me liar and traitor, so does Rome call you! Soon, too soon, she will take her vengeance for the choices you've made and the harm you've done to those who truly hold her dear—and not one soul, not one, will step forth to save you from her incisive punishment!

"Beware Gaius Horatius! You seal your fate by your own choice! Beware!"

Horatius looked like a man who'd entered a cave expecting to find a treasure, only to come face to face with the very angry dragon that protects it. Eyes wide and mouth tight, he staggered, white-faced, past the shocked guards, like one just managing not to bolt in absolute terror; a moment later, the door closed with the gentlest of thumps, as if those closing it feared to further disturb what they had, all-unprepared, awakened.

John sank to the floor as a great, whooshing breath deflated both his lungs and his all-encompassing ire. It seemed to him he should be sweating—or smoking, for that matter—yet he did neither. He wrapped his ragged blanket about his shoulders and shivered in a room suddenly grown too cool, lightheaded with the shock of the curse he'd just placed on Horatius's head.

For curse it was, undeniably.

He felt both elated and appalled, and it seemed to him the two emotions must either reconcile or tear him apart. How had Jeshua stood it? And why had *he* done it? Granted, Horatius, more than anyone John had ever met, deserved at least a goodly tongue-lashing. But to curse the man? As if one could be eternally cursed?

Yes, yes, Jeshua had called woe on the hypocritical rulers of Judea, for he'd abhorred those who claimed the authorization of God to take from others what they themselves would never give. Privately, however, Jeshua always insisted that the ability to eternally curse another did not exist...and that the twelve should never try to do so.

Truth to be told (and despite the Samarian incident), John had often been aghast at Jeshua's tirades, especially as his own awareness grew. His young heart, though quick to anger, felt sure his Teacher could have found less inflammatory ways to speak to the authorities. It never made sense to him that Jeshua would say the very things designed to make the leaders of Synagogue shut their ears to any possibility of accepting him.

But now, John himself had done exactly that, and he could not deny the sense of... *rightness* he felt at seeing the look of dismay, horror—and belief—on Horatius's face. Whatever Jeshua's comments to the contrary, the universe had heard, acknowledged and made John's words manifest; it could do no less. That curse was real, and unless the One Itself deemed otherwise, it would follow Horatius wherever he went.

John shuddered, chilled by what he'd done and where it would lead.

He closed his eyes and introduced one, and another, and then another technique. Slowly, the ropes of tension in his muscles slackened; he touched, then embraced, then submerged himself in the One. Both the muffled creak of the ship and the rush of the sea below his feet soon dissolved as John's awareness deserted his body's sensations; his consciousness stretched beyond the singular time and space he occupied...

...He looked down upon a billion, billion different lives as they lived out every possible drama. Time threaded through them, Its three aspects endlessly crossing, twining and mingling, first at this choice point, then at...this...and...at...this, but unlike the lives it flowed through, Time simultaneously experienced past, present, and future, the points where Its aspects converged being the most likely outcomes of actions once taken/being taken/to be taken by the myriad selves playing out those scenes. Only the phantom self saw Time as linear, as next and next and next, John suddenly saw—and therein lay the core of its ultimate powerlessness. For in truth, Time consisted not of separate aspects at all. Time was only and always here, only and always happening now.

And so in truth did not exist at all.

As he witnessed these lives, John discovered he had control over where he placed his focus, and played with shifting his awareness from one being's experience to another's and another's, literally *ad infinitum*. He saw the various possible outcomes of everyone's choices, even as they did not.

His attention was drawn to one particular point amongst those millions: it seemed somehow familiar. John stared curiously at that moment of happening, trying to identify it—and plunged toward it with such suddenness that he feared he would burn to a crisp, like a star falling to earth. Before panic could overtake him, however, he was there, in that moment.

As Gaius Horatius.

John felt the sinewy slenderness of Horatius's physical form surround his own consciousness, smelled as his own the scent that was unique to the Captain's body. Though the mind that hosted him did not, John perceived both the unconscious feelings and beliefs that controlled so many of Horatius's seemingly conscious actions...and for a startling moment, a greater, growing malevolence that grew behind them.

He watched in fascination as he/Gaius chose one path over another, experienced the results, reacted to them, then chose his next path. He saw both the history of John/Gaius as he was—and the unlimited histories of what he might have been:

he/Gaius remained as much the sum of his unchosen possibilities as the ones he'd chosen, even as they separated from the main timeline and dimmed into nonexistence. He saw as Time led him/Gaius to the makeshift cell aboard *Ares*, saw how his whole life had led to the moment where he/Gaius decided to menace the prisoner. John felt the soul-freezing terror of the prisoner's curse send him/Gaius lurching to the deck to vomit his dread into the sea below; he felt the intense shame and hatred that fueled his/Gaius's growing obsession with avenging himself on this Jew who behaved toward him as an Emperor...and in whose presence he felt so weak.

But unlike Gaius alone, John/Gaius also saw the results that would be born of this decision. He saw how the prisoner's curse would be made manifest by his/Gaius's refusal to choose the other possibilities that existed at the moment the curse had been spoken, saw how those outcomes could yet change, simply by him/Gaius choosing *this* over *that*.

John now understood what he'd previously only believed: neither he nor Jeshua nor anyone had ever called curses down on any other. There were no curses, only seeing clearly. His undue effect on Horatius's future was not his at all; he was but a messenger of fair warning that spoke in exactly the manner most apt to get the Roman's attention. John was, in truth, the Captain's own call to look to his heart and thus prevent any curse from coming true. Gaius Horatius truly was sealing his fate by his own choices —and yet, he could change that fate at any moment, simply by choosing differently.

With that realization, a sense of lightness suddenly filled John; Time and the multi-existent universes faded away. His consciousness once more slipped into *Ares's* cargo hold and The Comforter's warmth permeated his body, relaxing him so completely that he would surely have slumped sideways had there been room to do so.

Like a man falling into a deep well, John soon entered that place where no thoughts or considerations could exist, and knew only the unbounded joy of the Infinite.

Horatius did not return after their confrontation, but John still had more visitors than usual. At least three times a day, one or the other of the guards would come to peer unfathomably in at him, lantern held forth like some protective talisman. John ignored them in favor of remaining in the Silence; he came back to earthly consciousness only when *Ares* at last landed in Puteoli, the port city Rome relied on for its goods.

He was surprised when two guards came to retrieve him from his cell, for he certainly had no intention of resisting his removal from the cramped space and the truly horrible bucket. Nor would he try to bolt once he stepped ashore, for he could barely even stand. Though he tried to walk at his normal pace when he dizzily stepped into *Ares's* corridor, his escort ended up half-carrying him to the top deck.

Once there, Horatius spared him only the briefest of glances before ordering the guards to bring him along; the Emperor's representative already awaited them. John nodded to *Ares's* captain, whose left eye was still discolored from Horatius's punishment. The captain nodded back, then defiantly lifted his fist to shoulder height, knuckles facing downward and thumb out to the side.

It was the sign the Emperor used in the Arena when he chose to spare one from death.

John squinted against the brilliance of the wintry afternoon sun, finally able to manage a shambling walk...but on what would have been his last step on the tricky slant of the gangplank, his foot caught on one of the rough boards and sent him tumbling.

"By the gods. Are all Christine leaders such clumsy oafs? 'Tis a wonder they've managed to make any leeway at all in the jaded minds of the people...but then again, perhaps such simplicity is their charm."

The lazy, mildly sarcastic lilt did not in the least take away from the melodiousness of the voice. John realized he stared at the speaker's expensively sandaled feet and pushed himself into a kneeling position, wincing for his scraped knees and palms. He let his gaze rise until he could see the speaker's face.

Arius Galteus might not have been the most comely man in Rome, but finding the one who was would have been quite the task. His golden, broad-shouldered, well-honed form had the easy, relaxed grace of one who frequently tested his body's limits and found them high. His features, from his wavy, deep brown hair to his full, angel-bowed lips, fell together with magnificent symmetry, and his jewel-blue eyes glowed as if the sun lived behind them. Though he wore no uniform, John knew he was used to being obeyed. If a man's looks denoted his value, then here stood the one who should be Emperor.

But that, of course, was not the case. John knew there were those who'd considered Jeshua less than comely, plain, even. Yet look at what he had been and done. Arius Galteus was indeed handsome, but the cynicism he perceived in the masses was likely naught but a reflection of what he himself experienced.

Would John's death in Arena be the thing that alleviated his and Caesar's boredom?

The guards pulled John to his feet and Galteus looked him over, but though his manner seemed to confirm his boredom with all things, neither fear nor discomfort distorted the handsome official's features when their eyes met.

He did, however, wrinkle his perfect nose.

"I was given to understand that the Jewish people were stringent in matters of cleanliness. You, however, stink. Does not this ship have proper provisions for keeping crew and passengers presentable?"

"Prisoners are not given such privileges, Counselor. He has spent the journey in confinement, as is proper," Horatius answered.

"And you are...?" Galteus asked lazily, keeping his gaze on John.

"Captain Gaius Horatius, Counselor, personal aide to Governor Valerus of Athens."

"Ah. Well, Captain Horatius, aide to Valerus of Athens, were you so convinced this prisoner would jump ship and swim to safety that even the privilege of cleansing himself should be denied? Did you think he would take flight, like a bird? I hear tell the one who began this movement was capable of such miracles... Tell me, prisoner, can you fly?"

He did not wait for an answer, but turned to Horatius. "The Emperor sent orders that this prisoner was not to be harmed, and so I suppose he has not been, strictly speaking. But make no mistake, Captain, I am well aware this clumsiness is not inborn—and I am displeased by the delay his condition will cause in bringing him to Court.

"Patros," he said, turning to one of his own guards, "find us some transportation so we may get to Rome without having to carry him on our backs. Then you, Captain Horatius, will take the prisoner to the nearest bathhouse. I'll not present a derelict to the Emperor...no matter what his life expectancy may be."

So it was that John visited the famous baths of Rome. Heated water ran into the large, tiled communal tubs at all times, brought in by the amazing system of aqueducts for which the Romans were also famous. Despite his impending meeting with Fate and Her whims, and though the bath was a rushed-through thing, John so enjoyed the feel of clean water that he was able, after only a moment's trepidation, to set aside his cultural bias against exposing his nakedness to the soldiers who seemed to make up the bulk of the clientele at this particular bath. He could not resist a wry smile as he suffered the house slaves to hastily wash, dry and dress him in a clean, warm Roman-cut robe: Horatius might scowl, but he must be relieved there'd been slaves available to help clean and dress the prisoner so he wouldn't have to.

John was also fed his first decent meal in far too long. He was not allowed to dally over it any more than he was the bath, but it would not have taken him long to eat in any event. Though he'd enough of an appetite to eat a full meal and then some, he found his stomach simply could not take in much food after the long near-fast.

As he ate, John pondered Arius Galteus's place in the palace hierarchy. Horatius had referred to him as the "Emperor's representative", and John gathered he was not royalty. Yet the ease with which he gave orders, and the confidence with which he expected them to be followed, clearly indicated his status as Counselor was no token post, awarded for politics' sake. Galteus served the Emperor directly and on an ongoing basis.

The guards appeared and spoke briefly to Horatius, who in turn ordered the slaves to take away what was left of the meal. John wiped his face quickly and fell into step between the guards as they made their way through the crowded streets for the not-so-distant palace.

It was time to meet the First Citizen of Rome.

FORTY-ONE

Had *he been the* child of plebeians, or even of a mere senator, he would never have been allowed to live.

Limping, palsied, slack-faced, Tiberius Claudius Drusus Nero Germanicus had not even received his majority at age, but was left under guardianship as a woman would have been and kept from the public eye. He was a joke, a slow-witted deformity whose main purpose was to be the recipient of cruel comments and crude humor from the rest of the royal family.

When Claudius was forty-six, his nephew, the late and in no way bewailed Caligula, appointed him to a suffect consulship, for it amused him to give "The Half-Wit," one with such slurred, slow speech and a slurred, slow personality to match, such duties. It was the first time Claudius had been assigned any kind of public duty—and as it turned out, he was, emphatically, no half-wit.

"Murderer" he might be, the mind behind the eradication of Caligula—but Sovereign of Rome he most assuredly was as a result of Caligula's demise, so none had the audacity to say so aloud, nor even in whispers. Many were the ears that listened on Germanicus's behalf in the hope that he would favor them for their loyalty.

John entered a hall that could easily have held the largest of Jerusalem's synagogues, escorted not by the guards from *Ares,* but by members of the Emperor's

Praetorian Guard. Large as it was, the hall was still crowded, but John resisted the urge to peer at the elaborate array of statuary, tapestries and persons as he approached the dais on which Claudius' throne was seated. As he passed royalty, senators, rich merchants from other lands and slaves ready to do their masters' bidding, those closest to him stopped their conversations, their stares variously curious, annoyed and amused.

"He is tall for those people, is he not?"

"They say he is one of the original leaders of those Christines...as if it really matters."

"Supposedly, their leader could raise the dead and produce food from the air."

"Rank superstition! No doubt his only magic lay in his ability to use sweet-sounding words to part his followers from their hard-earned coins."

"How can he stand having so much hair? Does he think having a womanly appearance will save him from the Arena?"

Comments of that sort and more echoed through the hall as the crowd parted before, then closed after John. If the sound was anything to go by, however, the speakers did not go back to their original conversations, but turned their attention to the dais. They were curious to see what Claudius had in store for him.

"The Half-Wit meets the no-wit," someone said slyly, to the cautious titters of those around him.

They came to the end of the large hall where the Emperor slumped haphazardly, leaning on his throne's armrest as if he needed it to hold him up. If Galteus was the epitome of beauty, Claudius Germanicus was its polar opposite. He was old, yes, but he looked far older than he was rumored to be. His head swayed as if he had only minimal control over where it might go, and though he did not drool, he licked his lips constantly, as if holding his mouth closed was an effort. Everything about his face drooped with weakness.

That is, except his eyes.

Standing a bit behind and to Claudius's left was a woman dressed in such finery that she could only be his wife and Empress, Agrippina, daughter of his late brother and sister of Caligula. Her every nuance suggested deliberate ignorance of the Emperor's presence; her true, if discreet, focus was on the boy who stood next to her, a lad of thirteen or so summers who favored her strongly. Someone in the crowd referred to him as "that young Nero", followed by a carefully whispered commentary. Several men stood to the right of the throne, including Arius Galteus; John sensed within most of them a level of loyalty that went far beyond that of mere political cronies.

This one knows the value of every coin in his realm, be it metal or human, John thought, wondering how anyone could ever take him for a half-wit. He knew precisely which coins were his and which were owed to others. Claudius Germanicus might well forget what he was saying mid-sentence, as they said, but he never forgot what he meant to say.

"So, this...is the...disci-*pulh*...who walked with....the-e-e so-called *Chris*-tos."

Claudius stared at John, daring him to show surprise as his voice lingered over and expelled pieces of words with the explosive jaggedness only a stutterer could know.

"This one is called John Zebedee, First Citizen," a man next to Galteus said. He was around Claudius's age and had the look, not of royalty, but of one who had worked his way into his position. Claudius nodded without taking his gaze from John.

"Theeeey...say...your t-t-teacher could worrrk m-m-*mmmir*-acles. Diiiiid huh-he?"

"Yes, First Citizen, he did."

"Hee...c-could h-*heal*?"

"Yes." There were murmurs and a few nervous giggles.

"He pro-duced...fuh-fuh-ffood from th-eee...air?"

"When needed, he took two fishes and five loaves of bread and fed a multitude, far more than the amount of food should have allowed, First Citizen."

"Aaannd he....rraised the d-dead?" The snickering grew louder; Claudius ignored it.

"My fellow teacher and friend, a man named Lazarus, was dead for four days, First Citizen. But Jeshua, whom those in Rome call the Christos, called Life away from Death and Lazarus could not but answer."

"Aand....wh-what of y-y-*you*, Chrissss-*tine*? C-cann yuh-yooou...work m-*mir*-acles?"

"Though I by no means have my Teacher's consistency or skill, your Highness, the grace of the One has occasionally done what might be called miracles through me."

This claim caused outright laughter and fetched a number of derisive calls of "liar" and "charlatan".

"My Lord! My Lord, please! May I speak?"

Claudius looked about, seemingly confused as he tried to locate the voice through all the noise; John, however, recognized it immediately.

"And you are?" The older counselor said over the crowd's continuing murmurs, his tone regal where Claudius's could not be.

"Captain Gaius Horatius, aide to Governor Abunius Valerus of Athens, First Citizen. I had charge of the prisoner's transport here."

Claudius stared at Horatius as he stepped forward, calculating, perhaps, the worth of this particular coin to his Empire, then nodded for him to speak.

"It may please the honorable citizens assembled to laugh and take this Jew's claims as delusions, and so they may be. But I have traveled with him these several weeks. This man may seem 'as gentle as a lamb', as the Christines themselves would say, but I saw him take over men's wills with mere words. I saw men aboard the *Ares*, our transport, turn mutinous to Rome under his prodding."

The timbre of the murmuring changed as some in the crowd listened to Horatius's claims, and the few who laughed their responses now did so uncertainly. He seemed to grow taller, his diffidence subtly shifting to smugness as he pointed at John.

"His teacher was no charlatan, but a magician of great power who was rightfully executed for his treasonous behavior against the Empire. Like his teacher, this man would wrest power from the Emperor himself, if such were possible...and he and his followers think it is. He has even managed to corrupt high-ranking officers in the Army, officers who have in turn corrupted many of their men with this Christine cant."

Now there was genuine alarm. People looked nervously at each other, as if they should be able to recognize a Christine on sight. Cries of "who has he corrupted?" and "This must be stopped!" came from several directions. Horatius nodded in agreement.

"I tell you, good citizens and allies of Rome, this man and his ilk are as great a danger as any invading army, for they capture people's minds by stealth and convince them their rejection of the Empire's order will give them favor with the gods."

Now he faced the Emperor. "My, Lord. Were I your honored self, I would dispose of this one at once, then exterminate his followers to the man, just as you would any invader. Or any vermin."

Though they'd seemed indifferent when John entered the hall, in truth Horatius's words affected a crowd that was ready to hear them. Many were well aware of the fast-growing Christine influence, especially with Paul's journeys' throughout Asia Minor, and Horatius's comments only confirmed their apprehension over the growing sect.

One of the Emperor's advisors leaned toward him and they held a whispered conversation. Claudius nodded and looked at John, his eyes full of calculation.

"Y-y-*youu* s-say...yoou have d-d-done mmiraacles? Healed puuuuh-peopul?"

"I have, First Citizen. But as I also said, I have not my Teacher's consistency or skill in allowing the One to so flow through me."

"Thuh—en, best y-yooooou sh-shhould *gain* it. Wuh-wweeee orrder yuh-you to h-h-heeeal Us. Heh-*here* annndd n-n-nnow."

John looked at the floor to hide his disappointment as the room fell silent with shock and expectancy. He had known in his mind that his survival was unlikely, but his heart... his heart had hoped otherwise, and knew now there was no possibility it would be so.

The Emperor mocked him, and they both knew it. He sought proof of John's worthiness the way some sought proof of God's wrath by cursing others. Claudius had not just grown used to his defects, he'd learned to use them to great advantage. Taking those protections away would only cause John to meet death in some private place instead of the Arena.

Claudius mocked John and his Teacher, and that, in the face of his impending death, angered him. He locked eyes with the Emperor, letting his irritation show, and saw surprise flit across his face.

"My Lord, I will not heal you."

The uproar was tremendous...and made of equal parts of relief and anger.

"You refuse to heal your Emperor, though you say you can?" the outraged voice of the counselor who'd suggested John's test cried above the throng. The crowd again quieted, loathe to miss the prisoner's answer.

But John followed his Teacher's example with the Sanhedrin...and remained silent.

The advisor sneered as Claudius gave a bobbling nod. "Then you can take your miracles to the Arena, fool, for only they will save you. Remove this liar from our sight!"

The crowd chattered as the guards roughly grabbed John, but before they could drag him to the cells of the condemned, Arius Galteus stepped before Claudius.

"My Lord, a notion?" he said, his lazily melodic voice effortlessly stilling the room. Claudius seemed displeased by the interruption, for he'd just turned to his Empress, but nodded loosely. The guards stopped pulling at John.

"This man is a prominent Christine, one who walked with its founder as one of his closest companions. He is known, indeed worshipped, by all who follow this Way. To put him to death would be..." he paused as if thinking, "...a most unfortunate error."

"He is a traitor, Galteus, who seeks to destroy all we have built," the counselor who'd ordered John's removal said with stubborn annoyance. "His death in the Arena will make an excellent example of what happens to those who offend Rome."

Galteus shrugged, the gesture almost feminine. "It might be if this issue were only political in nature, Polybius, but it is not. It is religious, and as we both know, the religious can be irrational when choosing between their survival and their faith."

Galteus looked again at Claudius. "You have read the reports, my Lord. These Christines increasingly believe martyrdom to be a way to prove their dedication and gain entry to their paradise. Killing this one now will only intensify their fervor, not dampen it. We must find an alternative."

"If we kill enough of them, that will solve the problem, not?"

"That is not what the reports assert, Sepus. Many have converted to this sect because its members believe so strongly in their founder's values that they are willing to die without putting up a fight. I think it an odd and ridiculous trait in humans—yet have not we all heard of the power that one brave death can have on the battlefield? I say again, to kill one so prominent to this movement will only attract more foolish citizens to their cause. What now seems a small threat will become a definite one."

"Wuh-whaaat...then, do y-youuuu suggest, G-guuh-*gal*teus?" Claudius asked, interrupting a new round of volleys between his counselors.

"The galleys!" Someone called out, and many others followed suit.

But Galteus shook his head. "No, not the galleys—nor the mines," he sighed, before anyone could suggest it. "More than one of us has seen his like use mere words to sway men to revolt when before they showed only loyalty. Enslaving him will not work."

"Then what in Jupiter's Name are you suggesting, Galteus? If we cannot kill or enslave him, what is left?" Counselor Polybius asked exasperatedly. Galteus sniffed at the older man as if missing so obvious an answer was below him.

"Why, exile, of course."

That raised a number of brows. Common men who angered Rome were rarely exiled, for the mines, the galleys and the Arena needed them. And royalty never survived to be exiled; the danger of their returning with an army was all too real.

Polybius snorted. "And where would we exile him to? If you so fear his ability to affect slaves who have guards around them, surely he would corrupt those in other lands and come back to haunt our lenience. I say let us execute him and be done with it."

The room grew loud with the babble of debate; the Emperor's counselors' seemed evenly divided as to what John's disposition should be and contended earnestly for their particular solutions. John's own desires, of course, were quite clear...

...And, he realized suddenly, thoroughly caught up in the swirling energy that surged around him like an ill wind. He shuttered his eyes, not quite closing them, and focused more fully on the One's will, setting aside as best he could his own wishes.

All at once, Agrippina entered the discussion, the force of her bearing easily clearing a space in the midst of the men. She leaned close to her husband. Claudius listened raptly, then, looking a bit like a boy who has had his fun taken away, nodded and raised a wavering hand.

The talk fell to murmurs, then whispers, then silence. Her part in the debate over, Agrippina stepped away from the Emperor as if she could not do so quickly enough.

"G-galllteus innsists... thaaat to s-s-*send* yoou...to s-s-some distaant but p-po-*pop*-pulated land...would be ahhhssss dangerous as immm-*pri*-soning you. Th-that-t even c-c-cuttinnng out y-y-*your* tongue...w-w-would beeee a mistake, for y-your f-fuh-fol-lowers wuh-would only r-r-rally arounnnd...your ac-c-quired *de*-fect..."

John sensed the smile the Emperor concealed as he made this statement; he did indeed understand the power he wielded by virtue of his inabilities.

"But there are a number of places in this world that consist of little more than rocks, goats and scrub grass—or sand and sky," Galteus cut in smoothly, again waving his hand in that almost feminine manner.

"Our proposal is a simple one, John Zebedee of the Jews. We will transport you to one of those places and you will stay there, alone, for the rest of your life. And in exchange, we will not execute the Christines who hid you in Ephesus.

"We trust you find that acceptable?"

John could only nod his acquiescence, aware and thankful that what should have been his death had become a reprieve.

His audience with Claudius was now truly finished; this time the people ignored him as the guards propelled him back toward the hall's entrance.

That is, save for Horatius. Brave now in the presence of those who had the ear of the Emperor, he walked to the left of John so he could glare at him as he spoke.

"Do not think you and your followers have escaped, traitor. The Emperor makes a mistake condemning you to exile, and I mean to convince him of his error. Consider yourself always a prisoner condemned to death, Jew, for that is exactly what you are. Sooner or later, Rome will have her vengeance on you."

"As she will on you, Gaius Horatius," John replied. "The One in Her many guises is not mocked; She heard my words aboard *Ares*, just as you did."

The guards decided John was not moving fast enough and gave him a shove that almost brought him to his knees. But he did not miss how Horatius's face paled at his words...or lose the Calm that remained centered in the core of his being. So long as he had the One, John knew nothing Horatius or Rome attempted could daunt him.

Unfortunately, that did not stop Rome from trying.

The first thing John's jailers did once the guards brought him to the holding cell was strip him of everything save his loin wrap. Then, as their cackling laughter echoed sharply off the walls, each of them held John in a headlock and sheared him like a balky sheep, leaving him with naught but a fine, uneven fuzz to keep company with the numerous nicks and cuts they made on his scalp.

"Where now are your miracles, traitor?" they taunted raucously. "Why do you not save yourself?"

When John gave no answer, they beat him mercilessly.

It was not enough to simply pound him to the floor once and let be; lest he should escape their attentions too soon, his warders threw icy water on him when he threatened to lose consciousness, then resumed punching, kicking and even whipping him with the "soft" tail until he fell once more, then once more, and then once more again. The jeering went on; they repeatedly demanded he try to corrupt them with his magic, or raised their fists in mock-defense and invited him to fight back "like a true man".

Finally, John crashed to the rough floor yet one more time.

He heard the guards' murmurs through the roaring in his ears but was in no condition to understand what they said; he managed not to yelp as a toe punched his aching ribs and strong hands pulled him roughly to his knees. When he tried to stand, however, he was again shoved to the floor.

"You are a dog of a coward, Christine—so you can walk like one."

Harsh laughter rang out as they forced John to crawl on hands and knees to a deserted part of the holding pens, "To keep you from using your magic to corrupt others," they said. Someone promised there'd be more to come as his cell door closed.

But that would be later. Now, John rejoiced at being left in relative, if painful, peace.

His only company that night came a few minutes later; a warder dropped before him a slop-laden plate, and blessedly, the winter-weight toga they'd taken. John made no attempt to eat, but slowly and painfully wrapped the toga around himself like a cover. More than thankful for the Practice's simplicity, for his muddled brain could not have strung anything more complex together, John let their power touch mind and body. The pain of his rough treatment grew more distant and less cared about.

Then, for a time too long to count, he knew no more.

John returned to consciousness hours later, his toga-blanket askew. Though he shivered uncontrollably, he cautiously checked himself before trying to move. The cuts and contusions still hurt a great deal, as surface wounds will, but the piercing pain in his ribs and the ache of his thoroughly swollen face had lessened greatly. He felt sore all over, but it was the soreness of one healing, not one slipping from it.

Once John determined he'd do no more harm by moving, he slowly pulled his toga completely on and crawled to his dinner. He ate quickly, doing his best to neither look at, smell, or taste the rancid offerings, then lay back down to again embrace the Stillness.

Paradoxically enough, he had not entered the Practice with the intent of healing his body, despite its obvious need for it. As he'd explained to Prochorus on the road to Caesarea, one should never use the Practice for what they thought needed healing. After all, while the self insisted on trying to dissolve a blemish that seemed to mar its outer beauty, the One, with Its unlimited perspective, might be seeking to heal some poison in the blood. Entering the Stillness without ideas of what should happen was the best way to gain what one most wanted and needed—or better, to move beyond all wants and needs and know perfect Joy.

The continued healing of his physical body was not all John experienced as he engaged in the Practice this time. This time, his surface mind would not be still. His thoughts ranged from Mary, Ariadne and the rest of his companions, to Counselor Galteus's flippantly delivered but wholly serious threat against the Ephesian Christines, and back again, in an ever-widening circle of concern.

Usually, a city's tolerance for Jeshua's followers was determined by how the locals felt about the new Way. In Jerusalem and many small towns in Judea, of course, that tolerance had never existed, while cities like Athens and Ephesus had always been more lenient. In places like Corinth and Caesarea, where tolerance was waning, the local religious authorities usually condemned the Christines first, with some among their followers emphasizing that displeasure with violence.

But now Rome herself was taking a larger interest in the "Christine problem," developing an official willingness to deal violently with the new Way. The majority of those at Caesar's Court thought such violence inevitable—and far too many thought it long overdue.

A brief, confusing picture of Aggripina's son, Nero, suddenly flashed through John's mind, followed by a strong sense of fire and smoke; then came a sense of censure and persecution that would dog the Christines for literally centuries to come...

He sat at a sturdy oak table, the smell of lamb and lamp oil, sweat and wood smoke filling his nostrils. Though it was well past eighth hour, the summer sky was only now darkening toward the jewel-bright sapphire blue he so loved. His brother James sat to his right, quiet and thoughtful, his attention wholly focused forward; Judas sat to his left, not so quiet in his inner self, but just as taken. Nathaniel and Peter, Andrew, Simon, Matthew and Phillip, Thomas, Luke and Mark, were also present—in Martha and Uriah's house, John now saw. Mary and Martha, too, were here, as were Salome, Lazarus, Rachael of Caesarea and some of the Marys. And of course, Miriam stood by in all her highly distracting, womanly glory. The feel of homespun scratching his arms and the heaviness of his curly, nape-length hair filled John with an overwhelming sense of comfort and familiarity, even as he knew this to be another vision—or more correctly, the full reliving of an experience past.

Jeshua sat at the head of the table, the remains of his meal long ago set aside. His expression was serious as he wrapped his hands about his wine cup in this, the third year of his ministry. He was speaking of what was to come, and the why of it.

"Do you think this is the only home humankind has? That this is the only place the One seeks to reestablish the awareness of the Divine Mother in the heart of man? It is not. You do think my mission is to save humanity from the folly of following the phantom self, and I have told you that it is. I came, I said, that all might have Life and have it more abundantly.

"Yet, I tell you also that if you think that is your mission, you will fail utterly."

Murmurs of confusion followed Jeshua's words, some of them quite annoyed. Peter, as always, plaintively demanded an explanation: his fisherman's heart had no time for riddles; could not the Rabbi simply say what he meant? Jeshua chuckled and raised his hands before the company could work themselves into a full and indignant lather.

"I called you to be fishers of men, true—but I said nothing of the kinds of fish you'd take, or when the net would reach fullness. Sometimes the catch will seem sparse, or of a quality you would not feed to dogs. Other times, you will seem to catch good fish, but they'll choose to jump back into the water before they are fit to be eaten by the One." Jeshua's expression again grew serious as he gazed at these, his closest companions.

"And sometimes, it will seem as if the waters are poisoned, so that the good fish you catch die off in frightening numbers."

The murmurs that followed this pronouncement were subdued. Jeshua went on. "Yes, the Great Wheel will sometimes seem to turn outside the One's favor, dear ones, but do not let that appearance discourage you. Yours is not to save all men right now, but to give humankind the gentlest of shakes, so they may be distracted for a moment from this dream they think to be their lives. That little shake will plant a Seed, and that Seed will pass from father to son to grandson; from mother to daughter to granddaughter, until all this world at last awakens and blossoms forth as the perfection of the omnipotent, omniscient, omnipresent One.

"Until then, let no appearance that this work can be stopped deceive you. The One's will *is* done, and the Mother *has* returned..."

And so, now the Wheel was turning. John would live, but Rome's coming policies would soon jeopardize all who followed Jeshua's Way, not just the Ephesians. The waters, as Jeshua had said, were being poisoned and many of the "fish" he and the others had caught on the One's behalf would die.

He should not be discouraged, he thought. His Teacher had promised good would come from this approaching ill and he'd always kept his promises. Still, he found it hard to reconcile what approached with what would be in some distant time.

All at once, John's awareness began to fuzz away toward sleep.

He wanted to yell "Wait!" to his Self and Time, wanted to see what end would come from the Seeds now planted. Where would his companions end up in all of this?

But his Self and Time had other ideas; John's consciousness drifted completely away.

FORTY-TWO

The *guards came for* John at mid-morning.

He pulled the cowl he'd formed with part of his toga from his head and slowly stood, aware the chill he felt was not solely caused by the damp. Though he kept his focus on the Stillness, as they walked by the browning streaks of blood he'd left on the rough floor the day before and continued on past the oppressively empty cell they'd "questioned" him in, he couldn't resist releasing a small, relieved sigh.

That relief soon turned to surprise: John wasn't taken to another cell, but to the door of the prison itself. He raised his hands and squinted against the glaring brilliance of the mantles of two Praetorians—

—And saw that Arius Galteus stood with them.

The prison guards' response to seeing John in the full light of day was laughable: they fell away from him as if he was an apparition, their faces amazed and pasty with sudden fear. John had no bruise on him, no scab or scar. Save for the fact that his once shoulder-length hair now probably graced some artisan's shop, one would never have known he'd been the recipient of a severe beating only hours before.

Galteus raised a questioning brow...then sniffed and frowned.

"For a member of so cleanly a race, you do not do too well at staying clean," he said, shaking his head. "Unfortunately for all of us, we'll not have the chance to rectify the problem in the baths this time, for a ship leaves for your destination in short order and we must make haste to get you to Puteoli if it is to beat the tide."

Galteus invited John to walk beside him—downwind, he noticed—while the guards marched a few feet before and behind them, to clear the way of pedestrians and protect the Counselor's back. John basked in the fresh air and relative warmth of the morning sun; the calls of the people in the streets, the thunder of horses' hooves, the barking dogs and thrum of marching feet were welcome music, for he might never again hear them. He looked down a side street and smiled; each thing he turned his eyes on held a clarity he'd known only once or twice before, when he'd been with Jeshua.

He felt eyes on him and turned; Galteus stared at him, his confusion evident.

"I cannot decide if you are mad, or merely a simpleton who feigns a knowing manner," he said to John's inquiring gaze. "You are being sent to live the rest of your life away from all you ever knew, away from your very purpose, yet you smile like a boy receiving his first sword and shield. Does not the seriousness of your situation affect you at all?"

John's smile broadened. "Of course it does, Counselor—"

"Galteus. I've no great use for formalities."

"'Galteus' then. Of course the seriousness of my plight affects me. But as there is naught to do save to trust that things are going as the One plans, should I furrow my brow in worry, or enjoy those lovely scarves and the beauty of the girl who holds them?"

The Counselor turned to see an attractive girl of perhaps fourteen summers hawking an armful of many-patterned scarves from many parts of the Empire in a sweet, sing-song voice. "Troubles we will always have with us, Galteus, but beauty withdraws if we do not appreciate it. Or our ability to see it does, which is much the same thing."

Galteus seemed to consider John's statement, then nodded, no trace of his Court demeanor apparent. "I lived many years classed amongst the worst, as slave to Claudius, and now I am perceived as among the best, as a close advisor to him. Yet, with the intrigues of Court, I could find myself an entertainment in the Arena an hour from now.

"That is Life's way, I think, to take where it has given; the only question is, 'when and how much will It take this time?' Since that answer will be 'all' sooner or later, be you Emperor or slave, I choose not to spend my time finding new ways to protect myself from the gods' caprices, as Polybius and some other former slaves do."

Galteus gestured toward his guards. "Oh, I am not completely foolish about my safety. I carry weapons to defend myself, and these two are sworn by honor and friendship to protect me. But if, between the three of us, I cannot avoid the assassin's hand, it can only mean that Life sees fit to answer 'all' earlier than I might have liked. In the meantime, I too, would enjoy the wonders the gods send me."

"And are there those who consider you a simpleton?" John asked with a smile.

Galteus waved a hand and again adopted the lazy, indolent manner he'd used on the docks and at Court. "Why, of course they do,"—he dropped the façade— "But I am a simpleton whose power they fear. You realize, of course, that even after you left your audience with the Emperor, some continued to argue for your execution?"

"Hmm. I trust Gaius Horatius was one of them?"

"He further bespoke his concerns that you and your ilk will destroy the Empire quite eloquently; by the time he finished, more than one was anxious to dispose of the threat you signify as quickly as possible, despite the Emperor's decision."

"I see. Yet, even after hearing the Captain's pleas, you are still not of his opinion?"

"No. All I heard was the view of one who has his own ambitions and particularly hates you. Even so, his plea is the reason we head for the docks now. Accidents have been known to happen in the pens, only to be followed by lucre changing hands."

They came to the stables and the cart that would take them to Puteoli. Galteus was quiet, his beauteous countenance pensive as they left the city. Finally:

"And yet, I would ask: are you and what you represent a threat to Rome?"

John shrugged. "We have talked this half hour and more, and you strike me as being no mean judge of character. What do you think?"

The Counselor shook his head. "In honest truth, I do not know what to think."

John smiled. "Then what do you *feel*, Arius Galteus?"

Galteus looked a bit surprised at John's question, as if no one had ever asked him such a thing. Certainly none of those at Court seemed to appreciate him beyond his mask of indolent unconcern...that is, save for the Emperor himself.

"I serve the Empire more for what it can be than what it is, for I have seen both the lowest and the highest of Rome. I well know it can stand improvement. But your Way, should it truly catch fire, cannot but change the Empire enormously. My hope is that it would do so for good, but Rome thrives because of its strengths: of purpose, of focus, of action. In truth, I fear your Way's power to make us what we are not."

"Truth cannot destroy the truth, Galteus, only that which does not serve it." John couldn't resist a wry chuckle. "In fact, even that which does not serve sometimes falls by only slowly. Jeshua's Way, practiced from the heart of truth, can only fortify Rome."

But the Counselor shook his head at that. "That is well and good, but who defines 'from the heart of truth?' Certainly, the Emperor's definition varies from yours; indeed, yours varies from others who supposedly share your Way. No. I fear we cannot trust the wellbeing of the Empire to so wide a difference of opinion."

The sounds of other conveyances going by filled in for their conversation as they considered each other's comments. This time John broke the silence.

"Galteus, you did not know my views before you spoke on my behalf, yet you did so anyway. Why?"

"So many questions! Is it not enough that my decision saves your life? Are you not willing to attribute it to one of those 'miracles' your teacher was said to be so fond of?"

John's smile was more rue than relief. "I am glad indeed for the reprieve brought about by your mercy, Galteus, since I had no desire to serve the Emperor by being beheaded or skewered. Still—"

"Oh no. Do not mistake my reticence for mercy or even honor, Zebedee," Galteus interrupted. "Had I believed your death would serve, I would personally have seen you to the Arena, just as I personally see you into exile. But as I told the Emperor, whatever you may consider yourself to be, your followers deem you as being like unto your Christos. To kill you would be like chopping a head off the Hydra. Two—no, ten—heads would grow where one existed, and for each of those chopped off, ten more. It would be the death, not salvation, of Rome."

"And so you would exile instead of kill me."

"Precisely. Claudius and Polybius still think you seek political ends, despite what your people preach, but they have finally, if reluctantly, at least partially seen the logic of my argument. So we send you to an island still in the Empire. If they cannot kill you, then they would at least have you within their reach."

"And yet, you are not happy even with that solution, are you?" John's said, suddenly hearing in what Galteus said what he also did not say. The Counselor's frown spoke as eloquently as Horatius's words had reportedly done.

"I did not argue with Claudius' decision, for it was the best that was to be done; but no, I am not happy with it.

"Were it up to me, I would send you to the farthest ends of the earth."

The ship, named Ionus, was small, with a crew of less than twenty, plus two soldiers to serve as jailers. John was immediately led to a small cabin in the ship's stern that, compared to his most recent accommodations, was luxurious. It had a bed, blankets, a porthole through which the day's light shone, even a lantern.

"As was the case in the holding cell, you will not be allowed to speak to anyone, lest you should corrupt them with your speech," Galteus said when they entered the room.

"Do you truly believe I am some sort of magician, Galteus?"

The Counselor shrugged. "It is not my way to personally pay mind to the prisoners, but in your case, I wished to see for myself if Captain Horatius spoke the truth.

"And?"

"And yes...there is power in your words. I think it comes from what you believe you have experienced, not from any mystical powers, but Horatius convincingly conveyed the 'danger' to Claudius. I have never known the Emperor to be particularly superstitious, but he does understand how words can affect others. And like all royalty, he tends to be wary when it comes to anything that can adversely affect his status." Galteus shrugged again. "I am satisfied you cannot corrupt one who is not already so inclined, but your isolation during this trip comes by the Emperor's decree, not mine."

John nodded, but commented no further, for it was obvious Galteus did not realize the real reason he dealt so closely with this particular prisoner. Or better said, he was aware of only part of it. The full truth was that Arias Galteus, like Amadeon Iscariotus, saw in John's dedication to the One a mirror of his own dedication to the highest in Rome, and that reflection drew him to the Silence in John as surely as light drew a moth. It was a subtle effect; the ones thus attracted rarely knew what drew them, for their minds made plausible excuses for entering and staying in Its sight.

Galteus looked around the cabin, then at John; he cleared his throat awkwardly as the silence grew, his sudden discomfiture looking strange one so naturally graceful.

"I...enjoyed our talk and find myself wishing we had more time to continue it," he said at last, almost reluctantly. "It is a rare thing to find one who both sees the world and understands it."

"Even in the Emperor's Court?" John said, smiling as he asked it.

"Especially in the Emperor's Court," Galteus snorted elegantly. Then: "May the gods keep company with you in your exile, John of Zebedee."

"The One's blessings be with you, Arius Galteus," John returned with a small bow.

The door closed and its bolt struck wood; John heard Galteus give instructions to the guards, no doubt repeating Claudius's decree that none were to speak him. He again took in his surroundings, noticing touches he had not seen at first; in addition to the sleeping pallet and lantern, there was a chair to sit on and a small, if worn, rug before the bed. John sat, then lay down, suddenly aware of how tired he was...

...And scarcely made it through the first of his techniques before falling fast asleep.

John assumed his new home would be quite close to Rome, but it soon became obvious that that was not to be the case. The ship traveled south through the Strait of Messina to the Ionian Sea, thence from there back to the waters of Greece and Asia Minor. His guards spoke to him in little more than grunts, while the ship's company was never allowed close enough to exchange even the occasional "Good Morrow", and thus risk being endangered by his magical tongue. To his delight, however, he was regularly allowed on *Ionus's* decks deck to stretch his legs and enjoy the sea air.

John decided he'd not try to escape his exile, even should the chance present itself. Perhaps the Wheel had turned against Jeshua's followers and they'd soon know increasing persecution...but he'd already been a cause of death on this journey. True, he could no more have prevented those deaths than he could have stopped the Wheel's spin by demanding it; still, he would not be such a cause again if he could avoid it.

And yet, the idea of being alone for the rest of his days frightened him. His had been a life filled with human interaction; a life he'd not just enjoyed, but thrived on. How would he stand spending the rest of his days alone?

He realized he would especially miss the influence of the women in his life. Not just Ariadne—though her absence still felt to him as it must feel to lose an arm—but the Feminine energy itself. He'd constantly been in the presence, or more accurately, under the guidance, of women these last several years. Natter about it though he occasionally did (and what man did not?), the truth was he'd grown to rely on the softness of the Mother they embodied to soften the often impetuous sharpness of his Masculine. The stretching weeks of being only in the company of men who barely knew the One, and the knowledge that he would be forever sundered from that soft and loving guidance, told on John's sense of balance more than he'd expected...or liked to admit.

In truth, it sometimes filled him with an almost overwhelming sense of despair.

He didn't let those feelings become the belief that the reason for the despair, or even the despair itself, was real. After all, did the twelve think Jeshua's death served a purpose when it first happened? The answer seventeen years ago had definitely been "No". Despite their Teacher's promises, Jeshua's male companions had seen only failure in his ignominious death, an end to their glorious mission, not a beginning.

And yet, how many lives had Jeshua touched during and since his sojourn? How many lives had John touched on his? Had not the time he'd spent with the Ephesians, with the companions, with Mary, been worth whatever outcome?

Had not the incredible blessing of teaching and being taught of love by Ariadne been more wondrous than he could ever have asked?

John sighed, turned from his porthole and lay on his bed, not bothering to light the lamp in the darkening cabin as the evening sun dropped off the Mediterranean's distant blue-green edge to end yet another day.

Alone forever he might be, but never could he say this journey had not been worth it.

John woke in the dark of fourth hour to the sound of Ariadne calling his name.

He sat bolt-upright in the night-filled cabin, heart pounding, throat, chest and pit of his stomach suddenly aflame with a deep, elemental hunger. Someone awaited him; someone he'd known forever, someone he'd missed all his life without even realizing it, as he had missed Ariadne all his life without knowing it until he'd again seen her in Corinth. And this one, like Ariadne, promised an experience as great as what he'd experienced in again knowing his double.

The ringing tone of the voice—of Ari's voice—which even now was fading as sleep's muzziness dissolved, filled far more than just John's ears; it seemed to seize every inch of him, to be more than merely a voice. The yearning to feel—no, to be enfolded by, to *blend* with—the Feminine he'd so come to miss in these last weeks intensified; John eagerly waited to again hear, and so have the chance to respond to, the voice and the pull toward union it invoked. But as a minute, then ten, then a half-hour passed, he heard only *Ionus's* creak and sway and the thunder of the waves slapping her sides.

Finally, John lay back down on his pallet and stared disappointedly into the darkness. Surely the tail end of some dream had simply carried itself into his wakefulness. He closed his eyes and, after fitfully reentering the Stillness, drifted toward sleep.

The voice called again, again with his double's voice.

This time, John came up off his pallet, stalked to the porthole and leaned as far out of its confining frame as it would let him. His mind tried to tell him one of the sailors was relieving his boredom by playing some sort of prank, but his heart discarded that notion even before he confirmed no one camped beneath the opening.

Was he, perhaps, in the midst of a subtly manifesting vision? It would not be the first time in these many weeks that he'd thought himself fully awake and in the normal world, only to find he was sitting squarely in the middle of Somewhere Else. Still, John had grown used to feeling a difference in his visionary worlds, as if each dimension had a distinct, if sometimes subtle, "flavor", but that difference was missing here.

This was no vision.

Having ascertained that, John leaned back into the cabin and wondered at his response. Though he knew it was neither Ariadne nor the One, the voice filled him with the same sort of longing and eagerness that simultaneously emptied and filled his soul. Hearing it filled him with so much joy—indeed, with the threat of ecstasy—that it took his breath away; his skin burned with the same cold fire he'd felt on the Mount of Olives during Jeshua's transformation, during Mary's Ascension, and when first he'd met Ariadne in Corinth. No, it was not the Stillness the voice called him toward, or not solely That; yet he longed to answer it with the fervor of a thirsty man seeking life-giving water.

What was left of fourth hour came and went, as did the whole of fifth hour. Though the voice did not again speak, as John once more closed his eyes and simply waited, the sense of the presence behind it appeared. It remained distinctly feminine and continued to fill John's awareness with the sense of his double...yet he soon realized the caller's intelligence and beingness differed greatly from that of mere human sentience.

And that it wanted him as much as he was drawn it.

As he stood and stared out his porthole, John literally prayed *Ionus* would not change course, lest he should find himself pleading with the crew to turn back.

Morning came bright on the sea and found John there to greet its coming. As per Counselor Galteus's very publicly decreed orders, he was to be kept as healthy as possible while directly controlled by Rome: the guards brought his morning meal and bid him come out for his once every-other-day walk.

John ate quickly and practically ran over his jailers in his haste to get on deck. He walked straight to the bow to look out over the sea; his eyes unerringly sought and found a particular point on the distant horizon and he gripped the rails as if he feared he might fall—or jump—overboard. He could only see a faint suggestion of land, but he knew who-or-whatever so urgently called awaited him there. He turned to the guard closest to him and pointed, striving to keep the excitement in check.

"We head there? Is that the island I am to be exiled upon?"

The guard stared at John, thoroughly nonplussed, while his partner cautiously came closer. Though neither of them was unseasoned, their fear of what John might be able to do was plain. He'd not attempted to speak to them before because it seemed wholly unlikely there were no spies aboard *Ionus*; he had no desire to endanger these ones who sought only to fulfill their duty by tempting them to disobey their orders.

But he had to know. "Good sirs, do you truly think I would try to coerce you to free me—and thus put the entire Christine community in Ephesus at risk? I give you my pledge: I will not attempt to speak to you again after this, nor use this voice to divert you from your duty—but I must know the name of this place towards which we sail.

"Please, will you not break your silence long enough to tell me where it is I will be forever abandoned?"

The older of the two men looked about the deck, then, satisfied that no one was close by, nervously shrugged toward the almost invisible island.

"Patmos. The place where you will live out your days is called Patmos."

Ionus arrived in Patmos's waters shortly after Noon of a day made remarkable only by the fact that the sun saw fit to break through the clouds just as the ship dropped anchor in the small harbor. John and his supplies, which the Empire had so graciously provided, would be rowed to the island in the ship's two small boats.

And an abundance of supplies they were: tools enough to build a house, clothing and bedding enough for cold nights; the means to kill and dress the animals that dotted the island, and materials with which to fish. It need not be said that John wouldn't try to build a means by which to leave Patmos, though it was in fact surrounded by islands a boatman of his skill could easily reach. He was set for his new life.

Oarsmen in their places, the boats were lowered into the water; the first of the guards climbed down. John looked out at the island and sighed his relief, his whole body buzzing. "Home" his cells cried, and he believed them wholly. But as he made ready to follow the guard into the boat, something made him turn around.

Most of *Ionus's* crew had come forward, their stares reverent, even awed. They'd stayed away from John during the voyage under the threat of Rome's displeasure, yet he'd been aware throughout the journey that each time he came on deck, the sailors stopped whatever they were doing and gazed at him as if they saw a miracle.

Now *Ionus's* captain spoke. "Teacher," he said, "Sir. 'Tis likely treason to say it, but Rome makes a grievous error by leaving you to rot away on this island. Surely, those who so shamefully sent you forth could not've seen the Light so many of us have seen these many days, else, they'd know they imprison an oracle of Diana Herself...and that the goddess must be greatly displeased."

The Captain looked at his feet as if he, at least, felt the shame his Empire's leaders had not the wit to feel. "For our part in this, we've no right to ask it...but will you forgive us for bringing you to this barren end and give your blessing to this ship and crew?"

John looked to see how the remaining guard reacted to this breach, only to find the same reverent expression on his face; perhaps the fire he felt showed, as the halo of righteous anger had been visible to Horatius and his men aboard *Ares*.

"Feel free in your hearts, brothers," he smiled. "I understand duty of all things, for it is fulfilling the One's duty that brings me to Patmos. No man here has cause to feel shame, for no man here has wronged me. I can not but give the blessing you ask, and I do so gladly in the One's Name."

The air itself seemed to lighten with the sailors' relief as they bowed their thanks, and some among them even had tears in their eyes. John clasped the captain's hand and climbed into the bow of boat, followed by the second guard.

Soon, they were free of *Ionus* and heading toward Patmos.

FORTY-THREE

It might be, John bar Zebedee thought, that I will die on this barren rock called Patmos. More, he would do so far from friends, students, and the woman he loved more than his own physical life.

Yet all he could feel was joy.

The moment the guard spoke the small island's name, John knew it—*she*—was the source of the voice that called with such fervor. Patmos had waited years, perhaps centuries for him; his anticipation at finally meeting her grew with every pull of the oars.

Jeshua once told a story of being drawn in this way to a specific location: hungry, thirsty, very nearly delirious, he'd sought the place without ceasing for the last two weeks of his desert ordeal, stopping only when utter exhaustion forced him to. It was the place, he'd said, where he and Destiny had agreed to meet eons before, and any thought of ignoring the call had been out of the question. For with his arrival there, Jeshua had met and refused the three temptations to turn from his Path, and thus began to fulfill the Son of Man's destiny.

John was the first to jump ashore as the men's pulls drove the boats onto the sands —and he was almost brought to his knees by the power of the life force that greeted him when his foot splashed to ground. The guards and sailors stared as they dragged the boats higher onto the beach, but John was barely aware of their presence; he had to consciously focus on every move as he helped unload his supplies.

The business of unloading did not take long, even though they carried the supplies to the crown of a steep hill that boasted a magnificent view of the ship and harbor below. John did his part of the work with mixed feelings. It still frightened him to know he would soon be the sole inhabitant of Patmos, yet he was also anxious to be left alone with the island so her whispered secrets might at last be spoken to his heart.

He looked down at the carpet of winter-dun grass and slumberous, leaf-stripped trees that filled a small, rocky, bowl-like meadow; he'd be protected from all but the strongest winds that might visit during the rest of winter and spring. The knoll was situated so he could see the sea in three directions; in the fourth, he saw what looked to be the ruins of a small village in the distance. He'd easily find enough stones of suitable size to build a permanent shelter, but for tonight he would simply pitch a tent.

John turned, meaning to bid the oarsmen and guards farewell—but suddenly frowned with a half-remembered sense of familiarity at what he saw. The men were huddled together in earnest debate, the sailors gesturing back and forth while the guards half-heartedly shook their heads. Finally, the conference ended and the senior of the guards stepped forward, his face still holding the awe John had seen as they left *Ionus*.

And just as the Christines had in Ephesus, they offered to help him build a house.

Their offer touched John as much as they seemed touched by him, for his jailers in particular had no reason to make such an offer. He regretfully refused them, however; though some of them would likely seek more knowledge of Jeshua's Way when they got home, he feared what effects any returning word of these men's actions might have.

"I want you to know, the blessing I gave the crew of *Ionus* I especially offer to you," he said to the head guard, named Silvanus, and his partner, who was named Edigius.

"I've felt what it was to be treated as an enemy of Rome by other hands; that you have not done so is something neither I nor the One will forget."

Silvanus and Edigius did not bow as the crew of *Ionus* had, but gave John the highest tribute they knew: they saluted him as they would a fellow soldier and wished him the blessings of the gods as Galteus had done.

John did not wait to see *Ionus* fade from sight, but immediately began to explore his new home, smiling all the while. He'd thought the land spirits in and around Corinth wondrous, with their depth of Quiet and sense of long-accepted rightness, but next to those of Patmos, they were as children recently come to adulthood, quiet at last, but still unaware of the depth of Beingness that gave them succor, comfort and identity. John felt his life force take root in this place, embraced it as it welcomed him. He longed to sit and let himself experience what the island sought to share, longed to become one with the fullness of its center and knowledge.

Self-discipline, however, and the awareness that the sun would soon set into wintry, bone-biting darkness, stopped his indulgence.

Before taking such liberties, he needed first to set up camp and cook a meal. Then would he be ready to submit to Patmos's life force. He'd been led here expressly to discover such knowledge, after all; time enough to dive into it. A lifetime.

Setting up camp took longer than John expected. As the son of a once-nomadic people, the art of tent building seemed to be set in his bones—but as the son of Zeb bar Ezekiel the fisherman, he'd lived in houses, not tents. His experiences during Jeshua's ministry were no help; the twelve and their Teacher usually slept under the stars or stayed in others' homes, just as he and his companions had done on this journey.

Fortunately, and despite their many objections, John's father had insisted all his children learn to erect different kinds of shelters, for "with the Romans breathing ever more heavily down our necks, the ability might one day be useful. So quit your complaining and do it."

The tent finally came up just as darkness dimmed the land, and John cooked and ate a rudimentary meal of bread, rehydrated lamb and barley. He gathered the rest of his supplies so they would be close at hand, then leaned back against a large stone.

He stared at what promised to be a truly spectacular night sky, for the early afternoon clouds had long since blown away; as it faded from flaming gold to deepening blue to enduring ebony, First Star, and not long after, his many brothers, came forth to greet the earth and accompany the night sky on its rounds. Each star sang its own song, in its own language, yet the addition of new stars, each caroling their own and utterly different melodies, did nothing to diminish the glory of those whose songs had begun before. Indeed, each star's song only gained in depth and purity as another, then another distant sun joined the sky's chorus. Soon John, Patmos, and the surrounding sea vibrated with their joyful noise.

He remembered a certain story, "of a time from the Beginning Days," his mother Salome had been fond of telling...or perhaps it was that her children had repeatedly insisted on hearing it: when Adam and Eva walked the earth, she said, all humans could clearly hear the stars' song. All could hear the Lord El's loving words of reassurance and instruction on how to live with each other in peace and harmony. But with Cain's transgression, humankind began to turn away from their awareness of the Great

Self; each new generation birthed fewer and fewer who could Hear. By the time of the Flood, only the slightest few could still detect the stars' music—and fewer still of those ones chose to listen to the Wisdom that caused that music to be.

Like those ancient ones, all the Zebedee children had been born hearing the stars' music, but of the five of them, only John and his youngest sister, Abigail, never lost the ability. One night, as the twelve walked toward Bethany, Jeshua laid his hands on James's ears, and the elder bar Zebedee brother wept for joy, for suddenly he could again hear the music that had deserted him with the arrival of manhood. More, it was said that the children born of his followers could also hear.

Ariadne, too, had always heard the song of the stars—and of the grasses and trees and sea, for that matter. In the chill depths of morning, she and John often sat in the Karikos gardens, wrapped together in the heavy blankets from their bed, and shared the experience of touching into Infinity as the stars sang their Glorias to the One.

John missed her more than he could possibly say.

He missed them all in truth, and wondered how they fared. Ada and Hosea surely did well by them; John somehow knew in his deepest heart that though he could no longer sense Mary's presence, they, at least at some level, were still blessed by her guidance. Yet, still he wondered. By his reckoning, his companions would be finished with their training in another six or seven weeks...but what would be for next for them? He felt with a faith bordering on the fanatical that Ariadne knew he still lived and would forever wait for his return. But could he say the same of the others?

Should he expect to?

As if it knew his thoughts carried him away from it, the spirit of Patmos tugged at John's consciousness like a small child who's been promised a sweet if she eats all her dinner and now expects that promise to be fulfilled. He smiled his amazement at the sentience of the pull. It was not usual for devic entities, especially ones this big, to desire this level of communication with humans. The differences in their life spans and time sense was so great that they rarely gave more than the smallest amount of information to any but the most greatly gifted, those Mary had once called "natural Historians". Despite his recent experiences, John had never thought of himself as such...but Patmos obviously meant to prove him wrong.

So, with a deep, expectant, somewhat nervous sigh, he put more wood on his fire, wrapped a heavy blanket about himself, and settled comfortably against his rock. He felt a moment of trepidation, some small part reminding him that this which sought and was sought was not the One Itself and so could be a distraction or worse; but he set it aside and closed his eyes. He spoke a particular phrase of the Practice, his willingness to see what Patmos had to share with him complete, and entered the Silence.

Instantly, John dropped "down" into his Self and past it, straight to the center of the island's Knowing. As he fell, strings of light, millions of them, extended out from Patmos's heart and entered his essence through the base of his spine. He heard the echo of the stars' song in the strings; he vibrated with the beauty of each one's individual spirit. John exulted in it, opening ever more fully to the power that beckoned to him.

Suddenly, like sunlight exploding through the clouds, the strings filled, then burst through his body, radiating from his pores and pulling his awareness both "up" and "down" at impossible speed. They expanded, growing as large as tree trunks, and he expanded with them; he became a chain of brilliantly bright beams that in turn metamorphosed into individual particles larger than a man's head. John saw within each of those particles hints of what might be universes entire and was filled with the longing to visit those places as he had during his confinement aboard *Ares*, to know them more intimately...

...And to his overarching joy, his wish was suddenly granted. The Divine Feminine he'd so sorely missed was suddenly there, unreservedly offering him everything those universes held, and more; taking him deeper and deeper into the fullness of Her glory.

At some point in his other visions, John had always experienced at least one familiar sight, one sound or feeling he could identify from his own understanding. That was not the case now. As Patmos pulled him yet farther into her being and history, her rolling, soul-bright laughter at the silly notion that he *should* understand with something so paltry as mere human intelligence filled him. She flung him forth, to split into ever-smaller pieces of self, so that he might instantly know all she would give him; John witnessed what Patmos showed him—then became it.

He was a star, bright red and old as the galaxy, ready to die now that he had eaten his children, the planets that once orbited him. He was a slag-soft stone sitting beneath a ruby sky whose blazing, white-fire sun bleached everything around it to match its own lack of color. He was a creature shaped like a many-legged dragon, with fur the hue of deep waters, and he was the thing that killed him, a thing with too many limbs to be called human, but which nevertheless had human awareness. He was the molten lava that had destroyed most of what had once been the much larger island of Patmos, and a piece of space debris that would soon fall, burning, to the other side of the island.

He became a woman dying in childbirth, shrouded by the darkness of death even as she saw the beginnings of a light too bright to look on with mere human eyes; he was a burnt and broken tree, lying beneath a sea that bubbled and smoked and filled with ash. He became man and woman, Nubian and Greek, Jew and Barbarian. He was solid and gelatinous, vigorous as hope and silent as the mountains.

John was filled with an unbearable rush of ecstasy as Patmos awakened him to being all the Life that lived in time and space, as he became the billions upon billions of microscopic bits of awareness that lived within the infinite cosmos. He watched with unbounded elation as each particle folded into one form, then decayed away from it to take up residence in another, and yet another. He truly became a being of the universe, gloried in the knowledge that his body would never truly die. Parts of him would travel to the ends of the universe and back in an ever-repeating pattern; parts of him would stay on this earth. Whatever John, the son of Zebedee might do, *he* would continue on. It was all that was joy and beauty, this knowledge; all that was good and right...

...And yet, there was a shadow on it, the slightest blemish of wrongness, as if it was a secret he had no right to be privy to and he'd committed some awful breach in gaining it.

John's ecstasy whispered abruptly away as the small warning he'd felt before entering Patmos's presence stirred. The thought crept in, quietly, that he had, perhaps, gone beyond merely being one with the island's memories, possibly even to a dangerous extent. He felt a sudden, urgent need to step back from Patmos's intensity, to regain some semblance of his bearings. He started to throw off Patmos's visions, to again become solely his own identity, that of John bar Zebedee of Judea, sitting alone before a fire on the island of Patmos.

But then Patmos called his name, just as she had when he was aboard *Ares*.

The power that grabbed John from miles away and filled him with such longing that he'd actually prayed the ship would not turn from this place was, here within the being of Patmos, as great as an angel's strength was compared to that of an infant's. The island's call and her promise of a union that made even the completeness he shared with his double seem weak and trifling swallowed John; indeed, Patmos entered every cell, every fiber of his being with a rush of power so gigantic that it was, in truth, far beyond his capacity to manage as a human being.

The stars' music jumbled into clattering oblivion as time, space and matter disintegrated into uncountable lunatic fragments. John's sense of equilibrium and sequence fell to pieces as his self spread out into a nothingness that was not the Silence, into something that was neither thing, nor particle, nor thought, nor the Witness of them. John laughed and shuddered as his mind and body were flooded with Patmos's all-encompassing rapture; his last sliver of human awareness was the memory of Mary's warning that for him, Night might take a form that was completely unexpected.

And so it had, taking his sanity with it.

John wandered over Patmos through numerous turns of day and night, the unnoticed discomforts of rain and wind washing over him. He knew not how many of these cycles passed; his mind could no longer count days, nor even remember the words for light and wind and rain. He stood, walked, stumbled, fell down; he passed over the terrain about him like a tree that has suddenly learned to walk but cannot lift its roots high enough to get clear of the ground's obstacles.

Had others been on the island, they would surely have avoided him, for what they would have seen was a madman, his hair, though short, growing out in spiky, oily, muddy sticks. They would have seen a creature who alternately laughed, raged and cried as he wandered aimlessly from center to edge of the island and back again; they would have seen a naked fool shivering in the late winter sun, who lay down to shiver harder beneath the cold and rain of the island's nights only when exhaustion finally took him.

What his body experienced, however, John emphatically did not; he knew nothing at any time but overwhelming rapture.

Though his mind could no longer sense or understand the world his physical eyes showed him, John himself experienced only the caressing brilliance of swirling, tangible light...with Patmos as its source. To him, She had become the fullness of the Divine Creatress, the source of everything that had or would ever exist. The heights She took his heart and being to entangled him in an increasingly ecstatic dance; John was Patmos and She was he, wedded in a way his disjointed, quickly obliterated memories of another couldn't begin to touch. He walked with Her gladly, going wheresoever She chose, dancing whatever dance She bid; that he—or the "it" he'd become—did not fall into the sea and drown was due to sheerest luck...or perhaps the protection of the angels.

As time went by—hours or days or even weeks, he knew not which and did not care —a change came over John's incognizance; his awareness stepped slightly beyond the limit of being a thing that only experienced Patmos's dance within. Like a baby discovering his toes, John was suddenly aware of his body's most basic functions and observed them with microscopic fascination. He watched the flow of his blood, the beating of his heart, the movement of his atoms from organ to organ for hours, even days, with such complete focus that his breathing sometimes ceased for half-hours at a time. He understood the poetry of the rocks, grasses and sands without the need of translating it into cumbersome human language. John again had understanding of a sort, but the veil between what he experienced and what it meant still remained too thick for him to take volitional action.

He did manage one evening, wholly by accident, to wander into the camp he'd set up his first night on Patmos. He crawled under a blanket left among the things long since scattered by wind and goats and rabbits, to stop shivering for the first time in eons. Water he found by the simple expedient of tilting his face up when it rained, or stumbling into streams and swallowing what he did not choke on.

Food, however, did not fall into his mouth by sheer good fortune; he soon became an emaciated shadow of the man who'd stepped, healthy and well fed, from *Ionus's* dinghy.

John's heart experienced unbounded joy as the Island's song permeated his being, yes, but his body was dying of his spirit's neglect.

One day, in addition to Patmos's song and an odd keening that had daily grown more insistent, John awakened to find a new voice touching his awareness. Its call came to him with the light of morning, soft as the first spring breeze upon the land. He had to listen closely to hear its wordless invitation over the overpowering roar of Patmos's song. Still, though it had not the awe-inspiring vibrancy of Her music, its clarity pulled at his heart. It offered him an even greater experience than he was now having—if he would do what it asked—

—And for reasons John no longer had any consciousness of, he believed it.

He pulled himself up and followed, but it was a slow process: because of his body's condition, he had to rest frequently...and more than once he simply stopped, engulfed by Patmos's bliss. Near the end of the first day, he managed to stand and take a dozen steps in a row...but that triumph nearly ended in disaster. John's steps quickly degenerated into stumbles that finished in a sprawling fall; his cheek and chin slammed hard against a rock. He was unconscious for he knew not how long, was too stunned when he awoke to do more than lay the rest of the night in chilled, dazed misery. When morning finally came, standing made him horribly dizzy and caused his empty stomach to jump in sick alarm. The quiet voice seemed not to notice, but, pulling him as much by its Quiet as Patmos pulled him by Her ecstasy, urged him to keep moving.

Finally, late on the afternoon of the second day, he came to a cave.

John sat now, wholly exhausted, in the center of the largish cavern, and stared unseeingly out at the cold, powder blue sky. Had he been himself, he might have wondered at the impossible warmth of the cave, might have wondered at the cool, freshwater stream that cut through the rock floor next to where he sat. The quiet voice was nowhere to be found; the noisy "hallelujahs!" of the roiling brook joyously echoed Patmos's blissful presence and drowned it out.

All at once, John cocked his head like a puppy hearing a sound for the first time. The stream's song had changed to that of the voice, reminding his simple mind that he'd come to this place to receive some promised gift. He listened, nodded, then stuck his bruised and bloodied face full into the bubbling stream; he drank deep, following the quiet voice's instructions not to breathe in as he did so. When he sat back up, his body's thirst satisfied, water rolled down his face, carrying dirt and dried blood with it.

Then he frowned, and alarm overtook his features.

Patmos was gone.

John couldn't jump to his feet, but his panicked heart jolted as if someone had thrown him from a high cliff. The bliss he'd known for—what seemed to him—all his existence had disappeared. The anguished cry that broke from his throat bounced off the cave walls, multiplying and expanding until everything around him vibrated with his grief and horror. That grief echoed inside his mind, desperately calling, but there was no answering reassurance. Patmos was gone. She had abandoned him.

John had no words for anger or betrayal in his lost mind, but a sense of wrong filled him. He had done something wrong and She had left him. *He* was wrongness, useless and empty. He hunched in upon himself and clasped his arms around his stomach as if the emptiness within him was no longer caused by hunger alone—and belatedly discovered where the strange keening he'd heard over the last few days came from. He rocked back and forth, letting the sound roll from his throat; tears warmed his face, but he shivered as if chilled. Alone, he was alone...

But no. That wasn't true. Someone still spoke.

The quiet voice, now loud in John's mind, continued to gently entreat him. Sobbing uncontrollably, he threw his hands over his ears as if to shut it out; some part of him sensed or suspected that this was the cause of his anguish, the cause of all his misery. He would hear no more of the voice's promises, he would *not*. He hated the quiet voice, wanted it gone as Patmos was gone.

The voice did not heed John's wishes, but simply kept offering him the promise of, if not Patmos, then some beauty as great. And now it was augmented by another voice, one that somehow seemed familiar and yes, comforting, in a way that was different from Patmos, but which, even so, calmed his deserted soul. John's sobs slowly faded; he let his hands fall and listened.

There was a natural formation, a ledge, cut into the wall to his left; its roof was high enough that a tall man could lie on his back and stick his arms straight up without touching it. That was where John must go to receive the promised gift, the voice said.

John shook his head and whimpered. Though the water had restored him somewhat, he wanted nothing more than to lie down next to this stream right now and go to sleep. But the voice was having none of it; it prodded him, albeit gently, until he again got to his knees, made his long way to the ledge and slowly pulled himself onto it. Exhausted, John curled into a ball and waited, hoping for Patmos's return.

Patmos did not return; instead, the voice suddenly spoke to John in human words, using a series of short, simple phrases. He had the vague sense that he should recognize them, that he should understand their meaning, but doing so was still beyond him.

It didn't matter. A blanket of perfect Calm fell over John, Its cleansing Completeness entering at the top of his head and through the soles of his feet, to meet at his center in a brilliant (yet utterly Still) wave of rest. His battered mind struggled against the alien sensation, but the sudden sigh that took him was so deep that he completely relaxed.

Within seconds, John fell into the deep peace of perfect Consciousness and knew no more of Island Patmos, his body or the cave.

FORTY-FOUR

"Does he live?"

"I do not...yes...yes! See? His chest moves."

"Thank the One! Gods, look at him! He is naught but skin and bones—and skinned bones at that! What in the One's name happened to him? Where are his clothes?"

John heard the voices as if he was a disembodied spirit listening through the Veil. There was something strange about them.

"There was clothing at his campsite, and no harm to them or his tent, save being scattered around. I do not think the Romans did this, much as I think it possible of them... forgive me, my friend."

"Think nothing of it. I *know* it is possible of them. Do you actually think he has wandered around the island this whole time? Should we try to wake him?"

"Yes, I do think so...and no, let us let him be. Best I should work on these sores while he sleeps."

"Do they fester?"

"...Not that I can see...or at least, not seriously enough to take much worry for."

That was it, John realized. The voices spoke in *words*, just as the quiet voice had done before the Silence took him.

More, he understood them. John felt as if it had been centuries since he'd understood anything. Yet he also felt strangely bereft, as if he'd lost something precious, but could not remember what.

Pain there, came the thought, as something cool and wet touched his cheek. And not just there. He felt bruised and battered all over. He groaned, but could manage no words.

"He is coming to," one of the voices said. Then: "Rabbi—John bar Zebedee! Can you hear me?"

John frowned as the rush of realization and oblivion both claimed him. Not only were the voices speaking in language he could comprehend, but he knew them.

They belonged to Marcus Prochorus and Haifata Adan.

A full week passed before John was enough himself to either ask or answer questions. While he could not say how long he'd wandered about the island, based on the condition of his body, Adan suspected it had been a month or even as much as six weeks. Haifata and Marcus dressed his numerous wounds, then helped him into one of his now clean robes. John required the help; even standing was a major undertaking. Adan made herbed broths and cooked up a soft mush of grains and goat's milk so he could gradually get back into the habit of eating, but John found he had no appetite.

"Your hunger will come back, brother, fear not," Haifata gently told him. "The stomach goes to sleep when it has been long without food. It will waken in its own time."

But John knew his lack of appetite was not solely due to his shrunken stomach.

As reason slowly returned, he managed to tell Marcus and Haifata what little he remembered of his experience with Patmos. This was no small feat, considering the inherent impossibility of describing something so alien to human experience...but it was also true that John excluded a great deal, not least of which was the fact that Patmos's presence had returned, calling to him like a lover pining for her belovéd. John told himself he did not wish to alarm his friends with such news, but the truth was he was deeply, profoundly ashamed of all that had happened. It horrified him to know he'd allowed himself to be taken in so, had been so completely lost as to come to this point.

And it humiliated him to admit that Patmos's call still drew him.

His silence did not stop his friends from knowing something was wrong. During their first week on the island, the warriors took turns sitting by John's side, sometimes holding to his hand, other times holding to *him* as he thrashed in his sleep and sobs echoed through the cave. Most of the time, however, John simply sat quietly by, wrapped in a gauze of remorse that seemed to have no intention of ever lifting.

A great deal of his guilt lay in his realization that he hadn't really valued Mary's warning that Night might find him. Despite her comments, he'd assumed the passing of the doubts he'd experienced in Ephesus had left him in a stable state of wholeness, and his subsequent experiences had given him no reason to doubt that. After all, relinquishing identification with one's body was among the last and most difficult of the illusions to set by, and it appeared he'd done that, not only with Horatius's abuse aboard *Ares*, but during his beating in Rome.

He'd never considered that he might be deceiving himself.

Not that Patmos had intentionally meant to harm him, John knew. Jumbled though his memories were, he still sensed she was naught but an especially sentient devic being, that she had no malice in her. No, only hubris had led him astray; only his willingness to set aside the One in favor of a mere aspect of It had led him to this state.

I have been a terrible fool, was all he could conclude whenever his mind moved toward the subject of how he'd allowed himself to be swallowed by Patmos. And it never crossed his mind, addled as it still was by his personal Night, that perhaps his condemnation was itself an aspect of Night's influence; he couldn't see that his belief in his "foolishness" was simply a thought that had no more power to affect him than the belief that standing in the rain for too long might cause his body to melt.

Instead, he worried over what he would tell these, his companions. They had put themselves in significant danger to find the one he'd thought he was, not this husk who sat before them now. How could he tell them he'd been deceived, and that a part of him, a huge part, would willingly choose that deception again? How could he tell them that, had they not frequently engaged his attention, he would long ago have drifted back into Patmos's embrace despite knowing it would surely result in his being lost to earthly sanity forever?

Even John's body felt heavy with the shame of what he'd done, so that he wanted sleep more than he wanted to do the Practice. No, he did not avoid it or the Stillness altogether; he could never consciously go that far. Still, he often only looked *at* the One now instead of entering fully into Its embrace...and even that he did hesitantly, as if he somehow expected It would think him as full of folly as he himself did.

As if he feared It would reject him.

Though John found it as impossible to explain what had brought him to the cave as it was to fully describe his experience with Patmos, Prochorus and Adan were more than able to explain their presence.

"We heard rumors of everything from your summary execution to your enslavement in the Iberian mines," Prochorus said with his customary scowl. "Ada and Hosea—with the Karikoses' ready help—spent almost as much time trying to keep people away from us as they did teaching. We even discussed secretly moving from the cottages so we could continue our work without constant interruptions."

"So then, how did you discover my fate?"

"Titus and Iscariotus have friends in Rome. Though it took some time, they were able to discover what had really become of you and send word to us."

Haifata nodded. "Once we knew that, all else was easily decided. We left Ephesus immediately."

"But did not Ada, Hosea and the others object to your leaving? And what of Torer? I cannot believe he did not come, if only for the sake of the adventure."

"Oh, yes, Ada and Hosea objected strenuously," Prochorus said as if still amazed that anyone would argue against their task. "They insisted they were responsible for us by your charge and demanded we stay and finish the training as you asked." He snorted. "We ended that argument by the simple expedient of leaving in the night."

"You did not tell them you were leaving?" John was incredulous and more than a bit angry, but Marcus merely shrugged.

"We did tell them, bar Zebedee, more than once. Besides, we'd no more time to argue, especially after Haifata had his dream."

"The gods told me you needed help," Adan said at John's inquiring look. "They said I was to find you and render it as quickly as possible. I did so. Marcus decided to come along."

"But Torer decided to stay. Much to my surprise, I must admit," Prochorus said. "He seemed to feel the rest of the companions would be better served if at least one of 'the warriors' stayed with them."

John nodded, glad his admonition to the big man had taken root.

"If it will make you feel any better, we did not go without saying at least one 'goodbye'," Marcus suddenly chuckled. "Ariadne caught us leaving."

"And threatened to wake the others if we did not immediately explain ourselves to her satisfaction," Haifata continued, also grinning at the memory.

"Then she insisted on coming with us," Prochorus chuckled again, his admiration evident. "I tell you, bar Zebedee, that one is as stubborn a little thing as ever a man could hope to be cursed with, and it took some doing to convince her to stay. But she realized her lack of experience would slow us down and possibly put you in greater jeopardy..."

John knew Adan and Prochorus stared, but suddenly, he was barely able to breathe, much less speak. The sound of Ariadne's name had his heart thundering at battle speed; it drowned out his other senses and relegated Marcus and Haifata to the far background.

He stood in a space that seemed to have no ends. Patmos was with him, a shining, distant, womanly shape, arms spread wide as if She awaited only his will to plunge deep into the center of his being and once more thrust him into the center of Hers...

John shuddered and pulled away from Her plea by main force of will; after what seemed like hours, the feeling of being transported dwindled away.

He again saw Marcus and Haifata clearly, but could not shake the sense that the island had responded to his belovéd's name, that Patmos had in fact caused his reaction.

What did She want of him—and what did She want with Ariadne?

"Bar Zebedee?"

"I am...all right, Marcus." John spoke as if he'd been running hard, his voice hollow in his own ears. "It is just that...the ordeal of losing myself as I did...still seems to be with me. Fear not, my friends. It will pass."

Haifata continued to peer at him, his brows furrowed. He slowly shook his head.

"No, brother, I think not. I think it will not pass at all."

"What?" Prochorus said, alarmed.

Adan did not answer, but kept his eyes on John as if looking into the center of his soul. "You have told us much of what happened to you, brother, but there is also much you have not told, much you would not have us know. Why?"

Perhaps it was his weakened state. Or perhaps the directness of the question and the huge Stillness behind it, especially from this one, cut away all his protections and left John no place to hide the sense of disgrace that besieged him. Whatever the reason, tears suddenly filled his eyes. He tried to turn away from his companions, but Haifata, albeit with great tenderness, grabbed his emaciated wrist and forced him to continue looking at him. Prochorus nodded, his countenance also gentle with sudden understanding, and took John's other hand.

The three of them stood thus for several minutes, with naught but John's sobs and the little brook's praises filling the cave. Finally, Marcus spoke, his voice almost as soft as if he talked to himself.

"Do you remember, bar Zebedee, what you said the moment before you healed me in Bethany?" he asked. "You admonished me for throwing away the only other love of my life, my scribing, after Lydia and Tomus died.

"And that was exactly what I'd done, because, do you know? Though it seemed to be otherwise, the truth was, my wife and child were the ones *I* leaned upon. Their willingness to let me be their protector made me who I was, bar Zebedee, and I wholly believed it was incumbent upon me to keep them safe. When Lydia and Tomus died, I was so sure I'd failed them that remaining a scribe seemed like the greatest of desecrations to their memories. After all, I deserved no part of what I loved, since I'd so horribly failed what I most treasured. In fact, when I took the knife that took my legs, a part of me even rejoiced at that. It seemed a fit punishment, for just as with my scribing, I'd come to love being a soldier, and that was unacceptable. It was not until I worked with you, Mary and the Practice that I finally realized I had no reason to hold to fault for what happened to my wife and son, and never had.

Marcus suddenly smiled, the combination of joy and sadness filling his craggy face with surpassing beauty. "Do I still miss my darling ones? Yes, every day, even after all these years. And yet, bar Zebedee, as I step ever more into the Stillness you taught me to get to, I lately find myself thinking—often to my great surprise—that, considering where it has led me, I'd not change any part of what my life has been.

"Is it not possible, John, that Haifata and I, of all people, came to this place for you because we could forgive whatever happened here? More, is it not possible that whatever happened to you could not and should not have been avoided? That it was the very thing that had to happen for you to go where you must next go?"

John's brow furrowed as Marcus's words struck an echoing chord of memory. Adan saw it and raised a hand to forestall the Roman, but there was no need; Marcus's sensitivity to the shifts and flows of the energies around him had grown enormously.

It was hard at first for John to follow the threads of his budding memory, for the thick syrup of his humiliation made recalling anything of joy or beauty seem useless and unreal. Finally, though, Mary's words in Ephesus came back to him:

I will tell you this, Boanerge: what you recently experienced was not Night, only doubt. If Night does come for you, it will do so in a way you would never have imagined. In truth, I do not know if you will be able to avoid it—or even if you should. But if it does come, you need only remember your Teacher's words, 'Be still and know that I AM God'... And if that does not work, take the help that comes when it arrives. Do not, for any reason, rely solely on your own strength.

John at last did what he'd avoided doing since recognizing what had happened to him: he turned his focus fully inward. Marcus and Haifata also closed their eyes, and as was always the case when two or more gathered together, the strength of the three's focus on the Stillness soon generated a field of Wholeness that was far greater than the sum of Its parts.

John easily stepped onto the threshold of the One's Abode, only to be greeted as he always had: with joyful, eternal Welcome. The Love that forever created every form from Its unshakeable Center did not speak, being the Stillness from which all movement comes. Still, it made clear to John that if need be, It would wait forever for him to realize he had in truth never left It. The One was, always and forever, the faultless Mother/Belovéd that saw him in his perfection no matter what he thought he'd done.

As the welcoming Silence once more engulfed him...better, as he once more accepted the Beauty he was within Its Being, John knew this Belovéd would never intrude Its Self upon his. The One had no need to do so, after all: It already knew those places intimately, because It *was* those places. One could never lose Self or sanity by stepping into the One's embrace, only find greater wholeness. Whatever Patmos's allure, it could never be as great as the fulfillment the One offered in every moment, eternally.

And yet... John still felt Patmos's pull; still felt an overriding desire to return to her. Within her embrace lay something he needed, something he could only find by going back to her. But how could that be possible, especially now? It simply made no sense...

...And then, it made all too much sense.

Suddenly, John knew exactly why he'd been summoned to Patmos, knew who had truly sent Haifata—and Marcus in particular—to rescue him. He knew why hearing Ariadne's name had drawn Patmos closer to his awareness.

John opened his eyes. He was still weak, but the smile he bestowed on his friends was strong with gratitude. He told them at last of Patmos's original summons and of his irresistible, almost sexual, desire to answer it, spoke of her continuing call and how he'd longed to return to her. Told how, in defiance of Life Itself, he'd been willing to leave Ariadne and even Jeshua's charge behind for the sake of returning to her embrace.

Then he told them he intended to go back to her.

"By the heart of the Christos!" Prochorus's answer thundered off the cave's walls with the force of a sword hitting a shield, muting the small stream's hallelujahs. "You cannot actually mean that! You almost died from whatever that...that thing was, bar Zebedee—would be dead now, but for Haifata's willingness to listen to his dream! How can you want to...? It is insane! You cannot go back into that!"

"I must, Marcus. I have no choice."

Adan stared at John with grim concentration, but Prochorus began to pace and shake his head. The Roman turned to and away from John once, twice, three times, as if he meant to angrily berate him but couldn't manage to get words out. Suddenly:

"Damn it! Damn *you*...!" he said—then he did something John would forever hold in his memory. Instead of carrying on his angry tirade as old habit demanded, Marcus Prochorus stormed over to one of the many seat-sized stones in the cave, sat down, and began doing the Practice.

John couldn't help it; he grinned as the cave filled with Stillness. Truly, Marcus now had a new habit.

After a moment, the Roman opened his eyes, and though his voice was still passionate, his manner was much calmer. "You cannot allow yourself to fall into that vision again, you must not. John, look at yourself—and I do not just mean your body's condition! Both Haifata and I have feared this whole time to leave you alone, lest you should wander into the sea and not know—or care—enough to save yourself. Yet you tell us now that you mean to go back to the thing that caused it? *You* told us how dangerous it can be to follow the distractions of the phenomenal world, bar Zebedee. You told us to choose for the One over such things, not relish their attentions like some bored patrician's wife. You told us our good comes only from seeking the Source of all the beauty we might encounter on our journey.

"We valued your words so much that we followed where you would go and sought you in places where others would have you rot. Yet, you'd now ignore those words —your Teacher's words—and willingly enter a place you know is dangerous to your sanity and life? How can you expect us to accept this—to allow it, for the gods' sakes?"

In truth, the thought of returning to Patmos's embrace did send a chill down John's spine, for he couldn't deny that a part of him still desired to forget his Self in her. Might it be that he was lying to himself?

No, no. He would not step again into doubt, but into the heart of trust.

John gazed into Marcus's unhappy, stubbornly closed face and nodded compassionately, not sure if he did so for his friends or himself. "You are right to feel I betray your trust by seeking the very thing I warned you against, my friends. It does indeed seem to make none but insanity's sense, and I cannot prove in truth that it is not. I can only tell you that my reasons for reentering Patmos's influence are also the One's, and hope that you will trust me now as you did earlier in this journey. For make no mistake, I will answer Patmos's call again. To do otherwise will doom our mission before we even go forth, and that must not happen." John spoke to them both, but looked at Adan.

"Brothers, you must trust that I know what I am about."

Time seemed to attenuate as Haifata gazed intently into John's eyes; even the brook seemed to sing its hallelujahs at a more leisurely pace. John did not flinch from the African's stare as he had before; if any of his companions could see his true intent, could see beyond time and space and reason itself, Haifata could. And if he saw, he would, against all his own feelings and Marcus's objections, support John's choice.

Adan blinked. Time returned to its normal flow.

"Marcus, this is the reason we were sent here," the African said at last.

"What are you talking about?" Prochorus said, his eyes narrowing as if the light in the cave had suddenly grown too bright.

"What John speaks of doing is the reason—the true reason—we came to Patmos."

"No. Your dream said to come to Patmos because he was in danger."

"Yes. But that is not all I told you and you know it. We were also to do his bidding, to assist him in whatever way he required."

"Not this way," the Roman said, but Adan merely shook away his insistence. "Are you telling me we are supposed to let him go back into that...insanity?"

"Yes." Haifata's voice held an immensity of weary acquiescence. "If necessary, yes."

"Then you are as mad as he is," Prochorus said, but he suddenly sounded uncertain. He might believe John's brains to be addled, but nothing in his experience allowed him to think such of Adan. Haifata took advantage of that uncertainty to make his point.

"Though I like it no more than you, my friend, John speaks truly. I have no words for what I see when I now look into his eyes; the pictures that come have a veil before them that makes words impossible. What I can tell you, though, is that it is now more important than John's life or ours that he again seek communion with this place's spirit. If he does not, Marcus, the ill effects of that choice will ruin this world—not harm or slow its growth, but ruin it. There are powers involved in this that we know not of."

Adan shook his head, stopping further protest and attempting, John thought, to shake loose what he saw. Prochorus wanted to remain unconvinced, but his own soul felt the truth of the African's words.

"But what of the danger? You say this thing means you no harm, bar Zebedee. But only the grace of the gods brought you back from your last encounter, and that grace may not be with you next time. What then? We cannot reanimate the dead as your Teacher did. If you die, our quest will end anyway, for certainly none of us can lead it." Marcus began pacing again, running his fingers through his short hair as if he wanted to pull it out. When he again spoke, his voice was as close to pleading as John had ever heard it. "We could leave this place and continue on our journey, you know. Surely Claudius forgot you as soon as he put you here; the gods know, Rome has forgotten its exiles before. If we left this place now, they'd be none the wiser until it was too late.

"John, you do not have to do this!"

For the first time, John clearly saw the truth the Roman had never before let come forth: to Marcus Prochorus, John was no less than the savior Jeshua had been to many others. Yes, he knew Mary's blessing had made it possible for him to call forth the healing that let him regain his legs, but he knew, too, that the fullness of his healing could not have come without the completion he'd found in John's being. Whatever Adan said, it was literally true that Marcus wanted John's safety more than he wanted his own life.

John laid a hand on his friend's arm, both staggered and humbled by the enormity of Marcus's love for him, but still, he shook his head. His voice gentled as if he explained some difficult thing to a child who knew the truth but could not accept it.

"Listen to me, Marcus. Rome may not be so vigilant with its other exiles, but I guarantee they will be so with me. If I go from this place, they will quickly know of it, and the Emperor will then have his reason for openly persecuting the Christine population. Yes, perhaps we could reach our companions and save them from his wrath, but what of those who cannot travel with us? I told you of the Great Wheel brothers, of how it even now turns in a direction that will bring much sorrow to many. Still, I would do nothing to hasten its spin unless there is no choice."

John sighed. "Besides, can you truly believe, in the Stillness of your hearts, that my coming to this place is accident or coincidence? Whatever my experiences with Patmos, the One's Hand is thick in this mix. I have trusted It this far, not only with my life but with yours and the others'. Am I now to throw that trust away because there is danger of a kind I have not before experienced—or, more to the point, that I have? I cannot, you know I cannot. And so I ask you, brothers: will you stay with me while I return to Patmos's embrace?

"Will you guard my body while it sleeps?"

Haifata nodded as solemnly as one who knows he sends his best warrior to certain death. Prochorus looked as if he fought not to cry...but then, all at once, a look of surprise, followed closely by dismay, filled his features. He sighed, but his eyes shone.

"Very well...Rabbi. I promise I will support you in this thing—" his expression turned stubborn "—on one condition."

John's life force closed around and entered into Marcus's, even as it expanded out into the universe in unbounded waves. The depth of the ages and his and Marcus's place within them simultaneously enlarged their souls and shrunk them to the size of dust motes playing together in a field of Infinite Existence. Marcus Prochorus might well be the only man on the planet who dared make such total surrender sound like a demand—but then again, John never thought to see him concede such a thing at all.

And of course, there was no question of his answer.

"I agree to your condition, Marcus," John smiled. "And I thank you for the honor of serving thus."

Prochorus nodded, his face conveying more than a bit of shock. He still did not like the idea of John's return into Patmos's sway, but now he knew they could never truly be separated, any more than Joshua's death had separated him from his Teacher.

John clasped Haifata's arm, then embraced him. As he sat back on his ledge, he had a momentary urge to rush outside and survey the land, to stand beneath the clarity of the sharp blue sky and breathe in the spiky freshness of the sea. There'd been so little chance to do so since coming to the island, surely such a small delay would do no harm...

But no. Just as he'd resisted the urge to instantly fall into Patmos's embrace when first he'd arrived, John resisted the urge to delay returning to it now, aware that it came from no real need. It was just that the thought of again stepping into her power —and the thought that he still wanted to—made his breath go shallow with dread.

But then, perhaps such fear of returning to her is a good sign, he thought ruefully.

He lay down on the mattress of straw and dried moss wrapped in one of the blankets Prochorus had retrieved from his campsite, and forced himself to relax by saying the simplest of the techniques of the Practice. He was as ready as ever he would be.

"Keep the body safe, my brothers," he said, and silly though he knew it to be, John was glad his voice did not tremble. "If it dies before I can return, let it be buried on this island—and make sure Rome knows of it."

Patmos instantly washed over John as he closed his eyes. Even as his fear increased he could not stop the ecstasy that engulfed his mind and body...

... And yet, he had one more thing he needed to say, something that now meant infinitely more to him than the heart-pounding bliss inundating his soul and senses. John pulled against Patmos just long enough to be sure his words were clear, and this time he did not care if Marcus and Haifata heard the quaver in his voice.

"If I die, tell Ariadne I am sorry I did not keep my promise.

"Tell her I love her always."

FORTY-FIVE
Bethany

Miriam *of Midjel* was dreaming.

She was simultaneously falling and flying, forming and crumbling. The air around her was full with the swirl of distorted, half-coherent voices; she passed through places that were not places, felt feelings that were not feelings, saw things that were not things. All of them grabbed at her, trying to gain hold of her Self and scatter her understanding, but Miriam did not panic, for she was conscious in her dream. Rather, she chose a technique of the Practice and used it. The chaos did not stop or change, but she was soon anchored in the Stillness, a boat on a becalmed sea. She gently gathered her knowingness back into herself and waited.

She became aware that she was not alone: a being of brilliant, ever-changing light appeared before Miriam, Its joyous welcome threatening to break her heart. As the Power's wordless, soul-enfolding song vibrated throughout her being, she felt sure she had never heard beauty in any other language. It told her this place of impossibility was the only one that had ever truly been Home, that she'd been gone from It since Time Itself began and It had missed her dearly. It came toward Miriam, inviting her to rest in Its embrace and forever know the bliss that came of being one with It.

Miriam felt the Power's promise of eternal rejoicing sing in her cells like a lover's sighs rang in the ears. She wanted with all her heart to hasten into its embrace, to never again know the painful rigidity of the surface world...and yet, she hesitated. Though every sense told her the Power was not evil, the Stillness in her soul spoke even more clearly: she must not accept this invitation.

Grief-filled, Miriam willed herself to rebuff the Power's call and turned away from it with the intent of awakening from the dream...

...But like some men she'd had the misfortune of dealing with, "No" was not an answer It was willing to accept.

It was not offended, mind, for It had no capability of understanding such a concept. It simply sweetened its song and caressed Miriam's self with a shock of rhapsodic beauty that brought every memory of longing she'd ever experienced roaring into her veins to radiate straight into her heart and soul.

Miriam grew afraid. True, this sentience meant no harm. But she suddenly knew if she did not pull away now, she'd lose not just her self, but her Self. The Power drew ever closer, calling, calling, and even as Miriam's panic made her frantically scrabble for a door that wasn't there, her awareness drew rapturously toward It, overwhelmed by desire. At the moment Its touch pushed her to fall, drowning, into boundless delight, Miriam screamed, not sure if she did so in terror or ecstasy. She cried out to Mary, to Jeshua, to the One...

Miriam's eyes snapped open with the echo of the shriek she'd loosed in the dream rebounding off the walls of her room. Her shift was soaked with her own sweat, but she shivered uncontrollably; her blankets were bunched at her feet. She untangled them and covered herself just as Martha, Elior and Lazarus burst into the room.

A gaggle of students milled about in the hall behind her brother and sisters, eyes round with surprise, but none was foolish enough to breach her sanctuary, even under these circumstances. Officially, Miriam was gone, taking time away from teaching to rest and reenergize. She'd sequestered herself, giving instructions that no one was to bother her for at least a week—and those who well knew her knew she did not jest. Broaching this lioness's den without very good cause would be a grave mistake indeed.

Right now, however, she was glad for the intrusion, and gladder still she had not gone to Lazarus's small country house to take her sabbatical, as she'd originally intended. With what she now knew, that would have been the greatest of disasters.

"Miriam, what—?" Lazarus began, but she raised her hand, her face grave with the knowledge she now carried.

"John is lost."

Shocked silence filled the room as Martha and Elior pressed their hands to their mouths; Lazarus seemed suddenly made of stone, his face frozen with horror.

"John is dead?" Elior's voice came out in a strangled whisper. "The Romans—?"

"Not dead, lost," Miriam answered, suddenly impatient with the necessity of using words. The Power's doing? Probably. "We must help him."

"But how—?"

"Questions later. Now, we must act."

"But do you know what to do?" Martha asked, unwilling to let it go as her sister made a robe of her blanket and strode from the room.

"Yes. Whatever we are told."

Miriam entered the main room, shooing students before her. She sat in the chair that had been Mary's, feeling a kind of comfort in it—and wished just now that Mary herself was here. Though she'd spoken confidently of doing whatever the One asked, in truth she wasn't at all sure she could. Her double would have said just the right thing to awaken her consciousness to the right action.

But of course, Mary was dead now, come back to earth only to be taken by disease.

Miriam's uncertainty showed, not on her face, but in the room. Though the students had grown quiet, they could not completely still their nervous rustling. Under other circumstances, their many variations of curiosity and concern would have amused her—so unique, but so much the same!—but the phantom self made smiling impossible. It insisted she must act now, now, *now*; her very cells seemed to want to jump up and *act*.

She shook her head. The phantom self might have ideas of what to do, ideas that sounded very good. Still, bitter experience had taught her that what that self considered right action often led to catastrophe—and they'd have no second chance to salvage things if they failed in this task.

And so, Miriam closed her eyes.

"*Jeshua, amen,*" she said sometime later, her equilibrium reestablished in the One's utterly unconcerned Embrace. Even the most edgy of the students had calmed; now they were ready to do whatever the One directed. Miriam turned to her fellow teachers—

—Only to find that Martha, Lazarus and Elior had disappeared.

In their places sat three younger versions of herself, ranging in age from earliest womanhood to the time just after Jeshua' resurrection. Miriam started to exclaim at the strangeness of the sight, but then looked closer: the eyes that stared out of her younger selves were not her own once-jaded ones. These ones were Miriam, yes, but they were also still her sisters and brother.

What could this mean?

"Martha...?"

Martha/Miriam did not answer, but turned to the waiting students. They closed their eyes as if she'd spoken the command to re-enter the Stillness aloud; the room soon filled with the relaxed hum that typified a group in the midst of the Practice. Martha/Miriam turned to the other Miriams and they took each other's hands, then folded Miriam's hand in hers. She spoke no words, but Miriam could hear Martha's voice as clearly as if she did: Everything is ready.

Suddenly, Miriam was a disembodied beingness, zooming across the world at incredible speed. She flew over lands and waters she had never seen, yet, though the details were but a blur, she knew she would remember each and every bit of each place she passed over no matter how long she might live. She did not fly alone: Martha, Lazarus and Elior's beings flew with her, as did those of every one of the students. The vision of her various selves suddenly made sense: though she could feel the uniqueness of each person who was with her, she was the head, the consciousness of it all. She'd have access to their knowledge and talents when they came to where John now dwelled.

They knew of John's exile, of course; no news shared in one part of what so many called the Christine community took long to travel to the other parts. When news first came of his sentence, Miriam prayed the universe would at least tell her if he had been condemned to a desert or a paradise, for they'd not known when or where he'd been taken. That prayer was at last being answered, but now she feared rather than rejoiced at what she might find.

She/they came to a group of islands and, slowing, circled it like a hawk seeking prey. Miriam traveled from one island to the next, yet all of them seemed to be made of the same dull stuff. Winter's dreariness made rocks, rabbits and even goats difficult to distinguish from the gray grasses; only the tops of those trees which still had leaves were easily seen.

As she/they reached the seventh island, Miriam's eyes took in a figure. Naked, emaciated, dirty and stuporous, it lay on its side, covered with dirt and abrasions, as gray as the grass and stones around it. It hummed and keened to itself between shallow, ragged breaths, yet seemed wholly insensible of the harshness of the elements that battered it.

It was John.

The horror of the others who were now part of Miriam blew through her like hard winds through an ill-pitched tent; she "closed" her eyes, trying to calm herself and them before their collective fear prematurely returned them to Bethany. Despite their own shock, Martha, Lazarus and Elior also realized the danger: they reached out to the weaker links in the unit to radiate reassurance. One by one, the students turned their focus back to the Stillness; their horror eased to mere agitated waiting. Miriam turned her attention back to John and softly called his name, lest she should frighten him.

He did not hear. She called again, and yet again, eventually yelling into his mind; she even tried, to no avail, to grab and physically shake him. He was oblivious.

He is little more than a golem, Elior's voice said, and Miriam's horror returned to congeal into despair. Search for it though she might, she felt none of the familiar intelligence she had known as "John bar Zebedee". There was naught in that body now but a wild animal. No, not even that: this creature did not even have the sense to feed itself. It was dying of its own unawareness.

No, Miri, Lazarus traced. We mustn't see him that way, or all truly *is* lost. We must allow what is to make itself known, not be blinded what seems to be.

Miriam gratefully listened to her brother's advice and continued searching. Yes, a thread of intelligence did still live within the body; John was not a golem. She followed that thread, only to find the rest of John's mind was lost in an impossibly high ecstatic state—one whose source she recognized with a shiver made equally of fear and longing.

How could she possibly hope to lure him away from the Power's enticements when she herself still regretted, at least a little, not leaping into its embrace?

A memory suddenly flashed brief and clear: Martha bustled about with her usual quiet efficiency as she cleaned up after one of their dinners. Lazarus and Elior called her to come and sit, insisting that the dishes could wait, but Martha only smiled, shook her head, and cracked some joke about awakening in a goat's pen. Then, by focusing only on the task at hand, she cleaned up everything in a third of the time it would have taken Miriam, who had no more love for the art than she'd had in Jeshua's time.

Miriam understood. Yes, she had regrets—but they would never be great enough to draw her away from the One, so what value lay in giving them any mind? Best to give all of her attention to what she truly desired.

Compared to the rolling majesty of the Power's, the voice that came out when she once more called John's name was still a thin, reedy thing...but all the parts within Miriam sighed with relief as, this time, he slowly sat up and turned his attention to her. He might be gladly lost in the Power's devastating bliss, but some part of him still knew what it was to have More.

Miriam wordlessly offered John that more—if he did as she instructed.

Another part of her Self, meanwhile, extended outward and searched the island. It moved from John's old campsite, past a crumpled, weather-beaten robe and out along the edges of the island, only to find a cave fairly close to where John now sat. The cavern had no food, of course, but it was warmed by some source Miriam could not discern and, bless the One's miracles, a small freshwater stream cut through its floor.

It was perfect.

The Self extended its awareness further and made another discovery, one even better than the cave. A small boat headed for the island, and the light of the One that shone in its two occupants said they were very familiar with the Practice. Indeed, was not the white-skinned one (the other man was a Nubian) none other than Prochorus? Yes it was!

That caused a stir in the minds of the students! Let the critics tell these ones the Practice was a sham after this!

Miriam's amusement faded quickly. Prochorus, his companion and their help would not reach John for another two days. John, however, must reach the cave before the morrow's eve; else he'd not survive the cold snap her Self suddenly knew was coming.

So Miriam began to herd him to where he needed to go.

It was a long, heartbreaking, journey, for John fell near the end of the first day, knocking himself unconscious (and, they'd all feared for a long moment, dead). When he finally came to, he was too weak and sickly to walk, so he'd crawled most of the way over the rough terrain, worsening the contusions on his hands, knees and shins. They were all exhausted on the afternoon of this, the second day, but he finally sat here, on the floor of the cavern, lost again in the Power's bliss. Lazarus made them aware of a natural, ledge that was carved in the side of one wall. The clarity of the cave's life force was definitely strongest there; they all agreed it would be the ideal place for John to rest, heal and reawaken his consciousness.

Miriam managed to draw John's attention and made ready to point him toward it... but then reconsidered. Though there was no food, some water would surely help sustain him until his rescuers arrived on the morrow.

John cocked his head a little as she directed him, then trustingly dipped it into the stream and drank deeply.

At the moment he resurfaced, the excess water running brown down his bruised and wounded face, the air went suddenly, oddly, still; but before Miriam could determine what was different, John looked frantically around, his eyes widening in shock.

Then he began to wail like a terrified child.

Miriam tried to pierce his hysteria as he raved and flailed weakly about on the cavern floor, but to no avail. Panic pushed at her. Had some poison in the water finally carried away what little was left of John's sanity? Would Prochorus and the Nubian find nothing but a drooling animal—or a dead man—when they arrived? Had they come across time and space and selfness, only to fail after all?

Each of the four teachers called to John in turn, hoping to break though to him, but he clamped his hands over his ears to keep from hearing. Miriam felt desperation bud in all of them; the strain of holding to this place was beginning to tell. They had to get through to him, and quickly.

Suddenly, another consciousness joined the group, almost startling all of them out of their trance.

At first, Miriam thought it might be Mary, for it surely had her double's mark upon it, but she soon discarded that idea. This one used no words, seemed unable to do so; but the apology and urgency in its—no, *her*—manner showed she meant no harm...

...And all at once, Miriam realized who she could only be. She had Mary's mark upon her, yes—but she held John's heart and soul.

Miriam joyfully welcomed the newcomer, amused to feel her own wish to see what she looked like nosily echoed by Martha, Elior and Lazarus—and was thoroughly enchanted when the image of a small, shimmeringly lovely blue flower filled their vision.

Miriam's thoughts turned back to the problem at hand. If they did not act soon, John would never again know what it was to hold this radiant "Little Flower" who now lent her strength to theirs. But what to do? Even with his other, how could they help him find his soul when it was so thoroughly lost?

The Silence that anchored Martha's calm spoke.

No, sister, no. John is not lost...he merely *grieves* the loss of one he thinks important. Talk to him...there was a pause...no, *sing* to him.

Hope suddenly welled. Of course! John, in his insensibility, was bereft at the loss of the Power's presence, a state Miriam's dream experience gave her some understanding of. She began to croon softly into his mind, as a mother would to a sick child, and his double quickly joined her, gleaning the tune of one of Salome's old lullabies from Miriam's mind. Surely, surely, John would hear and respond to this!

Though it took most of an hour, John's hands finally fell away from his ears and his sobs died away. Lazarus was still adamant about the ledge, reminding them of its healing resonance... And more practically, the concern that John might fall into the stream, only to drown in his unconsciousness, was quite real. It took an agonizingly long, sobbingly painful time, but at last he reached the ledge...

...Only to have the Silence immediately, blessedly, send him into a deep, deep sleep.

Miriam wished she could do the same; she felt like she'd been awake for a million years.

John's double was just as exhausted, and Miriam was sure she would have cried if she could; her anguish, even through her relief, was tangible. And yet, her strength still shone clearly through as well, imparting itself, amazingly enough, to the Self Miriam and the others were in complete trust and generosity.

Miriam acknowledged the gift, sorry she could not comfort this Little Flower in person. She well understood how John could love such a one, even were she not his double...more, she saw the why, and the 'why' behind the why, that Mary had returned to earth. If ever this one discovered the location of this place, nothing, not the soldiers, not the elements, not the Emperor himself, would keep her from John.

Miriam wished she at least knew her name...

"Will he be all right?" Someone croaked.

Miriam looked around with startled eyes to see who else had come into the cave —but she was not in the cave any more. She was back in their meeting room in Bethany and alone within herself. Everyone stared at her; they'd all heard what she now realized was Elior's question, and awaited the "head's" answer.

She let her awareness drift inward once more. Prochorus and the Nubian would indeed reach John in time and bring him back from the brink of starvation, and she also strongly felt that the Power that had almost taken his life and soul would never again be such a danger to him. She even sensed, though not to the point of knowing, that John would find Vashti, just as his Teacher before him had—and it thrilled her that he finally understood the joy of being with one who loved the One *and* him with all her heart.

"Yes. Yes, I believe he will be all right," she said at last.

Miriam's assurance easily carried to everyone in the room, bringing smiles and congratulations all around. More, some part of her knew they had good reason to be assured.

So why did she still worry?

HEARTFELT GRATITUDE...

Creative endeavors (regardless of what the creator may want to believe): never occur in a vacuum. There are always people, some in the background, some not, who make what any writer or artist does far easier, if not, in fact, possible.

That is emphatically the case with *Son of Thunder*, and I want to acknowledge those people who made its creation possible.

First, tremendous thanks and blessings to the folks in Tacoma, Washington who put me up in their homes and hearts while I worked on the earliest drafts of this book: John and Jani Greer, Beatrice and Mike Petronelli, Francella and Dave Cozine, Wayne (Sahadeva) Cummings, Steve (Vidya) Bedell, and Margaret Jones. I especially want to thank Marilyn Robbins who, in addition to being incredibly cool, gifted me with the computer the first draft of this book was written on. Dulcie (Sanatakumari) Ponchot encouraged me to keep writing after the first five pages of the book poured out of my fingers at one AM one September morning.

My "readers," Ishaya monks all, gave me further encouragement and some excellent advice: Uśas, Sita Devi, Bharata, Amrita, and Sindhuma; Gargavan, Jaya, and Maharani. Special thanks and a really huge hug to Nandini; she knows why.

Two other people I most deeply want to thank, just for being there over of the last twenty years, are Suzanne O'Brien Cohn and Linda Hogan. Their recognition that the surface stuff is never where souls connect has made me feel boundlessly supported. I also want to again thank my parents, Ann and Marvin, for their boundless support in every part of my life. The Dedication says it all...but it can never be said enough.

Likewise, my Praise, Gratitude and Love for my Teacher, Gauri Ishaya, for Maharishi Krishnananda Ishaya, and for the other great Masters of every Age, including one Jeshua bar Josef, cannot be great enough. It is literally true that their unbounded love, patience and Knowledge of the inherent value of humankind—indeed, of the brilliance of God in each one's heart—along with their unwavering dedication to awakening each of us to the full awareness of that Perfection—is why this world still exists.

Last, but most assuredly not least, I want to thank John bar Zebedee, also called Boanerge. There are no words for what a shock it was hear his late-night demand to "Write my story", nor can I possibly convey what an honor and joy it's been to follow that instruction—and to engage in the Practice that's given me a means for doing so. It's been a wondrous experience, a blessing that daily leaves me wholly amazed.

A. K. Ishaya
November 23, 2005

...AND AN INVITATION TO LEARN "THE PRACTICE"

"**THE PRACTICE**" spoken of throughout *Son Of Thunder* is an actual meditation, a "prayer without ceasing" technique that exists in the world today exactly as it did two thousand years ago. It is called **The Ishayas' Ascension** and is taught by monks and teachers of the **Ishaya Order**.

Like the technique itself, the Ishaya Order has existed in one form or another literally since human beings first felt the desire to remember the Truth of who they are. Because the word "Ishaya" translates from the Sanskrit to "for Higher (or the Highest) Consciousness," the Ishaya Order can and does claim connections to every great spiritual tradition from Taoism to Zen to Hinduism; from Islam to Christianity and beyond.

The first four Ishayas' Ascension techniques are usually taught in a weekend course; participants to gain a deeper understanding the nature of the mind and discover what we Are beyond the mind. During the course, participants have several chances to directly experience the incredible ease and effectiveness of using this technique; even better, they become part of a growing community that increasingly experiences the truth of all Being.

The practice of the Ishayas' Ascension was reintroduced into world and brought to the United States in 1988 by an American-born monk of the Order, **Maharishi Sadashiva Isham (MSI)**. As stated in *Son Of Thunder*, it is the easiest and most joyful means for reaching the true goal of every human: to consistently experience the unbounded joy of the Infinite as ourselves. Successfully practicing the Ishayas' Ascension requires neither taking on nor giving up any spiritual beliefs; it is, if you will, the spiritual Rosetta Stone that allows people from every belief system and any walk of life to understand, and more, *experience* the fullness of the Infinite One we in fact are.

For more information on how to learn "The Practice", please contact the:

INTERNATIONAL SOCIETY FOR ASCENSION (ISA)
c/o Ishana Retreat and Yoga Center,
P.O. Box 429 Station Main,
Salmon a.m., BC Canada, V1E 4N6
(250)832-5088;
email: info@ishaya.org
Or visit **ISA** on the web at **www.ishaya.org**

ABOUT THE AUTHOR

A.K. Ishaya is a monk of the Ishaya Order and a teacher of the Ishayas' Ascension. A.K is fond of cats, loves the various incarnations of "Star Trek" without being the least bit reverent about it, suspects with some horror that John Denver's "Rocky Mountain High" may be the Song of the Universe, and has an ongoing love affair with God that has never been marred by a lack of wit. Home for A.K. is Northern California.

SON OF THUNDER:
Book I: A GATHERING OF COMPANIONS
A.K. Ishaya

Only Jesus' most trusted disciple can save his Teacher's most powerful and important Teaching—and humanity itself—from inevitable destruction ...because he is not a Christian.
7 by 10 inches, 368pages

Order Form (Please print clearly)

NAME_____

DATE ORDERED_____

ADDRESS_____Apt.#_____

CITY_____ STATE/PROVINCE_____

COUNTRY_____

POSTAL CODE_____

COPIES ORDERED_____@ $29.99USD, $28.99 CAD,   €20.99   £14.99
Please circle one.
Postage/Handling: Add $4.00 for US, $5.00 Canadian; £4.00 British
and €5.50 European orders per book.
For faster delivery, please visit us at www.ishayabooks.com for rates.

TOTAL COST_____

paid by CASH/M.O._____ CREDIT CARD (name):_____

Card #_____ Expires_____

E-MAIL_____

Please make a copy of this order form for your records
allow 4 to 8 weeks for delivery;
make checks or money orders payable to and send to
IshayaBooks
P.O. Box 2844
Fairfield CA. USA 94533
orders@ishayabooks.org • www.ishayabooks.com

ISBN 141206858-4